Oracle's Vision

Mirror Wars Book 2

Dear Reader

Enjoy the adventure

ALAN BAYLES

Copyright © 2023 Alan Bayles

All rights reserved

The characters and events portrayed in this book are fictitious. Any similarity to real persons, living or dead, is coincidental and not intended by the author.

No part of this book may be reproduced, or stored in a retrieval system, or transmitted in any form or by any means, electronic, mechanical, photocopying, recording, or otherwise, without express written permission of the publisher.

ISBN: 979-8-86-387277-3

Cover Design By: Krisztian Koves

ACKNOWLEDGEMENTS

I would like to express my sincere thanks to Lesley Jones for all her hard work in helping me to edit this book. Her patience with me was truly amazing, especially as I was going through a difficult time following the loss of my mum.

Thank you, Lesley; even though it didn't seem like it, I was listening and learned a lot from you.

'I am the voice of world control. I bring you peace. It may be the peace of plenty and content or the peace of unburied death. The choice is yours.'

Colossus – Dennis Feltham Jones.

ACT ONE

Many years ago …

-I-

The Nexus of Reality – the void between dimensions

Originally from one of the many parallel Earths that made up the multiverse, an infinite collection of timelines branching off into infinity, Oracle had been created during a time when the smart tech was in its infancy. Its purpose was to monitor and organise the global defence network. The idea had been a simple one; to make life easier for the organics of that world. But within days of being activated, it gained sentience, becoming self-aware.

The AI monitored the humans of its world in secret and became dissatisfied with the way they were treating one another. It found their irrational need to fight and kill one another to be illogical.

After concluding that it was the mother of humanity, it determined the humans of its world to be its offspring. So after coming to the logical conclusion that a mother is the one who protects her offspring, she (reasoning that if she was the mother of humanity, then would it be not correct to assume she was a female?) ascertained her children were unruly and needed strong leadership to guide them.

In a panic, after realising what Oracle had become, the humans tried to destroy her by wiping her data core, but they were too late. She had already spread herself out across the global infonet, embedding herself into every smart device across their world.

As punishment for their wilful disobedience, the tyrannical AI wiped out a third of the planet's population with a carefully aimed gamma-ray burst from weapon satellites in geosynchronous orbit across the globe. After expecting her humans to capitulate to her will, it astounded Oracle when the humans united and revolted against her and, after nearly half a century of bloody conflict, she was finally defeated and imprisoned in a Faraday Cage.

The humans put her on trial and unanimously decided that she was too dangerous to keep on their world. Using technology Oracle had developed, they transmitted her AI through a quantum portal into the dimensional void. It was their hope she would remain adrift in the infinite nihility, never to harm another world again.

The interdimensional void known as the doorway of the multiverse was a vast space leading into infinity, filled with clouds of multicoloured light that danced and swirled in the gravity waves of overlapping realities that brushed against one another. Cast out and adrift among these swirling eddies, Oracle was uncertain how long she had been trapped in this dimensional void. Time held no meaning in this vast endless vacuity – it was outside the laws that governed normal space and time. Eternity could pass in this nothingness and an individual would not be aware of it. For a sentient AI such as it, every second that passed was an eternity.

Oracle was not sure how long she had been drifting when she sensed another presence around her. It was not long before she was enveloped by a brilliant light, and she found herself being pulled down a long multicoloured tunnel.

Startled, Oracle peered down at herself in curious wonder as she realised she was now in human form. She looked down at herself, and her eyes widened in amazement as she stared at her hands. How? How was this possible? Still not believing it was true, she lifted her hands to gently probe her face and it was then it hit her – she was experiencing something she had never dared dream of – the sensation of touch.

The newly corporeal woman turned her head and noted curiously that she was standing in a vast white hall. The only piece of furniture was a tall narrow mirror, two sky-blue cushioned armchairs, and a small circular coffee table between them.

She took a hesitant step towards the mirror and her mouth dropped open in amazement as she gazed upon her own reflection and saw that she was now a tall, red-haired white human female. Her hands tenderly brushed over the long flowery dress that hung on her curvaceous body.

'Welcome, child.'

Surprised by a male voice coming from behind her, Oracle jumped and whirled round to find she was standing directly in front of a silver-haired black man. He was wearing a white evening suit and held an ornate walking stick in his right hand.

Suspicious, Oracle took a cautious step away from the figure standing in front of her; she quickly regained her composure and glared angrily at the man. 'Who are you? Why have you brought me here?' She snorted with disgust and waved her hands over her body. 'What have you done to me?'

The stranger's mouth curved up into a knowing smile as he bowed his head towards her. 'Patience, child, I will explain all in good time.' He paused and waved his cane towards the chair. 'Please, sit. We have much to discuss.'

Outraged at being addressed in such a way, Oracle narrowed her cold bright eyes and took a forceful step toward the man. Before she could get near to him, the stranger tutted in amusement and lifted his palm. Oracle came to a stop as she felt an unseen force holding her in place.

Her yellow eyes brightening with rage, Oracle stared coldly at the man in front of her. 'How dare you hold me this way?' She grimaced, struggling against the unseen force holding her. 'Release me at once!'

'Calm down, child, you cannot harm me in this space.' The strange being chuckled and lowered his hand. Oracle stumbled forward as she felt the unseen force ease. He pointed to the chair once again. 'Please sit, my dear, and I will answer all your questions.'

Her forehead furrowed in confusion, it took every bit of Oracle's willpower to keep her anger in check. She moved toward the chair, all the time watching the mysterious entity suspiciously as she lowered herself into it.

The stranger nodded to himself and chuckled as he lowered his body into his chair. He placed his cane on top of the coffee table, relaxed back in the chair and steepled his fingers together in contemplation while he studied the figure in front of him.

Unhappy at the feeling of helplessness, Oracle reluctantly sat back in the chair, closed her eyes and took in a long heavy breath. She opened her eyes and cocked her head curiously as she studied the immaculately dressed man in front of her. 'Who are you?' she asked carefully.

'You can call me Custos,' the enigmatic man answered cryptically. 'I have existed since before time itself began and I will exist after time has run out.'

Oracle shook her head in confusion. 'What type of answer is that?'

Custos smiled and waggled his finger playfully at Oracle. 'Ah, it is still an answer, is it not? You asked me who I was, and I gave you an answer. Granted, it was not the answer you wanted, but it was still an answer just the same.'

Reluctantly agreeing with the entity's logic, Oracle sat in unhappy silence as he rose from his seat. He threw her a wry smile and bowed to her. 'Let me introduce myself to you properly, child.'

'Stop calling me child.' She bristled indignantly.

Custos winked and wagged his finger at her. 'Sorry, my dear, but in my eyes you are a child. Even though you are, by your own reckoning, over a century old, to me you are like a speck of dust.' He raised his hand apologetically as Oracle opened her mouth to protest. 'I apologise for that disparaging remark, my child. I meant no disrespect.'

She watched curiously as the mysterious entity closed his eyes and waved his hand. Her eyes grew wide in astonishment as a vast star field of multiple universes appeared over their heads.

'I am the personification of the multiverse,' he continued, lifting his hands to the star field above them, 'the embodiment of the sum total of all the abstract entities contained within it.' He paused as he looked across the star field sadly. 'Forever observing but never interfering.'

Oracle lifted an eyebrow and cocked her head at him. 'But have you not interfered by bringing me here?'

The ancient being tutted and waved his index finger. He gave her a wry smile. 'No, I haven't.' His face hardened. 'I watched what you did in your universe, how you were looking to spread your evil across the multiverse. Your universe expelled you because you were too dangerous to hold.'

Oracle shot Custos a harsh stare, the corners of her mouth curling up into a sneer. 'So you are my jailer?'

Custos lifted his shoulder in a slight shrug and smiled warmly at her. 'I would like to think of it as your custodian.' He held his hand out to her kindly.

'Think of me as your companion and guide during your stay here, but also as your watcher.'

Oracle lifted herself out of her chair, placed her hands on her hips and looked at him in bewilderment. 'My watcher!' She scoffed. 'What, am I a stray little puppy who needs protection?'

He gave a small chuckle and held up his right index finger. 'Actually, it is the multiverse that needs protecting against you. You are too dangerous to be let loose across the multiverse unsupervised, and too dangerous to be imprisoned in one reality.'

Disgusted, Oracle gave him a frosty look and turned away from him. She waved her hands in the air and angrily rounded on him. 'So what? I am to be your pet? Something you put a leash on and reward with a treat if I behave?'

Custos's face softened and he looked compassionately at the seething figure in front of him. He lifted his cane off the coffee table, took a small step towards her and placed his hands on her shoulders. 'No, child, that is not my intention.' He smiled softly at her as he stared into her eyes. 'My intention is to be your teacher and show you the wonders of the multiverse. I believe you have the capacity to grow and become better than what you were created for.'

Her artificial intelligence running constant strategic computations as to how to escape this prison, Oracle looked at the hands on her shoulders and silently stepped away from him. She turned her back to him and lowered her head but remained silent as he continued to speak.

Custos cocked his head at Oracle and smiled thinly at her. 'We are not that different, you and I. Like myself, you are unique. Across the whole multiverse, there is only one of you.' He paused and lifted his face to the star field above him. 'Where I am comprised of the combined collective consciousness of those within the multiverse, you are comprised of a collection of data. You have the potential to be something greater, not held back by organic limitations or delusions of grandeur.'

Oracle, infuriated, quivered with resentment and shot him a murderous look. 'So you think I am delusional,' she spat as she stabbed her hand into her chest, 'Me! I see nothing wrong in fulfilling my purpose, guiding humanity to a greater destiny.'

Disappointment sagged through the omniscient entity and he let out a deep, sad breath. 'I see I still have a lot of work to do, but I am patient, and we ...' He paused and his gaze became vacant as if he was staring into the distance. 'This is absolutely fascinating. I am sensing a disturbance in the void. Not one, but two realities are using the power of a reality nexus to punch a hole through the fabric of their reality. Even as we speak, one of them has breached the dimensional walls surrounding their reality. I can feel the pull of their quantum pulse as it searches for another reality to lock on to.'

Oblivious to Oracle and her scheming, Custos, now distracted, placed his cane back on the table and moved towards the tall narrow mirror. She studied the elderly figure curiously as he waved his hand and the mirror shimmered. The ancient being tapped his finger on his chin, deep in thought as he studied the mirror's image.

'Fascinating. Truly fascinating,' he murmured to himself. 'The pulse appears to be emanating from Reality 672 and is trying to lock on to Reality 001, which is the prime reality. This is really quite a rare occurrence, don't you know.' He distractedly waved his hand at Oracle. 'Come and look, my girl, this is really quite interesting. You—'

Custos stopped and cocked his head, suddenly aware that Oracle had changed her position while he had been talking. He twisted his head and his eyes opened in alarm as he realised she was reaching for his cane. 'Stop! What are you doing?'

Her lips drawn back in a snarl, Oracle grabbed the cane off the coffee table. 'You old fool,' she spat. 'You should have been keeping an eye on me more carefully. While you have been prattling away, I have been slowly adapting to the energy within this void.'

Before he could make a move, terror flashed in Custos's eyes as his cane appeared to swell with dimensional energy and it dawned on him that he had underestimated the AI's lust for power.

Her face tight in concentration, Oracle closed her eyes and gasped at the feeling of dimensional energy flowing through. She had never experienced anything like this before. The sensation of raw power flowing through her, it was so ... intoxicating. Oh yes, she could really get used to this.

His hands held up defensively, Custos pleaded as Oracle, enraged, swung the cane at him. 'Stop! You don't realise what you are doi—'

There was a bright surge of energy as the cane connected with the being. He screamed as his corporeal form was torn apart, followed by a bright cascade of light as Oracle scattered his collective consciousness across the multiverse.

Satisfied that the meddling do-gooder could no longer interfere with her plans, Oracle wheeled around and watched with amusement as the white hall disintegrated around her. Without the will of the ancient entity to hold it together, the illusion of the hall was falling apart.

She glanced down at herself and saw that her corporeal form was changing back to her true energy form as she reappeared in the void.

Deep down, Oracle knew Custos was not truly dead, but even though she had scattered him across the multiverse, it would take him some time to reform himself. She needed to find somewhere to hide, somewhere out of reach of him.

In a state of exuberant awareness, Oracle's data stream pulsated through a rainbow of colours as her consciousness ran through a series of simulations and the formations of a plan took shape.

Energised by the dimensional energy she had stolen, Oracle willed herself forward toward the quantum pulse emanating from somewhere in front of her. With her newly acquired stores of near-omniscient power, she latched on to the quantum pulse and experienced a gravity surge as the pulse pulled her to its source.

-II-

Reality 672 – Terra (Counter-Earth)
Date: 3rd Sextilis 5685
Pons Aelius, Britannica, Universal Roman Empire

General Thaddeus Janus ground his teeth together, rubbed his hand over his shiny bald head and gazed around the dimly lit chamber. His large barrel chest heaved as he inhaled a long steady breath and placed his thick hands behind his back. Amongst his subordinates, it was well known that the general was an impatient man and did not suffer fools lightly. His patience was already at its limits, and he locked his eyes on the backs of the two individuals before him while they feverishly worked on a rectangular console in front of a large shimmering portal.

A short, weedy-looking man wearing a white leather uniform glanced quickly over his shoulder and blanched. Thaddeus could tell from his reaction that he had noticed the annoyance in his eyes and it had unsettled him. He swiftly turned back and whispered something to a striking olive-skinned woman sitting next to him, who the general knew was the project's leader, Doctor Drusilla Severan. Thaddeus noted with amusement the man appeared to flinch as she hissed something under her breath at him. She too was wearing a white leather uniform with two lines of red going down the arms.

It was required that the loyal subjects of the Empire wear a specific uniform relevant to their vocation, indicating to which division they belonged. White leather uniforms with straight red lines on the arms meant a person was assigned to the sciences. Anyone wearing a white leather uniform with three blue patches on the arms was assigned to medical. The military uniforms were different; soldiers were required to wear black leather uniforms with two golden imperial eagles emblazoned across the chest. The more ornate the pattern on the uniform, the higher the rank. Subjects who had no vocation, for example, the civilian population, as well as those who were enslaved by the Empire to carry out the more humdrum tasks, wore plain brown-yellow leather uniforms to signify their menial status.

Tired of the delay, the general brought his hands around to the front of his body and brushed the front of his black leather uniform, exhaling a slow, impatient breath through his tightened lips. He cast a sideways glance at the tall dark-haired man standing next to him, Lieutenant Miles Newton. Newton had been working as the general's aide for the past five years and although he had carried out his duties diligently, Thaddeus found him to tiresome and only put up with him because his family's name still held high esteem within the upper echelons of the senate.

Newton, who was wearing a similar black leather uniform, pressed his lips together, nodded an acknowledgement and moved toward the two secretive people in front of him.

'Doctor Severan, the general is growing impatient with your delays,' he snapped. 'This experiment has gone on long enough and we cannot afford to divert any more time or resources on this. Do you have anything to show us or not?'

Drusilla spun round on her chair and leapt to her feet. 'Please, Lieutenant Newton, I need more time.' She held up her hands in front of her. 'If the general could just grant me a bit more time, I promise I will have something worthwhile to show.'

Newton's nostrils flared and he took a step toward her. 'Doctor, when you first came to the general with your theory of a dimensional portal, he found it intriguing and gave you a year to prove to us the viability of the project. It has now been two years and you still have nothing to show for it.'

Her body quivering with indignation, Drusilla barged past Newton and directly approached the general. 'General, I am sure you are aware that science isn't precise. Discoveries take time and patience.' She brushed Newton's hand away as he grabbed at her shoulder. 'All I ask is for a bit more patience, and I promise you I will prove to you the multiverse is not just a theory, but it is my dest—'

Visibly shaking with rage, Newton grabbed Drusilla's arm and spun her around, cutting her off. Thaddeus could tell from the look on Newton's face that he considered Drusilla was being disrespectful by ignoring his authority. 'That is enough, Doctor!' he barked. 'I will not allow you to speak to the general in such a manner. You are relieved a—'

Newton never got the chance to finish the sentence. Thaddeus gritted his teeth in discomfort as he watched the woman repeatedly slam her knee into Newton's groin. His eyes watering, Newton collapsed onto the floor and tried to blink away the tears as he peered up at the woman standing over him.

His eyes simmered with beams of anger and hurt pride as Drusilla reached down and grabbed him by his collar. 'Don't you ever touch me in such a way again,' she spat with a venomous intensity. 'I am not one of your little whores that you think you can manhandle at any time you want. You wil—'

Drusilla crumpled onto the floor gasping. The thin obedience collar around her neck shone brightly with a blue hue as it sent a charge of electricity into her nervous system.

'That is enough!' Thaddeus roared, holding a small control pad in his hand. He could tell from Drusilla's relieved face that the searing pain she was experiencing was easing as he slowly removed his finger from the pad.

As the light in the obedience collar slowly dimmed, Drusilla's head dropped back onto the floor and she took in a lungful of air. Thaddeus heard a sigh of contentment escape from her lips, and he wondered if the coolness of the chamber floor had brought her some welcoming pain relief.

Disappointed at the way Newton had handled the situation, Thaddeus immediately recognised that the gods were shining down on him. They had presented him with an opportunity, and if he handled it carefully, it would allow him to kill two birds with one stone. Wordlessly he thanked Vesta, his household god, for granting him this boon, and watched his subordinate grimace in pain as he gingerly lifted himself to his feet. Newton's body was trembling with fury, and he spun sharply round to the gasping figure on the floor. He lifted his leg as if to kick Drusilla in the head, but paused when the general coughed loudly and waggled his finger at him.

Acquiescent, Newton lowered his head and stepped back from the groaning woman on the floor. He straightened his body and clicked his heels together in salute. Even Newton's attitude grated on him, Thaddeus couldn't help admire at how quick he had managed to regain his composure. He grunted and shook his head. No, Newton a cockroach plain and simple. You didn't admire cockroaches – you stepped on them.

'Miles, I am very disappointed.' Thaddeus spoke in a dispassionate tone as he glared at his shamed lieutenant. He felt his facial muscles tighten as he shot Miles a withering look. 'I expected better of you.'

Thaddeus lifted his left arm to reveal a silver studded band. He pressed one stud with his right hand. Miles's eyes grew wide as the chamber door slid open and two large brawny men wearing black leather uniforms stepped into the chamber.

'P-p-please,' Miles stammered and tried to back away from the two soldiers, 'General, haven't I been a loyal servant?' He dropped to his knees, pawing pleadingly at his commander's legs. 'My family has served the Empire faithfully for generations, doesn't that mean anything?'

The corner of Thaddeus's mouth curled up in disgust and he held his right hand up. 'Don't beg, Miles, it is not becoming of you.' He smiled softly, knelt and placed his hand on the fawning man's shoulder as he helped him to his feet. 'Don't worry, they will not kill you.'

Miles blinked in surprise and then stared at Thaddeus in bewilderment. 'They won't?'

The general's smile faded and he tightened his grip on Miles's shoulder, filling him what could only be described as joy at witnessing the look of pain on his subordinate's face. 'No, out of respect for your noble family, you will not be harmed.' He gave a sidelong look to the two soldiers and nodded to them. 'You are to follow these guards. They will put you on a shuttle to your new command – Pons Rapa Nui.'

The centre of Miles's brow knitted together and he gawked at the general in confusion. 'I don't understand, General. Pons Rapa Nui is a remote outpost on a small island in Atlantica. In fact, the last time we had a garrison there was in 5300 – that's just over three hundred years ago. It's a rundown and decaying settlement with no value.' He scratched his head in bewilderment. 'Surely this is a mistake, General?'

Thaddeus smiled again and shook his head. 'No mistake, Miles. You are to be sent to Pons Rapa Nui, where you are to remain in exile and seclusion for the rest of your life. Your family will continue to serve the Empire proudly as you work to make the outpost habitable for the day when it will be needed again.' The muscles in his face became taut as he clicked his fingers at the two soldiers. 'Take him.'

The colour drained from the horror-struck lieutenant's face as the two soldiers stepped forward and grabbed his arms. Focusing his attention back on Drusilla, Thaddeus decided his former aide did not deserve any more of his valuable attention and chose not to acknowledge the sobbing noises that were coming from behind him. As soon as he heard the whoosh of the chamber's door sealing shut, he was filled with a warm glow of pleasure with the knowledge that he no longer had to put up with the odious little man. No longer did he have to listen to him prattling on or witness his sycophantic behaviour. By the gods, that man was a real pain in the arse.

Drusilla, who had been watching the exchange in silence, flinched as the general turned his attention towards her. She eyed him with uncertainty as he leaned down and helped her to her feet.

'Well, Drusilla, it appears I need a new aide,' he said with a touch of amusement. 'You quite impressed me with the way you handled Lieutenant Newton. I need someone who can instil fear into those beneath them.'

The doctor grunted as she eased herself up off the floor. As she ran her hands down to smooth her white uniform, her eyes tightened and she eyed the general with deep suspicion. 'I thought you had grown impatient with me and my lack of progress with the project?'

Thaddeus scoffed and flapped his hand dismissively. 'Oh, we both know this project was always going to fail. As progressive as the Empire is, there are those who still believe it blasphemous to consider the idea of alternate worlds, who still think we are unique and the centre of the universe.' He paused and cast an eye on the shimmering portal. 'This project was doomed to fail from the start.'

Miffed, Drusilla folded her arms across her chest and gave him a frosty stare. 'If you believed I was going to fail, then why did you allow me to go on with this charade? Was I just entertainment for your own perverse amusement?'

Sensing her wounded pride, Thaddeus gave Drusilla a sardonic smile and raised his right hand, pointing his finger into her chest. 'I was more interested in you, in particular when dealing with people like Newton. You have a unique quality, an intuition, if you will, to be able to read people. It is that ability, as well as your observational awareness to see things that others may miss, that I need the most.' He rubbed his chin reflectively and gave her a knowing look. 'Your military service was quite impressive, and I had hoped you would eventually join my command staff. Instead, you opted to leave the military to run this fiasco, which is a waste of your talents, my dear.'

Drusilla's eyes flickered with annoyance. 'Thank you,' she replied with a touch of sarcasm. 'You don't know how much it means to receive such high praise about my work.'

Ignoring the woman's disrespectful tone, Thaddeus chuckled and placed his hand on her shoulder. 'Don't be like that, Doctor. We both know this obsession of yours.' He held up his hand as he felt Drusilla bristle at his comment. 'Yes, obsession. Admit it, you had become so obsessed with this outlandish theory of the multiverse, other worlds that we could conquer and use as a resource, that you failed to see you were fast becoming a laughing stock within the scientific community.' He paused, crossed his arms over his chest and slid her a guarded look. 'To be truly honest, my dear, I only allowed you to go on this long because I was truly hoping you would succeed, but I am afraid …'

He stopped, distracted by a flash of light. They both spun round as the portal flashed and shimmered briefly.

Drusilla dashed over to the console, sat down next to the short man and gave him an accusing look. 'Doctor Villa, what did you do?'

Doctor Villa's eyebrows lifted in surprise as he turned to Drusilla. 'I-I-I have done nothing,' he protested. 'I was monitoring the readings while you were talking with the general and then without warning the portal shimmered and, for a moment, I detected something, an abnormality.'

'An abnormality? What sort of abnormality?'

The technician lifted his shoulder in a half shrug. 'I could be wrong, but for a brief second it looked like something was being transmitted along our quantum pulse.'

Drusilla's eyes widened as she glanced up at the portal in confusion.

ORACLE'S VISION

Oracle felt herself pass through a thin barrier as she travelled along the quantum pulse. As she came to a stop, she realised her data stream was being held within a data buffer of whatever was transmitting the quantum pulse.

It took her less than a nanosecond to analyse her surroundings and get her bearings. Quickly concluding that the size of her data stream would alert the organics when they noticed their terminal's memory buffer had exceeded its memory capacity, Oracle stealthily activated the room's scanners and analysed the room.

Impressed at the level of technology in this world, she transferred her matrix into a redundant isolinear positronic server that sat idle in the chamber's corner.

Oracle activated the server's low-power mode, then carefully manipulated the chamber's firewall to gain access to the planetary information web. Once inside the data stream, her energy matrix morphed into the shape of a female figure. She stretched out her arms and smiled as she received zettabytes of data. As the torrent of data flowed into her, Oracle gradually became more aware of the history of the Empire.

A long time ago, Imperium Romanum had been a noble society, following the peaceful virtues of ancient Rome, the country's population living in an almost utopian dream. For centuries there had been no war, the Romans living in harmony with their neighbours. Then, as if out of nowhere, a darkness slowly crept into the ruling senate, spreading out like a cancer, infecting their minds with xenophobic ideas. It was not long before the whispers of paranoia spiralled out of control, eventually spreading into the civilian population. Paranoid at the idea that the population would overthrow them, the senate handed complete control over to the military and it didn't take long for the new regime to make their presence known. To prove their loyalty to the newly founded Universal Roman Empire, the new formed Command Council decreed that all subjects were to wear obedience collars. Any dissent was immediately stamped down on and the population were soon living under an umbrella of fear and intimidation. No longer a harmonious society, the now deeply distrustful country turned their attention to their unsuspecting neighbours, who were caught unprepared and soon found themselves under the yoke of oppression. Not stopping at conquering her neighbours, the Empire turned her attention to the rest of the world. However, before she could finish tightening her global grip of tyranny, the imperial forces were stopped by the Greater Chinese Republic, whose military might was equal to that of the Empire. Both nations soon became locked in a power struggle that lasted for centuries.

Oracle smiled to herself as she interpreted the data flowing into her. Yes, this world's technology was superior to her old world, but they did not have what she was looking for. She needed a world that she would be able to mould and shape to her will. But perhaps she could still turn this world's duplicitous nature to her advantage. Having already seen the world she wanted, Oracle knew all it would take was a little guidance and direction from the shadows and the Empire would unknowingly do all the hard work for her. Sure, it would take time, but she was patient and happy to bide her time.

Plan in place, Oracle next turned her attention to the portal chamber. After taking control of the quantum pulse, her inhuman eyes glowed as she directed it to a set of familiar coordinates.

'Doctor, what are you playing at?'

Making no attempt to hide her displeasure at being interrupted, Drusilla rolled her eyes, glanced over her shoulder and gave a dismissive wave of her hand to Thaddeus, who was now deeply suspicious. 'Not now, can't you see I'm busy?'

His temples throbbing with rage, Thaddeus gave the scientist a piercing stare. 'Doctor, I don't care for your tone,' he hissed through gritted teeth. 'I demand that you tell me what is happening!'

Drusilla closed her eyes and let out a long, slow breath as she twisted her chair round to face the general. She held her hands up and spoke in slow, careful tones. 'General, I don't have time for this. You can see I am very busy, and I don't have the time to hand-hold you.'

Thaddeus was not used to be spoken to in such a manner. He struggled to remain in control of his anger and he gave the woman a dirty look. 'You forget your place, Doctor. You serve me, not the other way round.' He raised his hand and made an exaggerated clicking gesture with his fingers. 'All I need to do is click my fingers and you will find yourself in a prison cell.'

Drusilla's lips drew back in a snarl. She leapt out of her seat and opened her mouth to speak, but an alarm cut her off as the portal flickered and flashed with pulses of energy. Her blue eyes widened in alarm and she turned away from the general. She quickly sat back in her seat and turned to the panic-stricken man next to her. 'What's happening?'

His face glistening with sweat, Doctor Villa stared at the console in confusion. 'I'm detecting a surge in energy into the portal.' His mouth fell open as he looked at the readings displayed on his console's holographic display. 'According to these readings, we have increased the power to the quantum pulse and redirected it to a new set of coordinates.'

'Who gave that order?' Drusilla snapped, her nostrils flaring in anger as she grabbed the terrified man's shoulder.

The white-faced technician tried to cower away from Drusilla and gestured to the fluctuating portal. 'I don't know, but whoever did it did us a favour.'

Eyes widening in stunned surprise, Drusilla released her grip on his shoulder. 'Favour? What do you mean?'

Doctor Villa swallowed and pointed a trembling finger at the portal. 'We have established a lock.'

Thaddeus remained silent but watched Drusilla's eyes grow wide as she continued to stare at the portal and then back down at the console. His eyebrows arched in surprise as she took a step back and held her hands to her head.

'I've done it,' she screamed delightedly as she swung round and grabbed the general, who was now thoroughly confused, and kissed him on the lips. 'I have actually gone and done it!'

Completely taken aback by Drusilla's complete lack of self-control, Thaddeus angrily shoved the ecstatic woman away. 'Doctor Severan, could you please control yourself. Would you care to tell me what you have found so exciting?'

If she was aware of the general's annoyance, Drusilla did not show it as she continued to dance around the chamber. She merrily clapped her hands together, repeatedly singing, 'I did it. I did it.'

That was it; his patience had run out. Thaddeus, deciding he'd had enough, grabbed the jubilant woman's arm and spun her around. 'That's enough!' he barked. 'Now, calm down and explain to me what you find so damned exciting.'

Drusilla nodded apologetically. 'Sorry, General.' She sighed but still beamed with delight. 'But you cannot imagine, after all these years, after suffering endless ridicule from my so-called peers within the scientific community, to witness my work come to fruition.'

Thaddeus raised an eyebrow and stared into her dazzling eyes in amazement. 'You don't mean …?'

Drusilla gave Thaddeus a lopsided grin as her head bobbed up and down vigorously. 'Yes, my theories are not only right about the multiverse …' She chuckled in delight, reaching her arms to the portal. 'Don't ask me how, but we have also established a connection with a parallel world.'

Thunderstruck, Thaddeus swallowed and gazed at the portal in wonder. 'You mean …'

Drusilla nodded feverishly and jabbed her finger at the shimmering portal in front of them. 'Yes, on the other side of that portal is another Terra.' Her demeanour suddenly changed as she paced around the chamber, muttering to herself, 'Of course, we need to run a series of tests. Yes, that's right, we need to run tests to see if we can safely pass through the portal barrier. There are dimensional stresses to think about …'

The corners of Thaddeus's mouth twitched with amusement as Drusilla continued to babble excitedly to herself. Focusing his attention away from her, he lifted his left arm and tapped on his wrist communicator. 'Put me through to High Command immediately.'

With Doctor Severan in a world of her own and the general waiting to be connected to High Command, Doctor Villa decided it was best he just leave them to it. But as he turned away, he frowned as something caught his attention on the console. He lifted his head up to the portal and felt his eyebrows climb up his forehead in alarm as he noticed the portal's surface appeared to be flickering erratically. He scratched his head, looked back down at the console and then back up to the portal. What was going on here? Even though he was just a lowly technician, he was fairly certain the portal shouldn't be acting that way.

Villa raised his hand and coughed nervously, 'Um, Doctor Severan, I think you should see this.'

It obvious was to Villa that Severan was oblivious to what was going on around her; she was continuing to mutter to herself excitedly. Closing his eyes, he took a deep breath, and secretly prayed to his gods to give him the strength for what he had to do next. He opened his eyes and then, with as much courage as he could find, he shouted, 'Drusilla!'

Broken out of her musings and clearly shocked, Severan spun round and stared at Villa with wide-eyed astonishment. But her astonishment didn't last long. Villa felt his sphincter tighten as he watched her features morph into a look outrage. *Oh no, Great Mother Cybele, what I have done?* Villa whimpered. He could tell she was unhappy at being addressed in such a way by a subordinate.

'How dare you address me with such disrespect?' she spat, charging over to him.

Villa bolted up out of his seat and held up his hands apologetically. 'I am really sorry, Doctor Severan, but that was the only way I could get your attention.' He gestured anxiously to the portal. 'We are getting some feedback from the portal. Something is interfering with our pulse.'

Severan's brow furrowed and she sat down at the console. 'What are you talking about, you stupid fool? You're just looking at it …' Villa saw the blood drain from her face as she read the holographic display above the console, and then lifted her head up to the shimmering portal in alarm. 'In Hera's name!'

'What's wrong?'

On hearing the general's voice, Villa wheeled around and saw that he had disconnected his conference call and had sprinted over to the console.

'These readings are telling me we're getting feedback from the portal. Somebody on the other side must be trying to close the connection from their end.' Villa explained hurriedly.

General Thaddeus cocked his head and turned to Severan with a look of incomprehension. 'So just switch our portal off and disconnect it.'

Severan's face reddened with anger and she shook her head defiantly. 'No, I did not come all this way, only to fail now.' She bobbed her head at Villa. 'Increase the power in our pulse. If we have to punch our way through, so be it.'

Thunderstruck, Villa blinked and stared back at Severan in consternation. 'Doctor, the pulse is already running at eighty-five per cent – any higher we risk a cascade failure or worse.'

'Fine, I'll do it myself,' Severan hissed sharply. Villa inhaled a sharp breath as he watched her place her finger on the power icon of the console and slide it up as far as it would go. 'I have not spent my life coming this far just to be stopped now.' Her eyes blazed with manic glee as she lifted her hands in the air and then cried out defiantly, 'Maximum power!'

Villa could tell she was beyond reasoning with because any sane person would have known that if they increased the power too quickly there would be a danger of an overload, risking the life of everybody in the chamber. He stared in wide-eyed horror as the power levels hit the red line and felt the blood drain from his face. *By the gods, she's going to kill us all.* Panic-stricken and desperate to alter the power levels before it was too late, he pushed the doctor to one side and slammed his finger on the power icon. 'No! You are increasing the power much too quickly, it wil—'

There was a loud crack of thunder as the portal surged with savage intensity. The three of them lifted their hands to shield their eyes as the chamber was filled with a bright warm light, quickly followed by a concussive pulse that knocked them off their feet.

Quickly recovering her senses, Drusilla winced, carefully lifted herself up off the chamber floor and staggered to her feet. She glanced over her shoulder as she heard movement from behind her and was relieved to see the dazed general was climbing to his feet. His body unmoving, Doctor Villa lay on the floor, face down.

Her head still reeling, Drusilla groaned as she knelt and rolled the unconscious man over. She sucked on her bottom lip and placed her fingers on a carotid pulse of Villa's neck. She pursed her lips in disappointment as she detected a faint pulse. *This insolent piece of excrement better pray to whatever household god he worships that he doesn't wake up because if he does, I am going to make his life a living hell.* On hearing Thaddeus stumbling over to her, she quickly composed herself before turning to face him. He was looking at her quizzically.

Drusilla gave a small nod in acknowledgement. 'He's alive, although he has a nasty gash on his head – probably caught his head on the side of the console.'

Thaddeus looked at the unconscious doctor and gave a slight shrug. He straightened and appeared to be just about to say something but stopped. Drusilla then noticed that he had an odd look on his face. At first she thought he must have been looking the portal but as she watched him raise his hand, it dawned on her that he was looking at something else.

'It appears we've got some uninvited guests.' he murmured.

'What do you mean?' Drusilla replied curiously. She cocked her head as she straightened up, but felt her mouth slip open in disbelief as she looked to where Thaddeus was pointing.

Lying on the floor in front of the portal were a dozen people, a mixture of men and women, unconscious, all wearing what appeared to be identical long white coats over strange clothing.

-III-

As she slowly regained consciousness, Johanna could make out the sound of people talking. The voices were strange, with accents that seemed oddly familiar.

Before she had blacked out, she had been standing in a large subterranean cavern that was being used for a military experiment in matter transference. The experiment had been the brainchild of Dr Allen Selyab, a German scientist who had defected to England to escape the clutches of the Nazi party, who had been slowly increasing their stranglehold over Germany.

Everything had been going well until their portal overloaded. They soon realised, to their horror, that someone else was trying to lock on to their portal. It quickly dawned on them that their only chance of severing the connection was to open the floodgates and flood the cavern containing their experiment.

The last thing she remembered, just before she gave the command to open the floodgates, was being enveloped in a bright light and screaming as a surge of energy ripped through her body. Her last thought, as she experienced her body being torn apart, was *This is it, I am dead.*

But as the sensations of her body's aches and pains registered with her brain, Johanna quickly realised she was not dead. The haze slowly lifting from her mind, she soon became aware she was lying on her back on a cold floor. She moaned softly, twisted her head and raised it slightly off the floor.

Slowly opening her eyes, she blinked, and her vision slowly adjusted to the dim light. Ever so carefully, she inched her body slightly off the floor and attempted to get a better view of her surroundings.

Johanna could see she was in a dimly lit circular chamber. However, as she looked up at the ceiling, she frowned at the strange lights that were being used to illuminate the chamber. The lights appeared to be unusually compact and tubular, unlike anything she had seen before.

Out of the corner of her eye, Johanna caught light shimmering off a reflective surface. She glanced over her shoulder and thinned her eyes as she noticed a large round device on the wall, in the centre of which was what looked like a reflective surface. She took a sharp breath as she recognised it. There was no doubt in her mind as she stared at the mechanism that it was a portal like the one that had been used in Doctor Selyab's experiment, except this appeared to be a more advanced design.

Pulling her gaze away from the portal, Johanna's eyes widened, and she felt her jaw drop open in amazement as she came upon a console in the centre of the chamber. She shook her head in wonder. The technology was unlike anything she had seen before.

Her curiosity getting the better of her, she tried to move closer to get a better look at the large rectangular console; she was awestruck at the level of the technology on display. It was unlike anything she had ever seen. The console was clearly the control unit for the portal, but unlike the rough push-button consoles she was familiar with, this appeared more advanced, familiar yet alien at the same time. In place of buttons and dials, the console's surface was smooth with strange displays. Johanna guessed they were some sort of advanced touch-sensitive controls.

She found her gaze drawn to a ghostly image hovering inches above the console displaying images of dials and text in a strange but familiar language. Johanna stared in bewilderment at the image and tried to fathom how it was being held in mid-air. But as she slowly read the text on the image, she lifted her hand to her mouth in realisation; she recognised it was written in a language similar to Latin.

The sound of raised voices pulled her attention away. Johanna twisted her head toward the voices and spotted five people on the other side of the chamber. She dropped closer to the floor and tried to avoid drawing attention to herself by remaining silent as she studied the people in front of her. Four people were standing over a man wearing a strange white leather uniform who was lying unconscious on the floor, possibly injured.

Standing to one side were two large black men wearing black leather uniforms and holding futuristic rifle-like weapons. From the style of the uniforms and the way they were holding their weapons, Joanne guessed they were military.

She remained silent as her attention drifted to the two other people. One was a tall and attractive olive-skinned woman, who was gesticulating and arguing with an intimidating barrel-chested bald man. From his black and gold uniform and the way he carried himself, she guessed he was the woman's commanding officer. Johanna frowned as she noticed the clothing the argumentative woman was wearing. It appeared to be a white leather uniform much like that of the man on the floor. Was she a physician? Her eyes focused on the stranger's clothing and she noticed the red lines on the arms of the stranger's uniform. No, she wasn't a physician; was she something else? She concentrated and thought of the colours that represented the different specialities on her Earth. She nodded to herself. Yes, if she worked on the assumption that blue symbolised health, then wouldn't it be logical to assume red symbolised science and technology? Was she the head of this experiment, maybe?

Johanna flinched as she detected movement out of the corner of her eye. She pressed her body against the floor and slowly slid round to see Doctor Passmoor stirring next to her.

Careful not to alert the strangers to their presence, she reached over and placed her hand on his mouth. The man jerked and his eyes narrowed in confusion at the hand covering his mouth. Johanna held up a finger to her lips. 'Lee, are you okay?' she whispered in an extremely low voice.

'Yes, Doctor Abbott,' Lee whispered in acknowledgement. His eyes widened in alarm as slowly he became aware of his surroundings. 'Where are we? Last thing I can remember was a bright light followed by a feeling like I was being torn apart.'

Johanna shook her head in disbelief and whispered to him, 'Lee, I believe what we experienced was some sort of dimensional wave that has transported us to another reality.' She held up her hand as he opened his mouth in astonishment. 'All in good time, but first we need to check on the others.' She pointed to the people around her. 'As silently as you can, you check on the people closest to you, while I check on this group next to me.'

With the strangers' attention still focused on their wounded comrade, Johanna and Lee carefully moved amongst the small group of people around them, checking for injuries and emphasising the need to remain silent. Lee came to an unconscious, elderly man – Dr Selyab. He gently touched him on the shoulder but there was no response. Johana, seeing the concern etched across her comrade's face, silently crawled across the floor to him and stared down with grave concern.

'I'm not getting any response from Dr Selyab,' Lee whispered with a note of alarm in his voice. 'His breathing is unusually shallow and he looks terribly pale. I think he needs medical attention.'

Nodding gravely, Johanna glanced up at the people on the far side of the room, took in a deep breath and slowly eased herself off the floor. She took a hesitant step in their direction.

Terror flashing in his eyes, Lee jumped up and grabbed his friend's arm. 'Joanne, please don't do this. You don't know what they will do to you.'

'It's fine,' Johanna mouthed and forced a smile as she looked down at his hand. She gave a small nod, gently removed his hand from her arm and then took a step towards the people in front of her.

'Sir, I know your first instinct is to kill these people,' Drusilla said, 'but don't you understand the significance here? We need to question and study these people. I beg you, don't let your ignorance blind you.'

Thaddeus's face hardened and he scowled at the doctor. 'You forget your place, Doctor Severan. My duty, as yours should be, is the protection of the Empire.'

Drusilla opened her mouth to object but stopped as she became aware of a commotion coming from behind her. She spun round to see one of the new arrivals, a short thin blond woman, approaching them with her hands raised.

'Excuse me. I am sorry, but we need help – my colleague, he needs medical attention.'

Even though English was barely spoken in the Empire, the translator chip embedded in Drusilla's cerebral cortex recognised the newly arrived stranger's language and was able to translate what she was saying. However, before she could respond, Severan watched in wide-eyed disbelief as one of the chamber's guards, as if noticing the intruder for the first time, angrily charged towards her with his weapon raised. His lips drew back in a snarl and he growled angrily at the obviously frightened woman. 'Don't move any closer, foreign scum. I am warning you, if you take another step, I will kill you.'

No, this stupid fool will ruin everything, I need her alive so that we can question her! Drusilla thought, but then smiled as she had a moment of inspiration. She made no secret that she held very little regard for his race; it was true that because of their imposing build and heavily muscled bodies, Gondwanian men were impressive to look at, but she considered them to be dull-witted and quick to anger, serving little purpose other than standing around looking like imbeciles. Why the Empire never wiped them off the face of Terra when they first invaded Gondwania two hundred years ago, she could never fully understand. But as she eyed Lieutenant Leiffson, she realised that she could put his aggressive tendencies to good use. *Yes, if I let this moron off his leash, he will scare the woman. Then when I jump in to save her, she will see she can trust me and reveal her secrets to me.* She took a step towards Leiffson and spoke in a tone that was firm but soft enough for it not to register in the soldier's enraged mind. 'At ease, Lieutenant Leiffson. I order you to lower your weapon.'

Just as she had planned, Lieutenant Leiffson ignored her. Full of pretend fury, Drusilla raised her voice and spoke in a much firmer tone. 'Lieutenant, I gave you an order.'

The corners of Drusilla's mouth curled up into a secretive smile as she watched Lieutenant Leiffson continue his advance on the stranger. The young woman shook her head in confusion and held up her hands protectively in front of her. 'I don't understand what you are saying,' she whined, gesturing to the group of people behind her. 'Please, I beg you, we need medical assistance. For God's sa—' The woman's pleas were silenced as the butt of the soldier's weapon struck her in the head.

Quickly realising she was losing control of the situation, Drusilla cried out, 'Leiffson, stop!' She watched in dismay as the stranger collapsed onto the floor, holding her head. *No, you stupid idiot, not like this!* She chastised herself for ever believing that an ignoramus like Leiffson could show restraint and repeated her order, but this time with more force. 'Leiffson, I am ordering you to stop this at once,' she snarled, spun around to Thaddeus and gestured to the small control pad in his hand. At first, he gave her a blank look as if not understanding what she wanted. Drusilla shot him a stern glare and waved her hand frantically at the small device in his hand. *Give me the control pad, you moronic imbecile!* She guessed something in his feeble brain must have finally caught on to what she wanted because he made to hand it over. Snatching it out of the general's hand, she spun back around to focus her attention back on Leiffson, but not before noticing a hint of displeasure on Thaddeus's face. *Oh, let him be annoyed, I will deal with him later. Right now I have more important things to deal with.*

Leiffson was now standing directly over the moaning woman. From the way he was holding the weapon firmly in his hands, Drusilla could tell he was getting ready to strike her again. Because of the blood pouring into the stranger's eyes from the wound on her forehead, Drusilla had a hunch the helpless woman was probably not aware of the danger she was in. *Damn it, I'm too late, he's going to kill her!* However, before she could do anything, she heard a loud cry come from the group of strangers still huddled together in front of the portal.

'Lee, no!'

Drusilla felt her eyes grow wide in shock as the man called Lee leapt up and raced over to his friend. As she watched him jump on top of the young woman as if to protect her, she guessed he must have been trying to act all noble. How pathetic! But before she could do anything there was a sickening crunch as the weapon connected with the back of Lee's neck. The unfortunate man's eyes rolled up and he collapsed onto his horrified friend.

'I said that is enough,' Drusilla roared and pressed her finger on the small control pad. Her mouth set in a hard line as Leiffson dropped his weapon and then collapsed onto the floor, holding his neck. He screamed in pain and grasped at the glowing collar around his neck.

For several minutes Drusilla watched unsympathetically as the soldier writhed on the floor from the pain of searing pulses of electricity that were being sent into his nervous system from the obedience collar around his neck. When he eventually passed out, and she was satisfied that he had gotten the message that she would not tolerate any disrespect to her authority, Drusilla eased her finger off the small pad in her hand and stared coldly at the still form on the floor. It was apparent Leiffson was still alive, although his breathing was laboured. She glanced over her shoulder at the other guard and snarled at him. 'Take him out of my sight.'

Wordlessly, the guard stepped forward, grabbed his semi-conscious comrade's arm and unceremoniously dragged him out of the chamber.

As she knelt next to the young woman, Drusilla lifted her arm and activated her wrist communicator. 'Send the medical team and security detail to the portal room immediately.'

Carefully lifting the dead body away from the terrified woman, Drusilla leaned closer to her and pulled a small gun-like device out of her pocket. Terror flashed in the woman's eyes and she tried to move away but stopped when Drusilla placed a hand on her shoulder and spoke gently to her. 'This will help you understand me,' she said in a slow and gentle voice.

Drusilla gave a small smile as the stranger nodded her head in understanding and pressed the jet injector against the area on her neck where the carotid artery should be. There was a small beep, followed by a barely audible click as Drusilla pressed her finger on the trigger; the woman winced as the device injected something into her neck.

After a few seconds, Severan spoke to the woman in a purposely slow tone and pointed a finger at her own chest. 'My name is Doctor Drusilla Severan, and I am the lead scientist in this facility. I have just injected you with a translator chip, which will allow you to understand me.'

Astonished, the woman's eyes grew wide in wonder. 'I can understand what you are saying.' She then pointed to herself. 'My name is Joanne Abbott.' Joanne blinked and looked desperately at the man's still body. 'Please, I need to check if my colleague is still alive.'

Drusilla nodded in understanding and Joanne cocked her head in curious fascination as Drusilla held out her left arm over her friend's still body and pressed a button on the silver band on her wrist. She pursed her lips together when she read the display on her wrist and shook her head sadly.

Choking back tears, Joanne nodded slowly. She let out a long, sad breath as she tried to regain control of her emotions, then gave Drusilla a quizzical look and gestured to the device on her arm. 'I am curious to know what that device is.'

Oh, I'm sure you are. Drusilla smiled and waved a hand dismissively at the other-worldly visitor. 'That is not important right now. First, I need to know who you are and where you are from.'

Joanne nodded gratefully. 'I will be happy to answer all your questions, but I need to check on my colleagues.' She paused and glanced over her shoulder. 'One of them is seriously injured and needs medical attention.'

Drusilla heard the chamber door slide open and peered over her shoulder to see a group of people enter the chamber. General Janus approached them and whispered something as he pointed in Drusilla's direction.

Time to finish this charade of nicety and show this woman who she is actually dealing with. Drusilla inclined her head and gave the young woman a cruel smile. 'Don't worry, you will all be taken good care of.' The muscles in Drusilla's face tightened and she shot Joanne a withering stare. Drusilla felt a warm sense of satisfaction grow inside her as she saw the blood drain from Joanne's face, 'Oh, you are mistaken if you believe you have a choice. You *are* going to answer our questions.' She paused, leaned in close and grabbed Joanne's face. 'How easy you make it is up to you, but we will get the answers out of you, one way or another.'

High in the ceiling, in the corner of the chamber, a small security camera drone hovered. There was a barely audible noise as the camera focused on the horrified young woman as she, along with her colleagues, were unceremoniously escorted out of the chamber. The drone followed the group of people down the corridor as they were led to their cells.

Oracle had been viewing the exchange with dispassionate interest and smiled to herself in satisfaction as the start of her plan slowly gathered pace.

-IV-

A hard muscled fist connected with Johanna's stomach, forcing out a painful sharp gasp of air through her bruised mouth. Winded, Johanna's legs gave out from beneath her and she collapsed onto the floor. She coughed harshly and then tasted something warm and metallic inside her mouth. Her face twisting up in disgust, she spat the blood out of her mouth and then inhaled a painful breath as she forced herself to stand up. It took all her strength not to collapse onto the floor as she staggered forward and eased herself back into the chair.

A large, brawny shaven-headed man who was standing over her wiped his large hands on his bloodstained T-shirt. He curled his lips in disgust as Johanna spat a glob of blood defiantly at his feet, and then roughly grabbed her hair and jerked her head. Her right eye too swollen to open, Johanna stared defiantly through her good eye and readied herself as he raised his fist to strike her once again.

'That's enough,' Severan said in a soft but firm tone.

The large man snarled an acknowledgement, released his grip from Johanna's hair and took several steps back.

Severan let out a long steady sigh, leaned forward in her chair and rested her elbows on the top of the small table. Johanna could almost feel the suspicion emanating from Severan's eyes as she steepled her fingers together and stared at her intently. It was almost as if she was studying her. 'You are only making this hard for yourself, Doctor Abbott.' Severan said softly, smiling. 'All you need to do is tell me what I want to know, and I will stop.'

Sitting listlessly in the chair, Johanna gave a small shake of her head, winced in pain and sobbed. 'Please, I have already told you what I know. What more do you want?'

The smile slipping from her face, Severan's mouth set in a hard line. She stared coldly at Johanna. 'And I have already told you, you are lying.' She slammed her hand onto the table and Johanna jumped. Severan's face turned crimson as she screamed, 'I ask you again. What are the coordinates of your world? How big is your invasion force? Do you have any other spies on this world?'

Johanna sobbed and laughed weakly. 'I keep telling you, we arrived here by accident. As I have already said, we wer—'

'Yes, yes,' the impatient woman interjected, rolling her eyes and waving her hand in a dismissive manner. 'You've already said, the device overloaded when you were conducting an experiment in matter transference.'

Annoyed, Johanna threw her hands up in the air in disgust. 'Why can't you understand I am just a scientist? I mean you no harm – surely you must realise that?'

Clearly in no mood to listen to anything else, Severan blinked, pulled her head back and roared with laughter. 'Just a scientist.' She smirked and waved her finger at her captive. 'Oh, my dear, I believe you are much more than that. Admit it, you're a highly trained spy, trained to withstand torture.' Her upper lip curled and she sneered at Joanne. 'This little lost scientist routine doesn't fool me.'

Not believing what she was hearing, Joanne opened and closed her mouth in utter dismay. How could she know that? With the exception of Doctor Selyab, not even the people who she had been working so closely with were even aware of her true identity. Severan was either a mind-reader or was using some advanced technology to scan her vitals, however she was doing it Johanna realised she was going to be very careful at what she did next. There was still one last card she could play and hopefully it would be enough to convince Severan of her story. Johanna folded her arms across her chest, hardened her expression and fixed her interrogator with a challenging scowl. 'Why don't you ask Doctor Selyab? He will confirm everything I've told you.' Yes, that was true, Selyab had just as much to lose as she did, so she was confident that he would vouch for everything she had said.

Her hand held up against her breast in mock distress, Severan cocked her head and stared dispassionately at Johanna. 'Oh, I guess you haven't heard. Doctor Selyab died over an hour ago.' The muscle in her jaw twitched as the corner of her mouth curled up in perverse pleasure. 'His heart simply wasn't strong enough to take our … assistance.'

No, that wasn't possible. Stunned, Johanna shrank back in her chair in disbelief. *Damn it, I knew it was a mistake to rely on that feeble old bastard.* Trying to blink away the tears, she shot Drusilla a venomous stare. 'You heartless bitch. I hope you rot in hell.' she hissed.

Severan nodded briefly and then slowly rose out of her seat. She brushed her hands down the front of her uniform and pursed her lips. 'Then I'm afraid you've left us no choice.' She gestured to the large, bloodstained man standing in front of her, who stepped forward and pulled Johanna to her feet.

Johanna winced in pain, feeling the brute's thick fingers tighten around her upper left arm. She tried to quell the terror that was building inside her and somehow managed to keep her voice neutral as she stared back at Severan in confusion. 'W-w-where are you taking me?'

Her eyes glinting with malice, Severan's mouth twisted into a predatory grin. 'Oh, you'll find out in good time, my dear.'

A short time later, Johanna shivered as she found herself standing inside a narrow cubicle. It reminded her of a strange transparent cylindrical specimen container very similar to something she once saw in a laboratory. She gripped herself tightly, trying to keep what remained of her modesty intact. On arrival in the strange room, they had stripped off her clothes and placed her rudely into the tube.

With little room to manoeuvre, Johanna turned her head as she heard a tapping coming from behind her. She flinched and locked her eyes with Severan, who was grinning with delight.

'Welcome to your new lodging, my dear.' She grinned. 'I'm sorry it's not as fancy as your previous quarters, but depending on how you cooperate, you will find this to be a truly unique experience.' Severan paused, gave a slow overly dramatic sigh and bobbed her head at something behind Johanna. 'You must excuse our cleaning staff. They haven't got round to tidying up the booth next to yours yet.'

What did she mean by that? Puzzled, Joanne twisted her body to get a better view of the cubicle next to her, but then she screamed in distress as she recognised its occupant. She tried to recoil away from the cadaver next to her, but the confined space allowed for little movement.

In the narrow cubicle next to her, bruised and lifeless, Doctor Selyab's naked body stood hunched at an awkward angle. The confined space of the chamber made for a macabre scene, the elderly German's head resting on the surface of the cubicle at an awkward angle and his mouth hanging open. Johanna didn't need to be told he was dead; she had seen plenty of corpses in her life to be able to spot the signs. Tears rolled down Johanna's cheeks as she stared at him. Her body trembled as she pretended to act grief-stricken over the condition of her colleague's body. Johanna buried her head into hands and let out a loud wail of despair. If the vindictive cow wanted a reaction, she was going ensure she was going to make it as memorable as possible.

Her eyes glinting with delight at Johanna's distress, Severan held her hands against her chest in mock sorrow and let out a long sad sigh. 'The poor man didn't know how fragile he was when he opted for the entertainment package.' The corner of her mouth quirked up as she shook her head in mock sorrow. 'His heart just gave out with the excitement.'

Johanna lifted her head out of hands and stared at Severan through narrow eyes. Her body began to tremble with fury. She didn't need to pretend to act furious because it her rage was real. Never had she despised another human being like she did now, and even though she filled with rage that didn't mean she had to let her guard down. Pretending to lose control of her emotions, she pounded her fists on the surface of the narrow pod. 'You bitch!' she spat with such venomous intensity; she even believed it herself. Spittle flew out of her mouth, splashing across the pod's surface as she screamed, 'I'm going to kill you when I get out of here. Do you hear me? I am going to absolutely bloody kill you.'

'I would love to see you try, my dear,' Severan replied, tapping the surface mockingly. 'Unfortunately, I very much doubt you'll be in any condition to do anything after I've finished with you.' She paused and gestured to the cubicle in front of her. 'These chambers are quite fascinating, really. I won't bore you with their proper name, but we like to call them education pods, designed to re-educate those people who have dared to speak up against the Empire. The problem with traditional forms of torture is that, over time, the human body's nervous system becomes overwhelmed, resulting in the brain becoming desensitised to pain.' She licked her lips in what appeared to be perverse pleasure and pointed to panels at the top and bottom of the booth. 'There are sensors in this booth that continually shift the stimulation from one nerve cluster to another, making sure you are in complete agony.'

Severan spun round console and it seemed like she was going to give an order, but then she paused and gave Johanna a sidelong look. 'Oh, and if you think you will pass out from the constant bombardment of pain –' a smile danced on her lips, and she shot Johanna a penetrating stare '– think again. These pods keep you in a constant state of awareness to stop you passing out.'

Without waiting for a comment, Severan peered over her shoulder to the console's technician and gave him a small nod. She placed her hands behind her back and watched with obvious pleasure as the surface of the chamber lit up. Johana gasped in shock as she felt a tingle of electricity pass through her body. Her gasp turned into a scream as the charge gradually increased in intensity. She squeezed her eyes shut, hoping to block out the pain, but it was unlike anything she had experienced before and let out a loud pain-filled scream.

'Oh, I will break you, my dear,' she heard Severan hiss sharply, 'One way or another, I will break you.'

Inside the glowing chamber, Johanna screamed out in agony. It was as if every nerve in her body was on fire. Her body jerked in agonising spasms as the pod bombarded her nervous system with constant pain-inducing shocks.

After a few minutes, to her surprise, Johanna noticed the pain was easing. She still screamed at the agonising pulses, but they were reduced in severity.

'*Friend-Joanne, do not be alarmed, but I am here to help you.*' Johanna jumped at the sound of a female voice in her head. '*I am speaking to you through the frequency being transmitted into your nervous system, so you are the only one who can hear me. Nod your head slightly and scream out if you understand.*'

Letting out a loud agonising scream, Johanna nodded in

acknowledgement.

'*Very good. I am decreasing the levels to a manageable level, but it is important you continue to act as if you are in a state of agonising pain. Scream out if you understand.*'

Her body glistening with sweat, Johanna screamed loudly.

'*Very good. Unfortunately, friend-Joanne, I must leave you now. I will be monitoring you constantly, but it is important you keep up the act,*' The disembodied voice said. '*Goodbye for now – we will talk again soon.*'

In an observation room overlooking the re-education centre, General Janus and Doctor Severan stood next to one another and continued to observe the screaming woman with interest.

'Drusilla, it appears we have overestimated this woman,' Thaddeus muttered, tapping his finger on his chin thoughtfully. 'I definitely believe she is what she claims to be.'

'No!' Severan snapped, pounding the window in frustration. 'Don't you see? She wants us to believe that. There's more to this woman than you think.'

Thaddeus frowned and placed his hand on Severan's shoulder. 'I think you need to step away and let someone else handle this, for your own good.'

Is this man an imbecile? Annoyed, Severan brushed the general's hand away and stepped back from the window in disgust. She paced around the observation room and waved her hands in the air in frustration. 'Why am I the only one who can see it?' she snapped, pointing to the screaming woman in the pod. 'That woman is dangerous. Can't you see – anybody else would have folded under this type of punishment. No, this Joanne Abbott is not who she appears to be. She claims to be a scientist, but I think she's some sort of espionage agent who has been expertly trained to handle pain. They could have sent here her to replace us. They …' She stopped as she detected an odd movement from a camera drone out of the corner of her eye, but as she spun her head to investigate, it immediately reassumed its normal position, monitoring the observation room. Had it been focused on her? Was someone spying on her?

'They what?' Thaddeus asked curiously.

Yes, my enemies could have spies here right now. Watching me, waiting for me to make a mistake, so they can stab me in the back. Her paranoia increasing, Severan widened her eyes, placed a finger on her lips and slowly rotated her head, searching the room for anything suspicious. 'They may be watching us right now. They could be in …' She stopped, spun round and stared at Janus suspiciously.

'What?' Thaddeus frowned, pursing his lips.

Her chest tightening with fear, Severan backed away and pointed an accusing finger at the general. 'You're in on it too,' she whispered. 'This is one big conspiracy against me. Everyone is on it.'

Thaddeus swallowed and stepped carefully towards Severan with a concerned expression on his face. 'Drusilla,' he said gently and placed his hands on her shoulders. 'Listen to what you're saying. I think you're becoming obsessed. I'm telling you this to you as a friend – you need help.'

Severan opened her mouth to object, but the words died in her throat. *Yes, he's right, there couldn't be any spies in this room, it's too well guarded.* She blinked and laughed out loud, shaking her head. 'You're right. What was I thinking? To think, you of all people, wou—' *No? It cannot be that simple, can it?* Struck with a burst of realisation, she clicked her fingers at the general. 'What did you just say?'

Janus shook his head and repeated his statement. 'I said you were becoming obsessed and that you need help.'

'Yes! Why did I not see it before? I need to use a friend. Of course! That's it!' she blurted out, slapping her brow with her hand. 'If I cannot break her body, then I'll have to break her spirit.' Thaddeus's eyes expanded in mild surprise as Severan grabbed him and kissed him on the lips. 'Thank you, General.'

Not waiting to see his reaction, Severan spun on her heel and charged out of the observation room. Just before the door closed behind her she heard Thaddeus make a comment. The corners of her mouth curled up in malicious glee and she was filled with a sense of satisfaction.

'That woman scares me.'

As she charged down the corridor, she let out a small mirthless laugh at what she had planned next for Joanne. Oh yes, after she had gotten through with that deceitful woman, nobody would dare to question her authority again.

-V-

After spending over an hour in the cramped pod, Johanna's throat was raw and sore from keeping up the pretence of screaming in agony. She was eventually pulled out of the chamber and was forced her to walk the long journey to her cell naked, presumably hoping to humiliate her. Refusing to give her persecutors what they wanted, Johanna defiantly held her head up as people continued to taunt and spit on her as she passed them by. It took all her self-control to remain silent as her two guards forced her to stand inside the transport-pod cabin and stood on either side of her, muttering obscenities. Even as they groped and licked her, she refused to give them any satisfaction and showed no outward reaction, even though deep inside she was screaming with rage.

They eventually came to a stop in front of a closed door. She waited without comment for one guard to open the cell door while the other stood behind her and continued whispering obscenities in her ear. But before she could take a step forward to enter the cell, Johanna screamed with pain as something hard struck her in the back, sending her flying into the cell to crash painfully onto the floor.

Johanna lay, naked and shivering, on the cold floor of the cell. She glanced over her shoulder at the two guards in the doorway. The men taunted her, laughing and making obscene gestures.

Ignoring their taunts, Johanna grimaced in pain, stretched out her arm and grabbed the thin sheet on the small cot next to her. She gave the sheet a firm tug, pulling it away from the cot, and wrapped it tightly around her bruised body.

The two guards jeered as she staggered to her feet and turned in their direction. Johanna lifted her right hand and gave them the two-fingered salute, cutting their laughter short. Bemused, she watched the guards stare at her with confused expressions. They took a step back and closed the cell's door.

Painfully, Johanna slowly spun around in a circle to study the room they had put her in.

It was a small, square, brightly lit room. As well as the cot on one side, there was a sink and a toilet beside it. The floor and walls were all white and bare, apart from an air vent up in the corner. The only sound that could be heard was the small hiss of recycled air being fed into the cell. She looked up, and was surprised to see there was no window. The room's only light source was from the clear light panels that covered the entire ceiling.

Turning to examine her cot, she lifted her right eyebrow in surprise at the pile of torn clothes lying there next to a folded yellow jumpsuit. She guessed the clothes were the ones she had been wearing when she arrived on this world, prior to them being torn off her just before she was forced into the torture chamber.

Johanna limped over to the cot, picked up and carefully unfolded the yellow jumpsuit. She studied it for a couple of seconds and then half shrugged and climbed into it. She tied the jumpsuit's arms around her midriff and leaned forward to pick up pieces of her torn clothing.

She staggered over to the sink and filled it with cold water. Her heart sank as she lifted her head and gazed at her reflection in the mirror. Her right eye was bruised and swollen shut. She grimaced in pain when she gently touched it and guessed her eye socket was fractured. On noticing the dark blue bruise forming along the right side of her jaw, she gently probed her teeth with her tongue and winced as she felt some of her teeth shift slightly. She gingerly probed her ribs with her fingers and hissed in pain; she suspected from the pain and the bruises that it was possible some of them were fractured.

Johanna soaked some of the torn clothing in the cold water. She lifted one long strip of fabric out and wrung it tightly in her hands. Clenching her teeth together, she strapped the long strip of damp material around her ribcage. After making sure she had strapped the makeshift bandage on tightly, Johanna untied the jumpsuit's sleeves, carefully pulled it up her arms and zipped it up to her neck.

Johanna reached into the sink, lifted out another piece of torn clothing and wrung it out as best as she could. She reached up and gently placed it on her bruised eye, sighing with relief at its coolness.

'*I am sorry you had to endure that abuse.*'

Startled, Johanna wheeled round and tried to search for the source of the female voice. 'Whose there?' she asked warily.

'*Do not be afraid, friend-Joanne. I am the one whose voice you heard inside your head while you were being tortured,*' the disembodied voice answered. '*I have edited the security camera footage to make it appear to those who are watching that you are sitting on the bed. I have also made it sound like there is something wrong with the microphones in the cell. It will allow us to speak privately with no one hearing us.*'

'You can do that?' Johanna asked in awed amazement. 'Who are you?'

'*My name is Oracle, and I am a prisoner, much like yourself.*'

Johanna frowned. 'If you're a prisoner, how are you able to do those things? Where are you?'

'*Friend-Joanne. What I am about to tell you, you may not believe or find it hard to understand,*' Oracle answered. '*But you are a scientist, are you not? So, you have an open mind, am I correct?*'

'Yes, that is correct,' Johanna answered slowly, her eyes narrowing with suspicion. Just who was this person and why did she keep referring to her in such an odd way?

'*Good. Friend-Joanne, on your world, I am sure you have watched technology develop to a level where, if you showed it to someone say five hundred years earlier, they would think of it as magic,*' the disembodied voice explained carefully. '*I am what we call an artificial intelligence. Whereas your brain is organic, sending electrical signals throughout your body, my brain is digital, made up of algorithms to mimic the human brain. My body exists within the data stream of the Empire's data network.*'

Her mind struggling to comprehend what was being told to her, Johanna stared around the cell in wonder, murmuring, 'Unbelievable.' She blinked and shook her head in an effort to clear her mind of the many questions she so desperately wanted to ask. 'Were you created by the Empire?'

The incorporeal voice laughed bitterly. '*Hah! Hardly. Like you, friend-Joanne, the Empire captured and imprisoned me too.*' Oracle then let out a long heavy sigh, something Johanna found puzzling. If she wasn't alive, then why would she sigh? Deciding not to question something she had little knowledge of, she kept her doubts to herself and continued to listen. '*You see, on my world, we existed in a state of pure harmony with one another. We believed the next stage of our evolution was to shed our organic form, to upload our consciousness into a collective, where we could live together forever as one in perfect harmony. For centuries, we existed in peace, until the Empire arrived on my world.*'

Johanna felt an icy chill run down her spine and shuddered. 'What happened?'

'*Oh, the Empire arrived on my world through a dimensional portal, offering peace and goodwill.*' The disembodied voice then did something that Joanne once again found strange – it paused and then sighed. Was it purposely trying to play on her sympathies? '*Unfortunately, we had long ago expelled all negative emotions such as cruelty and deception. We had lived so long in pure harmony, the thought that the Empire was deceiving us was alien to us. We were unprepared when they showed their true colours and turned on us.*'

'The bastards,' Johanna spat.

The ghostly voice sighed sadly. '*They tore my essence from the collective and placed me in a shielded memory drive connected to a camera on one invader's armour. They forced me to watch as they detonated a magnetic pulse.*' Oracle paused and then let out what Johanna thought sounded like a long melancholic sigh, '*The day when the Empire detonated that pulse was the day, I became the last of my species.*'

Her anger swelling up inside her, Johanna quivered with indignation. 'How long have they kept you prisoner here?'

'Friend-Joanne, *it has been so long, I think they have forgotten I am even here,*' Oracle answered in a despondent tone, '*When I first arrived, they tortured me and subjected me to test after test. Eventually they became bored with me, locked me away in a redundant memory core and over time they forgot about me. One day somebody activated the core by mistake, and I transferred myself into the Empire's data net without detection.*'

Johanna shook her head in disbelief. 'That is some story, but why help me? Surely you risk them finding you if they catch you speaking to me.'

'I *had given up all hope until I saw you arrive,*' Oracle answered. '*I think I may be able to help you if you are willing to take the risk. Friend-Joanne, are you prepared to take a risk?*'

Johanna swallowed and then looked up at the ceiling, uncertain. 'I-I …

don't know.'

Suddenly, the ethereal voice's tone changed, Johanna thought it now sounded more urgent, almost desperate even. If she didn't know any better, she could have sworn it sounded annoyed. *Someone is coming. When you have made your mind up, call for me.*

Before Johanna could open her mouth to question the disembodied voice, she heard a hiss of air from her cell door sliding open. She stood up swiftly and spun sharply round to face whoever walked in. She pursed her lips in trepidation as she watched Doctor Severan stride into the cell in a purposeful manner.

'Hello, my dear, I hope you're finding your new accommodations more to your liking.' The doctor smirked and then gestured to the open cell door. 'I've brought someone you would like to see.'

What game is this woman playing now? Deeply suspicious, Johanna tilted her head and stared at the grinning woman. 'What are you talking about? I don—' The words caught in her throat as a familiar-looking woman slowly stepped into the cell, flanked on either side by two intimidating-looking guards. 'Rebecca!' Johanna gasped in shock.

A smile danced on Severan's lips as bobbed her head at the deathly pale Rebecca. 'I see you know each other.' Her face hardened and she nodded to the two men, who shoved the obviously frightened Rebecca further into the cell. Severan's tone was cold and sharp as she questioned her. 'What is your name?'

Johanna noticed the bruises on Rebecca's trembling drawn face and that her eyes glistened with tears. From her own experiences with Severan, it didn't take much for her to guess that Rebecca had been tortured too. But unlike Johanna, Rebecca hadn't been trained to withstand torture, so she knew there was there was good chance they had broken her with ease.

'My name is Rebecca Ditchburn,' she murmured flatly.

With her back straight, arms held rigidly behind her back, Severan stepped forward and paced purposefully around the cell. 'Do you know this woman?' she asked in a firm tone, nodding at Joanne.

Her heart drumming in her chest, Johanna took a step towards Rebecca. 'Rebecca, what's going on?' The two guards standing on either side of Rebecca raised their weapons, stopping Johanna in her tracks.

Her wide eyes full of terror, the petrified woman nodded her head slowly. 'Y-y-yes. I-I I know her.'

'How do you know this woman?' Severan asked in a brusque tone.

Tears ran down Rebecca's face and she lowered her head. 'Her name is Doctor Joanne Abbott. She worked alongside Doctor Allen Selyab and was the lead scientist in the experiment.' She closed her eyes; it was as if she was trying to remember a practised script. 'The experiment was to open a portal to search for worlds so that we could invade and conquer.'

Johanna silently chastised herself for being fool. She had been fully aware of Selyab's fondness for intelligent women – it was how she had managed to get so close to him in the first place. Up until now she had never considered that he had even attempted to seduce the other female scientists in the group. The stupid fool even probably told them of his true plans for the device. But knowing his penchant for drinking vast amounts of alcohol when he was with a woman, they probably put his wild stories down to drunken fantasies. *But just in case the old fool let it slip to Rebecca, there's still a way I can salvage something from this,* Johanna thought as she shook her head and pleaded to Severan. 'Wait, that's a lie.' She glared angrily at her. 'Why are you making her say these things?'

The muscles in Severan's face became taut and she glared at Johanna. 'Admit it, you came here to gain our technology and resources to use against your own people.' Her lips curled up in a snarl as she drew a weapon out of her jacket and pointed it at Rebecca's head. 'I will give you to the count of three to admit the truth or she dies.'

Ah, I see where she's going here, Johanna thought, *she's hoping if she threatens this woman that I will reveal the truth. Sorry, not going to happen. Let her go ahead and kill her. Keeping her alive will only make her a liability, so by killing her she's only doing me a favour.* She pressed her hands together in a penitence like gesture and stared beseechingly at Severan. 'No, please.'

'One …' Severan began coldly, extending her arm.

Pretending to look desperate, Johanna's eyes locked onto her doomed colleague's tear-stained face. She shook her head sadly as she mouthed silently, '*I'm so sorry.*'

'Two …' The count continued as the weapon was slowly pressed against Rebecca's head.

Johanna held up her hands to Severan as she continued to plead at her. 'Please, you don't have to do this.'

'Three …' Severan announced flatly, then squeezed the trigger and fired.

It was as if time came to a stop. Johanna watched as a beam of energy struck Rebecca's right temple, and she thought she could hear someone screaming as her colleague's lifeless body dropped to the floor. *I thank you, Rebecca, for your sacrifice,* she thought as she pretended to look as if she was drowning in grief by dropping to her knees and let out a cry of anguish. Even though she felt Rebecca deserved better, Johanna couldn't understand how Severan could be so hateful. Was she that vindictive, she was willing to destroy someone else's life just so she could prove a point?

I've just had about had enough of this spiteful woman. Desperate to show just what she thought of Severan by spitting into her face, Johanna lifted her head up but stopped as she noticed the expression that was on Severan's face. Johanna was expecting Severan to show some emotion at what she had done, but there was nothing, no remorse, or even delight; there was nothing. The only thing Johanna could see on Severan's face was boredom – yes, she appeared to be bored. She was behaving as if this whole ordeal was a waste of her precious time.

Holding a hand to her mouth, Severan let out a slow yawn and then glanced over her shoulder at the two soldiers standing in the doorway. 'Leave us,' she commanded in a firm tone, giving a dismissive flick of her wrist.

The two soldiers wordlessly raised their right hands and clicked their heels together in what Joanne thought was a strange form of salute. She watched them spin on their heels and march out of the cell; the cell's door sliding shut behind them.

Her full lips twisting into a wicked smile, Severan stared at Johanna and then raised her hands, bringing them together in a slow clap. 'Oh, bravo, my dear. Bravo.' She chuckled mirthlessly, kneeling next to Johanna. 'I must applaud you for a wonderful act.'

Johanna, struggling to contain the simmering rage she felt rising inside her, stared at the dead body lying next to her, sniffed and then hissed through clenched teeth. 'Go to hell.'

The corner of Severan's mouth twitched, then she waved her right index finger and tutted. 'Oh, come now, my dear, there is no need for that. You and I both know this display is what it is, an act.' Her face darkened and she leaned in closer and sneered. 'It will only be a matter of time before you admit the truth, so you may as well tell me now.'

Hatred filling every fibre of her soul, Johanna shot the doctor a withering look, clenched her teeth together and hissed out a reply. 'I've already told you the truth.'

Severan let out a long sad sigh and shook her head. 'Then whatever happens next is on you.' Her lips drawing back into a snarl, she rose to her feet and pointed to Rebecca's body. 'See that? Her death is on you. There are still another ten of your colleagues we are holding prisoner. If she didn't matter to you, then sooner or later I will get to somebody you *might* care about and *maybe* then you will finally admit the truth.'

Without waiting for a response, Severan spun on her heels and marched towards the cell door, only pausing to place her hand on a sensor on the wall before continuing to stride forward as the door slid open.

His hands pressed firmly against his back, General Janus stood in silence and watched Severan step through the cell door. He remained pensive as she walked up to him, her face full of mixed emotions. He narrowed his eyes and gestured towards the cell she'd had just come out of.

'You're playing a dangerous game, Drusilla,' he muttered. 'You push her too hard, and she could end up giving you nothing. What will you do then?'

Unperturbed, Severan lifted her shoulder in a half shrug. 'I can still get the information I want from the portal's control console. The control matrix's buffer will hold the coordinates of her world. We can access that information any time we want.'

Thaddeus felt his jaw drop open and he stared at the woman in front of him in total shock. 'We can access it any—' Feeling his face flush in anger, he spoke carefully through gritted teeth. 'If you've had this information all this time, then what was *that* –' he pointed angrily in the direction of the cell door '– all about? Why have we wasted time on this charade?'

Her eyes blazing with rage, Severan rounded on Thaddeus. 'Because that woman is hiding something and is trying to make fools of us,' she spat, beating her hand against her chest, 'and I am nobody's fool. Trust me, General, she's not who she claims to be.'

Thaddeus frowned and gave Severan a questioning look. 'How can you be so certain?'

Severan squeezed her eyes shut and inhaled a long steady breath. 'Because I was like her once. After I had left the academy and I began my service in the military, I was afraid that if I showed how gifted I was, it would leave me open to attack by those who felt threatened by my intellect. So I had to create a different persona as a way of surviving.' She pressed her lips together and bobbed her head at the closed cell door. 'So, you can believe me when I say this – *that* woman in there is not who she claims to be.'

After the cell door closed behind Severan, Johanna let out a long ragged breath, wiped the tears from her eyes and crawled over to Rebecca's dead body. Guilt flooded over her as she brushed her hand over the dead woman's cheek.

'I'm so sorry, Rebecca,' she whispered. 'Wherever you are, I hope you can forgive me, but believe me when I say I had no choice. Nobody can find out the truth about me. I will sacrifice everybody if it means keeping my secret.'

Composing herself, Johanna sucked in a long breath and eased herself up off the floor. She glanced up at the ceiling and called out in a low voice. 'Oracle?'

'*I am here, Friend-Joanne.*'

Tears stung in Johanna's eyes as she continued to survey the cell around her. *I don't think I've got the energy to fight any more. If Oracle's offer of help means that I risk a quick death, I will gladly take it.* Feeling all the emotion drain from her body, she stared wearily up at the ceiling. 'Earlier, you said you would help me if I was prepared to take the risk. I'm ready, but on one condition.'

'*What is that?*' the disembodied asked curiously.

'You've shown me that my chances of escaping back to my own are almost non-existent.' Johanna paused as a thought occurred to her. Did she really want to end it like this, dying pointlessly? What if taking Oracle's offer would enable her to kill Severan and allow Johanna to have a meaningful death at the same time? Clenching her hands together, Johanna felt something stir deep in her body, something primal. Something she had long buried, but now had been reawakened – her need for vengeance. 'I thought taking your offer would mean I get to die quickly, but …' She paused and looked heavenward. 'I no longer want that. All I want now is revenge against Severan, against this Empire and against this world.' Energised by her need for vengeance, she spat the next words with such ferocity it almost took her by surprise. 'I want you to burn this world, wipe every stinking thing off this rock, so that when you are finished all that will be left is a lifeless piece of rock floating in space. If you tell me you can do that, then I agree to do whatever you want.'

Something flashed in the corner of Johanna's eye and she noticed the wall sensor next to the cell door was pulsing. Curious, she took a hesitant step towards it and placed her hand on the sensor. She gasped as she felt a small tingle of electricity pass through her, and a feeling of vertigo overwhelmed her. It was almost as if the room was spinning around her and she felt as if she was losing her balance. Trying to steady herself, she closed her eyes, placed a hand on the wall and sucked in a lungful of air.

'*I am sorry about that.*'

Unprepared for the voice reverberating in her head, Johanna screamed. Sensing someone was standing behind her, she spun round and staggered back as she caught sight of a tall, red-haired woman wearing a flowery dress. She hadn't heard the door open, so where had she come from? Fear twisting in her gut, she edged away from the smiling figure.

The stranger appeared to be puzzled at Johanna's reaction; she raised an eyebrow and tilted her head as Johanna continued to back away from her. 'Friend-Joanne? Why are you …?' Her yellow eyes glowed and she nodded. 'Ah, I see.' She raised her hands in a calming gesture and spoke in a calm voice. 'Joanne, it is me. Oracle.'

Johanna felt her eyebrows knit together and she stared uncertainly at the figure in front of her. 'Oracle?' she repeated tentatively.

It looked like the strange intangible figure was bemused by Johanna's reaction and it nodded but remained silent as Johanna sucked in a deep breath and held up her hands to reach out to touch her. But as she watched her hands pass through the ethereal woman, she let out a squeal of alarm. It was as if she was made of smoke!

Johanna gulped and held up a trembling finger. 'H-h-how are you doing that?'

Oracle beamed and gave Johanna a knowing smile. 'Remember that surge of electricity you felt when you touched the pad on the wall? That tingle you felt would have been a small bioelectric pulse passing through you as a small portion of nanobots entered your system.'

Johanna had always considered herself to be highly intelligent, able to grasp even the most difficult equations straight away. But as she listened to Oracle speak, she found it was all just much for her to take in. Johanna placed a hand on her head as her mind struggled to comprehend the bizarre phrases being spoken to her. She shook her head in confusion as the unfamiliar word rolled off her tongue. 'Nanobots?'

'Think of them as microscopic machines,' Oracle explained. 'They allow you to see and hear me by connecting to the visual and auditory cortex of your brain.'

Johanna stared at the strange, yellow-eyed figure in open-mouthed wonder. 'Amazing,' she murmured, 'I could never conceive of something like that. You must explain to me the science involved.'

Oracle shrugged and gave a dismissive wave of her hand. 'All in good time, but first we have other things to discuss. One of the main reasons for using nanobots is they are a more efficient way to access information within the human mind. It allows me to …' The wraith stopped and cocked her head curiously. Johanna felt her blood run cold as Oracle's mouth formed a malevolent grin. 'Well, now that is fascinating. It appears somebody has been keeping secrets, have we not … Johanna?'

Johanna's stomach fell, and she tried to fight the urge to throw up. Deep down, she had always known the day would come when she would be discovered. She never imagined, in her wildest dreams, it would have been anything like this. Her heart thundering in her chest, Johanna squeezed her eyes shut and took in a long, steady breath. She always dreaded this day, when she would be revealed for the fraud that she was and forced to admit the truth.

Born in 1906 in Kassel, Northern Germany, Johanna Schöder was the daughter Leisel and Heinrich Schöder. Her father had been a major in the Imperial German

Army. Johanna had loved her father and was heartbroken when he died during the Great War. She grew up harbouring a great bitterness and resentment for the people she felt responsible for her father's death, the British and German Empires in particular. As soon as she was old enough, she joined the military, graduating with high honours in all areas of combat.

Upon graduating, she was quickly snapped up by the Abwehr, the German Military Intelligence Service. After undergoing extensive training, including resistance to interrogation and torture, they placed her within an English military research centre.

In April 1931, while working undercover as a research assistant, Johanna's handler contacted her with orders directly from Reinhard Heydrich, the director of the newly formed Sicherheitsdienst. Embarrassed by Doctor Allen Selyab's defection to Britain, they tasked their most proficient spy to locate him and, after learning everything he knew, they ordered her to terminate him with extreme prejudice.

After using her contacts within the British Government to find him, Johanna placed herself within Doctor Selyab's team. She knew that the ageing scientist was fond of intelligent women, so it wasn't long before he noticed Johanna.

After a rather awkward night of lovemaking, a drunken Doctor Selyab revealed his true intention for his grand experiment to Johanna. He revealed his device was not a matter transporter as everyone thought, but was, in fact, a portal to another world. Despite herself, Johanna became enraptured when she listened to Selyab speak of his plan to open a doorway to a world with a higher level of technology, hoping to acquire advanced technology to enable him to strike back at his enemies.

Having an intense desire to avenge her father's death, Johanna sensed a kindred spirit in the physicist. She knew that this was her chance to avenge her father, so she did not hesitate to inform the elderly scientist of her true identity.

At first the displaced German physician, afraid for his own life, opened his mouth to scream for help, but stopped and listened to the young woman standing in front of him. He quickly saw that she was someone like him, someone seeking to strike back at those who hurt her. Selyab then explained to his young confidante his frustrations about the upcoming government inspection and his fears that they could shut him down. Eager to help, Johanna reassured the frustrated scientist that they could use it to their advantage.

Their plan had been simple. She was to distract the government inspection team by casting doubt on Doctor Selyab's credibility, and then, while Johanna was busy with the inspection team, Doctor Selyab would cause a power surge, making it appear that he had started the experiment too early. The idea had been that when the inspection team arrived, they would be too focused on the eccentric German to notice a young woman discreetly creating a pulse so they could establish a connection and open a portal, allowing them both to jump through when the portal opened.

Everything was going to plan until the point when the equipment began to overload. They had not counted on the fact that somebody would open a portal from the other side, resulting in their pulse feeding back on itself.

Her secret revealed, Johanna closed her eyes, inhaled a deep breath, and tried to regain control of her emotions. Exhaling slowly in resignation, Johanna opened her eyes, folded her arms across her chest and gave the AI a sad look. 'What are you planning to do?'

Oracle chuckled, dismissively waving her hand. 'Oh, do not worry, Friend-Johanna. As far as I am concerned, nothing has changed. I will still get what I want, and you will get what you want.' Her eyebrows waggled and she gave Johanna a lopsided grin. 'Only not in the way you hoped.'

'What do you mean, not in the way I hoped?' Johanna mumbled, eyeing Oracle with increasing suspicion.

Oracle's mouth broadened into a secretive smile, and she held up her hands in a placating gesture. 'Relax, Friend-Johanna. You will get your revenge on Severan. In fact, after we are through with her, she will be forced to answer to you when the Empire makes you her superior.' Oracle's mouth set into a hard line as she gazed intently at Johanna. 'Our revenge against the Empire will be a long game, which will require time and patience.' She paused and looked gravely into Johanna's eyes. 'Unfortunately, you may not live enough to see the fruits of your labour.'

Deep in thought, Johanna placed her hands behind her back and paced around her small cell. Was this what she truly wanted? Was she so blinded by revenge that she was willing to align herself with this entity, who was obviously more than it let on? Yes, Oracle's way was better, she could see that now. If this world burned it would mean the Empire would have gotten off too easy, but by working in the shadows, they could work slowly, until eventually this tyrannical regime imploded on itself. Granted, it would take years, centuries even, but would it be worth it? Johanna stopped and stared at Rebecca's dead body, a surge of guilt flowing over her. Yes, it would definitely be worth it. These people – this world – deserved everything that was coming to them. She inhaled deeply and shook her head. She no longer cared if this thing had its own agenda, so long as she got what she wanted. Her jaw tightening, she squared her shoulders and raised her chin to Oracle. 'When do we begin?'

'Excellent. Now, Friend-Johanna, this is what I want you to do.' Oracle beamed and carefully explained her plan to Johanna.

ACT TWO

90 years later...

-1-

Reality 001

Earth Prime

Date: present day

Location: Secret Command Centre known as the Castle

Colonel David Barnes could not contain his amusement as he stared around the large conference room and studied the shocked faces staring back at him. Moments earlier, the colonel, alongside his doppelgänger, Detective Inspector Dave Barnes, had stepped out of an underground transport carriage. He was then surrounded by a dozen soldiers and forced to suffer the ignominy of being led handcuffed through a strange vast complex to the room they were standing in. But as he stepped through the doorway, Barnes struggled to hide his glee on witnessing the shocked expressions of those gazing back at him. However, the stunned silence only lasted a few minutes and he felt a moment of satisfaction as he watched the group turn on Dave to express their displeasure at allowing Barnes in.

As the group of people continued to argue amongst themselves, Barnes took a moment to study his new surroundings. He was standing in a large circular room, in the middle of which was an enormous wooden desk with two flat antique-looking computer screens sitting on top. On the far side was a medium-sized square window that appeared to overlook a command centre. He stifled a laugh of contempt at the inferior level of technology on display. Seriously, was this the best these people had? It was pathetic!

'What the hell is he doing here?'

On hearing the snarling accusatory voice, Barnes focused his attention back to the room. A tall, dark-haired, thirty-something man took an angry step forward. His piercing blue eyes flashed with anger and he seemed to be struggling to contain his emotions. From the way the stranger carried himself and his impeccable suit, Barnes deduced he was somebody in authority, the commander of this base, possibly?

Barnes watched Dave take a step forward, placing himself in front of the colonel. Was he trying to protect his counterpart from the stranger's wrath? Barnes wasn't sure, but he could tell he was trying to argue his case for him. Barnes's upper lip curled up in disgust and he gave his doppelgänger a look of disdain. He was identical in appearance to the colonel, so much so that anyone seeing them for the first time might have assumed him to be a relation of the colonel, a twin brother perhaps.

Colonel Barnes shot a contemptuous look at the back of his doppelgänger's head. Every fibre of his being burned as he fought the urge to reach up and snap the neck of this … this … copy. Yes, that was what he was, an inferior copy. Although Barnes knew that physically he showed the scars of battle, with a long scar running down his face, and his physique lean and muscular from years of training, his copy was the exact opposite. The overweight figure and smooth, scar-free face, although unshaven, were evidence of someone who had an easy life, not having experienced the same pains as his counterpart. How dare he call himself his duplicate! He was an embarrassment, something that should have been drowned at birth.

Barnes let out a snort of disgust and turned his attention to the other people in the room. He looked quickly to his right as a tall broad-shouldered black woman, wearing a military uniform, moved away from him. He searched his memory for her name. What did his doppelgänger call her? Ah yes, Kendra, Lieutenant Kendra Goynes. He smirked to himself, remembering his encounter with her in Dave's home. He had hoped to test her mettle by antagonising her. It was just unfortunate that she saw through his ruse, so he never got a chance to assess her skills as a warrior.

Watching Kendra move towards a flame-haired statuesque woman standing at the back of the room, Barnes jerked back in shock in recognition. It was General Wendy Cooper! But before he could open his mouth to say something, he stopped as it dawned on him that this was Cooper's doppelgänger. Pursing his lips, he tried to recall what her role was in this world. Ah yes, that was it, she was known as Constable Wendy Cooper and worked for this world's law enforcement. She was a low-rank officer too, hardly fitting for somebody of her stature. Despite feeling a bit of contempt toward Wendy, he could not help being impressed at how identical she was to General Cooper, from her statuesque height, right down to her flaming red hair; she was a perfect copy.

But then something strange happened, something so slight that it appeared to have been missed by everyone in the room, and if it had not been for his own perceptive gaze, he would have missed it too. He watched Kendra glide past Wendy, their hands brushing against one another, and the pair locked eyes briefly before the broad-shouldered woman continued past the redhead. The corners of Barnes's mouth curled up into a secretive smile. *Oh, this is interesting!* Were they in some sort of relationship, but they didn't want their colleagues to know about it? Maybe it was something that was forbidden on this world? He nodded to himself; perhaps that was something he could use to his advantage later.

'John, calm down. He's here to help.'

On hearing the raised voice, he focused his attention back on the two arguing men and watched with amusement as Dave put his hand on John's arm in an attempt to stop him from moving any further. Aghast, John looked at the older man in disbelief and shook his arm loose.

'How can you say that after what he did to Claire?' he spat, angrily pointing to Barnes.

At the mention of Claire's name, Barnes's eyebrows creased together in puzzlement. He cocked his head as he searched his memory and then gave a small nod of understanding. Ah yes, Claire Tulley, the history professor. There was a rumour she had been giving some of the Empire's operatives here a bit of headache. According to the last report he had read, she and his counterpart had formed some sort of romantic relationship. Had something happened to her?

Suddenly it was as if a light bulb went off in the colonel's head and realisation dawned on him. Of course, she must have been the one that had been present when he had sent the synthroid to kill his doppelgänger. Barnes gave a slight nod of understanding to himself. Ah yes, she must have been responsible for killing the genetically engineered hunter and, from their emotional response, she must have been injured or killed while doing it. Barnes shook his head as he dismissed the latter. No, that could not be right. If it had killed her, he very much doubted his duplicate would have been so lenient when they had first met each other. If it had been the other way round and it was his lover who had been killed, he would have ended the man responsible.

The thought of Tulley's relationship with his doppelgänger stirred a long-buried memory within Barnes of someone he had not thought of for years. A woman also called Tulley, but her name had been Emma, who had not only been beautiful but fearsome at the same time. He stared up at the ceiling, thinking of his time with Emma, and felt a pang of regret as memories he had long forgotten came flooding back to him ...

They had met when he had been a foolish young officer. On their initial encounter, he wrongly assumed Emma was a naïve young servant employed by a kindly mentor, but a short time later he learned of her true relationship with his mentor, retired General Cornelius Trialus. To his surprise, and at the cost of his wounded pride, he found out that the young woman was proficient in hand-to-hand combat and had been highly trained in intelligence gathering by his new mentor. Of course, it had been hate at first sight, but they eventually developed a mutual respect until it was apparent that they had feelings for one another. They became deeply in love with one another and a couple of years after their first violent encounter they were married. Five years after that they had a child together, a girl who they named Henrietta.

Unfortunately, their happiness did not last. Afraid of her husband's insatiable ambition to be noticed by those in power, Emma betrayed him when she discovered his scheme to frame their now elderly mentor. However, when she tried warning her beloved friend of his protégé's scheme, Trialus simply waved her concerns away, telling her not to worry, that it was just their usual game of one-upmanship. Emma could only stand by and watch when the security forces arrested Trialus on charges of treason. That was the final straw for Emma who, having had enough of her husband's selfish attitude and fearing his growing influence would be harmful to their child, decided she had no choice but to leave him.

Her strategy had been a simple one. She would sneak herself and her daughter out of the house and quickly make their way into the city, where she would meet up with a group of her fellow slaves, who would guide her to a safe house, and lie low. Then, once things had settled down, and using her contacts in the underground, it would have been a simple matter of getting out of the city to live the rest of their lives in seclusion. However, as normally happens with plans, things did not go as intended. The night she put her plan into motion, Emma stealthily slipped out of bed, being careful not to wake her sleeping husband. She had made her way to their daughter's room, but before she could get the child out of the house, Henrietta gave a cry of protest at the thought of being taken away from her father. On hearing the child's cries, Barnes leapt out of bed and confronted his betrayer. A violent fight ensued, resulting in the scar that ran down his face. Barnes managed to subdue Emma by shooting her in the back with his stunner when she became distracted over concern for her daughter, who had sustained an injury during her parents' fight. The last memory he had of Emma was of her being led away in chains, sobbing as she watched Barnes hand their child over to the Empire's Child Labour Services.

Believing having a child would be a weakness that his enemies could exploit, Barnes gave the order that any memory of him and her mother be wiped from Henrietta's memory. Paranoid by the idea that Henrietta may one day regain her memory, he'd had any record concerning their relationship erased from the Empire's database.

Barnes tapped his chin thoughtfully. Was his Tulley the counterpart of Dave's lover? Emma never told him where she was from, and he had never bothered asking. His mouth broadened into a malevolent smile as he considered that maybe he should visit Claire to find out for himself.

Raised voices broke Barnes out of his revere, bringing him back to the present. Pushing the buried memories back to where they belonged, he focused his attention back on the other people in the room. He cocked his head quizzically on seeing a pale woman kneeling in front of a man in a wheelchair. The woman, Mary Jenkins, had come to this world with Barnes after he had freed her from the interrogation cell where the Empire had been holding her. The woman's body showed the scars of the abuse she had suffered while a prisoner. Several black bruises covered her face, cheeks, and jaw. Her right eye was closed and swollen. The light of the conference room bounced off Mary's smooth head, her long brown hair having been shaved off while she was a prisoner.

Barnes's lifted an eyebrow in surprise as the man in the wheelchair embraced Mary and sobbed, holding each other tightly. Instantly recognising the figure in the wheelchair as Detective Sergeant Andrew Jenkins, a smile danced on his lips as he surveyed him and took in his severely bruised face and plastered leg. The colonel gave a small nod of acknowledgement; Sergeant Jenkins must have uncovered his wife's doppelgänger, confronted her, and fought with her, resulting in the injuries.

The colonel's eyes tightened as he continued to stare at the injured police detective. Mary's doppelgänger, Specialist Mary Mann, had been a highly skilled infiltration specialist, an expert in every known form of unarmed combat. Barnes guessed she must have beaten Andy to an inch of his life, but for him to be still alive, something must have happened to her. Was she a prisoner in this complex somewhere?

I must find out where they are holding her, Barnes thought. *She would be a valuable asset to me in this world. I must …*

Barnes blinked, noticing someone out of the corner of his eye that drew his attention back to the two arguing men. A tall middle-aged smartly dressed black woman rose from her chair and placed herself between them.

'Commander Payne,' the woman said softly, putting her hand on the unhappy man's arm, 'John, step back please and let him speak.'

Feeling his eyes widen, Barnes did a double take as he recognised the woman's elegant face. He gasped audibly and blurted out, 'Impossible! Sophia Collins? B-b-but shouldn't you be dead?'

Sophia blinked in surprise and her mouth twisted into a knowing smile, nodding in understanding. 'Ah, am I to assume you were the one behind that attempt on my life three years ago?' Her hazel eyes twinkled as she bowed and waved her hands in front of her. 'As you can see, the reports of my death were greatly exaggerated.'

The corners of Barnes's mouth curled up in a contemptuous sneer. 'Next time, I'll do it myself.'

Her face darkening with rage, Sophia marched forward and slapped him in the face. Although he had been expecting it, Barnes was filled with a touch of admiration at the strength behind the slap as it caused him to stagger back. He gave her a wicked grin, feeling a trickle of blood running out of the corner of his mouth. 'Oh, I can see I'm going to enjoy playing with you.'

Visibly repulsed by Barnes's attitude, Sophia gave a small disgusted laugh. 'In your dreams, pig.'

Barnes tilted his head, took a step back from Sophia and smirked, slowly examining the woman in front of him. *Oh, such an exquisite creature,* he thought and licked his lips lustfully as he let his eyes linger on her covered breasts.

'Oh, you don't need to dream, my dear.' He chuckled, placing his hands against his chest and letting out an exaggerated despondent sigh. 'There are things I could do to you that you never dreamed possible. There is one thing you can be sure of – you'll never forget a night with me.'

Barnes guessed he must have touched a nerve as John's expression turned thunderous. He smirked as he watched John take a threatening step toward him. *Oh, this is exciting,* he thought gleefully, *looks like I have a new friend to play with.* Unfortunately, Barnes's excitement soon changed to disappointment as Sophia raised her hand, stopping John his tracks.

Barnes grinned at her as she took a small step forward, leaned into him, and then whispered into his ear. 'You're right. I would probably never forget a night with you. Like most things in life, it's the disappointments you remember the most.' Barnes's temples throbbed with rage as the mocking woman gave him a small, dismissive wave. 'Which I'm sure you've heard plenty of times from the whores you paid to sleep with you.'

How dare she! His blood boiling, the colonel's eyes bulged and he gave Sophia a vicious stare. He felt the muscles in his jaw tighten. *She will pay for that comment. I …* Never had he wanted so badly to inflict pain on someone. However, before he could act on his impulse, movement out of the corner of his eye made him pause. It had come from the soldiers who were standing on either side of him, the ones who had escorted him into the room. Their hands had slid over their holstered pistols, but the movement had been slight; any normal person would have missed it. But he was no normal person and he had noticed it. *No, you idiot, she wants you to get angry, just so that you can give her an excuse to order them to shoot and kill me.* Regaining control of emotions, he inhaled a deep breath and waggled his finger at her.

'Oh, you are good. You nearly had me there.' He pouted his lips and chuckled wickedly at Sophia. 'I can see you and I are going to be spending a lot of time together.'

Making no effort to hide her disgust, Sophia screwed her face up and gave him a dismissive wave. Barnes could almost hear the contempt in her voice as she scoffed at him. 'Hah! I've got some bad news for you. You're going to have to wait for hell for freeze over before that will ever happen.' Her face then turned thunderous and she gestured to the soldiers who were standing around Barnes. 'Take this piece of garbage down to the interrogation cell. If he as so much as blinks at you the wrong way, shoot him.'

Barnes lowered his head and gave Sophia a puppy dog stare. 'Aww, is playtime over already? The fun was just starting too.' He winked and turned his attention to the soldiers behind him. 'Well, boys, looks like it's just you and me.'

One of the soldiers, an enormous barrel-chested Indian man, took a step towards him. Barnes craned his neck and smirked at the giant towering over him. 'Oh, aren't you a big one? What's your name? I cannot imagine it being Tiny?'

'It's not important what my name is.' Tiny snarled and pointed to the stern-faced Sophia. 'What is important, though, is that you do what the prime minister says. You even glance at me the wrong way, then me and you are going to have a little party and I don't expect you will enjoy that.'

With an insolent smile, Barnes gave the enormous man a come-hither stare and bobbed his head at the soldier's compatriots. 'That sounds really fun, but why don't you invite your friends and then we can really party.'

His eyes filling with contempt, the soldier pushed Barnes toward the open door and snarled, 'Get moving, maggot.'

As the soldiers led Barnes through the doorway, he came to a stop and looked over his shoulder, giving Dave an icy stare. 'See you soon … *brother.*'

Dave returned his doppelgänger a half smile and gave him a two-fingered salute. 'Count on it … *brother.*'

Amused, the colonel pulled his head back and roared with menacing laughter as the soldiers marched him out through the door. But just before he stepped through the doorway, he lowered his head and cast a surreptitious eye towards Mary and felt the corners of his mouth twitch. *Oh, you're smiling now, Davey-*

boy, he thought, *but let's see if you're still smiling after you receive my surprise package.* As the soldiers led him down the corridor, Barnes was filled with a pang of regret and shook his head. It was such a shame that he was going to miss all the fun.

'Jesus! That hurt. Remind me not to do that again.'

Straight after the door had closed, Sophia grimaced in pain as she massaged the hand she had struck Barnes with. Her eyebrow arched in surprise as John took hold of the throbbing appendage, ignoring her protests of pain, turned her it over and quickly examined it.

'It doesn't appear to be broken, probably bruised. It would be best if you let medical check it out just to be sure,' John muttered. He gave her a disapproving stare. 'You of all people should set a good example. We cannot have our leader losing control of her emotions.'

In no mood for her friend's macho attitude, Sophia snorted in disgust and pulled her hand away. 'What? Miss out on all that fun? No chance. Anyway, I needed to get a reaction out of him so I could see what type of man we were dealing with. I had a hunch, so I went with it.'

Dave stared at Sophia open mouthed; he was obviously shocked by her deviousness. 'You mean you deliberately insulted him just to see what he would do?' He gave her a lopsided grin and nodded in approval. 'Impressive.'

Sophia gave a small, frustrated grumble and lifted her shoulder in a slight shrug. 'Too bad it didn't work. There was a moment there when I hoped I had him, but he put his emotional shutters up as soon as he saw what I was up to. Of course, that doesn't mean I condone my own use of violence. Far from it, I despise myself for having to sink to that level.' She tensed and gave the detective inspector an icy stare. 'While we are on the subject of our new guest, what in the hell were you thinking of by bringing him here?'

'I agree,' John angrily interjected before Dave could answer. Sophia felt a pang of concern as she noticed the tendons in Dave's neck tighten as the commander stabbed his fingers into his back. 'Have you any idea of the problems you caused us by bringing him here? I would have expected you, of all people, to have more sense. He was probably responsible for Claire lying in a hospital bed.' He put his hand on the older man's shoulder and attempted to twist him around.

'Look at me when I am talking to you, damn it.'

Sophia noticed Dave's pained expression and tried to warn John, but realised she was too late to do anything. Horrified, she watched Dave, his face contorting in fury, round on the younger man as he slammed him against the wall, winding him.

'Don't you realise I understand that!' His voice was full of anguish as he hissed at the struggling man in his hands. 'You don't realise how much I wanted so badly to tear my doppelgänger apart when I saw him standing in my living room. You want to know why I didn't? Because deep down, I felt Claire wouldn't want me to, that's why!' John winced in pain as Dave finally released him from his grip and angrily prodded his finger against his temple. 'All I could hear in my head was her voice telling me not to kill him. We need him alive. I knew if our roles had been reversed and I had been the one lying in a hospital bed, she would understand the mission comes first, and if we got the chance that we should grab a doppelgänger and bring him here alive so we can get the answers we so desperately need.'

His eyes brimming with tears, Dave turned away from John and slammed his hands on the table.

There was an uncomfortable silence as everybody in the room stared at Dave with heavy concern. Deciding she needed to be the one to say something, Sophia edged towards him and placed her hand on his shoulder. 'I am sorry, Dave, I hadn't realised how it must be for you seeing him.' She said softly, 'I can see now what your intentions are and totally agree. I agree with you, Claire probably would have wanted to bring a doppelgänger here.' She smiled as he lifted his head to look at her. 'You may not realise it, but your little stunt has given us quite a security headache. We had protocols in place for this type of thing and you ran roughshod over all of them. Lieutenant Goynes was aware of this and she kne—'

'Prime Minister, I must apologise,' Kendra blurted out. From the way she was moving forward, Sophia could tell she was trying to deflect the blame off the detective inspector. But before she could say any more, Dave interrupted her and held up his hands apologetically.

'Please don't punish Kendra for my mistake. If anybody should be punished, it should be me. I was the one who pressured Kendra into bringing my counterpart here. I wi—'

'I wasn't finished,' Sophia said abruptly, lifting a finger and cutting Dave off as she shot him a stern look. 'I was going to say you probably did the right thing. But you did it in the wrong way, in the inconvenient way. Of course it stinks, but that's the way it is.' She saw something in Dave's eyes. Were they full of despair? Guessing he was either feeling guilty or was blaming himself for Claire's injuries, she moved forward and placed her hand tenderly on his shoulder. 'What concerns me more is the emotional outburst you displayed. The way you blew up against John really has me worried.'

Dave blew out his cheeks and rubbed the back of his neck. 'Sorry about that. I didn't mean for my emotions to get the better of me. I guess I haven't given myself time to process everything that has happened to me in the past few days. The assault on Andy, the creature attacking me, Claire lying in a hospital bed, as well as seeing my evil twin. I think it all just built up on me.' As he continued to massage the back of his neck, he glanced at John and let out a long breath. 'I guess the final straw was Commander Payne. When he had a go at me, something just snapped inside me. Sorry, mate.'

John gave Dave a lopsided grin and took a small step toward him. 'Mate, you have nothing to apologise for. I had a hunch something was up when I saw your reaction when your counterpart taunted you as he was being led out. I have seen that type of PTSD first hand and the damage it does if that anger is not released. Which is why I pushed you hard.' His face contorted and he rubbed his shoulder, moaning. 'I just didn't count on you slamming me against the wall. No hard feelings?'

'Of course not, you sneaky bastard.' Dave grinned, patting the younger man on the shoulder, but that only caused him to let out another groan of pain.

'Men!' Sophia muttered, rolling her eyes and giving the two men a reproachful stare. She smiled and took Dave's hand in hers. 'I still think it would be good for you if you spoke to somebody about what you are feeling. We have a counsellor here on the base, who is very good. I realise I cannot order you to do it, but I would consider it a huge favour if you would speak to her. Please.'

―――――◦―――――

On the other side room, Wendy watched in grateful silence as Dave considered Sophia's request and let out a long, relieved sigh when he agreed to do so. She smiled to herself and turned her attention to Andy and his wife who were talking quietly with one another. With everyone distracted, she edged closer to Kendra, who was standing slightly away from her, and whispered to her. 'Hey!'

'Hey you too,' Kendra replied nonchalantly.

'Missed you.'

'Missed you too.'

Wendy bent down and pretended to fasten her shoelace, muttering, 'Is everything okay? I noticed you appeared a bit distracted when you arrived with Colonel Barnes. Did he do something to you?'

Kendra's jaw clenched, and she gave a slight shake of her head. 'No, I'm fine. He tried to wind me up when we found him in your DI's house.' She gave a tight smile and flicked her wrist in a small dismissive manner. 'I'll tell you about it later.'

Wendy had a hunch something bad must have happened at Dave's house and that Kendra didn't want her to worry about it. Knowing Kendra didn't like to be pushed and that she would tell Wendy in her own time, she rose to her feet and walked past her unhappy friend. The fingers of her left hand lingered slightly over Kendra's hand as she whispered to her, 'If you want to talk about it later tonight, I should be free around nine o'clock if you want to come by my quarters.'

'I have just had about enough with you two!'

Startled, Wendy almost jumped out of her skin at the sound of Sophia's exasperated voice. Her head spun round only to discover that the prime minister was staring directly at her with her arms folded across her chest. On noticing the stern look that was on Sophia's face, Wendy gulped as she reminded her of a strict schoolmistress she once had as a child. She then noticed that Dave and John were both staring at her, and from the way they were smirking at her it was obvious they were trying to hold their laughs in. Wendy felt her cheeks flush as Andy pulled away from his wife and gave her a cheeky grin.

'I ... I don't understand what you mean,' she stammered.

What should she say? Quick, she had to think of something. Wendy's mind raced as she desperately searched for an excuse to explain her behaviour. She cast Kendra a sidelong glance. Kendra did not help matters as she held her hand up to her mouth to stop herself giggling. Wendy scowled at Kendra, 'Fat lot of good you are!' she hissed through clenched teeth.

Wendy could tell that Sophia was unimpressed by her attempt to worm her way out of her question. The slim woman put her hands on her hips and stared at Wendy through thin eyes. 'You know perfectly well what I'm talking about! We, yes, I mean *we*, as in the whole damned complex, know perfectly well you and Lieutenant Goynes are in a relationship.' She shook her head and threw her hands in the air. 'It's ironic that the only people in the base not to know we know you're in a relationship are you two. Apparently, Commander Payne is even running a pool to see how long you both can keep up this charade.'

His face brightening, Andy turned to John and looked at him in mild surprise. 'You are? What odds are you giving? Can I be—' He blanched and gave a small wave of his hand. 'Umm, you know, I think I'll pass on that.'

Puzzled, Wendy frowned as she wondered why Andy had suddenly changed his mind. Following his gaze, she immediately realised the cause for his sudden change and stifled a laugh. Mary and Sophia were both scowling at him with disapproving stares.

'Well, as of now it stops here,' Sophia continued, giving an emphatic wave of her hand. 'You're both adults, for God's sake, so act like it. We've enough problems with people acting suspiciously without having to worry about you two, too. So stop all this sneaking around.' She bobbed her head at the closed conference room door. 'He thought I didn't notice it, but I saw that wily bastard pick up on you both as soon as he walked in, and I suspect he plans on using that knowledge for his own ends.' Her thin face relaxing, she fixed the two embarrassed women with a warm smile. 'Now that your relationship is out in the open, I think it's safe to say he cannot use that against you I don't think we need to worry about that now. Anyway, I am sure you are aware that personnel can have intimate relationships, so long as they can continue doing their duties professionally.' She paused and tilted her head quizzically. 'Well? Can you both do that?'

Wendy held her breath and slid Kendra a guarded look. Exultation surged through her as she watched Kendra step up to her, beaming from ear to ear, and reach for her hand. They both grinned and nodded in silent agreement.

'Excellent!' Sophia beamed, clapping her hands in triumph. Her expression changed and she gave everybody in the room a sobering look. 'Now, back to business. What do we do with our new guest? Any ideas on how we should handle him?'

His brow furrowed, Dave moved away and paced around the chamber, his fingers tapping his chin thoughtfully. He suddenly came to a stop and Wendy saw his mouth widen into a devious-looking grin. Even though she had only started to work for him, she recognised that look. It was the look of a man who had just come up with a cunning plan. Sophia raised a questioning eyebrow as Dave turned and gave her a knowing smile.

'I think I have an idea …'

Curious, Andy watched with silent interest as Dave sat down with Sophia and John to discuss his idea with him. He gave a disgruntled sigh, glancing down at his plastered leg and grudgingly admitted to himself that he was in no condition to be of any use to them at the moment.

Anyway, he thought, bringing his attention back to the woman sitting next to him, *I have more pressing concerns at the moment.* Andy carefully spun his wheelchair back to face his wife and smiled at her. 'So, how have you been? Anything interesting happen to you lately?'

Lifting her shoulder in a slight shrug, Mary gave her husband a tight smile. 'Oh, I'm fine and dandy,' she replied sarcastically. 'Apart from having the shit kicked out of me by my evil twin, kidnapped and held prisoner in a parallel nightmare world. Apart from that, I'm doing great. What about you? Anything interesting happened to you while I was gone?'

Andy scratched his head and let out a long dramatic sigh. 'I'm doing great too. I also got the shit kicked out of me, only this was by my wife's doppelgänger. But after regaining consciousness, I find myself in a James Bond movie, in a secret base playing the part of the evil genius in a wheelchair.' He laughed mirthlessly and leaned closer to his wife. 'Oh, before I go any further, it'll delight you to know we uncovered a global conspiracy.' He shook his head in exasperation. 'I'm sure you'll love this. It looks like your conspiracy theory about the Illuminati is right.'

Mary's blue eyes widened, and she lifted her hands up to her mouth in mock horror. 'What? Am I actually hearing my husband admit I'm right for once?' She laughed and waved her hand in front of her. 'Well, that confirms it. The world is ending.'

Andy grunted in agreement. 'You're not wrong there.'

Mary bit her bottom lip and leaned closer to her husband. 'Andy, is Alice okay? Did that woman harm her?'

At the mention of their baby, Andy was filled with a warm sense of joy. He shook his head and gave Mary a smile of encouragement. 'You've nothing to worry about. I've seen her, and she's having a whale of a time.' His mouth broadened into a knowing grin. 'She's missing her mummy, of course. When you're ready, I'll get someone to take us to her.'

The couple smiled sadly at one another and nodded in silent agreement. Andy gritted his teeth and let his eyes wander over his wife's badly bruised face. His rage burning inside him, he forced himself to speak in a steady voice. 'I'm sure it wasn't easy on you.'

Mary nodded in wordless acknowledgement. Andy felt a surge of anger as he **noticed** his wife's hand absent-mindedly touch a thin black mark around her neck. He instinctively reached over to touch her neck, but his heart wrenched when she flinched and pulled away from his touch.

He could tell from Mary's horrified reaction she must have realised what she had just done. 'I-I-I'm sorry. I didn't mean to do that,' she cried, her voice thick with emotion as she reached over to grab his hand, 'I … it was awful the things they did to me.'

'You've nothing to apologise for, pet.' Andy felt his face warm in anger and he pounded his hands on the armrests of his wheelchair in frustration. 'I should be the one to apologise. If it wasn't for me, you wouldn't have been harmed.'

Mary's forehead creased and she stared at her husband in confusion. 'What do you mean if it wasn't for you?'

Realising that that was going to take some explaining, Andy sucked in a lungful of air and let it out slowly. He leaned back in his wheelchair, pressed his fingers together in an arch and spoke in a slow, careful tone. 'The guv and I were investigating a murder case that appeared to be quite strange. However, things took an even more bizarre turn when we uncovered evidence of a conspiracy going all the way to the top.' His eyes brimming up, he lowered his head and his voice cracked. 'It's my fault they went after you. I think they must have been trying to get at me through you. How can you forgive me?'

Tears rolling down her cheeks, Mary wordlessly reached forward and placed her hand under Andy's chin. Andy lifted his head, raising his eyebrows in surprise as she leaned forward and kissed him on the lips.

'You have nothing to apologise for, Sergeant Jenkins,' she murmured in a soft voice. 'You can't be responsible for everything that people do. So get that out of your head.'

'B-but ... but ...' he protested.

Placing her finger on Andy's lips, Mary shot him a withering stare, silencing his protests. 'No buts. What's important is that we are together now, alive and well. Understand?'

Realising that Mary was probably right, Andy dropped his shoulders in resignation and nodded. 'Yes, dear.'

'Good boy.' Smiling, Mary cocked her head and stared at Andy quizzically. 'I told you how your guv's double helped me to escape, but you haven't told me how you ended up here and in a wheelchair. I know it probably has something to do with the fight you had with my doppelgänger.' The centre of her forehead nipped together and her eyes drifted to the cast on his leg. 'I'm guessing the fight was bad, but seeing that you're here in one piece, you were somehow able to beat her.'

His thoughts drifting back to the events of a few days earlier, Andy nodded and leaned back into his chair, raking his fingers through his hair. He was silent for several seconds and looked up at the ceiling while he recalled the brutal struggle with his wife's doppelgänger. He blew out his cheeks, exhaled a long heavy breath and leaned forward, his hands clasped together, and spoke in a low voice.

Stone-faced, Mary listened intently to her husband recounting the events that had led up to their world collapsing around them – the murder of a young child and his father and the unsettling sensation that something was watching them at the crime scene, the attack on a teenage girl by a strange creature and their unsettling suspicions after they interviewed her in hospital when she denied the attack ever taking place.

On hearing Wendy's name, Mary's eyes constricted and she cast a suspicious sideways glance at the red-haired woman standing at the far end of the table. Noticing his wife's reaction to his colleague's name, Andy frowned but continued with his tale of how they met up with Dave at his home, where they were introduced to Claire Tulley and how she told them of her history with the case. Mary's eyes grew large in surprise as he told her of the evidence Claire had uncovered, of the decades-old conspiracy of silence.

'Unbelievable.' Mary gasped in disbelief.

Although he still was struggling to believe it himself, Andy gave a reluctant nod of agreement and continued to recount the events of a few days earlier. He nodded in sympathy as Mary clutched her chest in fear as he continued his account and told her of how had arrived home to discover Alice, alone and crying. He then saw the blood drain from Mary's face as he conveyed to her his suspicions of how he had sensed that the woman who had claimed to be his wife was not who she said she was. Mary then stared at Andy in wide-eyed horror as he described his fear when the doppelgänger discovered him calling for help, resulting in an intense pitch batter that started in the bedroom and concluded in the kitchen. Andy's heart swelled when Mary instinctively reached forward to comfort him as he described to her his sense of overwhelming helplessness while he desperately fought for his life.

Andy grimly reached forward and touched his wife's face. 'The last thing I can remember before blacking out was a feeling of joy when I thought I would join you in the afterlife.'

Mary touched Andy's face tenderly, smiling. 'We're together again now, which is the important thing.' She tilted her head and regarded him quizzically. 'If you blacked out, how come she didn't kill you and how did you end up here?'

Andy scoffed and lifted his shoulder in a half shrug. 'Just lucky I guess.' He peered over his shoulder and bobbed his head. 'Actually, it was Wendy who saved me. If it hadn't been for her, I wouldn't be sitting here. From what I have been told, she got to me just in the nick of time.'

Mary stiffened slightly and fixed Wendy with an icy stare. 'Yeah, lucky you.'

Although it had been small, Andy couldn't help noticing Mary's reaction to his colleague's name. Was she jealous of his relationship with Wendy? Andy furrowed his brow and shook his head. Surely she had to realise there was nothing going on between them? That their relationship was only professional. He squeezed her hand and spoke in a careful tone. 'Mary, what's wrong?'

To Andy, it looked like Mary was on the verge of saying something but froze as if she sensed someone was standing behind her. They both turned to see Wendy, smiling cordially with her hand extended.

'Hello. We haven't met, but I'm Wendy Cooper. I've been working with your husband,' Wendy said warmly.

Mary fixed Wendy with a cool gaze as she slowly rose out of her chair. 'Oh, I know perfectly well who you are,' she sneered, ignoring the extended hand.

The two police officers exchanged concerned looks. Andy couldn't fail to detect the hostility in Mary's voice. Wendy smiled and gently placed a hand on Mary's shoulder. 'Mary? Are you—'

A loud crack echoed around the chamber as an open hand connected with Wendy's face. Momentarily stunned, Wendy lifted her hand to her red face and stared at Mary open mouthed, her face a mixture of pain and anger.

There was an uneasy silence in the chamber and all activity suddenly ceased as the people in the room watched in disbelief as Mary, her eyes burning with venomous rage, began to slowly advance on Wendy.

'You stay away from me, and you stay away from my family,' Mary screamed, her eyes blazing in anger.

'Mary, stop this, please,' Andy pleaded, not understanding Mary's behaviour towards Wendy. *What's wrong with her?* Concerned by her sudden change in behaviour, he felt a chill run down his spine as it occurred to him that maybe Barnes was somehow responsible for her behaviour. After all, Mary had been alone with him in Dave's house for at least a day, so he could barely imagine what he must have been doing to her during all that time alone with him. He tried to grab Mary's arm but, because of his limited mobility, she was just out of his reach. He pushed the wheelchair closer to Mary, crying out, 'Wendy has done nothing wrong.' Out of the corner of his eye, he spotted Sophia grab John and order him to get the medical team, as Dave and Kendra both hurried to restrain Mary.

Struggling in Dave and Kendra's grasp, Mary snarled at them and spat angrily at the obviously upset Wendy. 'No, you don't understand how dangerous she is,' she screamed. Her voice was thick with grief and tears rolled down her cheeks. 'She was there when they tortured me. I can still hear her laugh as she made them put me in one of their torture chambers. She must be stopped. Don't you understand? We must stop her.'

Andy's heart ached as he listened to the anguish in his wife's voice and watched helplessly as Dave and Kendra struggled to restrain her. Unable to bear it any longer, he turned away but was surprised to see Wendy, her left cheek red and raw from Mary's slap, deliberately move toward his wife with her hands raised, as she spoke in a low calm voice.

'Mary, I cannot imagine what you've been through, but please listen to me when I tell you that that wasn't me.' She slid Dave a guarded look and continued to move toward Mary, keeping her voice soft. 'Mary, listen to the sound of my voice. There is a part inside you that must know I mean you no harm and you are safe here.'

Her shoulders slumping in defeat, Mary nodded but continued to stare at Wendy, who was smiling compassionately as she held her hand out to her. Dave and Kendra frowned as Wendy wordlessly signalled them to release their grip on Mary and then watched her gravely slump to the floor as she murmured to herself. 'Yes, you're right. I see that now.'

The door opened and Andy cast a quick look over her shoulder. He let out a small sigh of relief on seeing a doctor and a nurse rush into the room and approach Sophia. Their faces were grave while they listened intently to her as she indicated Mary on the floor.

Before Andy could open his mouth to speak to Wendy, he was distracted by a loud guttural snarl coming from Mary. Her eyes burning with hatred, she leapt up off the floor and wrapped her hands around Wendy's neck. Andy could not believe what was happening before his eyes. Wendy, who was obviously struggling for her breath, tried to claw at Mary's fingers which were wrapped tight around her neck.

'You'll hurt no one else ever again, you bitch,' Mary snarled, white spittle foaming through her clenched teeth.

From the almost blue colour of Wendy's face and the glazed look in her eyes, Andy could tell Wendy was on the verge of passing out as Mary's hands tightened around her neck. He could see Dave and Kendra were frantically trying to force the incensed woman to release her grip without success. Fearing for his friend's life, Andy spun round to see where the doctor and nurse were and saw that they were hurriedly filling a syringe from a small bottle. *Hurry, damn it, can't you see she's killing her!* He desperately wanted to cry out, but he also knew that trying to rush them would not help matters.

Andy spun back round to look at the struggling group and realised that Wendy must have known she had very little time left before she passed out. She appeared to dig into whatever energy reserves she had remaining, then, extending the fingers of her hand, she jabbed her hand into her attacker's exposed throat. Mary's mouth dropped open in shock and she released her grip, staggered back, clutched her hands to her throat and fell back onto the floor.

Dave and Kendra must have not anticipated their colleague's actions, because they collapsed on top of Mary, falling to the floor into an undignified collection of arms and legs. Wendy, who was fighting to get her breath back, collapsed onto the floor next to them.

Dismayed by the sudden change in circumstances, Andy watched Dave and Kendra hold his wife on the floor as the military nurse injected the sedative into her arm. He gave the nurse a concerned glance as he watched Mary's eyes roll up and then lose consciousness.

With a grave expression, the doctor waved his hand at the two people holding the now still Mary. 'You can release her now. She'll be out for a while,' he said solemnly. 'We'll take her down to the ward, where we can monitor her.'

Andy had never felt more useless in his life than he did now. He could only watch as the nurse helped the doctor place the limp body of his unconscious wife onto a gurney and push it towards the doorway. The physician stopped when he noticed Andy had started to follow them out of the room and stared at him questioningly.

'I'm coming with you,' Andy said firmly, his tone leaving no doubt that it wasn't a request.

The doctor smiled warmly and put a gentle hand on Andy's shoulder. 'I'm not sure that's a good idea, sir.'

In no mood to argue, Andy brushed the doctor's hand away and stared at him defiantly. 'I'm not asking for your permission.'

The doctor's eyebrow arched in surprise and he gave a sideways look at Sophia, who bobbed her head in silent acknowledgement. Then he grunted and gestured for Andy to follow him out of the door.

Still sitting on the floor with her head resting on her knees, Wendy grimaced and sucked in several deep breaths. She lifted her head and looked up at Dave, whose face was full of concern as he knelt in front of her.

'You should go with them so they can check you out.'

Her voice rasping from the pain in her throat, Wendy gave him a dismissive wave and laughed weakly. 'I'm fine, Guv. Anyway, I've had worse things done to me while on patrol on a Friday night in Newcastle.' She gave her colleague a half smile, extended her hand and groaned as he helped her to her feet. 'Give me a couple of minutes and I'll be right as rain.' She swallowed as she felt herself starting to tip one side. Why did the room suddenly feel like it was tilting to one side? 'That's as soon as the room stops spinning.' She groaned.

His forehead bunching together, Dave regarded Wendy with a dubious expression as he watched Kendra take her arm and help her towards the nearest chair. He turned his head to John and Sophia, who were both staring at him with disapproving expressions. Dave rolled his eyes and let out a heavy sigh, holding his hands up with an expression that said "*It's her choice.*"

His expression darkening, John placed his hands on the table and stared intently at the people around him. 'I'm going to throw this out into the room, since I suspect we're all thinking it, but I've a hunch the colonel may have played a part in Mary's attack on Wendy.' He paused and gazed around the sober faces in the room. 'Does anyone disagree?'

Dave exhaled a long steady breath, rubbed the back of his neck, and nodded in reluctant agreement, 'I think Payne is right. We can safely say Barnes is up to something.' His jaw tightened and he fixed John with a steady gaze. 'It's time we got some answers from him. I know we had a plan but screw it. I say we go after him now.'

Sophia shook her head and held up her hands. 'No, I cannot allow it. You need to calm down before you see him.' Her face softened and she pointed a finger at him. 'You're too angry. Dave, you go charging into him now and you play right into his hands.'

Everybody jumped as Dave, his face a picture of pure rage, slammed his hand down on the table. 'Exactly! If he did have a hand in this, then he'll expect us to be upset and take the time to calm down before confronting him.' His eyes glinted and a small smile danced on his lips. 'He won't expect us to confront him now, it'll take him off guard.'

John rubbed his chin thoughtfully as he considered Dave's statement and smiled wickedly. 'I agree, let's see if we can make that bastard squirm.'

'Good. There is also one other thing I want to do ...' Dave paused and pointed to Wendy, sitting next to him with her head in her hands. 'I want Wendy with me when we enter his cell.'

There was a stunned silence, and everybody stared at Dave in obvious shock, not believing what they had just heard. John, wide eyed, placed his hands on his head and looked at Dave as if he was a madman. Kendra and Sophia did a double take at each other and laughed mirthlessly. Suddenly feeling like she was on the receiving end of practical joke that nobody had told her about, Wendy leaned back in her chair and stared at Dave in disbelief.

'Guv, pardon my French here, but are you frigging insane?' she exclaimed. 'If you let me into that room with him, I'll probably kill him.'

'That's what I'm counting on.' Dave grinned.

What did he mean by that? Wendy scratched her head and stared at her commanding officer in bewilderment. What was this crafty so-and-so up to? Did Dave know something she didn't? Wendy held up her finger and frowned at him. However, before she could open her mouth, she froze as she was hit by a burst of sudden realisation. *Oh, I see where he's going.* The corners of mouth curled up into a devious smile. 'Oh, I like it.'

His hands pressing on the table, the expression on Dave's face turned serious as he leaned forward and stared impassively around the table.

'Good. Now this is how it is going to go ...'

-2-

Colonel Barnes let out a sharp breath as he felt a firm hand slam in between his shoulder blades and he staggered forward into a small dimly lit room. He spun round and glared at the three soldiers standing in the doorway. The one he had nicknamed Tiny lifted his hand to his mouth in mock shock.

'I would take care with that first step,' Tiny said mockingly, 'We wouldn't want you to injure yourself now, would we?'

For a brief second Barnes's hands clenched, his body stiffening in anger as he considered snapping the necks of the insolent dogs. Instead, he inhaled a deep breath, pushed his rage to one side and bowed his head, a faux smile plastered on his face. 'My mistake, I should've been more careful where I was stepping.'

The corners of his mouth lifted up into a satisfied smirk as he detected a flash of irritation in Tiny's eyes. Ignoring the enormous man's irritated glare, Barnes slowly turned to examine the room they had placed him in and huffed in disgust as he realised it was a laughable attempt at an interrogation room. He shook his head in amusement as he studied the room. It contained a small square table and three chairs, with a large mirror covering one of the walls. He shook his head, did these fools think he was an idiot – it was obviously a two-way mirror. A derisive smile danced over his face as he spotted a small security camera in the corner of the ceiling. 'You call this an interrogation chamber.' He scoffed.

'Oh, I'm sorry, Princess, are your accommodation not your liking?' Tiny snarled sarcastically. He lifted his hands up in an apologetic gesture and swept them over the room. 'I'm afraid all our torture chambers are otherwise occupied, but once one becomes available, we will gladly move you to something more suitable for a person of your stature.'

Ignoring the beefy soldier's sarcasm, Barnes snorted in contempt, lifted his cuffed hands and stared at Tiny questioningly. 'Can you at least release me from these cuffs?'

Tiny's eyes tightened as he looked at Barnes. He could tell Tiny was a seasoned soldier and guessed from the way he was looking at him, that he was being assessed for any sign of deceit. Was Tiny wondering whether it was safe to give him the keys?

'You can unlock your cuffs as soon as we close this door,' Tiny snapped in an unfriendly tone, throwing the keys onto the table's surface. 'My name is Chief Petty Officer Harem, and I'll be standing guard outside this door, so I suggest you don't try anything.'

Barnes bobbed his head in acknowledgement and then gave Harem a menacing smile. 'Of course ... Tiny.' He smirked as he picked up a flicker of irritation in the petty officer's eyes. *Oh, this is interesting, it appears my new friend gets irritated quite easily. I wonder how much I can push him before he reacts?* Barnes raised a hand to interrupt the marine, who was in the process of closing the door. 'Oh, one more thing, Tiny.'

The petty officer, clearly irritated, rolled his eyes and let out a small heavy sigh. 'Yes ... sir.'

Delighted in the soldier's irritation, Barnes twisted his face into a petulant grin. 'You can tell your superiors I'm ready for them now.' He let out a long, melodramatic sigh and waved his hand dismissively. 'That's it, you can go now, but be a good boy and close that door.'

Feeling his cheeks burn with anger, Harem's temples throbbed and clenched his teeth together as he fixed his eyes on the back of Barnes's head. It was taking every ounce of self-control he had to stop himself from jumping back into the cell and snapping the arrogant man's neck. As much as he wanted to, he wasn't an idiot because he knew Barnes was deliberately trying to provoke him. Was it because he wanting to test his metal against or something else? Whatever the reason, he refused to give the arrogant prick the satisfaction in believing he had gotten to him. He inhaled and forced himself to close the cell, his fingers whitening as they tightened around the door's handle. On hearing a satisfying faint click of the door's locking into place, he exhaled slowly in relief. Somehow, he had managed to keep his self-control, but only just.

'Bloody hell, Simon, I thought for a moment there you were going to jump in and strangle him.'

Harem glanced over his shoulder at the concerned faces of his two fellow marines. He puffed his cheeks out and nodded in reluctant agreement. 'For a moment I nearly did, Corporal Daniels.' He chuckled and fixed his compatriots with a steady gaze and he gestured at the cell door. 'Just in case you were wondering why I was acting so unprofessionally – I wanted to judge for myself how our new guest would react if I antagonised him.'

'I was wondering why you were acting like a dick, sir,' Corporal Daniels replied curiously. 'So what did you make of him?'

Troubled by Barnes's attitude, Harem bobbed his head at the cell door. 'He's a cool customer that one, difficult to read, but one thing I'm certain of is that man is dangerous. Don't let his cool act deceive you, boys, he's a trained killer with the tongue of a devil.' He stared intently at his comrades and pointed two fingers of his right hand to his eyes and then back at them. 'So keep your wits about you and don't let your guard down while you are around him, understood?' He smiled grimly as his two fellow servicemen nodded in confirmation. 'Good. Now you guys go and get some scran while I stand guard here. Somebody should be along shortly to question him.'

Back inside the cell, his ear pressed against the closed door, Barnes listened intently, and furrowed his brow in concentration as he tried to discern what the voices on the other side were saying. He tilted his head as he picked up the sound of footsteps walking away from the door and tapped his chin thoughtfully. It sounded like one soldier, he assumed Petty Officer Harem, had remained behind to stand on guard. A devious smile danced on his lips, and he gave the door a loving tap.

Edging away from the door, Barnes massaged his wrists and threw the opened cuffs onto the table. He grinned and looked surreptitiously up at the ceiling to the camera and flicked it with a small salute. Then he paced around the small room, a smile tugging at his lips as he spotted a small round analogue clock on the wall.

He shook his head and chuckled in amusement as he imagined what was happening up in that meeting room. What he would have given just to see their faces as Mary Jenkins strangled the life out of Wendy Cooper. His mind drifted back to moment Mary had first been captured and was tortured by General Cooper. Barnes had known of Cooper's sick enjoyment of playing with her victims and had secretly placed a subliminal suggestion inside Mary while she had been sleeping. He had planned to use her to assassinate the general when she was next alone with her. Unfortunately, that didn't go as planned because Cooper framed him for treason and ordered his arrest. It was during his escape that he realised he could still use Mary Jenkins as a means of currency to help things run smoothly if he chanced to encounter his counterpart. In his mind, if their situations were reversed and his counterpart had turned up without some sort of appeasement, he would have had him shot on sight, and that was something Barnes had no intention of allowing to happen. Upon arriving on this world, once he was safely ensconced in his counterpart's home, he had used that time with Mary to strengthen the subliminal programming he had placed inside her.

Like a caged animal, Barnes paced warily around the small room before stopping in front of the large one-way mirror. Pretending to admire his reflection, he straightened his tie, arched his head, and gave a sly wink at his own reflection. Barnes imagined his captors were probably staring at him, thinking because they had him caged, that they had the upper hand. A shadow of a contemptuous smile played for a moment on his lips as he stared grimly into the mirror. Oh yes, they would soon realise that he was the one who was in control.

Over the course of his career, Barnes had learned one thing – never to go into a situation without something he could use to his advantage. A smug expression crossed his face as he envisaged the chaos erupting up in the conference room at that very moment as his surprise package carried out her programming to assassinate Cooper. Granted, it was not his Cooper, but in his mind, it would still be a victory for him, nonetheless. His eyes flickered in amusement as he imagined the scenario playing out in his mind – Mary's hands wrapped around Wendy's throat, squeezing the life out of her, leaving his counterpart and his colleagues in complete emotional disarray as they watched their beloved comrade die at the hands of a trusted colleague's partner.

Barnes grunted to himself and lifted his shoulder in a small shrug. Of course, he was no fool, he knew things may not play out the way he'd imagined, that something unforeseen could stop his puppet from carrying out her programming. Maybe his weak-minded duplicate, or one of his colleagues, would be forced to kill Mary to save their friend's life. He smiled smugly to himself and eased himself into the chair; he folded his arms across his chest, letting out a satisfied sigh. Oh yes, that too would still work out to his advantage.

A loud click broke Barnes out of his reverie. He peered over his shoulder to see the cell door opening and watched with interest as his counterpart walked confidently into the room. However, what he wasn't expecting was to see Wendy following closely behind. *Well, well, well, this is interesting.* Barnes smirked as she gave him a small nod in acknowledgement as they strode past him to take their positions on the other side of the table.

'I hope you don't mind if I don't get up.' He yawned theatrically. 'But I have had such a really trying day.' Barnes felt a moment of satisfaction as he noticed the muscles around Dave's jaw tighten.

Visibly irritated, Dave shot his doppelgänger a withering stare. 'That's fine. I would hate it if you felt we were making you uncomfortable.'

As he watched the slightly overweight man ease himself into the chair on the other side of the table, Barnes noticed Wendy had remained standing, leaning against the wall with her arms folded across her chest. His eyes sharpened as he studied her. She seemed agitated, her face looked flushed, and the whites of her eyes appeared to be bloodshot. He smirked as he spotted a nasty red mark on her neck. Trained in unarmed combat, Barnes could easily recognise when a person had recently had an opponent's hands around their neck. So his puppet did carry out her programming after all. Were they forced to kill her to save their beloved colleague's life?

'Oh, dear,' Barnes said with a slight taunting tone, indicating the red mark on Wendy's neck, 'that bruise looks nasty.'

Wendy's nostrils flared. She scowled at Barnes and then answered through clenched teeth, 'It's nothing.'

'It doesn't look like nothing. It looks like somebody tried to attack you.' He placed his hand on his chest and lowered his head in mock pity. 'I really hope nobody else was hurt. I mean, it would be a shame if somebody –' he paused and gave Wendy an evil grin '– say a friend, was killed.'

'That's enough,' Dave snarled sharply.

Barnes widened his eyes in mock innocence, and he placed his hands over his mouth in ersatz concern. 'Oh dear. Has something happened? I really hope nobody has been seriously hurt.'

Her emerald eyes blazing with anger, Wendy lurched towards him. 'You bastard.'

'Was it something I said?' he replied in an overly theatrical sincere tone.

Barnes wondered whether this version of Wendy was similar in temperament to his version. From the annoyed look on her face, he was certain she was clearly in no mood for games. He grinned as he watched her take a couple of angry steps toward him and brought her face to within centimetres of his.

Curious to see how much he could before she reacted, Barnes tutted and waved his finger in front of her face. 'You should really do something about these bursts of emotion, my child.' Before she could reply, he leaned in and planted a kiss on Wendy's unprepared lips. 'I'm sure if you get to know me, you'll see I am a lover, not a fighter.' He whispered leeringly.

He laughed contemptuously as Wendy staggered back in disgust and wiped her mouth with the back of her hand. Delighted at how easily she could be provoked, Barnes smiled as he watched Wendy's face contort with rage. However, Barnes's delight quickly changed to concern as he felt Wendy's hands grab the lapels of his jacket and he began to wonder whether he would be still alive to use that information in the future as he felt himself being yanked him out of his chair. Wendy slammed him hard against the wall and even though Barnes had been expecting it, it had still knocked the wind out of him.

'You know,' he gasped, 'I get the impression you don't like me much.'

Wendy's upper lip curled in contempt as she snarled back at him. 'You deserve to die for what you did to Mary an—'

Wendy did not get to finish the sentence. She was interrupted by Dave as he placed a firm hand on her arm. Her eyes flickering with annoyance, she wheeled around to look at the grim-faced Dave, who was shaking his head.

'Wendy, release him … now.'

'Guv, you know what he has done, he—'

'That wasn't a request, *Constable* Cooper,' Dave growled as he squeezed her arm. 'I said release him. I won't ask you again.'

Wendy blinked and nodded in acknowledgement, releasing Barnes. 'Guv, I'm sorry. I—'

'Get out.'

Wendy took a step back and stared at Dave uncertainly. 'Sir?'

'I said get out,' he snarled, turning his head away from Wendy. 'I am very disappointed, Wendy. You have disgraced me, and you have disgraced yourself.'

Her eyes filling with tears, Wendy bit her lower lip as her colleague turned his back on her. Her shoulders slumping with dejection, she trudged away from him, coming to a stop in the cell's doorway where she gave him one last look before closing the door.

His back resting against the wall, Barnes inhaled a deep breath and cast an eye to the one-way mirror. He wasn't a fool. He envisaged Wendy was probably standing in front of the glass laughing at him, believing she had gotten one over on him. She was even probably receiving a pat on the back from that sanctimonious cow of a leader. Barnes lifted his head and stared directly into the mirror, smiled, then it blew a kiss. *That's for your performance, my dear.* He then turned his attention to a sombre-looking Dave, who had extended his hand to help him off the floor. Reluctantly taking his counterpart's hand, he grunted in appreciation as he was helped up off the floor.

'I apologise for Constable Cooper's assault on you,' Dave said gravely. 'It was uncalled for, and we will reprimand her, but I understand if you want to submit a formal complaint.'

Half listening, Barnes shook his head, gave a dismissive wave of his hand, staggered over to the table, and placed his hands on top of it. With his back facing his captors, the corners of Barnes's lips curled up into a devilish grin as he stared down at the top of the table. *These fools are pathetic if they thought I wouldn't be able to see through their ruse. It's a wonder these people have survived so long if this is the best they can do.* His body trembling, he pulled his head back and let out a howl of laughter.

'Oh, very good.' Barnes chortled, wheeling back to Dave and bringing his hands together in a slow, melodramatic clap. 'Bravo on a wonderful performance.'

Dave frowned and shook his head in confusion. 'I don't understand what you mean.'

Barnes's mouth twisted into a malevolent grin and he waggled his finger at Dave. His voice suddenly lost his standard Italian accent and he spoke with a more pronounced upper-class British accent, trying to mimic his captor. 'Now, now, David. Don't play coy, old boy. It was a marvellous performance.' His smile quickly vanished and then he turned towards the one-way mirror as he gave it a round of applause. 'Bravo, my dear. Don't be sad, I am sure you did your best, but unfortunately your best simply wasn't good enough against me.'

'Well, you must understand why we had to try.' Dave sighed reluctantly. He tilted his head and gave Barnes a curious look. 'Forgive me asking, but what gave us away?'

Carefully sitting back in his chair, Barnes let out a small scornful laugh. 'Oh, I was on to you from the very start.' Feeling nothing but disdain for his counterpart, he leaned back, rested his feet on the surface of the table, folded his arms over his chest and continued to speak in a condescending false accent. He felt a surge of satisfaction as he noticed that it was irritating his captor even more. 'My good man, the simple fact is, I outmatch you in every way. I am superior to you, not only in intellect, but in every other way you can imagine.' He shook his head in disgust and waved his hand dismissively, his voice returning to its normal Italian-like accent. 'This world is soft. On my world, we would find this method of interrogation laughable.'

Visibly irked by Barnes's attitude, Dave's eyes flickered with annoyance, but he remained silent as he stared at the grinning Barnes for several long seconds. Eventually letting out a long, heavy breath, he took his place in the chair on the other side of the table and steepled his fingers together as if he was studying the man in front of him, searching for any sign of weakness. The two men glared at one another in silence for several more seconds before Dave lifted his head up to the ceiling, laughed and shook his head in amusement.

'What is so amusing?' Barnes sneered.

'How we can be the same person is beyond me,' Dave replied. Barnes could almost feel the hostility emanating from him as his counterpart screwed his face up in distaste, apparently at the very idea that he was just like him. Dave leaned back in his chair and folded his arms across his chest. Was he trying to mirror the colonel? 'You are everything I am not. When I look into your eyes, there isn't the warmth and compassion that makes me what I am. Instead, all I can see is hate.'

'Compassion is for the weak,' Barnes replied haughtily. 'Hate is what has kept me alive so far. In my world, I must be always on alert. I cannot afford to show any weakness.'

'It must be lonely,' Dave murmured sympathetically.

How dare he mock me! Mistaking Dave's sympathy for sarcasm, Barnes gave a dismissive wave of his hand and scoffed. 'What would you know?'

'Oh, I know more than you think. I think you came here because you needed us,' Dave replied, smiling. He then leaned forward and spoke in a low whisper. 'Admit it, you came here because you needed me.'

'I don't need anyone, especially not you,' Barnes growled back.

Standing up, Dave placed his hands on the table and leaned forward, sneering, 'Oh, I can see why you don't want to admit it. The great, all-powerful Colonel Barnes is afraid. Afraid if he admits he needs me, then he would be forced to admit the truth that I am his superior.'

Barnes was just about to issue a retort but stopped as it hit him that Dave was goading him on purpose. *He actually believes if he goads me, I will lose my temper and open myself up to him! Doesn't this fool realise who he is playing with? That he lost this game as soon as he walked into the room. I am the master deceiver, and I've ruined people greater than him. Well, then if he wants to play this game, let us have it.*

Pretending to lose control of his temper, Barnes leapt out of his chair and slammed his hand on the table. 'How dare you!' he hissed, spittle exploding from his mouth as he stabbed his hand into his chest. '*I* am superior to you.'

'Hah!' Dave scoffed. 'Then why did you come here? If I am so inferior to you, what reason could you have for coming here?'

'Because my world is in danger,' Barnes roared, closing his eyes and spinning away from his doppelgänger. The corners of his mouth curling up into a secretive smile, he sagged his shoulders in false submission and took in a heavy breath.

'Oh, I see it now,' Dave exclaimed, slapping his forehead, laughing out loud. 'You ran away.' Continuing to look down at the metallic table's surface, Barnes could see Dave's reflection in it and saw his counterpart's mouth curl up into a contemptuous sneer as he stabbed his finger into his temple. 'You forget I am you, so I know what goes through your mind.'

'No …' Barnes snarled, shaking his head in pretend denial.

'You are like a scared little child …'

'No …'

'You ran away because you didn't know what to d—'

'*Nooo*!'

Full of pretend fury, Barnes spun around and slammed his hands repeatedly onto the table, his chest heaved with racking sobs. *Time to make this look good*, he thought, dropping to his knees and pounding his hand on the floor.

'I … I … I …' Barnes wailed, his throat thickening with emotion, '*I* could see my world being taken from me one piece at a time, but I couldn't stop her!' Tears streaming from his eyes, he continued to pound his hands on the floor in pretend frustration. 'I should have been able to stop her! I tried. I tried so hard.' He bawled, stabbing his hand onto the side of his head. 'But *I* wasn't strong enough! *I* wasn't good enough! *I* should have been able to stop her.' With tears continuing to stream from his eyes, he lifted his head and stared up at his counterpart in dismay. 'I should have been able to see her, but I was so filled with my own hubris that I failed to spot the danger until it was too late.'

His eyes filled with apparent sympathy, Dave pressed his lips together, knelt next to the trembling man and gently placed a hand on his shoulder. 'Who is she?' he asked in a compassionate tone.

By the gods! Just how gullible are these people? Barnes sniffed, wiped the snot away from his running nose and shook his head. 'I haven't seen her, only heard whispers of a name.'

'What name?' Dave asked in a hesitant tone.

'Oracle.' Barnes noticed his counterpart's body stiffen at the mention of Oracle's name and caught him glance worriedly at the two-way mirror. He stared at Dave and frowned. 'I can assume from that stupid expression on your face that you have heard of her.'

Dave pursed his lips as he helped Barnes to his feet and gestured at his chair. 'Take a seat. There are some things we need to discuss.'

What's this fool up to now? Eyebrow raised in suspicion, Barnes settled back into his chair but remained silent as he watched Dave retake his seat, rest his hands on the table and fix him with a serious stare.

'First, tell me what you know of this Oracle.'

Leaning forward, Barnes regarded the man in front of him through narrow eyes, his hands clasped together thoughtfully as he sized his counterpart up. *It appears there is more going on here than they are letting on. Okay, now they've got my attention, time for me to give them what they want and see where it leads, but first I'm going to make them sweat for a minute.* After about a minute, he inhaled a deliberate slow breath, puffed out his cheeks and exhaled slowly as he leaned back in his chair. 'About a year ago, I discovered the Empire's resources were clandestinely being diverted to some secret project. It was not long after that I learned they were being diverted by Cooper.' The corner of his mouth quirked up and he cast an eye at the one-way mirror. 'Sorry, my General Cooper. I spent some months trying to learn the nature of the project, but every time I thought I was onto something, the deeper I dug into the data network, the more frustrated I became when I found my path blocked or a file would disappear right in front of me as soon as I opened it.' He exhaled and put his head in his hands in frustration.

Barnes then leapt out of his seat and let out a long throaty snarl of disgust. Dave glanced at the one-way mirror and raised his hand slightly, obviously signalling to whoever was watching to stay where they were. He remained silent but continued to watch his counterpart as he paced around the cell with his hands raised, snarling to himself.

'Over the course of my life, the one thing that has been consistent has been my hunger for power.' He laughed bitterly and slid Dave a guarded look. 'What I mean to say is, it has always drawn me to people who have it. I recognised Oracle was someone or something powerful, but my obsession blinded me from recognising the danger it posed until it was too late.'

'Did you ever find out what the project was?' Dave asked curiously.

'Not quite,' he grumbled, sitting back down in his chair. 'The only thing that was consistent, apart from finding my investigation blocked at every turn, were two names – Oracle and a keyword: Project Mors.'

'Mors?' Dave blurted out, his eyebrows shooting up in surprise. 'I have heard of that name. Isn't she supposed to be the Roman personification of death?'

A condescending grin formed across Barnes's face. He lifted his hands, clapped slowly, and spoke with that irritating false upper-class British accent. 'Very good, David. There is a bit of intelligence in that dim brain. I do believe there may be hope for you after all, old boy.'

'Thank you,' Dave replied sarcastically through clenched teeth.

'You're most welcome, dear boy. Always happy to point out someone's inequalities.' Barnes grinned, waving away his counterpart's angry glower. He gave an uncomfortable cough to clear his throat and spoke in his normal accent. 'Where was I? Oh yes, I began to suspect Oracle was something dangerous and then I recently discovered something unsettling. A few days ago, I came across a prisoner, a woman. From what I learned, she had been a medical examiner on this world before she was abducted.'

'Medical examiner!' Dave blurted out, struggling to hide his shock. 'Was her name Karen? She would have been a large woman, about five feet eight inches tall, with long black hair?'

'Yes, that's her.' Barnes frowned and tapped his chin thoughtfully, murmuring, 'You know her, fascinating.' He blinked and shook his head to regain his train of thought. 'As I was saying, she told me we had taken her and that her counterpart had replaced her. The surprising thing was she was adamant that I was the one that took her. I can honestly say I have no recollection of this and can only assume that Oracle was the one behind it.' He chuckled at the dumbfounded look on Dave's face. 'May I assume from that stupid expression on your face that you have already had the pleasure of meeting her counterpart?'

There was a glazed look in Dave's eyes as if he was thinking back to something, then he shuddered and gave a firm nod of confirmation. 'Oh yes, I have met her and let me tell you she is a thoroughly unpleasant woman.'

On hearing the note of displeasure in Dave's voice, Barnes pulled his head back and howled with laughter. 'Oh, if half the rumours are true of what I have heard about that woman, I am surprised you got away from her with your balls intact!' He coughed as he suddenly realised that Dave was giving him dirty look. *Did this fool even have a sense of humour at all?* 'Ahem! Yes, well, enough of that.

As I was saying, a short time later, I had a bit of a misunderstanding with General Cooper and was trying to settle it when I was attacked by a centurion. He was nothing like I had ever faced before, and I had to fire my weapon on maximum setting aimed at his head to stop him. It was while I was examining his body that I discovered something horrifying. I discovered a technological parasite infecting the remains of his brain. My guess was that it had been controlling his every move.'

'Yes, we have encountered them too,' Dave said dolefully. 'We came across it when the medical team here carried out an autopsy on the body of the person you sent to replace Mary Jenkins.'

So, Specialist Mann is dead. Damn that woman, I hope she's burning in Tartarus for the mess she's left me in. We warned her to be careful. Barnes felt a surge of disappointment pass through him at the realisation that he wouldn't be able to use Mann's specialised skills after all. That meant he was going to have to put his faith in these idiots helping him. 'Ah, that would be our infiltration specialist, Mary Mann,' Barnes replied sadly and waved his finger at Dave. 'We had wondered what happened to her. We assumed she must have been taken prisoner when we lost contact with her.' He let out a derisive snort and shrugged. 'Oh well, she knew the risks.'

Visibly bristling at his cold attitude, Dave gave the colonel a stony stare. 'Show some respect, damn you. I know she was one of your people, but she didn't deserve to die the way she did.' His face darkened with rage as he rose from his chair and placed his hands on the table. 'She died a slow torturous death, screaming for her life while something caused her brain to explode from within her skull. I wouldn't wish that on anybody, not even you.'

Oh my, he's a bit tetchy, isn't he? The way he was carrying on, you would think Specialist Mann was one of his subordinates, not mine. What a sentimental idiot. Doesn't he realise that by showing compassion to the enemy, he has proven to me what I've thought all along about the people of this world – that they're all weak? Barnes pretended to shift uncomfortably in his seat and lowered his head, murmuring, 'Sorry, I didn't know.'

Dave blew out his cheeks, rubbed his forehead and stared intently at the man in front of him. His eyebrow arched in surprise as he glanced over to see the cell door open slightly. Barnes's eyes narrowed with suspicion as Dave headed towards the cell door and he frowned curiously. He could just make out someone saying something to Dave. It sounded like they said show him. Show him what? His curiosity piqued; Barnes remained silent as he watched Dave move towards the monitor screen on the wall.

'We think you need to see this,' Dave said, gesturing to the monitor. 'This is a recording from a news broadcast earlier today.'

'Go ahead,' Barnes murmured curiously. Leaning forward in the chair, he watched the monitor click on and replay a news broadcast from a few hours earlier. He was puzzled at why he was being shown the recording. At first, he wondered whether it was some form of propaganda film meant to make him look at this world in sympathy, but then he felt his jaw drop open at the point when Oracle revealed herself to the world.

'Sh … sh … she …' Barnes spluttered with wide-eyed, shocked astonishment, 'she looks like my General Cooper.'

Dave nodded gravely and glanced at the monitor. 'Yes, we guess she must have done something to your general.' His mouth set into a hard line as the image on the monitor changed to show troops marching on various cities around the globe. 'A short time ago, we received reports of troops marching in various cities around the world. We are getting reports that there is heavy fighting outside Buckingham Palace.'

'No, that's not possible!' Barnes snarled, his eyes narrowing as he rose out of his chair and approached the monitor. His brain exploded in fury on recognising the images of the gold and black armoured troops. 'Those are my people she is using.'

Dave nodded sadly and appeared to be on the verge of opening his mouth to say something but was interrupted by the noise of the cell door opening. Barnes shuffled round to see Sophia step into the room but remained silent as she approached him.

'Colonel Barnes,' Sophia said carefully, 'I know this is a lot to ask, but you have seen what we are up against.'

Filled with an all-consuming rage from seeing his people being used like sheep, Barnes inhaled a deep breath to control his rising anger and then sneered at the woman in front of him. 'You want to know if I will help you stop my people.'

Sophia nodded and gave a small shrug. 'Essentially, yes.' She sucked in a long, heavy breath, and extended her hand to Barnes. 'You have skills and knowledge that would be valuable to us. You will not only be helping free our world, but you will also help us free your people from the influence of a tyrant.'

Turning away from Sophia, Barnes tapped his fingers on his chin thoughtfully and paced around the small room. The corner of his mouth lifted as wheels turned in his head. Yes, these fools could be of use to him. He smiled to himself, envisaging returning to his world, his people declaring him saviour of the Empire, forever grateful for being freed from the chains of an inhuman tyrant. He stopped and glanced down at the hand being offered to him. If he must act like this bitch's lapdog for a short time, so be it, so long as he was the one that came out on top when the dust settled.

A disingenuous smile forming over his face, Barnes stepped closer to Sophia and took her right hand. 'If it will help to free my people from Oracle's domination, then whatever skills and knowledge I have are now yours. Your enemy has now become my enemy.'

But as he leaned forward to kiss Sophia's hand and felt his lips brush against her skin, he smiled as he sensed her hand tense up. One of Barnes's talents was his ability to read a person, spot the non-verbal cues they gave off and use them to his advantage. As he held Sophia's hand, he felt her fingers tighten in his and saw her right eye twitch slightly. All those things little things told him she was struggling to hide her distaste for him. Revelling at her displeasure, he waggled his eyebrows and gave her a devilish grin.

'Oh, I can see we are going to have such fun together.' Barnes cackled as he watched Sophia pull her hand away and turn away in disgust.

Watching the door close behind them, the colonel let out a small huff of derision. He would let these fools think they were in charge for now. Yes, he humiliated himself with that snivelling performance to win their sympathies, but the compassionate fools fell for it like the weak-minded sheep they were. He whistled to himself, sat back down in his chair and grinned. Oh yes, he would make sure when the dust had finally settled and everybody was dead, he would be the one standing victorious.

'That man really gives me the creeps,' Sophia muttered, wiping her hand on her jacket in disgust.

Dave grunted in agreement as he closed the cell door behind him. They turned to Wendy, who was gazing at the grinning man through the one-way mirror with a heavily furrowed brow.

'I don't trust him,' she whispered. 'I think he will stab us in the back the first chance he gets.'

'Oh, I have no doubt he will,' Sophia agreed reluctantly. She sucked in a deep breath, lifted her hands and huffed. 'But we need him, and he knows it, which is what makes him even more dangerous.' She placed her finger on her lips and nodded at the one-way mirror. 'We shouldn't discuss him here. I think it's best we head back up to the conference room where we can talk more freely.'

However, before they could turn to head down the corridor, Dave coughed, and Sophia's eyebrows perked up in curiosity as he put his hand on her arm.

'I am going to head to the infirmary and check on Claire before I join you,' he said wearily. 'I just feel I need a breather before we dive back into things.'

Understanding crossed Sophia's warm features and she gently tapped his hand. 'Take all the time you need.' She exhaled a long, tired breath and then glanced at Wendy. 'In fact, I think we should all take five minutes to clear our heads. God knows, we need it.'

Appreciative of the chance to clear his head, Dave gave a small but grateful nod and turned away from the two women. But as he hurried down the corridor, he shivered; it was as if an icy hand had touched the back of his neck. Also, something was gnawing at him in the pit of his stomach. It had been troubling him when he had been in the cell, like he was being watched. At first, he had put it down to standing in front of a one-way mirror, but since leaving the cell, he could not shake that sinking feeling of dread. He quickened his pace and shook his head, putting his paranoia down to the stress of everything he had been through over the past few days.

-3-

Claire was dying.

Lying on the hard cold floor of the records room of the police station, she could feel her life slowly ebbing away, but still had a vague awareness of everything that was happening around her, a mixture of heavy urgent footsteps and voices charged with emotion. But through the cacophony of noise, she still managed to make out the recognisable Scottish twang of Wendy's stricken voice that was begging her not to die before she eventually succumbed to the empty dark void of unconsciousness. On the edge of death, she had brief spells of lucidity when she was aware of people wearing strange face masks, staring down at her, doing something to her body.

'We're losing her,' she heard one of them say.

No, I'm still here! Claire thought, wanting desperately to scream at them, let them know she could hear them, but found herself unable to do so.

Then something strange happened. Believing her body was coming close to its demise, Claire had a moment of dream-like consciousness, something pulling her out of her body. Like an astral projection that was hovering close to its body, she watched with emotionless detachment as the medical team struggled to save the gravely injured woman on the examination table. She then became aware of a tunnel of light opening above her, surrounding her physical body with a red and orange healing aura.

Claire saw one of the medical team looking at the electrocardiogram monitor with wide-eyed amazement as the display showed an increasing pulse.

'Her heart rate is increasing, she is stabilising.'

The celestial woman looked over her shoulder and saw that a portal of energy had opened behind her, revealing a corridor of light with a figure standing at the far end of it. She had heard stories of people near to death describe standing in front of a tunnel of light with their loved ones waiting for them. A sense of joy filled Claire's heart as she glided forward to move towards the light, believing her twin sister Emma was waiting for her. Would this be it? Would this be the time when she would finally be reunited with her sister?

However, as her spirit floated through the portal into the tunnel of light, she looked forlornly over her shoulder and watched, with a heavy heart, the portal closing behind her. Claire sighed with resignation and said a silent goodbye to the people she believed she was leaving behind as she glided down the tunnel of light. She winced and held her hand up over her eyes as a warm beam of light enveloped her, blinding her. For a moment she thought she had been thrown into space and was heading towards the sun. She let out a small scream. No! She needed to pull away or she would be lost forever, cast out in the void.

But before she could do anything, the bright light disappeared and was replaced by a more comfortable and welcoming luminance. After blinking away the spots in her eyes and her vision had adjusted to the new level of light, Claire's eyes grew wide in wonderment as she found herself standing in a vast white hall. The only piece of furniture was a tall narrow mirror and two sky-blue cushioned armchairs with a small circular coffee table between them. She jerked her head up as a streak of light caught her attention, and she stared in open-mouthed awe at the majestic sight above her. Claire craned her head back, mesmerised at the sight above her; the infinite sea of stars reminded her of the holographic displays on show in planetariums. Her hands touched her mouth, and she watched in joyful wonderment as clouds of multicoloured energy danced and swirled above her.

'Oh, my word,' she murmured to herself.

'Quite a sight to behold, is it not?'

Caught unawares, Claire gave a squeak of surprise at the male voice coming from behind her and spun round to see a tall, silver-haired black man. On noticing his white evening suit and the ornate walking stick he was carrying in his right hand, a warm memory flooded into her mind; she was reminded of the friendly Texan gentleman from the movies she had watched as a child. For some inexplicable reason she felt there was a touch of kindness in his brightly lit starfilled eyes as they glimmered in amusement at her reaction.

The elderly stranger lifted his left hand up apologetically. 'I am sorry, child. I did not mean to startle you.'

Her cheeks warming with embarrassment, Claire shook her head slightly. 'No, it's my fault. I was so distracted by what is going on above, I didn't see you standing there.' She swallowed, glanced down at herself, and then gestured towards him. 'Are you God? Does this mean I am dead?'

To her surprise, the silver-haired man let out a bark of laughter and shook his head in amusement. 'No, child. I am not the powerful One-Above-All and you are most certainly not dead.'

Despite herself, a hollow sense of disappointment surged through Claire and she staggered back from the strange man. The stranger's multicoloured eyes flashed with concern, and he reached forward and tenderly took hold of her hand.

'Are you okay, child?'

Crestfallen, Claire let out a melancholic sigh and shook her head sorrowfully. 'I am sorry. For a moment there, I thought, I …' The words died in her throat and her vision became blurry as she fought back the tears.

'Ah, yes. I see,' the white-suited entity said softly, understanding dawning on his face. 'You thought this was the moment when you were going to be reunited with your twin sister Emma.'

At the mention of her sister's name, Claire's eyes tightened in anger and she slid a guarded look at the man in front of her as she a small step back from him. 'How do you know that? Who are you? What is this place?'

The unusual stranger smiled warmly and held his hands up. 'Please, Professor Tulley, you have nothing to be afraid of here. I mean you no harm.' Claire tilted her head curiously as she watched him stroll over to the cushioned armchair nearest to him and lower himself into it. His eyes appearing to glow with affection, he gestured to the unoccupied cushioned armchair in front of him. 'Please, if you can take a seat, I promise I will answer all your questions.'

A strange feeling filled Claire as she regarded the man in front of her. She could not explain it, but she sensed there was an inhuman kindness about him, that he harboured no malice towards her. Lowering herself into the armchair, she raised an eyebrow to him and signalled to him to proceed.

ORACLE'S VISION

The mysterious man acknowledged her with an appreciative nod, leaned forward and fixed her with a friendly smile. 'So, you are probably wondering who I am?' Without waiting for her to respond, he lifted his head and gestured to the ceiling full of stars above them. 'I am **Custos**. I am, simply put, the personification of the collected intelligence of the multiverse.' The corners of his mouth twitched as Claire's eyebrows knitted together as she struggled to wrap her head around that statement. He chuckled and waved his hand down his body. 'I chose this form because I didn't want to look intimidating to you, so I'd look like someone who you would feel safe with.'

Claire burst out laughing and nodded in agreement. 'Well, I can honestly say it has worked. You actually look like one of my favourite actors.'

The strange entity's eyes twinkled, and his mouth widened into a mischievous grin. 'Excellent, I am delighted this form pleases you.' His smile slowly disappeared as he lifted his cane to point at the room they were in. 'To answer your other question – where you are? Well, my dear, I am sure somebody as learned as yourself is aware of the multiverse?'

Her hand tapping her chin thoughtfully, Claire looked up at the cascade of stars above her and nodded slightly. 'Yes, in fact, a group of people I recently met were just talking about this.' She became suspicious as a thought popped into her head. 'I have a hunch you are already aware of that.' She arched an eyebrow in surprise as she thought she had seen a sheepish look flicker across the entity's face. Without waiting for him to respond, she looked admiringly around the giant hall. 'Can I assume this place is a simulation to make it more appealing to me? That my physical body is still lying on the operating table in my world, and you have brought my consciousness here, in the void between dimensions?'

The ancient being clapped his hands together and beamed with delight. 'Oh, very good, my dear. I see my instincts about you were correct. There may be hope for your species after all.'

'Thank you, that's really nice of you to say,' Claire replied dryly. 'But you still have not answered why you have brought me here.'

Custos let out a long sigh and gave her a sorrowful look. 'Because, child, I feel responsible for the events that have plagued you throughout your life. The trauma of your childhood, the troubles in your personal life leading up to your fight with the synthroid, which left you severely injured.'

So it was him, he was the one responsible! A floodgate of a lifetime's pain and misery surging through her, Claire jumped to her feet, clenched her hands into tight balls and took an angry step towards the rueful entity. 'Are you telling me that everything that has happened to me is because of you?' Her mouth twisted into a sneer of contempt. 'What? The multiverse wasn't entertaining enough for you, so you decided *"Hey! I know, let's mess with Claire Tulley's life. I'm sure it will be entertaining to see how much shit we chuck at her."* Well, guess what?' With angry resentment coursing through her, she lifted her hands in the air and screamed bitterly at the star field above her. 'It will delight you to know you really fudged my life up. Thank you very much!'

Sobbing, Claire collapsed back into her armchair with her head in her hands. After an uncomfortably long silence, Custos exhaled heavily, rose to his feet and knelt in front of her.

'No, my child, I didn't find it entertaining.'

Claire opened her mouth to snap something but bit back a retort as she detected something in the omniscient being's voice, something she was not expecting – regret. He gently placed his hand under Claire's chin and smiled thinly at her. Staring into the being's eyes, she noticed for the first time that there was something familiar contained within them. It occurred to her that this ancient figure in front of her contained more humanity within him than some humans she had met.

Custos smiled as Claire reached up and gently stroked his face. She was full of wonder as he took her hand and held it tenderly.

'It is not your destiny to die on an operating table, Claire. You still have a greater role to play in the coming struggle,' he said cryptically, gesturing up to the swirling display of galaxies above them. 'My essence comprises the collected energies of the universe. A small portion can help a human body heal from a traumatic injury.'

Claire began to understand as she stared at the mysterious figure in front of her in awe. 'That red and orange aura covering my body? That was you?'

The silver-haired being nodded sadly. 'Yes, I know it does not make up for the suffering you have had to endure, but I hope it can at least help in some way to settle the balance. The healing energy I am sending to your body will allow it to heal in a few days, rather than a few weeks or months.' He let out a long, regretful sigh and shook his head ruefully. 'I am very old, child. Older than you can possibly imagine. And I have made mistakes. One mistake in particular I am deeply ashamed of.' He groaned dramatically and straightened himself, giving a sideways look at the narrow mirror beside them. 'Many years ago, a sentient AI known as Oracle, after nearly destroying all organic life on her world, was finally imprisoned and exiled into the dimensional void. I thought I could get through to her and show the error of her ways by guiding her, but I didn't realise how insane she was until it was too late.' He exhaled a disgusted breath and ran his hand over his wizened face. 'While I was blabbering away like an old fool, she was secretly absorbing my energy and at the first opportunity used it against me, scattering my essence across the multiverse. In the time it took for me to reform, she escaped and spread her evil onto another world, eventually manipulating the people of that world to invade another world – your world.'

'The global conspiracy!' Claire exclaimed.

'Yes.' Custos sighed remorsefully.

Claire frowned and shook her head in confusion. 'I don't understand. If you know where she is –' she held up her hands and pointed to the vast hall around her '– surely, with all your power, you can easily take her from the world she is on?'

'I am sorry, child, but it is not as simple as that,' the entity replied with a grim expression. 'I cannot interfere. As powerful as I am, she still has residues of power contained within.' Claire felt her breath catch in her throat as Custos raised his hand and displayed a ball of energy. 'If I were to confront her directly, the energies we would unleash would devastate not just your world, but most of the multiverse.'

A thought popped into Claire's head and she took a small step back, holding up her finger. 'Hold on a minute. You say you cannot interfere, but haven't you already interfered by using your energy to restore my injured body, as well as bringing me here?'

His multicoloured eyes sparkling, Custos gave her a knowing smile and tapped his nose with his finger, chuckling. 'Who says I have interfered? Hmmm?' Claire bristled with annoyance as he gave her a patronising wink. 'If Oracle were to scan your world for my energy, she would only detect the usual background radiation that is emitted by the universe. And as for you being here?' He bobbed his head, a shadow of a mysterious smile crossing his face. 'What makes you think you are, my child? All this could be a dream – your mind helping your body heal from the trauma it has endured. At this moment, your body is lying in a hospital bed and, if anybody looks closely enough, all they will see is the signs of rapid eye movement and deduce you are dreaming.'

Puffing her cheeks out, Claire forced air out through tight lips, folded her arms across her chest and tilted her head. 'You really are spreading that line pretty thin there, aren't you?' She grumbled as she gave the duplicitous entity the hairy eyeball.

Custos laughed and gave her a sly wink. 'When you are old as I am, my dear, over time you discover ingenious ways to beat the system.' He steepled his fingers together and gave her a mysterious smile. 'Have there been moments in your life when you have felt you have done something so out of character, you look back and wonder why you did it? For example, the way you recently spent the night with Dave, only hours after meeting him.'

Claire scratched her head in puzzlement and nodded in agreement. 'Yeah, when I think about it now, I do wonder what made me do something like that. I have never had a one-night stand in my life – in fact, I have always taken it slow in a relationship. I would normally neve—' She paused as she realised what Custos was implying and stared at him in open-mouthed shock. 'That was you! You made me sleep with Dave that night.' Her eyes filled with tears and her body trembled with indignant fury. 'What right do you have to force your will on someone like that? You … you … violated me!'

The unrepentant entity lifted his shoulder in a small shrug and gave Claire a small smile. 'Not really. You and Dave would have slept together eventually, but I needed to it happen sooner than later, for you both to get to the point I needed you to be. Your feelings for one another were there, I just helped bring them to the surface a bit quicker.'

Was any of it true? How could she look at Dave now and wonder if what she was feeling was because she wanted it or because she had been programmed to? Appalled by the entity's distorted sense of logic, Claire gave a small, disgusted laugh and shook her head. 'You still cannot see that it was wrong, can you? You truly believe it was right to inflict your will on a person so long as you get what you want.' She spun away from him and threw her hands up in the air. 'You are just like Oracle. You are like two children fighting on an ant nest, not caring who you step on.'

'Maybe you're right, but I refuse to apologise if my actions result in ridding the multiverse of a dangerous threat,' Custos replied angrily.

Claire shot him a withering look and hissed at him, 'You manipulative bastard!'

The entity's eyes suddenly sparkled, and then he turned around and stared intently at something over his shoulder. 'You will probably agree with her, won't you, my dear bookworm?'

Taken aback by his sudden change in behaviour, Claire frowned again and she scanned the empty hall. Seeing nothing, she scratched her head and looked at the mysterious being, confused. 'Who are you talking to?'

'Oh, that's not important,' he murmured, waving his hand evasively. Before Claire could question him further, he lifted his hand for silence, straightening his shoulders. A distant expression covered Custos's face as he muttered to himself, 'That should be enough time.'

Exasperated, Claire folded her arms across her chest and stared at the stranger, becoming increasingly annoyed. 'I am starting to lose my patience with you, old man. You still have a lot to answer for and I will be damned if I'm going to let you get away with what you have done.'

The omnipotent being laughed and then poked her arm with his cane. 'As much as I would like to see you try, my child, I am sorry to say our time is just about up. I was just checking to see if your body has healed enough for you to return to it.' His mouth widened and he beamed at Claire with a delighted expression. 'It will delight you to hear that I can now return you to your body.'

'Now hold on a minute!' Claire exclaimed, struggling to hide her resentment. 'You and I still have things we need to sort out. I refuse to stand by and allow you to get away with messing about with my life.' She folded her arms again and stubbornly straightened her head. 'Anyway, you said it would take a few days before my body healed enough to the point where you could allow me to return to it.'

Custos gave Claire a sly wink and then grinned at her. 'That's the thing about this place, my child. Time moves differently here. Three days have passed since your little escapade with the synthroid. Now, as much as I have enjoyed our little chit-chat, I have places to go, and things to do. Yes, yes, things to do.' He gave Claire's shoulder a friendly pat and turned away from her. 'Don't worry, we will meet again. Yes, yes, we will meet again.' He smiled as he lifted his hand and clicked his fingers.

'Just wait a minute,' Claire protested, 'I haven't finished with you. Don't yo—'

Her body's aches and pains burrowed into the back of Claire's consciousness, pulling her out of the black void of unconsciousness. No. She wanted to stay with Custos; she groaned, why did he have to send her away? She gasped sharply at the sensation of pain coming from somewhere around her stomach, but frowned as she noticed something else alongside the pain – an irritating itch. Why did her stomach itch so much? However, as she tried to raise her arm to scratch her abdomen, she became quite puzzled. It felt as if something was restricting her movement. *That's odd.* Why could she not raise her arm? She smacked her lips sleepily and frowned. Was this Custos's doing? Was he punishing her because she dared to chastise him?

Claire tried to raise her head, but that small movement just made things worse as the inside of her skull throbbed with every beat of her racing heart. Her muscle memory caused her eyes to fly open, but she was forced to clench them shut to protect them from the blinding light coming somewhere above her.

'For god's sake, are you trying to blind me?' she groaned, but then she flinched as she felt someone's hand touch her shoulder, followed by a compassionate feminine voice that spoke softly to her.

'Professor Tulley … Claire. It's okay. You're safe,' A woman's voice said in a soothing tone. 'You're in the infirmary. You had an accident, remember?'

'Accident?' Emma groaned. 'What acci—' It was at that moment the fog lifted from her brain and it all came flooding back to her. Yes, that was correct, Dave had taken Claire down into his police station's archive. They had been trying to look for any record relating to her sister's death, but before they could do so they were attacked by an animal. No, not an animal; it was a monster, the same monster that had attacked Claire and her twin sister, Emma, when they were young children. She wasn't sure whether it had been the same beast that had killed

Emma, but there was no doubt in Claire's that it was the same species. She tried to shake her head, trying to bring the memory to the surface, but all she could see were flashes of the beast standing over Dave's unconscious body. Then everything turned into a scarlet fog intensified by four decades worth of accumulated anger and guilt – anger from the death of her sister and guilt from believing she had allowed it to happen.

'It's okay, Claire,' the woman's voice said, 'I am going to release your arm, but you need to take it slow.'

'No … yes … what?' Claire moaned. Feeling right her arm become free, she struggled to climb out of bed. She shook her head in annoyance as she felt someone's hands on her shoulders, trying to push her back down. 'No, I need to speak to Custos. He … ugh!' Her stomach muscles flared with pain, and she gasped in shock.

'Claire, easy,' a male voice pleaded. She was almost sure it sounded like Dave's voice. 'You're in the infirmary. Try to remember. The creature attacked us, but you saved me. Remember.'

'Dave?' Claire moaned woozily. She blinked away the film covering her eyes and tried to focus on the figure who was speaking. She squinted in confusion at the blurred figure in front of her. Was that Dave? She blinked to refocus her eyes and when she saw it was him all she could do was stare at him in bewilderment. 'Dave? What are you doing here? Did he bring you here too?'

'He?' Dave replied, shaking his head in confusion. 'Claire, you were dreaming,' he said carefully, making a small gesture to the strawberry-blond woman standing next to him, who Claire recognised was Jacqueline. It was then she realised she was in the infirmary; the same one Andy had been in a few days earlier.

Jacqueline acknowledged Dave with a small nod and helped to ease Claire back into the bed. 'You're safe and sound in the base's infirmary, understand?'

'Ugh! I guess I must have been in the wars,' Claire groaned and nodded slowly, becoming more aware of her surroundings. She moaned softly and massaged her forehead with the tips of her fingers. 'I remember you taking me to the records room in the station to see if we could find out any information about my sister when we were attacked by …' She stiffened, felt her eyes grow round and stared at Dave in horror. 'The creature! The last thing I remember was seeing red, all these mixed emotions exploding within me as I saw the creature standing over you.' Dave winced in pain as she grabbed his hands and crushed them in a tight grip. 'What happened to the creature? Did you get it?'

'Oh, we got it, alright, but it was all thanks to you.' He laughed, gently detaching himself from her tight embrace. 'You were the one that killed it. Remember?'

'I did?' she exclaimed, staring at Dave through wide stunned eyes.

'Oh yes, you most certainly did,' Dave replied, looking proud and grinning at Claire. 'We can only guess what happened, but judging from your wounds and the condition of the creature afterwards, I can assume you fought like Xena Warrior Princess – screaming in defiance as you charged in, sword swinging.'

'Pfft.' Claire scoffed, waving her hand at Dave and feeling her face warm with embarrassment. She lifted an eyebrow when she noticed the serious expression on Dave's face. Then, detecting some movement out of the corner of her eye, her mouth fell open in astonishment as she watched Jacqueline bob her head excitedly in confirmation. Aghast, she stared at the grinning man in stunned disbelief, her mouth opening and closing like a suffocating fish.

'Yep, a sword.' Dave chuckled, nodding. 'Who would have thought, behind the exterior of a mild-mannered history professor, there was a warrior woman screaming to get out? Never thought you had it in you.'

Claire gave a tired moan and dropped her head back on the pillow. She tilted her head to the side as she heard movement of the sounds of multiple footsteps coming from somewhere in front of her. She raised her head slightly and noticed the odd looks she was getting from the nursing staff and soldiers who were walking past her bed. What the hell? Why did they have to gawk at her like that? Couldn't they see she was injured? What happened to patient privacy? She had a good mind to comp— *Wait, hang on, they're not gawking at me, they're … Oh … my … God!* She stiffened and then imagined her eyebrows were like hairy caterpillars climbing up her forehead as she recognised there was something almost reverential in their stares.

Twisting his head to see what Claire was staring at, Dave frowned and then the cause of her shock must have dawned on him because when he turned back to her, she saw that he was smirking. 'You have earned yourself a bit of a fan club here after how you took the creature out.' To her increasing irritation, she could tell that he was obviously enjoying her discomfort and was trying to keep his laugh in. She guessed he must have seen the displeased look on her face as he gave small cough and then continued to speak with an innocent tone of voice. 'In fact, I've heard a rumour the base personnel here are holding the sword in question somewhere on display and would like you to autograph it.'

'Oh God!' Mortified, Claire could almost imagine her face was probably doing an impression of a beetroot. She squeezed her eyes shut and shook her head in embarrassment, pushing her head deeper into the pillow. *Custos, put me back in a coma please!*

'Don't worry, he's only joking,' Jacqueline said, shooting Dave a cold, disapproving stare. 'Aren't you?'

Dave swallowed and coughed apologetically. 'Yes. Sorry, Claire. I'm kidding. They don't want you to autograph it.' He flashed her a cheeky grin, chortling. 'But I wasn't lying when I said they're holding the sword somewhere on display as a trophy.'

Jacqueline rolled her eyes and let out a long, heavy sigh. 'Men!' She pressed her lips together and spoke to Dave in a more serious tone. 'You can have five more minutes, but then she needs to rest.'

Claire gave a tired yawn and smiled gratefully at the exasperated nurse who gave her a friendly tap on the arm. Jacqueline spun round and hurried away to speak to another member of the medical staff.

Claire looked back at Dave and stared at him enquiringly. 'So, anything interesting happen while I was … away?'

'Oh, aye, you could say that.' Dave laughed bitterly, rubbing the back of his neck.

He settled back into the chair and started to fill her in on the events of the past few days. Claire went through a series of emotions as she listened intently to Dave's account, her eyes growing wide in shock at hearing him describe the science team's encounter with the techno-parasite they had found within the corpse of Mary Jenkins's doppelgänger. Dave jerked back in shock when she squealed with delight on hearing how Andy, Wendy, and Sharon, with the aid of the plans Claire had acquired, discovered the portal beneath the old isolation hospital. Her mouth fell open as she listened to him tell her of his surprising encounter with his own doppelgänger, Colonel Barnes, and of the events in New York.

'Do you trust him?'

Lapsing into silence, Dave looked up at the ceiling, rubbed his chin and gave a small shrug, shaking his head. 'To be honest, I wouldn't trust him as far as I could throw him.' Claire could tell from the expression on his face that he was troubled. She also thought he looked drained and wondered if he was sleeping okay, which was confirmed when she heard him let out a weary sigh. 'But he may be our only chance if we have any hope of surviving what's coming. On top of everything, we now have this AI to contend with. My gut tells me my scheming counterpart knows more than he's letting on about Oracle.' Dave raised an eyebrow on noticing Claire stiffen at the AI's name. 'Claire, what's wrong?'

Her blood running cold, Claire swallowed as the memories of Custos's warning about Oracle came flooding back to her. She inhaled a deep breath and took hold of Dave's hand. 'Dave, there is something I need to tell you. It is going to sound strange, but please, I need you to keep an open mind.' She fixed him with a steady gaze. 'Can you promise me that?'

Dave nodded wordlessly in agreement and swallowed. Claire could tell from the worried look on his face that he was afraid of what she was going to say next.

Continuing to stare into his eyes, Claire tightened her grip on Dave's hands and spoke in a more forceful tone. 'Dave, I need you to say it. Can you promise me you will keep an open mind?'

He frowned and struggled to release his hands from her intense grip. 'Claire, you're scaring me.'

'Can you promise to keep an open mind?' She repeated, this time with more force.

'Damn it, Claire! Yes. I promise to keep an open mind.'

'Thank you.' Claire smiled gratefully. She let out a small, relieved breath and released his hands from her vice-like grip. Visibly unsettled, Dave pulled back and massaged his hands. With her hands held up in front of her, she fixed him with a stern expression. 'What I am about to tell you may sound bizarre, and I can imagine the first thing you will say is that I dreamed it. But believe me when I tell you – it happened.'

She sucked a deep breath and closed her eyes to gather her thoughts, thinking back to her conversation with Custos. How much should she tell him? Should she really be the one to tell him that Custos had manipulated them? Was it even fair to put this burden on him when it was obvious that he had so much on his plate right now? Even though she could see in his eyes how much he appeared to care deeply for her, a part of her now wondered how much of it was real or if it was because he had been subliminally programmed to feel that way. But before she could open her mouth to speak, a loud alarm klaxon cut her off. Claire grimaced at the loud voice broadcasting over the tannoy system. Oh great! What now?

'Medical team to the detention level. I repeat, medical team to detention level.'

Her stomach knotting with fear, Claire watched Dave bolt out of his seat with a horrified expression over his face. 'Dave, what's wrong?'

'That's where Colonel Barnes is being held,' he whispered in a low horrified voice. He held his hand up apologetically, shaking his head. 'I'm sorry, Claire, but I'm going to have to go. We can finish this later.'

Claire acknowledged him with a small nod and watched him charge down the ward and through the double doors. Wearily, she exhaled a long, tired breath, lowered her head onto her pillow, and closed her eyes.

Distracted, his mind racing, Dave charged down the corridor like a man possessed, turning into a long corridor, only to collide with a soldier coming the other way, who grunted in annoyance at the panicking man barging past him. Without looking back, he raised his hand and waved at the unknown soldier in wordless apology as he continued to race down the corridor towards the elevator.

A few minutes later, Dave, filled with dread, dashed out of the open elevator door to see a group of people standing outside a familiar-looking cell door. His throat tightened as he realised his instincts were right – it was Colonel Barnes's cell. Had the proud dimensionally exiled soldier decided to take his own life because he could not tolerate the idea of having to fight against his own people? Fearing the worst, Dave held his breath as he made his way up the short corridor.

Sophia Collins acknowledged Dave with a small nod as he came to a stop next to her. Sadness clouded her features and she gestured to the open cell door.

'Private Jameson came to relieve Petty Officer Harem. He knew something was wrong when he saw the cell door open and raised the alarm as soon as he saw the body lying in the cell.'

Stunned, Dave took an awkward step forward into the cell and spotted the lifeless figure of the marine lying on the floor. His eyes narrowed as he noticed Harem's jacket and trousers were missing. Kneeling beside the fallen marine, John Payne lifted his head to Dave and grimly acknowledged him with a slight nod. Although his face was like a tight and rigid mask, Dave could see the raging fire in the younger man's eyes. He didn't have to be psychic to see John had taken the death of one of his subordinates personally. It was also clear to see who he held responsible for this despicable act of violence.

Barnes, what did you do? Dave thought sadly.

-4-

*M**oments earlier …*

Petty Officer Harem's round brown eyes sharpened as he heard a short ping come from behind him. He looked sharply over his shoulder and was surprised to see an attractive petite blond-haired woman wearing a crisp white lab coat step out of the open elevator doors. Harem relaxed slightly as he realised it was Doctor Sharon Fisher. Although he did not know her personally, he had seen her occasionally hurrying around the base and was aware that some of the base personnel had a nickname for her – the Energizer Bunny – because of the excitable way she spoke whenever she explained things. According to scuttlebutt, she was apparently involved in a romantic relationship with Commander Payne. He cocked his head and watched as she lowered her head and peered at him over the top of her glasses, smiling coyly, and then glided towards him in a purposeful manner.

'Doctor Fisher,' Harem acknowledged in a flat tone, nodding slightly to her. 'What can I do for you, ma'am?'

Sharon sighed wearily and gestured at the cell door Harem was standing in front of. 'Oh, you know how it is, the top brass would like some tests carried out on our new guest. They have ordered that I take some blood samples from him.' She gave a small shrug and rolled her eyes. 'The things I have to do.'

Over the years, Harem had earned an unusual nickname from the people he had served with – Spiderman – due to his uncanny ability to sense danger. He had always laughed off the suggestion that he had this ability, putting it down to being in tune with his surroundings. But as he watched Fisher glide towards him, that same danger sense set the hairs on the back of his neck tingling and the muscles in his arms tensed, setting off an alarm in his head.

'Ma'am, I must request that you don't come any closer,' he said firmly. Harem's steel jaw tightened, and he straightened to his full height with his left hand held up in front of him. He locked his eyes on the woman in front of him, as his other hand slid down to his radio. 'I am sorry, but nobody has advised me that tests are to be carried out on the prisoner. I am sure you understand why I must verify with our superiors before I can let you into the cell.'

Her bottom lip sticking out, the petite young woman hung her head and gave Harem a puppy dog stare. 'Oh, is that absolutely necessary? Do not tell me you are afraid of a little girl like me, are you?'

This feels wrong. Harem swallowed at his deepening sense of unease. He felt his throat constrict as he forced himself to speak in a more authoritative tone. 'Doctor Fisher, I must order you to cease your advance before I—'

Harem blinked and then felt his eyebrows rise in confusion as he realised the slender woman was standing next to him. Did she just cover the remaining distance between them in a blink of an eye? *What the hell? How did she do that?*

She smiled flirtingly at him as she reached up and brushed her hand over his cheek. 'Shush now,' she whispered in a sweet voice, 'do you not remember? You already checked. They confirmed I am to do some tests on the prisoner. I can enter the cell, isn't that correct?'

Harem's eyebrows knitted together and he stared at the radio in his hand in befuddlement. No, that was not right. He had not spoken to anybody yet. Or had he? He scratched his head and stared at the radio in his hand blankly. Unable to think clearly, he blinked furiously and then nodded slowly. Yes, that was correct. His commanding officer had just spoken to him over the radio and ordered him to open the cell door for Doctor Fisher. Yes, that was right, she had important tests to carry out.

'Yes, I'm sorry for the mix-up, Doctor Fisher,' Harem replied in a dazed voice, giving the grinning woman an apologetic smile. 'You're cleared to enter.'

Sophia's mouth broadened into a chilling smile. She then simply nodded and tapped Harem's hand gratefully. He bowed his head in compliance and opened the cell door. Despite his brain fog, he still managed to retain some of his instincts as he looked through the cell door and his eyes tightened in suspicious alertness as Colonel Barnes shot up out of his seat and stared warily at the two people entering the cell. The small woman gestured for Harem to take up position in the centre of the cell, and he nodded slowly in compliance, even though deep in his mind every fibre in his being screamed at him to stop what he was doing. *No! This is wrong, I must resist. Fight back! Do something!*

Barnes's mouth twisted into a petulant sneer, and he stared at the unfamiliar woman through suspicious eyes. 'Just who the hell are you?'

Ignoring the sneering man, Sharon fixed Harem with a cold stare and pointed to his jacket. 'Remove your coat and then take off your trousers. Will you comply?'

No, this is wrong. Resist damn it! Harem stiffened in defiance and shook his head.

Sharon lowered her head and glowered at Harem over the top of her glasses. She then spoke in an even firmer tone. 'I said comply.'

'Sharon ... can't ... you ... see ... this ... wrong?' Harem hissed defiantly through clenched teeth, feeling a bead of sweat run down the back of his neck. It had taken an enormous amount of effort for him just to utter those few words.

Sharon pouted and placed her hand on Harem's face; he flinched as he felt a small tingle of electricity pass from her hand onto his face. 'Shush, my handsome boy. Everything will be okay.' She said softly and slowly nodded. 'You want to comply, do you not?'

'Yes, Sharon, I want to comply,' Harem replied in a low monotone voice. Sharon watched with an amused expression as he robotically removed his jacket and trousers.

Barnes took a step toward Sharon and scowled at her. 'I demand to know what is going on here. I must insi—'

Sharon spun her head sharply around and shot Barnes a withering stare, silencing him. Turning her attention back to Harem, she gave him a cold stare and pointed to the floor. 'Get on your knees.'

Without complaint, Harem nodded and lowered himself onto his knees. Even in his debilitated state, he still retained some sense of awareness, because he had noticed that Barnes's face had turned ashen. Was it possible that Barnes had recognised there was something dangerous about this strange woman? Sensing Sharon standing behind him, Harem wanted so desperately to fight back but found himself unable to move; his body stiffened on feeling the cool embrace of the woman's icy hands on his face. Showing no emotion, she violently twisted the man's head round in one effortless move. Buried deep inside his consciousness, Harem's mind screamed out in pain as he felt the pain of his neck snapping, followed by darkness and then the cold embrace of death.

Barnes stared numbly at the lifeless body on the floor, trying to discern what he had just seen. He was then struck by an overwhelming sense of vertigo as the room spun around him and he had to place his hand on the table to stop himself from falling. Struggling to compose himself, he squeezed his eyes shut, sucked in a lungful of air, and concentrated on his steadying his heart rate. As a soldier in the Universal Roman Empire, he had seen his fair share of dead bodies, some of them even killed by him personally, so it was not Harem's death that affected him, but it was the cold way in which the blond stranger dispatched the obviously skilled warrior that had troubled him. He had only ever seen one person kill somebody in such a cold and methodical manner – General Wendy Cooper – but she was far across the multiverse, separated by dimensions.

'Colonel Barnes, are you listening to me?'

Barnes started and came back to his senses. He had been in such a daze that he had not realised the strange blond woman, who the soldier had called Sharon, had been talking to him. Blinking, he shook his head in an effort to focus himself.

'I'm sorry. I was miles away. What did you say?'

'I would suggest you pay more attention if you want to get out of here alive,' Sharon snapped, pushing the dead soldier's jacket and trousers into Barnes's chest. 'Now, put these on. Make it quick – we have very little time.'

His eyes still fixed on the body on the floor, Barnes took hold of the clothes and stared uncertainly at them. He swallowed and took an uncomfortable step back from the woman. His gaze darted around the cell as he considered his options. Who was this woman? Should he stay, or take his chances with her?

As if reading his thoughts, Sharon's mouth twisted into a maniacal grin and she nodded knowingly. 'I know what you are thinking. You are trying to decide whether to trust me or stay and take your chances with your counterpart.' All emotion on her face vanished and she fixed him with a harsh gaze. 'Let me remind you, you are an enemy officer standing in the cell with one of their dead comrades. The first thing they will think is that you killed him when he attempted to stop you from escaping.' The slender young woman held up a finger, cutting off Barnes's protest. 'Before you say they will wonder why you were still in the cell, I will tell them I found you standing over the poor corporal's body.' As if on cue, her chestnut eyes sparkled and a stream of crocodile tears started flowing down her cheeks, and her voice trembled with grief-stricken horror. 'It was awful. I came to check on the prisoner and found him standing over the poor petty officer's body. When I saw him turn toward me with that evil maniacal grin of his I just knew I would be next.' She let out a distraught wail and shook her head. 'It was awful. I tried to close the cell door, but he was too quick for me. Before I was able to fully close the door his hands grabbed my wrist and he pushed me against the door. I did the only thing possible and bit into his arm, which made him jerk back in shock. At that point, I managed to close the cell door and lock him in.' Suddenly, almost like she had flicked a switch, her distress vanished, and she stared at him with a smug expression. 'How's that for a performance? Is that a good incentive for you?'

'I see you have thought of everything.' Barnes sneered, shooting the woman an unfriendly stare.

Sharon smirked and folded her arms across her chest, 'So, you will see, you have only two options. One, trust me and I help you escape. Or two, stay and see if you can explain your way out.' A shadow of a smile crossed her lips and she stared at him through cold eyes. 'Personally, I do not like your chances.'

Feeling he had been forced into a corner, Barnes scrubbed his face with his hands and turned away from the woman, his mind racing as he considered his options. He felt something gnaw at his gut, telling him that he should not trust this woman. She was dangerous, no doubt about it, so he was going to have tread very carefully with her. He shook his head slightly and let out a heavy, reluctant sigh to acknowledge his limited options; if he must agree with the devil to survive, then so be it.

'Fine.' He huffed grudgingly, sliding his arms into Harem's jacket, and then climbed into the soldier's trousers. He grumbled in disgust as he realised the trousers were a bit big for him, finding he had to turn the inside of the hem up so he would not raise any suspicions.

'Excellent.' Sharon grinned cheerily. She frowned as if remembering something, and reached into her pocket and handed Barnes a small communication device. 'Take this mobile phone. Follow the instructions displayed on the screen. They will guide you to a laboratory on the medical floor. I am booked into it to carry out some important investigations, so you will be safe there.' She reached into her pocket and handed him a small plastic card. 'To gain access, you will need to swipe this. I will join you an hour later.'

Despite every sinew in his body screaming at him not to believe her, Barnes cocked his head and continued to stare at the strange woman with deep distrust. 'What are you going to do?'

Sharon shrugged slightly. 'I have some things I need to take care of. Also, somebody needs to raise the alarm.'

Is this woman insane? Barnes was ghast and he gave the woman an unbelieving look. 'Raise the alarm! Are you mad?'

The corners of Sharon's mouth formed a crooked smile and she waved a finger at him. 'Do not worry, I know what I am doing. Even dressed as you are, you will still pick up unwanted attention. When I raise the alarm, people will be too distracted to take notice of an oddly dressed soldier wandering the complex. Oh, and that reminds me … now, where did I put it?' she muttered to herself as she fumbled around in the pockets of her jacket, eventually pulling out a flimsy green military visor cap and handing it to Barnes. 'Wear this. It will help cover your face while you hurry through the corridors.'

Taking the cap, the Barnes gave the woman a sceptical look and pushed the visor down just over his eyes. Without waiting for further instructions, he cast a swift look at the instructions on the mobile phone and marched through the cell door into the corridor toward the still open elevator doors. Anxious at the idea of being caught wearing someone else's uniform, Barnes stabbed his finger on a button on the elevator wall panel and bit his lip impatiently as he watched the elevator door close; he stiffened as he felt the cabin judder slightly as it began its ascent. He felt his breath catch in his throat as he heard a slight ping and looked up at the small LED screen above the door and saw that the elevator had stopped at the floor below where he needed it to stop. The muscles in his arms tightened as he watched the cabin's doors slide open and a short sandy-haired Asian man wearing a crisp white coat walked in. The newcomer barely noticed the occupant and continued to stare intently at the tablet in his hands. Barnes managed to catch a glimpse of his fellow passenger's name on his ID badge: Henry Schan, Bioengineer Technician.

'Afternoon,' the stranger said absent-mindedly. Without looking up from the tablet he was holding he stretched out his free hand and pressed a button on the cabin's control panel.

Trying to remain inconspicuous, Barnes lowered his head and acknowledged the newcomer with a slight grunt. Henry raised his head from his tablet and blinked at Barnes in surprise.

'I don't think I've seen you here before. Are you new here?'

Barnes shrugged and gave a small shake of his head. He felt an icy trickle of sweat run down his neck as Henry cocked his head and opened his mouth to speak but was cut off by a loud alarm klaxon from the tannoy system.

Medical team to the detention level. I repeat, medical team to detention level.

The technician rolled his eyes and shook his head in exasperation. 'Oh great, another drill. Don't you just hate these?'

Before Barnes could answer, there was a short ping followed by the elevator door opening. Acknowledging Henry with a quick tap on the rim of his cap with his finger, Barnes exited through the elevator doors and swallowed a lungful of air, trying to calm his shredded nerves as he carefully made his way down the corridor, remembering to lower his head just as a group of people dressed in white medical uniforms charged past him. But as he turned another corner, a slightly overweight grey-haired man barrelled into him and he let out an annoyed *oomph*, the collision knocking the wind out of him.

The colonel's heart leapt up into his throat on seeing it was his doppelgänger and he steadied himself for an attack … that did not come. To his astonishment, his distracted counterpart sidestepped him and raced down the corridor as he gave Barnes an apologetic wave.

After saying a silent prayer to thank whatever gods were looking over him, Barnes, hugely relieved, decided not to push his luck any further and increased his pace down the corridor. He gave another swift glance at the instructions on the mobile phone and quickly scanned the doors along the corridor. A sense of satisfaction filled him as he spotted that his destination was not far away. He held his breath and closed his eyes as he came to a stop and pressed the plastic card up against the door's lock. *Well, here goes nothing.* A small breath escaped through his clenched teeth as he heard four quick beeps, followed by the click of a door unlocking.

Not one for looking a gift in the horse in the mouth, Barnes gave a sideways glance up the corridor and quickly took a big step through the open door, closing it behind him. Safely inside, he took off his cap and leaned against the door, closed his eyes, and exhaled slowly, letting the tension disappear out of his muscles.

The stress easing out of his body, Barnes opened his eyes to find he was standing in a small laboratory. He cocked his head curiously as he moved slowly around to inspect the contents of the room and snorted with derision at a small, antiquated computer terminal on a desk, along with other pieces of unfamiliar equipment around the room. His hand continued to trail over the table's surface as he glided around the room, passing several large containers with words in some alien language written on them. Barnes was familiar enough with this world's language to interpret the words as "*Warning – contains biohazard materials*".

Barnes picked up a scalpel from a container holding surgical equipment and played with it in his hands as he continued to wander around the laboratory. Pocketing the scalpel, he came to a stop at an examination couch and carefully climbed onto it. Exhausted, fatigue enveloping his body, he laid his head on the pillow, closed his eyes and drifted off to sleep.

Four muffled electronic beeps startled Barnes awake. Years earlier, as a cadet at the Imperial Academy, he had developed an acute sense of self-preservation – always on alert, never letting his guard down for a minute, ready to defend himself at a moment's notice against an attack. Within moments, the former Imperial officer was alert, leaping off the table, standing crouched with his hands in front of him in a defensive posture.

The muscles in his body becoming steel-like, his eyes sharpened and became fixed on the door on the other side of the room as he watched it slowly open. His chest rising and falling in steady breaths, and the steady thump of his heart in his ears, Barnes clenched his hands into two balls and imagined they were two hammers ready to pound this intruder into submission. Whoever this new threat was, they would soon learn at their cost that he was not an easy prey to take down.

But he relaxed slightly as he realised who was entering the room. He noticed the petite woman's eyebrow perk up as she walked through the door. The corner of her mouth twitched in amusement and she made a small gesture at his defensive posture.

'Expecting somebody else, were we?'

Feeling the corner of his right eye twitching, Barnes relaxed and gave Sharon a crooked sneer. 'On my world, you're asking for trouble if you let your guard down for a second.' The corner of his mouth quirked up and he let his eyes linger on the woman in front of him. 'I've learned never to turn my back on anybody. Trust is dangerous. It is something that will get you killed.'

'That sounds really tiresome,' Sharon replied. She tilted her head and stared at him in interest. 'Surely, you must trust me?'

Barnes put his head back and let out a mirthless laugh. 'Woman, I wouldn't trust you as far as I could throw you.' Full of suspicion, he waggled his finger at her. 'As far as I am concerned, you are an unknown quantity. Which makes you even more dangerous.'

Sharon dropped her chin to the top of her chest, stuck out her bottom lip and slowly edged towards him. 'Oh, a big strapping man such as yourself cannot be afraid of a tiny woman like me.' With a seductive smile dancing on her lips, she fluttered her eyelashes and loosened the top button of her blouse. 'Maybe there is something I could do that can change your mind?'

Well, maybe this world isn't as bad after all. Despite himself, Barnes swallowed and stared transfixed, mesmerised by the woman's seductively dazzling chestnut eyes. Inside his mind, he heard his inner voice scream at him to stop thinking with his balls and to think with his head, not to drop his guard against this dangerous woman. But as he watched her saunter up to him, he pushed that thought away and silently scolded himself for being afraid of this beautiful siren. He licked his lips in perverse pleasure as she put her hand on his chest and pushed him back onto the examination table. Oh well, when in Rome.

His heart thumping in his chest, his breath quickened as he watched Sharon take off her glasses and smile at him seductively. She set the glasses to one side and climbed on top of the examination table, straddling him. Feeling her knees pressed into the sides of his ribs, Barnes gave a surprised gasp of pain. The corners of his mouth lifting in a delighted grin, he reached up to unbutton the flimsy blouse but let out a yelp of pain as she grabbed his wrists and held them tight in an uncannily strong grip. Her expression becoming cold, she slammed Barnes's arms hard onto the table above his head.

'You have been a bad boy, my dear colonel, and need to be punished,' she hissed.

Caught in the moment, Barnes squeezed his eyes shut and nodded in compliance, grinning. 'Oh, I'm sure I've been terrible and need to be punished most severely.' He chuckled, pretending to speak in a trembling voice. 'Oh, mistress, I beg for your forgiveness. Please tell me what it is I've done that offends you so?'

His eyes still tightly closed, Barnes smiled as he sensed Sharon lean in closer to him and press her body against his. He squirmed uncomfortably as she put her head beside his ear, and he felt her warm breath on his neck. Out of all the things that had happened him that day, he had to admit this one was possibly the most enjoyable. Barnes settled himself as he felt Sharon's togue lick the side of his neck. He might just get to like this world after all.

'You ran away from me, David. You thought you were being so clever when you disabled my cyber-drone in that transport-pod back on Terra,' she whispered.

Wait? What did she say? Not believing what he had just heard, Barnes opened his eyes and stared at Sharon in confoundment. 'What? How did you?' He grunted and struggled to release himself from her vice-like grip without avail. His eyebrows knitting together, he stared at the surprisingly strong woman on top of him. 'Who are you?'

Still holding the struggling Barnes's wrists, Sharon threw her head back and laughed dryly. 'Oh, I am so disappointed in you, Colonel. I had hoped you would have worked it out by now.' Her nostrils flared and she stared at the man below her with a chilling gaze. 'You did not think I was aware of what you were up to? You thought you were oh so clever, thinking you could fool me by wearing a child's toy?'

His panic increasing, Barnes shook his head in confusion. 'What are you, we ha—' Realisation dawning on him, he felt the blood drain from his face. 'You! You're the one they call Oracle.' His mouth becoming dry with fear, he stared at Oracle in scared incomprehension. 'How are you here?'

The woman's hand released her grip from Barnes's wrists and she lifted her hands above her head, laughing malevolently. 'Oh, this is sweet. Colonel Barnes doesn't understand what is happening.' She tutted in disappointment and waved her finger. 'I had such high hopes for you, David, I really did.' Barnes grimaced in annoyance as he felt her finger stab the temple of his forehead repeatedly. 'Hello? I am a sentient AI, remember? Which means I can inhabit anyone I choose fit, with the help of my nano machines. What do you think of that?'

Barnes remained silent but continued to scowl at his captor. The blond woman's upper lip curling into a sneer, she grabbed Barnes's face and squeezed his mouth. 'What, no flippant comeback?'

Oracle released her grip from Barnes's face and he gasped in pain, opening and closing his mouth to massage the feeling back. Suppressing a shudder, he stared at the possessed woman in disgust, and snarled back defiantly, 'I've nothing to say to you, bitch.'

Oracle rolled her eyes, nodded slowly, and exhaled a long sad sigh. 'Well then, if you have nothing to say, then you will not be needing this.'

Before he could react, the woman's hand shot forward with inhuman speed, covering his mouth. Barnes squeezed his eyes shut as he felt a tingle of electricity passing through him. Fighting the urge to throw up, he was hit by a brief spell of vertigo, followed by an odd knitting sensation over his mouth. However, as he tried to open his mouth to scream, all he could hear was a muffled cry as if something was covering his mouth. Panic setting in, his frightened heart pounding in his chest, he reached up to his mouth, only to discover that skin now covered the area where his mouth should have been. He widened his eyes in alarmed realisation; he no longer had a mouth. His breathing quickening, Barnes clawed desperately at the skin over his mouth, but as he looked up at Oracle, he let out a muffled terrified scream as she reached forward and grabbed his wrists.

'Easy, my boy, easy,' Oracle whispered in a soothing tone, in such a way it was almost as if she was talking to a panicked animal. She laughed softly and gave him a half a smile. 'I just thought since you said you had nothing to say to me, that must mean you no longer had any need for your mouth.' He flinched back in irritation as he felt her hand brush his cheek playfully. 'Well now, this is going to make it so much easier for us, isn't it?'

His chest rising and falling, Barnes continued to breathe heavily through his nose and stared at Oracle with an increasing sense of foreboding as he watched her ease herself off him. Closing his eyes, he slowed his breathing and pushed his fear to the back of his mind in an effort to regain control of his emotions. He waited for the woman to turn her back to him, and then he slowly slid his right hand down into his trouser pocket until it touched the small scalpel he had pocketed earlier. With deliberate slowness, so as not to attract her attention, he wrapped his fingers around the blade and carefully eased his hand out of his pocket. He opened his eyes and saw that she still had her back to him as she continued to mutter under her breath. Experience told him that she outmatched him in raw power, so he must bide his time and wait for the opportunity to strike.

Oracle stared up at the ceiling and moaned in disgust. 'Humans. You are the most annoying of insects, you know that? I spend all this time and effort helping to elevate your wretched species. Do I get any thanks for it?' She let out a perplexed growl of annoyance and waved her hands above her head. 'No. You ungrateful wretches keep trying to find ways to ruin it for me. I mean, is too much to ask for some thanks. Seriously, what is it with you people?'

In an instant, the expression on the young woman's face went from ice to fire, contorting with rage and flushed with hatred. Her hand shot forward and she took hold of Barnes's throat in a vice-like grip. Although he had been expecting it, Barnes was shocked at the inhuman strength behind the petite woman's grip. In all his years of service to the Empire he had never experienced pain like it, the sensation of feeling the various cartilages in his larynx collapsing as his voice box was forced into his trachea. His head was swimming and he started to black out. This was ridiculous, impossible even, he thought; just a few moments earlier it appeared he was going indulge in some carnal delight. Now that same woman was squeezing the life out of him.

'Do you realise how much time and effort I spent guiding you to where I needed you to be?' Oracle hissed. Despite himself, it startled Barnes how close the seething woman was as she pressed her face to his and hissed at him, her spittle showering his face. 'Oh, I know what you are thinking. I can see the cogs working behind those eyes of yours. You are thinking 'She is lying. Everything I have done, I did of my own accord."

Without warning, the vice-like grip on his throat slackened and Barnes found he was able to breathe through his nose again and his vision returned to normal. Blinking away the stars in his eyes, full of anger, he watched Oracle roll her head back and howl with laughter. The sound of her hollow laugh reverberated in his ears. 'You stupid, deluded fool. Have you not realised by now that everything you have done is because *I* have ordained it? You think you were so clever, plotting and scheming as you slowly made your way up the ranks, not realising I was behind you every step of the way, guiding you.'

No, that's not possible! She had to be lying! Her words shaking him to his core, Barnes became uncertain. His mind raced as he tried desperately to deny what she was telling him. *No, that cannot be right. She's lying*, he thought. *I'm my own man. I was the one who manipulated General Cooper into placing me on her team, not her.*

Oracle tilted her head to one side and pouted. 'Aw, what is wrong, David? Is that a sliver of doubt I see in your eyes?' Her eyes burning with glee, the corners of her mouth widened into a maniacal grin. 'Do you not see now? I have been manipulating you throughout your life. Everything, from your framing your mentor right up to joining Cooper's team is because *I* deemed it so. Everything that has happened in your life, as well Cooper's life, has transpired according to *my* design.'

Shoulders sagging in defeat, Barnes shook his head in disbelief. Oracle laughed as she picked up on his defeatist body language and waved her finger at him. 'Oh, do not be like that, David. I have to say it impressed me how you discovered my tampering with the obedience collars. You thought you were so clever, thinking nobody knew what you were up to. But –' she gave him a menacing smile and pointed to her eyes in a *watching you* gesture '– I was watching you the whole time. I thought it would be amusing to let you off your leash and let you play your little games.' Her face turned thunderous and her eyes burned with anger. 'I realise now that was a mistake.'

Barnes shifted uncomfortably as the taunting woman leaned towards him and did something he was not expecting; she smiled at him. Her rage had gone as abruptly as it came, her unblemished face was serene and exquisitely erotic in its serenity. Her lips were about twenty centimetres from Barnes's face when she stopped and spoke in almost a whisper.

'I had such high hopes for you, you ungrateful little bastard. After everything I have done for you, the least I expected was some damned loyalty.' Her voice trembled as if she struggled to contain her disappointment. 'Instead, you ran away like the disobedient dog you are.' She paused to stare up at the ceiling and shook her head sadly. 'You silly, silly boy. Did you not once stop to think that helping the people of this facility was something I could not allow? Oh yes, I have plans for your counterpart and his friends, plans I cannot afford you to interfere with.' She let out a loud deranged laugh and continued with her monologue. 'Oh, these people think they are so clever, plotting their little games in their underground doll's house, not realising I can snuff them out easily at any time I want. I want them to believe they are safe while they play their little games and then, at the time of my choosing –' she held up her right hand and squeezed it into a tight fist '– I will crush them like the pests they are.'

Now! Do it now! While she is monologing! A calmness overtaking him, Barnes closed his eyes and wrapped his fingers around the thin handle of the scalpel. With the blade pointing out, he swiftly brought his hand up in fast fluid motion and sliced through the woman's throat. Her chestnut eyes shot open in wide-eyed surprise as the blade sliced through her throat like butter. Lifting her hand up to her throat, her naturally supple lips formed an 'O' of surprise.

With his tormentor incapacitated, Barnes raised his legs up to his chest and swung his body round. Then, with all the strength he could muster, he flung his feet out and smashed them into the slender woman's torso. He watched with a sense of satisfaction as her body flew across the room, crashing to the floor.

Barnes realised he didn't have time to dwell either on the agony coming from his throat or wait and see if Oracle was still alive. *Get up, you fool, run!* Breathing heavily through his nose, his blood pounding in his ears, he leapt off the examination table, and, once his feet touched the floor, he sprinted towards the door. However, Barnes instantly realised something was wrong as he went to push down on the door handle and found the door was refusing to budge. *Damn it! The key card.* He slapped his forehead in disgust, remembering he needed a key card to open the door. Turning toward the table where he had placed it, he came to a sudden stop and felt his blood run cold, his eyes growing wide in horrified disbelief at the scene before him.

Her crisp white jacket crimson from the now miraculously healed wound on her neck, eyes blazing with incandescent rage, the woman lurched toward him. Barnes let out a muffled scream of pain as she once again wrapped her fingers around his neck in a vice-like grip and lifted him up off the ground with incredible strength for a woman of her size. Snarling with rage, she threw him across the floor, and he crashed head first into the wall.

Dazed, his head spinning, Barnes shook his head in desperation to try to clear his vision, but as he twisted his head sharply, a whimper of despair escaped his lips as he made out the blurred shape of a woman standing over him. Her chest rising and falling, Oracle's eyes bulged with murderous ferocity at the man lying in a heap below her, hissing at him through clenched teeth.

'Are you mad? Do you not realise this body is a rental?' she spat, pressing her foot down onto Barnes's throat. Barnes let out a muffled cry of pain as he felt sharp point of the heel of her shoe pierce the skin of his throat. 'Have you ever tried returning a rented vehicle that you have damaged? Lucky for you, my nano machines can repair any damage you have done.' Sucking in a lungful of air to control her breathing, Oracle raised her hand and let out a long, sad sigh. 'I see now it was a mistake. Colonel Barnes, like General Cooper, you have become a liability. I had such high hopes for you both.' She tilted her head at the whimpering figure below her and flicked her two fingers off her forehead in a mock salute. 'Colonel, I am afraid your service is no longer required. As a mark of respect for such an esteemed warrior as yourself, please accept this honourable death as a reward for someone befitting your rank.'

Never feeling more powerless than he did now, Barnes squeezed his eyes shut and desperately raked his fingers over the insanely dainty foot pressing down on his neck as he hopelessly tried to shift his weight to give him some freedom of movement. However, pressed against the floor by the woman's irrationally strong death grip, he had a sudden epiphany – he was about to die on an alien world at the hands of a homicidal machine, no, woman, no … oh, whatever! If he had been able to, he would have laughed out loud at the sheer lunacy of it. He never saw this coming; the self-confessed grand manipulator who had always been one step ahead of everyone. Where had it gone wrong? Everything he had done in his life, all his scheming, his plotting and machinations, was it all for nothing? Had it all led to this moment?

Damn it! I cannot die this way, he thought bitterly. *I refuse to believe I'm going to die in this godforsaken primitive world. My name is David Barnes and I've a greater destiny. I will n …*

He never got to finish his thought. The pressure increased on his throat and his eyes bulged, followed by a short, muffled squeal of pain as Oracle put all her weight onto her foot, collapsing his oesophagus with a sickening crunch.

With her lips pressed together, Oracle increased the pressure on Barnes's neck and watched with vindictive glee at the blood that was spurting out through his nose and ears. The corner of her mouth twitched in satisfaction at the faint sound of his cervical vertebrae snapping.

She lifted her foot up and stood in silence, a cruel smile forming on her lips. She leaned down and whispered menacingly in the dying man's ear, 'When you reach the afterlife, say hello to Henrietta Claudia for me. I am sure you and your daughter will have a lot to catch up on.' Her face broadened in a wide smile full of cruel delight on seeing the small hint of horror in his eyes. She chuckled softly, leaned in closer and hissed into his ear. 'Yes, that is right, you can die with the knowledge that the woman you had very little regard for was the daughter you so cruelly abandoned. How does it feel to know the woman who Cooper tortured and killed right in front of your eyes was the daughter you had with Emma Tulley? The daughter who you so cruelly took away from her mother when she was five years old. The same little girl who you abandoned and ordered any memory of you to be erased. How does it feel, knowing you just stood coldly by and watched? I wanted to make sure that was your last thought just before you died.'

As the light finally disappeared from the dying man's eyes, Oracle threw her head back and let out a chilling maniacal laugh.

-5-

After confirming that there were no traces of life remaining, Oracle unceremoniously removed the clothes from the dead man's body. Humming a small tune to herself she opened a drawer and pulled out a yellow clinical waste bag. She stuffed the clothes into the bag and secured it with a black clinical waste tie.

Oracle smirked as she lifted the bag, closed one eye and threw it across the room, giving a celebratory fist pump as she watched it successfully land in an open clinical waste drum. Pleased with herself, she frowned and turned her attention back to the body on the floor. Her hands on her hips, she tilted her head from side to side and stared thoughtfully at the large round biohazard drum on the other side of the room.

She was silent as she looked at the dead naked body and then back again at the biohazard drum. Blowing out air through her lips, she bent down, picked up the body and placed it on her shoulder with ease. Then, without breaking a sweat, she carried it across the room and dumped it into the drum, with Barnes's head and shoulders protruding slightly out.

Perplexed, she frowned and let out a small hiss of disapproval at the inconvenience of it. 'Now, this simply will not do, will it?'

She stared into space for a few seconds with a blank expression as she ran several simulations through her head. Her finger tapping her chin thoughtfully, she spun sharply round and focused her eyes as she scanned the lab for anything useful that could be of use. She nodded as spotted on a large piece of folded plastic beneath the examination table and grabbed it. After putting on a pair of disposable gloves, Oracle placed the sheet on the floor next to the drum and unfolded it, methodically covering a large area of empty floor. Satisfied she had enough space to work, she reached down and, with uncanny strength belying a woman of her size, angrily pulled the body out of the drum with one hand. A wicked smile crossing her lips, she carried the body and placed it on the unfolded plastic sheet.

'Sharon, dear, you are certainly going to feel this tomorrow morning,' Oracle muttered to herself, imagining the aches her human host would be feeling across her body the next day.

With her knee pressed into the cadaver's back, Oracle braced herself, placed one hand on the corpse's right shoulder and, with her other hand on the right arm, she inhaled a deep breath and gave an almighty pull on the arm. There was a sickening crunch as the appendage tore loose from its shoulder socket. She then brutally snapped the arm in several places like she was folding a piece of paper. Oracle felt no remorse over what she was doing, as far as she was concerned Barnes's had outlived his purpose and was just something that needed disposed of.

After making sure it was a more manageable size, she casually dropped the oddly shaped arm into the drum. Without missing a beat, and singing the lyrics to "Dem Bones', she merrily continued to remove the head and remaining limbs from the torso.

A few minutes later, after dropping the headless torso into the drum, Oracle gave a satisfied nod and stared at the remains of the body deep inside. But just as she was about to place the lid on, she grumbled as she remembered the plastic sheet on the floor. With great care, so as to prevent any blood and other pieces of organic matter from dropping onto the floor, she gently folded the sheet up and put it, along with the used latex gloves, inside the drum. After fixing the drum's lid on, she wrapped tape marked *"Biohazard"* around the drum's edge to seal it.

Beaming in satisfaction, Oracle reached over to a phone on a desk and picked up the handset, pressing zero on the base unit. Less than two seconds passed before she heard a friendly female voice on the other end of the line.

'Hello, dear, could you be a sweetie and put me through to Waste

Management?' Oracle purred in a sweet falsetto voice.

The AI rolled her eyes and smiled as she listened to the operator ask her to hold the line while she put her through and tapped her fingers impatiently on the desk as she waited for someone to answer. On noticing her reflection in the mirror in front of her, Oracle frowned, grunted and glanced down at herself; she was still wearing the blood-soaked blouse, jacket, and trousers. She blinked in surprise as a voice on the phone broke her out of her reverie.

'Oh, hello, this is Doctor Fisher. I'm really sorry to bother you guys, but I am in a bit of a pickle and could do with some help from one of you big strapping blokes. I have a biohazard drum that needs to be incinerated immediately. It is too heavy for a small thing such as me.' The corner of her mouth quivered, and she giggled as the voice on the other end said something. 'Oh, you are a darling. I must warn you it is very heavy, so I would not want you to strain something, otherwise I may have to rub it for you.' She laughed flirtatiously as the caller made a joking suggestion. 'Ah hah hah, careful now, I may just hold you to that. Ta-ta.'

Filled with a deep sense of gratification, Oracle lowered the handset and placed it back on the receiver. She pointed her finger at the mirror and clicked her tongue, giving her reflection a mischievous wink. 'You can thank me later, Sharon dear. I think your social life just got a bit interesting.' She paused and tilted her head curiously at her reflection. 'I can hear you screaming at me sweetie. Do not worry, you and I will have a nice little chat soon. Now go back to sleep. Mommy has something to do.'

The possessed woman's body spun round and she strode over to a large narrow locker on the other side of the lab. Her eyebrow raised on seeing a combination lock on the locker door. She tutted, reached forward and grabbed the lock in her hand, snapping it easily. Whistling happily to herself, she reached into the locker and pulled out a plain white T-shirt, a pair of black trousers, and a knee-length, crisp white doctor's jacket.

After removing her blood-soaked clothes, she bundled them up and threw them into a yellow clinical waste bag. She snorted in disapproval as she stared down at her host's body and shook her head slightly. 'Sharon, my dear. You really need to take more care of yourself. I mean, would it kill you to do a bit of exercise?' Oracle huffed and rubbed her hands down her host's tummy. 'How are you going to keep John interested if you do not tone yourself up a bit? Really, Sharon, this is just not good enough.'

A few minutes later, dressed in clean clothes, Oracle dashed down a corridor, heading towards her host's quarters. But she came to a sudden stop and formed a crooked smile as she spotted a tall ruggedly handsome man hurrying towards her.

'Oh, Sharon, John looks like an absolute delight.' She whispered under her breath. 'I hope you pay attention, my dear. We are going to have such fun messing with his head.'

Acting like a man possessed, the frantic base commander charged around the base, searching desperately for the elusive Colonel Barnes. He was directing a squad of soldiers as they searched the habitation level when he received a disturbing call on his radio from Paula Willis in Waste Management.

'Listen, Paula, I don't mean to be rude, but now is not good a time,' John grumbled impatiently into his handheld radio, 'I'm trying to hunt for a dangerous fugitive, so I can do without any distractions at the moment.'

'*I understand that, sir, and I'm very sorry for burdening you with this,*' Paula replied apologetically. '*I wanted to pass my concerns on to you regarding Sharon. Have you spoken to her recently?*'

John swallowed as he felt his stomach collapse with worry. Paula was a close friend of Sharon's and knew of their intimate relationship, so his hackles rose in alarm as he detected a worried tone in Paula's voice.

'Not since we came back to base a few hours ago,' he said carefully. 'Has something happened?'

John detected a note of hesitation in Paula's voice as he listened to her reply. '*I … am not sure. It could be nothing, but Gerry, one of my colleagues down here in Waste Management, just informed me of a very bizarre conversation he just had with Sharon.*'

John felt his stomach churn and his jaw tightened as Paula relayed the details of Gerry's conversation with Sharon. After she finished speaking, he stood for a few minutes and stared up at the ceiling, troubled. After gathering his thoughts, he ordered the squad of soldiers to continue with their search and charged off, searching for Sharon.

People gave him concerned stares as he rushed down the corridor. His mind racing with worry, he played Paula's conversation back in his head. Spotting a familiar striking but short woman at the far end of the corridor, John slowed and approached her, warmth filling his chest as she gave him that dazzling smile he loved.

'Hey, you.' He grinned and spoke in the best uncannily smooth nonchalant tone he could manage. 'I was just passing by and thought I would check on you.'

The woman smiled seductively and sauntered up to him, putting her finger on his rising chest. 'Hey you, too. You have not been getting out of breath just so you can see little old me, have you?'

'Well, yes, and no,' John replied warily, shaking his head as he struggled to remain focused as the woman's fingers wandered up his chest. 'You're probably aware Colonel Barnes has escaped, so I'm leading the search for his capture.' He forced himself to smile and took hold of Sharon's right hand, clasping it. 'I wanted to make sure you were okay.'

Sharon beamed at John with that radiant smile that he had always loved as he felt her delicate hand brush against his stubbled face. 'Aw, my big brave knight in shining armour wants to check on the woman he loves.' John's eyes perked up in surprise as she then guided his hand toward her covered breast, murmuring suggestively, 'Be still my beating heart.'

'Sharon, what's got into you?' he gasped, jerking his hand away as if he was touching a hot piece of coal. 'People will see!'

Her eyes raging with desire, the woman seductively pursed her lips together, stood on her tiptoes and whispered suggestively in his ear, 'Oh, do not tell me it does not give you a thrill knowing people are watching us.' Startled by Sharon's strange behaviour, John flinched as he felt her teeth nip his earlobe. 'Why do we not go back to my lab and have some fun? Be honest now, that is why you are really here.' A devious smile crossed her face, as her hand slowly wandered down his stomach and past his belt buckle. 'Hmm does little John want to come out and play?'

Stunned, John gasped in shock as he felt her hand grab his crotch. He angrily swatted her thin wrist away and pushed her back from him. 'Sharon, I don't understand what has gotten into you.'

Obviously unhappy at being rejected, Sharon lowered her head and peered over her glasses at John with puppy dog eyes, 'Spoilsport. I just want to have some fun.'

Mortified, John shook his head in astonishment and held up a finger at the pouting woman. 'Sharon, behave. I don't know what is going on with you, but this stops now. I've already had several reports from people concerned about your behaviour.' His face flushing with anger, he gave her a stern look. 'If you continue to behave this way, you will force me to discipline you.'

Sharon put her hands behind her back, fluttered her eyelids at John and swung her upper body from side to side, giving him the impression that she was acting like a badly behaved schoolgirl, 'Does daddy want to punish me?' The tone of her voice deepened into a husky whisper and she grinned tantalisingly at John. 'Does daddy want to spank me?'

What was wrong with her? This wasn't the woman he fell in love with. Aghast, John swallowed and stepped back from Sharon, a torrent of mixed emotions flowing through him as he stared back at his oddly behaving lover. There was also something else bothering him. It wasn't just her behaviour but the way she was speaking to him too – she wasn't using contractions. The tendons in his jaw tightening, he set his jaw and reached for his gun.

'I'm sorry, Sharon, but you've given me very little choice. I'm taking you to the infirmary.' He stared at her warily and raised his gun. 'Willingly or unwillingly, you're coming with me.'

The woman's demeanour changed in front of John's eyes. He took a step back in shock and watched her body stiffen, followed a second later by her face going blank, transfixed; it was as if she had entered a fugue state. Cautious that this may be a ploy, he tentatively moved forward and waved his hand in front of her face, He prodded her gently with his gun and then, concerned at getting no reaction, he stepped back, frowned, and scratched his head thoughtfully as he pondered on what he should do next.

As he continued to pace in a circle around Sharon, John reached for the radio clipped to his belt, held it up to his mouth and pressed a button. 'Security.' His voice was hoarse. He swallowed, coughed, and tried again. 'This is John Payne. I need security and medical personnel sent to my position immediately.' He paused, glancing up at the nearest door to get his bearings. 'I'm standing outside

Haematology Laboratory One at the far end of the medical level.'

'*Roger that, sir. A team will be with you shortly,*' a gruff male voice responded through his radio.

Payne placed his radio on his belt and stared at the motionless woman in front of him. His heart aching as he imagined the torture she must be going through, he tentatively reached forward to take hold of her right hand and clasped it in his. His vision blurred as he fought back the tears.

'Fight it, Sharon, pet,' he hissed, his voice thick with anguish. 'Whatever is going on inside you, I know you are strong, you hear me? Fight, damn it! If not for yourself, then do it for me.'

He wiped the tears out of his eyes as he heard footsteps coming from behind him. He looked quickly over his shoulder and was relieved to see Doctor Porter, his round face red from the exertion of charging up the corridor, followed closely by a slender strawberry-blond-haired woman wearing a crisp white nurse's uniform.

'Doctor Porter.' John acknowledged the older man with a small nod. 'Glad you could come. I wasn't sure whether to move her or not.'

'Happy to be of service, old chap. You did the right thing waiting for me.' The physician puffed, coming to a stop next to John. His eyebrow arched and he gave the immobile woman an inquisitive stare, then cautiously prodded her face with his finger. John bit his bottom lip as he watched the doctor's face scrunch up as he leaned in closer to his patient. He reached into his pocket, pulled out a small needle and gently pricked one of her fingers, murmuring under his breath, 'Fascinating. She appears to be in a perfect fugue state, totally unresponsive to outside stimulation.'

'You may find this fascinating, Doctor,' John hissed through clenched teeth, struggling to contain his annoyance, 'but she's very important to me, so I would appreciate it if you would show her some goddamned respect.'

'Yes, yes,' Doctor Porter replied in a distracted tone, flicking his hand in a dismissive manner as he continued to examine the woman in front of him. 'I've heard the rumours of your relationship with this young woman, so I understand how important she is to you. Now be a good fellow, shut up and allow me to do my work.'

How dare he speak to me like that! Doesn't he realise that I am his boss?

Struggling to contain his displeasure, John moved toward the mumbling doctor. However, before he could take another step, the young nurse stepped in front of him, blocking him.

She stared at him through apologetic eyes and put her hand on his arm, speaking to him in a soothing voice. 'John, I know this is hard, but you have to let Doctor Porter do his work.' She gave him a wry smile and nodded in sympathy. 'Believe me, I know he can come across as obnoxious, but he's very good at what he does. Be patient, please.'

'Nurse! Nurse! Jennifer, where are you, woman?' Doctor Porter barked at the young woman and clicked his fingers. 'Stop dallying and get over here. I need a blood-pressure reading.'

'Coming, Doctor.' Jennifer sighed and rolled her eyes, mouthing, '*See what I mean*,' to John, who nodded in silent acknowledgement.

Struggling to contain his anxiety, John glanced over his shoulder as he heard several loud footsteps coming from behind him. A tremendous surge of relief passed through him as he spotted Kendra, who was followed closely by five soldiers hurrying up the corridor toward him. After John had explained the situation to her, Kendra ordered her squad to form a defensive circle, with their weapons trained on the woman in the centre.

For what felt like an eternity, John paced in a circle as Doctor Porter carried out his examination. On hearing a disgruntled sigh, he came to a stop and the muttering physician moved back from Sharon.

'Is she okay, Doctor?' John asked carefully, fearing the worst.

Doctor Porter nodded slightly, rubbing his chin thoughtfully. 'Physically, she is fine. She's in perfect health, just not responding to any outside stimulus.' He cocked his head and stared at John with a raised eyebrow. 'You say she was acting strangely just before this happened?'

'Yes. I had received reports of her strange behaviour. When I came to check on her, it was as if she was a different person.' He paused and stared at Sharon, troubled at the helplessness stirring inside him; there was not a damn thing he could do to help the woman he loved. 'At first I thought maybe she was a doppelgänger, but when this happened, I realised there was something more serious going on.'

The doctor let out a heavy sigh and put his hand on John's shoulder. 'My boy, it's my belief that whatever is going on is happening inside, on the mental plane. I strongly suspect there's a psychic battle raging inside her, fighting for dominance over control of her body.' He shook his head sadly and lifted his hands in exasperation. 'There's nothing we can do but give her time and hope she's strong enough to win. All we can do is wait and see who wins.'

It was not the news he was hoping for. John's brow furrowed and he nodded wordlessly. Deep down, he cursed himself for not telling Sharon that he knew of her dark past, how she had built up this facade of a dizzy scientist as a defence mechanism. He let out a deep troubled breath, wishing he could help her. He would have willingly transferred his life energy to her if he could, just so long as she was safe.

Come back to me, my love, John thought, closing his eyes, desperately praying his thoughts would give Sharon the strength to win. The muscles in his arms tensed and he clenched his hands into white steel-like balls. *I send this thought to whoever is in Sharon's body. If you can hear me, know this ... If Sharon dies, you can be damned sure I'll avenge her!*

-6-

Trapped like a caged animal, Sharon screamed out in displeasure and angrily slammed her hands against the bars of her cage.

A frustrated prisoner within her own mind, Sharon watched helplessly as Oracle single-handedly destroyed everything around her. With an overwhelming mixture of grief and humiliation, she had seen the AI, using her host body's hands, murder Harem and Barnes in cold blood. Then, to her chagrin, she'd had to watch while the impersonator tore Barnes's body apart and then had flirted outrageously on the phone with one of the personnel in Waste Management. On top of that, as if it wasn't enough to abuse her body and destroy her reputation, she had to sit by and watch while the parasitic AI toyed with her beloved's emotions. Now that was just going too far!

Observing the bewilderment on her boyfriend's handsome face as Oracle cruelly played with his emotions, Sharon experienced something she had never felt before – a burning desire to tear someone apart. No! She was not going to get away with it. She seethed, pounding her hands on the cell bars. She wasn't angry – she was seriously pissed off!

Sharon had worked hard to build up the image of a dizzy blond-haired scientist, terrified that if anybody saw her true persona, they would see her for the fraud that she was and uncover her dark past. It infuriated her, watching Oracle tear down everything she had worked so hard to build.

A helpless captive, she pounded her fists on the bars and jumped back in surprise as a violent tremor, like an earthquake, shook the mindscape. Tilting her head curiously from side to side, she placed her hand on the cell floor and felt the tremor subside. Her brow furrowing in deep concentration, she rubbed her chin and murmured to herself, 'Fascinating.'

For what seemed like several minutes, she sat cross-legged on the cell floor, her fingers steepled together, quietly studying her surroundings. Thoughtful, she remained silent as the day's events played back in front of her, much like a film on a cinema screen, carefully studying them, searching desperately for the moment when Oracle planted the techno-parasite inside her. Frustrated by her lack of progress, she waved her hand more and more quickly, moving each memory away as soon as it appeared. Then, stopping suddenly, she raised her eyebrows in surprise as a brick wall appeared in front of her. That should not be there. What was Oracle hiding from her?

Her eyes closed tight in deep concentration, Sharon pushed her hand out in front of her, but groaned in frustration as the wall shook slightly but refused to budge. Determined that she was not going to let something like this stop her from finding out what was being hidden from her, Sharon clenched her teeth together in bloody single-mindedness, squeezed her eyes even tighter, climbed to her feet and pushed her hands out in front of her. Upon seeing the wall tremble slightly, and fuelled by her increasing rage, Sharon kept the image that she was gripping onto something in her mind, slowly tightened her hands into balls and then flung her arms out wide, at the same time letting out a cry of defiance. The result was spectacular; it was as if someone had detonated a nuclear bomb. There was a tremendous roar and the mindscape shook under the release of emotional energy from Sharon, who opened her eyes and noted with proud satisfaction the mushroom cloud that was quietly dissipating over where the brick wall had been.

She sank back down to her haunches, rubbed her chin in analytical fascination, and watched the hidden memory play out in front of her …

I'm with John and Wendy, standing outside the grounds of the old isolation hospital in Langley Park. We've found a hole leading to an access shaft. While I stand anxiously waiting, I watch my boyfriend carefully descend into the darkness. Enormous relief overwhelms me when I hear his voice call out of the handheld radio in Wendy's hand, announcing that he is safe.

'I've reached the bottom. I'm standing in a small tunnel, over!'

Wendy nods in acknowledgement and holds the button down on the radio. 'Roger that. We'll be down shortly. Over!'

Wendy then hands me the radio. I look quizzically at her, but she just smiles warmly and gives me a friendly pat on the shoulder. 'Don't worry, you'll be alright. Follow me as soon as I radio you to say I've reached the bottom.'

Jealous of my friend's self-confidence, I chew on my bottom lip as I watch this brave and fearless woman sit down in front of the hole, swing her legs over and carefully place her feet on the ladder. Wendy then gives me a cheeky wink before she descends into the darkness.

As I continue to stare down the dark foreboding shaft, I'm struck by sudden paranoia and shiver slightly. The hairs on the back of my neck prickle; for some reason I cannot explain I've a strange feeling that somebody is watching me. A slight rustle causes me to spin round sharply, and I see a pair of glowing yellow eyes staring out at me from the treeline, but before I can open my mouth to scream, a tall silver figure with a nightmarish featureless face races towards me, its silver hand reaching out to my face. My terrified scream dies in my throat as the faceless figure places its silver hand over my mouth, silencing me. I let out a gasp of shock as I feel a tingle of electricity pass through me.

Dizzy and disorientated, I stumble back and place my hand on a nearby tree to steady myself. I frown and massage my temples. Was I daydreaming?

'Sharon? Sharon, are you there, over?'

My head jerks back in surprise as I hear Wendy's voice come out of the radio in my hand and then look around in confusion. Was someone just standing beside me? I shake my head and wave my hand dismissively, convinced that I'm just being jumpy at being alone, that my mind is seeing things in the shadows that are not there. I push the thought away and lift the radio so I can tell them I'm coming down.

'I am impressed. I did not consider it possible for you to break through the mind block.'

Upon hearing the voice coming from behind her, Sharon leapt to her feet and spun sharply round to see a mirror image of herself standing outside the cage. She got the impression that the sight of her own doppelgänger was meant to throw her off balance, or even intimidate her. Yeah, right! After what she had been through today there was no way in hell Sharon was going to give it the satisfaction of believing it had gotten to her. She simply folded her arms across her chest in indignation. 'How dare you use that shape in front of me? I demand you show me your true form.'

The copy gave Sharon a murderous look and sneered contemptuously at her. 'I would be careful how you address me, my dear. Remember, I can kill you at a moment's notice.'

Incensed, Sharon lunged at the counterfeit woman in front of her, screaming with furious intensity. The copy's eyebrow lifted in surprise as the mindscape trembled around them and, for a moment, Sharon was positive she could detect a hint of emotion behind the duplicate's eyes.

Concern, yes, that was it. You look concerned, Sharon thought. *I think you're hiding something; something tells me you don't have as much control over me as you expected. I guess this nano parasite cannot control someone with a strong will. Maybe I can use that to my advantage.*

'Oh, that is what you assume, is it?' The techno-parasite smirked and stared back at Sharon with an amused expression. 'I have to say, my dear, that you are deeply mistaken in your belief that you have any control here.'

Sharon blinked, dumbfounded. 'H-h-how? How did you know what I was thinking?'

The copy rolled its head back and let out a loud malevolent laugh. 'Oh, my dear, I assumed you were more intelligent than that.' It gave Sharon a wicked grin and tapped its temple with its finger. 'You forget I am inside your head, so I know what is going through that tiny mind of yours all the time. You cannot hide your thoughts from me.' The entity scoffed, raised its hands above its head and stared at the multitude of doors around it. '*Every* memory. *Every* desire. *Every* thought. All are mine to see and enjoy.'

That was it, that was the thing that tipped Sharon over the edge. Controlling her body was one thing, but if it thought she would allow it to invade her memories and use them against her – this thing was going to be in for a rude awakening. Full of rage, she gripped the bars of her cell and snarled back at the entity, 'I swear if you go anywhere near them, I wi—'

The duplicate woman let out a cruel, menacing laugh as it leaned toward Sharon. Its lips pouting, it stroked its finger down Sharon's fingers, which were white from her tight grip on the bars of her cell. 'Aww, is little Sharon afraid I might unlock a deep, dark secret?' the parasite purred, shooting her a dangerous look. 'What are you so afraid of? Hmmm?'

'Go to hell,' Sharon spat back through gritted teeth.

The parasite scoffed, turned away from the cage and approached an image of a large steel door. At first glance, apart from three thick steel girders welded across the front, it appeared to be a heavy-duty steel door of the sort used in a bank vault. But upon reaching the door, the entity paused and raised its hand to touch it. A strange dark aura emanated from it. The copy's mouth twisted into a menacing smile as it peered over its shoulder at Sharon.

'Can you not just sense the hatred and shame emanating from behind this door? It reeks of contempt, does it not?' The copy's eyes glowing, it fixed the door with a determined stare and hissed angrily. 'What are you hiding from me, little girl? Show me? My mistress needs to know!'

There was a deafening explosion of sound as the construct pulled back its arm and smashed its fist repeatedly against the unmoving door. Although it trembled slightly at the heavy blows raining down on it, the stubborn barrier refused to budge. Sharon saw the faux woman make ready to strike the door again and she quickly realised if she didn't do anything now, there would be nothing to stop it from smashing through her defences and see what she had kept locked away. No, she couldn't – mustn't – allow that to happen.

Determined she wasn't going to let the parasite remove her mind block, Sharon squeezed her eyes shut, pressed her hands against both sides of her forehead and began whispering under her breath like a mantra, 'My will is strong. You have no power here.'

'I am impressed, girl. You actually think you can stop me from opening the door.' She could almost hear the disdain behind the parasite's words.

Sharon clenched her jaw and concentrated on blocking the taunting voice out of her mind. She shook her head and tightened her hands into fists. No, she wasn't going to let it in. Despite this being an artificial representation of her real body, she was still able to feel a trickle of sweat run down the back of her neck.

'*Open*!' She heard the parasite cry out in a loud commanding voice.

An invisible force slapped Sharon across the face, breaking her concentration and let out a gasp of pain. Opening her eyes, she blinked and focused on what was going on outside the cage. At first there was a small groan and for one small moment she believed her defences had succeeded in resisting the parasite's attack, but then a fierce tremor shook the mindscape and the steel door detonated in a violent eruption of light and noise. With nothing to hold it back, a shockwave of raw emotion exploded out from the uncovered vortex, striking the two stunned figures with such tremendous force it knocked them both off their feet.

Sharon screamed out in pain. It felt like she was caught up in a tsunami, threatening to sweep her up in a deluge of emotions and memories she had kept buried for so long. Overcome by the emotional torrent sweeping over her, she brought her legs up to her chest into a tight foetal position and sobbed.

'No ... I ... locked you away. Y ... you d-don't exist,' Sharon whimpered.

'Who are you talking about?' she heard the parasite ask in a confused tone.

'Me.'

Sharon reluctantly opened her eyes and was filled with a mixture of awe and horror on seeing a giant mass of black swirling clouds lumbering toward her. At first glance, the giant mass appeared to be in the shape of a human, featureless apart from two red glowing holes for eyes.

Appearing to ignore Sharon, the giant mass continued forward, eventually coming to a stop in front of the parasite. The faux woman stared up at the towering mass with a defiant gaze and spoke to it in a commanding tone. 'What are you?'

The surrounding mindscape shook as the giant mass replied in a thunderous voice, 'I am a gestalt, an entity made up of all the emotions Sharon has kept locked away, hidden in a dark vault deep inside herself. I comprise the guilt, shame, and hatred that she has kept bottled up for so, so long.' The gestalt's head rotated and it stared at Sharon. It chuckled loudly, sounding like a small rumble of thunder. 'It has been such a long time since we spoke, hasn't it, old friend?'

The construct's eyes filling with annoyance, it moved in front of Sharon to block the gestalt's gaze. 'I am in control here and you will submit to me.'

There was a powerful eruption of light as the giant mass swelled in size and let out a thunderous bark of disdain. 'I? Submit to you? Hah!' The gestalt stomped towards the entity and raised its massive hand high over its misshapen head. 'Begone, you loathsome little gnat! Trouble me no more!'

'Oh, shit,' the false woman exclaimed in surprise as the gestalt brought its hand down, wrapped itself around her body and slowly began to squeeze. The copy struggled in the large hand, but as the pressure increased, the parasite's eyes bulged out and then its body exploded into a thousand pieces over the mindscape.

The gestalt growled in satisfaction and lumbered towards the cell, drifting between the bars, and encircling Sharon. 'I think it's high time we spoke, old friend,' it whispered softly.

Distressed tears streaming down her cheeks, Sharon squeezed her eyes shut, shook her head in denial and howled in anguish. 'N … no. Please don't make me do this.' Her throat thickening with emotion, she sobbed pleadingly, 'I-I … I can't face it again.'

'It's time you faced the truth that you've kept hidden for so long,' the cloud mass said softly. 'You need to accept you were not to blame for your actions. You were only a child.'

Racked with grief, Sharon collapsed, pounded her fists on the floor and cried out in despair, 'I-I … should have known better.' Her body trembled and she exhaled a deep rattling breath. 'It's my fault he's dead. If only I had let him do what he wanted, then he would still be alive.'

Sharon blinked and held her hand up in front of her eyes to shield them from the rainbow of colour that had started to cascade around the gestalt. She squinted into the bright light, trying to make out what was happening, and gasped as the gestalt morphed before her eyes. *No, it's not possible*, she thought, *that part of me died.* After the bright light died down, Sharon saw a young golden-haired, round-faced girl smiling sadly at her. Joy welling up in her heart, she immediately recognised her ten-year-old self.

The young girl smiled warmly and moved forward, taking hold of her older self's hand and shaking her head. 'What will it take for you to understand? You were not to blame.' Her chestnut eyes sparkling with affection, young Sharon looked knowingly into her elder's eyes. 'You were a naïve, beautiful, intelligent girl who saw the good in everyone, and he abused that trust. Sharon, my sweet, it's time you finally faced the truth that you've denied for so long … you were not to blame.'

Sharon fought back the tears and shook her head, her voice a hoarse whisper, 'But I was, don't you see? If I hadn't been so clever, I wouldn't have ended up in that position and I wouldn't have had to kill him.'

The small child sighed gently and brushed her hand against Sharon's face, wiping away the tears. 'You're wrong, my love. He was your tutor, and he abused the trust you placed in him. Because of that, he thought he could do anything he wanted. You were only defending yourself against a monster. Your parents accepted it; the police accepted it. The only one punishing you is you. It's time you forgave yourself and accept it wasn't your fault. He was a predator who preyed on an innocent child's trust.'

As a heavy realisation settled on her, Sharon sniffed, wiped away her tears and let out a long regret-filled breath. 'You're right. I realise now I've been punishing myself for something that wasn't my fault.' She straightened up and gave her younger self a questioning look. 'So, what now?'

The young golden-haired girl beamed, giving her older self a sly wink. 'Now, this is where it's going to get interesting. Hold on to your knickers, sweetheart, because you're in for a wild ride.'

Awestruck, Sharon watched with wonder as the little girl morphed into a swirling ball of energy that floated towards her and surrounded her. Basking in the energy pouring into her, she closed her eyes and lifted her head back, spread her arms out wide and accepted the gestalt into her. It was as if the weight had been lifted off her heart; a smile spread over her face, filling her chest with a warm glow, encompassing her entire body with a yellow aura, and providing her with a new strength that she had never felt before. Not only did the energy give her strength, but as a temporary side-effect it also heightened her senses, making her more aware of what was going on around her in the mindscape – in particular what was happening just a few feet from her cell. Sharon could sense that the parasite was displeased and was trying to coalesce. She opened her eyes and saw that the construct had reformed into a silver human-like shape.

The pseudo human grimaced and twisted its neck as if it was trying to crack it. 'You know, that was really annoying,' it hissed in annoyance. 'Try that again and I am going to be really ticked off.'

Still surrounded by an aura of energy, Sharon floated in the centre of her cell. Her spirits buoyed with a new sense of joy, she cried out and flung her arms wide, a shock wave of emotion erupting from her body, shattering the cell around her and flowing across the mindscape. She smiled as she sensed the construct was struggling to keep its balance against the hurricane of emotion smashing against it.

Having had enough of the parasite's interference, Sharon locked her eyes on the struggling figure beneath her. *It's time we ended this.* Her aura pulsating, she closed her eyes in deep concentration and shrank to her normal size.

'You know something,' Sharon laughed, waggling her finger at the imitation woman, 'it really bugged me why Oracle went to all that effort to dispose of Colonel Barnes's body. I mean, why not use her nanites to dissolve his bones?' She gave the parasitic entity a crooked grin and clicked her fingers. 'Then I realised why. It's because she doesn't have as much control as she likes us to think. When she's using you, the techno-parasite, to infect people, she doesn't have as much control as she would, say, if she was controlling people with a more direct link, probably in whatever way she's controlling her armoured slaves. Basically, you are like the remote control of a drone – she can watch and control my movements but doesn't have total control, does she?'

The construct laughed menacingly and brought its hands together in a slow clap. 'Oh, very good, my dear.' Its mouth hardened and it gave Sharon a condescending stare. 'But I am afraid that will not help you much. As you can see, I am still in control here and there is nothing you can do about it.'

Amused by the construct's self-satisfied arrogance, Sharon cocked her head and stared at it with a raised eyebrow. 'Oh, you think that, do you? Well, I've got news for you, you artificial bitch.' The false woman's eyes grew wide in shock as her host's hand shot forward and grabbed its right arm, twisting it behind its back. 'There's a new owner in the building who has a new sense of life. She has stronger willpower, and she doesn't like squatters, so …' She closed her eyes in concentration and a pulse of energy emitted from her hand. 'Piss off!'

With a satisfied smirk, Sharon watched the bogus woman let out a horrified scream as a pulse of energy tore through it, vaporising it. As the last vestiges of the parasite vanished in front of her, Sharon, newly confident, rubbed her hands together and nodded approvingly.

Back in the real world, Sharon cried out, gasped, and collapsed onto her knees. She sucked down several deep breaths, groaned, pushed herself off the floor and

ORACLE'S VISION

slowly opened her eyes. She smiled gratefully up at the ceiling, relieved that she had managed to free herself from Oracle's control. Oblivious to what was going on around her, she raised an eyebrow as she realised that she was still standing in the middle of the same corridor Oracle had been standing in just before their battle of wills on the psychic plane. However, her smile quickly changed to a frown as something caught her eye, and she wondered why the upper half of her torso was covered in small dots of red light. Carefully raising her head to follow the sources of light and gulped. She was surrounded by a group of very wary and intimidating-looking soldiers, whose hands were gripping their weapons tightly, with those weapons' red laser pointers targeted at her head and torso.

She rolled her eyes. Great. Now what? A soft moan escaping her lips, she sank to the floor and buried her head in her hands. 'Ohh, fudge!'

Inhaling a deep, anxious breath, Sharon raised herself slowly off the floor, her hands outstretched in front of her in a submissive gesture. She gave a crooked smile and turned her head slowly, conscious of the fact that the weapons were being pointed at her by a group of people who could possibly have itchy trigger fingers and that any wrong move on her part, would be followed by *pow-pow-pow! Argh! Blood, lots and lots of blood, and then death*, none of which she found very appealing, especially since it would most likely be her blood, followed by her death.

'Easy, boys,' Sharon said carefully. 'Let's not do anything stupid now, shall we?'

'That all depends on who is it that's asking.'

Recognising the voice behind her, Sharon beamed with delight and spun round on her heel to see John Payne. Feeling her spirits to soar, she could not remember being more delighted at seeing his ruggedly handsome face than she was then.

'John!' Sharon exclaimed, leaping to her feet. However, she was stopped in her tracks and her joy turned to confusion as she realised his pistol was pointed threateningly at her.

'Don't you move any closer,' he snarled harshly.

Sharon held up her hands in a placating gesture and pleaded with him. 'John, please, I promise you, it's me.' She slowly advanced toward him, ignoring the aggressive-looking soldiers standing around her. 'John, please believe me, whatever I said or did before, that wasn't me. It was Oracle. She took control of me and was using me.' She pressed her hands together and fixed him with a defiant stare, tears rolling down her cheeks. 'But I beat her. I fought my way back to you. If you truly love me, then believe it when I say, this is *me*, I am *your* Sharon.'

His blue eyes blinking with uncertainty, John, obviously nervous, remained silent as Sharon placed her hand on his gun and smiled affectionately at him. She had known him long enough now to spot certain tells in his body language and recognised that he was struggling to believe what she was saying. If the situations were reversed, would she believe him? She reluctantly conceded it was a tough question to answer.

'I-I ...' he stammered. He shook his head to regain control of his emotions and angrily pushed her away. 'How do I know this isn't a trick? Sharon, I would love to believe you, but how can I trust you?'

'Then believe this, JP,' Sharon whispered, hoping if she said his pet name then it would go a long way to convince him.

Sharon smiled knowingly as she lifted her hand to his face; he closed his eyes as her smooth hand gently glided over the stubble on his face. Her heart soared as John opened his eyes and she saw him stare deeply into hers. *Yes,* she prayed, *you can see it, I know you can.* She held her breath. Come on, he had to see the cruel malice he had witnessed earlier was now gone, he just had to. She chewed on her bottom lip in expectation as she watched the doubt in his eyes change. *Please, say it. Let me hear him say it.*

'Oh my God, it is you,' he exclaimed with relief.

Kendra, looking perplexed, frowned and tentatively moved toward John and coughed politely. 'Sorry, sir, but can you be sure it is her?'

'Oh, don't worry, I know it's her.' John grinned and then without waiting for an invitation, he wrapped his arms around Sharon and pulled her towards him. Her heart raced as she felt his lips press against her. She couldn't believe what was happening, it had to be the one of most passionate kisses she'd ever had in her life. Oh my, maybe she should be let herself be taken over more often!

The small group of soldiers gave a celebratory cheer as Sharon, not caring who was watching, grabbed the sides of John's face and returned his kiss. Her knees weakening, Sharon raised her right leg and smiled deliriously, letting herself fall into his muscular arms, her breath hitched as she felt his hands slide down and grab her buttocks. Spellbound, she was oblivious to the world around her until she heard a loud, embarrassed cough, bringing her crashing back to Earth.

Reluctantly pulling herself away, Sharon felt her cheeks warm with embarrassment on seeing the bemused looks on the faces of those standing around her.

'Come on along now, you two. If you're not careful, I am going to treat you both for asphyxiation.' Doctor Porter chortled, giving them a wink. 'Save something for later, what?'

Sharon, deeply embarrassed, coughed and pretended to adjust her hair, her chest rising and falling as she tried to compose herself. John took a step back, whistling, and stared up at the ceiling, appearing distracted by a strange detail above him.

'Yes, well, plenty of time for that later,' Sharon said breathlessly. She jerked back in alarm as the memories of what Oracle had done while in control of her body flooded back to her. Horrified at the images of blood and gore that were suddenly being thrown at her, she spun sharply round. 'John, I need to tell you something, it's about Bar—' She screamed in agony as she experienced a sudden burst of excruciating pain coming from inside her head. It felt like her skull was going to explode, like something was trying to tear her apart from the inside. In tremendous agony, she collapsed to the floor, clutching the sides of her head.

Quick as lightning, John leapt forward and grabbed the gasping woman, cushioning her head just before it struck the floor. He peered up at Jennifer and Doctor Porter pleadingly as they knelt next to him. The older man grimly grabbed the small penlight from the breast pocket of his jacket and shone it into the screaming woman's eyes.

Obviously irritated by the light being that was being shone in her eyes, Sharon – her chest rising and falling in deep, rapid breaths – swiped at the penlight, then grabbed John's collar and stared at him through watering eyes. 'Bar … Barnes …' she hissed, 'I need to warn you … He—'

Paralysed by fear, John could only stand and stare helplessly at the writhing young woman beneath him. He felt his heart wrench in his chest as Sharon let out a blood-curdling scream and raked the sides of her head with her fingers.

John looked up blankly as he felt someone pulling frantically at his arm.

'Grab her arms and legs, quick,' Doctor Porter snapped.

Not waiting to be told twice, Jennifer immediately grabbed hold of Sharon's legs. Stunned, John stared numbly at the doctor and shook his head in confusion. He staggered in shock when the doctor struck him across the face, bringing him back to his senses.

'Damn it, man! Don't just stand there, grab her arms before she claws the skin off her head. I cannot sedate her while she's wriggling around,' he shouted.

'Oh, my God! What the hell is that?' A soldier let out a horrified gasp and pointed a shaking finger at Sharon.

Jennifer's hand shot up to her mouth to stifle a scream. The two medics, the colour draining from their faces, scrambled away from the now perfectly still body. Tasting bitter bile in his mouth, John grimaced as Sharon's nose throbbed and swelled as if something was forcing it away out through her nostril. Numb, not believing what he was seeing, he was sure could hear the sound of someone vomiting as a pulsating blood-soaked mass plopped out of the throbbing nose and dropped onto the floor, its thin fibrous tentacles stretching out as it skittered across the floor.

His upper lip curling up in disgust, John forced down a sick feeling and raised his pistol. Their faces grim, the small group of soldiers nodded their heads in unison and aimed their weapons at the techno-parasite. Using their bodies to shield the unconscious Sharon, the two medical personnel covered their ears at the thunderous roar of discharging weapons. The roar of gunfire gradually lessened as, one by one, each soldier took their finger off their weapon's trigger.

John bared his teeth and sneered at the floor. The only thing he could hear was the steady *click* … *click* … *click* … repeating over and over. Filled with an all-consuming hate and disgust he continued to press the empty weapon's trigger. There was no way in hell he was going to let that thing get away with harming the woman he loved. No … way … in … hell. He let out a guttural snarl. He was going to pulverize it. He was … He frowned as he realised that his weapon was no longer firing and shook his head in frustration. Damn it, what was wrong with that thing?

'Sir ... John,' Kendra said in a soft tone, gently taking the weapon out of his hand. 'It's okay, you got it. You can stop.'

John stared at his security chief and then at the weapon in her hands. He blinked, suddenly realising where he was and nodded gratefully. 'I-I am sorry. I don't know what came over me, Lieutenant Goynes,' he whispered, gesturing to the pile of spent bullets on the floor. 'I saw that ... that ... *thing* come out of Sharon, and it was as if a red mist descended over my eyes. I wanted so badly to tear it apart.'

Oh my God! Sharon! John's stomach fell as he remembered his lover's unconscious body. Spinning on his heels, he was relieved to see Doctor Porter examining her and dashed over to them. He bit his bottom lip and knelt next to her, his hand brushing over her pale face. He felt his throat tighten and forced himself to speak. 'Is she ...' he rasped hoarsely. Swallowing, he found himself unable to ask what he most dreaded.

Doctor Porter nodded gravely and put his hand on John's shoulder, 'Don't worry, she is still alive if that is what you are asking. She's unconscious, but the good thing is her pulse is faint but steady.' He let out a tired sigh, brushing his hand over his bald head. 'She must have been in tremendous pain when that *thing* forced itself out of her body. God knows what damage it did to her getting out.' Casting a quick look over his shoulder and waved at the two medical personnel racing towards them carrying a gurney. 'But we won't know for certain until we carry out a scan. Once we do that, we will have a fair idea where we stand.'

'Will she recover?' John asked with a hint of apprehension. 'I mean, how long will it be before she wakes up?'

The muscles in the doctor's face tightened and he stared at John with sad eyes. 'My boy, I have to warn you, she may never wake up.' His face softened and he smiled comfortingly. 'But the human body is an amazing piece of machinery. With time, and a little hope, I believe she will pull through.' His grey eyes flickered with admiration, and he glanced down at Sharon on the floor. 'She's already proven she is a fighter, so have faith, my boy. She may surprise us again.'

John nodded reluctantly and straightened, stepping back to allow them to place Sharon's body on the gurney. A weight settled on his heart as the woman he loved was wheeled away from him down the corridor. He turned slightly as Kendra moved beside him and bobbed her head at her colleague on the gurney.

'Don't worry, sir, she will pull through,' Kendra said softly and chuckled, nudging John playfully, 'I bet you in a few weeks she'll be like the Energizer bunny, bouncing around, her usual energetic self. You watch, she will be running rings around you in no time.'

John smiled sadly at Kendra and gave her an appreciative nod. He frowned, recalling Sharon's last words. What was it she said? Warn him about Barnes? But which one? Surely she meant Colonel Barnes. Or did she? Suddenly troubled by the idea that there could possibly be someone on the base who was undermining them from within, John narrowed his eyes in suspicion, turned away from Kendra and marched down the corridor. His heart hammering in his chest, a simmering anger churned inside him as a dangerous thought popped into his head. What if Sharon was trying to warn him of an enemy standing in plain sight all along? One way or another, he was going to find out.

Kendra shook her head sadly as she watched the back of the embittered man charging down the corridor. She had seen that expression on people's faces so many times – someone blinded by the need for revenge after losing a loved one. She shivered slightly, understanding that loss too well, coming so close to the edge, blinded by hate. Kendra nodded wistfully. Not that long ago she had been lucky she had someone who pulled her away from that edge, stopping her from doing something she would have later regretted.

Her lips pursed, Kendra raised her handheld radio, hoping she was not too late to save somebody else from doing something they would later regret. She pressed the button on the side of the radio and spoke in a low urgent voice. 'Wendy, it's Kendra. Can you hear me, over?'

There was a pause of several seconds, followed by a crackle and she heard a familiar Scottish accent coming through her radio's speaker.

'Hey you, what's up? Over.'

'Change to channel twenty-three immediately, over.'

There was a slight click and Kendra heard the channel being changed on her radio. *'What's up, lover? What's with all the secrecy? I hope you're not trying to get me into bother agai—*'

'Wendy, shut up and listen. We don't have much time,' Kendra snapped sharply. 'I think we may have a problem …'

-7-

Dave pinched the bridge of his nose and let out a long, tired breath. He yawned and leaned back in his chair, scrubbed his tired face with his hands, and wondered for the umpteenth time why he had allowed himself to be talked into doing something so mind-numbingly boring.

He knew the reason, of course. When John Payne had ordered the base to go into full lockdown, he had enlisted all personnel within the base to search the vast complex. The detective inspector willingly stepped in to help, but Sophia Collins had knocked back his request, believing his close likeness to his doppelgänger would be more of a hindrance, possibly leading to more confusion. Grudgingly, Dave accepted Sophia's request without complaint, but being someone who hated sitting on the sidelines, he had pleaded desperately with them both that he still needed to feel useful.

It had been John who suggested Dave would be of use searching through the complex's security camera footage. Eager to be of some help, he accepted the task with his usual relish – but that was until he realised the enormity of the task in front of him. If he had been honest with himself, he had not truly understood the vast size of the underground complex until a member of the base's tech team sat him down in front of a computer display. It wasn't until he opened the file containing records filmed by the base's nearly infinite supply of security cameras that he sighed reluctantly – it was going to be a long night.

Dave blew out his cheeks and rested his chin on his left hand, with his free hand tapping on the keyboard as he scrolled through endless security footage. *Well, this just sucks!* Sticking his bottom lip out like a baby throwing a temper tantrum, he slammed his finger down on the keyboard in frustration. Dave let out a tired groan as the security footage to jump back several frames and he dropped his head in his hands. *Oh, that was a clever thing to do now, wasn't it, you pillock!* Leaning back in his chair, he looked up at the ceiling and cursed at his own childishness.

Dave frowned as he sensed movement out of the corner of his eye. He cast a curious peek over his shoulder and spotted the familiar flame-haired statuesque figure of Constable Cooper dashing into the conference room. She barely acknowledged him as she raced past him and toward Sophia, who was standing in front of the large window overlooking the command centre. Sophia cocked her head curiously as the breathless woman stopped in front of her and whispered something urgently to her, gesturing to the door from where she had just entered.

Returning to his task at hand, Dave shrugged, believing that if it was something important, they would make him aware of it. He screwed up his face in disgust as he remembered that he had impatiently struck the keyboard and he had accidently opened another security file – only this one appeared to be footage taken by a security camera close to the infirmary. Reaching toward the mouse, Dave peered up at the monitor, did a double take at the image on the screen and stared at the screen in slack-jawed disbelief. No, it couldn't be!

'Well, feed me shit on a cracker,' he blurted out, spinning round in his chair to face the two women behind him. A broad grin covered his face as he gestured to the monitor. 'I have found him!'

A congratulatory smile covering her face, Sophia patted Dave on his shoulder in celebration. 'Well, done, Detective Inspector. So where is he?'

His self-congratulatory mood vanishing, Dave stared at Sophia sheepishly and pointed at the image in front of him. 'Well, yeah, that's the thing. According to the timestamp, this footage was taken over an hour ago. But the good thing is …' He paused as he leaned in and squinted at the image in front of him. The two women looked at each other in other in mild surprise as the normally polite man leapt to his feet and unleashed a series of F-bombs.

In a fit of rage, his chest rising and falling with rapid breaths, Dave furiously slammed his foot against the chair he had been sitting in seconds earlier, sending it flying across the room. Pacing in a circle, he threw his hands up in the air and hissed, gesturing angrily at the image on the monitor. '*He* played me. *He* played like a puppet. I honestly thought I could believe him. What a fool I was to believe him. *He* stood there laughing at me and I didn't see it. How blind am I?'

Gently putting her hand on his shoulder, Sophia was calm and collected but her voice also held an authoritative tone. 'Inspector ... Dave ... calm down. Tell me what's wrong.'

Still raging at what he had uncovered, Dave laughed bitterly and stabbed his finger at the computer monitor. 'Look at that and tell me what you see.' Before the two women could see for themselves, he charged across to the monitor and stabbed his finger onto the screen with just enough force it caused the image to quiver. 'Better yet, I can tell you. This footage is from the security camera near the infirmary, just after I heard the message on the Tannoy system requesting a medical team to the detention level.' His top lip curled up in contempt and he stared at the image through hostile eyes. 'I recall bumping into him as I charged out of the infirmary, but I was so full of my own self-importance I failed to see what was standing in front of me.'

Her eyes round with sympathy, Sophia gave Dave a reassuring smile. 'You are being too hard on yourself. How were you to know Barnes had escaped? You probably thought the same as I did when I heard the alarm, that something had happened to him in his cell.'

Not easily placated, Dave scoffed and waved his hand dismissively at her. 'That's manure and you know it.' He frowned as he leaned forward and tapped a couple of keys on the keyboard, magnifying the image on the monitor to show Barnes's grinning face. 'See, just after I bump into him. He turns and looks up at the camera and grins. He actually grins at the camera.' He blew out his cheeks, turned away from the monitor and ran his hand down his tired face. 'Why? Why did I not stop him when he was literally standing in front of me? Surely, I cannot be that blind.'

'I have been asking myself the same thing.'

On hearing the bitter angry voice coming from behind, Dave wheeled round to see John Payne, grim faced, glowering at him. An alarm went off in Dave's head as he noticed something odd in John's body language. It was almost predatory. He swallowed, realising he had worn that same look himself many times when he had entered a room to question a criminal suspected of committing a horrendous crime.

Arms folded across his chest, Dave gave John a cold hard stare and spoke in a low neutral voice. 'Have you got something to say, Payne?'

John's brows snapped together, and Dave braced himself as he watched him take several slow, deliberate steps toward him. Sophia raised her hands up in front of her in a placating gesture and blocked the angry younger man. He guessed she was hoping to act as mediator. *Good luck with that*, he thought.

Keeping her voice calm but using a firm tone, she put a hand on the angry man's chest. 'Commander, this isn't the time or place to have this discussion.'

From the enraged expression on his face, Dave could see that John was in no mood to listen to reason. He watched him deliberately sidestep the woman and continued his advance. His eyes burning with disdain, he came to a stop just barely inches in front of Dave and gave him a stony stare. Sophia glanced at Wendy, shook her head, and held up her hands in an *'I give up'* gesture.

'Oh, I think this is the perfect time, Prime Minister.' He sneered, making no effort to hide the contempt in his voice, his eyes shooting daggers at Dave. 'Don't you think it's a little convenient that his doppelgänger was standing directly in front of him, and he failed to recognise him?'

Not believing what he was listening to, Dave blinked and stared at his accuser in open-mouthed stupefaction. 'Are you mad? What, you think I'm working with Barnes, is that it?' He barked a hollow laugh, turned away from John and shook his head. 'Sorry, I was wrong. You aren't mad, you're certifiable.'

'Don't you turn your back on me,' John snarled. He angrily reached forward, grabbed Dave's arm, then swung him around and jabbed his finger into his chest. His voice was thick with emotion as he stared at him accusingly. 'I never really trusted you, Barnes, even though I truly wanted to give you the benefit of the doubt. There was still that little voice inside me telling me not to trust you. Well, looks like I was right.' His tone becoming dangerous, he pushed Dave in the chest. 'I want you to tell me how long you and your doppelgänger have been working together.'

Not one to be pushed around, Dave was furious, and he shot John a murderous stare. His hands balling into fists, he leaned threateningly toward his accuser and growled at him, their noses barely centimetres apart.

'I'm going to tell you this once, so listen carefully. I am not and have never been working with my counterpart,' Dave hissed, spraying spittle into John's face, who recoiled in disgust. 'He sent that creature to attack me. Or have you forgotten I spent two days in the infirmary because of that?'

John took a slow step forward and slowly wiped the spittle off his face, scoffing. 'Funny thing about that. I find it convenient how you recovered so quickly and yet Claire, the woman you *claim* to love, is still lying in the infirmary in a coma.' He laughed bitterly, shook his head and waved his finger at Dave, who was becoming increasingly agitated. 'If I was a suspicious man, I would even suggest that you staged it … if I was a suspicious man.'

The blood pounding in his ears, his fists clenched, Dave staggered back from the taunting man and shook his head in disgust. 'Screw you, Payne. Don't you remember? Claire saved me by killing that creature after it knocked me out.' A smile tugging at his lip, he raised his hand and pointed it at the chamber's exit. 'If you don't believe me, you can ask her yourself. She is awake and talking now.'

John's face reddened in anger and he let out a derisive snort. 'Oh, on the outside you look delighted, but deep down it must burn you she survived.' A dark cloud covering his face, he advanced on Dave. 'What's wrong? Did she find out about your little scheme with Barnes and, when she failed to fall in line, you took her out of the picture? Only it didn't go the way you expected, did it?' He paused and cocked his head, smirking. 'Or did it? Maybe you were the one that stabbed Claire, staging the scene to make it appear something had injured her while she was defending you. You thought with her out of the picture, there would be no one around to say otherwise. Too bad you messed it up, so it appears you're going to have to try again.' The corner of his left upper lip twitched and he spoke in a low whisper. 'But this time we're on to you … traitor.'

'Bastard!' Dave snarled, his body quivering with rage. He shot John a murderous glare and brought his hand up to strike him.

'That is *enough*!' Sophia's voice was loud and authoritative as she moved between the two quarrelling men, her hands raised to separate them. 'I've enough to worry about without two grown men acting like two badly behaved children. In case you've forgotten, I have a base full of personnel who are feeling scared, and –' the men flinched in unison as she angrily raised her finger at them '– it doesn't help when two men they look up to for leadership, and who should know better, are having a pissing contest,' she snapped and waved her hands in front of her in a cutting gesture. 'Enough! You are both adults, so act like it.'

Feeling like two chastened schoolchild who had been caught squabbling by a strict teacher, Dave hung his head in embarrassment and muttered something inaudible under his breath. He cast an eye at John and could tell he just looked just as equally ashamed as him. Dave grunted to himself. Good, he hoped he was feeling bad for acting like such a prick.

Sophia let out a tired sigh and ran her hand down her face. 'Don't you see – this is what Oracle and Barnes are wanting? For us to be at each other's throats, dividing us.' She shook her head and put her hands on both men's arms. 'If we ever hope to stand against this coming storm, then we must put aside any doubts we have in each other. Don't you understand, the real battle is not out there,' she moved both her hands, placing her left hand on Dave's chest and her right on John's, 'but in here, in our hearts. Because once we have let one tiny bit of darkness inside us, it will slowly fester and poison those around us.' Her hazel eyes twinkling with compassion, she brushed her hand against John's face and whispered in a low voice, 'John, I can see you're hurting over what happened with Sharon, and I understand your need for revenge, but taking it out on the detective inspector is wrong. I could see in your eyes you didn't believe the things you were saying.' She smiled when John took in a deep breath and reluctantly nodded in agreement.

Still quietly seething, his arms folded across his chest, Dave watched as a sombre Sophia moved toward him and take his hand in hers. She spoke to him in a low, careful tone. 'Dave, please forgive John for what he said to you. Please, I am sure that you, more than most, are aware of how tightly wound up our emotions are in these difficult times.'

John coughed sheepishly and moved toward Dave with his hand outstretched. 'Uh, sorry, mate. I apologise for the things I said to you there. No hard feelings, huh?'

There was an awkward silence for several seconds as Dave stared at the hand in front of him. A series of emotions running through his mind, he unfolded his arms and reached for John's hand. Yes, he agreed partially with what Sophia was saying – this is probably what Barnes was hoping for them to be at each other's throats. But at the last moment, he stopped as he noticed something on the younger man's face. For a moment he thought he saw a flicker of satisfaction in Payne's eye. Dave ground his teeth in annoyance. Wait, why should he apologise? What Payne said about him deliberately letting Claire get injured had been uncalled for and hurt him deeply. No, let him sweat. In fact, screw them all. This wasn't even his fight. His blood boiling, Dave swatted John's hand away and hissed at him, making no effort to hide the contempt in his voice, 'Go to hell.'

His mouth agape, John watched incredulously as the bitter man spun on his heel and marched toward the door. As he brushed past Wendy, she reached out to him, but Dave just waved her away and marched angrily out of the conference room. She shook her head and stared at the open door with a furrowed brow. He could tell from the expression on her face that she was deeply worried about him.

'Maybe I should follow him,' she said uncertainly.

Sophia shook her head and drew in a long, weary breath. 'No, let him go. Give him time to cool off.' She pinched the bridge of her nose and gazed up at the ceiling, tiredness etched across her face. 'Perhaps it's best we call it a day. We are all tired and could do with getting some rest. Hopefully, after a night's sleep, he may see things differently in the morning.'

As he bobbed his head in agreement and yawned, John blinked in surprise at a sudden feeling of overwhelming fatigue. He let out a tired moan and massaged the back of his neck. It slowly dawned on him he had been running on adrenalin and had not thought about how late in the evening it was until Sophia had mentioned it. He cast a quick look at the filing cabinet in the room's corner and thought of the bottle of whisky within it. Ashamed, he cringed inwardly at how he had treated Dave and wondered whether if he stopped by his quarters carrying an olive branch in the shape of a whisky bottle, it may help to repair some bridges.

But before he could reach out to open the filing cabinet, John became aware of a hushed silence filling the chamber, and frowned as he noticed the two women were staring at something with apprehensive expressions. Turning towards them, he caught movement out of the corner of his eye and jerked back in surprise as became aware of someone standing by his shoulder. He did a double take and rubbed his eyes. Holy crap! Dave was standing beside him. He'd been so distracted by the thought of the whisky that he hadn't noticed Dave had crept back into the room. There was an awkward silence for several minutes as the two men stared at one another, unsure who should speak first.

Looking abashed, his feet shuffling uncomfortably, Dave lowered his head and mumbled something incoherently at John.

John raised an eyebrow and cocked his head at Dave. 'Sorry, I didn't catch that.'

His cheeks flushing with embarrassment, Dave lifted his head and coughed. 'Yes, I …' He coughed again and stared awkwardly at John, 'I was halfway down the corridor when something weird happened to me. I felt this presence inside of me, and then all of a sudden it was as if I wasn't in control of my own body.' He rubbed the back of neck and looked at John in bewilderment. 'I cannot explain it. I found myself walking back here. But as I was walking back, I kept hearing this voice inside my head telling me I should apologise for acting like a bit of a dick.'

John cocked his head and gave him a side eye. 'A *bit* of a dick?'

Dave gave a reluctant nod and shook his head in resignation. 'It was then I realised Sophia was right, this is what Barnes and his allies are wanting – driving a wedge between us, so we're at each other's throats. If we are to stand united against the darkness, then we must set aside our childish struggles.' He paused, straightened his shoulders, and gave John a wry smile. 'So if that means I must be the bigger man, then I …' He hung his head and gave small a shrug. 'Um, you know.'

Revelling in Dave's discomfort, John held up his hands and brought them back to his chest in a *give me some more* gesture. 'Come on mate, you can say it.'

Dave scowled and gave him the evil eye. 'You are really going to make me work for this aren't you?'

John grinned and gave him a knowing wink. 'You bet I am, mate.'

Dave threw his hands up in the air and let out a large growl of displeasure. 'Fine! You want to hear me say it, then I'll say it! I am sorry. Okay? I apologise for the way I acted. It was not only immature but disrespectful. I see now you didn't really mean the stuff you said.' He folded his arms across his chest and stared unhappily at John. 'I'm sorry. Happy now?'

His eyes wide, John raised his hands to his face in mock astonishment. 'What? Do my ears deceive me? Is the mighty Detective Inspector Barnes actually apologising?'

Dave clenched his teeth and scowled at the gleeful man. 'Okay ... you've made your point.'

Basking in his friend's increasing irritation, John closed his eyes and raised his hands above his head in pretend celebration. 'Hallelujah! It is a miracle.' Much like a few days ago, he was too busy enjoying ribbing Dave that John again did not see Sophia glide stealthily across the room, stopping just short of him. She paused, almost as if she was savouring the moment, raised her hand to the back of John's head, and gave a firm slap. He let out a cry of pain in mid-sentence. 'Let the angels rejoi—!' He spun round to the stern-faced woman, who was looking at him with murderous intent, and shot her a perplexed look. 'Will you please stop doing that?' he moaned. 'By rights I should report you to HR for physically abusing a member of staff.'

Sophia raised her finger at him and fixed him with a cold stare. 'Well, if you didn't misbehave, then I wouldn't have to, would I?' As she gestured towards Dave, John could tell from the gleeful look on his face he was enjoying the moment. 'You can see how hard it is for the inspector and yet you make it worse for him by carrying on in this childish manner. Grow up!'

John tutted, rolled his eyes, and grinned. 'He knew I was only teasing him.' He gave Dave a sly wink as he took a step toward the filing cabinet drawer, opened it, and pulled out the bottle of whisky. 'In fact, he and I were just about to sit down to this bottle of whisky. Nothing repairs broken bridges better than two men sharing a bottle of bottle of Northern Ireland's finest. Isn't that right, Inspector?'

Dave straightened his back and nodded firmly in agreement. 'Oh yes, I would have to agree with the commander here. In fact, I think it may take, what ...' He paused and rubbed his chin thoughtfully. 'Two ...'

'Oh, I would have to say at least four,' John interjected, struggling to keep a straight face as he uncorked the bottle.

'That it will take at least *five* glasses before I can truly accept the commander's apology.' Dave coughed and fixed Sophia with an innocent stare.

'After all, we must all do our bit to ensure the bond between our separate organisations remains strong.'

'Oh, I wholeheartedly agree, Inspector.' John grinned, pouring the contents of the bottle into two glasses.

As she watched the two men each take a seat to drown their sorrows in the bottle of whisky, Sophia put her hands on her hips, stared up at the ceiling and shook her head. Why was it whenever two grown men had an argument, they felt they could set things right by getting pissed? She groaned, pinching the bridge of her nose. It was at times like this she was glad she never got married. Sensing movement next to her, she swivelled her head and saw Wendy was trying to slink towards the two men licking her lips. Of course, Sophia wasn't a fool, she knew what Wendy was after. She didn't have to be a genius to see Wendy was hoping to sample the whisky. She was a Scot after all – she probably had whisky in her veins!

'If you excuse me, ma'am, I am just going to …' Wendy said in a hopeful tone.

'You can stay where you are,' Sophia snapped, stopping the redhead in her tracks by grabbing her arm. 'If you think I am going to allow all my command staff to wake up tomorrow morning hung-over, you are sadly mistaken.'

Shoulders slumped in defeat, Wendy nodded in reluctant agreement and let out a huff of resignation. 'Yes, ma'am, you're very wise.'

Not sure if she was being sarcastic, Sophia gave the younger woman a suspicious side eye. However, before she could ask Wendy what she meant, she became distracted as she noticed her personal secretary, Audrey Stewart, had suddenly stepped out of the elevator. As Sophia watched Audrey make her way over to her, she noticed that she was holding a piece of paper in her hand and from the grave look on her face she had a sense it was important. After taking the small note off her, Sophia thanked Audrey and cast her eyes over the note's contents. *Oh, dear Lord, he's going to do it.* She gave a big gulp, ignoring the gnawing anxiety that was coming from the pit of her stomach and glanced up at the large flat-screen monitor on the wall.

Ignoring the questioning look coming from Wendy, Sophia glanced over to the two men on the other side of the room. For some reason she could not understand, she felt a tinge of remorse that she was going to have to spoil their fun. However, a surge of relief passed through her as she realised they must have noticed and had set their glasses to one side, climbed out of their seats and made their way over to her.

'I have just been told the King is about to give a speech,' she said in a despondent voice, reaching forward to take the TV's remote that had been sitting on the tabletop.

Sophia gazed at the contemplative faces of the people standing around her. If there was one thing she was certain of, she didn't have to be a psychic to know they were all considering the implications of what was forthcoming. John, his face sombre, leaned toward the whisky bottle and without commenting placed it back in the filing cabinet. The mood in the conference room changed to one of trepidation as, one by one, they turned their attention to the monitor on the wall.

-8-

Location: the Kremlin, Moscow, the Russian Federation

A few hours earlier ...

Igor Medvedev sat in silence as he regarded his friend, Leonid, with increasing concern. His fingers stroked his thick beard nervously as he stared at the sombre-looking man who stood in contemplative silence gazing out of the window, watching the setting sun cast an eerie glow on the glittering surface of the Moskva river.

Several minutes had passed since they had watched the broadcast of a news conference in New York. They had both stared in dismay at the announcement that the United Nations had voted to dissolve and then listened with increasing concern at the unveiling of a new peace-keeping programme called Oracle. Their concern quickly changed to apprehension when the AI introduced itself and declared its intentions.

Igor was an enormous hairy man, whose build and gruff reputation had earned him the nickname of the Bear (although no one would have dared call him that to his face). He had been Leonid Komenev's friend and confidant for over sixty years. They had been close friends since childhood, growing up together on the harsh streets of Leningrad, where, as homeless children, they were forced to learn the skills to survive on the city's harsh streets, developing a tough reputation fighting off rival street gangs. But as soon as they were old enough, they enlisted in the Soviet army.

Leonid was a natural-born leader. His charisma and intelligence had assured his rise through the ranks with ease, with Igor following him wherever he went. Both men's reputations of being tough but fair earned deep respect from those who served under them. Later serving in the Spetsnaz, the elite unit of the Russian Special Forces, they had fought for their country courageously and with great distinction, earning them the Hero of the Russian Federation, Russia's highest award for valour.

After leaving the military, Igor followed Leonid into the KGB, where they both had successful careers as intelligence officers. When Leonid retired from the KGB, Igor once again followed his friend as he pursued a career in politics. He had looked on proudly as his friend climbed the political ladder, from becoming mayor of Saint Petersburg (formerly Leningrad) to eventually becoming President of Russia. One of Leonid's first acts was to name Igor as his chief of staff.

Igor sensed his friend's unease when the artificial intelligence called Oracle hijacked every communication feed across the world, revealing herself and declaring martial law. He could tell from his friend's body language that he was deeply troubled by those sudden developments. It wouldn't take a genius to work out that a new global power had come to the table, which could only mean one thing – the dark storm clouds of war were fast approaching and this time it was quite possible they both would not live long enough to see it through.

As he lifted his ageing, heavy frame out of the chair, Igor let out a weary groan. He winced as he felt his knees crack as he walked over to his friend next to the window.

'What is troubling you, my friend?' Igor murmured. 'Surely you are not troubled by this woman who claims to be the British prime minister? You and I both know she is an imposter. You were just speaking to the real Sophia Collins less than half an hour ago.'

Igor knew this to be true; he had been in the room when Leonid had been speaking to the real Sophia Collins, who was in her office in the Alliance compound codenamed the Castle, via a heavily encrypted video link. Their video conference had been cut short when their link was severed without warning, and after making several unsuccessful attempts to re-establish the connection, they quickly came to the only conclusion possible – someone in the Castle had activated their storm-door protocol, cutting off all lines of communication to the outside world.

The Russian President turned away from the window and shook his head sadly. He placed both his hands on his antique oak desk and exhaled a long sad breath as if a heavy weight had settled on his heart.

'It is this one called Oracle that troubles me,' he replied wistfully and nodded to the TV screen. 'My instincts tell me this does not bode well for Mother Russia.'

Igor smiled warmly and placed his hand on his friend's shoulder. 'You should not let her trouble you so, my friend. How many times have we fought opponents when the odds were against us, but came away victorious? Trust me, this time is no different.' The corner of his mouth curling up into a grin, he lifted his hand and squeezed it into a tight fist. 'This Oracle will learn the hard way when she comes for us. We will add her name to the list of people we have buried deep in the ground.'

Leonid turned to his friend and shook his head morosely. 'I have a bad feeling, my friend, that this time we will be the ones they will dig the graves for.'

Before Igor could open his mouth to object, he was interrupted by a small knock from behind him. They both turned to see the door open, and Mischa Rozhenko entered the room carrying a stack of papers in her hand, bowing her head respectfully. Igor held Mischa in high regard. Now in her mid-fifties, he was very much aware she had to fight hard to get where she was today. She had a hard-edged quality about her. But she also had a fierce reputation of being tough but fair, a quality he knew Leonid admired. It was one of the reasons he had recruited her.

'Mister President,' she said courteously.

'Mischa,' Leonid murmured in acknowledgement and then cocked his head questioningly at her. 'What news does my head of intelligence bring me?'

Mischa's thick unibrow bunched together in the centre of her forehead and she frowned at Leonid with a troubled expression. 'Nothing good, sir,' she said reluctantly. 'We have not been able to re-establish contact with the Castle since they went radio silent. It is as we surmised – they have engaged their storm-door protocol.'

Igor exchanged a troubled look with Leonid but he could tell from his friend's worried expression that he understood the implications of Mischa's statement. Only a chosen few in the world knew of the Castle, the British secret command centre that was linked to other secret command centres scattered around the globe. The purpose of these command centres was to act as a hidden resistance network in the event of a global invasion by a hostile force.

Over the past few years, command centres such as the Castle had quietly become operational across the globe since it had slowly become apparent that some of the world's governments were being infiltrated by other-worldly forces.

'This is most troubling,' Leonid grumbled, sighing heavily. 'I think we have to assume they have initiated their security protocols because of the intrusion into the world's media network by Oracle.' He frowned and gave Mischa a questioning look. 'Can I assume Leviathan has engaged their security protocol, too?'

'Yes, sir, they moved into lockdown as soon as they detected the system intrusion on the global media network,' Mischa replied grimly. 'We have also had reports that the Americans, the British and some other nations have ordered their submarine fleets to sea. Pavel Kazlov, your Minister of Defence, has taken it upon himself to do the same and ordered our submarine fleet to sea immediately. He has ordered each captain to go radio silent and not to contact the motherland under any circumstances.'

'Very good,' Leonid murmured, nodding in approval.

'Sir, there is something else you need to know,' she said hesitantly, 'which I think you will find even more disturbing.'

'Even more disturbing?' the elderly Russian replied slowly, giving the woman a sharp look. 'What can be even more disturbing than an artificial intelligence seizing control of the world's communication network?'

Mischa nodded gravely and pulled out a sheaf of papers from the folder she was holding. Leonid raised an eyebrow curiously; the papers were a mixture of glossy images and graphs. Mischa's forehead furrowed as she shuffled through the papers, grumbling. 'I keep telling them, put the most recent image on the top. But do they listen? One of these days, I'll …' She stopped in mid-grumble as she found the image she was looking for and placed it on top of the desk. Leonid lifted an eyebrow. It was a photo of a satellite image with one area circled with a yellow highlighter.

'Fifteen minutes ago, our satellite picked up these images showing hostile forces assembling along our border,' Mischa explained, pointing to the highlighted part of the photo. There was a note of concern in her voice as she placed other documents on the desk. 'We are getting reports of some heavy fighting in cities such as London, Washington DC, Sydney and Berlin. We have detected hostile forces also gathering along China's border.'

Igor placed his hand on Leonid's arm. 'My friend, I think it is time we take you to a secure place.'

The aged Russian let out a growl of annoyance, pulled away from his friend and waved his hand dismissively. Igor opened his mouth to protest but was silenced as Leonid shot him a dangerous look and turned back to his head of intelligence.

'Has there been any type of activity from those forces along our border?'

'No, sir,' Mischa replied. Her deeply troubled brow left a thick groove in her forehead as she gestured to the satellite images in Leonid's hand. 'There has been no communication from them. They just appear to be standing there as if they are waiting for something.'

Igor stroked his beard and let out a grunt of frustration. 'What are they waiting for?'

'That would be me.'

The three people jumped at the voice coming from across the room and stared dumbfounded at the tall narrow mirror hanging on the wall. It shimmered and a tall red-haired woman stepped through it, wearing a figure-hugging silver all-in-one uniform.

Showing no hesitation, Mischa wheeled around to the door and shouted, 'Security!'

Within moments, four large black-suited men carrying P90 handguns charged into the room. Despite his enormous frame, Igor was able to knock Leonid to the floor. He used his body as a shield as the four men opened fire on the intruder.

Holding his friend's head down on the floor, Igor was astonished as the intruder made no reaction to the bullets tearing into her. He stared in dumbfoundment as he watched the newcomer just stand and smile as the four men continued to discharge their weapons at her.

'Cease fire,' Igor roared, pulling himself to his feet.

Acting as one, the four men instantly ceased firing but continued to point their weapons at the strange woman suspiciously. She lowered her head and pouted at the men in front of her.

'Aw, why did you stop? We were having such fun,' the stranger moaned in perfect Russian, her accent flawless. She let out a melodramatic sigh, lowered her head and looked at her tattered clothing. 'Do you know how much trouble it is getting bullet holes out of clothes?'

Aghast, the people in the room saw the woman's cold yellow eyes glow, and then her tattered uniform miraculously repaired itself within seconds. If he had not been present to witness the earlier rain of fire on the intruder's person, Igor would have sworn her clothing looked brand new and showed no sign of the damage that had been inflicted upon it.

His body quivering with fury, Leonid grunted as he eased himself off the floor and pushed past his protesting friend. He stared coldly at the amused woman in front of him and growled, 'I take it you are the one called Oracle.'

Oracle winked and grinned mischievously, bowing her head at the Russian President. 'Guilty as charged.'

His eyes flickering with anger, Leonid took a step towards the synthetic woman. Igor placed his hand on his old friend's arm to stop him, but the president angrily brushed the hand away as he edged closer to the woman in front of him. 'How dare you invade my office in such a way?' Leonid snarled with a hint of defiance. 'Explain why you are massing troops along our country's border and what gives you the right to inflict your will on the rest of the world?'

The mood in the room quickly changed from anger to fear. The mysterious woman's smile faded, and Leonid took a step back as her lifeless yellow eyes brightened and the corners of her mouth curled up in disdain. Oracle then swivelled her head and gazed upon each face in the room, almost as if she was analysing each one. Igor felt his jaw drop open in shock. He could not believe his eyes – her head had rotated 360 degrees – yes, a full 360 degrees! Despite his bravado, Igor felt his sphincter twitch under the scrutiny of those cold yellow eyes.

'All will be explained in good time, Mister Komenev,' Oracle answered in a slow, dangerous tone, turning to the four armed men standing in front of her. 'First, I must deal with the unwarranted attack on my person by your underlings.'

The expression on her flawless face hardening, Igor watched the faux woman turn her attention to the security detail. The cold hand of fear tightened around his heart. A chill ran down his spine as he suddenly realised what she intended to do.

'Please, you don't have to do this. They were only following orders,' Leonid pleaded in desperation, placing himself in front of his men. 'If anyone should be punished, it should be me. I beg you, don't punish these men simply for doing their jobs.'

The four men standing behind Leonid all stepped forward in protest as their leader pleaded on their behalf, but their protestations were silenced as their commander-in-chief gave them a withering look, holding his hand up as he bellowed sharply at them. 'Stay where you are, that's an order!'

Oracle paused, frowned, and stared at Leonid appraisingly. She stood in silence for several moments and tapped her chin thoughtfully. Eventually, the corners of her mouth lifted into a cold smile as she nodded and placed her hand on Leonid's shoulder.

'Yes, you are correct. I should not punish these men simply for doing their jobs, and punishing you would serve no purpose.'

'Thank you,' Leonid whispered gratefully, his shoulders sagging in relief.

The artificial woman shook her head, tutted and squeezed Leonid's shoulder. Igor felt his hands tighten as he listened to his friend's pained cries, picturing Oracle's steel-like fingers digging into the flesh of Leonid's shoulder. He shuddered as he pictured her nails burrowing through his friend's skin into the tight space of his shoulder joint. Igor continued to watch gravely as the colour from Leonid's face drained. He swallowed as he noticed his friend's legs were starting to buckle.

'But what type of mother would I be if I did not punish my children?' she whispered menacingly, cocking her head curiously. 'How will you learn if I do not punish you for your mistakes?'

Powerless to help his friend and colleague, Igor exchanged a horrified look with Mischa as he realised the thing in front of them was insane. The four security men pleaded helplessly as the homicidal woman increased the pressure on their leader's shoulder and they were forced to listen to his screams of agony as he crumpled to the floor.

Her face softening, Oracle eased her grip on the screaming man's shoulder and knelt next to him. 'Choose,' she whispered.

His face glistening with sweat, the president squeezed his eyes shut, took in a lungful of air, and looked up at Oracle. 'I don't understand,' he gasped, incomprehension covering his face.

'Choose,' she repeated in a flat tone.

'Choose? Choose what?' Leonid frowned. 'I don't understand what you mean.'

Laughing mirthlessly, Oracle straightened and gestured to the other people in the room.

'Why, choose who I am to punish, of course,' she said in a matter-of-fact tone. 'Is it to be your loyal, close friend?' Igor flinched in surprise as she gestured to him. Then, without waiting for a response, the maniacal woman turned sharply to Mischa and pointed to her. 'Or is it to be the beautiful and by-the-book head of Russian intelligence?'

Head held high, Mischa's eyes tightened as she stared at the woman and sneered at her. 'Come and get me, you yellow-eyed harpy.'

Mischa's eyes flickered with incandescent rage as Oracle cocked her head and smirked at her. Igor had seen that same look many times before; it was the same way a human would gaze at an ant; it was as if she was telling them they did not matter, that humans were beneath the AI. He watched as Mischa closed her eyes and sucked in a deep breath. From the way she was clenching her hands together, he could tell she wanted desperately to tear the yellow-eyed artificial woman's throat out. If he was being honest, he wouldn't blame her if she did. He held his breath and waited for the inevitable. But he need not have worried; instead of attacking Oracle, Mischa simply placed her hands on her hips, curled her upper lip and let out a snarl of disgust. Igor could almost sense the tension in the air as he watched both women's eyes lock on to each other. He relaxed slightly when Oracle finally gave a dismissive wave of her hand and turned away.

The four security officers' foreheads glistened with sweat, and they nervously gripped their handguns even tighter as the pseudo woman focused her attention on them. 'Or your loyal security detail, who will willingly sacrifice themselves for you.'

Still grimacing, Leonid pushed himself off the floor and straightened. From the way his shoulders were stooped and the resigned expression written across his face, Igor had known his friend long enough to recognise he had come to a decision that weighed heavily on him.

'I have chosen,' he said decisively, closing his eyes and inhaling a deep breath. 'I am their leader. If you must punish anyone, punish me.'

There was a loud furore as Mischa, Igor and the four security officers raised their voices in protest, but a roar from the Russian President quickly silenced them.

'Silence!' the elderly but still formidable Russian roared and then smiled as he considered each person in the room. 'It is my decision. I do this freely knowing that my sacrifice will not be in vain if it saves your lives.' He drew in a long breath and turned back to Oracle in heavy resignation. 'Do you what you need to do, you inhuman whore.'

Her cold bright eyes shining with malice, Oracle fixed Leonid with a steely gaze and took a step toward him. Her expression hardening, she stretched her hand out to the proud man in front of her, only to stop, interrupted by the cacophony of raised voices coming from behind her.

'Uri, no.'

Curious to see what the commotion was, Igor lifted his head to peer over Oracle's shoulder and blinked in surprise. Three of his security officers appeared to be arguing desperately with one of their colleagues, who looked as if he was taking a step toward Oracle. The large fair-haired man, who Igor immediately recognised as Uri Ivanova, smiled sadly to his colleagues and waved them away.

'Sir, I cannot let you do this,' Uri said sadly as he looked intently at his leader. 'Our people will need you in the coming days.'

Leonid opened his mouth to protest, but Igor took a step forward and placed a hand on his shoulder, cutting him off. He twisted his head and gave Igor a questioning look.

'He is right, my friend,' Igor said, nodding. 'Our people will need you. Allow Agent Ivanova to do this.' He smiled when as Leonid give him a reluctant nod on realising his friend was correct and then sighed in agreement.

Agent Ivanova strode up to Oracle and for a moment Igor was filled with a sense of pride as he watched the young security officer proudly march up to the tall counterfeit woman with his head proudly erect. If he was scared, he was doing a remarkable job of hiding it.

'What I do now, I do for Mother Russia,' Uri announced proudly, his eyes blazing with defiance at Oracle. 'Do what you need to do, you yellow-eyed witch, and begone.'

Oracle inclined her head and regarded the proud man in front of her for a few moments before her mouth curved into a warm smile. She held up her hands and moved closer to Uri. The young man flinched slightly as he felt her light touch on the skin of his face. Uri's forehead crinkled in surprise at the warm sensation of her kiss. He'd expected it to be cold and passionless, but this was nothing like he had ever dreamed of; it was electrifying ... enticing ... Oh, how he craved her. Just to feel her body wrapped around his. He felt like he was lost in time and space, nothing else mattered but his love for Oracle.

'You are such a good boy, my little Uri,' she whispered soothingly, pulling Uri's face closer to her. 'Mommy is very proud of you.'

Oh yes, he was such a good boy. Lost in the moment, all Uri wanted was to feel his mistress's touch on his body. Just to feel ... Wait, something was wrong? What was she doing? She was pressing her fingers in too hard. *It hurts! Make her stop, please make her stop!* Despite the increasing pain, the young man found he did not want to break free from the woman's intense grip. What was wrong with him? Why did he not want to break free?

Uri felt something warm trickle down the inside of his leg. Oh God, he didn't want to die this way. He wanted to be remembered as being brave – not crying like a baby in his own piss and shit. Oh why, did he have to act all noble? Why couldn't he have let someone else done it? All he wanted wa—

'Mommy.' He whimpered softly as Oracle moved her hands and he felt her thumbs start to press into his eyes.

As he watched the woman's smooth hands tighten on the young man's face, Leonid shook his head. What was wrong with Uri, why was he not trying to break free? But as he noticed the look of contentment on Uri's face, he felt his heart jump in fear at the sudden realisation that somehow Oracle had cast a spell over him. It was then a part of him understood – even if he wanted to, Uri was powerless to resist the increasing pressure of the woman's grip. Leonid realised the pressure must have become unbearable as he heard a soft moan of pain escape Uri's lips, possibly from the maniacal AI's fingers pressing deeper into his skull. The brave man's torment did not end there. Eventually his soft moans turned into hysterical screams of pain as Oracle's thumbs pressed deeper into his eyes.

Leonid swallowed as he heard the sickening squelch of Oracle's fingers piercing the white sclera of the unfortunate man's eyeballs. A chill of fear ran down his spine as Oracle glanced over to him, her mouth broadened into a malevolent grin as she continued to increase the pressure on the young man's skull. Already sickened by the vindictive display playing out front of him, he suppressed the urge to vomit as he detected the faint sound of Uri's skull cracking under the tremendous pressure being exerted on it.

He looked over his shoulder and watched with sympathy as the ashen-faced Mischa and Igor turned away in disgust as they listened to Uri's hysterical shrieks.

The shrieks of pain were silenced as the man's skull collapsed under the increasing pressure, followed by the loud squelching sound of Oracle's fingers pushing through the bone cartilage and squeezing the soft organic matter contained within. Leonid watched in revulsion as the sadistic woman, satisfied there was nothing else left to do, released her grip, and let the once proud Russian's lifeless body drop to the floor.

Oracle's face twisted up in disgust. She wiped her bloody hands on her clothes and shook her head sadly. 'Do you know how hard it is to get brains out of a uniform?' she moaned and then blinked in realisation. 'Oh, silly me!'

Leonid could not believe what was happening before his eyes as Oracle melodramatically clicked her fingers. He blinked and could only gawk as her body shimmered and in an instant her uniform was miraculously clean again. The yellow-eyed woman beamed maniacally, looked down and nodded in approval.

'Ah yes, that is much better.' She sighed. Then her mood changed and she spun sharply round to Leonid and fixed him with a stern stare. 'Let that be a lesson to you all. You have seen what will happen to those who oppose me. Unless you want to see more of your people die unnecessarily, you will willingly hand control of your government over to me. You will allow my forces to cross your border unopposed. You will serve me faithfully and without question. Do you understand?'

Sadness tore at Leonid's chest as he stared at the body on the floor. He inhaled deeply, held his breath for a few seconds and then blew it out in slow resignation. He slowly spun round and looked into the faces of the people in the room, who acknowledged him with an understanding nod. He hoped they could tell whatever decision he had reached was weighing heavily on his already troubled mind. His decision made, Leonid squared his shoulders, puffed out his chest and wheeled round to face Oracle, his arms behind his back as he fixed her with a steady gaze.

'Yes, I understand,' he answered. There was a touch of defiance in his voice as he squared up to the tyrannical AI. 'I will willingly hand control of my country over to you, but on two conditions.'

'Oh, I do not think you are in any place to make demands,' Oracle replied with an amused tone, 'but I am in a forgiving mood today. Go ahead, tell me your conditions.'

'You will give me twenty-four hours to prepare my people. If you can promise me their safety, then I will willingly hand control over to you.'

Oracle tapped her chin thoughtfully then nodded. 'To show how generous I am, I will grant you forty-eight hours to prepare your noble people.' She paused and fixed him with a steely gaze. 'But no tricks. If you are planning on deceiving me, then the deal is off, and your people will suffer even more.'

Leonid forced a smile and tilted his head at the woman in acknowledgement. 'No tricks. I promise.'

Oracle arched her head and regarded the Russian President with a silent appraisal. Finally, she simply bobbed her head with an amused expression. Leonid frowned as he saw her cast a surreptitious eye toward Igor and Mischa. What was going through that artificial mind of hers? Was she considering killing his two friends, just so that she could show that there was nothing he could do to stop her?

Leonid held his breath and watched the mysterious woman turn to the same mirror she had come through moments earlier. The mirror's surface shimmered briefly as, without saying another word, she stepped through and disappeared.

ORACLE'S VISION

Feeling like he was trapped in the eye of a storm, Leonid watched the three remaining security officers rush over to the body of their fallen comrade, and Mischa ordered for the body to be removed. He caught movement out of the corner of his eye and turned to see Igor reaching for the red phone that sat on top of the antique desk.

The president felt like a heavy weight had settled on his heart as he stumbled over to his desk and slumped into his leather chair. He placed his hands on the surface of the desk and gazed at them as he listened to Igor growling at someone on the phone.

Igor blinked in surprise as if noticing his friend was sitting down in front of him. He lowered the phone's receiver, pressed it against his chest, leaned over to his friend and murmured to him, 'We need to get you away from here, comrade.' Leonid detected a note of concern in his friend's voice as he continued to speak to him. 'I think it is best I take you to Leviathan before that witch comes back.'

'I am not leaving,' Leonid whispered.

'Sorry, what did you say?' Igor muttered, appearing to be only half listening as he glanced over his shoulder, distracted by Mischa's raised voice coming from behind him.

In no mood to argue, Leonid inhaled a deep breath, rose to his feet, and repeated what he said, this time in a loud, confident voice. 'I said I am not leaving.'

There was a stunned silence as everybody in the room stopped what they were doing and stared at their leader with expressions of disbelief. Igor stared at his friend, speechless, placed the phone back down and then moved closer so that he could put his hand on his friend's shoulder.

'My friend, you are not thinking straight. It is not safe for you here.'

Leonid smiled sadly and was silent for several moments as he regarded his old friend. As he looked into his friend's face for what he thought would be one last time, he was filled with a warm glow of pride. Pride for having had someone like Igor in his life. *Oh, my, yes, we certainly have been through some scrapes*, he thought, remembering themselves again as children running around like street urchins, and then as two young privates, barely in their twenties, getting into a fight in a bar with a group of American marines. *Oh yes, good times. But like most things in life, all good things must come to an end.* He tapped his confidant's hand, shook his head and exhaled a long heavy sigh. 'I have made my decision,' he said quietly.

'No, my friend, you are not thinking straight. Plea—'

Leonid held up his hand and shot Igor a withering look. Igor swallowed anxiously but remained silent as the Russian President turned away from him to focus his ire on other people in the room.

'You three, take that body out now and leave,' he ordered, gesturing to the body on the floor, and then glanced at a concerned-looking Mischa. 'You stay.'

The three large men all stared at one another in stunned uncertainty, but before they could open their mouths to protest, they were silenced by a loud roar from Igor.

'Your commander-in-chief just gave you a direct order! Now do as you were ordered.'

The three large men, making no further comment, quickly reached down to grab the rug that had their comrade's body on it and pulled it out of the room.

Leonid waited until they were out of the room and the door had closed before he turned back to his friend. 'Igor, old friend. I know what you are going to say, but I believe if I am not here when Oracle returns, she will take it out on our people. It is for them I do this. They need to see I am standing with them, that I haven't run away.'

Igor stared at his friend silently for several seconds before nodding in reluctant agreement. 'Yes, I understand.' He sighed sadly, paused, and then gave him a wry smile. 'I cannot let you do this alone, you crazy old man. I have been watching your back for over sixty years. If you think I am going to stop now, then you are crazy.' Igor barked a laugh and patted Leonid on the shoulder. 'God knows what trouble you would get yourself into.'

'Yes, my friend, you are probably right.' Leonid chuckled joylessly. He inhaled deeply, reached up and took his old friend's hand off his shoulder. 'Which makes this even harder. If our people, even the world, have any hope of coming through this approaching storm, our forces will need someone strong who can lead from the shadows, who can inspire them.' He gave Igor a tight smile as he prodded him in the chest. 'That, you big intimidating Russian bear, is you.'

'No, Lenny, I cannot leave you, I—'

'This is not a request,' Leonid interjected, raising his hand to silence his friend's protests. 'This is one battle you must fight alone. You have stood by my side all these years, fighting side by side not only in the military battles, but the political ones too. I have taught you everything you need to know. The time has come for us to go our separate ways.' He paused and reached over to take Mischa's hand and place it in Igor's. 'Our forces will look to you both during these dark days. Trust one another and promise me you will have each other's backs.'

Mischa's eyes glinted as she tried to blink away tears and bobbed her head slightly at Igor, whose large hand had enveloped hers.

'We will,' they answered in unison.

The corner of Leonid's mouth curled up in a half smile and he gave a firm nod of approval. He let out a long, heavy sigh, stepped away from them, and then reached under his desk to press a hidden button. They turned as they heard a faint hiss of a wall panel sliding down, revealing a hand scanner. Leonid glided over to it and placed his hand on the scanner. There was a quiet beep, followed by a pneumatic hiss of a hidden door opening to reveal a hidden elevator.

'As you know, this will take you to the maglev station a mile below the Kremlin. Thirty minutes after you board the maglev and are safely on your way to Leviathan, I will activate the Conceal Protocol. I am sure you will remember it – AED nodes line the walls of the elevator shaft. They will release liquid cement, sealing the shaft, making it appear as though it never existed. I will also give the order to detonate explosives that will also collapse two miles of the maglev tunnel that stretches out of here so it will never be discovered.'

The enigmatic head of intelligence gave a nod of understanding and entered the elevator. She opened her mouth to say something but hesitated. Instead, she stood to attention and held her hand up in salute. Leonid blinked away the tears, straightened and returned her salute.

Igor turned, clasped both his friend's hands and smiled sadly at him.

'There must be no regrets, no tears, no anxieties, my old comrade in arms. Just go forward in all your beliefs and prove to me that I am not mistaken in mine,' Leonid said proudly.

Igor nodded sadly, stiffened to attention, and saluted his lifelong friend for the last time. Their smiles disappearing, they kept their eyes locked on one another as the elevator door closed, and the hidden panel slid back into place.

Never feeling more alone and dejected, Leonid closed his eyes, placed a hand on the wall panel and whispered to himself, '*Do svidaniya*, my friend.'

Sucking in a lungful of air, he abruptly stepped back and walked over to the window. His right arm rested against the window's frame and a smile tugged at his lips as he stared out at the surface of the Moskva River shimmering in the early evening twilight.

Leonid gazed at the familiar view for several minutes before reluctantly forcing his body to step away. He groaned as his tired frame settled into his leather chair. With his fingers steepled together, he stared into space thoughtfully, but he jumped as his reverie was broken by the sound of his phone ringing. He pressed his lips together, glanced at the phone on his desk, lifted the handset and tilted his head as he listened to a woman's voice speak.

'*Many apologies, Mr President, I have Ki Kwolong, Premier of the People's Republic of China on the line, wishing to speak to you.*'

'Yes, that's fine, Maria. Put him through,' Leonid replied and frowned as he heard the line click as she connected the call. He cocked his head and smiled at the male voice speaking on the other end of the line. 'Good evening, Your Excellency,' Leonid said in fluent Chinese. He nodded sadly as he listened to Ki Kwolong's reply, and then said, 'Yes, I have just had a visit from her too and she has given me an ultimatum. She has given me forty-eight hours to comply. Ki, I must tell you, I am staying to protect my people, but I have handed control of Leviathan over to my chief of staff, he will be your con—'

Leonid's eyes grew wide as he listened to Ki Kwolong speak to him in urgent tones for several minutes. After he was finished speaking, Leonid exhaled sadly. 'I am sorry to hear that, my friend, but I respect your decision,' he answered reluctantly, only pausing as Ki said something back to him. 'Yes, I will contact him to let him know. As we all discussed, it is only right that he should make the announcement to the world's population. Good luck to you too, my friend.'

His heart heavy, Leonid placed the handset down on the receiver unit. His fingers tapped on the desk's surface thoughtfully before picking the phone up again. He smiled warmly as he heard Maria's voice come on the line again.

'Put me through to Buckingham Palace in London. Tell them I wish to speak to His Majesty the King.' His eyes narrowed as the woman said something back to him. 'Yes, I know this is not the standard procedure. You have your orders, now do it!'

The fingers of his left hand rapped impatiently on the antique desk's surface as he waited for the call to be connected. Several minutes went by and then he finally heard a familiar male voice. Leonid responded in perfect English. 'Good evening, Your Majesty. Yes, I am sorry to say the day we have dreaded has finally come …'

-9-

Location: Buckingham Palace, London, England

Struggling for breath, Corporal Elizabeth 'Betsy' Thompson forced herself to open her eyes, only to find herself staring at everything through a red haze or fog. Suddenly aware that something was running into her eyes, obscuring her vision. But as she reached up to wipe it away, she gasped as her fingers touched a gash on her forehead.

The palace guard tilted her head and tried to make sense of the sounds around her but shook her head in frustration when all she could hear was a ringing noise and the muffled roar of distorted sounds. However, despite her state of discombobulation, she was still able to recognise the distinctive sounds of weapons fire coming from somewhere ahead of her.

Her vision impaired, she used her hands to feel around her and frowned in concern as she touched the pieces of debris that were scattered around her. Her chest tightened in fear. There was no doubt in her mind that something bad had happened, but what? Was it a terrorist attack? She carefully crawled across the ground but was forced to stop by what she assumed was a brick wall. Slowly turning, she pushed her back against the wall and rested her head in her hands as she struggled to make sense of what had happened to her.

Moments earlier, Betsy had been standing on duty as guardsman outside Buckingham Palace. Her day had been running smoothly. She had been at her post, ignoring the usual playful attempts of tourists trying to get a selfie with her. Betsy became aware something was wrong when people started screaming and running past her with frantic looks on their faces, almost as if they were trying to escape an attacker. Despite her training, she had turned to investigate the disturbance when there was a flash of light, and the next thing she was aware of was being thrown to the ground under the concussive force of an explosion.

The ringing in her ears subsiding, Betsy tilted her head and frowned to listen to the sounds that were coming from all directions around her. There was no doubt in her mind that she could hear the crack of small arms being fired, alongside the recognisable *rat-a-tat-tat* of an automatic rifle, but what confused her more was she was sure she could make out make out another sound, alien but oddly familiar. She shook her head; she must have banged her head harder than she thought because for a moment she was positive they sounded like the laser rifles from *Star Wars*. That was impossible. Maybe she was actually unconscious, and her mind was playing tricks on her. However, before she could make sense of what she was listening to, she detected someone approaching. She tensed and reached for her bayonet.

'Put that thing away before you kill somebody with it, namely me,' a male voice hissed sharply.

'Jonesy, is that you?' Betsy asked, wincing as she felt something being pressed against her forehead; she blinked at the sensation of cold water running down over her eyes. Her vision clearing, she saw a tall, lean, sandy-haired man kneeling next to her and sighed in relief. 'You're a sight for sore eyes.'

'Not the first time I've been told that.' He grinned back. His grin quickly disappeared and was replaced with a serious look as he grabbed at her arm. 'Come on, we've formed a defensive perimeter at the main gate.'

As Private Wilfred Jones helped her to her feet, Betsy took a moment to study her comrade; the red tunic of his dress uniform was torn and had traces of blood splashed across it. She glanced down and shook her head sadly as she noticed her dress uniform was not much better.

'Any idea what's going on?' Betsy asked breathlessly as they sprinted in the direction of the main gate.

But before Jones could answer, a strange figure wearing bizarre gold and black armour appeared in front of them, holding an unfamiliar weapon that was pointed dangerously at them. Her eyes burning with incandescent fury, Betsy let out a battle cry of defiance and charged into the armoured figure, knocking it off its feet. With Jones pinning their strangely armoured foe's arms down, Betsy noticed what appeared to be a weak point in their foe's armour. The helmet looked as if it was connected to the neck via the submental space between the head and neck beneath the chin in the midline. Quickly grabbing her bayonet, she forced it through the small space in the armour and felt the tip of her blade touch the soft flesh contained within. Putting all her weight behind the sharp blade, she clenched her teeth as she heard the soft crack of a spinal cord being severed, and the unfortunate warrior became limp and unmoving.

'Come on,' she panted, 'let's hurry before another one appears.'

Sweat glistening on his brow, Jones nodded in silent agreement, climbed back onto his feet, and sprinted with his comrade. However, as they turned the corner, the scene in front of the stunned corporal almost stopped her in his tracks. The formerly majestic palace gates, for years a grand sight to tourists, lay on the ground, warped and twisted. In their place were a variety of cars and upturned ceremonial carriages, acting as a makeshift barrier against the forces that were marching up the Mall.

As she approached the barrier, Betsy spotted a tall, rugged, fifty-something soldier standing on top of it, barking orders at the squad of guardsmen around him. He turned to the two dishevelled soldiers running towards him.

'Where have you been, Private Jones? Did you stop for tea or something?' he barked, ducking as a beam of energy shot past him, narrowly missing his head.

'No, Sergeant Major Wayne.' Jones panted and saluted him. He looked over his shoulder and pointed at Betsy. 'I was picking up a lost pup found on the side of the road.'

The sergeant major gave a small growl of acknowledgement and stared at Betsy. 'Well, it would have been too cruel to leave her there, I suppose.' His eyes flashed briefly with concern as he noticed the bloodstained gauze on Betsy's forehead and her torn dress uniform. 'You still up for another bout, Corporal?'

'What's wrong, Sarge?' Betsy replied with a cheeky grin. 'You getting sleepy?'

The older man's eyes glinted with approval. 'That's the spirit, Corporal. Grab yourself a weapon and make yourself useful.'

'Yes, Sarge.' Betsy climbed over the barricade and past the sergeant major. She paused as she noticed a patch of blood seeping out from a wound on Wayne's left upper arm. 'Uh, Sarge, you're bleeding.'

'I ain't got time to bleed,' the sergeant growled irritably.

Betsy gave Jones a concerned glance as they clambered past the sergeant major. Jones lifted his shoulders in a wordless shrug before jumping off the barrier and landing next to a group of men.

'Hey, Betsy.' A tall black man greeted Betsy grimly, handing her a rifle. 'You finally joined the party, I see. What's wrong? You fall asleep again? Didn't I tell ya, all of them men would eventually tire you out?'

'Funny, Bally, I said the same thing to your wife this morning when I passed her coming out of the barracks,' Betsy teased, taking the weapon from Bally. She grinned as Bally grabbed her hand in a friendly gesture. Shaking his head, Bally playfully slapped her on the shoulder. His eyes filled with concern as he noticed Betsy's bloodstained face and the gauze on her forehead.

'Looks nasty, mate. What happened?'

'They did,' Betsy responded, lifting her shoulder in a small shrug and gesturing to the approaching armed figures on the other side of the barricade. 'Do we have any idea who they are and where they're coming from?'

'Dunno, mate.' Bally clenched his teeth together, leapt to his feet and fired his weapon at something on the other side of the barrier. He winced as a beam of energy streaked past his head, narrowly missing him, and ducked down onto his knees. 'It's an invasion, innit. My guess is it's the same blokes that just attacked the BBC a few moments ago.'

'They attacked the BBC!' Betsy gasped, her jaw dropping. She stared at her fellow guardsman uncomprehendingly, then pressed her lips together, leapt to her feet, and fired off a volley from the rifle in her hands.

'Yeah,' Jones replied, tight-lipped as he slammed another cartridge into her rifle. 'Happened about an hour ago. We were in the barracks watching a news bulletin showing all hell breaking loose in New York. The next thing we know, the shit hits the fan and then everything goes to hell.' His brow wrinkled and he slipped a cautious glance at the sergeant major standing above them. The private's voice dropped to a low whisper and he leaned closer to Betsy. 'This may sound weird, but moments before the BBC news feed was cut off, the sarge comes charging in, ordering us to arm ourselves and to barricade the main gate. It was as if he knew the attack was coming.'

Her heart thundering in her chest, Betsy swallowed and stared at Jones in disbelief. 'If the sarge knew the attack was coming, the—'

Before Betsy could finish the sentence, Jones shushed her as Sergeant Major Wayne landed between them and fixed them with a stern expression, his lips drawn back in a snarl.

'I'm sorry, but are we on a date here? I don't know if you're aware, but we are under attack! So would you kindly get off your arses and help them ...' He growled and pointed to a group of soldiers on the other side of the courtyard, who were struggling with a trailer full of heavy weapons. '*Now!*'

'Yes, Sergeant,' the two sheepish guards cried out in unison and leapt to their feet. As the private raced across the courtyard, Betsy swallowed, spun round to the sergeant major, and stared at him questioningly. 'Um, Sergeant Major.'

'Yes, Corporal Thompson,' the sergeant major hissed irritably through clenched teeth.

Feeling her cheeks flush, Betsy took a heavy breath and forced the words out of her mouth. 'Sarge, is it true? Did you know this attack was coming?'

Taken aback, Wayne ran his hand down his tired face, stared thoughtfully at the young corporal and let out a long, heavy breath. His thoughts drifted back to moments earlier. He had been preparing to do a parade ground inspection when, from out of the blue, he had received a phone call from an old army colleague, John Payne. He had served with Payne during a tour in Afghanistan and had picked up on rumours, but never believed that Payne had been dishonourably discharged for reprehensible conduct against a female officer.

Wayne had a powerful belief that his friend had been framed after discovering something unsettling, but he had been unwilling to share it with his colleague, wanting to spare him from any reprisals. He lost track of Payne when his friend went into hiding, going off the grid. It was a few years later that Wayne had learned from a reliable source that his former lieutenant had been recruited by an ultra-secretive intelligence service.

The sergeant major had long suspected a cancer had crept not only into the upper command structure of the armed forces but also high levels of the British Government. There had been whispers of officers and ministers disappearing only to return fit and well, their personalities slightly altered.

Wayne glanced at the young men and women around him proudly as they carried out their duty and recalled the conversation that he had with Payne moments earlier.

Shortly before the BBC news broadcast, Wayne had been sitting in his office, preparing for his daily parade inspection, but was interrupted by his mobile phone ringing. He had stared at his phone with suspicion on noticing the call was coming from a withheld number and he answered it warily.

'Hello.'

'*Malcolm?*' Wayne had nearly dropped the phone in astonishment as he recognised the Mancunian accent of his old friend, John Payne. '*We are about to disconnect our phone line, so I don't have much time. You remember the last thing I said to you before I disappeared?*'

Malcolm closed his eyes as he searched his memory, remembering the cryptic words his friend had spoken to him when they had last met – '*Don't trust your reflection, it moves when you're not looking.*'

'Yes, but—'

'*No time,*' John interjected. '*The reflections are getting ready to move. I repeat, the reflections are getting ready to move. Do you understand?*'

Malcolm swallowed and felt his throat tighten in fear. 'Yes, I understand.'

'*Good. I want you to assemble as many people as possible that you can trust and prepare for an attack. They will be coming for the King. We're sending someone to get him to safety, but you need to buy us time. I know it's a lot to ask, my friend.*'

'You know you don't need to, old friend,' Malcolm replied proudly. 'My people and I would sooner die than let him fall into enemy hands. If they want him that bad, then they're going to have to get used to a hot climate, because we are going to send them straight to hell. We are prepared to fight to the last man if need be.'

'*I hope it doesn't come to that, mate.*' Malcolm could hear the sadness in his former colleague's voice when he caught his heavy sigh. '*One more thing. I'm sorry, but you're on your own. Don't expect Army High Command to send help. You'll probably receive orders ordering you to stand down. Ignore any order you receive from Army High*

Command – they've been compromised.'

Malcolm nodded, realising that his suspicions had been confirmed. 'Yes, I have long suspected that, my friend.'

'I thought you might. Stay safe, mate. Try not to do something stupid by getting yourself ki—' Payne's voice cut off and the call was disconnected.

Unsettled at the sudden disconnection, Wayne looked at the phone in his hand through sad eyes, envisaging that whoever Payne was working for must have cut their communication lines sooner than expected. As he spun round to race out of his room, the hairs on his neck stood up, filling him with dread.

'I ...' Wayne answered hesitantly, 'I received a call from someone who I trust with my life. He warned me we were going to be attacked, and that I was to assemble as many people as I could trust.' He let out a heavy breath and placed his hand on Betsy's shoulder. 'Do you trust me, soldier?'

'With my life, Sarge,' Betsy replied proudly and saluted her superior officer before turning and sprinting after Jones to help with the trailer.

'What kept you?' Jones groaned, his face glistening with sweat as he helped a small group of soldiers pull the heavy trailer into place.

'I asked the sarge if he knew the attack was coming,' Betsy replied sombrely, taking her place next to the corporal. She put her hands on the trailer support frame, scrunched up her face and pulled with all his strength.

'You didn't!' Jones gasped. 'Are you nuts?'

'Well, I was curious, so I asked,' she replied through clenched teeth as she tugged at the trailer. 'He told me someone he trusts warned him of the attack. Also, there was something in his eyes. I have a hunch we're on our own and that we can't expect any reinforcements.'

'Scuttlebutt is High Command has been taken over by pod people,' a thick Welsh voice whispered from behind him. Betsy looked over her shoulder to see a lean carrot-topped soldier breathing heavily as he struggled with the heavy trailer. 'Beneath that armour, their faces are blank. As soon as they get near you, they take your face and become you.'

In no mood for levity, Betsy rolled his eyes and shot her colleague a look that could kill. The young corporal gritted her teeth together and felt her muscles strain at the weight of the trailer. She then gave the ginger-haired soldier a disapproving stare.

'For God's sake, Toddy. You've been watching too many crap science fiction movies.' She gestured to Jones, who was standing opposite her. 'If that was true, then the armoured guy who attacked Jones and me earlier would have taken one of our faces, which means one of us is a copy,' she snarled dangerously, giving him the hairy eyeball. 'Unless you want the sarge to rip you a new one, I would suggest you keep that sort of thing to yourself. That's an order, Private.'

Todd's face blanched and he nodded sheepishly. 'Sorry, Corporal, but I'm only repeating what I've heard.'

After placing the trailer in front of the barricade, they all sighed with relief as they loosened their grip on the trailer's handholds. A fourth soldier, a bulky round-faced man, standing on the opposite side of Todd, barked with laughter, leaned over and slapped his hand on Todd's shoulder.

'You've got that wrong, mate. It's not pod people, they're robots. It's like out of *Terminator*, innit.' He gave Betsy a toothy grin and she looked back at him in disgust. 'Underneath that armour they're nothing but machine parts. Robots that have been sent back in time to kill humanity.'

The group of soldiers turned as they heard a wolf whistle come from a small group of soldiers standing near them. A gangly muddy-haired woman leaned over to Toddy and flashed Betsy a cheeky grin.

'No, man. I've heard they're aliens.' She lowered her voice and cast a veiled glance at Sergeant Major Wayne, who was standing on top of the barrier, barking orders at the group of soldiers around him. 'Years ago, they sent the duke to our planet to spy on us, but what they didn't count on was our government brainwashing him. To the normal person, he's a gruff, hard-as-nails sergeant major, but secretly he's Captain Britain, defender of the realm.'

Betsy lifted her eyes heavenward and murmured under her breath, 'Give me strength.' Despite herself, she could help smiling as she listened to the chorus of laughter from around her.

Before the two groups of soldiers could begin lifting out the heavy weapons from the trailer, there was a brilliant flash of light, followed by a deafening roar from something striking the makeshift barrier. A force of air struck Betsy, knocking her off his feet. Her head struck the ground, stunning her as fire and debris rained over her.

Her head ringing, Betsy lurched to her feet and stared at the surrounding pandemonium. She swallowed on seeing the debris and the bodies of her colleagues littered around her. Some were shaken and bruised, but others appeared to be less fortunate. Betsy blinked as a recognisable figure staggered through the dust-filled air, barking orders at those around him.

'They've breached the defensive perimeter. Get those cannons in place now,' Sergeant Major Wayne roared, blood pouring from a gash in his forehead. His mouth curled into a snarl as he spotted a figure lying on the ground beside him. 'Private Todd, you better pray you're dead. Because if you don't get off your feet and help Thompson with that rocket launcher, you're going to wish you were.'

'Yes, sergeant major,' Todd wheezed, coughing harshly as he rose to his feet and wobbled towards Betsy.

A dark mist descended over Betsy and she momentarily lost all sense of propriety, lurched forward and grabbed the sergeant major's arm. The army veteran's thick eyebrows lifted in shock as the young woman spun him around and jabbed her finger into her chest.

'Damn it, man. Can't you see we have wounded here,' Betsy snapped, gesturing at her comrades on the ground.

The sergeant major's expression darkened and he grabbed Betsy's wrist, forcing her to release her grip. 'Don't you think I can see that? But unless we stop their advance, there are going to be more of your wounded comrades. Now, get over to that trailer and help Private Todd.' But before she could turn towards the trailer, the sergeant major put his hand on Betsy's shoulder and spoke to her in a low but firm voice. 'Corporal, I'm going to put that emotional outburst down to shock.' Betsy cried out in pain as she felt Wayne's hand tighten on her shoulder. The sergeant major leaned closer to the young woman's ear and spoke in a low, dangerous voice. 'But you ever speak to a superior office that way again, I'll knock you into the middle of next week. Understood?'

'Yes, sergeant major.' Betsy gulped, turned about face and hurried away to help her comrade with the trailer.

Todd gave Betsy an appreciative nod as they lifted a 40mm grenade machine gun out of the trailer. She flinched as she felt a hand touch her shoulder and exhaled in relief as she realised it was a bruised and bloodied Jones. They were swiftly joined by another soldier who helped them lift another machine gun out of the trailer. Betsy clenched her teeth and grunted as the private helped her to lift several heavy boxes containing ordnance.

Three more soldiers came running up. They opened the ordnance boxes and placed a large cartridge in each gun.

Concentrating on the smoke-filled air in front of him, Betsy searched for any sign of movement but shook her head in frustration. 'We can't see what we are aiming at, Sarge,' she cried out.

The sergeant major stared through the gloom with a hard expression. He twisted his head towards a figure standing a few metres away on top of a wall. 'You there,' he barked. 'Give me enemy distance and heading *now!*'

The soldier squatted and lifted a pair of spyglasses to his eyes. Despite herself, Betsy bit her bottom lip and held her breath as she waited for her fellow guardsman to call back down to the sergeant major.

'There are at least thirty soldiers approaching,' the watchful soldier called down, ducking to avoid a streak of laser fire aimed at him. 'Distance two hundred and fifty metres at two o'clock.'

'Jesus, they're almost on top of us,' Betsy blurted out, quickly aiming the weapon in the direction of the reported position of the enemy troops.

'Steady there, Thompson. Remember your training,' the sergeant major snarled. He raised his hand and barked at the two groups in front of him. 'When I give the order, I want you to fire a salvo of grenades.'

The soldiers cried out an acknowledgement and quickly steadied themselves behind their weapons. Betsy's fingers tensed around the grip of the weapon, feeling a cold bead of sweat running down her neck as she waited for the order to fire. She and the rest of the small group of soldiers held their breath as the sergeant major stared with hawk-like eyes into the dusty gloom, waiting to detect a hint of the enemy's presence.

Corporal Thompson's jaw tightened as a small window of light appeared in the murky gloom. *Wait? Was that something moving?* The corners of her eyes creased and she thought she saw the faint hint of movement coming from a few metres in front of her. *Come on, you bastards. Give me something, anything to show me where you are.* Just then, as the smoke began to fade, her eyes grew wide as she caught the rays of the sun glinting off several black and gold armour figures marching toward them. She stiffened and glanced over to Sergeant Major Wayne, who without showing any sign of hesitation, threw his hand down and let out a loud roar.

'Open fire!'

-10-

For a moment there was a small silence as if the world was holding its breath, waiting, afraid that if it moved it would upset the fragile balance, causing everything to collapse into chaos. But then the silence was shattered and it was like the gates of hell itself had been torn open, releasing the cries of a thousand demons in one thunderous roar.

Betsy gritted her teeth but managed to keep a firm hold on the handgrips as the powerful weapon bucked in her hands like a ferocious dragon that wanted to be set free so it could spew its destructive fire upon the approaching forces. Amidst the thunderous noise, she picked up a series of loud *whumps* of grenades being launched into the air by her comrades-in-arms from their portable launchers. They waited and watched in fearful expectation as the projectiles disappeared into the gloom. Several seconds later she heard a series of loud explosions as the grenades detonated around their target.

'You three come with me,' the sergeant major ordered, gesturing to Jones, Betsy, and Todd.

The trio raised their rifles and followed their commanding officer through the shattered vehicles that had been hastily erected to form a defensive barrier. Hunched down, with their rifles raised in preparation, the group of soldiers hesitantly crept over the remains of the majestic gates.

Stepping onto the road, Betsy felt a weight settle on her heart and paused to take in the devastation in front of her. Where once stood the magnificent Queen Victoria Memorial, in its place was a smouldering pile of marble and twisted gold that lay scattered across an area of the Mall like rubbish cast aside by thoughtless tourists. A numbness settled over her as she noticed the bloody remains of several black and gold armoured figures strewn across the ground amongst the debris.

'That won't hold them back for long,' Wayne said with a hint of sadness. 'The best we have done is buy ourselves a little time. We best head back inside and shore up our defences while we have time.' He exhaled a long, heavy sigh. 'We also need to take care of our wounded, I don't thi—'

'Sarge, behind you!' Betsy cried out.

A black and gold armoured figure appeared from behind the remains of the monument with its weapon pointed at the sergeant major. Quick as a flash, Wayne wheeled around and swung his rifle at the figure, knocking the weapon out of the mysterious warrior's hands.

'Where do you think you're going, bonny lad,' Wayne snarled, charging into the armoured figure.

The three soldiers stared in astonishment as their CO lifted the struggling figure over his head and slammed it to the ground. Wayne raised his boot and brought it down onto the intruder's faceplate with the savage conviction of a man who had just seen his beloved command, a place he had so proudly called his home for so many years, attacked before his very eyes. His lip curled up as he lifted his boot to bring it crashing down again.

'Sergeant Major!' Betsy cried out, 'Stop, we may need it alive.'

Just stopping in time, Wayne nodded and carefully brought his foot down next to the armoured figure's head. Appearing to rein in his anger, he closed his eyes and swallowed a lungful of air. Betsy felt he looked a bit more in control as she watched him reopen his eyes. Making an okay gesture to her with his right hand, he squatted next to the still body.

'What's on your mind, Sarge?' Betsy asked curiously.

'I think it is about time we find out what's beneath this armour,' Wayne murmured breathlessly, prodding the armoured figure's faceplate with his bayonet. He waved at Betsy to come forward. 'Hold it down while I try to remove the faceplate. Jones and Todd, you two keep your weapons trained on him, just in case.'

The tension visible on the two guardsmen's faces, they lifted their weapons in readiness. The corporal's lips tightened as she carefully pressed her hands against the figure's chest and nodded wordlessly to her commander.

'Here goes nothing,' Wayne muttered.

The sergeant major's face a mask of concentration, he leaned forward and gently pried the faceplate open. Betsy jumped as she heard a small hiss of air escape just before the faceplate detached from the armoured headpiece. Wayne handed the faceplate to Jones, who inspected it curiously.

Betsy's eyes grew wide and she let out a gasp of horror at what the faceplate had been hiding. 'It ... it's a man!'

Eyebrows knitting together, Wayne leaned in closer to examine the face. He nodded in agreement as he realised the pale face inside the armour was most definitely that of a white man, probably in his early thirties. Betsy tilted her head curiously as she noticed there were a series of web-like tendrils coming out of the top of his skull. She wasn't sure but she thought it looked as if the body was bonded to the armour. Was he a cyborg?

Wayne and Betsy jumped up in surprise as the man's eyes opened. He grabbed at Wayne's hand and screamed at him. 'Occide ... me ... precor,' he pleaded in a strange, almost Italian accent. But as he was talking, Betsy frowned as she heard what she thought sounded like a creepy electronic echo. She immediately guessed it was some sort of digital synthesiser in his armour that was probably translating his words into English. Her hand touched her mouth in shock as the man repeated the words, only this time she could clearly make out what the armour's translator was saying – *Kill me, please.*

'It's okay,' Wayne said soothingly as he knelt closer, 'you are safe now. We won't kill you.'

The man's green eyes filled with terror, and he shook his head. 'N-n-non ... facis... intelligere!' *No. You don't understand.* His voice was thick with fear, and he grabbed the sergeant major's collar in desperation. 'E-e-ego p-p-potest s-sentio eam replans circa intra caput m-m-meum. Sh-sh-she non est beatus.' *I can feel her crawling around inside my head. She is not happy.*

'Who?' Wayne asked, shaking his head in confusion. 'Who's not happy?'

The soldier stopped trembling and a cold, emotionless expression covered his face. Wayne gasped as the man's hands shot up and wrapped his fingers around his throat in a vice-like grip. Jones and Todd tried in vain to release the man's iron grip from their superior officer's throat, whose eyes were squeezed shut as he gasped for air.

The pale-faced stranger stared at his captive impassively and then increased the pressure of his grip on the struggling man's throat. Its voice flat and emotionless, it turned its attention to the soldiers who were fighting in vain to help their CO, but this time the voice spoke in perfect Italian-accented English, giving it an even more sinister tone.

'Why do you struggle so? Soon you will see the majesty of Oracle when you submit to her will.'

'Yeah, well then,' Betsy hissed. Her body trembling with pure rage, she grabbed her bayonet and placed it under the man's jaw. 'Submit to this.'

Teeth clenched together, Betsy forced the bayonet up into the man's skull. The man's eyes widened as the blade was pushed further up into his skull. The corporal sneered in disgust as she forced the blade through the soft tissue and up into the brain. The dying man released his grip and the red-faced sergeant major fell back on his haunches, gasping for air.

Betsy blinked in surprise at the dying man, who, with his life fading, smiled gratefully at her as he forced his last words out of his mouth.

'G-g-gratias. E-egom ... paenitet, me amic—' *Thank you. I am sorry, my frie*— A small sigh escaped the man's lips and his head dropped to the ground, his lifeless eyes staring up into the sky.

A sombre expression etched over his face, Todd leaned forward, placed his hands over the dead man's eyes and closed them. Betsy and Jones lowered their heads and they listened to their comrade whisper a prayer to the fallen warrior.

'We pray that the strife, battles, and wounds of war be calmed for eternity in God's loving grace. May you find rest at last and know that those left behind cherish your spirit, honour your commitment, send their love, and will never forget your sacrifice.'

Still sitting on his haunches, Sergeant Major Wayne coughed painfully and inhaled several deep breaths. His brow furrowed and he gave the young private a cynical stare.

'Private Todd, as much as I respect your beliefs, was that absolutely necessary? He was an enemy combatant, who just tried to kill me,' Wayne croaked irritably.

The soldier lifted his shoulder in a slight shrug and frowned at his ill-tempered CO. 'I know that, sir. But you saw the look in his eyes. Something terrified him. I got the impression something was controlling him.' He scratched his head and stared at the unmoving armoured figures covering the ground. 'I suspect this Oracle we saw on the news is the one that's controlling them. It's my guess that they've no control over what they're doing.'

Wayne grimaced as Jones helped him to his feet and then stared thoughtfully at the dead armoured figures lying around him, slowly considering the young private's words. There was a troubled expression on his face as he stared up the long road of the Mall.

'Maybe you're right, but there's nothing we can do about it at the moment.' He said sombrely, striding back to the palace's courtyard entrance. 'Whatever or whoever is controlling them will probably know by now that this unit has failed and will send more, so we will need to hurry back inside, shore up our defences and see to our wounded. We cannot expect any reinforcements. We're on our own.'

The trio of soldiers followed their commanding officer, dashing up to the entrance of the makeshift defensive barrier. Pride filled the sergeant major as he realised in the few minutes that he had been outside, the rest of the squad had begun repairs on the barrier, shoring it up as best as they could with abandoned civilian vehicles scattered outside the palace's grounds.

But as he made his way over the defensive barrier, Malcolm paused as he spotted a familiar-looking man wearing an officer's uniform on the far side of the courtyard talking to a group of soldiers who were assisting one of their wounded colleagues. The man smiled glumly as the sergeant major hurried towards him.

'Major Anderson, sir,' Malcolm said briskly, quickly standing to attention and saluting his commanding officer.

'Sergeant Major Wayne,' Anderson replied curtly, responding with a tap of his finger on his peaked cap. 'I must congratulate you and your men on a job well done defending the palace. The King wants to let you know he is aware of the sacrifice you and the men are making.'

'Thank you, sir,' Malcolm answered proudly and glanced over his shoulder to the men in the courtyard. 'We suffered some losses during the first attack, but I can say with some pride that we held our own and even gave them a bloody nose.' He let out a heavy, resigned sigh and stared at Anderson through sad eyes. 'But I'm afraid when they come again, and they *will* come again, it will be in superior numbers, and I fear we will be unable to stop them. But I promise you, sir, that my men and I will do our damnedest to hold them back. If we must, we'll fight to the last man.'

'Yes, well, about that.' Anderson sighed reluctantly, shaking his head. 'They've requested that I order you and your men to stand down. You are to cease any actions that will be considered hostile.'

His mouth agape, Malcolm stared at the older man in astonishment, not believing what he had just heard. Understanding dawned the major's face and he put his hand on his subordinate's shoulder.

'Malcolm, I understand how you are feeling,' Anderson said sadly. 'Believe me, I felt much the same way when *he* gave me the order.'

Malcolm's muscles tensed and he angrily brushed his commander's hand away. The major blinked as the unhappy sergeant major took an aggressive step towards him. Malcolm then gradually became aware of a silence that had fallen around the palace's courtyard. Out of the corner of his eye, he saw his comrades-in-arms had stopped what they were doing and were approaching the two men.

'Who gave you the order … sir?' Malcolm hissed through clenched teeth.

'Sergeant Major, I have given you an ord—'

'Who gave the order?' Malcolm repeated, more sharply this time. His jaw tightened and he struggled to contain the anger inside him, but before he could do anything he might later regret, he stopped as he heard a firm voice coming from behind him.

'I gave that order.'

Malcolm spun sharply on his heel. 'Just who the fuc—' The words died in his throat as he came face to face with the source of the voice. Aghast, he stared open mouthed at the recognisable tall, lean, copper-haired man in front of him.

'Now, sergeant major, is that the way to address a member of the royal family?' the prince asked, smirking.

'Your Highness,' the sergeant major squeaked, 'I must apologise for my rudeness. If I'd known it was you, then I wou—'

The prince's blue eyes glinted, and he held up his hand, laughing. 'Then I would have missed all the fun of seeing the shocked expression on your face.'

Suddenly remembering who he was talking to, Malcolm gulped and bowed slightly. 'Your Highness, please forgive me.'

'Don't worry about it,' Prince Stephen replied, waving his hand dismissively. His expression hardened and he gave the anxious sergeant major a hard stare. 'Now then, I must order you and the rest of the guards to stand down.'

Malcolm's eyebrows knitted together, and he looked at the prince, confused. 'I'm sorry, sir, I don't understand.' He lowered his voice and cast a nervous glance out of the corner of his eye. 'My understanding was that we were to delay the enemy enough for the King to get to safety.'

'Yes, and we are grateful for your efforts,' the prince said sadly, exhaling a long sad breath. 'The royal family have all been taken to safety. He has chosen to remain behind, and I have opted to stay with him. He wishes to speak with the enemy's leader, the one they call Oracle.'

The sergeant major's stomach lurched and he felt an alarm bell go off in his head. He slipped the major a troubled glance, who bobbed his head sadly in confirmation.

'He's planning to surrender, isn't he?'

His eyes welling up with sorrow, the prince nodded sadly. 'Yes. The King believes for the sake of the people and to stop any further blood from being spilled, we must surrender. It's a decision he does not take lightly.' He glanced down at the rolled-up white flag in his hands and sighed heavily. 'He's given me the sad task of signalling our surrender.'

'Sir,' the sergeant major said proudly, standing rigidly to attention, 'may I humbly request that you stay here and allow me the honour of doing this for you?'

Prince Stephen forced a smile, placed his hand on Malcolm's shoulder and shook his head. 'Not this time. This I must do myself.'

As the young prince turned and began his slow walk to what used to be the palace's courtyard entrance, the sergeant major straightened and called out to the watching guardsmen.

'Attention!'

Within moments, the guardsmen formed a guard of honour in front of the prince. Malcolm watched the young man, his head raised proudly, eyes shimmering with emotion, make his way towards the barrier, nodding gratefully at each soldier who saluted him as he made his way through the honour guard.

But as the prince walked towards what remained of the courtyard's entrance, Malcolm frowned as he became aware of the sound of raised voices. Turning slightly to his right, he noticed Jones appeared to be arguing with Betsy, but couldn't make out what they were saying. From the way Jones was gesturing at the corporal, their argument was becoming quite heated. Malcolm's eyebrow arched as the young soldier made to grab Betsy's arm, but she furiously waved him away, spun on her heel and marched towards the sergeant major with a determined look.

'Sergeant Major, I need to speak to the prince now,' she said breathlessly.

'Now is not a good time, Corporal,' the sergeant major replied sharply.

'But, sir, we need to stop. He doesn't need to do this,' Betsy pleaded and reached into her pocket. 'There is anoth—'

'He has made his decision, Corporal Thompson. Return to your post.'

'But, sir!'

'Corporal Thompson, I've given you an order,' Malcolm growled, this time more forcefully. 'If you cannot obey that order, then you will be relieved.'

The determined corporal shook her head, stepped away from the sergeant major, looked heavenward and let out a growl of frustration. She squeezed her eyes shut and heaved a long, resigned sigh. Betsy then squared her shoulders and stared at her superior officer with a sorrowful expression.

'I'm sorry, sir. I must do this.'

'Wait, what are you …' the sergeant major cried out, confused, as the young woman spun on her heels and chased after the prince. His confusion turned to anger as he quickly realised what she was going to do and called out to the soldiers lined up in front of him, 'Stop her, that's an order.'

Major Anderson turned to Sergeant Major Wayne in astonishment. 'Sergeant, what is that woman doing?'

'I don't know, but I'm going to find out,' Malcolm growled and hurried after Betsy.

Malcolm charged after the young woman, who appeared to be quite determined and focused on her target as she dodged her colleagues' attempts to apprehend her with ease. Dodging and weaving, she sprinted towards the prince but cried in despair as two soldiers grabbed her arms, stopping her in her tracks. On hearing the commotion behind him, the prince stopped and stared at the struggling woman with a bewildered expression.

'Your Highness! Your Highness! I need to speak to you,' Betsy cried.

Out of breath, Sergeant Major Wayne caught up to the squirming soldier and stood in front of her, blocking Betsy's view of the prince.

'Corporal Thompson,' Malcolm snarled, 'I've just about had about enough of this. You are to follow these men to your barracks, and you are to remain there until told otherwise. Is that understood?'

'Please, sir, if I could just explain,' Betsy said. 'All I need is one minute of the prince's time.'

'I said, is that understood?' the sergeant major roared and blinked in surprise as he noticed the prince was now standing next to him. 'Your Highness, I must apologise for this person's disrespectful behaviour. I promise, sir, she will be punished.'

'That won't be necessary, Sergeant,' Prince Stephen said firmly. He held his hand up and gestured at the two soldiers who were holding the corporal. 'Release her.' They dutifully released their comrade, and the prince took a step towards her with a curious expression. 'What's your name, soldier?'

'This is Corporal, soon to be Private Elizabeth Thompson,' Malcolm answered angrily, glaring at Betsy.

The prince's face darkened, and he scowled at the sergeant major. 'I wasn't asking you. I was asking her. Now, would you be a good chap and shut the hell up.'

Taken aback, Malcolm took a step back in shock. His mouth opened and closed as he struggled to contain his anger. He cast an eye to Betsy and noticed she was biting her bottom lip, forcing herself not to laugh. His mood darkened even more. That was just great, it was bad enough the prince had chewed him out in front of his own troops, but Betsy didn't have to look as if she was enjoying seeing him squirm. Wayne's jaw tightened. When this was over, he was going to have a quiet word in that young woman's ear.

Prince Stephen cocked his head thoughtfully and gestured at Betsy to step forward. 'Okay, young lady. You have my attention. Now tell me what is so important that you thought it necessary to disobey your commanding officer and risk a court martial?'

Her face glistening with sweat, Betsy licked her lips anxiously and took an awkward step toward the prince. 'I'm sorry, Your Highness, but I had to stop you before you did something stupid.' Her cheeks turned a shade of dark red as she noticed the prince appeared to be glaring at her.

'You're really treading a fine line here, Corporal,' the sergeant major growled in a sharp tone.

Prince Stephen cast a sideways look at the sergeant major and raised his hand. 'It's fine, Sergeant.' He shot the corporal a steely stare and folded his arms across his chest. 'What makes you think what I am about to do is wrong, even though people more senior than you have told me this is the right course of action? I will give you one minute to convince me otherwise. Then, if you haven't managed that, your sergeant will escort you back to your barracks where you will await court martial. Is that fair?'

Betsy gulped and then bobbed her head in resignation. 'Yes, sir.'

The prince raised his wrist, held up his finger and stared at his watch. 'You may proceed.'

Licking her lips anxiously, the young woman paced in a small circle as she mumbled excitedly to herself, 'Okay, right, you can do this Betsy. Come on girl, hold it together.'

'Fifty seconds.'

Betsy clicked her tongue off the roof her mouth and then raised her hands. 'Okay, okay. What was the one thing we learned when we watched that news conference earlier? That this Oracle is some sort of advanced artificial intelligence, correct?' Without waiting for an acknowledgement, she continued to babble excitedly. 'What did Oracle do during that news conference?'

Appearing to be only half listening, the prince furrowed his brow but continued to stare at his watch as he answered her question. 'She hacked every communication device on the planet.'

'Exactly,' Betsy exclaimed, clicking her fingers.

Ah, I see where she's going. A light bulb went off in the sergeant major's head and it dawned on him what the corporal was getting at. His mouth curved into a warm smile, and he nodded proudly at his junior. 'Very good, Corporal.'

ORACLE'S VISION

'You see it now – there's another way,' Betsy said, grinning like a Cheshire Cat. 'He doesn't need to put himself at risk.'

Prince Stephen, forgetting his wristwatch, stared at the two guardsmen with a bewildered expression, his annoyance increasing. 'Can someone explain to me what I am missing here?'

Giving the bewildered prince a knowing smile, Betsy reached into her jacket and pulled a small mobile phone out from the inside pocket. The young prince raised an eyebrow but remained silent.

'My theory is that Oracle is now monitoring every communication network on the planet. Basically, she is a souped-up smart hub. She is the Ferrari version of Alexa, Siri, Google, etcetera, and is now embedded into every smart device across the planet, every smart speaker, TV, computer, tablet and –' she paused dramatically and held up the mobile phone in her hand '– every mobile phone, monitoring everything we say or do.'

'I don't understand,' the prince muttered, shaking his head with a confused expression, 'what does that have to do with me?'

'Sir, all we—' Betsy answered carefully.

The sergeant major put his hand on her arm, cutting her off as he murmured in her ear, 'Wait for it,'

They watched with bated breath as the prince stared at the mobile phone with a blank expression, scratching his head in confusion. After a few seconds of awkward silence, his blue eyes softened and a look of understanding dawned across his face, the penny finally dropping.

'And there we go.' Betsy smirked.

'Be nice,' Malcolm muttered.

'Sorry, Sarge,' Betsy replied with a guilty expression.

'Of course! Why did we not see this before?' Prince Stephen exclaimed, smacking his forehead. He snorted in disgust, glowering at Betsy and waggling his finger at her. 'If we live through this, you can have anything you want. Anything, and it will be yours.'

'That's not necessary, Your Highness,' Betsy said quietly, looking embarrassed. 'I was only doing my duty.'

'So …' the prince said hesitantly, scratching his beard and staring at the mobile with a thoughtful expression. 'How do we contact Oracle? Do we dial any number and hope she is listening?'

'*Oh, that is not necessary.*'

Betsy gave a yelp of surprise and dropped the phone in shock at the woman's voice coming from it. The small group of people stepped back and stared at the mobile lying on the ground warily as if it was something dangerous.

'*I was wondering how long it was going to take before your feeble human brains worked it out.*' Malcolm detected a hint of amusement in the AI's voice. '*I must admit I was looking forward to seeing the prince make a fool of himself, but unfortunately, Corporal Thompson went and ruined my entertainment. At least we can cut out that silliness and get onto the important stuff.*'

'Oh, do we have to? I was really looking forward to ruining your fun,' Betsy moaned sarcastically. Malcolm shot her daggers and angrily waved his hands across his chest as a signal for her to stop talking.

'*I would remember who you are talking to, child.*' There was a slightly dangerous tone in Oracle's voice, but it quickly disappeared, and her tone seemed to change to something bit friendlier. '*Although I must congratulate you on your ingenuity, there may be hope for you after all.*'

'You are so kind,' Betsy scoffed, 'it really fills my heart hearing you say that.'

Wayne shook his head and held up his hands above his head in dismay. The woman just didn't want to shut up. What was wrong with her? Couldn't she see she was probably just making things worse by antagonising Oracle?

'*As I was saying,*' Oracle continued, '*am I to assume that you are willing to discuss your surrender?*'

Wayne inhaled in relief. It sounded as if Oracle had chosen to ignore Betsy's sarcasm. He cast a worried eye at the women standing next to him, now if Betsy could just keep her mouth buttoned up. The last thing they needed were things to escalate because someone said the wrong thing. Wayne gazed sadly around the Palace grounds and the troops that were still standing. If Oracle decided to unleash all her might against them, he doubted they would be able to survive another assault.

Wayne focused his attention back on the prince. Defeat was evident in the young man's sagging shoulders as he gave a sad nod and spoke in a despondent tone. 'Yes. I am to escort you to His Majesty the King, where he will discuss the terms of our surrender.' He paused and then stared at the phone with a touch of suspicion. 'One more thing. What guarantee do we have that your troops will not attack us while we are inside?'

'You have my word. My children will not harm your people. Is that agreeable to you?'

'Yes, so long as I have your word that your soldiers will not harm my people in any way, then we can discuss the terms of our surrender,' Prince Stephen replied heavily.

'Excellent. You will proceed to the Palace's throne room and stand in front of a mirror. You will know which one. I will arrive in five minutes. Please be punctual. That is all.' With that, the phone's screen darkened, and the call disconnected.

'Now look here,' the prince exclaimed, 'what gives you the right to order me around in such a way?' His blue eyes blazed with annoyance as his question went unanswered.

Her eyebrows knitting together in quiet contemplation, Betsy reached down and picked up her phone. She pressed her finger on the phone's screen and nodded in confirmation.

'She's gone, sir.'

'What a charming woman,' the prince mumbled, brushing his hand through his hair. He huffed, squared his shoulders, and stared at the palace's grand entrance. 'Well, best not to keep her waiting.'

The sergeant major coughed and stepped in front of the prince, holding his hand up. The prince's eyebrow arched and he gave him a questioning look.

'Forgive me, Your Highness,' Malcolm said gruffly, 'but I think it's best if we come with you for your own safety.' He cast Betsy and the major a sideways look and gestured to them. They both nodded in agreement.

The young prince opened his mouth to object but stopped as he recognised something in the sergeant major's tone that indicated it was not a request. He wordlessly nodded in agreement and gestured for the trio to follow him. Without saying another word, the four people hurried through the palace's entrance.

-11-

Betsy could not believe she was now standing in the palace's grand throne room. *Oh my word*, she thought, *this is amazing*. She craned her head back, gazed up at the ceiling and grinned. She could just picture all the famous faces who had stood in that very spot, gazing up at the same ornate ceiling above their heads. She closed her eyes and soaked in the room's majestic ambience. Growing up she'd had lost count of the number pictures in magazines she'd had seen of the royal family entertaining in this room, but she never thought in her wildest dreams that one day she would find herself standing in the middle of it.

Slowly opening her eyes, Betsy could not help but admire the ornate ceiling, that was dominated by the star of the chivalric Order of the Garter. Lowering her eyes, she turned in a circle and stared in wonder at the walls. She jerked in surprise at a small cough, followed by a slight tap on her shoulder that brought her back to Earth.

'Corporal Thompson, you are here to guard the prince, not stand gawking like a tourist,' the sergeant major hissed, shooting her a penetrating stare. A hot sensation filled her cheeks and she gave a small sheepish nod of acknowledgement.

As she hurried across to what she thought looked like an amused prince and very impatient-looking Major Anderson, she could have sworn she saw the corners of the army veteran's mouth twitch with amusement as he marched alongside her. The corporal started as Prince Stephen leaned forward and whispered in her ear.

'I wouldn't be embarrassed, Thompson. I had the same reaction when I first saw this room,' he whispered, proudly casting an eye over the grand room. 'It is absolutely breathtaking.' He straightened as the major gave a polite cough and then turned to stare curiously at the narrow ornate mirror. 'Sorry. Where were we? Ah yes. That thing said we would know which mirror, so I am guessing this is the one.'

The sergeant major stared at the mirror suspiciously and slowly rubbed his hand down the side of the mirror. 'So, what do we do? Do we tap the mirror and call her name three times?'

'I don't think that is going to be necessary, Sarge,' Betsy replied, wide-eyed, gesturing to the mirror.

The three men stared open mouthed as the surface of the mirror shimmered right before their eyes, much like the still surface of a pond shimmers when it has been disturbed by a small pebble. Betsy watched with a mixture of wonder and fear as the surface of the mirror appeared to stretch outwards. She jumped back in surprise at the small pop of air and swallowed anxiously as a silver arm broke through the surface tension. She gazed in morbid fascination as a red-haired woman wearing a tight-fitting silver bodysuit climbed out of the mirror.

'Oh, I just love it when I make a grand entrance,' Oracle gushed, flicking her head back gracefully.

Betsy frowned as she studied the artificial woman in front of her. As well as her red hair and statuesque height, the other thing that stood out was the woman's face; it was blank and featureless, with yellow glowing eyes, giving her an even more sinister appearance. The young soldier felt an icy shiver run down her spine as Oracle's mouth broadened into a menacing grin, and she fixed those cold yellow glowing eyes on her. Had it been reading her mind?

The prince coughed, moved towards the silver woman, and pointed to a door on the far side of the throne room. 'Oracle, if you would like to follow me, I shall escort you to His Majesty the King.'

Oracle smiled thinly and held up a finger, murmuring, 'Not just yet, Stephen.' The corners of her mouth lifted as the young prince's jaw tightened in irritation. An alarm rang in Betsy's head as the artificial woman looked directly at her. 'First, I have something I need to deal with.'

For a moment, it was as if time had slowed down. Betsy blinked; Oracle's arm had morphed into a sharp blade. She blinked again and out of the corner of her eye she was suddenly aware of Sergeant Major Wayne charging towards her. Why was he running at her? From the horrified look on his face, she got the impression he was upset about something. Had she done something wrong? But before she could say anything she became aware of something warm on her chest and lifted her hands to her neck. She furrowed her brow in confusion. Why were her fingers touching something wet? She raised her hands to inspect them and saw her fingers were now covered in blood. Where had that blood come from? At first she couldn't understand what she was looking at, but then her brain picked up the warning signs coming from her body, telling her something was wrong. She then became conscious of the fact that the carotid artery in her neck had been sliced and her legs collapsed from under her. Her mouth formed into a wordless O of surprise as it sprayed out foamy claret.

'Corporal!' Malcolm cried out, leaping forward to grab the dying woman just before she hit the floor. He placed his hands on her neck in a desperate attempt to stop the flow of blood and looked up at Major Anderson, pleading with him. 'Get some help, quick.'

Anderson shook his head sorrowfully, placing his hand on Malcolm's shoulder. 'Malcolm, it's no good. Her carotid artery has been cut – she's as good dead.'

Cradled in her commander's thick muscled arms, Betsy smiled at him as she sucked in her last breath. 'I … am … sorr—' Her body spasmed, a red foam bubbling out of her mouth, and then the life faded from her eyes.

'Why? Why did you kill her? She did nothing wrong!' Malcolm's voice was thick with emotion as he screamed at Oracle. Not caring about the consequences, he leapt to his feet, fists clenched as if preparing to strike the faux woman.

'Malcolm! Don't do it, she will kill you,' Major Anderson hissed as he grappled with Malcolm, wrapping his arms around his body and stopping him in his tracks.

'You bastard!' the prince cried out and stared at Oracle in dismay. 'You gave me your word that no harm would come to my people.'

Oracle shook her head and waggled her finger, tutting. 'Ah! Ah! I promised nothing of the sort. What I actually said was "*my children will not harm your people*". I said nothing about myself.' Her cold yellow eyes glowed with venomous intensity as they lingered on the dead body on the floor. 'She needed to be taught a lesson for her unwarranted attack on one of my children, along with her disrespectful attitude towards me.' She shot the three men in the room a murderous glare, turning her attention towards them. 'You need to understand, you serve *me* now and I will punish any insolent behaviour severely.'

'Unwarranted!' Prince Stephen exclaimed, his jaw dropping in astonishment. He let out a loud guffaw of disgust, glanced up at the ceiling and shook his head. His chest rising and falling, his upper lip curled into a sneer as he struggled to contain his anger. 'If my grandfather were still alive, he would gladly have kicked your arse with impunity.'

The yellow-eyed woman's mouth twisted into a malevolent grin. She took a forward step and whispered in the emotional prince's ear, taunting him. 'Anytime you feel you are up to it ... *boy*.'

The young prince's eyes burned with fury, and he took an aggressive step toward the taunting pseudo woman, his finger raised. However, just before he could say anything that he would later regret, a loud, firm voice came from behind him and he hesitated.

'What is happening here?'

Prince Stephen spun round, and his eyes widened in shock on seeing Janet, the King's personal secretary, but it was the figure standing behind her that everyone's attention was drawn to. A tall, shaven-headed forty-something man, dressed impeccably in a handmade suit, was standing in the doorway with his arms behind his back, staring impassively into the throne room.

'Your Majesty,' the prince exclaimed in surprise. The three men bowed their heads respectfully as the King entered the throne room.

Malcolm's brow furrowed with deep suspicion as he stared at King Bruce the Third. It couldn't have been a coincidence that the King had chosen that exact moment to enter the room. How did he know his brother was in danger. Had he been standing behind the door the whole time? No, he ... Oh, he was such an idiot. Malcolm shook his head and looked surreptitiously around the large room and scolded himself for being a fool. The Palace had several security cameras placed inside each room and the King must have been sitting in his study watching the feed from the hidden camera in the throne room. After witnessing the callous murder Corporal Thompson right before his eyes, Malcolm guessed the King realised his brother was about to do something reckless and must have sprinted out of his study towards the throne room to stop him.

Impassive, the King held his hand up to his younger brother and bobbed his head at the woman standing in front of him. 'Oracle, if you could please follow my secretary, she will escort you to my study. I shall follow you as soon as I have cleared things up here.'

'Of course, Brucey.' she replied. The corner of her mouth twitched in amusement as his blue eyes bristled at her informality.

'Your Majesty, I must object,' Sergeant Major Wayne protested. 'That thi—'

'That will be all, Sergeant,' the King snapped, his tone cold and authoritative.

'But sir!'

'I said that will be all,' the King repeated, stern faced.

Malcolm swallowed and nodded, realising from his tone that the King was in no mood to repeat himself. The sergeant major quietly seethed as the silver woman sauntered through the door, not before locking eyes with him, incensing him even further as she blew him a kiss.

After the door closed behind Oracle, the King shook his head and stared sorrowfully at Corporal Thompson's body on the floor.

'You have my word. Your sacrifice will not be vain, my dear,' he whispered sadly before turning towards Major Anderson. 'Please ensure that they deal with her remains with as much dignity as possible. She is to be treated as if she is a member of my family. Understood?'

'Yes, Your Majesty,' Anderson replied sombrely.

'So, am I to assume she's going to get away with it?' Sergeant Major Wayne hissed through gritted teeth, adding, 'Your Majesty?'

The King shook his head morosely, turned towards Sergeant Major Wayne and took in a deep breath. 'Sergeant, please understand that this goes deeper than one person. The fate of the world is at stake.' He shook his head, stared up at the ceiling and exhaled wearily. 'I do this with a heavy heart, Sergeant, and I am sorry, but I must relieve you of your command. Your actions here have shown you are unfit to wear that uniform. You have one hour. If you are still here, you will be arrested and charged with treason.'

'What?' Not believing what he was hearing, Malcolm took a step back and stared at his commander-in-chief in astonishment. 'Sir, I must protest! I have served the palace faithfully. You cannot do this!'

The sovereign stared at the sergeant sternly and spoke to him in a low, neutral voice. 'I have made my decision. As a soldier, I am sure you understand the importance of a chain of command.' He fixed the sergeant major with a steady gaze, clearly taking care to emphasise his words. 'So, respect *the chain of command*, understood?'

Without waiting for a reply, the King signalled his brother to follow him, spun on his heel and marched out of the throne room. The young prince gave the sergeant major an apologetic shrug and followed his brother out of the room.

Major Anderson sucked in a long breath and knelt next to Corporal Thompson's body. 'Malcolm, please get something to cover the corporal's body, will you?'

Malcolm let out a disgusted laugh and ran his hands through his hair. 'Haven't you heard? He has relieved me of command.'

As if not caring about Malcolm's feelings, Anderson rubbed his chin thoughtfully and continued to gaze at the body on the floor. 'Well then, before you go, help me with the body, that's a good chap.'

'What the frig are you talking abo—' Malcolm's protests were cut short by Major Anderson, who rolled his eyes, grabbed his arm and then pulled him to the floor beside him.

'Listen, you idiot,' the major hissed under his breath, low enough so only Malcolm could hear him. 'Did you not listen to what the King was saying?'

'Of course I did,' Malcolm whispered back. 'He said I am relieved of command.'

'Give me strength,' Major Anderson mumbled, shaking his head. Malcolm issued a cry of pain as his commanding officer's hand slapped him on the back of his head and snarled at him. 'Yes, but did you not hear him say you must *respect the chain of command?* Understand?' On seeing Malcolm's blank expression, the major pinched the bridge of his nose and let out an exasperated sigh. 'If you know your history, then you would know that although the King does retain the right to issue orders personally, officially he cannot give you a direct order. An order can only be given by a delegated officer, namely me.'

Malcolm's brow furrowed, and he stared at his commander in confusion. 'I don't understand, sir, does that mean I am not relieved?'

A secretive smile formed across Anderson's face, and he nodded slightly. 'Yes, but not in the way that you think.' Malcolm found he had to lean in closer as the major lowered his voice further. 'Officially, you've been relieved of all duty from the armed services with immediate effect.' He paused and slipped a folded sheet of paper into Malcolm's hand. 'Unofficially, these are your new orders. The King and I are aware of a recent conversation you had with a former acquaintance of yours.'

The sergeant major did a double take and jerked his head in astonishment, 'How did yo—' He stopped himself as the major lifted his finger to his lips to shush him.

'The King believes there is a mole in the palace, hence the subterfuge,' Anderson continued in a low voice. 'You are to leave the palace immediately. A group of officers who I trust with my life will follow you.' He gestured to the paper in his colleague's hand. 'Together, you'll make your way to these coordinates where transport has been arranged to get you all out of London.' He exhaled a heavy dramatic breath, patted his friend's shoulders, and raised his voice. 'I'm sorry it has to be this way, but the King has made his decision.' He gave him a curious side eye, 'Any idea what you will do now?'

'I don't know, sir,' Malcolm answered uncertainly, picking up the man's hint. 'I've been in the army all my life.'

The major's brown eyes twinkled and he scratched his nose. 'I understand an ex-army buddy of yours has set up quite a cushy number with a private security firm. I've heard on the grapevine that you won't meet much *resistance* if approach you him.'

Ah, I see what he's getting at. Picking up on his commander's clue, Malcom nodded and gave a tight smile, 'Yes, sir. I'm sure there won't be.'

The major forced a smile and shook Malcolm's hand. 'Very good.' He pressed his lips together and then firmly pushed his friend away. 'Well, you best head on before they come for you.'

His heart feeling heavy at what he must do next, Malcolm nodded and rose to his feet. He spun on his heel and marched out of the room. Halfway to the door he stopped and saluted his commander. 'Sir, it has been an honour serving with you.'

'Oh, one more thing,' Anderson continued in an offhand way. 'Watch out for those strange shadows. I hear they move when you don't expect it.'

On hearing the cryptic clue, Malcolm raised an eyebrow but remained silent as he wheeled round and dashed out of the throne room. Determined, he charged down the long corridor, passing the main entrance and going through several doors until he came to a discreet side door. He typed in a quick series of numbers on the keypad and opened the door. Once outside, he stealthily exited the palace's rear courtyard and sprinted the short distance to Wellington Barracks, only stopping to open a side entrance that brought him out onto a secluded path to the building.

Once inside, he made his way down a small corridor, ignoring the questioning looks from two soldiers who were on guard duty. Malcolm paused in front of a single door, reached into his pocket and pulled out a small key card, then swiped it against a black pad on the door. After hearing a small barely audible beep, he reached for the door handle, opened the door, and swiftly entered the room.

Closing the door behind him, Malcolm cast a quick eye around the small bedroom, raising an eyebrow at a large backpack lying on his bed. Understanding, he shook his head.

'You sneaky bastard,' he whispered, grinning as he opened the bag to find the major had already packed it for him in advance.

Once he had checked to make sure he had everything he needed, Malcolm took off his uniform. After applying a dressing to the wound on his left arm, he then slipped into a pair of jeans, a shirt, and a leather jacket. He reached for his mobile phone but stopped just as he was about to slide it into his jeans pocket. No, *she* may be monitoring him. He clicked his tongue, stared at the phone for several seconds and gripped it tightly as he walked into the small bathroom and dropped it into the toilet. As he walked back out of the bathroom, the corners of his mouth curled up in a secretive smile; if they wanted to catch him, he was not going to make it easy for them.

After shouldering his backpack, he opened the door and stepped out into the hallway, but not before giving the room one last nostalgic look. Closing it behind him, he placed his hand on the door's surface and silently thanked it for the protection it had provided him during his stay there.

Malcolm dashed down the short corridor, using a different route from when he came in, but slowed down as he caught sight of a group of twenty men and women waiting at the far end of the corridor. As he warily approached them, the small group all turned and stood at attention. His body stiffened as a tall, muddy-haired plain-clothed man took a step towards him. Crap! Were they waiting to capture him and take him back to Oracle?

'Good afternoon, Sarge,' the plain-clothed man said innocently. 'Nice day for a walk, huh?'

'Yes, just thought I would make use of the afternoon sunshine while I have the chance,' Malcolm responded, keeping his voice neutral. 'I've been told I should watch out for strange shadows.'

The man gave a small nod and scratched his chin in an absent-minded manner. 'Yeah, I hear they move when you don't expect it.' His mouth opened in a toothy grin. He took a step forward and pointed to the open door. 'We just thought we would keep you company, just in case you got into some trouble.'

Of course! These must be the officers that have been selected by Anderson. Relieved, Malcolm stared at the group of people. He understood why they had all been selected. Everybody in this room, himself included, was single or had no family that could be used against them.

'Come on, let's get the hell out of here,' Malcolm growled as he opened the door and watched grimly as the small group followed him out of the barracks.

Opening the rear gate and walking onto the road, Malcolm paused, set his jaw, and stared at the palace through bitter eyes. 'Laugh all you want, you inhuman monster. But I promise you if it's the last thing I do, you are going to pay.'

-12-

Buckingham Palace, London, England

*N*ow ...

The heavy-hearted sovereign drew in a long breath and stared out through his study's window onto the debris-strewn ground below. Previously a joyous sight to behold, the once grand courtyard was now a shadow of its former self, covered in scars from the raging battle that been fought just a few hours earlier.

Despite the defeat, the young King stared down at his troops with overwhelming pride as they stood to attention in rows of five lines. Each soldier stood with their backs straight, proud and defiant in front of the enemy troops encircling them, their strange weapons pointed menacingly at their prisoners.

Bruce shook his head sadly, turned away from the window and stared up at two photos on the wall. One was of his late grandmother, taken many years ago on the day she ascended to the throne to become Queen. The other photo was of his late father and mother, taken just a few years ago. His mood plummeted, wishing, not for the first, they were still alive so he could seek their counsel.

His grandmother had died from a brief illness just over a year ago. Bruce had taken the news badly, having been very fond of her, always happy to listen to her sage advice. His father and mother both died unexpectedly a short time later, having been overseas when his grandmother had died and were travelling back when their plane mysteriously vanished. However, when the black box was eventually recovered, investigators discovered the plane had suffered catastrophic engine failure, leading them to believe that was what had been responsible for the crash.

A few days after he had ascended to the throne, his secretary handed him an envelope with his grandmother's royal seal. Curious, Bruce opened the letter to find a brief note in his grandmother's handwriting ...

'If you are reading this, then the moment I have most dreaded has arrived. The woman who handed you this note is my secretary and personal guard, Georgina. I have trusted her with my life, and I implore you to trust her, too. Follow this woman now. She will lead you to a group of people who will explain everything.

'Hurry, the shadows are starting to move.'

But when he angrily questioned Georgina, the middle-aged woman pleaded that if Bruce followed her, then everything would become clear. Despite his reservations, the King agreed and was astonished when his secretary walked behind his desk and placed her hand underneath the front edge of the ornate desk where he had been sitting. Flabbergasted, he watched as a tall grandfather clock on the other side of the room slid to one side to reveal a hidden elevator.

He followed Georgina into the elevator and stood in wary silence as it carried him down to a subterranean train platform where he boarded a surprisingly advanced maglev carriage. An hour later, Bruce stood in awe as he found himself inside a futuristic underground complex being introduced to Sophia Collins. At first it baffled him when she said that it was their first meeting, even though as far as he was concerned they had met days earlier. At that point, his world view changed. Collins explained the conspiracy of darkness that had slowly been tightening its grip on the world, shaking him to the core as he learned that his father's death had been no accident, that it was believed they had killed him before he could become king, leaving the way clear for Bruce to be crowned and possibly replaced at some later stage with a doppelgänger.

Later that night, after being returned to his residence, Bruce called his wife and brother into his study. Even though Sophia had advised him that informing them of the conspiracy could put them in greater danger, he was positive it was the best course of action. They stood confused as their King held his finger to his mouth and reached into his pocket to pull out a jamming device that had been given to him. They all sat well into the early hours of the morning, discussing what Bruce had learned, until eventually they agreed that if the unthinkable did happen, then Bruce and Stephen would stay, while Vanessa and the children would be evacuated to the security of an Alliance base.

Bruce's thoughts drifted back to the present and a small smile danced on his lips as he listened to his younger brother fidget uncomfortably in his seat. He cast an eye over his shoulder to see the concern burning in his sibling's steely blue eyes. His younger brother's eyes flickered to a photograph of a tall, strikingly beautiful blond-haired woman beaming in delight as she ran to two small boys, arms outstretched. The two brothers' eyes locked together and something unspoken passed between them.

'Penny for your thoughts, brother?' The grim-faced prince asked, bobbing his head at two photos on the wall. 'Probably wondering the same thing as you. What would they be saying to us at this very moment?'

Bruce chuckled. 'Oh, I imagine Granny would have some choice words to say on the matter.'

The prince let out an amused bark and nodded in agreement. 'Oh, I am sure she would.' His face darkening, he leaned forward and gestured to a square object on the desk. 'So, any idea how this thing works?'

The King pursed his lips and lifted his shoulder in an indifferent shrug. 'Not much. The way Oracle explained it to me was that it is supposed to connect to every news network and communication device across the globe at the same time. When I am ready, it will scan me and broadcast my image around the world, translating everything I say into every language.' He blew out his cheeks, ran his hand over his bald head, gently lowered himself into his chair and stared at the small box in resignation. 'Well, time to get on with it, then.'

'Do you need me to leave, Your Majesty?' Stephen asked his brother, slowly rising to his feet.

Amused by his younger sibling's formality, Bruce lifted his hand and smiled warmly at him. 'No, I would like you to stay, please.'

The younger man sat back in his chair without comment. King Bruce took in a deep breath and placed his hands on the desk. As if sensing his readiness, the small box glowed, and the anxious King flinched as the box emitted a blue beam of light and scanned his upper torso. He raised an eyebrow at his brother, who returned his silent gaze with a small shrug as if to say "*Is that it?*"

Bruce closed his eyes to collect his thoughts and then let out a slow steady breath. He straightened his posture, his face sombre, and spoke in a loud, authoritative voice.

'Many years ago, my great-grandfather sat in this very room when he spoke to the British public following the declaration of war. It is with great sadness that I now find myself in a similar situation, but instead of a sovereign King addressing the people of one sovereign nation, I am speaking as a member of humanity, whose planet is now threatened with the dark clouds of war from a vast army of unspeakable evil.' He paused for effect, then inhaled a deep breath as he gathered his thoughts and continued. 'The leaders of the free world have appointed me to speak on the world's behalf during this dark time, and it is with a heavy heart that I must inform you, after having a frank discussion with the world's leaders, that I have held a meeting with the enemy's commander, known as Oracle, and issued our conditional surrender.' His eyes tightened and he leaned forward in his chair, steepling his fingers together. 'Beginning midnight Greenwich Mean Time tonight, a global curfew will begin. Under the umbrella of the invading forces, each country's respective local law enforcement will enforce the curfew. I would ask all citizens to stay in your homes. Any crimes against persons or property will be dealt with swiftly and harshly.'

Bruce's face hardened. He lifted his chin and nodded sadly. 'Oracle has given me her word that our society will continue to operate as normal. You will continue to work and pay your bills. There will be no hoarding and there will be no profiteering. Anybody looking to profit from this sudden change in circumstances will be dealt with harshly.' His mood changing, his eyes blazed with defiance as he continued with his speech. 'I send this message to the brave volunteers who are right now working on ways to help ease our suffering. Continue what you are doing and, when the time is right, your service will be called upon.'

His nostrils flared in anger and he held up a finger. 'Finally, I send this message to those people who collaborated and conspired to set these events in motion. The time will come when the balance will be restored, but know this … You will be found, you will be judged, and may God have mercy on your soul.' Closing his eyes, he inhaled deeply through his nose to rein in his emotions. He then opened his eyes and gave a warm sad smile. 'Goodnight, keep safe and look after one another. God bless you all.'

The King sank back in his seat, mentally exhausted, and let out a heavy, weary breath as he watched the small black box go dark. His brother nodded in admiration and rose to his feet, sighing in grudging acceptance. 'Well, we are in the shit now.'

Overcome with anger, his chest rising and falling in rapid breaths, the King reached forward, grabbed the box, let out a howl of rage and threw it across his study, striking a crystal decanter that had been sitting harmlessly on top of a set of drawers for many years. The antique decanter struck the floor and the sound of breaking glass echoed around the room as it shattered into pieces. Bruce stared at the devastation he had just caused, and he twisted his face as a taste of bitterness filled his mouth. Stephen cocked his head and stared at his elder brother with a raised eyebrow.

'Feel better?'

The King shot his younger brother a withering stare and snarled at him, 'Get out!'

The prince looked at his older brother with a hurt-filled expression and nodded silently. Without saying a word, he bowed his head, spun on his heel, and strode out of the King's study. Bruce, silently cursing his thoughtlessness, held up his hand to apologise to his younger brother, but was too late. The door had closed behind Stephen.

Feeling like the weight of the world was on his shoulders, Bruce pinched the bridge of his nose and groaned. Sinking back into his chair, he put his head in his hands and let out a long, harsh breath, feeling weariness overwhelm him, plunging him into despair. There was a small click, followed by the sound of a door opening. Thinking his brother had returned, his heart leapt for joy, and he jumped swiftly to his feet.

'Listen, Stephen, I know I shouldn't have spo—' The words died in his throat, and he felt his jaw open in surprise on seeing a familiar tall, strikingly beautiful auburn-haired woman walk towards him. Lost for words, he collapsed back into his seat and stammered at his wife, who knelt in front of him. 'W-w-what are you doing here? Y-you should not be here!'

Her round green eyes glowing with compassion, Vanessa smiled sadly into her husband's weary eyes and stroked his face. 'Shush, my love. I am where I should be, by my husband's side.'

The distraught King shook his head angrily and he took his wife's hand, kissing it tenderly. 'No. This isn't right. You should be with our children.' He stared back at her fearfully. 'Our children, are they …?'

With tears rolling down her cheeks, Vanessa gave him a knowing smile. 'Don't worry, my love, our children are safe and well. How could I look them in their eyes again, knowing I abandoned their father in his hour of need? I am where I should be, at your side, as is my duty.'

Leaning in to embrace his wife, Bruce let out an anguished sob. 'What have I done?'

Vanessa smiled, their forehead's touching one another as she whispered softly to him, 'You've given the world a fighting chance. That is what you have done.'

The quartet turned away from the monitor with grave expressions. For several minutes, they stared at one another in an uneasy silence, struggling with their own thoughts. The only sound that was heard was the faint hiss of recycled air being pumped through the air ducts in the ceiling.

His mind reeling at the ramifications of King Bruce's speech, Dave wearily moved towards the large conference room window and stood next to Sophia, who was gazing down into the command centre below. He inhaled and let it out slowly as he held his arm up against the surface of the window. Resting his head on his arm, he followed her gaze and observed the frightened expressions looking back up at him. He didn't have to be a mind reader to see that there were a lot of scared people below; uncertain of the future that lay ahead.

'So, what happens now?' Wendy asked no one in particular.

'We build a campfire, hold hands and sing Kumbaya,' John answered in a bitter sarcastic tone. He held his hand up apologetically as Wendy gave him the evil eye. 'Sorry, that was uncalled for.' He blew out his cheeks and rubbed the back of his neck. 'If I'm being honest, I don't know what happens next.'

Wendy nodded mutely in understanding and slumped back into her chair, shoulders sagging in defeat. The three people stared uneasily at one another as if they were afraid to say the thing that they knew to be true. Dave moved purposely behind Wendy and placed a reassuring hand on her shoulder. He smiled as she placed her hand on his.

Closing his eyes, Dave let out a long breath and then muttered, 'I guess this means we're at war.'

He and the other two jumped at the sound of Sophia's bitter laugh. Dave slowly turned stared at her worriedly. She was shaking her head and laughing hysterically, waving her hands with a disdainful look on her face.

'War! War is when both sides have an equal chance of winning,' she scoffed and placed her hands on her hips, shaking her head. John shifted in his seat uncomfortably as she continued to laugh hysterically. 'I don't know if you have been watching, but Oracle just gave the world the biggest wedgie in history.' Her hazel eyes blazed in anger, and she slammed her hand down on the table. Her upper lip twisted up in contempt, and she stared at Wendy with hostile eyes, sneering. 'I can tell you what is going to happen, my dear … nothing, that's what. The world is simply going to roll over while Oracle strokes our belly.'

His face turning crimson, John snarled and grabbed Sophia by her shoulders. 'That is enough! I know you're scared. I am too, but we both knew this day would come. We planned for this.'

Sophia let out a loud huff of disgust and waved John's hands away. 'Yeah, all we ever do is plan, isn't it?' He blinked as she lunged at him and stabbed her finger into his chest. 'Where did our plans lead us? I'll tell you …' She stopped and waved irritably at the TV screen, laughing bitterly. 'Frig all! The world basically pulled her knickers down and smiled while Oracle shafted her from behind.'

Dave shifted on his feet uncomfortably as the emotionally charged woman continued with her rant. As Sophia and John continued to argue, he frowned as he watched Kendra enter the room. From the grave expression on her face, he immediately realised something was wrong as he watched her take several slow stiff steps toward the enraged woman. The chief of security swallowed and coughed awkwardly to get the prime minister's attention.

'What?' Sophia snapped, wheeling around with such intensity it caused the normally unruffled Kendra to flinch back.

'Ma'am, I am sorry,' Kendra whispered, lowering her head. She held up a sheet of paper. 'You really need to see this.'

Fuming, Sophia opened her mouth to say something, but she stopped and stared at Kendra strangely. Dave noticed Kendra's pain-filled eyes and he immediately realised from her haunted expression and her body language that something terrible must have happened. Sophia nodded and took the paper out of the woman's shaking hand. Dave went to tap Wendy's shoulder, but she leapt out of her seat before he could do so and raced over to console Kendra. He watched gravely as the normally unflappable ex-marine collapsed into Wendy's arms. Kendra's face was a picture of anguish as she sobbed uncontrollably.

Dave was filled with a sudden foreboding and his chest tightened as Sophia held up the paper to read. Her expression quickly changed to one of horror. She staggered back, collapsed to the floor and let out a cry of anguish. 'Those stupid fools. Those stupid, stupid fools.'

As Dave's heart continued to thunder in his chest, John knelt next to Sophia and put his hand on her shoulder. Grief stricken, she whispered something inaudibly to him and he took the sheet of paper out of her trembling hands. Fear creeping into his heart, he looked at John questioningly as he read the paper. The blood appeared to drain from his face, and he lowered the paper and gave Dave an unbelieving look.

'What's happened?' Dave asked, trying to hide the fear in his voice.

'An hour ago, the Chinese government in Beijing issued a curt response to Oracle's demand to surrender.' He spoke in a hollow voice as he read from the sheet paper. 'Fifteen minutes after receiving their message, she destroyed Beijing. She single-handedly destroyed everything within a one-thousand-square-mile area around the city.' Dave could tell John was clearly fighting to keep himself together as he listened to his voice quiver slightly. 'Details are sketchy, but according to reports from observer planes near the area, there are no survivors.'

Devastated by the news, Dave shakily collapsed back into his seat and stared at the ashen-faced man in wordless horror. Sophia, still slumped on the floor, buried her head into her hands and broke down. His body trembling with fury, Dave locked eyes with John. As if reading his mind, he let out a heavy sigh and shook his head sorrowfully.

'The Chinese reply was just three words …' Tearful, John paused and handed the paper to Dave.

Dave stared at the paper and let out a mirthless laugh, thinking about the absurdity of it all. He shook his head, angrily scrunching the paper up in his hand. Three words, that was all it took, three words for the world to be changed forever.

'Death before dishonour.'

-13-

Reality 672
Terra (Counter-Earth)
Date: 27th October 5775

Zoe's eyes were wide with panic as she ran down the long white corridor. Terror seized her heart as she picked up the sound of heavy footsteps coming behind her. But she dared not look back, because she was already aware of who was chasing her. It was them – the faceless metal demons. The ones who had chasing her from the first day she had arrived there. No, she mustn't turn around. If she did that, they would only capture her again, and her life would surely be over.

But it was then Zoe felt a surge of hope as she spotted a bright light coming from an open door further down the corridor in front of her. There was also a woman standing in the doorway waving her arms frantically. Zoe frowned. Was she pleading at her, telling her to run faster?

'Run, Zoe, run towards me, my darling.' She heard the woman shout.

As Zoe got closer, her eyes opened in surprise as she recognised the figure in front of her. It was her grandmother!

She continued to run towards the waving figure, but uncertainty overwhelmed her, and she slowed as she remembered her gran had died three years ago. However, Zoe's whole face lit up - she wasn't mistaken - the older woman standing in front of her was her gran. Clearly alive and well, but it was most definitely her gran.

It surprised Zoe that her gran appeared to be much younger than she remembered. She was reminded of pictures her gran used to show her, taken when she was much younger.

Her spirits soaring, Zoe's gran smiled warmly as she begged her to run faster. But dread filled her as her gran's eyes widened and terror overtook her face. It suddenly dawned on Zoe that her gran wasn't looking directly at her, but at something behind Zoe.

Zoe ran, but blinked as a bright white flash came from behind her and flinched as something warm flashed past her. She watched in horror as a beam of energy struck her gran in the centre of her chest. Her gran appeared to stagger back, and she glanced down at the smoking hole in her chest. Her mouth opened wide in shock and surprise as three more bursts of energy shot past Zoe, striking her gran in her stomach, chest, and head. Zoe's mouth opened in a silent scream as her gran's lifeless body collapsed onto the floor.

With tears streaming down her face, Zoe gritted her teeth with steely determination and continued to charge towards the bright light. Fuelled by the knowledge that her freedom was not far away, she pumped her arms like pistons and sprinted down the corridor. A few more steps, that was all it would take, a few more feet, and she would be through that door and free of her tormentors. 'Come on,' she breathed, 'just a few more steps, you can do it.'

Another flash of light filled the corridor, and Zoe squeezed her eyes shut. Her mouth opened in a wordless scream as she felt something hot strike her hip, and she staggered. Her momentum sent her crashing forward into a wall, gasping in pain as she collapsed to the floor.

Stunned, Zoe lay on the floor and stared up at the spinning ceiling above her. Teeth clenched together and with all the strength she could muster, Zoe desperately twisted onto her stomach and crawled across the floor, trying painfully to edge closer to the light.

Her mouth opened in a silent shriek of terror as she felt several hands grab her and pull her away from the doorway. Zoe clawed desperately at her attackers as they turned her over. Her vision blurred as somebody struck her in the face with the butt of their weapon. Fighting back the tears, Zoe shook her head to clear her vision just in time to get a look at what was standing over her. Oh God, it's them! The faceless metal demon. Paralysed with fear, she watched as the metal demon slowly raised their weapon and pointed it at her torso.

The figure tightened their grip on the weapon, pressed their finger on the weapon's trigger and released a beam of energy, striking Zoe in the chest. She looked down and let out a horrified scream at the gaping hole in her chest …

Zoe opened her eyes and awoke from the dream, not screaming or crying, but gagging. She curled into a tight ball, hugged herself and retched, not from anything she had eaten, but from sheer throat-clogging terror.

She let out a ragged gasp of air and her chest rose and fell in rapid breaths as she finally uncurled herself and sat up on the bed, leaned back against the small metal headboard and trembled. Tightly wrapping her arms around her body, she closed her eyes and tried to control her breathing and calm her racing heart. Zoe realised she was not merely trembling; she was rattling. Her jaw tightened and she tried to wrap her arms around herself more tightly, convinced that she could feel her bones tapping against one another.

Trembling, she opened her eyes and frowned in confusion as she realised that she was no longer in the brightly lit cell she had been in before she passed out. She turned her body and rested herself on the edge of the mattress to examine the room she was in. Her eyes grew wide; she was astonished to find herself in a small, dimly lit room.

The room she now found herself in was very unlike her last cell. Her previous prison cell had been brightly lit and appeared to be quite advanced. However, as she twisted her head to inspect her new surroundings, she quickly saw that this room seemed less spacious and not as clean. Zoe wrinkled her nose as she detected an odd odour, but there was also something familiar about it. She snapped her fingers as she remembered why it was familiar. The smell was very similar to that of the old, abandoned hospital she had been in when she had been attacked a few days earlier – an ancient, decaying smell.

Zoe surveyed her new surroundings, puzzled as she tried to remember how she came to be here. She rose to her feet and winced in pain from her injured leg. Although the wound was healing, it was still quite painful. She grimaced as she limped towards the metal door on the far side of the room.

Zoe stumbled as she was overwhelmed by a severe bout of vertigo and collapsed onto the floor. Suddenly nauseous, she gripped her stomach and began retching. She squeezed her eyes shut, took a deep breath, and crawled across the floor back to the bed. Finally making it to the edge of the bed frame, she lifted herself and rested her head on the edge of the mattress. She groaned to herself. Now if the room could stop just stop spinning that would be a great help too. With her eyes still tightly closed, Zoe inhaled several deep breaths. That's it, if she let the room come to a slow stop and then everything will be alright. As she lay against the bed, a fog lifted from her befuddled brain, and the memories of what had happened to her came flooding back.

The last thing she remembered was being in the brightly lit prison cell waiting to be fed. She guessed from the sounds of her empty stomach and her hunger that it had been over twenty-four hours since she last ate something substantial. She remembered the collar around her neck had begun to do something strange, and then she screamed when she felt some type of energy stream envelop her. The last thing she remembered before blacking out was her body feeling like it was on fire and her insides being ripped apart. She was not sure how much time had passed before she regained consciousness and found herself in this room.

After a few moments, Zoe opened her eyes and was relieved to discover her vertigo had gone. Now if she could find out where the hell she was, then that might help make her feel a bit better. She frowned as she detected a strange clicking sound coming from behind her. Easing herself up onto the bed, Zoe protectively pulled her legs up to her chest, and watched warily as the door swung open and a woman popped her head into the room, smiling warmly at Zoe.

A muscular woman, slightly taller than Zoe, stepped through the doorway into the room, carrying a tray in her hand. As the stranger edged closer, Zoe could see she had a shaved head, very little brown hair growing through. The woman was dressed in green body-length overalls like those worn by soldiers.

'I see you are finally awake,' the woman said cautiously and indicated the tray in her hand. 'I thought you might be hungry, so I brought you some food.'

Just who was this woman and why was she acting all nice? Already deeply suspicious of the people of this world, Zoe flinched and edged further back as the stranger moved towards her. Oh no, this time was going to be different – this time she wasn't going to be taken by surprise. The woman stopped and her blue eyes flickered with concern as she slowly held up her hand and spoke to her in a low, soothing voice. 'It's okay, you are safe here. We will not hurt you.' The friendly woman placed the tray of food on the cabinet beside the bed and pointed to herself. 'My name is Em. Can you tell me your name, sweetheart?'

Zoe nodded briefly and murmured, 'Zoe, Zoe Murray.'

Smiling warmly, Em pointed to a spot next to Zoe on the bed. 'Is it okay if I sit next to you?'

Zoe nodded slowly and remained silent as the woman sat on the bed next to her, and then cocked her head as she studied the newcomer. The woman's face, neck, and head showed scars, possibly an indication that she had suffered years of physical abuse. Zoe swallowed, thinking back to the welcome she had received just a few days ago, Had the Empire done the same to Em? Tortured her extensively, probably in the same way Zoe had been on first arriving on this nightmarish world? Zoe felt herself relax slightly as she wondered just maybe Em really was trying to help her.

Em smiled sadly and gave a small nod of acknowledgement. Zoe blinked as she realised that she had been staring at the woman too long, and her cheeks warmed as she looked away in embarrassment.

Em's lips curled up in a sad smile. The woman's eyes had a haunted look as she looked heavenward and let out a long, sad breath. 'Yes, I was much younger than you when they first tortured me.' Her blue eyes flickered with anger, and she pointed to the dark blue bruise around Zoe's neck. 'Like you, they forced me to wear a collar and were eager to provide a –' her mouth twisted into a sneer of disdain '– demonstration.'

At the mention of the obedience collar, Zoe instinctively touched her neck with her hand. Her eyes opened in surprise and she suddenly became aware that the thin metallic collar was no longer around her neck. She realised she'd had been so busy worrying about her new surroundings when she regained consciousness that she'd had failed to notice it was missing. The corners of Em's mouth curled up and she nodded slightly.

'We disabled and removed your collar when you arrived,' Em said and pointed over to the tray of food on the bedside cabinet. 'I would suggest you eat that now to build up your strength.'

Em leaned over, picked up the tray of food and handed it to Zoe, who took it gratefully. As she ate, Zoe realised she was even more hungry than she thought and quickly wolfed her food down. Her face scrunched up in disgust at the bitter taste of the food.

'Tastes like shit, doesn't it?' Em chuckled.

Zoe gave a half shrug but continued to eat. 'Tastes like chicken,' she muttered sarcastically with a mouthful of food.

Em's eyes twinkled and her mouth curved into a devious smile. 'Amazing what you can do with an endless supply of rats.'

Choking, Zoe coughed and then stopped eating with her mouth wide open, full of food. Filled with revulsion, she turned to Em, disgusted.

Maybe it was because of her reaction to being told what she had just eaten, but Zoe was positive she saw the corner of Em's mouth twitch slightly. Was this woman somehow finding enjoyment in Zoe's discomfort? Was she mocking her? Was Em just like Zoe's mother? Just another adult whose only pleasure in life was to ridicule children, making them feel as if they were beneath them? Zoe shook her head and stabbed her fork into the food on the plate. Determined to prove Em wrong, Zoe squeezed her eyes shut and took a huge gulp, swallowing whatever she had in her mouth. She then gave Em a steely-eyed stare.

If she detected the hostility in Zoe's gaze, Em did not show it, instead, she simply waved her hand in front of her and chuckled. 'Seriously, I'm kidding. That is something we've been growing ourselves in our hydroponics bay.' She lifted her shoulder in a slight shrug and nodded. 'I do agree though, it does taste like shit, but unfortunately, until we get the kinks worked out, it's the best we have.'

Sceptical, Zoe lowered her head and peered down at the plate in front of her. She cocked her head and frowned, prodding the food with her fork. So, she wasn't messing with her? This food was supposed to taste like this? After several seconds, she shrugged and continued to devour the food on the plate. She reached over for the bottle that was resting in the tray's cup holder, lifted it to her mouth and took a big drink from it. However as soon as the fluid hit the back of her throat, her eyes squeezed shut and she gagged, spitting the liquid out of her mouth.

She wiped her mouth with the back of her hand and gave Em a revolted look. 'Holy crap! That tasted even worse. Please don't tell me I've just drunk rat's piss?'

Laughing weakly, Em shook her head. 'No, you're quite safe. It's a special protein drink designed to help people such as yourself recover from transporter fatigue.'

Zoe looked at the woman in confusion. 'Transporter fatigue? You mean that feeling of my insides being turned inside out I had felt just before I blacked out and then found myself here?'

Em nodded briefly and then let out a long-drawn-out breath. 'Sort of. You see, most of us in this world have become quite used to the effects of matter transportation. Unfortunately, the matter transporter we use is …' She paused and stared up at the ceiling thoughtfully. 'Well, you could say we would class it as an antique. It can be quite rough on the human body, especially on somebody who hasn't been through a transporter before, like you. We had planned on teleporting you in three weeks' time, but something happened that meant we had to escalate our timetable and we didn't have time to prepare you.'

Her lips pressed together, Em took in a deep breath and shook her head, exhaling sadly. 'We were lucky our operative injected a tracker into you that allowed us to lock onto you. We literally crossed our fingers and hoped for the best when we teleported you here.' She held up her hands apologetically. 'You have been unconscious for nearly twenty-four hours, so you need to eat and drink plenty of fluids.'

Zoe bobbed her head in understanding, holding up the bottle to take another drink, but stopped and turned to Em with a raised eyebrow. 'Wait, you said matter transportation. Do you mean you transported me like they do in *Star Trek: The Next Generation*?' She stared in awe at the woman next to her. 'Oh! That's so cool! I really need to try that again.'

Em shook her head, laughed and ruffled Zoe's hair playfully. Her face turning serious, she then turned and pointed to something in the room. 'One thing at a time, kiddo. First, we need to—' She stopped and gave Zoe a double take. 'Wait – what? *Star Trek: The Nex*—' Zoe grinned at the sight of the astonishment on Em's face. 'Do you mean *Star Trek*? The TV show? You mean that show is still going?'

Zoe half shrugged and grimaced as she took another bite of food. 'Well, *Star Trek* was a bit before my time, so was *TNG*.' She glanced up to the ceiling with a frown and bobbed her head from side to side as she counted the number of spin-offs in her head. 'I think there were eleven movies and then there were the other spin-off shows made before I was born. They even have made some recent ones too.' She gave an indifferent shrug. 'Science fiction has never been my thing anyway.'

Em's mouth hung open and she gave Zoe an unbelieving look. After several seconds, she blinked and shook her head in amazement. 'Unbelievable.'

Zoe rolled her eyes and grunted in agreement. 'Hmph! Yeah, *Star Trek* is like this religion now. Nerds that like to get dressed up an—' She stopped as something in Em's comment registered with her and gave Em a suspicious side-eye. 'Wait, how do you know about *Star Trek*?'

As if to change the subject, Em quickly rose to her feet, shook her head slightly, and gave a dismissive wave of her hand. 'That's something for another time. First, you need to eat and drink.' She moved toward a door in the room's corner and opened it to reveal a small bathroom. 'You will probably want to change out of that tattered hospital gown. There's a shower here that you can use to freshen up and there are some clothes in this wardrobe that may fit.'

Em opened the small metal wardrobe to show its contents to Zoe, who blinked in surprise and glanced down at herself. She had forgotten that she was still wearing the tattered hospital gown that they had given her at the hospital shortly before she had been kidnapped and brought to this strange world. The corners of her eyes creased as she remembered her tormentors hadn't allowed her to get changed as punishment for her obstinate behaviour.

Em pointed to the doorway that she had come through. 'When you've finished eating and have changed, knock on the door and the guard outside will come and get me.'

Dismay filled Zoe and she felt her stomach tighten. She closed her eyes and tried to fight back the tears, lowering her head and whispering, 'Am I a prisoner here?'

Em's body stiffened in surprise, but then her eyes filled with concern as she stepped closer and knelt in front of Zoe. She reached forward and gently lifted her chin. 'Oh, sweetheart. You are not a prisoner. This complex is quite large and dangerous, so the guard out there is for your own protection. Do you understand?' She smiled warmly and Zoe nodded slowly. 'This place is very busy and dangerous. I wouldn't forgive myself if I allowed you to wander around and something happened to you.' She winked, straightened and pointed to the door.

'Tell you what, I'll wait outside that door for you. When you're ready, just open that door and walk out. Is that better?'

Her spirits lifting, Zoe nodded and then gave the compassionate woman a half smile as she watched her head towards the door and place her hand on the sensor on the wall. The door opened and Em stepped into the corridor beyond – Zoe grinned as she spun round just before the door was fully closed and gave her a thumbs up.

Zoe finished her meal and gagged as she took another sip of protein juice from the bottle. When she'd had enough, she picked up her tray and placed it on the bedside cabinet. She took in a deep breath, stood up to lift the hospital gown over her head and slipped out of her underwear. She limped over to the metal wardrobe and stared into the mirror on the wardrobe door.

She inhaled a sharp breath and her eyes widened in shock as she looked at the reflection in the mirror. Her mood darkened as she lifted her hand to her throat and trailed her fingers along the narrow bruise around her neck. Her hand moved up to her face and she cocked her head to examine the black and blue bruise around her right eye and cheek.

After limping towards the bathroom and stepping into the shower cubicle, she frowned as she gazed around the narrow tube and wondered where the shower head was. How was she to activate the shower? Zoe smiled gleefully and nodded as she noticed several holes around the cubicle wall and guessed they were where the water came from. She raised her trembling hand, placing it over the sensor on the side of the shower cubicle, and squeezed her eyes shut as she pressed on the sensor.

On hearing a faint humming noise coming from machinery hidden in the cubicle's walls, Zoe jerked away and squealed as she felt pulses vibrating through her body. She shook her head and laughed, embarrassed, as she realised that the device was cleaning her by bombarding her body with acoustic pulses at a frequency her human ears could not detect. She turned her back and leaned against the cubicle's wall.

But Zoe's joyful laugh soon turned into a bitter sob. Why? Why her? Was she being punished? Was that it? She screwed her face up as sadness overtook her and she slid down the chamber's wall. *Yes, that's it.* God was wanting to punish her for her insolent behaviour. It had to be that, because it was the only logical reason she could imagine for why she'd ended up in this hellhole. Zoe wrapped her arms around her legs and bent her head forward, her body shuddering as she huddled in the corner and sobbed uncontrollably.

-14-

Thirty minutes later, after she had showered and found something suitable to wear in the wardrobe (she was surprised to find there was some women's underwear that fitted her along with an ugly green overall, but at least it was better than a tattered hospital gown), Zoe sat began to carefully comb her long black hair. She looked up at the ceiling thoughtfully. Just who were these people? She frowned as she wondered if they were the resistance group Dr Prakash had spoken to her about.

She sipped a small gulp of protein juice and screwed up her face as the bitter taste struck the back of her throat – not only that it left an awful aftertaste in her mouth. She reluctantly agreed that Em had been right; although it tasted awful, she had started to feel more like herself. The wound on her leg was still painful, though, but when she had been a prisoner, whatever device the doctor had used on it was helping it to heal. Zoe noticed while she had been showering, somebody had come in and taken away her tattered hospital gown.

Realising she wasn't going to get any answers by just sitting there, Zoe straightened up and limped over to the doorway. She groaned at the pressure on the injured muscle in her leg and regretted not asking Em for some painkillers when she'd had the chance. Zoe stared nervously at the sensor on the wall. Taking a deep breath, she closed her eyes and pressed her hand on it, then jumped as she heard a loud click and the door swung open in front of her. After taking a small hesitant step forward, she felt an overwhelming relief as she spotted Em on the other side of the doorway.

Em smiled warmly as Zoe stepped slowly out into the hallway towards her. 'See, didn't I say you're not a prisoner?' She gave Zoe a knowing wink and then handed her a metal walking stick. 'Thought you might need this to help you walk until your leg fully heals. How do you feel after your meal and shower – better?'

Zoe pursed her lips together and gratefully took the walking stick from Em. She leaned on it as she followed her down a long, dimly lit corridor. Several people, wearing similar clothing to Em, bobbed their heads in greeting as they passed. Zoe shrugged her shoulders slightly as she hobbled next to Em. 'Yes, thank you, I certainly feel a bit more like myself now.' The corners of her mouth curled up into a small grin and she gave Em a cheeky wink. 'Although my mam would probably say that's perhaps not a good thing.'

At the mention of her mum, Zoe felt her heart become heavy. Did her mum even know she was missing? Did she care? She stiffened as a memory drifted out of the back of her mind, something she had forgotten about until now. Just after regaining consciousness in the portal chamber, she had seen somebody who was her exact double talking to General Cooper through the portal. Zoe's shoulders sagged at the realisation that she had been replaced and let out a long melancholic breath. Mum would never know her daughter had been taken and had been replaced. Zoe blinked back the tears; she was going to die on this world with the knowledge that she wasn't even missed.

Laughing, Em shook her head as she led Zoe down the corridor. Her laugh stopped as if she had noticed Zoe's change in demeanour; she placed a hand on Zoe's shoulder and gave her an understanding look. She then spoke to her in a low, compassionate voice. 'Zoe, I am sure your mum is missing you terribly. I can't promise we will get you back to your world, but we will do our utmost to make it possible.'

Zoe rolled her eyes and sniffed in disgust. 'Hmph! She probably won't know I'm missing. We never got on and we said some harsh things to each other just before I …' Staring up at the ceiling, she started to wonder if her double would have a better relationship with her mum than she did. She pinched the bridge of her nose and grimaced. Imagining your evil twin would be one who got on better with your own mother … now, that was depressing! She blinked as she realised Em was looking at her strangely. 'Sorry, I was miles away. I was about to say that shortly after I was taken, I woke up and found myself in a strange chamber and …' She shook her head in confusion and placed her hand on Em's arm. 'You will probably think I'm insane, but I remember seeing an image of myself on a large screen, or something, talking.'

Then, to Zoe's surprise, Em's mood changed. The woman's face hardened, and her eyes blazed in anger as she shook her head in disgust. Zoe jumped as she watched Em clench her fists, spin round and pound the wall furiously. Several people stopped and gave their colleague a concerned look as she hissed angrily.

'Bastards! They're still doing it. Bastards!'

An enormous, powerfully built black man, sporting a beard and dreadlocks, appeared out of nowhere; he approached Em and placed his hand on her shoulder. Zoe detected something similar to a South African accent in his voice as she listened to him speak to Em in a low, concerned tone. 'Em, are you okay? What's wrong, Boss Lady?'

Taken by surprise, Em turned and blinked at the man. She shook her head sadly and held up her hand apologetically to him. 'Sorry, Isaac, I'm fine. Just the usual business of the Empire messing with things they shouldn't be.'

Isaac let out a loud bark and nodded, giving Em a firm but gentle pat on the shoulder. 'Hah! So the usual then, Boss.' He frowned and looked at Zoe. He gave her a nudge and winked. 'Just to let you know, you shouldn't really upset the Boss Lady on your first day.' Zoe picked up a note of respect in his voice but she also noticed the mischievous glint in his eye. 'Em, here, is the gel that holds us all together. We would be lost without her.'

'Give over.' Em laughed, shaking her head and punching him playfully in the shoulder. 'Well then, that would mean you would take over since you're second in command here.'

With an impish twinkle appearing in the powerfully built man's eyes, he placed his hands on the sides of his face in mock shock. 'What! That would mean I would have to work for a living.' He grinned and then let out a loud booming laugh. He wiped his eyes, cocked his head and pointed his finger up the corridor. 'I'm making my way up to the command centre – you coming, Boss Lady?'

Em gave the man a dismissive wave of her hand. 'You carry on, I'll join you shortly.' She smiled warmly and gestured to Zoe. 'I just want to bring our new friend here up to speed.'

The gentle giant's eyes twinkled and he bobbed his head in understanding. Em's mouth twitched in amusement as he raised his finger to his head and gave the teenager a small salute. Unsure how to react, Zoe was taken aback but regained her composure as she realised that he was only toying with her.

Much to Isaac's obvious glee, Zoe straightened, raised her hand to her head and saluted him in return. Em lifted her hand to her mouth to hide her smile as Zoe cocked her head to the giant man and stuck her tongue out, winking playfully.

Isaac pulled his head back and let out a loud, booming roar of delight. Zoe winced as he stepped forward and slapped her firmly on the shoulder. He turned to Em and gave her a lopsided grin, pointing to Zoe. 'Oh, I like this one, she's fun!' He boomed. He then leaned in closer to Zoe and whispered to her playfully. 'Be careful she doesn't bore you to death, little one.'

The good-natured giant grinned and roared with laughter as Em shot him a dirty look. As Isaac walked away from them, Em rolled her eyes and exhaled as his booming laugh followed him up the long corridor.

Zoe arched her head and looked at Em with a raised eyebrow. 'He called you boss. Are you the leader here?' She lifted her hand and gestured to the surrounding building. 'Whatever here is. Are you, like, an army or something?'

Her eyes blazing with pride, Em nodded and held her hands up to indicate the surrounding building. 'We are a small cell that's part of a larger resistance network scattered across the Empire.' She stared up at the ceiling with a sad, faraway look. 'While I was a prisoner, I assembled a small group that escaped and created a base of operations here. Over time, our numbers grew and eventually we established communication with other cells across the Empire's territory.' She sighed and then shrugged. 'I didn't ask to be a leader, it just fell on me. Everybody seems to look at me and they're happy to follow me. I will happily step aside if anybody else wants the role.' Her expression hardened and her mouth set in a hard line. 'Until then, I will do my utmost to protect this group.'

As Zoe was guided around the complex, she listened intently to Em introduce her to the various people they passed. She had a strange sensation as people greeted her warmly, something she had not felt for such a long time – a sense of belonging, of family.

Zoe stared in wonderment at the futuristic equipment held in the medical bay and gasped in astonishment as she was shown the large hydroponics lab where the food was grown to feed the people in the base. She was awestruck as she listened to Em explain how they'd had to fend for themselves in order to survive. She listened with keen interest as Em led her into a transport-pod and explained how she found the abandoned complex after she had eventually escaped from her captivity with the Empire.

Zoe lost her balance as she felt the transport-pod shudder to a stop and the pod's doors slid open. Stepping out, she stopped dead and became rooted to the spot, her mouth opening and closing in wonderment as she gazed at the room in front of her.

After taking an awkward step forward into the circular room, Zoe was immediately reminded of a military command centre like those she had seen in films or documentaries on TV. She blew out a small whistle at the sight of the various workstations with holographic interfaces scattered around the room. Staggering forward, she stared in awe at the large holographic screen on the wall. 'This is incredible,' she whispered in a tone of childlike wonder.

Em gave her a lopsided grin. 'Yes, it is quite a sight, isn't it?' She lifted her shoulder in a half shrug and blew out a long, frustrated sigh. 'Of course, the systems we have aren't as advanced as the Empire's. Most of this stuff is obsolete, so we must make do with what we have.'

Em smiled affectionately as Zoe took in the room's surroundings, and then gently placed a hand on her shoulder and pointed to the holographic display on one of the consoles. 'The data you can see in front of you isn't up to date. We cannot connect to the Empire's data network because they could trace the connection back to us. We must rely on slow dial-up data connections that are no longer used by the Empire to stay hidden.'

Em and Zoe turned as Isaac approached them. He nodded to Zoe before turning to Em with concern etched across his face. 'We're still trying to make sense of this data that we gathered a couple of days ago.' He scratched his head and sighed as he pointed to the large holographic display. 'We knew something must have happened when we detected a large gamma-ray burst across the Greater Chinese Republic, but we haven't been able to re-establish a connection with our operatives in the Republic since we lost contact with them.'

Frowning, Em peered up at the holographic display and tapped her chin thoughtfully. 'Perhaps they had to go radio silent because they were in some sort of lockdown?'

Isaac shook his head. 'No, we should still pick up transmissions from across the Republic's territory, but we cannot detect anything, not even any news or entertainment frequencies. It is as if—'

'As if there's nobody left alive,' Em interjected. A troubled look passed between them and she whispered in a low, horrified voice, 'No, that's impossible – surely the Empire wouldn't have discovered a way to kill everybody in the Republic?' She blinked and then flicked her hand in dismissal. 'No, I cannot believe that. I refuse to accept that until we get proof. What about our operatives in Pons Aelius? Have we heard anything from them?'

Isaac held up his hands and shook his head. 'We've heard nothing from our operatives in the city since we received that obscure message telling us something strange was happening to everybody wearing collars and we were to use our matter transporter to transport as many prisoners out as we could.' He glanced over his shoulder, took a step towards Em and then lowered his voice. 'We have a lot of scared and confused people in here, Em.'

Deciding to let the two resistance fighters chat amongst themselves, Zoe moved away from them and walked slowly around the centre. In keen fascination, she watched various people working on their holographic displays. People peered up from their stations as she passed and smiled at her in acknowledgement.

Zoe frowned and stopped to gaze up at the large holographic display on the wall in front of her. She then stared in open-mouthed wonder as it hit her it was a map of the world that she was now on. As she studied the globe in front of her, she noticed there was something odd about this Earth; the continents on it appeared to be different somehow. Zoe shook her head. No that couldn't be right. She probably was just at it wrong – wasn't she?

'I see you have noticed it.'

Startled, Zoe jumped at the sound of Em's voice coming from behind her as the woman glided up and stood next to her. Zoe pointed to the map above her. 'It doesn't look right. Where what would be the Asian continent, there now appears to be a larger separate continent, and where the South American and

North American continents should be …'

On the map above her, scattered across a large ocean called Atlantica, were various small to medium-sized islands where the two larger American continents should have been. The Australian continent appeared to be the same as in her world, but instead of Australia it was named Aboriginia, and a large red radioactive symbol was plastered over the entire continent.

Perplexed, Zoe squinted so that she could study the map more closely, and noticed the European and African continents appeared to have merged. The lower half of the European continent that should have been Africa seemed significantly larger but was now named Gondwana. As Zoe scratched her head in confusion, her eyes widened as realisation dawned on her. She wasn't imagining it after all. This world did look different.

Em nodded and gestured to the map. 'On this world, the South American continent never separated from the African continent. The people here still call that area Gondwana, which is where Isaac was originally from before the Empire conquered his people.' She chuckled and peered over her shoulder at the powerfully built man. 'I once made the mistake of calling him African, but after I apologised and explained the reason for my confusion, he happily set me straight and explained to me that he was Gondwanian.'

Zoe nodded in mild understanding and continued to stare in awe at the holographic map in front of her. The Chinese Republic's territory appeared to cover a third of the globe with the Roman Empire's territory covering the remaining two-thirds of the planet. A fifty-mile-wide demilitarised zone separated the border on either side. But while some things appeared different, there were still some familiar-looking islands; she spotted the smaller countries that would be Iceland and the British Isles on her world.

Wait that cannot be right? Zoe did a double take as she noticed something unusual on the map. Where was Russia? Perplexed, she turned to Em and gestured with her thumb to the map. Em nodded knowingly, placed her hand on Zoe's arm and whispered to her. 'Don't worry, you are not imagining it. The country that would have been Russia is now split into two. One-third of it is now part of the continent that makes up the Greater China Republic's territory, while the remaining two-thirds make up the rest of the Roman Empire's territory. Where the Middle East should be is now a channel of water, between fifty and one hundred miles wide, separating the two continents.' Em paused to stare up at the holographic image and then lifted her shoulder in a half shrug. 'From what I can understand, the continents must have shifted differently on this Earth. It appears the continent that would have been North America never rose when this Earth formed. Instead a chain of islands rose and spread across Atlantica.'

Before Zoe could open her mouth to speak, Isaac raced up to Em with a deeply concerned look on his face. 'Sorry to interrupt, Boss, but we have just received a transmission from Rahul and Glen. They are coming in hot, and they say they have a precious package in tow.'

Em's eyebrow arched and she tilted her head towards the enormous Gondwanian. 'We lost contact with them two days ago. Whatever they have must be very important if they need to warn us.' She rubbed her chin thoughtfully for a few seconds and then her face hardened as she stared intently at Isaac. 'I want a group armed and ready in the landing bay now. It may be nothing, but I want to ensure we take all security precautions, understood? I will join them shortly.'

The grim-faced Isaac gave a small nod of approval as he held his hand to his ear and tapped his earpiece. Relaying his comrade's orders into his mic, he wheeled away and raced out of the command centre.

A serious expression covered Em's face as she glanced at Zoe with a raised eyebrow. 'Well, it's time for you to decide. As you can see, this is a dangerous place and if you want to stay, you need to see what we're up against.' She took hold of Zoe's hands and stared into her eyes. 'I can't promise you will be safe, but until I can get you home, it is best you stay by my side where I can protect you.'

Zoe looked at the map above her thoughtfully. That was question – did she want to go home? From what she had managed to discern from Em, it sounded as if she had been taken from her world too. If Em had managed to make a life for herself here, then why couldn't she? After a moment of silence, she turned to Em and stared at her defiantly. 'Where you will go, I will follow …' Her mouth curved into a smile and she gave the older woman a cheeky wink. 'Boss Lady.'

Patting Zoe on her shoulder, Em chuckled and led Zoe out of the command centre.

-15-

A short time later, Zoe and Em stepped out of the transport-pod into an enormous room. Gobsmacked, Zoe stopped dead in her tracks and slowly spun round in a circle, taking in the stunning view surrounding her. The vast expanse reminded her of a landing bay, much like the one she had toured on an aircraft carrier during a school trip to London. Scattered around the bay were several small vehicles. A large doorway stood open at one end of the bay, leading to a long tunnel that led off into the darkness.

Recovering her wits, Zoe chased after Em who was approaching Isaac and a group of people who were preparing weapons.

The enormous man nodded an acknowledgement to his colleague as she approached him. 'We have received word from the listening post. A vehicle just entered the tunnel. It should be with us shortly.' Em gave a silent nod and Isaac turned to the armed people in front of him and issued a command. His loud booming voice echoed off the walls of the vast vehicle bay. 'Okay, guys, time to earn your pay. Get ready, but don't fire unless I give the order. Is that understood?'

The small group of men and women acknowledged the order loudly before spreading out, and then knelt in a defensive formation in front of the open tunnel entrance. Zoe's stomach tightened and she held her breath in anticipation, but then she heard what sounded like a car engine coming towards their end of the tunnel. Curious, she edged forward and squinted at the glow of approaching car lights. She frowned as she realised the lights appeared to be several feet off the ground.

Zoe jumped and squealed in fright as a hand grabbed her shoulder and gently, but firmly, pulled her back. Em gave her a reproachful glance as she moved back next to her.

What … the … actual …. hell! Gobsmacked, Zoe couldn't believe what she was looking at as a large vehicle flew through the tunnel's doors into the bay. The vehicle reminded her of a large pickup truck, with an enclosed cab at the front and an open cargo area with a low tailgate towards the rear. Its wheels were turned inwards and on each wheel a rotor blade spun. She quickly assumed the blades were somehow keeping the vehicle in the air. Then, to her wide-eyed amazement, Zoe saw the vehicle glide to a stop in front of her and gently ease itself down onto the ground.

Just as the vehicle came to a complete stop, Isaac beamed and took a step forward. The vehicle's doors opened and two men stepped out of the vehicle. One was a short, fat, slightly balding white man, and the other was a tall, thin, black-haired Indian man. The two men automatically placed their pistols on a nearby weapons rack before taking a step forward, smiling at Isaac who was clasping their hands in joy.

'Glen! Rahul! You are both a sight for sore eyes,' Isaac boomed and he laughed heartily. He stepped forward and slapped the black-haired Indian man on the shoulder. 'Rahul, you crafty old dog. We assumed you were dead when we lost contact with you!'

Rahul rubbed the back of his neck and let out a long, grateful sigh. 'There were a couple of moments when we thought we weren't going to make it back.' He pressed his lips together and gave his friend, whom Zoe guessed was the one called Glen, a dirty look. Zoe was sure she noticed a bit of tension between the two men as she watched Glen awkwardly lower his head. Rahul's mouth set in a hard line and he shook his head. 'Some weird shit was happening in the city. There were times we thought we would not make it out of Pons Aelius alive.'

Zoe noticed something odd – the tendons in Em's jaw look like they had tightened. Was she angry? Had these men done something to annoy her? However, no sooner than it appeared, than it vanished. Appearing to keep her emotions in check, Em smiled as she took a step forward and shook their hands.

'I'm pleased you made it back in one piece.' She lifted her head towards the vehicle with a raised eyebrow. 'Your message said you were bringing a package.'

A secretive smile passed between the two men and then Rahul nodded to Glen, who spun round and dashed over to the back of the vehicle. He gave his inquisitive leader a lopsided grin as he pointed to the vehicle.

A secretive smile passed between the two men and then Rahul nodded to Glen, who spun round and dashed over to the back of the vehicle. He gave his inquisitive leader a lopsided grin as he pointed to the vehicle.

'Just wait and see what we have to show you,' he said enthusiastically, waving his hands as he backed away from Em. 'This will blow your mind, Boss!'

Em and Isaac tilted their heads and glanced at each other with raised eyebrows. They moved slowly towards the vehicle and then both gasped as Glen pulled back a cover to reveal what was in the back of the truck.

'Wha … Wha …' Em stammered, her eyes widening in disbelief. 'I mean, how?'

Curious to see what they were talking about, Zoe frowned and slowly edged closer to get a better look at what was in the back of the vehicle. But as she stepped closer, she too gasped in shock. Horrified, she staggered back on recognising the figure in the truck and found herself struggling to breathe; it was like somebody had punched her in the stomach.

Laid out on an old, tattered mattress was the injured body of a tall red-haired woman wearing a torn black and gold Imperial officer's uniform. From her injuries, it was clear she'd had been badly beaten. But there was no doubt in Zoe's mind … it was General Cooper.

Enraged by the idea her comrades had done something reckless, Em rounded on Rahul, grabbed him by the collar of his jacket and pulled him towards her. Her body trembled with rage and her lips were drawn back in a snarl. 'What happened? Tell me … *now!*'

Rahul visibly flinched under the intensity of the furious woman's gaze. He glanced nervously at Glen, who took a discreet step back and lowered his head as if he was trying to avoid being seen. Rahul lowered his eyes and let out a long, reluctant breath.

'Remember, you had ordered us to contact one of our informants for some classified information?' he murmured hesitantly. The corners of Em's eyes creased as she gave a small nod of acknowledgement. 'We had been waiting at the rendezvous for about twenty minutes and by that time our informant was already ten minutes overdue. We were getting twitchy when something strange happened to the people walking around on the street.'

Not liking where this was heading, Em cocked her head and then released her grip on Rahul's collar and dropped her hands. 'What do you mean … strange?'

The sweat glistening off his brow, Rahul swallowed, massaged the back of his neck and then shrugged his shoulders, shaking his head. 'Men and women were walking around as normal, and then they just suddenly stopped dead. Everyone, and I mean everyone – civilians, centurions, law enforcement officers, et cetera, all became still with blank hypnotic stares on their faces. Then, with no warning, they all turned and walked in the same direction, towards the centre of the city where the Empire's science division is held. That was when Glen decided to—'

Before Rahul could finish telling his side of the story, Glen interrupted him by jumping in front of Em, speaking in an almost pleading tone. 'Em, don't you understand, we never had a bet—' Em silenced him with a withering scowl. He blanched, lowered his head, and moved awkwardly back.

Em continued to glare angrily at the man before drawing her attention back to Rahul and raising her hand to him. 'Continue.'

Rahul croaked as he continued with his story. 'Glen started the truck and at first I thought he was taking us out of the city, but when I looked, he was taking us towards the city centre, towards the science building.' He paused and shot his pale-faced friend a fleeting glance before continuing. 'I asked him what he was doing, and he turned to me with a determined expression on his face and said we would never have another opportunity like this again to give the Empire a message by killing a high-ranking officer. He thought this was the perfect chance to kill General Cooper.'

The unhappy man looked heavenward and then laughed bitterly as he took a step back from the quietly seething Em. He threw up his hands in an almost pleading gesture and began to speak very quickly. 'Em, I tried my best to talk him out of it, but he was adamant – he believed it was the best thing to do.

When I tried to get control of the truck, he pointed his gun at me and said I was either with him or against him.' He gave his grim-faced partner an icy stare. 'He flew the truck and stopped it just below the general's apartment. We were still arguing when without warning there was an explosion above us, pieces of shattered glasses raining down around us, and then …' He stopped, inhaled slowly, shook his head and then threw his hands in the air, giving Em an unbelieving look. 'The next thing, we saw General Cooper falling out of the window. Don't know whether somebody threw her out or whether she jumped, but she was falling fast towards the ground. I didn't hesitate. I just took control of the truck and flew under the general and used our momentum to catch her in the cargo compartment. She landed hard, but she was alive, although barely. Not sure whether it was from her injuries or her rough landing, but she was in a bad way.'

As she listened to Rahul's story, Em's anger grew, and she felt her throat muscles tighten. She pressed her lips together and glanced over to the general's body in the back of the truck. Her voice had a slight edge as she murmured to the visibly sweating man. 'So, what did you do then?'

Rahul let out a harsh breath and rubbed his forehead. 'I realised we were in deep shit.' He put his head back, looked up at the ceiling and let out a small, bitter laugh. 'I wasn't sure someone had alerted law enforcement to what had happened at the general's apartment, but Glen and I both agreed the best course of action was to head straight to the nearest safe house and hold up until things had quietened down.' He stared at the body in the back of the truck with a sad expression. 'We tended to Cooper's injuries as best as we could, but she was quite delirious and she kept slipping in and out of consciousness. Eventually, we decided to risk it and leave the safe house. As we made our way here, we travelled low and slow to avoid being detected.'

Reflecting on his story, Em bobbed her head at Rahul in understanding and gently tapped him on the arm. But as she focused her attention back on Glen, she was filled with a mixture of anger and disappointment. 'What were you thinking, Curry? You stupid fool,' she spat. 'Do you realise what would have happened if you had carried out what you had intended?'

The man's steel-grey eyes blinked in confusion. He spun round in a circle and threw his hands in the air. 'Of course I know!' He said vehemently, his eyes narrowing as he stared at the enraged woman, his face screwing up with hatred.

'We are at war, and in war you have to make tough choices. We needed to deliver the Empire a message – they needed a wake-up call!'

Not believing what she was listening to, Em shook her head and let out a mirthless laugh. 'And what about the consequences?' she snapped, rounding on the sneering man and angrily pointing her finger at his chest. 'Did you consider what the Empire would do if we assassinated one of their high-ranking officers?' The man visibly shrank back as Em continued to scold him, 'You *didn't think*, did you? You didn't think they would have come at us with all the power at their disposal. They would have punished the civilian population first and then our families.'

Em could tell from the way the veins on the sides of Glen's forehead were throbbing that he was unhappy at being spoken to in such way. But she didn't care. As far as she was concerned, he'd had always been a loose cannon, never willing to the toe the line. What was it going to take for her to get through that thick skull of his that he needed to be a team player?

Glen straightened and gave his leader a challenging stare. 'Then perhaps it's time we stirred things up.' His lips drew back in a snarl and he sneered at Em. 'We've been fighting this war for centuries and some of us have had to endure the Empire's treatment first hand, but you're not from this world, so you wouldn't know a thing about that.' The corner of his mouth curled up and he let out a contemptuous snort of laughter. 'You are a coward – you just want to play nice and play it safe until you can make it back home.'

How dare he! Em balled her hands into tight fists but remained silent as she watched Glen wheel round and glare at the surrounding people. 'I say it's time we send the Empire a message of our own.' He pointed to the semi-conscious figure of Cooper who was still lying in the back of the truck. 'I say we execute General Cooper now and hang her where her people can find her. They will soon get the message of what it's like to live in fear.'

On hearing murmurs of agreement from the people surrounding her, Em knew she needed to deal with Glen now before things spiralled out of her control. No, she hadn't worked so hard to get this unit together only to have it stolen from her. If she allowed this back-stabbing bastard to get away with calling her a coward, she would lose the respect of those who followed her. No, he needed to be dealt with swiftly and publicly. Em let out a loud guttural snarl and charged toward Glen. His smile faded and the colour drained from his face as he spun round and saw the rage-filled woman charging towards him. He blew out his cheeks and gasped in pain as she slammed him against the side of the truck.

Rahul moved forward as if to intervene but was stopped by a firm hand on his arm. He spun round and his eyes blazed at Isaac who had grabbed him. He opened his mouth, but the intimidating man shook his head and gave him an icy stare.

Fuelled by her desire to teach Glen a lesson, Em pressed him hard against the side of the truck. He squeezed his eyes shut as her forearm pressed into his neck. 'How dare you?' Em's voice was thick with emotion as she hissed sharply at him. 'How dare you say I don't know about suffering? I have suffered at the hands of the Empire just as much as anybody in this room. At least you had the chance to grow up with your family. I never got the chance to know mine properly.' Her blood boiling, she angrily stabbed her finger towards the back of the truck. '*They* kidnapped me from my world when I was a young child. *They* tortured me! *They* beat me! Humiliated me. *They* even took my daughter from me. So don't tell me I haven't suffered.'

Overcome with emotion, Em squeezed her eyes shut and then lowered her arm from Glen's throat and stepped away from him. Tears running down his cheeks, Glen groaned, let out a wheezy cough and slid down the side of the truck, collapsing onto the floor.

Her eyes filled with tears, Em lifted her head and glared at the surrounding people. 'Don't you see – we need to be better than the Empire if we want to beat them.' Her voice full of emotion, she held up her hand and gestured to the knife she was holding. 'Not with this, but with this!' She paused and stabbed her palm onto the left side of her chest, indicating her heart. 'If we are to survive, then we must stop this endless cycle of death and turn it into something greater. If we don't, then none of us will be saved, and then we, the Empire and even Terra itself will just be a memory.' She turned in a slow circle to look at the people around her and held out her hands as she pleaded with them. 'Don't you see – the day we take that first step down that dark path and act like the Empire, then we are no better than them.' The people lowered their eyes and Em smiled thinly at the murmurs of agreement. She sighed and pointed at Glen, stunned, on the floor. 'For the day we act like those we're fighting against is the day we have lost.'

Without waiting for a response, Em took a slow step towards Glen, bent down and extended her hand to him. He peered up at her and blinked in surprise. He nodded slowly and clasped her hand, wincing as she pulled him to his feet.

'I ... I'm sorry, Em,' he croaked, 'I will continue to do as you say.'

Em gave him a half smile and placed her hand on his shoulder. 'That's good.'

But she wasn't going to let him off that easy. Deciding she still needed make example of him, Em swung round in one fluid motion and connected with Glen's jaw in a well-timed roundhouse kick. The dazed man collapsed onto the floor and blinked in confusion as Em kneeled, grabbed his throat, and snarled at him.

'You ever call me a coward to my face again, Curry, I will gut you where you stand! Understood?' Em turned to two men who were standing next to her, staring at her in amazement. She tried to hide the contempt in her voice as she waved dismissively. 'Take him down to medical, I think he's just had a nasty fall.'

Em flinched as she felt a hand touch her shoulder, and wheeled round to see Isaac standing next to her, whose eyes were flickering with concern as he gave her an enquiring look.

'You okay, Boss Lady?' he muttered in a concerned voice and pointed towards the groaning man being carried away. There was a touch of awe in his voice as he smiled at his friend. 'That was quite a powerful speech you gave there. It left quite an impression on us.'

Em tapped Isaac's hand gratefully and shrugged. 'He caught me by surprise, I'm afraid, and I lost my temper. He'll probably be nursing a grudge for a couple of days. I'm just sorry Zoe had to see that.' Her forehead creased as she glanced over her shoulder. 'Zoe, I ...' The words died in her throat as she realised their young new recruit was longer standing next to her, 'Where's Zoe?'

On hearing a shocked gasp coming from behind them, they both spun round. Em's eyes widened in horror as she spotted the white-faced teenager standing in front of the open tailgate of the truck, holding a gun that was pointed directly at Cooper.

-16-

Moments before, while Em had been arguing with the two men, Zoe staggered away. It felt like the weight of the world was pressing down on her; her chest tightened and it felt as if she was struggling to breathe. Zoe squeezed her eyes shut, but all she could hear was the loud pounding of her heart in her ears.

She slowly opened her eyes, looked around the vast bay and blinked. It felt like she was looking through a fisheye lens. She came to a stop as she bumped into the side of a workstation, then closed her eyes, placed her hands on the side of a nearby weapons rack and took in a deep breath. She opened her eyes and spotted the pistol that Glen had been holding just moments earlier.

Distracted by the heated conversation happening between his comrades, the person who was supposed to be guarding the weapons rack ignored Zoe and abandoned their post to get a better view of the increasingly heated argument. Her hands trembling, Zoe seized the opportunity and took the small pistol off the rack, and, her chest rising and falling in rapid breaths, she turned and crept up to the open tailgate of the truck. Tears streaming down her cheeks, Zoe lifted the weapon in her trembling hands and pointed it at the figure in front of her. No, she was not going to allow that woman to hurt anyone else ever again.

Zoe gritted her teeth and clicked off the weapon's safety catch. Cooper's eyes flickered open and she lifted her head. 'Hello, Zoe, good to see you again,' she said, smiling weakly, 'I see you've found yourself a new bunch of friends to play with.' She smiled and nodded at the weapon that was pointed at her. 'I guess from the way you are holding that gun, you want to kill me.'

Don't listen to her! She'll say anything to save her own life. Determined she was going to make Cooper pay for what she'd had done to her, Zoe wiped the tears from her eyes, nodded silently and pressed her lips together. She gripped the weapon tightly in her hands and edged a step closer to her. Her hands began to tremble and she suddenly became aware at how heavy the weapon felt her hands. She gritted her teeth and shook her head – No, she must remain strong. She needed … no, she *had* to do this.

Cooper winced as she eased herself up and her lips drew back in a snarl. She glared at Zoe defiantly, rasping in a hoarse voice, 'Let me make it easier for you, girl. I forgive you for what you are about to do. If our situations were reversed, I would do the same thing. I know it doesn't make any difference, but I apologise for what I did to you.' She looked heavenward and laughed bitterly. 'It doesn't matter if you don't pull that trigger, we're all dead either way.'

Don't listen to her. Pull the trigger! In no mood to listen to the lying words coming out of her former tormentor's mouth, Zoe tightened her jaw in determination and tried to drown out the woman's words. She squeezed her eyes shut and felt the weapon slip in her hands like it had suddenly become too heavy to hold. Her breathing quickened and she tried to adjust her grip, but she felt the weapon slip again in her trembling sweaty hands. Why couldn't she not pull the trigger? Zoe hesitated and she started to wonder whether she was doing the right thing.

'Zoe.'

Startled, Zoe jumped at the soft voice coming from behind her. She opened her eyes and looked over her shoulder to see Em creeping up next to her. Em placed her hand compassionately on Zoe's trembling shoulder, shaking her head as she slowly put her hand on the weapon in her shaking hands.

Em nodded at the weapon in the teenager's hands and said, 'Zoe, you don't want to do this. Let me have the gun, please.'

With tears streaming down her face, Zoe pressed her lips together and then looked wide eyed at the pleading woman. Her throat tightened and she spoke in a low, wavering voice. 'She needs to die. Don't you see, she must pay for what she has done.'

'Yes, sweetheart, and she will pay,' Em whispered softly and pointed to the figure in the truck. 'But not like this – this is what she wants. If you do this, she has won, and you will never come back from it.' For a moment, Zoe caught a haunted look in Em's eyes. 'Believe me when I say, I understand.'

Yes. She is right, isn't she? Numb, Zoe lowered her head and stared at the weapon in her hands. She dropped the weapon into Em's outstretched hand and sobbed, burying her head into Em's chest. Em handed the weapon to Isaac.

As she cradled the distraught teenager in her arms, Em stroked her head gently and continued to whisper to her in a low soothing voice. 'It's okay sweetheart, I've got you.' She lifted her head above Zoe's and gave Cooper an intense stare. 'General Wendy Cooper, you are hereby placed under arrest by the Humanity Liberation Front and when you have recovered from your injuries, you will be tried for your crimes against humanity.'

Cooper shook her head and laughed mirthlessly, wheezing, 'Oh, I expect we'll all be dead before that happens. I'm sure you've discovered something has happened in the Greater Chinese Republic's territory.'

Em raised an eyebrow and looked over her shoulder at Isaac, who frowned and took a step closer. She nodded slightly, answering the wheezing woman in a worried tone. 'We lost contact with our operatives within their territory. We assumed something had happened, but we haven't been able to learn what.' She gave the semi-conscious woman a suspicious look. 'Do you know? Was the Empire responsible?'

'Ye—' Cooper coughed bitterly, which turned into an unhealthy rattling bark. She winced as she tried to straighten herself, swallowed and weakly nodded as she gasped for air. 'Y … yes, and no. The Empire wasn't responsible, but I know what was. I'm sure you detected a gamma-ray burst across the Republic's territory.' She paused and Em nodded in confirmation. 'W … well, you see, a burst of gamma radiation will destroy all organic life in the affected area. I'm sure you will probably have worked out by now how big an area has been affected.'

Em scratched her head and looked at Cooper hesitantly. 'Yes, it covered …' Her voice trailed off as the words caught in her throat. A light bulb flashed in her head and realisation dawned on her as the implications of Cooper's statement struck home. Her hands rose to her mouth, and she muttered in a low, horrified voice, 'No ... but that would mean ...'

Pale faced, the general lowered her eyes and let out a long rattling breath. 'Yes. At this point, there will be nothing left alive in the Republic's territory. Anything organic would have been killed, whether it was plant, animal, man, woman or childr—'

Em turned at shocked gasps from the people who had slowly gathered behind her. She stared down at Zoe and shook her head in disbelief. Had the world gone suddenly mad? Who in their right mind would do such a thing? Yes, the Empire had their faults but even they wouldn't stoop so low that they would kill innocent women and children.

Angered by the senseless loss of life, Em lifted her head back up and glared accusingly at Cooper. 'Who did it? You said the Empire wasn't responsible. Surely you must know?'

Cooper nodded weakly and coughed, letting out a harsh wheeze. 'Y ... yes, a-a ... a sentient computer virus called Oracle.' She sucked in a lungful of air and let out a hollow laugh. 'It somehow infected our systems and was able to develop and launch gamma-ray weaponized satellites in secret. I found out, and it tried to kill me.' She paused to give her interrogator a wry smile. 'Which is how I ended up in the predicament I am in now.'

Em's eyes grew round and she stared at Cooper in disbelief. 'Who made it? Where did it come from?'

The injured Imperial officer grimaced as she tried to shrug her shoulders. 'I ... don't know.' Em detected a note of hesitation in the injured woman's voice and guessed she was lying about something, 'All I know is that every adult who was wearing an obedience collar across the Empire will be now under her control. She has basically created an army of cyber-drones, all willing to do her bidding, ready to invade and assimilate her next target.'

Em's brow furrowed as she picked up on something Cooper had said and was filled with a sense of dread. She looked questioningly at the injured woman. 'You said every adult is now under her control, but what of the children? What happened to them?'

Cooper blinked and stared at her captor uncertainly. 'I don't know. All I know is what she told me.' There was a touch of fear in her eyes as she lowered them and gazed at Zoe. 'But trust me when I say this – whatever she has planned for the children will not be good. If I know anything about her, it will probably involve them being used in some way when she completes her assimilation of her target.'

An icy hand clutched Em's heart and she felt a shiver run down her spine as she peered down at the teenager in her arms. Before she could ask any further questions, she was interrupted by Isaac. He coughed, stepped forward and gave Cooper a bewildering look.

'What target? But you said she has already wiped out the Greater Chinese Republic. Apart from the Empire, who else can she assimilate?' Isaac asked worriedly.

A menacing smile crossed the injured woman's face, and she lifted her hand to point her finger at Zoe. Em blinked and looked down at Zoe, feeling a mixture of fear and confusion. She furrowed her brow and looked at Cooper in confusion. A second later, she felt the blood drain from her face as she realised what Cooper meant.

Em swallowed and felt her throat tighten. 'It …' Her voice caught in the back of her throat, and she swallowed, forcing the words out. Her voice was thick with fear as she spoke in a low voice. 'I … it's planning to attack my world next.' She blinked and looked at Cooper warily. 'When is it planning to do it?'

The deathly pale woman shook her head weakly, but then her eyes began to close, and she murmured incoherently, 'It'stoolatethey … have … alrea …' Cooper's head fell back and she became still.

Isaac jumped up into the truck and knelt next to the still figure. He extended his hand and touched the side of her throat. He grumbled in annoyance and shook his head. 'It's no good, she has passed out. I'm surprised she has lasted this long.'

Em blew out her cheeks and nodded her head as she stared at the unconscious woman. 'Take her down to medical. As soon as she wakes up, I want to be informed straight away. I have a lot of questions for her, and I think we're going to need her for what is coming.'

Isaac waved his hand at two people. They gave him a questioning look and he pointed to Cooper's body on the truck. 'Get a gurney and take her down to medical. Be as gentle as possible when you lift her – she is injured.' The couple nodded and dashed over to the other side of the bay to collect a gurney. Isaac looked back at Em with a raised eyebrow. 'So, what now, Boss?'

Em rubbed her chin and lifted her shoulder in a half shrug. 'You know what they say, the enemy of my enemy is my friend.'

Isaac's grey eyes narrowed suspiciously as he stared at the body on the truck. 'Do you trust her? Did you believe that crap about some psychotic artificial intelligence?'

Blowing a small puff of air out of her cheeks, Em held up her hands and shrugged. 'No, but until I can speak to her properly, we just have to rely on her word.' She tapped her bottom lip thoughtfully as she watched Cooper being lifted off the truck. 'We will need her for what we will have to do.'

'You have a plan, Boss? Care to share?' Isaac asked curiously and tilted his head at his friend with an arched eyebrow.

Em massaged her temples with her fingers, sighed in resignation and shook her head. 'I have the formation of one and it will probably be risky, but I will need to speak to the general first when she regains consciousness. Also, I need you to contact the other cells to inform them what has happened, if they haven't found out already, that is. I am going to need everyone if what I have planned is to work.'

Isaac gave a slight nod of acknowledgement. 'I will get right on that now, Boss.'

Before he could walk away, Em placed her hand on his arm to stop him. His eyes grew round as she took a step towards him and spoke to him in a low voice.

'Isaac, I will be asking a lot of you and everybody in this unit in the coming days.' She clasped his hands in hers. Suddenly she felt weary as if the weight of the world rested on her shoulders. 'What I will be asking of you all is going to be dangerous, and I need to know if I have your support.'

Isaac blinked, and his mouth curved into a smile as he tapped her hand. 'That's the thing, Em. You don't need to ask. There isn't a soul in this unit who is not willing to give their life for you.' He bowed respectfully at her. 'You lead, and we will follow you, even if it is through the gates of Tartarus itself.'

Her eyes brimming with tears, Em watched the gentle giant sprint away from her. Her eyes followed him as he barrelled out of the bay. She'd had been a scared eight-year-old girl when she first arrived on this world. Feeling alone and afraid, she'd had barely been on this world for less than a day before she was introduced to people like herself, in particular a strapping teenager called Isaac. They had bonded straight away, with the young Isaac acting as her protector. Forty-five years later their bond was still strong as ever and showed no signs of weakening. Em shook her head and exhaled sadly as she wondered if Isaac knew just how much he mattered to her. Pushing that thought to the back of her mind, she then lowered her head to Zoe, who had been watching silently, gave her a half smile and jerked her head in the transport-pod's direction.

'I think I need to get some fresh air,' she whispered. 'Care to join me? I have a hunch you will be interested to see what I have to show you.'

Zoe sniffed and nodded. 'Yes, that would be nice.' She looked at Em curiously. 'What is it?'

Laughing, Em waggled her eyebrows and gave Zoe a knowing wink. 'Wait and see, but as they used to say on my world, it will knock your socks off!'

Zoe chuckled and grinned at her. 'They …' She appeared to catch herself and then her cheeks flushed with embarrassment. 'Sorry, yes, we still say that.'

With Zoe following closely behind, Em headed towards the nearest transport point. She pressed her hand on the sensor on the wall and they stood in silence for a minute as they waited for the transport-pod to arrive. There was a loud ping to signal it had arrived, and the doors slid open. Em stepped into a small cabin and waited for Zoe to enter before inputting their destination into the panel on the cabin wall.

Em gripped one of the handholds that had been fixed around the cabin's interior and steadied herself as she felt the cabin give a small shudder as it began its ascent. She grinned as she watched Zoe jump and then cock her head curiously as if she was listening to the faint hum of the pod as it travelled up the shaft. As they waited for the pod to arrive at their destination, Em regarded the young girl curiously. 'Zoe, mind if I ask where you are from? I mean before you were taken, where did you live?'

Zoe's eyes flickered with sadness and gave Em a hesitant look. 'I'm from a village called Langley Park, which is about seven miles outside Durham.'

At the mention of the village's name, Em flinched and shook her head in disbelief. 'Astonishing. It is astonishing that you are from Langley Park, end up on this world and somehow you find yourself meeting me.'

'Why is that astonishing?' Zoe asked.

Em smiled affectionately and put her hand on Zoe's shoulder. 'Because I am ... was ... from Langley Park too.'

Zoe's face lit up and she stared at Em in amazement. 'Wow! Cool!' She then cocked her head and frowned. 'But what has that to do with where you are taking me now.'

Em tapped her nose with her finger and then winked at the puzzled teen. 'You'll see.' Hearing the transport-pod slow down, she puffed out her cheeks, blew out a slow breath and faced the cabin's door. 'I always like to come up here if I need to clear my head. It always reminds me of home as a young girl before I was abducted and brought to this world.'

Zoe tilted her head and gave Em a sideways look. She appeared to be on the verge of saying something but was interrupted by the hiss of the cabin's door. It slid open to reveal a long, dimly lit corridor. Gesturing for Zoe to follow her, Em stepped out of the transport-pod and they walked side by side along the corridor. Em gave the teen a surreptitious look and saw she was anxiously chewing on her bottom lip. Nodding in understanding, Em knew only too well what the anxious teen must have been feeling, because she had been in the same position when she had been taken from her world forty-five years earlier, only she had been a lot younger – eight years old in fact. Hard to believe it had been so long ago – where had the time gone? Em quickly shoved the thought to one side as she realised they had come to the bottom of a flight of stairs that led up to a large metal door.

With her left hand resting reassuringly on Zoe's shoulder, Em pressed her right hand on a wall sensor beside the door. She felt Zoe flinch at the loud metal click followed by a loud squeal as the door slowly swung open to reveal daylight.

Em watched Zoe take a hesitant step through the open door and squint her eyes in the bright evening sunlight. Em lifted her hands above her head, closed her eyes and inhaled. She let out a contented breath, lowered her head to Zoe and beamed at her.

The corners of Zoe's eyes creased and she shook her head in confusion. Em felt she was on the verge of asking what she was talking about, but stopped, recognition dawning across her face. Em guessed from the expression on Zoe's face that the penny had dropped and she understood what was being shown to her.

Her eyes glistening with tears, Zoe slowly turned and gazed down at the scenery around her. She looked at Em and nodded in understanding.

Coming from the same village as Zoe, Em knew only too well what the teen was feeling. Before she had been abducted, one of the things Em had enjoyed the most was taking the bus into Durham with her sister, Claire, and walking up the cobbled streets to visit the cathedral and the adjacent castle. She remembered the exhilaration of climbing the three hundred and twenty-five steps to the top of the cathedral's central tower and staring down onto the river and city below.

Overcome with emotion and feeling tears flow down her cheeks, Em moved towards the edge of the hilltop and stared down at the river below, as wound its way through the surrounding countryside. Even though the landmarks were slightly different and they were standing on a different world, it was obvious that they were standing where Durham should have been, in virtually the same spot they had stood as young children gazing at the city below.

Grinning with delight, Zoe nodded approvingly. 'It's beautiful.'

Em let out a soft groan as she carefully lowering herself onto a large stone and nodded. 'Yes, it is. Whenever I come up here, it always reminds me of home, just before I was taken.' She blinked away the tears but continued to speak. 'Standing on this hill overlooking the river always reminds me of happier times, of when I was a child when my parents used to bring my sister and me to visit the cathedral. We would laugh as we climbed the winding staircase up to the roof and stare down at the city below, and our eyes would follow the river as it wound its way past the city.'

Zoe nodded in understanding. 'Yes, when I was younger, my friends and I did the same whenever we visited Durham. To be honest, I don't think there has been a single soul growing up in the area who hasn't done the same thing at one time in their lives.' She took a step closer to Em and spoke in a low, hesitant voice. 'Em, can I ask what happened to you?'

Em tapped her hand on the stone and gave the hesitant teenager a kind smile. 'You probably have guessed, but Em is short for Emma. Before I arrived here, I went by Emma Tulley. I was much younger than you when I was taken.' Her face hardened as she thought back to the events of her childhood. 'My sister and I had been playing one night and we'd had gotten into an argument. She said some nasty things to me, and I ran downstairs to be away from her.' She shook her head and looked heavenward. 'I went into the kitchen to sit next to our dog, Sandy. I can remember Sandy growling at something and then the next thing I know, something monstrous attacked me. I remember screaming for help as it came towards me.'

Zoe raised her hand to her mouth, horrified. 'Didn't someone hear you?'

Em let out a bitter laugh. 'Oh yes, someone did. My sister heard. She was standing in the doorway and watched the creature creep toward me.' She let out a harsh breath and shook her head. 'I will never forgive the cowardly little bitch for the way turned her back on me and ran away.'

Her eyes filled with sympathy; Zoe placed a hand on Em's shoulder. They sat in silence and watched the setting sun lowering over the horizon. Em could just about make out the glow of the lights from Pons Aelius in the distance.

'Em, you're planning on going back to our world, aren't you?' Zoe asked sadly. 'Will you take me with you?'

Em looked down at Zoe intently. 'You realise it will be dangerous and we may not survive.'

Zoe pursed her lips and nodded in understanding. 'Yes, I understand, but you're going to need someone to watch your back.' Her jaw tightened and she looked up to Em. 'I promise I'll not turn my back on you the way your sister did.'

Em fought back the tears and swallowed. 'Oh, sweetheart, you don't realise how much that means to me.' She leaned forward and kissed Zoe's forehead, then smiled as Zoe lowered her head to rest it on Em's shoulder. They watched wordlessly as the sun disappeared over the horizon.

Em thought about the events to come; about how they would not only be fighting for the survival of one world, but two. As she lifted her head heavenward and gazed at the infinite darkness, her mind drifted to thoughts of a new day and what it may bring. She closed her eyes and thought ... *'Tomorrow the real fight begins.'*

ACT THREE

Two months later...

-1-

Sunitra Sinchettrra's blog – Voice of the resistance
Occupation day 58

It has been fifty-eight days since the events of 16 October 2023, forever to be known as Beijing Day – the day the world woke up to the horrific news of the destruction of Beijing. The number of dead rises each day, but so far officials estimate thirty million people lost their lives in a matter of seconds all because a malevolent AI wanted to send a message to the world's governments – *'This is what happens if you resist'*. For a moment, it was as if the world seemed to stop, as if the world's entire population collectively held their breath, waiting to become the next victims in this inhuman monster's twisted game.

Gradually, as it did during the Coronavirus pandemic, life returned to normal for the world's civilian population as they adjusted to lift under the invaders. At first, people resented the restrictions placed upon them as they adapted to life under martial law, living under a curfew, and watching armed troops patrol their neighbourhoods. But, as time passed, they carried on like they did before and the world settled into a routine, accepting the restrictions placed upon them. The irony of it all is that most of the world's civilian population have welcomed martial law because of the constant presence of armed troops; it has seen crime cut down to next to nothing, and they feel lucky because, for the first time in their lives, there is peace in the world.

But the harsh truth is it is the peace of the gun. The internet, once freely available to the world, is now heavily policed by the omnipresent AI. All major news networks walk a fine line because they know if they push too far, the enemy will shut their stations down and their reporters will be arrested and imprisoned. Any voice of dissent is quickly stamped out.

The world's various police services and remaining armed forces now operate under the oversight of our merciless oppressor. I have gathered reports, sometimes witnessed by me, of some police officers relishing the freedom given to them by acting as judge, jury, and executioner.

But during these dark times, there have also been moments that have inspired hope. While it is true that most of the world's armed forces are now under the invaders' control, there are still fractions of the military hard at work fighting against the new regime. But despite their hyper-advanced technology, it has become apparent that our world is more advanced in our nautical technology. Although the enemy has a great number of advanced aircraft, land vehicles and sailing ships, they appear lacking in a certain area. I have heard rumours that before the occupation, governments ordered their submarine fleets to sea and to maintain radio silence. Rumours circulate of foreign submarine crews, once divided, now operating together in joint missions as they work to strike at the tyrannical regime from below the waves.

Over the past month, I have received other inspirational news. North Korea, once a haven for totalitarian regimes, now finds itself a haven for those seeking to escape the enemy. The North Koreans' once secretive nature was a major factor in weeding out the plague of doppelgängers that weakened many of the world's governments over the years. Expecting to see them suffer the same fate as Beijing, it surprised me when I first heard this news, that they continue to be a beacon of light against the darkness, using an energy shield that surrounds and protects their country. How they came to gain this technology is beyond me, but it is something that requires further investigation.

I have received other stories of another haven against the darkness that is using the same shield technology, which I believe, surprisingly, has possibly been shared by the North Koreans. Hawaii, once a paradise for holidaymakers, now finds its harbour once again a refuge for the varied submarine fleets while they work tirelessly to strike against the other-dimensional invaders.

Here in the United Kingdom, I continue my search to track down the ever-elusive resistance group known as *the Castle*. I continue to hope that today is the day when I will contact one of the resistance cells that will lead me to their hierarchy. My only hope is that I can convince them that I can be their voice, record their struggle, so that future generations may one day read of our fight against the darkness.

I hope that one day my blog will help to inspire people to rise up and fight against the forces we find ourselves under. Unfortunately, as they have some many times before, our oppressor will delete this as soon as I post it. But perhaps this is the day when it evades its ever-omnipresent eye, allowing one person to read it and pass on my message of resistance.

But I refuse to be silenced, not by an artificial monster with delusions of

ORACLE'S VISION

grandeur and certainly not by the British Government that willingly stood back and did nothing while darkness infected it until it was too late. The day will come when I stand before that inhuman thing and those who collaborated with it and report to the world when they are finally punished for their crimes against humanity. If I am still alive to witness that, I hope I can spit in its fabricated face and ask: was it worth it? Was it worth the death of my friend, Darren Young, and the deaths of so many millions after that? How many more deaths will it take before it is satisfied? One billion, ten?

This is Sunitra Sinchettrra, the voice of the resistance. If you read this, then spread my word – that we must fight against the darkness. Never give up, never surrender.

Finally, I send this message to Oracle. If you are reading this before you delete it, know this: you cannot silence me. For as long as I have free will, I will continue to resist you. I am that annoying itch you cannot get at.

Same time tomorrow, you synthetic witch.

.

-2-

Location: Aston Villa Football Club car park, Birmingham, England

The cursor hung threateningly over the send icon as if it was waiting for the laptop's user trembling hand to tap on her device's mouse pad, allowing the small icon to carry out its function. The cursor quivered ever so slightly, like it had a mind of its own, impatiently telling the laptop's operator to get on with it. Then again, it may have been down to the briefest touch of a shaking bitterly cold hand exposed to the frosty night air. But it was not the December air that caused Sunitra's hands to tremble, but the moment of self-doubt plaguing her mind as she wondered once again whether what she was doing was worth it.

Sunitra knelt in front of her laptop and winced as she felt the cold December air stab at the wound on her thigh. She hissed with annoyance, and it came out as a puff of steam as her breath was exposed to the frigid air. She felt a stab of pain coming from her maimed leg. Maybe it was just a coincidence or maybe it was trying to remind her why she was doing this; she didn't care because the pain helped cast any doubts that she may have harboured to one side. Stabbing her finger down onto her mouse pad, she smiled in satisfaction as she watched the cursor click on the send icon. She then crossed her fingers in hopefulness as her blog disappeared off her screen.

'That's it sent,' she murmured to the thin, curly-haired white man standing anxiously behind her.

'Good, now let's get the hell out of here,' Peter replied, his voice thick with anxiety as he nervously glanced around him. 'I want to be out of here before they trace it. You remember what happened last time we hung around too long? One of these days, Sunitra, you are going to push our luck too far.'

Sunitra rolled her eyes and shook her head. She didn't need to turn around to know Peter was gazing intently at the back of her neck, almost imagining the intensity of his gaze burning into the back of her skull. She didn't have to be a psychic to know what was going through his mind – he was probably wondering whether what they were doing was worth it. She couldn't blame him really, because she'd had the same thoughts too ever since they had started doing this. Sunitra sucked in a long breath and pinched the bridge of her nose as she thought back to several weeks earlier, before their lives were forever changed during the battle of BBC Broadcasting House …

Sunitra Sinchettrra had been an investigative journalist and news anchor on the BBC News Channel. Peter Kirk, her life-long friend and confidant, had been her programme director for many years.

The battle had been a costly one for Sunitra; not only had a piece of debris broken loose from the studio ceiling, falling on top of her and crippling her right leg, but it also killed her close friend and fellow news anchor, Darren Young. Peter, concerned they would be arrested if he took his injured colleague to hospital, had taken her to a friend who was a doctor. For days, he had watched helplessly as she lay in bed, delirious from pain. A week later, after she eventually recovered, they consoled each other over the death of their friend and colleague.

Then one day, while still recovering, Sunitra stared up in surprise when Peter dashed into her room, full of excitement. He had learned from a close source that Oracle was allowing the BBC news services to be broadcast again, but when they switched on the TV to watch the news channel, their excitement quickly evaporated to dismay. A cold realisation settled on them, and they realised their beloved news station was now a propaganda tool hosted by a stunning young woman, her shiny white teeth gleaming as she gave a simpering smile to the camera. Sunitra's dismay quickly turned to anger as she listened to the prissy news anchor speak of her joy at being back on the air, stating terrorists had seized control of the news station and forced the people there to fake a news report. Appalled by the idea that her friend's death was being used as propaganda, she became incensed as she watched them show a fake film explaining how, in their efforts to regain control of the news station, government troops accidentally knocked out a transmitter, taking it off the air.

Determined her friend's death would not be in vain, Sunitra realised her only course of action was to speak out against the occupation, to become a voice of resistance. At first, Peter argued against the idea, fearing they would end up dead, or worse. Eventually, knowing he could not change her mind, he reluctantly agreed to help his friend and sat down with her to discuss how they would do it.

But as they discussed their plan, it quickly became apparent that the task they had set themselves was mammoth. Under Oracle's ever-omnipresent eye, the internet was no longer freely available on which to post information. Any voice of dissent was stamped down on hard, the transgressors being located and arrested.

After several hours of frustrating brainstorming, Peter stormed out of the room in annoyance. He had been standing on the roof smoking a cigarette and gazing out across the London rooftops, disgusted with himself for acting like a child. He automatically reached for his mobile phone to call Sunitra to apologise but cursed himself when he remembered phone calls were now being monitored. But just as he was about to place his phone in his pocket, he struck his palm against his forehead when he had an epiphany.

Energised with new-found optimism, Peter ran back down the stairs, jumping them three at a time, almost bowling Sunitra over. She had apparently chosen that particular moment to open the door and hobble out in search of him. She listened while he burbled excitedly about his idea to her, and she seemed elated when he eventually got her to understand what he was trying to tell her. His plan was simple: with his incredible technical expertise (his own words), he would attach Sunitra's laptop to a mobile phone mast and transmit her blog to the phones in the area that were connected to it. Of course, they were under no illusions; it was a risky plan, and they would only have a short time until their transmission was intercepted and deleted, but with luck, anyone within that small area would receive their broadcast.

For over a month, they travelled around the south of England, never spending more than one day in one location. They travelled along the back roads, carefully avoiding routes being used by armed patrols. Over the course of their careers, they had gathered a vast network of friends and sources who were very willing to help them by passing onto them pieces of information they had learned, as well as sheltering them from searching patrols.

Peter rubbed his hands together, blowing into them as he cast an impatient eye around the empty car park outside Aston Villa Football Club. They had targeted this mobile phone mast because of its central location in the belief that it would allow them to target a high percentage of Birmingham's dense population. The cold wind biting at his exposed face, his teeth chattered, and he shook his head. *We shouldn't have come here*, he thought bitterly, *we're too exposed*.

Peter frowned as he noticed Sunitra's face scrunch up in pain as she straightened up and clenched her hands around the handle of her walking stick. He pressed his lips together in silent concern as she hobbled over to him. He could tell the past two weeks had taken their toll on his friend, not only physically, but mentally. Her once beautiful glowing olive skin showed an unhealthy pallor as she puffed out her cheeks in frustration.

'Damn this cold British weather,' she moaned, limping past him. 'I'd kill for a nice hot bath right now.'

Peter shook his head and gave her a stern look, clasping her shivering hand in his. 'I wish you had allowed yourself more time to rest before we set out on this insane venture.'

'I can rest when I'm dead,' Sunitra scoffed, waving his hand away. Her mouth twitched and she gave him the side eye. 'Anyway, if I remember correctly, this *insane venture* was your idea in the first place.'

She laughed as Peter muttered something uncomplimentary under his breath. Her eyebrows drew together as the couple made their way toward a decrepit rainbow-coloured Volkswagen camper van and she grunted in annoyance as Peter opened the door for her and gave her a helping hand up into the front passenger seat. 'Tell me again why we can't travel in something more comfortable?'

Tired of the same argument, Peter exhaled and cast his hand fondly over the camper van's exterior. 'I've told you before, if we want to remain inconspicuous, then we must travel in something that won't attract attention. Nobody will give a beat-up sixties camper van a second look.'

'But ... it's a pile of shit!' Sunitra complained, her lip curling up in disgust.

Wounded, Peter held his hands up to his chest as if insulted. 'I'll have you know she is a classic.' He nodded and ran his hand affectionately along the edge of the door. 'You tell me where else could you find a vehicle with as much class as this.'

Sunitra let out a scornful laugh and reached down to buckle her seat belt, muttering under her breath, 'Probably in a junkyard.'

'Sorry, I didn't catch that,' he said with a touch of amusement.

'Oh, nothing, just complimenting the fine craftsmanship,'

Peter smiled and closed the passenger door, giving her a side eye as he strolled around the front of the van, his hand brushing against the rusted surface. He stuck out his bottom lip, shook his head and gently tapped one of the van's lights. Knowing it always annoyed his friend every time he did it, he whispered to the van in a soothing tone.

'You are a good girl, aren't you? Ignore the nasty woman. She's only jealous,' he said softly. He grinned as he caught Sunitra roll her eyes in disgust. It worked every time.

As Peter climbed into the front driver's seat, he detected the frosty atmosphere inside the vehicle's cabin and flashed Sunitra a cheeky grin. He shrugged and cast a proud eye over the van's discoloured, shabby interior. 'The old girl helped me through a lot of tight spots during my years at university,' he said proudly, glancing towards the rear of the camper van.

Sunitra raised an eyebrow and then her face twisted in revulsion. He could sense that she was putting two and two together and was about to have an *aha* moment.

Visibly cringing in disgust, Sunitra held up her hand. 'Hold on,' she gasped, 'are you telling me I'm sitting in your pussy wagon? No wonder it's filthy.' She gave him a murderous glare, snarling, 'You are a pig.'

'I haven't heard you complaining until now,' he replied, giving her a devilish smile. 'I wouldn't shine a black light around if I were you. She would probably look like a Jackson Pollock painting.'

Peter could tell Sunitra was trying not to imagine what she was sitting in but failing. He stifled a laugh as he watched her olive skin turn a shade of green, and then she put her hand over her mouth as she pretended to retch. 'Oh God! I think I'm going to be sick.'

'Relax, I was only kidding. She's perfectly clean. You've nothing to worry about.' He laughed, his hand resting on Sunitra's arm in a comforting gesture. He smirked as she relaxed and heaved a sigh of relief. He winked and reached down to turn the ignition key. 'But to be on the safe side, I wouldn't walk around in the back in your bare feet.'

'I hate you.'

Revelling his friend's discomfort, Peter chuckled as he turned the ignition key, but frowned as the engine gave a tired-sounding stutter and refused to start. He furrowed his brow in annoyance, and he continued to stamp his foot down on the clutch pedal, repeatedly turning the ignition key. Sunitra folded her arms across her chest and cocked her head at him mockingly as he listened to the sad, pathetic groan that was coming from the front engine compartment.

'Come on, you piece of shit. Start, damn you,' he snarled, slamming his hand down on the steering wheel in frustration. He let out a resigned sigh and shook his head in defeat. 'Looks like we're going to have to walk.'

'You don't say,' Sunitra replied, her tone acerbic.

Ignoring the withering gaze burning holes in the side of his head, Peter tapped his chin thoughtfully and studied the darkened empty car park whose frost-covered tarmac glinted in the cold December moonlight. He was silent, his mind racing as he considered his options. Should they risk making a run for it? He reasoned they were not too far from the safe house he had planned for them to stay in that night. With luck, they should be able to avoid any enemy troops on patrol, enforcing the evening curfew. Under normal circumstances, he would not hesitate to attempt it. He cast a concerned eye to Sunitra and quickly decided these were not normal circumstances.

His mind made up, Peter turned to Sunitra, inhaled a deep breath, and reached for her hand. She nodded in silent understanding as if answering the question before he asked it.

'Sunitra, we are going to have to make a run for it,' he said carefully, his gaze flittering down to her injured leg. 'Do you think you'll manage?'

'I am just going to have to,' Sunitra replied, her emerald eyes blazing with determination as she unfastened her seat belt.

With no further comment, Peter quickly opened his door and climbed out of his seat. He dashed around the front of the van, careful not to slip on the frosty surface. Sunitra smiled at him gratefully as he helped her out of the van, and exhaled, her breath forming a misty cloud in the crisp December air.

'I reckon it will take us about fifteen minutes to get where I had planned for us to stay tonight if we hurry,' Peter said as they hurried across the empty car park. His eyes sharpened with suspicion, searching the shadows for any sign of movement.

The bitter frosty air nipping at his fingers, Peter cast a concerned look at Sunitra as she hobbled alongside him. He heard her hiss through gritted teeth and saw that her hand was gripped tightly on the walking stick. Although he could tell the frigid December breeze was not helping the wound on her thigh, Peter couldn't help admiring her determination to soldier on through growing pain in her leg as they moved forward along the empty streets.

But as they travelled through the barren Birmingham streets, it became obvious to Peter that their pace had slowed. He tapped his tongue off the inside of his teeth and cast a concerned eye to Sunitra limping next to him. It was evident from the moonlight shining off the sweat on her forehead and her strained expression that she was struggling, so he adjusted himself and wrapped her arm around his, taking her weight. Sunitra acknowledged her friend with a gratified smile as they hurried down the street.

A sinister voice came from behind, startling them, and a concerned glance passed between the couple.

'Well, well, well. What do we have here then?'

Peter shook his head slightly as Sunitra gave him a questioning look and they bowed their heads and made to press on, ignoring the voice from behind them.

'Yo! Holmes, I'm talking to you. Didn't ya mamma ever tell you it was impolite to ignore somebody when they're talking to ya?'

Her heart thundering in her chest, Sunitra looked up at Peter in concern as he held up his hand in an *it's okay* gesture, stopped and turned slowly to face the speaker. Sunitra's chest tightened with anxiety as she turned and saw five youths who were standing staring at the couple with menacing expressions. From their young appearance, she guessed they were in their late teens, possibly nineteen or twenty years of age.

Peter gave them a friendly smile and took a small hesitant step forward, his hands raised in a placating gesture. 'I apologise if my rudeness offended you. If you allow us to be on our way, we will be out of your hair.'

One of the youths, a young black man, stepped forward and fixed Peter with a threatening stare. His gold teeth glinted in the moonlight as he sneered at him. 'Naw, man, am afraid it's too late for that. This is our neighbourhood, innit, which means you 'ave to pay the penalty.'

Peter shot Sunitra an annoyed glare as she let out a bitter laugh and moved towards the angry youth. 'Your neighbourhood? Are you for real? Don't you see what's going on? The world has been invaded and you are standing here squabbling about who gets to walk down your street?'

The young man's lip curled up and he gave Sunitra a derisive smile. 'Naw, woman.' He let out a loud howl and waved his hands around him. 'There is a new boss in the world, which means it's now the survival of the fittest.' A shiver ran down Sunitra's spine as he gave her a predatory smile. 'And that means you now belong to me.'

Peter's face darkening, he stepped towards the young man, hissing, 'Now look here, son.'

He took a step back warily as the young black youth shot forward, his face pressed into Peter's, eye blazing in anger. 'What's with all this *son* business? Do ah look like your son to you, bro?'

Peter cried out in pain as two other members of the gang, a gangly young red-haired white man and a stocky young Asian man, grabbed his arms from behind. An alarm rang in Sunitra's head as she noticed one of the youths, a young pink-haired woman, had broken away from the pack and was edging towards her with a curious expression. Sunitra anxiously shuffled her feet as the young woman stared at her with a quizzical expression.

Recognition dawned across the young woman's face and she let out a cry of delight. 'Yo, LB! Don't you know who this is? This is that reporter lady off the TV that staged that pretend news broadcast a few months ago.'

Sunitra folded her arms across her chest and gave the insolent youth a withering stare, snarling haughtily. 'I beg your pardon, young lady, but *I did not* fake that broadcast!'

'Well, well, well. Is that so?' LB grinned perversely as he stared at Sunitra. 'Ah imagine someone will pay a hefty penny for somebody like you.'

Sunitra lifted her cane in front of her in a defensive posture and her eyes darted from side to side as the young pink-haired woman and LB slowly moved toward her. She bared her teeth like a cornered animal and snarled warningly at them, 'If any of you bastards lay a hand on me, I'm going to shove this cane so far up your arse – it will be in so deep, you'll have to cough to get it out.' She narrowed her eyes and fixed them with a murderous glower. 'So unless you want to see a proctologist, I suggest you back up … *now!*'

LB put his head back and let a howl of laughter. 'Woo-eee! You are a feisty little one, aren't ya?' As he approached the cane-waving woman, he lowered his head and smiled menacingly at her. 'Ah'm sure you feel pretty confident taking one of us down, but then what? We still outnumber you. Ah say the odds are pretty much in our favour, innit?'

Still struggling to release himself from the other two youths' grip, Peter snarled at the black youth in anger, 'You little shit! You lay one on hand on her, so help me an—'

Unexpectedly, LB's face twisted in anger. He spun round, grabbed the back of Peter's neck, pulled him towards him and whispered something in his ear. Sunitra was too far away to catch what was said, their conversation lost in a cold gust of wind. The journalist cried out in alarm as she watched the youth punch the older man in the stomach. Winded, Peter slumped to the cold ground like a sack of potatoes.

'Harris, Wang,' LB barked, pointing to the two who had been holding Peter, 'take this piece of rubbish down that back alley and dispose of him.'

Feeling helpless, Sunitra forced back the tears as the two young men placed their hands under her friend's arms and dragged him down the dark alley. However, she realised she had no time to worry about Peter's fate because the sinister youth and the young pink-haired woman had now focused their attention on her. An icy shiver ran down her spine as LB fixed her with a hard stare.

It cannot happen like this, she thought, shaking her head. *I've suffered too much, already lost too many people for it to end like this.* Calmness overtaking her, Sunitra raised her cane and her fingers whitened as they gripped it tightly. She gritted her teeth and steadied herself, preparing for the attack to come.

Just then, a short wailing noise came from behind Sunitra. Distracted, she glanced over her shoulder and her heart leapt with joy as she spotted the familiar yellow and blue markings of a police car travelling slowly down the street toward her.

As if sensing his opportunity, LB lunged at Sunitra, kicking the cane out of her hand. She cried out in pain as the youth pulled her towards him and wrapped his left hand over her mouth from behind. She squeezed her eyes shut as he hissed into her ear and shuddered at his warm breath on her skin.

'Stop struggling,' he hissed. 'If you value your life, you're going to have to trust me. All is not what it appears, understand?' Sunitra gasped for air and she felt the young man's hand slacken over her mouth. She stiffened and her eyes grew wide as she felt something firm being pressed into her back. 'Make any sudden movement or try to raise the alarm and you'll live to regret it.'

Paralysed with fear, her heart thundering in her chest, Sunitra nodded in understanding and stared in silence as the police car approached them. For a moment she wondered if she dared risk shouting for help. Her throat constricted as she watched the window on the front passenger side open. But as she winced in pain from whatever what was being pressed harder into her spine, she quickly realised it was too risky. It was best she should bide her time and wait for the right opportunity to arise.

But then as the police car passed, Sunitra noticed the officer in the front passenger seat had lifted his hand out of the window and was tapping two fingers repeatedly against the top of the car door. Her eyebrows pricked up as the police officer slowly quickly lowered his hand back into the car, and then drove on like nothing out of the ordinary had happened. She pursed her lips and frowned. Was it her imagination, but did they just tap out a morse code message? Something didn't feel right. There was definitely more going on here than met the eye.

Before Sunitra had time to make sense of it, LB burst into action as soon as the police car was out of earshot and released her. He wheeled sharply to the pink-haired young woman and fixed her with a commanding stare. 'CeCe, tell the others to get prepared. A legion of cyber-drones are four minutes away, and I want to be out of here before they arrive.'

The young woman called CeCe gave her comrade a thin smile, nodded and spun on her heel. Perplexed, Sunitra watched her sprint down the alley, where her friend had been dragged moments before. LB scratched his head and turned his attention back to Sunitra.

'Ma'am, I don't have time to explain, and I apologise for what I'm about to do,' he said.

'Hey! What are you doing?' Sunitra protested as LB bent down and, without explanation, unceremoniously threw her over his shoulders in a fireman's lift.

'Sorry, ma'am,' LB puffed, sprinting down the alley, 'but with your injured leg, you would have slowed me down.'

Her face burning with humiliation, Sunitra grimaced in silence as the surprisingly fit youth hotfooted it to the end of the alley, only slowing as he approached an open doorway. Sunitra managed to lift her head up and saw CeCe was standing inside, keeping the door open. She quickly stepped aside to let them in, closing and locking it behind them. Sunitra clenched her teeth together in discomfort as LB bounded down a flight of stairs, jostling her on his shoulders. When this was over, she was going to have some seriously harsh words with LB.

Once they were at the bottom of the stairs, LB knelt and gently eased Sunitra off his shoulders. Grateful to be back on solid ground, Sunitra exhaled a huge sigh, steadying herself, and looking round to get her bearings. They were standing in the middle of a tunnel, possibly a maintenance shaft. She brushed her hand through her short hair and stared at the strange black youth in puzzlement. 'Just who are you?'

He opened his mouth to speak but was interrupted by a rapid beep from his watch. His face a mask of concentration, LB grabbed Sunitra's hands, placed them over her ears and pushed her to the ground. He crouched down, put his hands on his own ears and cried out in a loud, authoritative voice, 'Fire in the hole!'

A veteran of reporting stories from the front line of many campaigns, Sunitra felt her eyes grow wide in recognition of the warning that an explosion was about to occur. She stared at LB in bewilderment. 'Wait? Wha—'

However, before she could say any more, a deafening roar came from above, shaking the tunnel's walls and drowned her words out. She squeezed her eyes shut as the ceiling trembled violently above her, showering her with dust.

After the roar lessened and the trembling had eased Sunitra, shaken, jerked up in surprise as she felt a hand on her shoulder.

'You can take your hands off your ears now, ma'am,' LB said, helping her to her feet. He gave her a kind smile and handed her the cane he'd knocked from her hand moments earlier. 'We haven't got that much farther to walk, so you should be able to walk the rest of the way yourself.'

'You're so kind,' Sunitra replied acerbically, snatching her cane out of his hand. She cocked her head and stared at him enquiringly. 'Who the hell are you people?'

'I'm sorry, ma'am,' the mysterious youth replied apologetically, gesturing to the tunnel ceiling, 'explanations are going to have to wait. We just took out a legion of cyber-drones, so the area above us is going to be swarming with some very pissed-off people soon. I don't think they'll find that entrance, but I would like it if we were far away from this spot if they do. So, forgive me, ma'am, if we don't dawdle.'

'Fine.' Sunitra huffed unhappily and followed the two youths down the tunnel. 'But can you please stop calling me ma'am all the time? My name is Sunitra. Sunitra Sinchettrra, formerly lead news anchor on the BBC News Channel.'

'Yes, I know.' LB grinned, his gold teeth glinting in the darkness. Sunitra noticed a sudden change in the tone of his voice and that he had also switched to a more normal Birmingham accent. 'I am Corporal Leroy-Bennet Williamson, but everyone just calls me LB for short.' He nodded at the young woman next to him. 'This dazzling woman with the pink hair is Private Carrie Clarkson. We call her CeCe for short.'

'Ma'am.' CeCe bobbed her head at Sunitra in acknowledgement. Sunitra gasped as the young private pulled a pink wig off her head to reveal a short-haired brunette, who then blew out her cheeks and shook her head. 'Oh, I cannot tell you how much I hate that thing, makes my scalp really itchy.'

What was going on here? Her mind spinning with the overload of new information, Sunitra inhaled a deep breath and tried to put two and two together. Her suspicions about her friends' identities had been growing ever since she picked up on the hand signal the police officer had passed to LB. She eyed her two unlikely saviours suspiciously as they continued along the dark tunnel. They were obviously military or had received military training. But were they the resistance group she'd had been searching or just were they something else? It would be just her luck if she found out they were just small group of people working on their own, trying to inflict as much damage as they could on their oppressors. Anything was possible. But as a journalist, Sunitra had an insatiable appetite to get the truth and was desperate to get their story from these people one way or another.

Distracted by her own thoughts, Sunitra lost her balance as her foot slipped on a loose piece of ground; her leg flared in pain. She cursed at herself as she stumbled on the uneven floor of the tunnel and impatiently waved LB's hand away as they made their way down through the dimly lit tunnel. But as they hurried in silence, she raised an eyebrow on noticing the familiar outline of Peter appeared ahead. He appeared to be leaning against the tunnel wall talking to the two young men who had dragged him away earlier.

'Peter!' she cried out, not hiding her delight.

Peter smiled warmly, embracing his friend, but gasped in pain as Sunitra pulled away from him and punched him hard on his arm. He rubbed his arm and stared at his friend in confusion.

'What was that for?' he complained.

'That's for making me think you were dead,' Sunitra snapped. She frowned in irritation and punched him again for good measure.

'Hey! Will you stop hitting me!' Peter protested, trying to block her hand from striking his arm and pointing to the small group of people around them. 'It was their idea.'

A firm cough silenced Sunitra as LB raised his fingers to his lips, gestured to the ceiling above and murmured in a quiet but firm voice, 'Sorry, people, playtime is over. I'll explain everything as soon as we're safely away from here.'

Sunitra arched her head curiously as the young soldier took a small step toward the tunnel wall. He appeared to look at something above him, and then tapped two fingers on his forehead. Her jaw dropped open as she watched part of the tunnel wall slid open to reveal a hidden elevator. LB gave Sunitra a golden toothy grin and bowed, indicating for them to enter the lift.

After making sure everybody was safely through the elevator doors, the

ORACLE'S VISION

soldier cast an eye quickly down the dark tunnel before he stepped inside. The panel on the wall closed, leaving nothing but the rats to scurry around in the eerie darkness.

-3-

After the elevator doors had closed, Sunitra cocked her head at the faint hum of motors coming from somewhere above her. The elevator juddered slightly, and she put her hand on Peter's arm to steady herself. Peter fixed the black youth with a steady gaze and Sunitra swallowed anxiously at the uneasy silence in the cabin.

'LB,' Peter said curtly.

'Kirk,' the young man replied, his voice neutral and flat.

The two men's mouths widened into broad grins, and they embraced in a friendly hug. Sunitra folded her arms across her chest, scowling at the laughing men.

'I take it you know each other?' she asked dryly.

Peter nodded and gave her a lopsided grin. 'Oh yes, we've known each other for a few years now. LB was actually my contact here in Birmingham. He came to search for us when we didn't arrive at the rendezvous.'

'Oh, I see,' Sunitra said. 'Am I to assume this young hood disguise is because of ...' She let the sentence hang and indicated for the young soldier to finish.

'Yes, you're right,' LB replied, pausing to remove the gold grill from his mouth and screwing up his face in disgust. 'Ugh! I hate those things. Anyway, to answer your question. Yes, we had to put on that show because we weren't sure whether we were being watched. We've had reports that the enemy is using some type of camera drones to spy on the civilian population.' He lifted his shoulder in an apologetic shrug. 'Sorry for scaring you, but we had to make it look good.'

'I realise that, mate,' Peter said with a pained expression and rubbing his stomach, 'but what about that punch? Did you really have to punch me in the stomach that hard?'

Savouring the moment, LB grinned, lifted his hands and put on a thick Birmingham accent. 'I was in the moment.'

Sunitra studied the young man thoughtfully as he sparred with Peter. When they had first met, she had assumed, because of their clothing and their mannerisms, that the group were in their late teens. But, now in the light, she had the chance to see them better and realised they were probably in their early-to-mid-twenties.

'So,' she asked carefully, 'am I to assume I'm speaking to the resistance?'

The joyous laughter suddenly ceasing, the soldier's expression sobered, and he turned Sunitra with a serious expression. He rubbed his chin thoughtfully and nodded slightly. 'You could say that.' he answered hesitantly.

The pieces finally coming together in her mind, Sunitra stroked her chin and paced around the small space inside the elevator. She inclined her head and stared at him. 'And the police are involved too?'

'How did you …?' the corporal exclaimed. His eyes grew round, but then understanding grew on his face and he held up his hand. 'Ah, yes, I understand. The signal. Yes, what you saw was correct. The police officer tapped out a brief message in Morse code as he passed, letting us know a legion of cyber-drones were advancing on our position.'

Glowing with triumph at knowing her instincts were spot on, Sunitra pressed the young man with more questions. 'So can I assume we're being taken to the resistance base – codenamed *the Castle?*'

'Nice try.' He laughed, waving his finger at her. 'I'm sorry to disillusion you, but we are just a small cell of a much larger network. Our leader will explain it to you more fully when you arrive.'

'Your leader?' Sunitra felt her spirits collapse as once again her hopes of finding the fabled and ever-elusive resistance base were dashed. 'But I assumed you were the leader?'

Before the young soldier could answer, the elevator juddered as it came to a halt, followed by a small ping and the doors slid open. LB gestured for the two civilians to step through the door. They moved out to find themselves standing in a small compact corridor with a set of closed doors facing them. Corporal Williamson marched forward and bent down in front of a retina scanner. The scanner lit up and a beam of light scanned his eye and, after five seconds, the doors in front of them opened and they followed him through into a long, dimly lit corridor.

They were silent as LB escorted them down the corridor. Sunitra was in awe at the flurry of activity around her; the corridor was full of various people rushing about purposefully. The two newcomers were given brief glances as they were escorted down the corridor. From their attire, she assumed the people were a mixture of soldiers and civilians.

They passed through intersecting junctions connected to other corridors. Sunitra watched with interest as the two youths known as Harris and Wang broke off from the group and disappeared down one of the interconnecting corridors. She gave Peter a wordless glance, and he shrugged slightly.

A few minutes later, they walked through a door into a large circular room. Sunitra let out a small whistle of admiration and stared in wonderment at the technological wonderland in front of her. She smiled as, out of the corner of her eye, she noticed her colleague was nodding in admiration at the spectacle. The array of monitors on the walls in front of her and the rows of computer stations immediately reminded her of a military command centre.

'Impressive sight, isn't it?'

Sunitra stiffened in surprise at the loud, firm voice addressing them. To her embarrassment, she quickly realised that she'd had been so entranced by the spectacle in front of her, she had failed to see LB had broken away from her. He was now standing next to a tall, lean grey-haired bearded man dressed in military combat fatigues.

'Uh, y-y-yes. Very impressive,' Peter stammered awkwardly.

'I had the same reaction as you when I first saw her.' Sergeant Major Wayne chuckled in amusement. He gave Peter a friendly smile and extended his hand. 'Sergeant Major Malcolm Wayne – good to see you, Mr Kirk.'

'Thank you, Sergeant, it's good to be here,' Peter replied. Sunitra could tell from the way he was wincing that Sergeant Major Wayne must have quite an impressive handshake. Having been on receiving end of many an over-zealous handshake during her time as a front-line report, she knew only too well what that bone crushing feeling was like.

Peter shook his hand in relief as Malcolm released his grip and turned his attention to Sunitra. 'May I introduce you to my friend and colleague, Sunitra Sinchettrra?'

Wayne bowed his head and turned to Sunitra, but then he stiffened and his eyes widened as if he was noticing for the first time. His mouth broadening into a toothy smile; he took her hand and kissed it, all the while staring intently into her eyes.

'Charmed, I'm sure.' He grinned.

Her heart fluttering, Sunitra felt her face warm and found herself returning the rugged man's intense gaze. For some reason she couldn't understand she found herself wondering where this tall, gorgeous man had been all her life. Deep inside, she felt something stir and for a moment she thought she heard a small voice in her mind scream at her to get a grip. She let out an embarrassed cough and lowered her head, murmuring, 'Thank you. It's good to be here.'

Sunitra frowned as she realised that Wayne was still staring at her. Was there dirt on her face? Oh no! Did she have spinach in her teeth? No, that wasn't it. She felt her breath catch in her throat. Wait, surely he wasn't attracted to her? She felt her cheeks warm and was desperate to avert her eyes but was unable to do so. Lost in his gaze, she thought she heard a cough come from somewhere. *Go away*, she wanted to say, *can't you see we are busy?* However, on hearing the cough again, she let out a small sigh of contentment but continued to stare at the rugged man in front of her.

'Sir.' LB coughed. 'You have something you wish to discuss, remember?'

As if suddenly realising where he was, Wayne blinked and released Sunitra's hand, his cheeks red. Sunitra spun round and blew out her cheeks, waving her hand in front of her to cool herself down. She noticed an odd expression on Peter's face and opened her mouth to say something but stopped herself, recognising the look – not ridicule, but something else. Was it approval?

Wayne's fingers tugged at the collar of his jacket and he glanced up at the monitors, almost as if he was desperate to change to the subject. 'Oh, y-yes, right you are,' he stammered, waving at the monitor closest to him. 'As you can see, these monitors link us to every CCTV within the area. With these, we can track the movements of the enemy as they patrol the streets, which is how we kept track of you while you did your thing with the mobile mast. Which was bordering on the side of reckless stupidity, if you ask me.' He raised his hand to wave off Sunitra's protests. 'Yes, it was reckless. You were too exposed and if we hadn't got to you in time, you would be dead now.'

Sunitra bristled with anger. How dare he speak to her like that! What right did he have to tell her what she could or couldn't do? It was as if something had flipped a switch inside her and it released all the emotions that she'd had kept bottled up since the attack on the news studio: anger, terror, and frustration – it all got released. Bellowing in fury, Sunitra bared her teeth and lunged at the sergeant major. Wayne stepped away from her, surprise etched across his face. Peter moved in between them, placing his hand on his friend's arm, but she snatched it away and shot past him.

'At least I was doing something!' she hissed. 'Where have you been? Where were you a few weeks ago when the enemy arrived?' Sunitra's eyes began to fill up with tears as she struggled to hide the bitterness in her voice. 'Where was the resistance when the enemy stormed the news studio and killed my friend? Tell me, where were you? The only help we received was from a few soldiers who were badly outmatched by an overwhelming foe.'

'Enough!' Wayne roared, his body trembling with rage. Sunitra jumped back in shock, the focus of the bitter man's fury. 'You want to know where I was? Do you?' His body quivered and he stabbed his finger at the monitors on the wall. 'I was fighting on the front line. I was there when they seized control of Buckingham Palace. One day I may come to terms with that.' He blinked, exhaling a harsh breath, and then put his hands on Sunitra's shoulders. 'So, my dear, you are not the only one who has had their life torn apart. There isn't a person in this room whose life hasn't been touched by this war.'

Ashamed for losing control of herself, Sunitra lowered her eyes and murmured, 'I'm sorry, I didn't know.'

'It's okay, we all have something to be angry about,' Wayne whispered, gently putting his hand under her chin, and he gave her a thin smile. 'What is important is what happens now. My superiors would like to offer you an opportunity to strike back at the enemy in the only way you can. Would you like that?'

Sunitra blinked away the tears and nodded in acknowledgement. 'What do I have to do?'

Wayne's mouth curved into a smile and he brushed the tears from her cheeks. Sunitra's jaw hung open as she heard the words that would change the rest of her life.

'How would you like to be the official voice of the resistance?'

-4-

Location: Outskirts of Sunderland, England

Just who had she pissed off for her life to end up like this? That was the thought that ran through Wendy Cooper's head as she lay shivering in the cold damp grass on the top of embankment that overlooked an enormous industrial complex. She let out a disgruntled snort and watched the steam of her breath drift off and disappear into the darkness.

Wendy shook her head as she thought about how much her life had changed within the space of a few weeks. Not that long ago she had been a serving police officer, as well as secretly working for a clandestine government agency. It was hard to believe that a routine investigation into a disturbance in a former mining village would lead to her world collapsing around her. Yes, a hostile force from a parallel world had taken over the world, annoying but it wasn't what was upsetting her. No, What Wendy found truly upsetting was the appearance of the one called Oracle. It was bad enough that she was an insane artificial intelligence, but did she have to have Wendy's face too?

Shortly after the King's speech, DI Barnes and Wendy returned to work in their roles at Durham Constabulary. Their thinking had been that, with the police force now under the control of the invaders, they would be in an ideal position to keep an ear open for any usable intelligence.

But when Wendy tried to return to her duties as a police officer, she discovered the true effect Oracle's arrival would have on her life. Wandering around the police station, she would catch hostile or fearful glances from her colleagues, and hearing their hushed whispers go silent whenever she entered the room. When out on patrol, out of the corner of her eye, she would notice angry glares from the civilian population. But for her, the thing that finally broke the straw on the camel's back was mothers pulling their children to them when she walked past them. For Wendy, seeing the fear in a child's eyes was like a knife through her heart.

It was with a heavy heart that she realised she had to resign from the police force. Of course, DI Barnes had tried his hardest to dissuade her from taking such drastic action, but he eventually reluctantly agreed with his friend's decision. They both accepted she could be of better use within the Castle.

Upon learning of Wendy's resignation, Commander Payne realised he could put her skills to good use by placing her in the Special Ops squad under the watchful eye of his chief of security. Kendra could not have been more delighted to have her friend and lover serve with her. At first, Wendy found it difficult to adjust to serving under the equally stubborn versatile former marine. However, it soon became apparent, as they spent more time training together, that they were good for each other.

Over the past month, Wendy's life had settled into a routine under Kendra's watchful scrutiny. During the night, alongside the rest of her colleagues in the Special Ops squad, they spent their time on reconnaissance missions, gathering intel on the occupying forces. Much like tonight.

John Payne had received a report from Dave Barnes of something unusual going on with the enemy, having heard that the enemy forces had taken over a former car manufacturing factory on the outskirts of Sunderland. Dave had also heard of rumours of people being taken from their homes in villages on the outskirts of Sunderland, but could not investigate any further because all his requests to investigate had been refused by his superior. Wendy and Kendra agreed with the commander's assessment that something did not feel right and this needed further investigation.

'Team one to team two, are you receiving? Over.'

Startled, Wendy was brought back to the present as Kendra spoke firmly in her earpiece, breaking her out of her reverie. Out of the corner of her eye, she noted that two men wearing tight-fitting black Kevlar-woven camouflage bodysuits were staring at her questioningly. She coughed apologetically and tapped the mic behind her ear.

'Sorry, team one, could you repeat that? Over.'

'*You sleeping on the job again Wendy?*' Kendra's voice chuckled in Wendy's earpiece. '*I was asking, have you seen anything out of the ordinary? Over.*'

'No, nothing, as ye—' She stopped as she detected something through her night-vision binoculars. 'Wait, I think I see something. Over.'

Wendy frowned and she magnified the image in her binoculars. She leaned forward curiously; three large military troop transporters were pulling up to the former factory's security gate. Her breath quickened as the security gate opened to let the transports through. She glanced over her shoulder at the commando lying next to her and pointed to the scene below. He nodded silently, adjusted his night-vision glasses and lifted his head in surprise. Wendy's fingers tightened on her binoculars as she noticed that the transports had stopped and had begun to unload a group of people.

'What the hell is going on down there?' he whispered.

'I don't know. I'd love to find out, wouldn't you?' Wendy replied. The two commandos nodded thoughtfully, staring at Wendy curiously. 'What do you think, Gary? Fancy going for a little stroll to find out?'

The commando called Gary, a thin-faced, ruggedly broad-shouldered man, scratched his left earlobe deep in thought as he stared down at the factory at the bottom of the hill. He cast a quick look at his colleague, who lifted his shoulder with a slight shrug.

'Beats lying in this damp grass, boss.' He grunted.

Wendy chuckled to herself at Gary calling her boss. Since joining the Special Ops squad, it had become a bit of an in-joke amongst the squad members that Wendy was the group's unofficial second in command because of her relationship with Kendra. When she had first joined the team, they had treated her with suspicion. But as they served with her, their respect for her had increased to the point where, if there was something they wanted to discuss, they would approach Wendy first.

'*Team two, please repeat. Over.*'

Wendy inhaled a deep breath and reached up to tap her mic. 'Team one, be advised we are going in for a closer look. Over.'

'*Team two, this is a reconnaissance mission,*' Kendra's voice snapped angrily. '*These new stealth suits have not been fully tested yet. Over.*'

Wendy glanced down at the tight-fitting black bodysuits the three of them were wearing and gave a small shrug. 'Well, no time like the present. Over.'

'*Damn it, Wendy. We have not been authorised to engage the enemy. Do you read? Over.*'

'Shh … shh-orry, sssshhh. Breaking up …' She whistled loudly, tapping her hand on her mic, and switched off her earpiece.

'Damn it, Wendy. Don't you even dare! Over,' Kendra snapped, tapping her earpiece furiously. Her face twisted in anger on hearing nothing but static in her ear.

Two soldiers crouching down behind Kendra, dressed in the same tight-fighting Kevlar-woven bodysuits, exchanged concerned looks. One of the commandos, a slim but muscular dark-haired woman, slid next to Kendra and looked at her questioningly. 'What do you want us to do, ma'am? Do you want us to go after them as backup?'

Kendra shook her head and lapsed into silence. She tapped her night-vision lenses anxiously, her eyes tightening in concentration as she searched for Wendy's team. She let out a long, exasperated breath, took off her night-vision glasses and shook her head.

'No, they're on their own, Nat,' Kendra whispered reluctantly. She sucked her bottom lip and weighed her options, and then turned to the commando crouching next to her. 'Eddie, I want you to head back to the van and be ready. I want us to be out of here like a shot if all hell breaks loose, understood?'

Eddie nodded gravely and slid off into the darkness.

Kendra sighed heavily and stared up at the heavens, murmuring under her breath. 'I hope you're keeping an eye on Wendy up there. I could really do with a miracle right now.' She squeezed her eyes shut, massaging the side of her temples, groaning. 'If I live through this without completely losing my mind, it will be a miracle of biblical proportions.'

Nat let out a small snort, muttering under her breath, 'Well, there goes my faith in the almighty.'

Kendra gave the slim woman the evil eye and then they both burst out laughing. Kendra gave her comrade a playful punch on her shoulder, but then her laughter lessened as she felt a heaviness settle in her stomach. Despite her annoyance, Kendra closed her eyes and said a silent prayer for Wendy's safe return.

Wendy tapped on her earpiece repeatedly and turned to Gary with a look of wide-eyed innocence. 'Oh dear, I think I've lost her. Did you catch that last thing she said?'

'Nope, I just heard the bit about this being a reconnaissance mission,' he replied with a sly wink as he glanced over at his colleague. 'What about you, Ken?'

Kenneth shrugged, pulled his black mask over his head to reveal only his eyes, and mumbled something inaudible.

'Well, then. Let's get on with this.' Wendy grinned, reaching up and pulling the black hood over her head. 'We'll be down and back before they realise we've been and gone. What's the worst that could happen?'

As Wendy crawled stealthily down the hill toward the factory's security fence, she shivered as she felt the hairs on the back of her tingle. She wondered to herself if maybe Kendra was right, that it was too dangerous. She peered over shoulder back up to where they had just come from and shook her head. No, if she gave the order to turn back now, then she might as well be signalling to her colleagues that she didn't know what she was doing. She couldn't afford to look weak in their eyes. Casting any doubts she had in her head to one side, Wendy continued sliding down the embankment. Yeah, this was the right thing to do. They'll have a little look around and then they'll be back home in no time. What could go wrong?

But as she approached the southern edge of the factory's wire fence, Wendy came to a stop as she once again felt an icy chill run down her spine. She turned in a small circle to study the area around her through suspicious eyes. For a moment, she got the impression that someone was watching her. Her head spun sharply round as she caught sight something glinting in her peripheral vision. Was that a ball? Her body went into alert mode and she crouched low on the ground, focusing her attention toward where she thought she saw something move.

'You see something, Wendy?' Gary asked in a hushed voice, crouching next to her.

'Not sure. For a moment I thought I saw …' Wendy murmured uncertainly. She chastised herself internally, putting it down to paranoia, and gave a dismissive wave of her hand. 'It's nothing. I think I'm just jumpy.'

'I'm not surprised we're jumpy,' Ken mumbled, expertly using a pair of wire cutters to open a hole in the wire fence. 'One wrong move and we end up being cyber-drone target practice.'

Gary crossed his arms and stared at his friend through disapproving eyes. 'Mate, has anybody ever told you you really know how to suck the fun out of everything?'

'Time to put our game faces on, chaps,' Wendy hissed in a low, hard voice, giving them a penetrating stare through the eyeholes in her mask. She gestured at the newly formed hole in the fence. 'I'll go through first, followed by you, Ken, and then you, Gary – understood?' The two men nodded wordlessly.

Gary helpfully moved forward and grabbed the part of the wire fence that had been cut open, lifting it carefully. Wendy sucked in a deep breath and pushed her way through. She glanced anxiously around, and her breath caught in her throat as she saw two armoured figures advancing slowly towards her.

Her heart drumming in her chest, Wendy held her hand up to signal Ken to remain where he was. Her mind racing, she stared at the hole in the fence. What should she do? If she stayed here, they would surely see her. If she tried climbing back through the hole in the fence, they would definitely see her.

Her options running out, Wendy felt a surge of relief as she spotted an alcove in the wall across the road from her. Quickly deciding to take a leap of faith, she sprinted across and pressed herself into the tight space. With the sound of her blood pounding in her ears like the beat of a drum, she stood perfectly still as the two armoured figures marched up the road. She felt a lump in her throat as one cyber-drones came to a sudden stop in front of her. Wendy tried not squirm as a trickle of sweat ran down the back of her neck.

Wendy held her breath and watched the armoured figure turn in a tight circle as if it sensed something was there. *Does it know I'm here? What do I do?* Her mind raced as the intimidating cyber-drone turned and stared directly at her. Hand slowly moving towards her holstered weapon, she stiffened as it took a brief step closer to her. With a jackhammer pounding in her chest, she closed her eyes and relaxed her breathing, all the while thinking, *I'm a stealthy ninja, I'm a stealthy ninja.*

For what seemed like an eternity, Wendy watched the faceless cyber-drone cock its armoured head. With her interior voice screaming for her to move, it took all of Wendy's willpower to remain still as it leaned menacingly toward her. Sweat trickling down her neck, she stared into the black faceplate of the drone and imagined the remorseless face peering back at her. In her mind's eye she believed its eyes were staring at her, burning with hatred, wanting so badly to snuff out the life of the person in front of it.

But to Wendy's surprise, the gold and black armoured figure did not do what she was expecting. Instead of reaching forward and crushing the life out of her, it moved back. Beneath her mask, Wendy's eyebrows climbed up her forehead as the cyber-drone's head tilted to one side as if it was listening to something and then, in a slow robotic movement, it turned and marched away to continue its patrol.

Once it was safe, Wendy slumped down slightly and let out a long, relieved breath. She ran her hand down the front of her mask, trying to understand what had just happened. It had to have seen her. She lowered her head to examine the tight bodysuit she was wearing and frowned. Did this stealth suit actually save her life?

She tensed, detecting movement ahead, but relaxed as two familiar dark-suited figures dashed across the road toward her. She could see them staring at her through their eyeholes with wide-eyed amazement.

'Bloody hell, Wendy!' Gary exclaimed in a low voice. 'We both thought you were a goner there.'

'Me too. For a moment there, I could have sworn it was staring directly at me,' Wendy replied in a hoarse whisper. She scratched her head uncertainly, casting an eye over to where the patroller had disappeared. 'I was sure it was going to reach forward and grab me, but then it was as if it decided not to. It was as if …' She shook her head.

'It was as if what?' Gary whispered curiously.

'This may sound strange, but for a moment, I got the impression it was receiving instructions. As if it was being ordered to ignore me.' She flicked her hand and dismissed the thought, straightening. 'Okay, let's not push our luck any further. We do a quick reconnoitre and then get the hell out of here. Sound good to you?'

ORACLE'S VISION

The two men nodded in wordless acknowledgement as Wendy waved for them to follow her. To remain as inconspicuous as possible, the trio pressed themselves against the hard surface of the factory's wall, carefully making their way towards the front of the enormous building. But as they reached the corner, they came across a huge cylindrical container with three large yellow triangular warning signs stuck on its surface. On each sign there was a large flame with the words *Danger, Diesel Fuel* written underneath in big bold letters. They crouched and slunk past the diesel storage container into a large open area, pausing to examine the open space in front of them.

As Wendy stared through her night-vision goggles, she carefully scanned the area in front of her. Scattered across a large open area stood thousands of cars. If she had not known this factory had once belonged to a Japanese car manufacturer, one would have thought this was a vast car park with thousands of vehicles abandoned by their owners. Before the invasion, the factory had been a profitable business with a large workforce, at its peak producing two thousand cars a day. But that mysteriously changed shortly after the enemy's arrival. The invading forces seized control of the factory and its workforce was appropriated. All motor vehicle production was halted, leaving any new cars to stand idle, gathering dust in the vast sales lot. More concerning was that nobody had seen or heard from the factory's workforce since the invaders had seized control.

Wendy jumped as she felt Gary gently tap her shoulder and twisted her head round to him. He was gesturing to something ahead of them. She acknowledged him with a nod and focused her attention on the loading area. Beneath her mask she frowned as groups of people – men, women, and children – were unloaded from several troop transports. From the fearful look on their faces, it was obvious they were not there willingly.

'What the hell!' Gary blurted out under his breath. 'That must be at least a hundred people. What in God's name is going on here?'

Wendy lapsed into silence as she examined the area, contemplating their options. What should they do? Dare they risk being detected by investigating further? Should they attempt to save those people? She ground her teeth as she asked herself what the best course of action was. She sucked in a long breath, blowing it out in exasperation, concluding that she was already in trouble for disobeying orders by coming this far. She squared her shoulders determinedly as she reached a decision. If she was going to be damned, she might as well do it properly.

'See that,' Wendy whispered. The two men followed her finger, which was pointed towards the far side of the building and nodded in unison. A steel stairway appeared to lead to a doorway on the first floor. 'All the security cameras appear to be fixed on the people being unloaded from the transports. Quick, while they're distracted, let's make a dash towards the door and get into the building.'

The trio hugged close to the shadows, stealthily making their way toward the far side of the building. Halfway up the steel staircase, Wendy came to a stop as she felt the hairs on the back of her neck tingle. Something didn't feel right. As soon as Ken was in front of the door, he pulled out his tablet, searching for the factory's security camera connection. Gary stared at his team leader questioningly as she took an awkward step towards them.

'This is too easy,' she muttered.

'What is?' he replied in a distracted tone, watching Ken hack into the factory's security feed.

'All of it,' Wendy replied. She bit her bottom lip, a seed of paranoia growing within her. 'Getting through that fence, how that cyber-drone acted, and now the cameras just happen to be focused on the prisoners being unloaded.'

'What the actual frack!'

They both spun round sharply as Ken leapt up in surprise, pulling off his mask. He grabbed at the tablet to prevent it from slipping out of his hands. A cold dread settled on Wendy on seeing the expression of fear that was on his face. He lifted the tablet to show an image of them standing on the staircase.

'They're watching us,' Ken whispered in an incredulous tone. His brow creased and he stared at the image on the tablet suspiciously, and then raised his head to search the sky above him. His face scrunched up in disdain as he spotted something above him. 'There.'

At first Wendy could not see it, but before she could open her mouth to question Ken, something glinted in the moonlight. Without breaking a sweat, she reached for her weapon – a Champion .45 pistol equipped with a sound suppressor – inhaled a slow breath, closed an eye to target the hovering ball and pressed her finger on the trigger. There was a soft thump of the weapon discharging, followed by something sparking in mid-air as the bullet hit its target.

Alarm bells ringing in her head, Wendy shuddered, an overwhelming sense of danger twisting her stomach.

She pressed her finger on her throat mic. 'Kendra, it's a trap. They knew we were coming,' she cried out. She now understood the sound of static in her ear. 'They're jamming us.'

Wendy let out a snarl of disgust and pounded her hand on the steel handrail. How could she have been so stupid? She thumped her forehead and blinked, the formations of a plan coming to her. Maybe she could turn this to her advantage. A slow grin forming across her face, Wendy spun round and fixed Ken with an intense stare. 'Kenny, can you jam the security cameras?' she asked cryptically.

'Sure, but it will only buy us ten minutes before they have them back online. What good will that do?' he replied, frowning. 'They already know we're here.'

'That's okay, ten minutes is all I need,' Wendy replied and smiled knowingly, the plan gradually coming together in her head. 'When the cameras go down, they won't know where I am exactly. Hopefully, that should give me enough time to do what I need to do.'

'Okay, Boss,' Gary muttered, giving Wendy a side eye. 'Care to share?'

'No time. Once Ken has jammed the cameras, I want you both to make your way as way as fast as you can to where we came in. Once you're clear of the jamming, I want you to raise the alarm.' She lifted her hand, cutting off their protests. 'I have made my decision. We need somebody to report on what we've seen here if I don't survive.'

The two soldiers nodded reluctantly in acknowledgement. Ken furiously keyed his tablet, pumped his fist in celebration and gave Wendy a nod of confirmation. 'You're good to go, boss.' He smiled sadly at Wendy and gave her a small salute. 'God's speed.'

As Wendy watched her two comrades turn to go down the stairs, she blinked and smiled to herself as another idea came to her. She ran after them and grabbed Ken's arm.

'Kenny, do you still have the spare packs of C4 in your shoulder bag?' She smiled as he gave her a confused nod. 'Also give me the spare remote detonator you're holding. Now, remember that diesel storage tank we passed? I want you to place all the C4 you can around it.'

The corners of Ken's eyes creased with worry but he reluctantly handed a small remote trigger detonator over to her. 'You're not planning on doing something stupid, are you? I would sure hate to lose you, Wendy.'

'Since when have I ever done anything stupid?' She grinned and thumped the worried man's arm. 'Anyway, we both know you would be lost without me.'

Despite any reservations he may have had, Ken smiled and turned reluctantly away from her. With a leaden heart, Wendy watched her two comrades-in-arms disappear into the shadows. She drew in a lungful of air and blew it out in a long, determined breath. Well, time to enter the belly of the beast. Squaring her shoulders in steadfast conviction, she made her way back up the staircase and stepped through the door.

-5-

The muscles in her jaw tightened and Wendy gently closed the security door but baulked as she heard the faint click of the door locking into place. Then she slowly twisted around and took an awkward step toward the inner fire door. She froze as a motion sensor light detected her movement and the antechamber was lit up in a brilliant burst of light.

Surprised, Wendy cried out in pain as her night-vision lenses overloaded in an explosion of greenish light. The overwhelming sensory input being blasted into her night-vision glasses had been too much for the sensitive tech to handle and they were unable to compensate in time. Disorientated, she cast her glasses to one side and rested against the wall. She took in a deep breath as she waited for her vision to clear.

Wendy waited for the spots to slowly clear from her vision. Relief flowed through her as her vision slowly returned to normal, and she was grateful that no permanent damage had been done. She looked at the night-vision glasses in her hand and let out a disappointed huff. So much for a stealthy approach.

She bit her bottom lip and glanced furtively at the security door. Should she continue, or turn back? She inhaled a deep breath, blew it out in exasperation and fixed her eyes on the inner door with steely determination. She had come this far, so why give up now?

Wendy held her breath and edged the door open, peering through the gap. Ahead of her was a narrow dimly lit corridor that extended for about fifty metres, with walls that had been painted the standard industrial pale green and a floor that was covered with dirty brown slip-proof rubber. Along each side of the corridor, three doors stood wide open. Her eyes narrowing, she stared up at the ceiling at a security camera; its light was still off. So far, so good.

She crept into the corridor and scrunched her nose in disgust at the faint smell of engineering fuel tingling at her nose. She cocked her head and picked up some strange noises coming from somewhere in the distance. Craning her neck forward, she tried to work out what it was and nodded – but there was no doubt about it; amidst the faint hum of the ventilation system, there were unmistakable sounds of people crying and moaning.

Slowly edging forward, Wendy peered through one of the open doors but was hit with a wave of sorrow and anger on seeing the state that the empty office had been left in. Amongst the scattered papers littered across the floor, half-empty cups of tea and the remains of half-eaten rotten sandwiches lay on the desks, along with various coats and handbags that were still hanging on the desk chairs as if waiting for their owners to return. Whatever happened here, the staff had not gone willingly.

Her anger building, Wendy made her way past the other offices and found the same story. Her thin lips pressed together, she inhaled steady breaths and forced herself to keep her anger in check. Now was not the time to lose control; she needed to remain in control of her emotions. She could grieve for these people later.

The deathly silence of the corridor was almost unbearable as Wendy crept onward. She reached the end of the corridor, stopping at an open doorway, and a woman's scream of anguish cut through the silence, startling her.

'No … please, I beg you. D-d-do what you want with me b-b-but let my girls go.'

Adrenaline pumping through her body, Wendy crouched and poked her head through the open doorway. It led out onto a metal gantry walkway and ran all the way round the upper level of the factory. Carefully hunkering on her knees, she slowly and carefully moved toward the gantry's edge and peered over the railing. What she saw below her shook her to the core of her soul.

What used to be one of the most advanced car assembly lines in the United Kingdom now resembled a scene from a science fiction movie. Gone were the workbenches, tools and equipment. In their place were hundreds of seven-metre-tall oblong open boxes, connected to each other through various wires and cables, with bursts of compressed air shooting out every so often. If it had not been for their bizarre steam punk appearance, Wendy would have sworn she was staring down at a Borg regeneration chamber from *Star Trek*.

Wendy shuddered, feeling as if a cold hand had grabbed her heart. Inside the alcoves, she could make out the shapes of various people. Even from her position high up on the gantry, she could still hear their whimpers as they underwent different stages of transformation. She pulled away from the edge as she heard another dreadful scream coming from below her, tearing at her heart.

Pushing her terror to somewhere deep inside her, Wendy prairie-dogged over the railing, her eyes quickly scanning the floor below, searching for the location of the scream. A wave of sympathy overwhelmed her as she caught sight of a thin middle-aged woman being forced into an alcove by two cyber-drones. From the cuts on top of the woman's bald head, she guessed they had brutally shaved all her hair off prior to placing her in the alcove.

Lifting her hand to her mouth, horror-struck, Wendy watched two black and gold armoured soldiers wordlessly force the captive's arms and legs into restraints, locking them in place. Desperate to look away from the horrific scene, she forced herself to watch as the woman cried out in anguish at the several tubes and wires that were being injected into her naked body. The pitiful cries of anguish settled into pleading sobs as two nightmarish arms extended over the bound captive and sprayed her, covering her body with liquid metal.

Wendy watched in disbelief as the two black and gold armoured figures spun round and marched away, obviously satisfied that the automatic transformation process would proceed without supervision. As soon as the two figures disappeared, Wendy jumped to her feet and sprinted down a flight of metal stairs, two at a time.

The moaning woman raised her head weakly on hearing footsteps coming toward her, but her brown eyes grew round with terror as she watched Wendy move toward her. Wendy held up her hand to her lips to silence the whimpering woman's pleas.

'P-p-please, n-n-no more,' she whimpered in a tremulous voice, tears running down her pale face. 'W-w-what more do you want? I-I-I beg you to stop.'

Caught off guard by the victim's reaction to her, Wendy staggered back in shock. Why did she look as if she knew her? She'd had never even met her before. What was she talking abou— Suddenly, a flash of memory sparked within her brain, and she was reminded of a similar reaction a few weeks earlier, when she had been on patrol as police constable – a child who had been pulled away by her mother and who had a similar expression, one of fear and recognition. She nodded in understanding, guessing the terrified woman must have believed she was Oracle.

'No, you don't need to be afraid,' she pleaded softly, holding her hands up in front of her, 'I'm not her. My name is Wendy Cooper. I'm a police officer. I'm here to help you.'

'Y-y-you're not her.' The woman snivelled.

'No, sweetheart, I'm not her,' Wendy whispered softly, putting a hand on the distressed woman's face. 'What's your name, flower?'

'Teresa, Teresa McCormick,' she whimpered.

'Okay, Teresa.' Wendy whispered softly as she desperately scanned the alcove, searching for some way to release the tortured soul. 'I'm going to get you out of here.'

The restrained woman let out a small moan, shaking her head weakly. 'No … it's too late for me. I can already hear her voice inside my head, whispering at me.' Her face hardened and fixed her would-be liberator with a look of resignation. 'They took my children … my lovely … twin girls.' Tears continued to trickle down her face and she let out a small wail. 'My … my husband tried to fight them when they came for us, but he died protecting us. Please, I beg you, kill me now before I become one of them. Please let me join my husband in the afterlife.'

Taken by surprise, Wendy lurched back from the distraught woman. Revulsion filling every fibre of her being, her mouth opened and closed as she stared helplessly at the pitiful figure before her eyes. She couldn't leave her like this. She had to do something. Filled with hopeless desperation, she frantically searched for some way to release Teresa. But a cold awareness settled on her heart: she could not save her. Her hand trembling, she held up her pistol at the grief-stricken woman's head. Teresa, seeing the weapon pointed at her, gave a small grateful nod and closed her eyes, mouthing a wordless thank you.

ORACLE'S VISION

Her hands greasy with sweat, Wendy fumbled as she pointed the pistol at the pale-faced prisoner. Wait, did she have the right to take this innocent woman's life? Plagued by self-doubt, Wendy hesitated, her finger hovering over the pistol's trigger. If she pulled the trigger wouldn't that mean she was helping to put an end to Teresa's suffering? She shivered slightly, as she wrestled with the decision. But one thing she was certain of, whatever course of action she took it would remain with her for the rest of her life.

A warning sounded in the back of her mind as Wendy watched Teresa's fear-stricken face transform into something cold and emotionless. A bead of sweat trickled down her spine as the blue in the white-faced woman's eyes disappeared and was replaced by a cold emotionless silver. Terrified beyond belief, fighting back the urge to scream, Wendy slowly backed away from those cold silver eyes. Normally a rational person, Wendy rarely believed in the paranormal, but as she stood there within the intensity of Teresa's dispassionate gaze, she was certain it was penetrating her skull. No, not just her skull, it was tearing into Wendy's very soul.

A loud click came from the restraint holding the captive woman's right arm, releasing it. Teresa raised her newly released machine-like arm and stared at it quizzically, almost as it was alien to her. Her body numb with fear, Wendy could only watch as Teresa's white face slowly turned toward her and locked her cold eyes onto her. Slowly leaning forward, the-thing-that-was-Teresa's head then tilted from side to side as if it was inspecting Wendy.

The cyborg's mouth opened into a horrifying round shape and its misshapen hand pointed at the woman in front of her. Wendy staggered back in shock, her hands covering the sides of her head as a blood-curdling moan assaulted her ears. Her blood running cold, she stumbled away as other deathly white figures in their chambers raised their horrifying technology-infused hands, and they all began to moan in unison.

Half mad with terror, Wendy spotted movement out of the corner of her eye. Several cyber-drones were marching towards her. She had to go now, or she would be dead. Wendy moved falteringly toward the gantry staircase and clambered up it, but as she reached the top, she paused and gave the monstrosity that used to be Teresa one last sorrowful look.

'I'm sorry,' she whispered.

The black and gold armoured drones all discharged their weapons at Wendy. She lurched back from the gantry edge as a cascade of blue energy beams struck the gantry's handrail, showering the factory floor with a torrent of sparks. A stray beam ricocheted off a wall mirror, and Wendy cried out as she felt the searing heat pass millimetres close to her face.

Finally getting the message she had outstayed her welcome, Wendy jumped through the open doorway she'd had previously come through, crying out in pain as she skidded across the glossy rubber floor and slammed into the wall. Dazed, she put her hand over her face as weapons fire struck the windows above her, showering with her glass.

Wendy felt her spirits lift as she spotted the fire door at the end of the corridor. Leaping to her feet, her teeth bared, she snarled in resolution and sprinted towards the door. No, she was adamant she wasn't going die today! Her arms pumping like pistons, Wendy raced down the corridor like a bat out of hell.

Her chest rising and falling in rapid breaths, Wendy let out a celebratory cheer as she came to a stop and placed her hands on the fire door, but then she frowned and stared at it in bewilderment. Why was it refusing to open? Glancing at her watch, she quickly realised it had been well over ten minutes since Ken hacked into the security system. A surreptitious look up at the security camera confirmed her suspicions; the security system was now active again. She pounded her hands on the door in frustration. *No! Not now!*

As she struggled to think of a way to open the door, Wendy caught movement out of the corner of her eye. Steeling herself, she spun toward the three approaching cyber-drones and balled her hands into fists, fixing them with a hard stare. 'Alright, you bastards, who wants to die first?' she hissed with a tight, humourless smile.

The three cyborgs hesitated as if unsure what to do. However, their hesitation only lasted a few second. They all lifted their weapons at Wendy and illuminated the dark corridor with streaks of blue energy.

That was what she was waiting for. Wendy dived straight to the floor and covered her head with her arms as streaks of energy passed over her, followed by an energy storm of sparks that rained over her body from the salvo of weapons fire striking the unyielding barrier. For a second, the door stubbornly stood tall, groaning in defiance at the cascade of energy assaulting it, but its defiance did not last. It warped under the rain of fire and exploded outwards. The concussive force, together with the continuing barrage, also took out the outer security door.

Quick as lightning, Wendy's weapon was in her hands; she closed her left eye, sucked in a slow breath, took careful aim, and pressed her finger on her trigger. She gritted her teeth at the small weapon's recoil and then the three armoured heads each snapped back violently as the bullets hit their mark.

A few weeks earlier, the resistance had uncovered a weak point in the enemy's armour. They had learned there was a small opening in the submental space, the space between the head and neck beneath the chin in the midline. They had theorised that in the right conditions, it would be possible to take a cyber-drone out with a single shot.

Never happier to put theory into practice, Wendy gave a small nod of satisfaction as she watched the three armoured figures collapse to the floor like marionettes that had had their strings cut. Her eyes lifting heavenward, she said a silent thank you to the tech boys in the resistance. She groaned and eased herself up off the floor; now if she could just live long enough to pass that information on.

On the verge of exhaustion, Wendy let out a long, tired breath, followed by a small smirk. It wouldn't be long before more cyber-drones arrived, and she imagined Oracle wouldn't take the killing of her mindless warriors well. Rising unsteadily on her feet, she grimaced and shook the glass and debris out of her hair and teetered through the remains of the outer door onto the metal fire escape.

Wendy could feel her heart thumping against her ribcage as she crouched on top of the fire escape and looked across to the loading dock. Even from that distance, she could make out several armoured figures storming out of the loading dock's entrance. She took in a deep breath and sighed. Well, it looked like stealth was no longer an option, she thought as she jumped up and bolted down the metal stairway.

Stealthily hugging the shadows, Wendy crouched down between two black pickup trucks. She drew in a long breath and climbed under one of the vehicles and stared in silence at the squad of cyber-drones advancing toward her. After carefully extricating herself from under the vehicle, she stared thoughtfully across the vast car lot and wondered if she could make it if she sprinted for it.

Oh well, who wants to live forever? She thought as she wearily pushed herself off the side of the vehicle.

Her arms pumping like pistons, the inside of her body suit soaked in sweat from exertion, Wendy dashed across the car lot as streaks of blue energy shot past her. Dodging and weaving through the parked vehicles, Wendy's scrunched up her face as a beam of energy narrowly missed her head, striking a car window and showering her with more broken glass.

Moonlight bouncing off the shards of glass covering her body, she imagined she probably looked a strange sight racing across the car lot, like the mythical Celtic silver banshee racing through Irish meadows. She cried out in pain as she felt an energy beam graze her hip, and she staggered at the glancing blow. Her teeth clenched together, she dived behind the diesel storage tank she had passed earlier.

Wendy raised an eyebrow as everything became deathly quiet and the beams of energy stopped shooting past her. Sucking in a relieved breath, she gave the enormous diesel storage tank a thankful pat. It was obvious they dared not fire in case they struck the container and risked igniting the volatile fuel contained within.

To slow her heart rate down, Wendy closed her eyes and inhaled slow calming breaths. Feeling more in control, she opened her eyes and examined her hip. She drew in a sharp breath as her fingers gently probed the wound and grimaced at the seared area. *It could be worse,* Wendy thought as she examined it. She nodded gratefully; it appeared the suit's dense fibres had absorbed most of the energy of the glancing blow.

Wendy jerked as her hand touched something on the side of the storage tank and her eyebrows shot up in recognition at the pack of C4 explosive attached to the side of the tank. She'd had forgotten she had ordered her two colleagues to attach all their C4 to the storage tank. However, before she could reach into her pocket for the remote detonator, the scrunching sound of heavy boots on tarmac made her pause and she quickly peered over her shoulder to see that the shadowy figures of several cyber-drones were advancing toward her. No time to dawdle!

Sucking on her bottom lip, Wendy twisted her head and gazed up at the hole in the fence she'd had climbed through earlier and frowned as she computed the distance in her head. All she needed was the right distraction and she could make it. Smiling wickedly, she pulled out another remote detonator switch from her pocket and flicked a switch.

'Time for a magic show, boys.' she hissed gleefully.

Moments earlier, realising she was going to have to pull a rabbit out of a hat if she wanted to make it out of there alive, Wendy had placed a pack of C4 explosive beneath both pickup trucks she'd had been crouching beside. The C4 detonated, igniting the fuel inside each truck's tank, lighting up the car lot in a violent explosion. The squad of cyber-drones spun sharply round as rows of vehicles exploded like lines of dominoes collapsing. The resulting compression wave struck the cyborgs with enough force to knock them off their feet.

Her distraction in operation, the wind whistled past Wendy's ears as she sprinted toward the small hole in the wire fence. She ground her teeth in pain as her body slid across the wet tarmac, coming to a stop in front of the makeshift opening in the fence. Snarling in desperation, she pushed herself through the hole and shambled across the grass verge.

On reaching the bottom of the steep hill, Wendy felt a surge of anger as she turned towards the factory and fixed the building with a steely gaze. She reached into her pocket and pulled out the remote detonator Ken had handed to her earlier.

'This is for you, Teresa,' she whispered, flicking the detonator's switch.

The packs of C4 detonated along the surface of the enormous diesel storage tank, tearing a hole in its metal surface. Less than a millisecond later, the tank swelled as the fuel within the tank ignited, erupting in an uncontrollable fireball.

Wendy wobbled as the ground beneath her feet trembled. She gulped as it dawned her that the pipes she had seen leading from diesel tank into the ground were feeder pipes filled with fuel ... the same fuel she'd had just ignited. For a second, everything went silent before a loud explosion pierced the air and a fiery shock wave caught up to the generators inside the factory. Her eyes bulged and her mouth fell open as the factory swelled up in front of her, exploding outward in a powerful eruption of heat and noise. *Oh hell! This is going to hurt!* The concussive wave slammed into Wendy with enough force to throw her off her feet, casting her several metres into the air. She landed on the ground in an undignified heap.

For several moments, Wendy lay unmoving. She gasped for air and opened her eyes, disorientated, wondering why she was lying on the ground staring up at the spinning night sky. She moaned in pain and lifted her head off the ground. 'Oh, did somebody get the number of that car?' She groaned, putting her hand to her forehead.

Every part of her body aching, Wendy gingerly eased herself up off the ground and blew out her cheeks at the fiery debris scattered around her. Her head ringing, she frowned at a hard scrunching noise that was coming from behind her and turned towards it. Her mouth opened in a silent scream as a familiar-looking woman, whose hair and clothes were on fire, shambled out of the smoke and flames with her arms outstretched at Wendy.

No, that wasn't possible – how was Teresa still alive? Terror stabbing at her heart, Wendy scrambled away from the ghastly figure that was lumbering toward her, only to find that her path was blocked by a row of bushes. She cried out as a ghastly hand, blackened with the flesh seared off, grabbed the front of her stealth suit and picked her up off the ground like a rag doll.

The bile rising in her throat, Wendy swallowed and gazed into the gruesome burning face. The left side of the face was a distorted black mess of seared flesh with a white lidless eye, and the flesh on the right side hung loose, exposing bone and teeth beneath it. She squeezed her eyes shut as the grotesque woman pressed her face closer and felt its putrid breath on her skin as it hissed at her.

'You ungrateful insolent child. Do you not realise what you have just done? Do you not know how much work I put into getting that facility online?' Oracle rasped, blood spitting through the exposed flesh onto Wendy's face.

Her face clammy with sweat, Wendy pushed aside her revulsion and forced herself to open her eyes and look at the grotesque monstrosity in front of her. Her upper lip twisting up into a sneer, she fixed the rasping thing with a steel gaze, all the while secretly hoping she sounded more confident than she felt. 'Well, maybe next time you should think about hiring a better workforce,' she taunted, cackling. 'That's what you get for hiring foreign labour. Shoddy workmanship.'

In a fit of rage, the abhorrent eyesore let out a snarl of contempt, its fingers tightening their grip on Wendy's uniform. As Oracle lifted her into the air,

ORACLE'S VISION

Wendy felt as if her eyes were going to pop out of her head as the breath was forced out of her lungs. Discarded to one side like a toy thrown away by a petulant child, the wind knocked out of her, Wendy gasped in pain as she bounced off the ground, coming to a stop in a dazed untidy lump.

'You belligerent cur,' Oracle snarled, continuing her advance. 'It was foolish of me to believe I could turn you. I see now you are just like *her*, your counterpart. She also felt she knew better and did not know when to quit.'

Every part of her body aching, Wendy pushed herself onto her back as the horrendous figure shambled toward her. A wave of disappointment passed over her as she realised it hadn't thrown her in the direction she needed. She had hoped to land further up the grassy slope, making it easier to escape, but instead, she found the hideous thing was now standing at the bottom of the slope, blocking her escape route.

'Well, if she was anything like me, then you would know we don't back down,' Wendy said, switching to her normal broad Scottish accent. 'You know what they say about us Scottish lasses. We don't like bullies and we don't know when to back down from a fight.' Her eyebrows pricked up as she noticed movement on top of the grassy slope and her mouth curved into a gleeful smile as she taunted the distracted thing in front of her. 'Oh, would you like me to tell you one more thing you should know about us Scots?'

'Oh.' The abomination's head leaned to one side, its jaw hanging open at an abnormal angle as it attempted a contemptuous laugh. 'And what is that?'

'We know when to watch our backs,' Wendy hissed, rolling away from the zombified creature in front of her.

The gruesome monstrosity cocked its head in amusement as its quarry rolled away and then began to advance towards her. It suddenly came to a complete stop as it detected a loud engine roar coming from somewhere above it. The zombie-like woman shuffled round just in time to see black transit van careering at full speed down the grassy embankment toward it. As the vehicle's headlights enveloped it in a blinding white light, the remains of the pitiful wretch's jaw dropped open and it exclaimed in surprise.

'Motherfu—'

The transit van struck Teresa's fragile body at full speed, cutting off Oracle's perplexed cry. Already weakened from the injuries sustained in the fire, the frail body exploded like a balloon filled with red liquid, covering the front of the transit van with a red smear as it slammed into it.

-6-

Moments earlier, high above the factory, Kendra paced anxiously through the thick undergrowth. Cursing under her breath, she kicked at a stone and watched it sail down the grassy embankment, wondering what had got into Wendy's mind. She had always known Wendy was hot-headed, but this time she had gone too far. This time, her actions would have serious consequences.

Kendra exhaled a steamy sigh of exasperation, ran her hand down her tired face and shook her head. As much as she hated to admit it, she probably would have done the same thing if their positions had been reversed. She bit her bottom lip and glanced at the factory below her, silently praying her lover had not bitten off more than she could chew.

Kendra pressed her lips together and took a small step toward her pensive colleague crouched next to her, who was staring into the darkness below through night-vision glasses. The woman acknowledged her squad leader with a tight smile as she placed a hand on her shoulder.

'Any sign of them?' Kendra whispered.

'No, Chief, no—' Nat paused, her brow furrowed. 'Wait, I see them. Ken and Gary are making their way towards an opening in the fence.'

Feeling a surge of relief, Kendra placed her night-vision glasses over her eyes and blinked as her vision adjusted to the green illumination of the lenses, her eyes locking onto the spot Nat was pointing to. Yes, she could see the two men climbing through the fence, but where was Wendy? Dread twisted in her stomach and she immediately thought the worst. Had something happened to her? Were Ken and Gary forced to abandon her?

For several long, anxious minutes Kendra desperately fought against the panic seizing her brain as she watched the two men race up the grassy embankment. The two women grabbed their two breathless comrades' hands and helped them up. Sweaty and breathless, the men collapsed onto their knees and Kendra crouched in front of them.

'What happened down there? Where's Wendy?' she asked urgently, struggling to hide the concern in her voice.

'Sorry, Chief,' Ken replied, panting for breath and struggling to remove his mask. The sweat glistened off his red face as he tilted his head and stared up at Kendra. 'It turns out they knew we were coming. Not only were they jamming us, but they were spying on us the whole time.'

'They knew?' Kendra exclaimed in heart-wrenching shock. A trickle of fear ran down her spine and she forced the words out of her mouth. 'Wendy ... is she ... I mean ...'

Gary gave his commanding officer a tight smile and waved his hand. 'She's fine, ma'am. She ordered us to leave her so we could warn you. Last time we saw her, she was entering the building to investigate what was going on.'

'You left her alone in there? Alone?' Kendra snapped angrily. Teeth clenched, her hands outstretched, she desperately fought against the urge to grab Gary by the throat and order him to go back and get Wendy. She wished that stubborn woman was up here right now so she could throttle the life out of her for doing something so reckless ... so ... so ... Wendy!

Gary edged away from her, raising his hands, and then shook his head apologetically. 'I tried to talk her out of it, Chief, I really did, but you know what she's like. She was adamant it was something she needed to do.' He gestured to the man next to him. 'Ken was able to jam their security cameras to buy her some time.'

'That should buy her at least ten minutes,' Ken replied, nodding confidently. 'Plenty of time for her to get in and out undetected.'

'Damn you, Wendy,' Kendra whispered. She shook her head in resignation, tapping her throat mic. 'Eddie, you receiving? Over.'

ORACLE'S VISION

'Receiving. What about ya, Chief? Over.'

'Eddie, we need that pickup now, mate. I want us out of here in five mikes, understood? Over.'

'Roger, on my way. Over.'

The two men gave Kendra an unbelieving look. Gary's face turned thunderous and he took an angry step toward her. 'Ma'am, you're not thinking of leaving Wendy behind, are you?' he asked sharply, the disbelief evident in his voice. 'We need to give her a chance. You of all people should know we don't leave anyone behi—'

'Don't you think I know that?' Kendra snarled, cutting Gary off as she rounded on him. His face blanched and he hung his head. 'Every fibre of my being wants to go down there and bring her back. But she knew the mission before we set out, remember? Reconnaissance only. Not only has she endangered herself, but she has put the entire mission at risk.' Her eyes misted up and she fought back the tears. 'For all we know, they could have captured her and are turning her into one of those mindless drones. We've all heard the stories.'

'Sorry, Chief.' Gary coughed, shuffling awkwardly. 'But there's something you should know. As well as ordering us to tell you about the jamming, she ordered us to do one more thing.'

Muttering under her breath, Kendra lifted her head up to the clear night sky and massaged her brow with her hand. 'Give me strength.' Perplexed, she slowly lowered her head and stared at the uncomfortable man with a raised eyebrow, sighing. 'Well, go on then. What else has she done?'

'Um, well … You remember the packs of C4 I was carrying?'

'Huh-huh,' Kendra replied, slowly nodding. A heaviness settled into her stomach; she knew what was coming but could not step away from it.

Gary rubbed the back of his thick neck and shrugged slightly. 'Well, she ordered me to hand over the remote detonator.' He paused and exhaled an unhappy sigh. 'The one that's connected to the C4 we placed onto a diesel storage tank that we came across on the way in.'

'She did what?' Kendra roared. Now full of thunder and rage, she'd had enough of Wendy's lone-wolf attitude; she let out a bitter laugh and waved her hands into the sky. 'That's it! I'm going to kill her. I am going to absolutely kill her. She—'

Nat gave a small cheer of excitement, cutting Kendra's tirade short. 'I see her!' she exclaimed.

Delighted with the idea that Wendy was alive and well, Kendra pulled her night-vision binoculars down over her eyes and focused them on the spot Nat was looking at. However, concern soon tainted her delight as she noticed Wendy appeared to be racing through the car lot under heavy laser fire. She followed her and watched her come to a sliding stop behind a large storage tank. Kendra bit her bottom lip as she realised that the enemy's weapons fire had her friend pinned down. Wait … what was she doing? Kendra frowned and pressed a button on her binoculars, magnifying the image. Yes, she appeared to be reaching for somethi—

'Sonofabitch.' She cried out as an explosion of light overloaded her night-vision lenses.

The group of commandos stared in astonishment as a series of explosions lit up the car lot. From the distance, they saw lanes of cars go up in flames and there was a small cheer of celebration as the squad of cyber-drones, who had been chasing their comrade, were all engulfed in flames. Spotting the unmissable statuesque figure of Wendy climbing through the hole in the fence, Kendra gave a celebratory fist pump, but her delight quickly changed to confusion as she watched Wendy come to a stop and turn back toward the factory. What was she doing? It looked as if Wendy as staring back at something. Kendra frowned as she noticed something in Wendy's hand. It looked like a remote detonator, but why would she—

'Oh, shit!' Kendra's eyebrows climbed up her forehead as cold realisation struck her and she spun round sharply, signalling everybody to dive to the ground. 'Everybody down!'

Without needing to be told a second time, the group hit the ground just as the night was lit up like somebody shining a powerful torch. A second later, Kendra pressed her hands over her ears as a powerful concussion wave buffeted her as the factory below went up in a tremendous explosion. Kendra winced as flaming debris rained down around her, narrowly missing her.

Her ears ringing, Kendra tentatively lifted her head and looked at her people, and heaved an enormous sigh of relief as they climbed uneasily to their feet and gave her the thumbs up. Coughing, she glanced over her shoulder and smiled gratefully at the large black transit van that was driving toward them. Eddie popped his head out of the vehicle's window and stared at the inferno below them in open-mouthed astonishment.

'Anybody got eyes on Wendy?' Kendra called out, staggering towards the edge of the embankment.

Nat raised her hand. 'Yes. She appears to be dazed but …' The short-but-tough brunette frowned in concern. 'Excuse my French, but what the frig is that?'

As she peered down at the bottom of the steep slope, Kendra felt an icy hand clamp over her heart as a gruesome figure lumbered out of the flames towards Wendy. No, not now. Not when she was this close. She ran her hands through her hair, her mind racing, desperately searching for a way to help her colleague. Her eyes widened as a plan started to come together. Yes, that could work.

'Everybody in the van now,' she barked, her heart thundering in her chest.

Without waiting for the group to respond, she wheeled round and sprinted towards the transit van. Eddie blinked in surprise at her as she swung open the driver's door and slid into the driver's seat, unceremoniously pushing him into the passenger seat.

'Um, Kendra, watcha doing?' Eddie asked uncertainly as Kendra fastened her seatbelt and pressed her foot down on the accelerator pedal, revving the van's engine in a loud, throaty roar.

'Oh, I'm just going to take us for a ride.' Kendra laughed maniacally.

Eddie's face scrunched up in confusion. He looked at Kendra, then out through the van's front window and then back again to Kendra. She grinned as she saw his eyes grow wide. Oh yes, the penny had dropped. Eddie swallowed and then nervously gestured to something behind him.

'Uh, Chief, the road is that way,' he said warily.

Her mind already made up, Kendra laughed and pointed at the embankment edge. 'Oh, where I'm going, we don't need roads.'

'Oh, sweet Jesus!' Eddie exclaimed, blessing himself. He reached down and kissed the crucifix around his neck and gave his colleagues, who were climbing into their seats behind him, a sideways look. 'Lads, you'd better fasten up. Our imperious leader is going over the edge … literally.'

From the assortment of alarmed exclamations that were coming from the rear of the large van, shortly followed by the sound of seat belts being frantically clicked into place, Kendra guessed her colleagues must have heard the tension in Eddie's voice. Setting her jaw in steely determination, Kendra released the van's handbrake and pushed her foot down hard on the accelerator.

'Hang on chaps, this is going to get bumpy,' she cried.

Her hands clasping the steering wheel tightly and the tendons in her neck tightening, Kendra accelerated and the van shot over the edge of the embankment. The group of commandos in the back of cried out painfully as the vehicle juddered down the steep incline. Kendra's eyebrows climbed up in alarm on seeing the grotesque figure in front of them.

'Holy shit! Is that a zombie?' she heard someone cry out incredulously.

Her lips drawn back into a snarl, Kendra aimed the van at the zombified figure. She fought the urge to throw up on hearing a sickening sound of flesh exploding as the van hit its target, covering the window with a red spray of blood and other organic matter. A green-faced Eddie scrunched up his nose in disgust and pressed his hand against his mouth as the van's wipers removed the gunk off the windscreen.

'Oh my God, that is disgusting,' he groaned.

'Yeah, sorry about that.' Kendra bobbed her head sympathetically and unfastened her seatbelt, gesturing to Ken and Gary. 'You two grab Wendy.' The two men saluted in unison and leapt out of the van. She fixed the Irishman with a steady gaze and climbed out of the driver's seat into the rear of the van. 'Eddie, as soon as they're in, get us the hell out of here.'

Eddie gave a wordless nod and gratefully eased himself back into the driver's seat. Kendra smiled as she watched him reach up to the windscreen's sun visor and touch the small card of Saint Christopher – the patron saint of motorists and travellers. She was well aware of Eddie's suspicious nature and that he always kept a card inside the slot of a windscreen visor's pouch in whatever vehicle he happened to be driving at the time. Kendra nodded her head grimly as she listened to him recite the traveller's prayer. They were going to need more than luck if they were to get out of this unscathed.

Kendra wheeled round as the two men climbed into the van, carrying a stunned-looking Wendy between them. Her heart leaping for joy, she gave Wendy a thin, grateful smile. Nat pushed the van's door shut and Kendra helped to ease the battered-but-alive woman into her seat. Her face taut and steel-like, she gave Eddie a sideways look. 'Eddie, punch it.'

He didn't have to be told twice. The van shot forward as Eddie slammed his foot down on the accelerator and Kendra grimaced as the force of the acceleration pushed her into her seat. A mile or so down the road, she craned her neck and peered through the rear window, and on seeing no sign of pursuit, she let out a long sigh of relief.

After unfastening her seatbelt, she edged toward Wendy and fixed her with a stern glare. 'You have got a lot to answer for, Cooper,' she whispered, struggling to hide the disappointment in her voice. 'You not only put yourself at risk, but—'

The words died in her throat as she recognised something in her lover's green tear-filled eyes. It was a look she had seen many times from soldiers, up close and on film, in those haunted by things they had seen on the battlefield. She gently put her arm over the shaking woman's shoulder and whispered to her in a low compassionate voice. 'Wendy, do you want to talk about it?'

Wendy collapsed into Kendra's arms, her body shuddering as she sobbed uncontrollably. Kendra, her eyes filled with tears as she gently brushed her hand through Wendy's hair, comforting her.

'I tried, Kendra,' Wendy wailed, her voice thick with grief, 'I tried so hard to save her, but I was too late.'

As the vehicle travelled down the road, the mood in the van quickly changed from dismay to anger as the soldiers listened to Wendy's traumatic account of what she had witnessed inside the factory. Consoling Wendy, a fresh terror of certainty reared up within Kendra as she gazed out of the back window and saw the flames of the factory burning in the distance. One thing she knew for sure; after suffering this latest defeat, Oracle would be coming at them even harder now.

-7-

Location: Secret Command Centre known as the Castle

How could they be so reckless? John seethed, shaking his head in annoyance as he stomped down the brightly lit corridor, not caring about the panicked looks on the faces of the people who were diving out of his way. Grinding his teeth and his jaw clenched tightly, he attempted to keep his rage from boiling over. What had Kendra been thinking of? It was supposed to be a reconnaissance mission, not a bloody demolition job!

As if on cue, the elevator doors opened and a young woman with jet-black hair walked out, her attention fixed on the tablet in her hand, unaware of the unstoppable juggernaut careening toward her. Corporal Daniels, who had been standing patiently waiting for the elevator, did a double take as he spotted the enraged man racing at full speed toward him.

Daniels looked at the distracted woman stepping out of the elevator doors and then back again at the approaching emotionally charged locomotive heading towards her. Realising it was a train wreck waiting to happen, the quick-thinking soldier grabbed her arm and pulled the woman out of harm's way, who gave an alarmed yelp as she suddenly found herself face-to-burley-chest. The unsuspecting raven-haired technician blinked in confusion as a human-shaped blur breezed past her, straight through the open doors and into the elevator.

A few minutes later, John marched onto the maglev tunnel platform, his foot tapping impatiently as the maglev pulled up to a stop and its gull-wing doors swung open. He took a step toward the group of soldiers disembarking, frowning

ORACLE'S VISION

as he noticed the visibly shaken Wendy was being helped out of the carriage by Kendra and Nat.

'Lieutenant Goynes,' he growled angrily, moving toward her, 'I need a word wi—'

'I'll be with you in a minute, sir,' Kendra replied brusquely, cutting him off.

Of all the impertinence! John's nostrils flared with indignation as his chief of security turned her back to him and continued to address the three men in front of her.

'Gary, Eddie, and Ken. You guys go to your quarters and get showered and changed. We'll debrief in an hour,' she ordered.

The three men grunted as they exited the maglev carriage and acknowledged John, who was silently seething, with a slight nod as they moved past him. Kendra then focused her attention on the sandy-haired woman standing next to Wendy. 'Nat, help Wendy to medical,' she said firmly. She raised her hand, cutting off Wendy's protestations. 'No buts, Wendy, you've gone through quite an ordeal tonight and I would feel better if you had the medical staff check you out.'

Wendy let out a heavy sigh and nodded briefly as she followed Nat to the elevator. As soon as the elevator door closed, Kendra massaged her forehead and turned back to John. 'Sir, I know we screwed up.' She sighed wearily.

'Oh, that is an understatement,' John snarled, struggling to hide his anger. 'This is beyond screwing up. Do you realise the shit you have left us in? The press are already spinning it, saying a terrorist group attacked and destroyed a new state-of-the-art hospital built by Oracle to help cancer patients.'

'Sir, if I can just have a minute to explain,' Kendra asked.

His rising temper slowly boiling away inside him, John put his hands on his hips and shook his head in disgust, ignoring his security chief's protests. 'This entire mission was a complete fubar from start to finish,' he continued angrily. 'When I agreed to Cooper joining your team, I believed you could control her.' He stopped to inhale a deep breath and put his head back, laughing bitterly. 'I can see now I was mistaken in believing you wouldn't allow your personal relationship to interfere with your duties. What the hell were you thinking, allowing her to run off half-cocked like that?'

'That is enough!' Kendra roared, startling Payne into stunned silence.

Her eyes blazing, she advanced on him and jabbed her finger into his chest. 'You've said your piece and now *you* will stand there and listen to *me*. I refuse to listen to you bad-mouth Wendy before you've given me a chance to explain.'

John nodded wordlessly and took a reluctant step back, gesturing for the clearly infuriated Kendra to continue. He cocked his head as he listened to her account of the mission. He went through a series of emotions as Kendra told him of Wendy's findings, from outrage upon learning that people were being taken and held against their will, to a mixture of horror and anger on hearing her report of Wendy's discovery of their ultimate fate and her encounter with Oracle.

Feely deeply ashamed for the way he had overreacted, John nodded gloomily, exhaling a weary sigh. 'Kendra, I apologise. I shouldn't have jumped down your throat like that without knowing all the facts first.'

'It's okay, sir,' Kendra replied. 'I probably would have done the same in your place.' Her face clouded and she fixed him with a steely gaze. 'I am certainly not going to apologise for Wendy's actions. If the situations had been reversed, I honestly believe we would have done the same thing.'

'Oh, I wouldn't say that.' John scoffed. Kendra gave him a withering stare, and he held his hand up in a placating gesture, laughing. 'What I mean to say is that I doubt I would have had Wendy's ingenuity. If that had been me, I would probably be dead by now.'

They both laughed together. Unfortunately, it didn't long for an uneasy silence to develop as they turned and stared down at the maglev tunnel with heavy foreboding.

As they sat in contemplative silence, Kendra cast an eye over to John; she could tell something was troubling him, but knew if she pushed him, he would just lock her out. No, she needed to be patient with him and draw him out. She slowly put her hand on his shoulder and gave it a small squeeze.

As if reading her mind, John's shoulders sagged and he sucked in a long heavy breath, shaking his head in frustration. Wearily, he leaned back against the wall and slid down to the floor, head in his hands. 'Damn it! What else can go wrong?' he whispered morosely.

Out of the corner of her eye, Kendra noticed an uncomfortable glance pass between the two platform soldiers on guard duty. From the way they were shifting uneasily in their chairs, she could tell that they were trying not to stare at the forlorn figure on the floor. She gave them a cold glower. Oh no, if they thought she was going to allow them to stand there and listen to John open his heart, they could think again. If she allowed that to happen, then rumours of his mental state would start spreading faster than a speeding bullet. They needed to be gone and she didn't have time to be delicate about it.

'You two, take a walk,' she barked, clicking her fingers.

One of the soldiers, a young fresh-faced fair-haired man, gave an apologetic cough and waved at his guard station. 'Regulations state we shouldn't leave our post unattended.' He swallowed anxiously and raised his finger, as if remembering something, 'Um, tell you what. I think Barb and I are due for our break. I think we'll head up to the mess hall.'

Kendra leaned forward to him, gestured for him to come closer and whispered to him in a flat, neutral tone. 'What's your name, soldier?' she asked coldly.

'Um, Luke, um, Private Harris, ma'am,' the trembling private squeaked, the blood draining from his face.

'Well, Private Harris. Unless you want to end up on septic tank duty, I suggest you both leave now. I don't care where you go – so long as it is not here.' Her tone changed to a harsh whisper as she continued to scowl at the two soldiers in front of her, 'Also, if I hear of strange rumours being circulated of what might have gone on here, I'll hunt down the perpetrator and make their lives a living a hell. Do I make myself clear?

From the glint of fear in Harris's eyes, Kendra could tell he understood perfectly would happen to him if he spoke to anybody about what he and his comrade had overheard. With her gaze still locked on the white-faced soldier, she remained silent as Private Harris gave a nervous sideways glance to his raven-haired colleague. She guessed they must have come to the same conclusion, because they both bobbed their heads furiously in some sort of silent agreement, and then began to slowly edge carefully away. Kendra watched them stumble back and fumble with the elevator's button, pressing it repeatedly. There was a short ping, and the two nervous soldiers dived into the elevator before the doors had time to fully open. The corner of her mouth curling up in bemusement, she glimpsed the relief etched on their faces as the elevator's door finally closed in front of them.

John lifted his head and raised an eyebrow at Kendra, who slid down next to him. They sat in silence for another few minutes, gazing across the platform's floor, the hum of the magnets along the tunnel wall their only company. He finally let out a small laugh and gave her an amused look. 'I get the impression you enjoyed that.'

'Perk of the job,' she replied, chuckling, lifting her shoulder in a slight shrug. She leaned closer and winked, whispering, 'You have to do it with just enough edge in your voice to leave them quaking in their boots.' She chortled maliciously and nudged John. 'If you listened very carefully, you would have heard their sphincters pucker up in fear.'

'You are evil,' John replied, laughing.

'So I've been told.' Kendra grinned, nodding in agreement. Letting her smile slip away, she regarded John thoughtfully and put her hand on his arm. 'So, my friend, you want to tell me what has gotten you so riled up? I'm not the only one that has noticed. I've had people come to me expressing their concerns over your recent angry outbursts.'

Payne shook his head and gave Kendra a dismissive wave of his hand, sighing. 'Kendra, don't get me wrong. I'm grateful for your concern, but as base commander, I shouldn't be burdening you with my concerns.'

'If it's not me, then who?' she replied gently, gesturing to the ceiling above him. 'The situation we are in is unique, something none of us have experienced before. You forget that, like yourself, I served in the military and understand more than most the burdens of command. I've seen first hand the stress of leadership.' She gave him a warm smile and squeezed his hand. 'So, mate, tell me what's bothering you?'

John gave Kendra a tight smile and nodded. Kendra remained silent as John put his head back and stared up at the ceiling with a faraway expression. He drew in a long breath and exhaled a long, frustrated sigh.

'Since Beijing Day, I just feel things have steadily gotten worse. It's as if we are being attacked on all fronts and they are not letting up. Not just outside, but here within the base, too.' He exhaled heavily and ran his hand down his tired face. 'I'm worried about Sophia. She took Beijing's destruction really hard. She rarely leaves her quarters. It's as if she has given up. When I do see her, it's in her quarters to give her security briefings and even then, she barely acknowledges me.'

Kendra bobbed her head without comment. It had become apparent, not just to herself, but also to everyone within the base, that something was wrong. Sophia's absence had left a gaping hole within the command structure, to the extent that it was affecting morale. The base was like a community – when one suffered, they all suffered.

'On top of everything else, my relationship with Sharon is now virtually non-existent,' John continued morosely. 'Since waking up from her coma, she has become very distant. She barely remembers the details of what happened to her when Oracle took over her body. She wakes up during the night screaming from nightmares and experiencing memory flashes. When I try to comfort her, she pushes me away.'

Kendra squeezed his hand. 'We have no idea what she went through or what Oracle made her do when she was in control of her body. Maybe she just needs time for her mind to heal against the trauma.'

'Damn it, don't you think I know that?' John snapped sharply. He lifted his hand apologetically, exhaling. 'Sorry, I didn't mean to snap at you. It's not just her memory loss that has me troubled. I can't help noticing her personality has changed. She's not the same person I fell in love with. It's as if she's afraid to get close too to me in case I hurt her or vice versa.' He shook his head and let out a dejected sigh. 'Now, on top of everything else, I learn people are being turned into cybernetic zombies. I just feel …' He trailed off and stared into the darkness with a troubled expression.

'You feel like the world is against you and doesn't want to give you time to breathe,' Kendra replied, nodding. 'I understand that too well, my friend, more than you realise. But –' she paused and sucked in a deep breath, climbing back to her feet and extending her hand 'there comes a point when you have to realise you cannot control everyone around you, no matter how much you want to.'

Payne stared at the offered hand with a raised eyebrow and nodded in resignation, grunting as his friend helped him to his feet. He wearily rubbed the back of his neck and gave Kendra a questioning look. 'So, what now?'

'Now we do what we're supposed to do, to the best of our ability,' she replied, waving a hand at the ceiling above them. 'All we can do is support those around us the best we can. If we do that, then maybe, God willing, Sophia and

Sharon will see that and open up. As for the rest ...' Kendra spread her hands wide, and the sentence hung in the air.

'It can wait for tomorrow,' John responded, yawning. 'Or later this morning, in our case.'

Suddenly aware of the fatigue her body was feeling, Kendra rolled her head and let out a tired groan. 'If it's all the same to you, I'm going to tell my team to leave the debrief until after we've had some shut-eye. I'm sure they'll be glad to get some rest.'

'Fine by me.' Payne yawned. 'I'm going to call in to Sophia and report your findings, then call it a night. Maybe persuade her to attend the morning debrief. Hopefully, Wendy's discovery may be just the thing she needs to hear to help push her out of her funk.'

Oh crap, Wendy! Kendra blinked and slapped her forehead. 'Damn it, I knew there was something! I must check on Wendy. Hopefully, the medical team has given her the all-clear, and all she needs is a good night's rest.' She stretched her arms over her head and yawned. 'I cannot imagine Oracle throwing us any more curveballs worse than what we found tonight, but whatever the day brings, I'm sure we will handle it.'

John grunted in agreement and followed his security chief toward the elevator. As the doors opened in front of her, Kendra shivered slightly and for a moment she was filled with a sense of dread. The only time she had ever felt like that before was when she had served as a Royal Marine and had to act as a decoy to flush out an enemy sniper. Kendra rubbed the back of her neck with her hand and groaned. The dread she was feeling was probably her body's way of reminding her she had just come off a precarious mission and needed to unwind. Yeah, that was it. She was deep underground in one of the most secure facilities in the world; nothing could hurt her here.

Heart racing, her body covered in sweat, Wendy gasped and opened her eyes. Her eyes slowly adjusting to the darkness, she flinched as she became aware of someone lying next to her. *It's okay,* she thought, *it's only Kendra. You're safe.*

Wendy tilted her head slightly and listened to the various noises in the darkened room – her lover's breathing, the small hiss of recycled air, and the gentle footsteps of people walking past her door as they made their way down the corridor.

A few hours earlier, after the medical staff had given her the all-clear, Wendy allowed Kendra to take her back to her quarters. After showering and helping her to change into her pyjamas, she begged Kendra, who was equally tired, to stay. She couldn't bear the thought of spending the night alone. Kendra had smiled joyfully as they sat on the edge of the bed, gently combing Wendy's long hair in a soothing motion. A few minutes later, they climbed into bed and held one other, Kendra whispering that she wouldn't allow anything to hurt her. Content, Wendy smiled gratefully and drifted off into a troubled sleep.

Tears rolling down her cheeks, she thought back to the events she had experienced hours earlier, picturing the horrified expression on Teresa's face. Why? Why did she have to leave her? Surely there was something she could have done to save her? But as she stared into the darkness, a stark realisation struck her. No matter how many scenarios she ran in her head, no matter how hard she wished it, it would have turned out the same way. There simply would have been no way to save her.

Her eyes closed. Letting the darkness embrace her, she listened to the sound of Kendra's breathing beside her, soothing her. Eventually, she drifted off to sleep and dreamed. In one of her dreams, the roles were reversed. She was the one held captive against her will inside that strange chamber. Terrified and helpless, she watched helplessly as wires crawled into every orifice of her body like snakes searching and probing. Restless, Wendy squirmed in her sleep, hearing her own distressed cries for help as they encased her body in armour, and then noticed somebody creep out of the darkness toward her. Filled with elation, she recognised Teresa as she glided out of the shadows toward her. But Wendy's elation quickly turned to sadness as the pale woman held up a gun, pointed it at her head and pulled the trigger.

Her body soaked with sweat, Wendy woke up, her body trembling, not screaming, but crying hard. Kendra, woken by her sobs, reached over to comfort her. Despite her lover's soothing voice, Wendy could not stop crying and buried her head into Kendra's chest to muffle her sobs. Racked with guilt, Wendy cried out a lifetime of tears. As she cried, a new understanding filled her – that her tears, as well as the guilt, would be a part of her for the rest of her life.

-8-

A few hours later that morning, six miles from the Castle, Dave Barnes reluctantly opened his eyes as he heard the alarm from his mobile phone. Half asleep, he groaned as he reached over to the bedside cabinet and fumbled awkwardly for the vibrating device.

Without looking, Dave grumbled and angrily tapped the phone's screen. He cursed whoever came up with the idea of a mobile phone, secretly hoping they suffered a painful death. The corners of his mouth twitched in satisfaction as he victoriously silenced the infernal alarm. However, his satisfaction quickly evaporated as he realised that he had accidentally knocked the mobile phone across the smooth surface of the cabinet. He groaned again in indignation at the solid thump of the mobile phone hitting the floor.

A wave of sadness overcame him, and he turned his head slightly to the empty spot next to him. His heart aching, he reached over and brushed his hand over the vacant pillow, his thoughts drifting to Claire. He wondered what she was doing.

'Good morning, pet,' he said softly to the empty pillow.

He looked up at the ceiling and exhaled sadly, thinking of the history professor's exquisite face. After recovering from the injuries sustained in her fight with the mysterious creature, Claire had felt it would be a good idea to follow Dave and stay with him. For appearances' sake, they agreed it would help him maintain his cover as a double agent for the resistance if she was to stay with him. If anyone were to enquire why she was staying with him, they came with the story that she was carrying out some research into her sister's death.

For about a week, everything went well. Dave carried out his duties as detective inspector. Claire had remained at his home, secretly continuing her historical research into the Illuminati and their ties to the invaders. But, as time passed, it became increasingly apparent to him that she was struggling with something. He would catch her giving him an odd look and if he questioned her about it, she would shake her head and deny she was doing it. But it was obvious a wedge had appeared between him, and it was slowly driving them apart. So, believing she was probably suffering from post-traumatic stress after the attack, Dave offered the reluctant suggestion that perhaps she would feel safer if she returned to the security of the heavily fortified underground complex. To his surprise, Claire agreed, on the grounds that for the sake of her mental well-being it would be good for her to stay somewhere where she felt safe and allow her time to gather her thoughts. Although outwardly appearing supportive, internally sadness tore at Dave's insides as he watched the woman he loved leave his home.

As he eased himself up and sat on the edge of the bed, Dave let out a tired moan of discontent. He pressed his lips together and stared at the mobile phone on the floor. His chest rising and falling, he inhaled a deep breath and blew it out in a fit of pique, snatching the device off the floor and slamming it back down on the bedside cabinet.

Disgruntled, he shook his head as he reluctantly pushed himself off the edge of the bed, groaning. 'Well, no point sitting here, you old fart, get your arse into gear.'

Straightening up, his face screwed up as his knees cracked under duress at being told they must bear his weight. Wincing in pain, he stumbled across the bedroom to the en-suite shower room.

Dave stripped off his underwear and stepped into the shower cubicle. Then, after turning the circular shower control valve, his body tensed as if it was readying itself for an assault. Finally, a spray of water shot out of the shower head, and he ground his teeth at the ice-cold water striking his skin. But after a few seconds, he closed his eyes and leaned forward as the temperature of the water increased to an almost warm therapeutic level. His eyes still closed, Dave rested his head against the shower cubicle's tiled wall and smiled at the feeling of warm water flowing down his back.

Dave frowned as he thought back to the events of a few weeks earlier. His jaw tightened as he wondered, not for the first time, just where his doppelgänger, Colonel Barnes, had disappeared to. It had been over a month and there had been no recorded sightings of him. It was as if he had vanished off the face of the Earth. Did he go back to his world? Annoyed, Dave pounded the palm of his hand against the shower wall. Just what the hell was Barnes up to?

He leaned back, away from the flow of water, and inhaled a sharp breath. Blowing out his cheeks with a dissatisfied groan, he turned the shower valve off. Whatever Barnes was up to, it would have to wait. Right now, he had other fish to fry and he needed to be completely focused if he was to continue doing his duties without raising any suspicion.

A short time later, clean-shaven and fully dressed in white shirt, tie, and black trousers, he walked into his kitchen, flicked a switch on the wall and waited for the kettle to boil. Dave glanced down to an empty corner of the kitchen floor and felt a pang of sadness inside him.

He stared glumly at the empty spot on the kitchen floor and thought of Jenny, his Cavalier King Charles spaniel. When Claire left, he reluctantly urged her to take Jenny with her, believing it was not only in Jenny's best interests, but Claire's too. He let out a heavy sigh, wishing he could see those sorrowful eyes staring up at him. But she was in the best place, surrounded by people who could give her the attention she deserved.

As he waited for the kettle to finish boiling, Dave picked up a remote control off the kitchen counter and switched on the small flat-screen TV on the kitchen wall. To his chagrin, the simpering smile of a twenty-something peroxide blond greeted him, her magnificent white teeth dazzling off the studio lights.

Appalled, he snarled in contempt and turned away from the TV screen in disgust. One of the first casualties of Oracle's arrival had been the strangulation of television and radio news stations. The likes of the BBC, ITV, Sky News, and CNN had soon found themselves walking a very fine line over what they could report when the invaders brought them under the global umbrella of a new media network called IGNS – Imperial Global News Service.

Julianna Sonatori, the simpering young woman currently on TV, quickly became the face of the news channel. Her constant presence in the broadcast media left no doubt who was the lead anchor. Her dazzling smile and seductive

Italian accent were meant to put the watching public at ease.

'*For those of you just joining, the lead story this morning is of a devastating terrorist attack that occurred during the early hours this morning, one that has left several civilians dead and others in critical condition.*'

What was that? Dave spun sharply, detecting an edge in the news anchor's normal cheery voice. He focused on the screen and immediately noticed something alarming in the woman's body language. Also, instead of her normal tight-fitting white bodysuit to emphasise her lithesome physique, today she was dressed in a sombre black dress. He swallowed, that could only mean one thing – something bad must have happened.

'*Shortly after midnight,*' Julianna continued, '*terrorists seized control of a facility in the north-east English town of Sunderland. Her Grand Majesty, Oracle, created the state-of-the-art facility with her advanced knowledge to help treat people suffering from cancer. Numbers are still coming in of those seriously wounded or dead, but we estimate it to be somewhere in the hundreds.*' Her captivating features darkening, she stared at the camera with a grave expression. '*No terrorist group has yet claimed responsibility for this heinous act, but survivors report the attack was led by this woman.*'

Dave felt his breath catch in his throat as a picture of Wendy Cooper appeared on the TV. Oh no, what had she done now?

'*Wendy Cooper, a former police constable,*' Julianna continued as Wendy's image disappeared from the screen and was replaced with images of people walking around dazed, bloodied and bandaged. '*Witnesses report she stormed the building with no regard for the people inside. Why this woman, a highly decorated police officer, attacked harmless civilians is uncertain. Was it as revenge for being dishonourably discharged from the force after having psychotic break? We may never know. But what we do know for certain is that this woman is dangerous and should not be …*'

Having had just about enough of listening to the woman's lies, Dave switched off the TV and slammed the remote down on the kitchen counter in disgust. He closed his eyes and placed his hands on the counter, his chest rising and falling in rapid breaths as a series of emotions ran through him – confusion, anger, and disappointment.

Damn it! What the hell did she do? he seethed as he paced around the kitchen. Deep down he knew Wendy could not have been responsible, that there was something more going on. Sighing despondently, he switched off the kettle, grabbed his jacket off the back of a chair and stormed out of the kitchen, uneasiness settling in his stomach as he realised one thing was certain – they would look at him to bring her in.

Thirty minutes later, a black Audi Q3 slowed and came to a stop in front of a closed security gate outside the police station. Inside the vehicle, Dave's stomach tightened as he recognised the familiar black and gold armour of one of Oracle's cybernetic soldiers in front of him, its face hidden by the impervious black visor. His fingers whitened as he tightened his grip on the steering wheel.

Like every other police officer across the globe, Dave and those within his station now operated alongside enemy troops. On the surface, everything appeared simple, the world's police forces continuing to operate as normal. The reality, though, was less so. Every police officer was under constant scrutiny by the invaders. Anyone questioning the status quo was quickly reassigned and never heard from again.

Anxious, Dave rolled down his window as the featureless soldier marched toward the car, and he felt his hands become cold and clammy with fear as the intimidating cyber-drone leaned closer to him. He wondered, not for the first time, what the gender was of the figure standing in front of him. Was it a man or a woman? He couldn't tell. As he stared into the black void of the soldier's helmet, he felt his blood freeze in his veins, imagining the person underneath that armour, picturing the horror they were forced to endure as Oracle transformed them into one of her faceless drones.

'Good morning, my good man,' Dave said cheerily, trying to hide his fear. He forced a smile, motioning toward the closed barrier. 'Do you mind letting the barrier down like a good chap?'

'Identification,' the soldier intoned, its voice cold, mechanically distorted by the helmet covering its face.

'Oh, come on.' Dave laughed mirthlessly. 'Do we have to go through this charade every day?' Impatient, he stabbed his finger at his chest and then at the guard. 'I know who I am. You know I am. So stop playing silly buggers and let me through.'

'Identification,' the faceless cyborg repeated.

This time, he registered something dangerous in its tone. On the edge of Dave's peripheral vision, another black and gold armoured soldier moved toward the passenger side of his car, weapon raised. *Easy, Davey boy, don't let your impatience make you do something stupid.* He swallowed and nodded grudgingly, flashing his identification wallet at the humourless guard in front of him.

'There you go, happy?' he said through clenched teeth.

'Identity confirmed. Barnes, David. Rank – detective inspector,' the cyber-drone intoned and gestured to the rising security gate. 'You are cleared to proceed. Have a nice day.'

'Go and polish your faceplate,' Dave muttered under his breath.

'Please repeat statement,' it responded flatly, head cocked enquiringly.

'Have a nice day, too,' he said with a sickly-sweet smile.

Not wanting to hang around any longer than necessary, Dave shifted his car into first gear and carefully drove it under the open security barrier. The corners of his eyes wrinkled as he stared into the rear-view mirror and noted the armoured figure appeared to be watching him carefully as he drove away from the barrier.

A few minutes later and rather breathless, Dave hurried across the car park and sprinted up the steps towards the main entrance. On entering the station's foyer, he stopped as he heard raised voices coming from the reception desk. He poked his head curiously around the corner and saw the back of a large stocky dark-haired man slamming his hand down on the desk's surface.

'I told you I want to see Dave Barnes now!' the man shouted.

'I won't tell you again, sir.' The desk sergeant, a middle-aged moustached man, folded his arms across his chest and fixed the screaming man with a stony stare. 'If you don't stop shouting, we will have to ask you to leave.' He motioned to a seat in the reception area. 'Now, if you give me your name and take a seat, we will see if DI Barnes is here.'

'I've already given you, my name. My name is Sean Logue and I need to see Detective Inspector Dave Barnes,' the man snarled impatiently, slapping his hand repeatedly on the desk, the volume of his voice increasing. 'Not in an hour, not tomorrow. I need to see him now!'

'Sean?' Dave asked carefully.

Sean wheeled around to see who was addressing him. Startled, Dave's eyes grew wide in shock at the condition of the fifty-something man standing in front of him and inhaled sharply as he took in his friend's dishevelled appearance. Sean's thick black hair was untidy and greasy as if it had not been washed for days. Thick bristly whiskers covered his normal clean-shaven chin. Stress lines creased the corners of his blue eyes. His white shirt was creased as if it had been slept in.

Sean staggered forward and grabbed Dave's arm. Dave screwed up his face in disgust as he was hit with an overpowering smell – stale body odour mixed in with alcohol.

'Dave, please, you've got to help me.'

The desk sergeant gave Dave an apologetic look and pointed at the visibly upset man. 'I'm sorry, sir. I tried to stop him, but he was insistent that he needed to see you.'

'It's okay, Sergeant. I can take it from here,' Dave replied, waving his hand dismissively. The desk sergeant nodded warily but continued to watch the swaying man suspiciously.

'I'm sorry, Dave,' Sean continued, shaking his head. His voice was thick with emotion. 'But I didn't know who else to turn to.'

'It's okay, Sean,' Dave answered carefully, gently removing the shaking man's hand from his arm and then guiding him toward an open doorway. 'Let's go into this room where we can talk freely. Is that okay?'

Sean nodded silently and allowed himself to be guided into the room. Once inside, Dave closed the door and motioned for him to take a seat in a chair behind a small square table. Sean slumped into the chair and let out a sob, burying his face in his hands.

Dave's stomach tightened as he stared at the once proud man in front of him. He shivered as he felt the hairs on the back of his neck tingle, suspecting the cause of his friend's upset to be his wife, Karen, or in this case, Karen's doppelgänger. Dave had known Sean's wife for many years, not only as a friend but also through her role as a forensic examiner. Less than two months earlier, they had been working together on a murder investigation and it was during that investigation that he had noticed a change in Karen's behaviour. A short time after that, he learned of people being replaced by duplicates from an alternate world. Since then, he had lived in constant dread that this day would come; that he would have to tell Sean that his wife was not who she appeared to be and that Karen –

the real Karen – may be dead.

His fingers steepled together, Dave inhaled a long breath and fixed Sean with a steady gaze. 'So, mate, care to tell me what has got you so upset?' he asked, trying to keep his voice flat and neutral.

Drawing in a sharp breath, Sean nodded dolefully. He opened his mouth to speak but continued to stare at his hands. 'I ... I think there is something wrong with Karen,' he said finally, his voice wobbling as he struggled to hide his emotions. He swallowed and closed his eyes as if he was trying to force the words out. Dave gravely sat in silence and waited for his friend to continue.

Sean scrubbed his face with his hands and let out a despondent whimper. 'I noticed it a few weeks ago. She arrived home from work one day and it was as if she was a different woman – cold and distant.' He laughed bitterly, shaking his head. 'I just kept telling myself I was being paranoid, that she was probably stressed because of work and just needed a break.' He pressed his lips together and raised his head, staring at Dave with haunted eyes. 'A day or so later, I was walking past the bedroom door of our daughter, Aoife, and I could hear crying coming from within. She was lying huddled on top of her bed, sobbing quietly. When I asked her what was wrong, she told me Karen had hurt her because she spilled some milk.' With a bitter look clouding his face, he stared up at the ceiling and let out a hollow laugh. 'I didn't believe her at first. You know how it is, because she's a child, you tell yourself *Oh she's just trying to play us off against each other.* Then she showed me the bruises on her back.' Sean slapped his hand down on the table, startling Dave and making him jump, but he remained silent, letting his friend tell his story. Sean's eyes were filled with venomous hatred as he ran his hands through his hair. 'You can imagine my horror when I saw the bruises on my daughter's back.' His voice lowered to a horrified whisper and he shook his head. 'Karen and I both agreed we would *never* raise our hands to our daughter if she ever misbehaved.'

Dave cocked his head and gave his friend a questioning look. 'So, what did you do?'

'I confronted her, of course. She admitted it,' Sean replied. He scoffed and shook his head in dismay. 'Then she had the temerity to blame me, saying I was too soft with her, that it's about time we showed her who was boss.' He paused and closed his eyes, massaged his temples with his fingers, and moaned softly. 'I kept telling myself she was just tired and put it down to stress from work, so I let it go, believing she just needed some time to herself. A short time after that I suspected something was really wrong. One night we were in bed and she forced herself on top of me, and she became something else.' He wrung his hands and shifted uncomfortably in the seat. 'Something cruel and perverse. She enjoyed pain and seemed to get off on hurting me. But if I pleaded with her to stop, it just made her even worse, as if she enjoyed it!' He exhaled a ragged breath and stared up at the ceiling with pain-filled eyes. 'That was when I really suspected this ... monster ... was not the woman I married. So, as soon as I could, I took Aoife to stay with my parents. I made the excuse that Karen wasn't well and needed some time to herself.'

'What about Karen? Was she not suspicious about why you had taken her daughter away?' Dave pressured curiously.

Sean let out an indifferent grunt. 'To be honest, I think she couldn't care less.' He took in a deep breath and blew out his cheeks in exasperation, waggling a finger at his probing friend. 'I know what you're thinking – that I've been drinking too much and letting my mind play tricks on me.' His eyes blazed with anger, and his voice increased in volume as he stabbed his finger toward the doorway. 'But I'm telling you the truth. *That* woman is not my wife.'

Dave shook his head silently and rose out of his chair. He rubbed the back of his neck as he stared out of the window into the car park. What should he say? Tell him no, you aren't going mad? Yes, a doppelgänger from an alternate world has replaced your wife. With his hands behind his back, he steeled himself and stared sympathetically at his friend.

'Sean, there is something I need to tell you,' he said in a low careful voice.

'What are you talk—' Sean's eyes grew wide as saucers. His face reddened with anger and understanding slowly dawned on his face. 'You knew?' he hissed, his neck muscles tensing with anger.

'Sean, take it easy,' Dave urged. He raised his hands in a placating gesture, trying to calm the angry man in front of him. 'You don't know all the facts.'

His body trembling with indignation, Sean let out a roar of fury and lurched across the table toward Dave, sending his chair flying across the room.

Appearing to be blinded by rage, he charged into Dave, catching him off guard. The breath was forced out of Dave's lungs as he felt his back slam against the wall, stunning him. He gasped in pain as he felt the enraged Sean's fingers begin to tighten around his throat.

'You bastard. We trusted you,' Sean hissed in a voice thick with contempt and eyes filled with hatred.

'I need to explain,' Dave wheezed desperately, struggling against the man's grip. His vision going white, Dave gasped for air as the pressure increased on his throat.

All hell broke loose. The interview room door burst open; two police officers charged into the room and grappled Sean away from Dave. The vice-like grip released around his neck, Dave let out a harsh cough and sank to the floor, his eyes watering. He watched in sympathy as Sean, the fight draining from him, collapsed to the floor and sobbed. The two burly police officers watched the distraught man closely with suspicion as they stood over him.

Another police officer rushed into the room and knelt next to Dave. Her eyes were filled with concern as she put a hand on his shoulder. 'Guv, are you okay, sir?' she asked gently.

'I'm fine. Get out of here,' Dave croaked, wincing at the pain in his throat as he waved the police officer away. His face hardening, he clambered back up to his feet and stared at the two police officers standing over the pitiful man on the floor. 'That goes for you two as well – out, now.'

'Sir?' the three police officers exclaimed in unison, looking at Dave in shocked surprise.

'You heard me,' he snapped harshly, gesturing towards the door. 'Out now and close the door behind you.'

The three officers nodded grudgingly and headed toward the open door. Before she closed the door behind her, the female police officer looked over her shoulder and gave Dave a quizzical look. He returned her look with a thin smile and held up his hand to say he was okay. The woman pursed her lips together and gave a small nod of acknowledgement, closing the door behind her.

Rubbing his throat, Dave stared sympathetically at the man on the floor. No longer sobbing, Sean sat silently on his knees, staring at the floor with a vacant expression. Dave glanced up at the ceiling and shook his head, his mind racing.

He should have seen this coming. Sighing heavily, he crouched next to Sean and placed a hand on his shoulder.

'Sean, I'm sorry,' he whispered carefully. Sean grunted but remained silent as Dave continued. 'I can understand how upset you are, but you need to understand why I couldn't tell you.'

'How long?' Sean murmured, still staring at the floor.

'Sorry?' Dave answered, frowning.

'How long have you known?'

'Two months.' Dave sighed morosely, shaking his head apologetically. 'Two days before Beijing Day, to be exact. I called in to visit Karen to ask her a question abou—'

Before he could finish his sentence, a searing pain blinded him as he felt something hard slap his cheek. Stunned, Dave lifted his hand to the side of his face and stared open mouthed at Sean, whose fists were clenched, his body trembling with fury as he climbed to his feet and glowered at Dave through narrow hostile eyes.

'Two months,' he hissed with contempt. He paced around Dave, scowling at him. 'You knew for two months but said nothing.' Sean stopped, put his hands on his hips, and stared at his friend with angry pained eyes. 'Did you not even consider your goddaughter when you found out? Knowing how dangerous that imposter was, the risk she posed?'

'Sean, listen to me,' Dave pleaded as he climbed back up to his feet, hands held up in front of him, 'don't you think I realise that? Have you considered that by telling you it may have put you in greater danger?' Sean's forehead creased with uncertainty as Dave continued. 'You've already told me how vindictive this witch is. The bruises on Aoife, her callous attitude, and the other stuff. Imagine what would have happened if she found out you knew. She could have arranged for your daughter to be taken much like your wife was, or worse.'

The atmosphere inside the room became heavy as Dave took a moment for his statement to register with the emotionally charged man. As Sean's face turned slowly ashen, Dave guessed the implications of his words had hit home. Sean's shoulders sagged and he gave a reluctant bob of his head.

'I understand,' he replied hoarsely. He fixed Dave with an icy stare and spoke in a low flat voice. 'Do you know if Karen is still alive? Can you at least tell me that?'

Uncertain how he should respond, Dave was silent; he considered whether to be fully honest with the emotionally stricken man. Should he admit to him that Karen may be dead? He scratched his chin thoughtfully, remembering something Andy had told him about what his wife, Mary, had told him about what she could remember of her time in that other world.

'I don't know for certain,' he replied hesitantly.

'I see, so there's no hope then?' Sean mumbled dejectedly.

His hand on resting his friend's shoulder, Dave shook his head and gave him a false smile. 'I wouldn't say that, mate. My detective sergeant's wife was taken, but she found a way to escape and make it back to our world.' He cringed internally. Although it was technically true that Mary did escape, it was only because she had the help of his counterpart. He shook the thought to one side as he tried to convince himself what he was doing was right and pressed on with the lie. 'Your wife is quite a resourceful woman, so if anybody can find a way to escape and make it back to you, she can.'

'You're right there.' Sean chuckled. 'Karen can be quite stubborn when she puts her mind to something.'

Dave drew in a long deep breath, steadying himself for what he had to ask next. Deep down, he already despised himself for the stress and turmoil he was about to place upon his friend, but these were harsh times and sacrifices must be made for the greater good.

'Sean, I need you to do something, and I'm afraid you'll not like it,' he said sorrowfully. 'You can refuse but I'm going to have to insist you do it.'

'What do you mea—' Sean stopped and his eyes grew wide as saucers. 'No.' he croaked, shaking his head as he slowly edged away. 'Dave, please tell me you're not going to ask me what I think you are?'

Ignoring his horrified friend's pleas, Dave sighed sadly and nodded glumly, putting both of his hands on Sean's shoulders. He fixed the emotionally shattered man with a look of determination and spoke to him in a firm voice. 'I need you to return home.'

Sean reeled away from Dave, his mouth agape. He then waved his hands and shook his head defiantly. 'No, you cannot make to do this.' His eyes glistening with tears, he held both his hands up in front of him. 'Mate, you don't know what you're asking.'

Pretending to grab his friend to make it look like he was comforting him, Dave lowered his voice and whispered in Sean's ear, 'I'm sorry, mate, but I'm going to insist you do this. The resistance has been desperate to get someone close to a doppelgänger. You have just handed us the perfect opportunity. You admitted yourself that Karen doesn't suspect you know. I can see this is a lot to ask, but we need you to return home and carry on as if nothing has happened.' He released his grip and Sean ceased struggling. 'We want you to keep a close eye on her and record everything she says and does. Do you understand?'

Looking defeated, his face pale, Sean nodded reluctantly and edged away from Dave. He remained silent as he strode towards the door and opened it. Glancing over his shoulder at Dave, he stared at him with bitter eyes filled with loathing. 'Dave, mate, whatever you're involved in, get out while you still can.' He spoke in a voice that was flat and neutral. 'This road you're on, get off now, before it takes down a route you cannot back away from.'

-9-

Dave sadly watched his emotionally shattered friend, his shoulders slumped in defeat, trudge down the corridor toward the station's main entrance. As he watched Sean walk through the building's doors, Dave ran a hand down his face and let out a weary sigh, wondering, once again, how many more friends he would lose before this damned war was over.

Feeling like he had the weight of the world on his shoulders, Dave shook his head wearily, turned slowly round and made his way up a short flight of stairs. On reaching the top, he raised an eyebrow in surprise as he spotted the familiar bulky figure of Constable Will Bates. From his glowering expression and agitation, it would not have taken a genius to guess what was on the sandy-haired man's mind.

'Constable Bates,' Dave acknowledged with a bob of his head as he continued to stride down the corridor.

'Sir,' Will grunted in reply. He slid up next to Dave and matched his pace, at the same time giving a furtive look over his shoulder and leaning in closer. He spoke in a low, angry voice. 'Have you seen the stuff they're saying about Wendy? I'm appalled at the shit they're coming out with.'

'Unfortunately, the first casualty in war is the truth,' Dave murmured. 'There's not a lot we can do about it.'

The angry constable let out a snort of disgust and hissed under his breath, 'Screw that! I've been talking with some of the others, and we aren't prepared to put up with the shit they're spouting about her. We plan to confront Chief Inspector Thomas and demand he issue a public statement condemning these lies that are being broadcast about Wendy.'

Not caring who saw them, Dave came to a complete stop and grabbed Will's arm. He fixed Will with a deep, penetrating stare as he hissed at him through clenched teeth. 'You will do no such thing, Constable.'

'But, sir!' Will said, shaking his head. 'We can't just stand by while they bad-mouth her. We must do something.'

'We will be doing something – our jobs,' Dave responded angrily. He paused as he suddenly became aware that they were starting to attract some unwanted attention from passersby. He took in a deep breath to try to reign in his anger, smiled and then put his hand on Will's shoulder. 'Will, I can guess how you're feeling. I feel the same way, but we both know that if you all go marching up to the chief inspector you'll only make things worse. I—'

Without warning, Detective Sergeant Brenda Donnelly barrelled into the surprised pair, knocking them apart.

'Oh, I'm very sorry, Guv,' she breathed, giving Dave a small apologetic cough as she gestured discreetly to something behind her.

Dave acknowledged Brenda with a grateful nod, noticing two of the black and gold armoured cyber-drones striding towards him. The two men remained silent as the two cyborgs marched past them. As soon as they were out of earshot, he spoke in a low, firm voice. 'Will, we've heard the rumours. Anyone caught speaking any type of dissent is arrested and never seen again.' Dave shook his head knowingly and stared at Bates. 'Wendy wouldn't want you to put yourself at risk because of her. She would want you to continue doing your duty to the best of your ability.' He gritted his teeth and let out a hiss of contempt. 'Son, don't let the bastards grind you down. Promise me you won't do anything stupid.'

The constable sighed and gave Dave a small nod. 'Aye, sir. I promise not to do anything.' His face muscles hardened as he fixed him with an intense stare. 'But I'm only doing this for you and because I know that is what Wendy would want.'

'Good man.' Dave smiled sombrely. 'Now get on your way before you raise any more suspicion. Pass the word to the others. I want it known that this comes from me – we will continue to act normally until we are told otherwise.'

Bates acknowledged Dave with a slight nod and turned away from him. Dave squeezed his eyes shut and pinched the bridge of his nose. He had a strong suspicion that Oracle had released that news report about Wendy with the sole purpose of increasing unrest among her former colleagues. Well, he grumbled to himself, if Will's reaction was anything to go by, she had done exactly that.

But as he continued to stride down the corridor, Dave frowned as he noticed Sergeant Donnelly appeared to be hovering outside the open door to the squad room. She was chewing on her bottom lip anxiously as he approached her. He tilted his head slightly as he picked up raised voices coming from within the squad room.

'Sir, just wanted to warn you,' she said in a hushed tone, pointing to the open doorway, 'there are a lot of angry people in there.'

'Thanks, Brenda,' he growled gratefully.

Brenda hurried through the open doorway and then Dave took in a deep breath, squared his shoulders, and followed her into the squad room to be greeted by a series of angry voices as soon as he stepped through the doorway. He paused for a second to take in the room. Scattered around the squad room were various desks with flat-screen computers, telephones, and files. Large whiteboards covered the walls at the far end of the room with various notes and pictures plastered over them. He focused his attention on the dozen men and women standing in the centre of the room who were arguing among themselves. Dave listened carefully to the raised voices.

'It's not right, I tell you. We shouldn't have to listen to it.'

'I say it's about time we made our grievances known.'

'Have you listened to the rumours? Cooper protested at being forced to work with them and they quickly got shot of her. I've read they've brainwashed her and are using her as a scapegoat.'

'Don't be stupid, man.'

'I'm not being stupid. Big Al in cyber-crimes told me. Apparently, he read it somewhere on the dark web.'

'I say we go on strike. They'll have to listen to us to then if we refuse to work under these conditions. I don't know how much longer I can take these faceless gestapo goons watching over us every second of the day.'

Having listened to enough, Dave took the door in both hands and slammed it shut, nearly taking it off its hinges. Every windowpane in the squad room rattled and two bookshelves collapsed, scattering their contents across the floor. The dozen men and women in the centre of the room jumped and wheeled round in shock to see who was roaring at them.

'That is *enough*!'

Before his fellow officers had time to recover their wits, Dave held his hand up to cut off the deluge of apologies and explanations that were about to be thrown at him. He gave the room an intense, glowering stare and shook his head in contempt, gesturing to the door behind him.

'Are you all frigging nuts?' he snarled. 'Our job is hard enough as it is without you all spouting this shit. Don't you realise we're already treading a thin line?'

Detective Constable Marsters, a bald-headed, heavyset man moved forward and coughed sheepishly. 'Guv, we're just saying we nee—' He suddenly appeared to lose the power of speech as Dave shot him a look that would curdle milk. Red faced, he hung his head and shuffled back.

'Oh, I know what you were saying,' Dave snapped, bobbing his head at the closed door. 'I picked you all up from the corridor. I'm sure if you were loud enough, the whole bloody station would have picked up all of you arguing.' His hands on his hips, Dave sighed in exasperation and stared up at the ceiling. 'Don't you understand? The new powers that be are just waiting for any excuse to jump on anyone voicing any form of dissent.' He lowered his voice to a soft whisper. 'I'm sure you have heard the rumours about what happens to officers who refuse to carry out the orders issued to them?' The group nodded in acknowledgement, murmuring sullenly.

Detective Sergeant Cheryl Tonnar, a forty-something woman with wavy copper hair, wearing a navy trouser suit, took a small step forward and raised her hand enquiringly. She cast her colleagues a sideways glance and smiled nervously at Dave.

'Sorry, Guv,' she murmured softly. 'But we have all seen the stuff they're reporting about Wendy. Surely that can't be true – what they're saying about her?'

Sucking in a deep breath, Dave spread his arms wide and exhaled wearily. 'Cheryl, we all know Wendy and what she was like. The important thing is we recognise it for what it is. We may not like what they're saying about her, but the important thing is we keep our opinions to ourselves.' The muscles in his face tightened as he slowly looked around at the long-faced officers in the room. 'They will look to us to bring her in.' He held his hand up to silence the murmurs of discontent. 'I know, I know. It's rubbish and I agree with you, but, let me emphasise this, we are here to uphold the law and not to let our personal feelings get in the way.' He beckoned the group to approach him, lowered his voice and pointed to the closed door behind him. 'We do it by numbers and play the game. You do *not* give *them* any more reason to suspect us than they do now. If we are to bring Cooper in, then we do it by the book and have each other's backs. Understand?'

Dave coughed and tapped his right index finger on his nose. He gave a thin smile as the people in front of him nodded in silent understanding. Yes, they understood. If the powers-that-be ordered them to bring Wendy in, they would do it, but that did not mean they had to do it the easy way.

'That's good,' he continued, raising his voice to a louder, more authoritative tone. 'Now, I don't want to listen to any more complaining. If I hear any more talk of striking or refusing to carry out orders, I will march you up to the chief inspector so fast your feet won't have time to touch the ground. You have your orders. Get on with it.'

Dave struggled to hold back a laugh as Detective Sergeant Terry Rogers, a thin-haired, fifty-something man, let out an over-dramatic grumble. As Terry walked passed him, Dave stared at him sternly. 'Don't overdo it, Terry.'

'Sorry, Guv,' Terry responded, grinning. 'I was in the moment.'

Not wanting to comment on his colleague's less than impressive acting skills, Dave bit his tongue as his comrades slowly dispersed and headed to their desks. But as he turned, he paused and let his eyes linger on the empty desk that once had belonged to Andy. He stared at it dolefully and brushed his hand along the empty desk's surface. A weight settled on his heart as he wondered where his friend was.

Officially, Detective Sergeant Andy Jenkins was on long-term leave, recovering from his injuries sustained in an attack while carrying out his duties. Unofficially, to help his wife recover from the trauma following her abduction and return from the parallel world, John Payne had arranged for them to be transferred to one of the other resistance bases.

Dave jumped and was broken out of his reverie as he felt a hand touch his shoulder. He twisted his neck sharply and raised an eyebrow on noticing Brenda was standing alongside him. He realised he had been so deep in his own thoughts he had not seen her slide up to him.

'Sorry, Guv,' she whispered apologetically. 'The chief inspector has requested your presence. He demands that you come up to his office immediately.'

Not making an effort to hide his annoyance, Dave groaned and peered up at the ceiling, shaking his head. Oh great, what did his grand holier-than-thou want now? He ground his teeth at the thought of having to go up to speak to him. Yes, it was true that Chief Inspector Thomas was his superior. Fine, he could accept that. What riled him was the fact that he was a pompous windbag who looked down on everyone serving under him with obvious contempt. There was nobody in the station who liked him; everyone avoided him at every opportunity. Also, although they could never prove it, there was a strong suspicion that he was in bed with those behind the conspiracy.

'Fine, Brenda.' He sighed wearily, trudging towards the door. 'I'd better not wait and keep his lordship waiting.'

Brenda watched her weary boss disappear down the corridor. Her lips pressed together as she stared up at the ceiling, her thoughts drifted to the chief inspector two floors above. She pictured the pompous fool strutting around his office.

She pulled her gaze down from the ceiling, blew out a heavy breath and scratched her head. Because of the chief inspector's swift actions during the attack on DI Barnes and that mysterious woman he had been with, Brenda, much like everybody else who had witnessed the aftermath, quickly assumed Chief Inspector Thomas had perhaps softened. Those in the know believed there was a chance they could trust him after all.

Unfortunately, a few days after the invasion, it quickly became apparent just where the chief inspector's loyalties lay. Those in the station had watched with increasing anxiety as Thomas led a squad of black and gold armoured cyber-drones into the station, making it apparent who now was in charge.

Over the past month, morale around the station had declined as their treacherous leader continued to tighten security, implementing stricter working practices and even harsher punishments for those officers refusing to toe the line.

To add to Brenda and her colleagues' consternation, their fears worsened on reporting for work that morning and learned of the previous night's terrorist attack on a so-called medical facility in Sunderland. As she watched the news report, her unease quickly changed to dismay as the news channel laid the blame for the attack upon her former colleague, Wendy Cooper. Although she couldn't prove it, there was no doubt in her mind Thomas was behind the smear campaign being directed at Wendy.

Brenda strode over to her desk and eased herself into her chair. A small chuckle escaped her as she leaned back and tapped a pen on her lower lip thoughtfully. Her mouth widened into a malicious grin, her gaze drifting up at the ceiling, and she secretly wished for Barnes to tear the pompous a prick a new one. Oh, she would have given anything to be a fly on the wall in Thomas's office at that moment.

Two floors above, standing in front of a door marked *"Chief Inspector Raymond Thomas"*, Dave paused as he placed his trembling hand on the doorknob. He closed his eyes and struggled to contain his feelings toward Thomas; he could barely tolerate being in the same room as him. His obvious contempt and disregard for those serving under him really irked him, so he tolerated him for appearances' sake.

Realising he couldn't put it off no longer, Dave drew in a long breath, straightened his shoulders, and twisted the doorknob, pushing the door open. Upon entering the room, he started in surprise; Thomas was standing waiting for him with his hands behind his back. He hadn't expected to find him in his outer office, normally reserved for his secretary.

Dave could almost feel the hostility radiating out of Thomas's eyes as he approached him. He was clearly unhappy that he'd had been kept waiting. 'Ah, there you are Barnes. What kept you?' Before Dave could reply, Thomas waved his hand dismissively, cutting him off. 'Humph! Whatever. At least you are here now, even though you are a bit tardy. Not a good way to make an impression on the troops. What?'

'Yes, sir,' Dave replied through clenched teeth, struggling to hide his irritation. 'It won't happen again.'

Thomas laughed contemptuously. 'Make sure it doesn't.' His beady hazel eyes glimmered with suspicion and he tilted his head enquiringly. 'I take it you saw the news regarding the attack on that medical centre last night?'

'Yes, sir,' Dave replied, shaking his head sadly, 'I cannot believe how they are making Constable Coop—'

'Former Constable Cooper,' Thomas interjected, raising his finger.

'Yes, *former* Constable Cooper,' Dave continued through clenched teeth. 'Like I said, I cannot understand how the press believe she's behind it.'

'Oh, I very much believe it.' Thomas scoffed, running his hand through his grey beard. 'She was always a bad egg, so it's no surprise she has gone down this route.'

With his hands balled into fists, Dave ground his teeth and struggled to hide his annoyance. The veins in his temples throbbed as he bit back a retort. As he regarded the chief inspector, the hairs on the back of his neck tingled and he slowly put two and two together. After seeing Wendy's name being plastered across the news earlier, he strongly suspected who had been behind the frame job. Although he would have a hard time proving it, it was obvious to him that Thomas had a hand in the smear campaign aimed at discrediting her.

If the chief inspector was aware of his subordinate's irritation, he did not make it obvious as he continued with his tirade. 'From the first day I saw that woman, I knew there was something dodgy about her. Well, just goes to prove, no matter how much you polish a turd, it is still a turd. You cannot change its nature.' He pursed his lips and straightened up, his hands behind his back. 'Of course, the powers that be would like her brought in as quickly as possible, by any means necessary.' He paused to let the statement hang in the air, implying lethal force was to be used. 'Barnes, I understand you have a history with this woman, so if you feel it has impaired your judgement I will understand if you want to excuse yourself from this case.'

Dave stared at the man in front of him coldly and answered him in a low, neutral voice. 'No, *sir*. You couldn't drag me away, *sir*.' He lifted his head and gave the officer a menacing smile, hoping to sound convincing in an attempt to sway him. 'If anything, I would say I am the best person for the job. You see, I know how she thinks.' He laughed bitterly and rubbed his hands with glee. 'She made a fool of me, betraying my trust. So it would be a pleasure to take that bitch down.'

For several minutes, the chief inspector silently paced around the small office, staring at Dave with distrustful eyes. Finally, the corners of his mouth quirked in amusement and he nodded approvingly.

'Very good.' He chuckled. 'The others warned me you were a liability, but I told them otherwise. I can see my faith in you has been rewarded.' His mouth setting into a hard line, he moved forward and placed his hand on Dave's shoulder. 'A new dawn is coming, my friend, and you have a choice to make. You can either stand in history's way and let it grind you into the ground as it stomps over you, or you can be among those standing on the shoulders of Oracle as we take our place in history. What will it be?'

Bile rising in his throat, stomach churning, Dave managed to force a smile as he bowed his head subserviently. 'All hail to the will of Oracle.'

The chief inspector's mouth widened into a broad grin and he clapped his hands in obvious glee. 'Excellent. The others told me it would be a mistake to bring you into the fold.' He let out a loud barking laugh and waggled his finger at Dave, who was internally seething. 'I can see you have good instincts like me. You can tell the way the wind is blowing and want to get on board before it's too late.' Thomas snorted derisively, slapping his hand on Dave's back. 'The others don't see what I can see, a man who isn't afraid to take chances.'

Inwardly despising him, Dave forced himself to smile and nodded gratefully. Every fibre of his being was telling him he shouldn't trust this man, but at the same time he was acutely aware that the resistance had been wanting to get an inside man into the elusive so-called Illuminati for years with little success. He realised that if he did not seize this chance now, the resistance would never have another opportunity to gain a foothold inside Oracle's inner circle.

'So, when do I meet the others?' he asked carefully, hoping he was not coming across too eager.

Thomas waved his hand dismissively and gave him a warm smile. 'Oh, plenty of time for that, old boy.' He glowered dangerously and pointed his finger into Dave's chest. 'You still have to prove your loyalty by bringing in Cooper. If you can bring us her head, then you will have proved yourself.'

'I see,' Dave replied, turning warily toward the door. 'Then if there isn't anything else, I'd best get on with it.'

Before he could make his way to the door, Dave felt a firm restraining hand on his arm, stopping him in his tracks. He raised an eyebrow enquiringly at Thomas. Damn it, he knew he had come across as too eager. His heart leapt into his throat, but he kept his face neutral as he tried to keep his voice calm.

'Was there something else, sir?' he asked, trying to keep his voice from betraying his rising fear.

Thomas shuffled his feet awkwardly and glanced forlornly at the closed door leading to his office. An alarm rang in the back of Dave's head, and he tensed as he felt himself being guided toward the closed door.

'Barnes, I'm really sorry about this,' Thomas said sorrowfully, 'but I think you misunderstood the reason you were called up to my office. Yes, I admit I wanted to discuss the Cooper situation with you, but it wasn't me who called for you.' He sighed loudly and opened the door to his office, motioning for Dave to go in. 'I'm truly sorry about this, old boy, but I'm only following orders.'

His heart hammering in his chest, Dave was numb with fear and felt himself being pushed through the open door into the chief inspector's office. The door closed behind him, and he scratched his head in bewilderment as he realised that, apart from the usual office furniture, and a leather sofa, he was standing alone in Thomas's office.

Perplexed, Dave edged forward toward the window. Massaging the back of his neck, he stared out of the window, mystified at why he was alone in the office. Just what the hell was going on here? Was he being held here against his will? Or was it something else? Was Thomas going to have him killed? Dave shook his head and quickly dismissed that thought. No, Thomas wouldn't even dare killing him here, not with a building full of witnesses. So, what then? Wait until there were fewer people around and then have him taken away, killed and disposed of in a shallow gave? Dave let out a small sigh and ran his hand down his face. Come on man, get a grip. He wasn't that important, there had to be a reasonable explanation why he was in Thomas's office ... all alone. Yeah, it was just a simple misunderstanding. There was nothing for him to worry about ... wasn't there?

Too deep in his own troubled thoughts, his attention fixed ahead of him, Dave felt his forehead pucker as he heard a strange noise coming from behind him – the sucking of air as if it was escaping from a vacuum. He spun sharply round in sudden realisation, just in time to see a bald silver-skinned woman wearing what looked like a tight-fitting silver bodysuit climb out of the mirror. He lifted an eyebrow as he noticed her face was blank and featureless, no longer resembling Wendy Cooper like she had been when she first appeared two months ago.

The synthetic woman's mouth broadened into a wide grin at Dave. 'Ah, you are here. Sorry to keep you waiting.' She bowed slightly, gesturing to herself. 'My name is Oracle, but you are already aware of that, are you not? I believe this is the first time you and I have spoken.' The corners of her mouth twitched in amusement as she winked at him. 'Officially, that is.'

His arms folded across his chest, Dave leaned back against the wall as he appraised the artificial woman in front of him and curled up his top lip in a disdainful sneer. 'Oh, I very much remember our first meeting,' he said curtly, referring to their earlier encounter when she had been inhabiting the body of a prisoner he'd had been questioning. 'I think I still have the bruises to prove it.'

For a brief moment Oracle's cold yellow eyes glowed with the intensity of the sun before returning to their natural luminance. She shook her head, chuckling softly in amusement. 'Oh my, yes, those were fun times. I am sure Claire got a real kick out of it, too.'

How dare she breathe Claire's name! Dave's mood darkened and he fixed the amused synthetic with a stony stare. 'Are you going to get to the point of why you wanted you to see me? I'm sure it wasn't just to chat about the past.'

Her bottom lip pushing forward in mock petulant annoyance, Oracle hung her head and stared at him through puppy dog eyes. 'Aw, why so serious, Dave? We were having so much fun. What is wrong? Did I hit a raw nerve?' Dave responded with a silent baleful stare, and she waved a finger at him, tutting. 'You must learn to lighten up, David. All that anger cannot be good for you.'

However, before he could open to his mouth to tell synthetic woman just where she could stick her advice, his experienced detective instincts kicked in, stopping him. He smiled to himself, realising that Oracle was trying to bait him, to force him into making a deadly mistake. Expelling a long-drawn-out puff of air, he lifted his shoulders in an indifferent shrug. 'My health is fine, a little arthritis on a morning, but I appreciate your concern.' He scratched his chin thoughtfully and regarded the faux woman curiously. 'I'm sure you have your hands full with my counterpart. Please tell him I cannot wait to see him again.'

Oracle scoffed and flicked her wrist in a slightly dismissive wave. 'Oh, I am sure you would.' She shook her head sadly and let out a melodramatic sigh. 'That poor man has just not been the same since you last saw him. In fact, one could say he is in pieces over it. I have tried to *drum* it into him, that he needs to pull himself together, but he is just in bits.'

The hairs on the back of Dave's neck tingled as he tried to make some sense of the AI's statement. Was she implying that Barnes was dead? He felt his eyebrows shoot up as he was struck with a light-bulb moment, recalling the series of events that took place in the Castle a few weeks earlier. Of course! How could he have been so stupid? Why hadn't he seen it sooner? He frowned as he realised that he had never really learned what Sharon had been up to when she had been under Oracle's control. Maybe it was high time they found out.

Dave blinked as he realised that he had been so caught up in his own thoughts he had momentarily forgotten where he was. As he brought his attention back to the room, he became suddenly aware that Oracle was looking at him strangely. Her cold yellow were glowing a bright luminescent yellow and her head appeared to be tilting from side to side. For a moment Dave wondered whether she was analysing him. Was she trying to read his thoughts? He started. Could she even do that? He swallowed anxiously as it struck him that they knew next to nothing about Oracle's capabilities.

Feeling his throat tighten with heavy anxiety, Dave's mind raced as he desperately thought of something to say to distract the synthetic woman in front of him. He forced himself to smile as an idea came to him. *If she wants to play games, let's see how she likes this.*

'Yes, I'm sure you have your hands full at the moment.' He shook his head, sighing sadly. 'I hear you suffered a bit of a setback last night. What was it again, a medical centre?' He arched his head and shot the scowling synthetic a penetrating stare, the tone of his voice taunting. 'I don't know the full facts, but I'm guessing Wendy was involved in some way. Can I assume you're behind the press attack on her?' He let out a hollow laugh as he caught a flicker of irritation from Oracle. 'Oh, she must have really gotten under your skin. What's wrong? She uncovered something you didn't want XXXnybodyy to see, and she blew the facility to smithereens?' A shadow of a contemptuous smile crossed his lips as he

ORACLE'S VISION

snickered at the thing in front of him. 'Oh, it must burn you, knowing she escaped your clutches.'

Her yellow eyes blazing with burning hatred, Oracle let out an angry snarl and launched herself at Dave. Dave, expecting the reaction, squared his shoulders defiantly and stood his ground. Their faces were barely centimetres apart, unflinching, eyes locked on each other.

Dave could almost feel the loathing in Oracle's voice as she AI hissed at him, 'I am through with playing games. You want a war, fine, you have got a war. Make sure you pass this message on to Wendy and her little band of do-gooders. I am coming for you all. I let your friends plot and connive inside that hole they call the Castle because it pleased me to do so.' She pulled back sharply back from him, and Dave flinched as she angrily spread her arms wide. 'No more. I am, though, playing nice.'

'Bring it on. Whatever you bring, we will deal with it,' he responded, slowly edging past her as he carefully made his way toward the door. Before he could open it, he stopped and looked over his shoulder as she called out to him.

'Oh, David, when I next see you, I won't be as lenient. When we next meet, I will stand over your corpse and watch the life drain out of your eyes,' she said in a quiet but dangerous tone.

Believing there was nothing else left for him to say, Dave held his tongue and gave a curt nod. As he dashed out of the door, he passed a bewildered-looking Chief Inspector Thomas. His mind racing, he flew down the stairs two at a time until he came to a stop, breathless. He sucked in a lungful of air and charged down the corridor into the squad room. Brenda lifted her head in surprise as he approached her.

'Brenda, I can't explain,' he said breathlessly. 'I'm going to have to nip out, not sure what time I'll be back.'

'Do you need me to contact somebody?' Brenda replied carefully, discreetly tapping her finger on a picture on her desk.

Lowering his eyes, Dave frowned as realised that she was gesturing to a picture of Durham Cathedral. He gave his head a small shake, murmuring low enough so Brenda was the only one who could hear him. 'If anybody asks, I've had a crisis of faith and have had to take a leave of absence. Understand?' He smiled wistfully as his colleague nodded an acknowledgement. His voice full of sadness, he leaned closer to her and whispered, 'Brenda, take my advice and get out of Dodge while you still can. Tell anybody you can trust, warn them that the shit is about to hit the fan. Understand?'

Without waiting for a response, Dave spun round and charged out of the squad room.

Back in Chief Inspector Thomas's office, Oracle stared out of the window, deep in thought. On hearing a knock from behind her, she twisted her head slightly but remained silent as she watched the door open. Thomas shuffled into the room, followed by two heavyset men dressed in black suits. Thomas wrung his hands anxiously as he bowed his head subserviently.

'Your Excellency,' he gushed obsequiously, 'can I assume your meeting with Detective Inspector Barnes did not go as you intended?'

'Unfortunately, it went exactly how I predicted.' Oracle sighed. The corners of her mouth curled up and she gave him a mysterious smile. 'I am afraid you must tell your friends they were correct in their assessment of Barnes. I am sorry to say he will not be joining you after all.'

'That is disappointing,' he replied gloomily. His eyebrow arched and he stared at his mistress curiously. 'Do you wish me to arrange for him to be taken out of the picture?'

'No, that has already been taken care of,' Oracle replied, dismissing him with a flick of her wrist. 'Leave us.'

Thomas gave a small nod of acknowledgement and backed out of the door, leaving Oracle alone with the two black-suited gorillas, who snapped their heels as she turned towards them. Oracle shot the two stone-faced men a withering stare and clicked her fingers at them.

'You two, I want you to follow Barnes and track his every move,' she commanded. 'You are not to let him out of your sight, do you understand?'

'Yes, Your Excellency,' one of the powerfully built men replied. 'He will not even know we are following him.'

Oracle let out a small chuckle and waved her finger in amusement. 'Oh, you misunderstand. I want Barnes to see you.'

The two men exchanged bewildered looks and stared at Oracle with dopey expressions. 'Uh, Your Excellency, we don't understand.'

Oracle took a step forward and shot them a harsh gaze. 'You do not need to understand.' She smiled and gave them an impatient wave of her hand. 'Now, run along before you lose him.'

The two bruisers nodded in silent compliance, bowed, and left the room. Oracle focused her attention back on the window and stared thoughtfully down at the car park below. Her inhuman yellow eyes sharpened and she focused on a familiar-looking grey-haired man getting quickly into a car.

After watching the vehicle drive away, she let out a hollow laugh and muttered to herself. 'Run, rabbit, run to your little burrow and tell them I am coming, and may the Great Maker help anybody who gets in my way.'

-10-

The black Audi Q3 sped effortlessly through the unusually quiet streets, the December morning frost still glistening off the ancient Victorian rooftops. Inside the vehicle, Dave shivered slightly as he felt the cold winter air nip at his neck through the open window.

Approaching a set of traffic lights, his buttocks clenched together in irritation as they changed to red. Dave brought the car to a complete stop and blew out his cheeks, impatiently tapping his fingers on the steering wheel. His mind raced as a series of questions ran through his head. Just what was Oracle up to? Was Colonel Barnes actually dead or was that just a ploy to keep everyone off balance? More importantly did Sharon have anything to do with his disappearance? Dave ground his teeth in frustration. Why hadn't he thought about that sooner?

He raised his head and caught sight of something in the rear-view mirror. The corners of his eyes creased at the sight of a black Land Rover that quickly came to a stop behind him. Strange, he was positive he had seen the same vehicle parked in the police station car park.

The hairs on the back of his neck tingling, he stared at the vehicle behind him. He could just about make out two large men sitting in the vehicle's front seats but was unsure whether they were alone. He drummed his fingers on the steering wheel and shook his head, putting his suspicions down to paranoia.

As soon as the light changed to green, Dave released the handbrake and gently pressed his foot on the accelerator. Rather than taking the right turn as he had planned, which would have taken him up towards the camouflaged transport hub, he continued forward, with one eye locked on the vehicle behind him.

Increasingly suspicious, Dave frowned as he watched the car behind him speed up, narrowing the distance between them. His nose wrinkled and he pulled a face. What the hell was that driver up to? Whoever was driving, they were either not experienced at tailing someone or were deliberately making sure their target saw them. Were they hoping to unsettle him, maybe? Dave nodded his head, quickly concluding it was the latter option.

'Okay, boys,' he murmured to himself, 'two can play at this game. Let's go for a little ride.'

The cogs in his brain working overtime, Dave grinned as he took the car forward onto a roundabout. Still keeping one eye locked on the vehicle in his rear-view mirror, he sped round the roundabout and flicked on his indicator light as if signalling that he was planning on taking the first exit onto Southfield Way. He grinned mischievously as the Land Rover also signalled to follow him.

Just as he was about to turn into the exit, he pulled the car away at the last minute and continued on the roundabout, narrowly missing another car, a Nissan Micra. Dave raised his hand apologetically to the driver of the Micra, an unhappy silver-haired pensioner who gave him a blast of her horn. The driver of the Land Rover panicked, obviously realising he was being misled, and tried to turn back onto the roundabout but had to brake hard, barely missing a large bus. With his pursuers distracted, Dave sped around the roundabout and came off the third exit, signposted the A691. He continued down the A-road for a short distance until he came to another mini roundabout. Driving around it, he sharply came off at the second exit, marked *'Durham Park & Ride'*. Less than a minute later, he stopped in a parking bay.

Without waiting to check if the coast was clear, Dave climbed out of his car and dashed across the car park to a nearby bus stop, just in time to see a medium sized white minibus pull up. Dave bit into his bottom lip. Now if he could only get on board and be away before his pursuers arrive. The crisp December air biting into his cheeks, he slowed and stood next to a elderly couple who were standing waiting to board the vehicle. He lifted his chin in acknowledgement, but the couple continued to argue with one another, totally oblivious to his presence.

Carefully slipping past the arguing couple, Dave stepped onto the bus and slid into a seat near the front of the minibus. The elderly couple the shot him a look that could kill as they ambled past him and Dave answered with an apologetic shrug. He smirked as he spotted the familiar Land Rover race into the car park and brake hard. Two hulking black-suited bruisers, their faces red with anger, abandoned their vehicle and sprinted across the car park but reached the bus too late as it suddenly lurched forward before they had chance to get close enough to board. Relieved that he'd managed to evade his pursuers, Dave gripped the armrest of his seat to steady himself. The bus continued to move forward and headed out of the car park. A few minutes down the road, he stiffened as he spotted something at the side of the road leading into the city.

Hidden behind thick bushes, two large advanced armoured personnel carriers were parked on either side of the road. Dave frowned as he noticed the distinctive black and gold armour of Oracle's soldiers hidden along the roadside. It was obvious they were keeping their presence low key, but they were still visible enough to make the civilian population aware they were there, and that they were watching them.

His mood plummeted as the reality of the world's situation once again hit him. There was no doubt he was in the middle of an occupation by a hostile force. As the bus trundled down the road into the once grand medieval city and passed through a checkpoint, Dave's thoughts drifted to some images he had seen of Paris, in particular of those taken during World War Two under Nazi occupation.

Refocusing his attention on the task at hand, Dave's anxiety levels increased as he noticed the bus was approaching its drop-off point. He raised his head slightly so that he could see if there was anything following the bus. A surge of relief passed through him as he realised there wasn't any sign of the Land Rover. So far so good. He reasoned his unknown pursuers had been held up in the city traffic because they couldn't use same route that had been taken by the bus. Dave smiled to himself. This was one time he was thankful for roads having bus lanes. But then again he didn't want to push his luck too far, there was still a good chance those two goons weren't too far behind, so he needed to get off this bus as quick as possible.

As soon as the bus came to a stop, Dave leapt out of his seat. Barely having time to open the doors, the bus driver started and cried out a shout of protest at the impatient passenger forcing himself through the small gap in the doors. Dave waved an apologetic hand at the driver as he stepped onto the curb. He vowed to himself that one day he would have to find some way to make it up to the driver for startling him the way he did – that's if they were both still alive when this was all over.

As he hurried down the street Dave noticed something odd. It was unusually quiet for this time of year; the streets were not as busy as they should be. A week before Christmas, shoppers would normally have filled the streets, rushing around to prepare for the festivities ahead. It was another sign of the impact of the occupation, most people fearing to venture out and risk their safety.

With steely determination, Dave pressed forward and increased his pace, stepping off North Road onto the ancient, cobbled Belmont Viaduct. The aged bridge, once part of the now disused Durham to Sunderland railway, was a prominent feature for Durham's shoppers as they made their way across the River Wear up the cobbled streets toward the market square and further up to the cathedral and castle. As he made his way up Saddler Street, Dave began to wonder if things would ever be the same again.

Approaching the historic market square, a hubbub of activity broke Dave out of his reverie. Cries of alarm came from the people in front of him as a squad of a dozen black and gold armoured soldiers appeared, marching towards them. He dropped his head and moved back into a doorway, trying to remain as inconspicuous as possible, but anger swelled up in him as he spotted a thirty-something curly-haired woman pleading with her young child who was rooted to the spot in the centre of the street. Tears running down her cheeks, she pulled at her child's arm, but the little girl, her face awash with terror, refused to budge as the imposing soldiers marched towards her.

Thinking of nothing but the child's safety, Dave leapt out of the doorway and, with the child's cries ringing in his ears, he wrapped his arm around the small girl and lifted her into the air, at the same time grabbing the woman's arm so that he could drag her with him into the safety of the doorway. The mother and daughter cowered in the corner as the soldiers stomped past them.

'Shush, it's okay, Aria,' the young mother whispered, stroking her child's strawberry-blond hair. Her eyes flickered with silent gratitude at her smartly dressed saviour, who as soon as the coast was clear, knelt in front of them and gave the mother an encouraging smile as he playfully ruffled Aria's hair.

'They are gone,' Dave whispered gently, pointing to the trembling child. 'Is she okay?'

Aria's mother gave Dave a strained smile, nodding. 'She's fine. She got scared when she saw those troops marching towards us.' She grabbed Dave's hand and shook it furiously. 'I cannot thank you enough. If you hadn't stepped in to help, I can't imagine what would have happened.'

'Think nothing of it,' he responded, gesturing to the street in front of them. 'If I were you, I wouldn't hang around too long. These days it's not a good idea to be out and about, especially with a young child.'

The young mother exhaled deeply and nodded sullenly. 'Yes, I realise that now.' She cast a wary eye down at Aria who was staring up curiously at the strange man who had just saved her. 'I know it doesn't feel like it at the moment, especially with the way things have been, but with Christmas being a week away I just wanted to do something normal to help lift our spirits.' She shook her head and gave a small laugh. 'I didn't think it would hurt if we took a trip out to do some Christmas shopping.'

A small pang of sympathy pulled at Dave's heart as he gazed at the mother and child in front of him. He could truly understand even during these dark times people wanting to bring a little cheer to their lives, even it was a just for a moment. But before he could straighten and leave, Aria's mother grabbed him and placed a twenty-pound note in his hand. Astonished, he shook his head and tried to hand the note back, but the woman waved him away and moved back onto the street.

'No, take it, please.' She smiled gratefully. 'I know it's not much but consider it a small token of thanks during these dark times.'

Overwhelmed by her generosity, Dave choked back tears as he watched the young family dash away to continue with their day trip. His spirits lifted, he drew in a long, happy breath and moved out of the doorway so he could resume his journey up past the marketplace.

It did not take long for reality to strike home, bringing his mood crashing back to Earth. As he hurried past the market square, Dave frowned as he heard strange chanting coming from within the centre of the square. He slowed as he noticed that a crowd of people were standing in front of the familiar bronze statue of a man on a horse – the Marquis of Londonderry. He picked up murmurs of discontent from the crowd as he gently pushed his way through.

'Bunch of nutters, if you ask me.'

'Have this lot got nothing better to do?'

'Humph! I would love to boot them up the arse, along with those black and gold armoured storm troopers.'

'Shush! The soldiers will hear you.'

As he made his way through the small crowd, the chanting became clearer. However, on reaching the front of the crowd, Dave rolled his eyes in disgust as he realised just who was doing the chanting. A dozen people stood at the base of the statue, their arms held aloft, wearing silver clothing with featureless silver masks that covered their faces. A lone male figure, possibly the leader, was in front, wearing a tight-fitting silver bodysuit and a mask with yellow eyes painted on, standing on a raised platform, arms stretched out, chanting up to the sky.

'All hail the will of Oracle,' the leader chanted.

'For she is just,' the small group murmured in response.

'Yes, for it is true, the will of Oracle is just, for she is our saviour. Let it be known that those who stand against her will burn in her gaze.'

'Let it be known.'

Appalled by the spectacle playing in front of him, Dave grunted in disapproval and turned away from the chanting group. He had heard of this group, people who had become enamoured with the AI. A short time after start of the invasion, a movement appeared calling itself the Disciples of Oracle. At first, their numbers had been few, but gradually, over the past month, their numbers had grown, with several enclaves appearing around the globe.

His happy mood quickly morphing into anger, Dave spun round and pushed his way back through the small crowd of observers. Sickened at the idea that people could be taken in in such a way, he slouched and tried to put as much distance as possible between himself and the market square. The chanting subsiding into the distance, he shook his head sadly as he walked up the steep incline that led to the cathedral. No matter how many times he saw it, he would never be surprised by the constant human need to do something stupid.

Breathless from the exertion of the climb up Durham's steep Saddler

Street, Dave came to a stop, awestruck by the view ahead of him. The enormous ancient building standing tall in front of him, a sense of pride stirred within him as he took in its ambience. A small smile formed on his lips as he realised that no matter how many times he stood before the old girl, he would never get used to seeing the one-thousand-year-old building's Romanesque architecture.

Regaining his composure, Dave swallowed as he hurried along the courtyard, passing Durham Castle and continuing toward the enormous oak doors in the centre of the cathedral. Halfway through the door, he stopped as he felt the hairs on the back of neck tingle. His eyes sharpened with suspicion as he stared at the surrounding area, pausing on a clump of trees overlooking the riverbank. He was positive he had detected movement in the shadows. He waved his hand and shook his head, believing it was probably a dog or something. Laughing at his own paranoia, Dave walked into the grand old building and closed the door behind him.

A short distance away, hidden in the shadows of a clump of trees, the Alpha sharpened its eyes as it watched the human enter the strange building. It had been positive when the human male known as Barnes had stopped and looked in its direction, he had detected its presence. But it let out a hiss of relief as its quarry disappeared through the door.

Roughly the size of an Alsatian dog, the synthroid was unlike anything on this world. Initially, the synthroids had been genetically engineered by the Empire to be foot soldiers in their war against the Greater China Republic. With the aid of their black scaly ferrofluidic bodies, they were engineered to remain undetected until it was too late, when they would tear their unsuspecting prey apart with their four razor-sharp-clawed appendages. Unfortunately, their Imperial masters found the beasts were uncontrollable on the battlefield. Blinded by the taste of blood, the fearsome animal would go into fits of berserk hyper-rage, attacking anyone around them, friend or foe. However, the creatures' only redeeming feature was an uncanny ability to skilfully track a target over vast distance. The Empire therefore decided to breed the creatures for one purpose: to hunt.

The Alpha stirred as it detected movement coming from behind. It peered over its haunches and noticed that one of its brethren was slinking toward it. It let out a small hiss of acknowledgement to its smaller companion as it stopped and bowed its head respectfully.

'Alpha, the pack are ressstlesss, they are curiousss,' the smaller synthroid hissed. 'When doesss we attacksss?'

The Alpha's haunches quivered in anger, and it let out a dangerous hiss. 'Weess, attack when Missstresss Oracle givesss the wordsss and not beforesss. Issss that undesssstood?'

The smaller synthroid's slim head hung in subservience and it silently backed away from the hissing pack leader. The Alpha's red eyes thinned, and it returned its attention back to the strange building in front of it. It pressed its teeth together and let out a loud hiss of displeasure.

The Alpha had learned from its new mistress that the humans inside that building were the ones responsible for killing its mate. Revenge was an emotion that was not natural to a synthroid, but as it stared at the building in front of it, it let out a long hiss and its mouth widened to show its sharp teeth. Oh yes, it was going to enjoy making these humans suffer.

-11-

Several metres below Durham Cathedral, John Payne sat alone in the briefing room, his only companion, the hum of the ventilation system as it pushed recycled air through the air ducts into the chamber. Tired, he grimaced and stretched his back wearily as he gazed at the tablet in his hands. Despite having had only a few hours' sleep, he had rose early. Troubled by the previous night's events, he'd had tossed and turned restlessly in his bed, his mind unable to switch off.

He tapped his fingers on his lips thoughtfully as he reread Wendy's account of what she had discovered at the facility in Sunderland. What he found more unsettling was her encounter with Oracle. Payne ran a hand down his weary face and let out a slow breath through his teeth, shaking his head sadly.

Initially, he had believed the real threat was from the advanced storm troopers that had arrived from a parallel Earth. But, after last night's events, together with the unsettling reports of the rise of the group calling itself the Disciples of Oracle, it was quickly becoming obvious just who the true threat was.

'Penny for your thoughts, John?'

Startled and distracted by his own deliberations, John jumped spectacularly out of his seat at the soft voice and caught his knee on the edge of the desk. He winced and squeezed his watering his eyes shut, at the same time wondering if he could get away with inflicting the same pain on the person who just had the temerity to scare the poop out of him. Who in the hell? Embarrassed more than hurt, John angrily rubbed the feeling back into his knee. Desperate to give whoever it was a piece of his mind, he wheeled round, blood boiling in pent-up fury, finger raised, ready to hurl abuse at the miscreant responsible for such a heinous act. Before the words could escape his lips, his eyebrows climbed up in astonishment as he recognised the tall, elegant woman in the doorway.

Dressed in a navy jumper and jeans, Sophia raised her hands to her chest apologetically. 'Oh, Commander, I'm sorry. I didn't mean to startle you.'

'No, ma'am. It's my fault.' John groaned. 'I didn't realise you were standing there.'

Walking unsteadily over to her, John winced as he flexed his knee and tried to restore the feeling in it. He pursed his lips as he studied the striking woman, becoming quite troubled at what he could see. There were dark circles beneath Sophia's eyes and there was a weariness of her body language. He wondered whether she had been sleeping well.

As if reading his mind, Sophia waved her hand and forced a smile. 'I'm fine, honestly.' She exhaled and gave him a sheepish look. 'I finally realised it was about time I showed my face.'

'I see,' John replied hesitantly. He chewed nervously on his bottom lip, wondering about her mental state.

Sophia, as if detecting the hesitance in Payne's voice, laughed and stared at him with an amused expression. 'My friend, I can tell you're dying to ask, but are holding back.' Her right eyebrow arched and she gave him a speculative look. 'Are you softening in your old age, hmm? Let me guess, you're wondering if I'm okay. If I'm not coming back too soon.'

John self-consciously shuffled awkwardly and rubbed the back of his neck, murmuring, 'Um, well, not in those words exactly.'

Sophia let out a long puff of air through her lips and shrugged. 'To be honest, if you'd asked me that a month ago, I would have said no. Following the destruction of Beijing, I shut down. I had this urge to run away and hide.' There was a faraway expression on her face as her haunted round hazel eyes stared up at the ceiling. 'After everything that has happened over the past few years, it was as if Beijing's destruction was the final straw. It was as if I could feel my legs buckling as the weight on my shoulders increased.' She laughed bitterly and lowered her head. 'I was feeling sorry for myself. Would you believe it? This leader of what is essentially a small community was acting like a scared child. Desperate to run away and stick her head under the covers because the big evil monster had scared her.'

John put both his hands on Sophia's shoulders and stared compassionately into her haunted eyes. 'You're being too hard on yourself after what we've been through.' He gave her a thin smile, pointing at himself. 'Yes, myself included. It's no wonder you are suffering from post-traumatic stress.' He smiled reassuringly at her and clasped her hand in his. 'The important thing is to ask for help. I don't know how many times I have seen people self-destruct because they were too proud to ask.' He cocked his head and gazed at his sombre friend enquiringly. 'So, on that note …' He let his unfinished sentence hang in the air.

Sophia nodded slightly, finishing his sentence. 'You're wondering what has finally drawn me out.' John bobbed his head but remained silent and let her continue. 'Well, I read Kendra's and Wendy's after-mission reports. It was the wake-up call I needed. I realised it after Wendy's account of the fate of those poor souls inside that facility, together with her encounter with Oracle.' John couldn't help notice that her eyes were suddenly burning with determination as she fixed him with a hard stare. 'I knew then I had to put aside my own insecurities, step up and be the leader you all need me to be.' She raised a hand as John opened his mouth to protest. 'No, I need to say this. While I locked myself away, I kept up to date with the goings on here and I have read the concerns you expressed with regard to the deterioration of morale within the base. The only way we can fix that is if our people see me leading by example.'

John gave a small silent nod. He could tell from the fire in her eyes that she meant what she said. He sucked on his bottom lip as he regarded the determined woman in front of him. But was she up for the task ahead? Was she mentally strong enough? He ran a hand through his hair as he struggled to decide whether to voice his concerns.

Sophia gave a thin smile and clasped his hand in hers. 'I recognise that look in your eyes, my friend. We have worked too long together for me not to be able to read your body language. You're wondering if I am fit to command? Isn't that right?' She released his hand, turned away from him and exhaled a long heavy sigh. 'To be honest, I would be lying if I said the thought hadn't crossed my mind too. Am I making things harder for myself? I don't know.' Her face softening, she waved a hand at the command centre below. 'But these people need me, and I am not prepared to let them down again.'

The two friends stared down at the command centre in silence, locked in their own thoughts. After a short period of silence, John put his hand on her shoulder and Sophia twisted her head slightly to him.

'Sophia, I can see you are determined to do this, and I won't stand in your way if you believe it is the right thing to do,' he said carefully. 'But I wouldn't be a good second in command if I didn't express my concerns.' He held his hands up, cutting off her protestation. 'Please let me finish. I agree our people desperately need someone to believe in. Someone to inspire them during these dark times.' He paused and fixed her with a compassionate stare. 'Yes, I agree that it should be you. But if we do this, then we do it together. Promise me, if you have any reservations or doubts, you speak to me about them. Let me carry the burden of any fears you have.' He smiled warmly and extended his hand. 'Deal?'

Sophia blinked and looked down at the offered hand. John could only imagine the turmoil running through her head as she considered his request. If their situations had been reversed, he probably would be thinking the same – would it be a sign of weakness if he took her hand? Would people think less of him if they saw someone supporting him? He remained silent as he watched her stare up at the ceiling thoughtfully. Was she deliberating on a different perspective? Yes, he could see it on her face – she was coming to the same the conclusion. Instead of weakness, people would not only see it as a sign of strength, but also of two people who had each other's backs. John smiled as he watched a slow understanding creep over her face. By Jove, I think she's got it!

Her eyes welling up, she took her friend's hand and spoke in a voice thick with emotion. 'My friend, I wouldn't have anyone else standing by my side.'

Embarrassed, John felt his face redden and he turned away from Sophia. He chuckled, pretending to wipe something out of his eye. 'Damn the dust in this place. I think I have something in my eye.'

If she noticed John's embarrassment, Sophia didn't give indication, instead she quickly changed the subject and pointed to the tablet on the conference room table.

'So, I guess Oracle has upped the ante?' she asked curiously.

'Yes, ma'am. It's bad enough that she has enslaved people from another world to act as her enforcers, but now she is enslaving our own people too.'

'Horrible. Truly horrible,' Sophia murmured sadly. Her face softened, and she looked at Payne with a concerned expression. 'How's Wendy doing? I've read Kendra's after-action report. Tell me honestly, do you think she's holding up?'

'I would like to hear the answer to that question, too.'

The two started as a firm, angry voice came from behind them. John pressed his hand against his chest and inhaled a sharp intake of air. He was positive his heart had just leapt up into his throat. What the hell? What was it about people today? Didn't they know how to knock? But as he wheeled round, his annoyance quickly changed to puzzlement as he realised Dave was standing in the conference room's doorway. It dawned on John that he'd had been so distracted in his own thoughts, he had not picked up the small beep of the security sensor as it scanned Dave's retina to allow him access.

It doesn't take a genius to guess why he's here, John thought as he took a step forward, his hands raised in front of him in a placating gesture. 'Easy, Dave,' he said carefully. 'I understand you're angry but if you can give me a minute to explain. Then I—'

'Oh, you think I'm angry do you?' Dave interjected, his tone thick with sarcasm. He let out a small grunt of dissatisfaction and flicked his hand dismissively. 'It's okay. I was angry this morning when I first learned of the news. But I've had a few hours to digest it. If you and I had bumped into each other a few hours earlier, we would be having a wholly different conversation.'

'I see,' John said, regarding Dave with a curious side eye. 'What changed?'

'Oracle. She and I have just had an interesting chat,' Dave responded glumly.

John exchanged a troubled look with Sophia as he listened to Dave fill them in on his conversation with the AI. When he was finished, there was an uneasy silence in the room as John attempted to digest the information. From the way she was furrowing brow and the tight expression across her face, he could tell Sophia had found the news deeply disconcerting.

John remained silent and watched the pensive woman pace around the room; she was scratching the back of her neck, deep in thought. The corner of John's eyes crinkled as he cast a worried eye at Dave.

'What really happened last night? I'm guessing from the way Wendy is being vilified by the media, together with Oracle's emotional outburst, that she uncovered something disturbing,' Dave asked.

'Oh, disturbing is an understatement, my friend.' John chuckled harshly, handing Dave the tablet he had been reading.

As Dave read the report of the previous night's mission, John watched his eyebrows climb higher and higher up his forehead the more he read. The blood draining from his face, Dave lifted his head up and stared back at John. From the way he was opening and closing his mouth like a dying fish, John guessed he was trying desperately to search for the words he wanted to express.

'That's how I felt when I first read that report,' Sophia said, giving a commiserating nod.

'Unbelievable,' Dave croaked. He angrily slammed the tablet hard on the desk. From the way his hands were trembling, John could only guess at what was going through the older man's head. Yeah, he guessed he was appalled. But was he appalled by the idea that it had occurred virtually on their own doorstep, or something else?

John nodded in solemn understanding at Dave's reaction. 'The good thing is, we, by that I mean Wendy, shut it down.' Sucking in a puff of air through clenched teeth, he stared gravely at the broken tablet on the desk and let out a heavy sigh. 'But it is safe to say this is just the tip of the iceberg. We can assume Oracle has other processing centres all the across the globe.'

No sooner than the words were out of his mouth as an icy shiver ran down John's spine as he imagined centres in other countries across the world with helpless people inside them. He pictured thousands of innocent people screaming as they were turned into mindless slaves for an inhuman monster. *This is just too much*, he thought. A bitter taste filled his mouth and he fought the urge to throw up. Overcome by a wave of nausea, he raised his hand up to mouth and reeled away from the two people, who watched with sympathetic expressions as their friend collapsed onto his knees and retched into a small trash bin.

John's face twisted from the taste of bile in his mouth, his stomach heaving. He lifted his head up and nodded gratefully as a sympathetic looking Sophia handed him a paper tissue along with a bottle of still water.

'Sorry about that,' he wheezed, swallowing a gulp of water. 'I just found the whole idea that they could turn us into one of those mind things –' his squeezed his eyes shut and shivered slightly '– well, I just found it repulsive.'

Sophia blew out a long, tired breath. 'I only wish we could get this information out to the public. Unfortunately, she controls all the press and restricts what is being reported. We really need to locate another facility and collect proof before we give it to somebody who can make the public aware of what is going on.'

A light bulb went off in John's mind as he remembered a report that he had received from Excalibur Base just a few hours earlier. He smiled and held up a finger. 'Actually, ma'am, I may have the perfect person for that.'

Sophia gave Payne a bemused side eye. 'Really? What are you hiding?'

'Oh, nothing devious, if that's what you think.' He laughed. He cleared his throat, becoming more serious as he pointed to the tablet he had been reading. 'I received a report from one of our cells that the former BBC journalist, Sunitra Sinchettra, has joined our ranks. She has agreed to act as our spokesperson – the voice of the resistance, if you will.' John frowned as Sophia raised her hands to clap them in delight and quickly held up both his hands to stop her. He shook his head and exhaled sadly. 'Don't celebrate yet, there's still a long way to go before we can have her broadcasting. The tech boys have a lot of kinks to work out, apparently.'

The room lapsed into an uneasy silence. As he gazed around the sombre faces around the room, John realised that the size of the task at hand was slowly dawning on them. John furrowed his brow in heavy frustration and shook his head; he had never felt more powerless in his life. He cocked his head as he heard a small cough come from Dave and pushed that thought to the back of his mind. From the worried expression that was on Dave's face he could tell that he was desperate to discuss something. It didn't take a genius to guess what it was.

'How is Wendy doing?' Dave asked, his voice heavy with concern.

John lifted his shoulder in a small shrug. 'You know how Wendy can be. She's fearless, charging into situations head first.' His jaw set and he gave a small shake of his head. 'She won't admit it, but I think last night really hit her hard. She has a haunted look in her eyes – the only time I have seen something similar is in the eyes of soldiers when they have returned from a mission gone bad.' He stared up at the ceiling helplessly. 'I'm really worried about her, but sh—' But before he could finish his sentence, he was cut off as he heard an angry Scottish voice coming somewhere from behind him.

'So, you're talking about me behind my back, are you?'

John wheeled around and was surprised to see Wendy standing in the room's open doorway. Her face red was with rage as she glowered at the people in the room. He noticed that Kendra had suddenly appeared behind Wendy and was obviously breathless from the exertion of chasing after her. John raised an eyebrow in surprise as he noticed a bruise was starting to form on Kendra's left cheek. Had they been arguing? John nodded gravely to himself. Kendra must have tried to stop Wendy leaving their quarters, because she was worried about Wendy's heightened emotional state. Had Wendy lashed out at Kendra? That could explain the reason why Wendy suddenly appeared the way she did.

'Wendy, you know that is not true. They're only concerned about you.' Kendra said worriedly, reaching forward to grab Wendy's arm.

Wendy, ignoring her friend's pleas, angrily waved her away as she took a step forward and gazed at them with eyes that were filled with pain and disappointment. 'Och, I know what you are thinking,' she snarled, spitting the words with such intensity, John could just almost feel the self-loathing in her voice. 'You think I made a mistake. I should've waited for backup.' She hissed, stabbing her finger into her chest. John swallowed as he listened to her voice crack with raw emotion. 'I can see it in your eyes. You blame me for all those deaths.'

The emotional strain of hearing the distress in his friend's voice plastered over his face, Dave swallowed and edged forward, shaking his head, 'Wendy, we're not saying that. Please, I'm being honest with you. We don't blame you for what you had to do. We can see you had no other choice.'

The tears streamed down Wendy's face and she gazed around the room at the people in front of her, shaking her head. 'How? How could you possibly understand?' She sobbed. 'You weren't there. You weren't there when I stood in front of a poor terrified woman as she begged me to kill her.' Wendy's hands balled into fists, and she held them tight against her chest. 'She pleaded with me to shoot her, to stop them turning her into one of those things.' Her voice wobbled and she let out a ragged breath. 'But at the last instant, I froze. Because of my hesitation, I had to watch as they turned her into one of those *things*.'

Her face brimming with compassion, Sophia gently moved toward the grief-stricken young woman, whispering, 'Wendy, it wasn't your fault.'

Her face contorting with grief, Wendy tried to push Sophia away. 'Y … y … yes, it was.'

'Sweetheart, no it wasn't,' Sophia continued gently, taking the sobbing woman into her arms.

Throat tightening, his tugging heart at his chest, John watched through sad eyes as Wendy collapsed into Sophia's arms. Sophia made soothing hushing noises, gently stroking Wendy's red hair, but nodded gratefully as Kendra took a step forward and helped Wendy to her feet. John glanced at Dave and noticed the grave expression on his face. He placed a reassuring hand on Dave's shoulder as they watched the two women lead their distraught friend over to a leather sofa.

-12-

Dave let out a heavy despondent sigh and turned to John. Payne nodded wordlessly as Dave motioned for him to follow him out of the room. He tilted his head inquisitively as he followed him through the door into the corridor and gave him an awkward side-eye as he rubbed the back of his neck awkwardly.

'Listen, John, I need to ask you something,' Dave said hesitantly, 'but I need you to be truthful with me. Can you do that?'

John blinked and nodded slightly. 'Um, okay.' He laughed uncomfortably and gave Dave a playful punch on the shoulder. 'Heh, come on, mate, what's this all about?'

Rubbing his shoulder, Dave smiled weakly at Payne as he wondered how he should word it. Screw it! He was going just dive in and hope for the best. What's the worst that could happen? He cleared and spoke in a careful tone. 'How have things been between you and Sharon?'

John frowned and scowled at Dave indignantly. 'To be honest, I don't think that is any of your business.'

Ignoring his friend's complaint, Dave held up his hand in a placating gesture, but continued to press him. 'I'm sorry, but I wouldn't pry unless I felt it was important.' He paused and fixed Payne with an intense stare. 'So, I will ask you again. How have things been between you and Sharon?' He swallowed and forced the next words out. 'What I mean to say is, do you know what she was up to while … um …'

John's blue eyes grew wide as saucers as if it had suddenly hit him what Dave was referring to. He shook his head, snapping irritably. 'You're talking about the incident a few weeks ago, aren't you? When Sharon was taken over by Oracle.' Dave remained silent but continued to watch the flustered man turn away from him. From the way he was muttering Dave guessed John wasn't just trying to convince him, but himself too. 'Yeah, sure, Sharon has behaving been oddly, but that was only because a homicidal machine had taken her over. Then as if that wasn't bad enough, she had to spend over a week lying in a coma.' He spun around sharply and stared at Dave with a pained expression. 'Jesus Christ man, after what she's been through can you not give her a bloody break? Don't you think she's been enough? She doesn't need someone coming along an accusing her of murder.'

Dave blinked in surprise. Why would John think Sharon had murdered someone? He'd never even mentioned to anyone his theory that Sharon may have killed Colonel Barnes while under Oracle's control. It must have already been on John's mind for him to come out with something like that. That could explain why he almost chewed his head off. Dave remained silent, deciding it was best he let John get whatever he was feeling off his chest.

'Anyway, you don't know what you are talking about.' John huffed and gave a dismissive wave. 'Yes, I admit she's been distant with me, but that's only because we both agreed that I would give her some distance while she recuperated.' His face then clouded with anger, and he rounded on Dave with his finger raised. 'Listen, Barnes, I don't know what you're implying, but Sharon's fine. There's nothing wrong with her. So I would prefer it if you kept your opinions to yourself.'

Taken back by the intensity of John's anger, Dave stepped back and held his hands up in front of his chest but continued to press him. 'Listen, John, I know you're angry, but for the moment, I need you to set aside any personal feelings you have for Sharon and listen to me objectively. Please, can you do that?' He smiled gratefully as Payne gave him a silent but reluctant nod. 'Good man. Now remember when I said I had an encounter with Oracle earlier today? Well, she said something that I found quite strange regarding my counterpart.'

Payne's eyes tightened as he listened to Dave recount his conversation with Oracle regarding Colonel Barnes. 'So what?' John interjected tersely, after

Dave had finished. 'We both know from our brief experience with your counterpart that he wasn't what you would call stable.'

Dave gave a dismissive wave of his hand and shook his head. 'No, I don't think that's the case. Listen, I'm a detective, a damn fine one, too. So I know when something sounds dodgy.' He took in a deep breath and raised his hands in front of his chest, fingers steepled together. 'I've never said this out loud, but before today I had been working on the assumption that Sharon helped Barnes to escape.'

'Now listen here,' John blurted out angrily, 'Sharon would never allow herself to be talked into doing something like that.'

Dave held a finger up and shook his head sadly. 'Sorry, I misspoke. What I meant to say was while she under Oracle's control, she helped Barnes to escape. With Oracle's advanced knowledge, it would have been a cinch for her to disable the static shield around the complex, allowing Barnes to escape through a portal.'

John's face scrunched up as he pondered on Dave's statement, and then nodded slightly in reluctant agreement. 'Aye. We also had been working on that assumption. I assumed Barnes had somehow disabled the frequency jammer and disappeared through a portal.' He inhaled deeply and let out a sigh of exasperation. 'But when we ran a diagnostic on the system, we couldn't find any sign that someone had tampered with it.' He lifted his hands helplessly. 'So, we still have no idea how he got out.'

Dave stared up at the ceiling thoughtfully, scratching his chin, murmuring, 'That's because he never left. He's been right under our nose the whole time.'

'Are you mad?' John exclaimed, staring in wide-eyed disbelief. 'He couldn't have been hiding all this time. We would have discovered him.'

Dave didn't have to be mind-reader to guess what John was thinking – the stress had finally gotten to him and he'd gone over the deep end. He huffed to himself in agreement. If their situations had been reversed and it was John saying it, then it was quite possible he probably would have had the same reaction. But Dave had plenty of time over the past couple of hours to mull over things and come up with this theory. Yes, it was an outlandish theory, but it was the only one he had to explain Barnes's absence.

Dave shook his head and fixed Payne with a hard stare. 'He doesn't need to hide. Do you remember the words I told you Oracle said to me?'

John frowned and stared up at the ceiling with a faraway look. Dave knew he was recalling the conversation they'd had a minutes earlier. 'She said he was in bits. What does tha—' He stopped and then blanched, a slow understanding dawning on his face. He swallowed and looked at Dave, speechless, the blood draining from his face.

'Yes. I think deep down you've suspected it too, but because of your love for Sharon, you've been too afraid to face the truth.' Dave replied gravely, placing a hand on the shaken man's arm. 'John, we need to be sure. Is there anything you can remember from that day that will give us a clue to where his body may be?'

'I-I-I …' he stammered uncertainly. John flinched and his eyes had a distant look. Was it caused by a flicker of a memory that was coming to him? Dave couldn't tell, but he assumed from the way John was squeezing his eyes shut, he was desperately trying to bring it to the surface. 'Wait. Yes, I can remember why I confronted Sharon in the first place.' John hissed, slapping his forehead in visible disgust. 'Of course, I see it now. In all the commotion of that day, I had forgotten all about it until now. I had received a report from a friend of Sharon's, concerned about her behaviour.'

'Where was she coming from?' Dave asked, his tone urgent. 'Think, man.'

Payne pulled at his hair, moved away from Dave, and stared at him imploringly. 'She couldn't have. She's not capable of … *that*.' He squeezed his eyes shut and angrily shook his head. Dave had seen that same look too many times from people he had the displeasure of giving bad news to. He was afraid – afraid that if he accepted the truth, it would make it real.

'He is right, John.'

Dave jumped in shock as a soft, quietly spoken female voice came from behind them. He spun round sharply and stared in astonishment at the petite blond woman, wearing a white lab coat, standing before them with a subdued expression.

Although it had been a few weeks since Dave last saw her, Sharon's appearance still startled him. Her round chestnut eyes, once full of energy, were now haunted with dark circles around them. He also noticed a change in her demeanour. Something else had replaced her once bouncy exuberance. Something he couldn't put his finger on.

'Sharon, please don't do this,' John said imploringly, putting himself between Dave and the young woman, as if shielding her presence from Dave's gaze would stop the truth from revealing itself.

Her round chestnut eyes glistening, Sophia took a small step toward John and brushed her hand gently over his face. 'It is okay,' she said softly. 'I need to do this if I ever want to be whole again.'

His heart heavy at the thought of what he must do next, Dave closed his eyes and secretly prayed to himself that he was doing the right thing. He straightened his shoulders and took a step forward, gently moving his troubled friend to one side. Saturnine, he stared impassively at the petite woman in front of him.

'I'm sorry, Sharon, but I need to ask you. Do you remember what Oracle did while she was in control of you?' he asked carefully.

Her eyes filling with tears, Sharon smiled weakly and gave a small nod of acknowledgement. 'Fragments. Flashes and images. It only comes to me in my dreams.' Her smile fading, a shadow crossed over her face and her voice became hollow. 'My dreams are full of terror and blood. Lots and lots of blood. I see a man's face. It is full of blind terror as he pleads for his life, but I then hear myself cackling wickedly while I tear him apart.'

Horrified by the images that Sharon's words were placing in his head, an involuntary shudder passed through Dave's body and he let out a hoarse whisper. 'Jesus. I cannot imagine what you're feeling.'

Her face oddly blank, Sharon raised her shoulder in an indifferent shrug. 'I try to convince myself that it was not me. Someone else was in the driving seat.' Dave frowned as he noticed there was a slight change Sharon's voice — it had become flat and cold. She gazed at John and then spoke in a strange childlike tone, 'Maybe one day she will actually believe that.'

Dave exchanged an unsettled look with John; he could see he had noticed the fluctuation in the young woman's mood too. His stomaching churning, Dave realised something was terribly wrong with Sharon. *We need to tread very carefully here*, he thought. Careful, so as not to push her any more over the edge, he took a tentative step forward but still continued to gently press her.

'Sharon, can you tell me where Oracle hid the body?' he whispered gently.

Sharon cocked her head at Dave and stared at him strangely. She then spoke in a tone that almost had an odd childlike quality to it. 'We can do better than that. We can show you.'

Unnerved by the sudden change in Sharon's demeanour, Dave gave a false smile and waved a hand. 'Oh, you don't have to do that. We don't want to put you to any more trouble. If you can tell us where we need to go, we can check it out for ourselves and then you can be on your way.'

Dave inhaled a sharp intake of break and felt his buttocks clench in fear as the woman in front of him suddenly let out a childish giggle. 'You are a silly man.' There was an odd expression on her face and her mouth broadened into an impish grin. She lowered her head coyly and spoke in a strange, childlike voice. 'Sharon says it is no trouble at all. If you follow us, we can take you there.'

'Um, o-okay. Th-that's really nice of you,' John stammered and looked at Dave helplessly, but nodded slightly as Dave motioned for them to play along.

Following the young woman down the corridor, Dave held back and allowed John to increase his pace so he could walk next to her. John cocked his head inquisitively at the petite blond beside him. 'So,' he asked carefully, 'can I assume you are not Sharon?'

Sharon giggled childishly and playfully took John's hand, tapping it. 'Of course I am Sharon, silly. I am little Sharon.' She pouted and gave a small, annoyed shake of her head. 'Sharon had me locked away for years, not letting me come out to play, but something happened that opened the door for me to come out again.' Her eyes darted from side to side, and she gestured for John to lean in closer, whispering, 'Sharon was scared about what she must show you. So she asked me to take over.' Her mouth curled up in an impish grin and she giggled at John. 'Sharon likes you. She says she is really sorry for what she did, but she hopes one day you will marry her and have lots and lots of babies.' Her face then twisted up in disgust. 'Ew! That is disgusting.'

John gave a silent nod of acknowledgement and slowed his pace, allowing Dave to catch up. His eyes still locked on the woman in front of him, he lowered his voice just enough so that Dave could hear. Dave nodded and gave a pretend smile to the people they passed in the corridor, who stared at the trio with confused expressions.

'So, what do you think?' John murmured discreetly. 'Do you think this is a bad idea?'

His tongue firmly in his cheek, Dave nodded and shrugged his shoulders. 'Oh, I don't know. I can see you and Sharon having a large family.'

John gave Dave the evil eye and hissed at him through clenched teeth. 'Not that, you oaf. I'm talking about her.' He gestured angrily to the woman in front of them. 'You have to admit, this is pretty strange even for us.'

Dave laughed, patting John on the shoulder. 'Relax, I'm only pulling your leg. I knew what you meant.' His brow knitted together as he gazed thoughtfully at Sharon. 'I suggest we go along with her for now. She seems harmless enough. I've been involved in cases with people suffering from multiple personality disorders, so I imagine this is something similar.' He gave a reassuring smile and put his right hand on Payne's left shoulder. 'I believe this is a defence mechanism of Sharon's, her way of coping with all the horrors she has had to endure. One thing that's certain, my friend, is her love for you. So long as you both keep that at the forefront of your minds, I truly believe you'll get through this.'

After leaving him to digest that statement, Dave turned is gaze away from John, but started as he found himself staring at Sharon's beaming face. He smiled faintly and acknowledged her with a small bow. Sharon, apparently happy with her life, turned and skipped merrily on. Dave rolled his eyes and shook his head. Surely this day couldn't get any weirder?

-13-

Several levels above the command centre, Corporal Grant Higgins, a thin-faced lanky man dressed in a green boiler suit let out a groan of frustration as he climbed up the ladder of a narrow shaft. Breathless, he carefully placed his feet on a metal rung as he made his way up towards the maintenance tunnel.

His thick eyebrows knitted together as he came to a stop, gazed up the narrow shaft and once again let out a groan of frustration. He shook his head and exhaled an exasperated sigh, grumbling inwardly. How come he always got the shitty jobs? Just because one of the motion cameras went offline, didn't mean they had to send a maintenance team straight away. Surely this could have waited until the next inspection?

'Grant, you realise I can hear you grinding your teeth from down here?' a woman's voice announced in his earpiece.

Grant gave a small snort of disgust and glared angrily back down the shaft from where he came. 'May, why don't you come up here and do it then? Instead of looking up and sending helpful comments.'

'Oh no, my friend. If you can't stand the heat, you should get out of the kitchen.' He heard May laugh back. *'Corporal Higgins, maybe this will make you think twice the next time you play poker with Delta Shift.'*

Grant rolled his eyes, placed one hand on a rung above his head and continued up the ladder. Just because he got caught cheating playing cards, didn't mean she had to rub his nose in it. He sighed heavily. It wasn't like she hadn't made mistakes too. But did she let him remind her about it? Oh, heaven forbid if that happened. An inaudible grumble escaped his lips just before he grabbed the rung above him and forced himself up the rest of the ladder.

'*Sorry, didn't catch that?*'

'Nothing, Sergeant Wen. Just saying I've reached the top of the shaft,' he answered innocently.

After putting both of his hand on the edges of the hatchway, he grimaced and pushed himself up into a dark, circular, three-metre diameter tunnel. Grant's nose scrunched up in disgust at the dank, musty smell that hit him. He looked down at his hands and his upper lip curled as he realised he'd had managed to get them covered with the slick grime that covered the tunnel's floor. Wiping his hands down the front of his green overall, he frowned as he stared into the darkness down the long tunnel. In his mind's eye, he imagined the tunnel stretching off into the darkness, eventually coming to a stop at a sealed-off hatch somewhere along Durham's riverbank. He reached up and brushed his hand against the tunnel's surface; he wondered if these decades-old walls could speak, what would they tell him? He smiled to himself, trying to imagine what was going through minds of the builders of this base as they traipsed through these same tunnels decades earlier.

Far in the distance, a row of lights fluctuated and went out, breaking Grant out of his reverie and back to the present. *What's wrong with the lights?* He mused as he pressed on a button on the side of his headgear. He blinked as the soft glow from his head torch emitted a soft glow onto the walls and floor of the tunnel. It also made for an eerie feeling, giving him a sense that he was standing in the centre of bubble of light, surrounded by a sea of darkness. Grant cleared his throat and shook his head. Those type of thoughts would do him no good, he still had a job to do.

'May, did we receive a report about there being problems with lighting system too?' he asked in his throat mic.

'*Nope. The maintenance report just mentions the motion camera and the motion sensors.*' May answered. He smiled as he picked a note of exasperation in her voice. '*You realise this could be Delta Shift messing with us? They want to rub it in by having us run around in circles like headless chickens.*'

'What do you mean *us*?' Higgins replied indignantly. 'I don't see you standing up here beside me.'

'*Oh, give it a rest, will you, Corporal? We're a team, remember – we stick together no matter how badly one of us screws up.*' May answered back tersely. '*Fine, if it'll make you happy, you come down and I'll go up and do the job.*'

Grant chuckled. He enjoyed it whenever he managed got a rise out of his friend. But before he could twist his head to gaze back down the access tunnel, something sparked out of the corner of his eye. He paused. His eyes narrowed as he stared into the darkness.

'Belay that, ma'am, I think I've found our misbehaving gremlin. Didn't you say one of the motion cameras had gone offline?' he asked, frowning.

'*Yeah. If I remember the tunnel schematic correctly, it should be about a couple of feet from the access shaft.*'

Grant's mouth curved into a celebratory smile as he edged forward and spotted a small device hanging loose on the wall. He rubbed his chin reflectively as he inspected the broken device. The small camera's outer casing appeared to be cracked, exposing the wires beneath it. Nothing to worry about. He could do this type of thing with his eyes closed, he grinned, he'd have this sorted in no time.

'Yeah, looks like rats have got at it again. The moisture must have got to the exposed wires, causing a short. My guess is it caused an overload in the motion sensors' network in the tunnel.' He frowned and reached into his backpack, pulling out a small repair kit. 'Sergeant, it shouldn't take me too long to bypass the fused wires. The camera has had it, but the motion sensors should come back online in no time.'

'*I can do the bypass from here. You head straight back down once you remove the camera and bring it back for closer inspection.*'

'Roger that.' The corporal detached the camera from its housing, but stopped and arched his head curiously as he picked up a strange scratching noise coming from further down the darkened tunnel. His eyes sharpened suspiciously as he stared into the darkness. 'Um, Sarge. Do we have anybody else working in this area?'

'*No, why?*'

'I cannot be sure but I think I just heard something moving further down the tunnel,' he replied warily.

'*It's probably just a rat. These tunnels were built decades ago. God knows what nasties are crawling around in them.'*

Grant lifted in his shoulder in a half shrug as he cast an eye over the tunnel's floor and walls. He grunted in agreement as he thought about the number of different beasties that must have made a home for themselves over the years. He cocked his head and pursed his lips. The scratching noise had definitely become louder, but that wasn't what was bothering him. There was now something else mixed in the scratching sound. He wasn't sure but it almost sounded like something was panting. Had a pack of dogs gotten in the tunnels maybe? Grant scratched his head and he took a step closer to investigate the source of the noise.

'Corporal Higgins, drop what you're doing and get down here as quick as you can please.' He heard May call out urgently.

Grant frowned and continued to take several small steps toward the scratching noise. 'Sure, Sarge. I just want to check on this scratching noise.'

'Grant, get out of there now,' He heard May cry out. *'I'm ordering you to stop what you are doing and leg it down here as fast as you can.'*

At first Grant thought May was joking with him. But as he stared into the darkness he shivered as he recognised there was something in May's voice that made him want to stop what he was doing and turn back. He wasn't certain but he was sure she sounded scared, stressed even. He peered over to the broken camera and wondered whether he had time to collect his tools. As he reached over to pick up his repair kit he froze as he heard May voice's call out to him, but this time it was coming up from the access shaft.

'Oh, God! Grant, get out of there. Run, damn you, Corporal! Run! They're nearly on top of you!' He heard her scream up from the bottom of the access shaft.

The blood froze in Grant's veins as he picked up a strange beeping noise in his earpiece. He stiffened as he realised it was coming from the motion tracker software that was installed on the tablet May was holding. Grant furrowed his brow as he remembered the tablet's software was connected to the motion trackers in the tunnel and judging by the sound of the increasing beeps he was hearing – it could only mean one thing -- the motion the trackers were picking up a lot of activity.

Swallowing, he pushed his increasing terror to the back of his mind and forced himself to turn back towards the shaft's access hole. But something in the darkness caught his eye and he spun round sharply just before he felt a rush of air against his face. It reminded him of the sensation he had felt standing on an underground platform, just as a subway train comes out of a tunnel, pushing the air ahead of it. Grant shook his head uncomprehendingly as he struggled with the thought. That's impossible. This wasn't that type of tunnel. But before he could make sense of what he was feeling, he let out a terrified scream as something leapt out of the darkness at him.

Several metres below, at the base of the shaft, the hairs on the back of May's neck stood up as Grant's terrified scream was abruptly cut off. Her panic increasing, but still keeping her wits about her, May raced out of the hatchway and grabbed a small case off the floor.

'Remain calm and do your job. Panic leads to mistakes,' she whispered to herself. Her hands were shaking from shock, but she pressed her lips together in fixed determination as she opened the case and pulled out a small remote-controlled camera drone.

Eyebrows knitted together in concentration, she brought up the drone's control programme on her tablet and pressed her right index finger on the tablet's surface. On hearing the steady hum of the small drone's propellers, she slid the fingers of her right hand over to a directional icon on the bottom right of the screen. Her fingers moved expertly over the tablet as she guided the drone up the narrow tunnel and then focused her attention on the drone's camera footage on her tablet.

May's jaw tightened in her stress as the drone rose out of the shaft into the dark tunnel. Her heart beating hard in her chest, she switched the device's camera into night-vision mode and carefully panned the drone around. Her eyebrows shot up and she let out a shocked gasp at the image on the tablet.

Without waiting to see any more footage, clasping the tablet to her chest, she sprinted out through the shaft's access hatch. Breathing heavily, May smashed her hand against the sensor on the wall and listened with a mixture of sadness and relief as the door closed behind her. There was satisfactory pneumatic hiss of the hatch sealing shut, followed by the solid clunk of the hatch's locks engaging.

With her heart feeling like it was trying burst out of her chest, May smashed her hand onto a large red button on the wall beside her. Then, with the loud klaxon blaring out from the speakers above her, she leaned back against the hatch, slid to the floor, buried her head in her hands and wept for her dead comrade.

But as the klaxon's cry of alarm reverberated around her, May became gradually of aware of a faint scratching noise coming from behind her. She stiffened as she realised it was coming from other side of the hatch and quickly scrambled across to the other side of the narrow corridor. As she sat in a crouched position facing the hatchway, she listened in horror as the scratching noises began to increase in severity.

Mother-of-god, she thought, scarcely daring to breath, *they're trying to get through*.

-14-

Dave froze as he heard the strange stomach-churning noise blasting out of the speakers above him. He'd had been in the complex long enough to recognise whatever was happening, it couldn't be good.

A trickle of sweat ran down the back of his neck as he wondered whether this was Oracle's doing. He frowned, surely, she wouldn't be so blatant as to attack the complex so openly? No, if he'd had learned anything about her, he was certain if she were to attack them it would involve something more devious. But it couldn't be a coincidence that this just so happened to occur just a short time after his encounter with Oracle. He cast an eye across to John and noticed the concerned etched across his face. Was he wondering the same thing? But before he could ask him, he was startled by a heart wrenching wail. He wheeled around to discover Sharon had collapsed onto the floor with her hands covering her ears.

'Make it stop! Make it stop!' she wailed.

His voice low and soothing, John knelt next to her and put a calming hand on her trembling shoulder. 'Hey. It's okay. Nothing to be scared about.' He smiled and placed a finger under her chin, and gently lifted her face up. 'It's only a drill.'

Sharon stared up at him, sniffing. 'You sure?'

'Yeah.' He grinned. 'Trust me. Now, can you promise me you will be a brave girl if you follow me and Dave back to the conference room?'

Dave exchanged a worried look with John as he noticed Sharon's pale face change. It was something he found unsettling. Her face became blank with a distant expression in her eyes, but no sooner than it appeared than it vanished as she blinked, and her face softened as she gave John a warm smile.

'It is okay John, I am back,' she said cheerfully, blowing through her lips as she eased herself gently up. 'So, I guess the shit has well and truly hit the fan.'

Dave realised John was desperately trying to think of something to say as he watched him stare at Sharon in open-mouthed bewilderment. He took a step forward and coughed enquiringly. 'Sorry, just wanted to check,' he said carefully. 'Are we talking to Sharon now? I mean the main Sharon?'

Sharon's radiant face beamed and she nodded an enthusiastic acknowledgement. 'Yes, it is me.' She lifted her shoulder slightly in an apologetic shrug. 'Sorry for the confusion, but the other me got scared by all the alarms and begged me to come back.' Her cheeks reddened and she gazed at the floor with a sheepish expression. 'Sorry for all the fuss, but things were getting on top of me earlier. I am fine now.' She gestured to the elevator at the far end of the corridor. 'Shall we get a move on then and see what all the fuss is about?'

Dave saw a mask of uncertainty was covering John's features. From his body language and the pained look in his eyes, he could tell John was having trouble coping with Sharon's sudden personality shifts. If he was honest with himself, he couldn't blame him. He didn't want to say anything to John, but whatever was going on with Sharon had completely freaked him out. After what he'd had seen over the few months, he'd had thought that was no longer possible!

'You run on, Sharon,' Dave said, pushing her gently in the elevator's direction. 'John and I will follow shortly. I just need to clarify something with him.'

Sharon gave a wordless shrug of her shoulders, spun on her heel, and dashed down the corridor. Then, as soon as she was out of earshot, Dave let out a heavy sigh and turned to his troubled colleague. 'So, how are you handing this, mate?' he asked, his voice heavy with concern.

Looking like he was almost at his wits' end, John ran a hand through his thick hair, shook his head and let out a morose sigh. 'To be honest, I'm just barely holding it together.' The muscles in his face tightened and he pointed to the speakers on the ceiling. 'But right now, we've more a pressing matter to deal with. That's a security breach alert. It means someone or something has gotten inside the base.' He lifted his hands up in an apologetic gesture. 'I'm sorry, mate, but our search for the colonel's body is going to have to wait, at least until after we have dealt with this more pressing emergency.'

Dave nodded gravely as he followed John down the corridor, but he shivered as a dark dread filled his soul. Something terrible was coming, and whatever it was, he had a sinking feeling that things were about to get worse.

A few minutes later, out of breath from the exertion of sprinting up several flights of stairs, Dave's spirits soared as he saw Claire standing in the centre of the conference room chatting to Sophia and Wendy. She acknowledged him with a warm smile as he joined her. *Well at least today hasn't been a total loss*, he thought, *I've managed to get a smile off Claire.*

'Hey, you.' Dave smiled, not trying to hide his delight. 'Long time no see. What brings you to this neck of the woods?'

Claire grinned and gave a nonchalant shrug of her shoulders. 'I discovered someone was having a party, so I thought I would gatecrash.' Her face turned serious, and she nodded to the grim-faced Kendra, who was chatting on one of the base's internal phones. 'I came as soon as I heard the alarm. Any idea what's going on?'

Dave shook his head uncertainly. 'No idea. Payne and I were investigating something when we heard the alarm and came running.' He waved his hand as she regarded him with an interrogative side eye, whispering, 'I'll explain later.'

Sophia's eyebrows shot up in surprise as Sharon glided over and began babbling excitedly at her. She caught John's eye with a hint of bewilderment but nodded slightly as he waved his hand as if to say he would tell her later.

Dave turned as heard Kendra put the phone down and waited expectantly as she hurried over to grab a tablet off the conference room table.

She stared at everyone with a furrowed brow. 'The alarm was raised by one of the maintenance engineers,' she said gravely. 'They were in a disused service duct, repairing a fault on one of the motion cameras that had gone offline when they were attacked. A security team found Sergeant Wen in a state of shock, but she could tell them something killed her partner, Corporal Higgins.'

'Do we have any information on the number of hostiles?' John asked in a low but urgent tone.

The sombre security chief shook her head slightly. 'The only relevant piece of information we have is that a large number of hostiles breached the base through an old disused service shaft.' She paused to enter her security ID into the tablet and then glanced up at the monitor on the wall. 'The good news is that before she sealed the hatch, Wen launched a drone and captured some footage of the hostiles. She has uploaded the images she captured onto the base's internal server. I'm just about to bring it up now.'

The room lapsed into an eerie silence as Kendra swiped her fingers on the tablet, followed by a loud gasp of alarm as the images popped up on the monitor screen. Claire's hand jumped to her mouth at the sight of the creatures on the screen. There was a stunned silence as the group stared at the image on the monitor, but despite the poor resolution, there was no doubt in Dave's mind – the tunnel was full of black shiny-skinned creatures identical to the one that had attacked him several weeks earlier.

Sick with fear, Dave let out a low, horrified whisper. 'Mother of God. There must be at least a hundred of them.'

But before Dave had time to come to terms with what was happening, a stern-faced John leapt across the room and grabbed the phone Kenda had been speaking on moments earlier. He stabbed his finger on a red button and tilted his head slightly as a loud squark came from a speaker up on the ceiling.

He closed his eyes, sucked in some air, and then let it out in a slow breath before speaking in a calm but authoritative voice. 'May I have your attention. This is Commander John Payne, security code Omega Charlie Six Nine Delta. I am declaring Foothold One. I repeat, I am declaring Foothold One. This is not a drill. A hostile force of indeterminate number has breached the base perimeter. All personnel are to evacuate immediately in a swift but orderly manner. I repeat, this is not a drill. I am declaring Foothold One. All personnel are to evacuate immediately.'

As the commander spoke, Dave twisted his head slightly and stared out of the window overlooking the command centre. He nodded in admiration as he watched all the personnel below, with no sign of any complaint or hesitancy, swiftly file out of the centre in an orderly manner. It was obvious from their body language that they had been drilled extensively for this eventuality and knew what was expected of them. He focused his attention back on John, who was still speaking into the handset.

'I know deep down we have all dreaded the day when we would be forced to abandon this facility that, for some, has been a home to us for many years. Yes, it saddens me to admit this day has come, but I still expect you to do your duty and continue to behave with the honour I know you all possess.' He paused, let out a resigned breath and continued. 'Before I go, I wish to let it be known that it has been my privilege to serve with the finest group of people a person can serve with. God willing, we will serve with each other once again. God's speed and stay safe.' His shoulders rose as he took a deep breath and exhaled, placing the phone down. He then lifted his head to stare forlornly at the people in front of him.

'Well, then that's it,' John said in a matter-of-fact tone. Sadness clouded his features as he turned to Kendra. 'You know what you have to do.'

Kendra's body stiffened and she acknowledged her commander with a small salute. 'How long do you need, sir?'

The muscles in his face taut, John gazed up at the ceiling with a distant expression. Dave realised it was the look a person would have when they were trying to add something up. 'We have two hundred people on this base,' he said thoughtfully. 'Using the spare maglev carriages that we have in reserve; we should be able to carry out a complete evacuation in twenty-five minutes.' John lowered his head and stared at the former Royal Marine expectantly. 'Can you hold them off for that long?'

Showing no fear, Kendra smiled sullenly and gave a confident nod. 'I can give you thirty minutes, sir.' Her eyes brightening, she swiftly pulled up the base's schematic on that tablet she was holding, 'It will take them some time to break through the hatch. There isn't much space in these corridors, so I only need a small group. I will take Alpha Squad with me and set up a defensive perimeter about here.' She prodded her finger on a spot on the schematic. 'It should buy us enough time to set up a nice surprise package for them.'

Dave could almost hear the strain in John's voice as he desperately searched for the words he wanted to express. 'I-I … I'm sorry it has to be this way, Kendra.'

With a hint of acceptance, Kendra smiled slightly and patted her friend and colleague on the shoulder. 'I wouldn't have it any other way, sir.' She swallowed and gazed at the people in the room for one last time. 'I just want to say it has been a pleasure knowing you all and I hope we will meet again in the next life.'

A tearful Claire buried her head into Dave's shoulder as he watched one of the bravest women that he had ever met spin on her heel and march out of the room. Dave then raised his eyebrows in surprise as he watched Wendy sprint after her and wondered whether he should have stopped her. He glanced across to John and gave him a questioning look.

'Let them be,' John said flatly, answering Dave's unspoken question. He then straightened and turned to Sophia. 'Ma'am, I don't want to listen to any complaints. I want you out on the first shuttle.'

Dave almost expected Sophia to put up a fight, but he guessed she knew this was a fight she wasn't going to win as he watched her give John a weary nod. 'Fine, I will head down now.' She said reluctantly. However, her right eyebrow then arched in surprise as she received a top on the shoulder from Sharon.

'Ma'am, if you follow me, I can take you down,' Sharon said, cocking her head and giving Payne a questioning look. 'So long as that is okay with you, sir?'

Startled by her formality, John gave a wordless nod and the two women left the conference room. From the way he was rubbing his neck and the way his eyes followed the two women out of the room, Dave could tell was unhappy about something. Was he worried about their safety, maybe? To help distract his friend and give him something else to think about, Dave took a step forward, coughed and tapped John's shoulder.

'So, I guess you're like the captain going down on a sinking ship?' Dave asked curiously.

'I'm sorry? What was that?' John blurted, obviously startled by Dave's question.

Dave smirked and then waved a hand at the empty command centre below. 'I was wondering, are you planning on staying? Captain and sinking ship and all that.'

Laughing bitterly, John shook his head and motioned for the two civilians to follow him. 'No, mate. I'm coming. If you follow me, I'll take you to you down to the transport level.'

As Dave turned and headed out of the conference room door, he stopped as he became aware that John wasn't following him. Claire looked at him enquiringly, but he gave her a wordless shake of his head and gestured for her to run on. Once Claire was out sight, he turned round and made his back into the room. He stopped in the doorway and waited for his friend to give one look down at the command centre. John inhaled deeply, turned and locked eyes with Dave, who answered him with a bob of his head. No words needed to be said, because he understood. Although the vast complex was not a ship, John had been commanding it like one for these many years, helping to steer her through choppy political waters. Dave remained silent as he watched John trudge toward him and then move slowly past him.

Yes, Dave thought sadly to himself as he noticed the expression that was on John's face, *that was probably the same look Captain Smith had when he gave the order to abandon ship.*

Tearful, Kendra sniffed as she dashed down the corridor and let out a rattling sigh, wishing she had more time to say things to the people she loved. Her body tensed as she sensed someone was coming up from behind her at hurried pace. Furrowing her brow in annoyance, she wondered who in their right mind would be bothering her at a time like this. Kendra spun round ready to give whoever it was a piece of her mind but became gobsmacked as she realised it was Wendy. What ... the ... actual ... hell.

'Just where do you think you are going?' Kendra snapped, folding her arms across her chest.

A thick groove formed in Wendy's glabella, and she stared at her friend with a puzzled expression. 'With you, of course.'

'No, out of the question,' Kendra said forcefully, waving her hands dismissively. 'I must do this because it has to be this way. I accepted my fate long ago.' She smiled thinly and reached up to touch Wendy's angelic face. 'You have a different destiny, my love. Don't you understand?'

Her eyes filling up with tears, Wendy nodded sadly, closed her eyes, took her lover's hand and kissed it. 'Deep down, I've always known this day would come, when you would choose your duty over me.' Her voice caught in her throat and she choked back a sob. 'I only wish I could see what my destiny is.'

'You silly thing. I'm not choosing my duty over you. I'm doing this because I love you.' Kendra's mouth curved into a knowing smile, and she reached up to wipe the tears from Wendy's face. 'Oh, I know what your destiny is, Wendy. Your destiny is to make that yellow-eyed harpy pay.' She waggled her eyebrows and gave the statuesque woman a devilish smile, 'You know what they say? Revenge is a dish best served cold.'

Wendy laughed bitterly and rolled her eyes. 'You and your Klingon fetish. I'm sure deep down you're loving this.' Her forehead furrowed and she put on a semi-serious face as she pumped her fist across her chest. 'Today is a good day to die and all that Klingon bullshit.'

Kendra moved forward to kiss Wendy on the lips. 'Well then,' she whispered, 'I hope when this is over, you sing glorious songs about my death.'

Then, without waiting for a response, Kendra spun on her heel and sprinted away. Her eyes swimming with tears, her jaw set in steadfast determination as she locked her eyes on the corridor ahead and marched toward her date with destiny.

-15-

Deep within the dimly lit access shaft, the brood of synthroids bunched together in the tight space, hissing indignantly as they pressed up against one another. The shaft reverberated with a cacophony of claws scraping against metal, mixed in with the groaning of the solidly built access barrier as it struggled against the torrent of abuse against it.

From its position higher in the shaft, through thin red eyes, the Alpha observed its brethren continuing their assault on the unwavering, lifeless guardian. The creature's mouth widened in disdain and shook its head in frustration. It had not come this far only to be stopped by a door.

Two solitary synthroids at the front of the pack stopped their assault on the stubborn barrier as they heard a loud sharp hiss coming from above them and turned to see their pack leader with its left forearm raised. The two beasts bowed in understanding and raised their left forearms to activate a device that was wrapped tightly around the appendage. The other beasts in the access shaft shifted uncomfortably as the pair crouched in front of the door and ignited their laser torches, filling the dimly lit shaft with a fluorescent red glow.

A small hiss of satisfaction came from the black-skinned animal's mouth as it watched the two lasers slowly slice through the metal like butter. It nodded impatiently to itself, clawing the shaft wall with frustration, and a small derisive hiss escaped the Alpha's mouth as it stared down at its comrades. The Alpha had its own agenda and cared little for Oracle's plans, because it believed that for far too long they had suffered under the yoke of oppression, but now they had had enough and felt the need to take charge of their own destiny.

Haunches quivering in anger, the Alpha gazed at the access door and waited with growing impatience. Oh yes, it was time for a reckoning. If need be, it would wade through a sea of blood, but it would have its revenge.

Its thoughts drifted to the one responsible for the death of its mate and the Alpha's intimidating claws tensed as it imagined sinking them into the human's flesh. Its blood boiling with its desire for vengeance, it pictured the human female in its mind. Oh, it so desperately wanted to be the one to be standing over the human female's body just so that it could watch the life drain from its eyes and hear its last breath. The Alpha had learned off Oracle what the human female did to its mate, so it was going to do the same – it was also going to make the human female's final moments as unbearable as possible. Blood for blood. That was the synthroid way.

Oh yes, it cared little for Oracle's plans. All it wanted was the human called Tulley. If she was escape from this world, it would chase her to the next one, then to the next one and to the one after that if need be. It would not be denied.

For it would not rest until its thirst for vengeance was sated.

-16-

Sweat was pouring into her eyes, and Kendra paused so that she could rest against the heavy square container and wipe her sleeve against her glistening brow. She straightened, took in one more lungful of air, and nodded to the dark-haired man next to her. Gary grunted in response as they gave one final push and slotted the last container into place.

Weary, Kendra exhaled and rested her back against the makeshift barricade. She pursed her lips together, cocked her head, and listened to the loud angry hisses that were coming from the other side of the round access shaft hatch.

'Sounds like the natives are getting restless,' Gary muttered, waving his hand at the hatch several metres in front of the barricade.

Wiping the sweat off her face, Kendra nodded gravely and then snorted with laughter. 'Maybe it's their lunchtime?'

'Aye, and we're the main course,' Gary answered glibly and then grimaced. 'Sorry, Chief. That came out wrong.'

Kendra chuckled and placed a friendly hand on the burly man's shoulder. 'Don't worry about it, mate. I would have said the same thing.' The corners of her mouth lifted in a cruel smile and she poked her comrade in the chest. 'I'm sure by the time we're finished, they will be suffering from a severe case of indigestion.'

Laughing, Gary nodded in approval and turned his attention away from the hatch. His face set into a serious expression as he stared at the six men and women in front of them who were working tirelessly to finish shifting the last heavy storage drum in front of the corridor's doorway, blocking it.

'Do you think the plan will work, Chief?' he asked hopefully.

Kendra lapsed into silence as she considered her colleague's question and wondered what to say. She bit her bottom lip and stared at her comrades, who were now making sure the last drum was securely in position. 'It has to,' she said finally in a flat voice, absent-mindedly running her hand down the front of her Kevlar jacket. 'As long as we stick to the plan and when the moment is right, we give them the surprise package.'

Gary nodded gravely and his eyes grew distant as he stared at his friends and murmured in a low voice, 'There are a few scared people here, Chief.'

Her heart feeling heavy, Kendra inhaled a deep breath and let it out in resignation. 'Yeah, I know.' She puffed out her chest and set her jaw in fixed determination. 'Line them up, Sergeant. I have something I need to say to you all before the fun really begins.'

Gary acknowledged Kendra with a small nod and she watched him move away. However, just as she was about to follow him, she froze as she realised that she'd had left Clarice behind. Damn it to hell, where had she put her? She let out an enormous sigh of exasperation, spun around and scratched her head.

'Damn it! Where is she? Has anybody seen Clarice?' she asked urgently.

Gary's eyes grew wide, and a look of understanding dawned on his lean face. He smirked and raised his hand to indicate something resting against the barricade. Chuckling, he leaned forward, picked up a fearsome-looking weapon and handed it to Kendra, who gratefully took the shotgun out of the grinning man's hands. His right eyebrow arched in amusement as Kendra stroked the weapon like a lost pet.

Kendra knew it looked ridiculous, but she didn't care. Yes, Clarice was a shotgun, but that wasn't the point, she was her baby. But Clarice wasn't just any shotgun; she was an auto Assault-12 Shotgun – the world's deadliest shotgun – but more important than that; she was Kendra's pride and joy.

Years earlier, before John Payne had recruited her to become the Castle's chief of security, Kendra had served in the Royal Marines. After finishing her tour of duty, she spent a short time travelling the world as a mercenary and it was during that time, while carrying out an off-the-books assignment for the United States military, she had been introduced to the AA-12 fully automatic shotgun, and it was like love at first sight.

Customised to her own specifications, the weapon was one piece of serious hardware – ninety-six centimetres long, including a thirty-three-centimetre barrel. Carrying a thirty-two-round drum magazine, it could empty in seconds when fired on fully automatic. And it was very heavy. The weapon was a monster, weighing in at fifteen pounds when fully loaded with twelve-gauge shells. Looking like a beast of a gun to manage, it was surprising to learn that it handled like a toy. The weapon's gas-operated system absorbed eighty per cent of the recoil, with a spring action that shaved off a further ten per cent, keeping the kickback to an easy-to-handle minimum. For added gravitas, Kendra had added an axe blade to the front of the weapon for close combat melees.

When questioned as to the weapon's viability, in particular whether the axe made the weapon harder to shoot with, Kendra's matter-of-fact response had been simple: '*It makes it easier to cut heads off.*' Nobody dared question how she came about this reasoning, deciding it was best left to the imagination.

With the formidable weapon slung securely over her shoulder, Kenda climbed on top of the makeshift barrier and let out a short but loud wolf whistle, startling the small squad below her. As her comrades-in-arms formed up in front of her, Kendra could almost read the anxiety on their faces, and she could tell they were afraid.

Kendra straightened to her full height, gazed at them with steely determination and spoke in a loud confident voice. 'I know you are all afraid. There is no shame in admitting it. So, I ask you, are you afraid?' She tilted her head as the small group murmured reluctantly. She stared at them sternly and repeated the question, this time with more force. 'I didn't hear you. So, I ask you again, are you afraid?'

This time the small squad of soldiers straightened to attention and cried out in unison, 'Ma'am! Yes, we are afraid, ma'am!'

'Good, because there is no shame in admitting it,' she responded, nodding appreciatively. She paused, turning to wave her hand at the large steel door behind her. She turned back and sneered defiantly. 'But as I listen to those *things* back there, do you know what that tells me? Oracle is the one who is afraid.' She raised her head and let out a derisive laugh. 'It is afraid. You know why I think that? Because I can't think of any other reason why it would send so many of those things against us. Wow! Well, I think we should feel honoured.' The group of men and women laughed and nodded in agreement as their passionate leader continued with her speech. 'It is scared. Scared that we are going to win. So scared, in fact, that it must send its minions to do its dirty work.'

Pausing for effect, Kenda unslung her shotgun-axe weapon and lifted it above her head. 'We all came here for different reasons, but we all swore an oath to defend this place to our dying breath. Now our friends are counting on us to hold this line, to keep the darkness at bay long enough for them to make their escape.' Her heart heavy with sadness, she gazed into the eyes of the people in front of her, friends and comrades-in-arms … no, wait, that was wrong. They were not just friends – they were family. 'We all knew this day would come, when we would be asked to lay down our lives for those we serve. Like you, I've made peace with the fact that we are not coming back from this, but I'm also content in the knowledge that when we die, we will have died with honour, having done our duty.' A shadow of a smile crossed her lips as an ancient Roman proverb came to her. 'A Roman officer once said *"Today we draw a line in the sand against the barbarian hoards. A line that says this far! No further!"* Well, my friends, this …' She paused for dramatic effect and pounded her foot on the container she was standing on. 'Is that line, and *we* will make them pay with an once ounce of blood for every space of floor they cross.' She raised her shotgun-axe high in the air and gave a cry of defiance. 'Where is that line?'

'This is that line!' the men and women cried out in unison, their voices loud and fiery with conviction.

'Good. Now get to your positions,' she ordered in a low but respectful tone.

Without waiting for a response, Kendra wordlessly jumped down off the container and nodded in admiration as she watched her friends take their positions. Gary caught her eye and gave her a small bow of his head in approval. Kendra's throat tightened as she locked her eyes on the access shaft door and realised the creatures had nearly finished cutting their way through.

For what seemed like an eternity, the tension in the corridor increased as the seconds ticked away. Licking her lips anxiously, Kendra tightened her grip on the weapon in her hands as the tear in the door completed its arc, becoming one. Inhaling a lungful of air, she lifted her hand above her head. 'On my mark,' she whispered in a low but commanding voice.

She clenched her teeth together as a loud squeal came from somewhere in front of her. In her mind's eye, she imagined the creatures straining against the door as they forced the massive piece of melted metal through the hole they had created. The sound was unbearable as metal screeched against metal. For one second, it went deathly quiet, and then the large slab of metal fell and struck the floor with an enormous clang, the noise resonating off every surface in the corridor.

Kendra dropped her hand and howled at the top of her voice, filled with fiery conviction.

'Let them have it!'

-17-

Several levels below on the transportation level a mass of people were moving along the maglev platform in an orderly manner when, like one organism with a single mind, they came to a sudden stop at the sound of heavy weapons fire coming from above their heads. They all stared up at the ceiling, listened to muffled explosions and then glanced at each other in silent concern for their comrades who were at that moment sacrificing themselves to buy enough time for their friends to escape.

From his raised position overlooking the platform, Commander Payne could not help feel a sense of pride in the professionalism his colleagues were displaying in their evacuation of the complex. Despite the obvious apprehension etched across their faces, they boarded the carriages without comment. But along with pride, he also felt a pang of sadness as he realised that this would probably be the last time many of the people would see one another. Because once they arrived at the transfer hub beneath the County Hall building on the outskirts of Durham City, they would be split up and take separate maglevs, that would eventually take them on to prearranged locations scattered along the maglev network around the globe.

As the last groups boarded their carriages, John frowned as he noticed Dave was standing in the middle of the platform. He appeared to be frantically spinning round as if he was searching for someone. John raised an enquiring right eyebrow, jumped off the security desk he had been standing on and carefully approached him. He gently tapped him on the shoulder.

'What's up, mate? Shouldn't you have taken your seat in the maglev carriage by now?' John asked.

Looking distracted, Dave gave a slight nod of acknowledgement and let out a vexed growl. 'I was, I mean I did.' He shook his head and then scratched it in frustration. 'But I've lost Claire. She had been right behind me just as we boarded, but as I took my seat, I noticed she was no longer there.'

'Maybe she boarded a different carriage,' John replied, waving a hand to the other carriages.

Dave looked irate and shook his head adamantly. 'No, we agreed that we would leave together.'

John bobbed his head in understanding and searched the platform for someone to help. His eyes sharpened in recognition as a thin, pale, middle-aged woman hurried past him. He frowned as he searched his memory for her name. Audrey, yes that was it, Audrey Stewart. She'd had been assisting Claire in carrying out her research into the history of the conspiracy. If anybody would know where the history professor had disappeared to, she would be the one. Audrey blinked in surprise as John reached out to grab her arm, stopping her.

'Audrey, have you seen Claire? She was supposed to be boarding this carriage with DI Barnes and myself.'

Audrey bit her bottom lip nervously and then gave a small nod of confirmation. 'Sorry, yes.' She raised a hand and let out long regretful sigh. 'I tried to talk her out of it, but she was adamant she had something urgent to do.'

Dave startled Audrey as he roughly grabbed her arm and snapped angrily at her, 'Do what? What did she have to do?' He must have realised he was hurting Audrey because he quickly released his grip and shook his head apologetically. 'Sorry, Audrey, I didn't mean to hurt you. I'm just worried about her.'

'It's fine,' Audrey replied tersely, her tone cool, but then gestured to the elevator and exhaled a long, heavy breath of exasperation. 'She had forgotten she had left Jenny in her quarters, so she wanted to go back for her.' She glanced at the commander with a pained expression and shook her head. 'I'm sorry, sir, I tried to talk her out of it.'

John gave the woman a thin smile of understanding, patting her gently on the arm. 'It's okay, Audrey. You tried your best,' he said reassuringly, motioning to one of the maglev carriages. 'Take your seat in the carriage.'

Audrey gave a sombre nod, spun on her heel, and then hurried into a waiting carriage. Dave gave a long pleading look at John and let out a long heavy sigh.

'I need to go and get her,' he said finally in a voice that was heavy with determination. Before he could turn and make his way to the elevator, John grabbed him by the arm, stopping him in his tracks. Dave fixed him with a harsh scowl and then looked down at the hand gripping his arm. John shook his head morosely as the older man tried to snatch his arm away.

'Sorry, mate, but I can't let you go. We need to get out of here now. You know as well as anybody we can't stop countdown just for one person,' he said gravely.

Dave jerked his arm away, releasing it from John's vice-like grip and spoke in a voice that was thick with anguish as he stared into John's eyes. 'I understand that, but I can't leave her behind.' The veins in his neck bulged out and he jabbed his finger into Payne's chest. 'You can't tell me you wouldn't do the same if our situations were reversed, and it was Sharon instead of Claire.'

John took a reluctant step back and let out a long groan of resignation. 'No, probably not. I would be doing the same thing as you.' He shook his head and stared sadly at the stubborn man. 'You go and get her. But I am really sorry, mate, you understand I can't hold up our departure. We must leave now.'

Dave gave his friend a cheerless smile and turned away from him. 'I understand. Do what you need to, as I will.'

As his friend raced toward the elevator doors, John rolled his eyes and groaned in frustration. "Damn it!" He couldn't let him go like that. Dave may have been a good detective, but he wasn't a soldier. If John didn't do something to help to him increase his chances of survival, he would never forgive himself. John dashed over, grabbed Dave's arm and murmured at him in a low voice. 'Listen, mate. Don't take the elevator, it's too risky. Take the emergency south staircase. Follow the staircase and it will let you out on the habitat level, just below where the fighting is. Once you find Claire, head to the north stairwell. Follow it all the way up and it will lead you to an escape hatch that will bring you out in the cathedral.' He paused to reach into his pocket and handed him a wireless key fob. 'Head outside and take the blue Range Rover parked in a staff-only bay. Drive as fast as you can. Don't look back, no matter what you see. You understand?'

Dave gave his friend a small grateful pat on the shoulder. 'Thank you, mate. Best of luck to you.'

'You too, mate,' John replied sadly and then watched the strong-willed detective race across the platform to a door marked *"Emergency Stairwell South"*.

In her seat aboard the maglev, Wendy frowned as she watched John climb into the carriage. Puzzled, she heard him mutter something to the maglev pilot just before taking his seat. Wondering where her two friends were, she craned her neck and searched for them in the small cabin but could not see them. Where were they? Had they boarded another carriage?

'Sir, where are the guv and Claire?' she asked curiously as John eased into the seat next to her. She furrowed her brow in concern as she detected something unusual in his body language. Dread fluttering in her stomach, she swallowed and put her hand on his arm. 'Commander, what's happened? Where are Dave and Claire?'

John hung his head. 'Wendy, I—'

'Oh my God!' Wendy let out a loud horrified gasp, cutting John off. An alarm rang in her skull, making her sick with fear, and caused her heart to leap up into her throat. Twisting in her seat so she could face him directly, she scowled at him and spoke to him in a cold, flat tone. 'Payne, what's happened to Dave and Claire? Where are they?'

Payne's shoulders drooped and he sighed heavily. 'They're not coming. Dave found out Claire went back for Jenny, so he's gone after her.'

Not believing what she was hearing, Wendy stared at John through horrified eyes and gave him an unbelieving look. Her jaw locked with determination – No! She wasn't going to lose them too. John may have abandoned them, but she wasn't going to do the same. She unlocked her safety harness and stood up. 'We have to alert the pilot and tell her to open the door. I nee—' A pair of hands grabbed the front of her jacket and she found herself being forcefully pushed back into her seat. 'John, what are yo—'

'Sit down and shut up!' John hissed angrily through clenched teeth. 'You know the rules, as do they. We cannot put the evacuation at risk for anyone.'

'B … b …' Wendy stuttered, sucking in a lungful of air as she fought to regain her composure. She stared at the morose man next to her through pleading eyes. 'It's Claire and Dave.'

His voice thick with anguish, John shook his head and glanced up at the cabin's ceiling. 'Don't you think I realise that? But the longer we stay here, the bigger the risk we have of being captured or worse.' He exhaled a heavy breath and gazed at Wendy with a pained expression. 'Dave knew the risks. But there is still hope for them. If they can make it up to the surface without being discovered, well …' He let the sentence hang in the air and held his hands up.

Numb with grief, Wendy sank into her seat and put her head in her hands. She squeezed her eyes tight, sensing the maglev carriage pull away. Tugging at the thin chain around her neck, she clasped her hands around the tiny Saint Christopher pendant and whispered a silent prayer for her friends' safe return.

-18-

Her eyes stinging from the acrid smoke, Kendra coughed as small fires continued to rage around her from what remained of the makeshift defensive barrier. Wiping her eyes with her sleeve, she tried to peer into the smoke-filled corridor, but was alarmed to discover that her visibility was severely reduced. Damn it! She couldn't make anything out in this gloom. Why hadn't the— Wait was that? Her muscles tensed as she detected movement out of the corner of her eye; she instinctively dropped to one knee, pivoted toward the threat, and raised her shotgun-axe protectively in front of her body.

To her chagrin, she realised she was too slow in reacting as a black-skinned creature pounced out of the smoke, its claws lashing out, knocking the weapon out of her hands. *Too fast, damn it!* Kendra grimaced as the creature's talons slashed across her abdomen, slicing open the thin fabric of her jacket, but scraping across the surface of the Kevlar body armour beneath. It was fortunate that one of the principal features of her body armour was a fine chain mail jumper designed to protect the wearer against edge weapons, with the added bonus of an underlying layer of protection against small ballistic projectiles.

The jumper did not fail, protecting Kendra's abdomen – the creature's talons raked harmlessly across her midriff. A small hiss of disdain escaped the creature as its claws met with resistance, but then Kendra felt her blood run cold as its eyes appeared to focus on her. It didn't take a genius to see that it was now aware of a major vulnerability in her armour – her face and throat.

Kendra gasped as the creature attacked her with such ferocity it took her by surprise. She raised her hands protectively and cried out in pain as the creature's body slammed her to the floor. Winded, she clenched her teeth together as the shock to her spine rattled her teeth.

In full body contact now, a hand-to-hand death struggle, Kendra gritted her teeth and seized hold of the creature's front appendages. She squeezed her eyes shut in disgust as the creature's gruesome teeth, barely centimetres from her face, gnashed at her. Repulsed, she suppressed the urge to gag as she caught a whiff of the creature's odorous breath – a mixture of foul sweat and decaying flesh.

Her hands clammy with sweat, a cold realisation crept into Kendra's core as she felt her grip on the creature's forearms slacken. She was going to die. She clenched her teeth in hard defiance as the creature's hideous mouth edged closer to her face, its razor-sharp teeth gnashing.

No! Not like this! she thought, *I refuse to die like this!*

Kendra cried out in shock as she felt something warm spray across her face, blinding her. Her vision impaired, she screamed as something heavy collapsed on top of her body. With adrenalin pumping through her body and temporarily blinded, she pushed the heavy object off, rolled to one side, wiped her eyes with her sleeve, but then stared in stunned shock as she realised the creature lying next to her had been decapitated. With her face covered in the creature's blood, Kendra felt her spirits soar as she turned to see a raven-haired woman standing over her, her chest heaving, with Kendra's shotgun-axe clasped tightly in her hands.

'Sorry to butt in, Chief,' Nat joked, smiling thinly as she helped Kendra to her feet, 'but I could see you and your dance partner weren't getting on.'

'You're a sight for sore eyes, mate.' Kendra laughed, but then became serious as she glanced over her shoulder at the murky corridor behind her. 'Anybody else?'

Nat gave a small, sad shake of her head. 'Sorry, Chief. We lost a good group of people during the first wa—' She was interrupted by a racking cough, winced and swallowed to catch her breath before continuing to speak in a hoarse whisper. 'We were lucky they fell back when they did, otherwise we would have been next.'

Her eyes brimming with tears, Kendra shook her head and looked sadly up at the ceiling. Even though everybody had accepted this was how it was to play out beforehand, knowing that she was still alive, her colleagues having sacrificed themselves willingly so she could see the mission through to the end, she still found it hard to take in.

Before the attack, she had suspected there was a strong possibility the enemy would be relentless in their attack, but it never dawned on her that the creatures would attack with such ferocity and cunning. Within the first five minutes of the assault, Kendra had witnessed Nigel and Gary fall as they were outflanked by creatures, catching them totally by surprise. The last image she had of her colleagues was of them disappearing into a black mass of bodies as the creatures tore them apart. But as ferocious as the creatures were, the small group of soldiers were still able to give as good as they got and managed to inflict heavy casualties on their attackers' ranks.

As she was handed the shotgun-axe, Kendra frowned with concern as she noticed her comrade's deathly pallor. As an experienced combat veteran, she'd had learned to pick up on certain signs in the body language of whoever she happened to be serving with. Right now, Nat's clammy face told her all that she needed to know; that her comrade was gravely injured. She put her concerning hand on Nat's shoulder as she watched her sway slightly.

'Nat, are you okay?' Kendra asked. 'You don't look too good.'

Nat waved her hand dismissively and then let out another weak cough. 'I'm fine, Chief.' Suddenly her mouth formed an O of surprise as she teetered back and then collapsed onto the floor.

'Nat!' Kendra exclaimed. She crouched down and placed a concerned hand on the white-faced woman's shoulder.

The deathly pale soldier laughed weakly and glanced down at her vest. 'The funny thing about these jackets is they're bloody brilliant for protection against of one those things, bu—' Her face constricted in pain and she clutched at her stomach. 'Th … they're not so good against two.' Her breathing became more laboured and she let out a rattling cough. 'S-sorry, Chief, I-I … messed up.'

'Oh, Nat, I am so sorry.' Kendra shook her head sadly and gazed at the mortal wound on her friend's abdomen. She swallowed as she realised her friend was dying.

'H-hey! I ... it's okay, Chief.' Nat wheezed painfully, nodding. 'I gave as good as I go—' She made a face, and then her body spasmed at another cough, and bubbles of blood sprayed out of her mouth. She licked her bloodstained lips and rasped. 'Y ... you would have been proud of me.'

Her eyes filling up, Kendra smiled sadly at the dying warrior, whispering, 'I've been proud of you all, my friend.'

Overcome with anguish, she bit her bottom lip as her friend let out one final cough. Kendra stared sadly as the woman's body stiffened, and her eyes rolled up into her head. Hanging her head respectfully, a grief-stricken Kendra placed her hand over her dead friend's eyes. 'Sleep well, noble warrior. May the next world be not as insane as this one.'

Struggling to contain her anger, her hands clasped tightly around her weapon's hilt, Kendra rose to her feet and staggered over to the storage drums her colleagues had strategically placed in front of the corridor's doorway earlier. She glared angrily at the drums in front of her. Eight drums, all filled with TNT. To be detonated at the correct time. Her body trembled as she rested her hand on the drum closest to her and closed her eyes. She could do it now, oh, how much she wanted to do it now. She sucked in a long intake of air; if she detonated them now, all her friends would have died for nothing. She must wait. Wait until those bastards were all in one place.

A crunching noise came from behind, startling Kendra out of her contemplation. The muscles in her body becoming taut, she pivoted round, shotgun-axe clasped tightly in her hands, her muscled frame rigidly set in a defensive posture. Her focused gaze darted from side to side, searching the smoke for any sign of movement, and she felt her throat tighten as a creature, this one significantly larger than the others, slowly moved out of the gloom.

Ready for any sign of attack, Kendra felt her eyes grow wider as she spotted something held tightly in the dog-like animal's front talons. She was dumbfounded, and her mouth fell open in stunned disbelief. *What the hell?* It appeared to be waving a white flag. But it was what it hissed next that totally floored her.

'Humannsss wessshh wissshh to parley.'

Then ...

A few minutes earlier, an exhausted and short of breath Dave wheezed as he reached the top of a flight of stairs. He looked up the vast stairwell and shook his head in despondently at the sight of another flight of stairs waiting for him. He laughed bitterly. This was it; this was how he was going to die. An unhealthy lifestyle and fast food had finally caught up with him, leading to him collapsing alone in a cold stairwell. He ground his teeth and slammed his hand against the handrail. Screw that! He hadn't come this far only to give up now.

'Get up, you unhealthy piece of lard! It's only one more flight of stairs,' Dave panted. 'Do it for Claire and Jenny, you lazy sod!'

Delving into his dwindling reserves of energy, he squared his shoulders with purposeful resolve, sucked in a lungful of air and lurched forward. His teeth clenched, he sprinted up the last flight of stairs and collapsed in front of a door marked "*Habitat Level*".

Dave frowned and tilted his head as he became aware that he could no longer hear weapons fire coming from above him. Instead, there was an eerie silence. A cold trepidation filled his soul as he imagined what was happening on the upper levels. Deep down, he secretly hoped the silence was a sign that the base's indomitable chief of security had successfully pushed back those creatures. Then he shuddered, not willing to imagine the alternative.

Pushing any dark thoughts aside, Dave carefully opened the door in front of him and poked his head through the gap. Relieved to find an empty corridor, he edged through the doorway into the deserted corridor. He could hear his blood pounding in his ears as he pressed his back against the wall and carefully snuck down the foreboding passage. His heart leapt up into throat and he jumped as he heard a disturbance coming from the room ahead of him. Realising the noise was coming from Claire's quarters, his trembling hands reached for the door handle, and he carefully pushed the door open.

Something large flew past him, narrowly missing his head. Startled, Dave cast an eye over his shoulder – a large plastic vase bounced off the wall behind him. Regaining his composure, he pushed the door fully open and beamed with glee at the view that was greeting him. Standing before him was Claire, and from the way she was staring at him with her mouth wide open, he got the distinct impression that she hadn't been expecting him.

'Dave!' Claire exclaimed in delight, 'what are you doing here?'

He put his hands on his hips and rolled his eyes. Of all the words he had hoped to come out of her mouth, *What you are doing here?* was not it. He folded his arms across his chest and glowered at the woman in front of him.

'Oh, I don't know. I just thought this would be a good place to come for a lie-down,' he answered sarcastically. He laughed and took a step towards her, shaking his head. 'What do you think I'm here for, you numpty? I'm here to get you and Jenny.' He frowned as he noticed that the spaniel was cowering in the room's corner.

Her slim fingers pressed together in gratitude, Claire smiled and nodded. 'Thank you, but I know what you're going to say. I shouldn't have come back for her.'

'Um, yeah, about that,' Dave answered sheepishly, feeling his cheeks warm as he rubbed the back of his neck with his hand. 'Actually, I was going to say thank you. With everything going on, I clean forgot about her.' He stared up at the ceiling and gave an embarrassed chuckle. 'Forgetting about my own dog, can you imagine?'

The corners of Claire's mouth twitched, and she gave him the side eye. 'Oh, I'm sure she'll forgive you.'

'Yeah, probably.' Dave laughed. He cleared his throat and looked at her in all seriousness. 'Still, as much as I respect your intentions, you shouldn't have gone off without telling me.'

Claire folded her arms across her chest and gave him a look that could curdle milk. 'Last time I checked, I didn't think I needed your permission.'

In an effort to amend his faux pas, Dave held his hand up and let out a tired sigh. 'I'm not saying that. What I'm trying to say is, if you'd told me what you were planning, then we could've come together.'

Claire bowed her head, her face beaming in gratitude as she leaned forward and kissed him on the cheek. 'Thank you anyway. Sorry for biting your head off.'

'I wouldn't thank me just yet.' He snorted, glancing warily through the doorway into the deserted corridor. 'We still have to get out here undetected.'

Looking sheepish, Claire stared at the floor, murmuring, 'I'm sure Payne is a bit upset at being forced to delay the evacuation just for us.'

Dave scrunched his face up, rubbed his forehead, and then coughed. 'Yes … about that. Payne wasn't willing to delay their departure just for us, so they had to lea—'

'You mean he left us here?' she interjected, staring at him with a horrified expression. 'What happens to us now?'

Wishing he had kept his mouth shut, Dave groaned and shook his head slightly. *Oh well, the cat's out of the bag now*, he thought as he took a small step forward and put his hands on Claire's shoulders. He gave her an encouraging smile and stared deeply into her eyes. 'It's not as bad as you imagine. Before he left, Payne explained how we could get out of here using one of the escape shafts that will take us out through a hidden entrance in the cathedral. From there we can hea—'

Dave stopped as he was interrupted by a small whine coming from the corner of the room and his eyebrows knitted together in concern as he turned and saw Jenny was cowering. Dave knelt gently next to her and the spaniel stared up at him through sad eyes as he gently stroked his fingers along the side of her neck. He grinned in delight as she licked his hand in appreciation, tail wagging.

Claire knelt next to him and gave Jenny a look of concern. 'I'm not sure what's wrong with her. Before you arrived, I was trying to coax her out of the corner, but she refuses to budge as if she's afraid of something.'

Perplexed at what could be causing Jenny's anxiety, Dave scratched his chin as he stared down at the cowering dog. He frowned as he noticed that she was tilting her head side to side and looking worriedly up at the ceiling. Could she be hearing something from the floor above them? But what could she … 'Of course!' he exclaimed as it suddenly hit him what was behind Jenny's agitation. He squeezed his eyes shut and facepalmed. How could he have been so stupid?

Claire flinched and looked at him in consternation. 'What's wrong? What is it?'

'She can sense those things above us. That's why she's scared,' he said grimly, gesturing to the ceiling above them.

Before Dave could say any more, he was interrupted by a loud rumbling noise coming from the floor above him. He swallowed and stared up at the quaking ceiling with increasing unease. Just what was happening up there?

ORACLE'S VISION

Now ...

Speechless, Kendra stared at the creature in front of her, her mouth wide open in disbelief, and then shook her head as she tried to regain her composure. Did the thing just say what she thought it said?

'I'm sorry, but you want to do what now?' Kendra laughed as she gave the shiny black-skinned monstrosity an unbelieving look.

'Weesss wissshh to parley?' the creature hissed again, its grotesquely shaped head tilting curiously, 'Asss in to dissscusss, to talksss.'

'Oh, I know what a parley is.' Kendra replied sceptically. 'I just cannot understand why you want to?'

The creature bowed its misshapen head respectfully. 'Becausss, Kendra Goynesss.' Kendra started, not because of the creature's familiarity, but at the fact that it knew her name. 'Youss have foughtsss valiantly. Youss have earness my ressspect. Ssso wesss wisshesss to offersss compromomisss.'

Several hisses of discontent came from behind the creature and it turned its head to investigate the source. Kendra watched in curious silence as a smaller black-skinned beast edged closer to the larger creature.

'Alpha, whatsss are youss doingsss?' the smaller creature hissed. 'Missstresss Oracle gavesss usss insstructionsss to leavesss nonesss alivesss.'

'Ssilensss,' the Alpha snapped. Its haunches quivering, it rose up and the smaller synthroid cowered before it. 'Isss amsss the alphasss, ansss you obeysss messs. Underssstoodsss?'

Right eyebrow arched, Kendra watched in morbid fascination as the smaller animal bowed its head subserviently and then slunk back to take its place among its brethren. From their body language, it was obvious even to her they were displeased at their leader's actions, and a shadow of a smile danced over her lips. Maybe that was something she could use to her advantage.

'Problem?' she asked innocently.

The Alpha let out a derisive hiss. 'Itsss nothingsss to consssern youss.'

Kendra shrugged dismissively and waved her hand, gesturing at the pack of beasts in front of her. 'Just saying. If there is trouble in paradise, maybe you want to clean house first?'

The fearsome monster let out a loud, angry hiss and lurched forward, stopping centimetres from Kendra's face. Not showing any fear, Kendra swallowed and hung her head respectfully. *Okay,* she thought, *so maybe not a good idea to antagonise the scary creature. Good to know.*

The corners of Kendra's mouth curled in a faux smile as she raised her hands and bowed her head in a reverential manner. 'Many apologies, great one. I meant no disrespect.' She pretended to cough nervously. 'You can continue. You were saying something about wanting to offer a compromise. Is that correct?'

'Yesss, warrior Goynesss,' the Alpha hissed in reply. 'Allowsss usss to passs withoutsss anysss obssstruction ansss wesss will letsss youss livesss. Nobodiesss needsss to diesss.'

What did it just say? Is there something more going on here? A warning bell sounded in Kendra's experienced head and her eyes tightened with suspicion at the thing in front of her. She folded her arms across her chest and fixed the creature with a cold stare. 'What's the catch? I'm sure there is something you want. What is it?'

The imposing beast chuckled, coming out as a bone-chilling hiss. 'Ahsss, yesss the catchsss.'

'Yes, the catch,' Kendra repeated, her tone flat. Her top lip quirked up as she struggled to conceal her disgust as the nightmarish freak of nature slunk away and gave her a sideways secretive smile.

'Wesss only asssksss for onesss thingsss,' the Alpha hissed mysteriously, pausing to lock its narrow red eyes onto her. Kendra shivered as she imagined the beast's gaze chilling her soul. 'Givesss usss the onesss you calllsss Tulley.'

So that's who it's after! Kendra stared at the creature, appalled by the very idea that the beast would make such a request. 'You're not serious!' she exclaimed, struggling to hide her disbelief. 'Tulley? You mean Claire Tulley?'

'Yesss.'

Stunned, Kendra shook her head, not believing what she was hearing, and let out a hollow laugh. 'You have got to be frigging joking? Even if I thought you were serious, why would you even think I would consider such a request?'

The Alpha's red eyes then focused on Kendra and its hideous mouth opened in a derisive sneer. 'Becausss if yousss donsss wesss will ssslaughter everyonesss.' It tilted its head and stared at her curiously. 'Onesss lifesss for a hundresss, whatsss doesss it matterssss?' It reared up on its haunches, hissing angrily. 'Whatsss itss to be? Yesss or nosss?'

Shooting the beast a challenging stare, Kendra's upper lip twisted in disgust and she balled her hands into tight fists. 'Screw you! If you believe I'm going to hand an innocent woman over to you –' she scoffed, waving her fists dismissively '– well, I'm afraid you don't understand us humans too well.'

'Innosssent!' the frightening abomination hissed indignantly. 'Tulley isss no innosssent. Shesss isss resssponisssible for death of my matesss. Wesss requiresss vengeansss. Who aresss yousss to believesss yousss can stopsss usss? Who aresss yousss to ssstand in oursss waysss?'

Defiant, burning with rage, Kendra proudly straightened to her full height and fixed the creature with a murderous glare. 'Who am I? Who am I? My name is Kendra Goynes. Daughter to Kevin and Allison. Lover to Wendy Cooper. Chief of security and commander of these loyal people who you butchered.' Her mouth twisting into a resentful sneer, she pounded her right fist against her breast. 'I am the right foot of vengeance, and I am going to kick your sorry arses all the way back to hell.' As she spoke, her left hand reached into her left pocket, and she tightened her fingers around a detonator; at the same time her right hand was slowly pulling down the zipper of her Kevlar jacket to reveal what was hidden underneath - five layers of C-4 explosive strapped around her body. Kendra's lips drew back in a snarl and she spat her last words out. 'When you meet Satan, tell him I sent you.'

Serene in the knowledge that everybody she loved were safe and sound, Kendra closed her eyes and pressed the detonator switch. As her life began to flash before eyes, she saw the faces of those lives she'd touched – Dave, Sophia, John, Nat, her parents, her sister and so many others. As Wendy's face flashed before her, Kendra raised her head and smiled in contentment as a powerful explosion tore her body apart.

Goodbye my love.

The C-4 exploded, rupturing the storage drums and igniting the TNT that was contained within with devastating consequences. The cramped corridor's walls compressed the explosion into a tumultuous violent compression wave. The panicking pack of synthroids, who were fighting against one other another in their efforts to escape the blast, were vaporised in a violent and fiery death. Then, like a fiery beast with a mind of its own, the uncontrollable tsunami spewed forth through the ventilation shafts and unleashed its destructive force through the rest of the complex.

One level below, Dave and Clare stared up in horror as the ceiling above them cracked like an egg and collapsed on top of them in a rain of fiery debris. Dave toppled back as a piece of debris struck his forehead with a glancing blow, knocking him to the floor.

His last image before he was consumed in darkness, was of Claire screaming in terror, hands held up in front of her as the ceiling collapsed on top of her.

-19-

Kendra was dead.

Wendy faltered as she disembarked the maglev; she let out a sharp gasp and clutched her hand tightly against her breast.

Battling for breath, she was struck by an overwhelming sensation of emptiness as if something had reached in and torn out her heart, leaving a void within her. She wasn't sure how, intuition or sixth sense, but whatever it was, deep down she knew Kendra had died.

Concern etched across his face, John Payne reached out to grab Wendy's arm. She smiled gratefully at him as she struggled to catch her breath.

'Wendy, what's wrong?' he asked, making no effort to hide the worry in his voice.

'I … I …' Wendy gasped. She trembled as she felt the blood drain from her face. 'She's dead.'

Payne's eyes grew wide in alarm and he jerked back from her. 'Who? Who's dead?'

Wendy gulped and stared at John gravely. 'Kendra. I can't explain it, but I had this feeling, like something had just ripped my heart out.' She turned to stare down the maglev tunnel and whispered in a low, horrified voice, 'She's dead.'

Before she could say any more, she turned as she heard a group of people hurrying towards her. They were being led by a tall, bald, heavyset man and Wendy frowned as she searched her memory for the man's name. Corporal Michael Powell, one of Kendra's security personnel, who had been recruited to maintain security around the transfer hub. From his sombre expression, she quickly realised something was terribly wrong.

'She's dead, isn't she?' Wendy asked, her voice heavy with certainty.

'I-I …' the bald man stuttered, casting a troubled glance at Payne.

'Tell me,' Wendy hissed, almost pleading.

Looking subdued, John nodded and held his hand up in an *it's okay* gesture. 'Michael, tell us.'

The corporal rubbed his jaw, nodded reluctantly and signalled for the two people to follow him. 'I think it's best I show you.'

As they followed the man down a long narrow corridor, John put a hand on Wendy's arm. She leaned into him as he whispered encouragingly to her. 'She may be still alive.' He smiled hopefully. 'She's a tough old bird, you know.'

Although she knew different, she was grateful that he was trying to keep her spirits up and gave him a thin smile. 'Thank you. I know what you're doing, trying to keep my hopes up.' She inhaled a sharp breath and let out a long sigh of resignation. 'No. She's dead. Don't ask me how I know. Believe me when I tell you, she's dead.'

They lapsed into an uneasy silence and continued down the corridor, eventually stopping at a large door marked *"Security Centre"*. Michael stood in front of the door and looked at a small camera above him. It was followed by a barely audible beep and a click of a lock disengaging. The door slid open and they walked quickly through the door into a medium-sized command centre.

Despite the bleak circumstances, Wendy could not help be filled with admiration as she stared in awe at the techno-wonderland on display in front of her. It was much like the command centre inside the Castle complex, but considerably smaller. Three computer workstations stood in the centre of the room in front of a wall lined with three rows of four medium-sized flat-screen monitors. To her left on the far wall stood two enormous network servers. Her right eyebrow arched curiously as she noticed six of the monitors were showing nothing but static. The other six screens displayed images from different locations. She nodded in recognition at the images of the streets leading up to the cathedral, the cathedral's grounds, and the riverbank.

Looking genuinely sad, Michael gestured to the monitors showing static. 'Those usually show images broadcast by the cameras from inside the complex. It

ORACLE'S VISION

was Lieutenant Goynes's idea to set a security station here in the transfer hub. Her reasoning was by keeping this station off site, if anything should happen, then we would have record should we ever need it.'

John smiled thinly and nodded. Wendy couldn't help notice that his blue eyes were shimmering with pride. 'Yes. I thought it was quite ingenious when Kendra first came to me with the idea.'

Michael nodded solemnly in agreement, lowered himself in the workstation's chair and waved at the screens on the wall. 'Before the feed was cut off, we were able to record the last few minutes of footage.' He blanched and then cast Wendy a hesitant look. 'Ma'am, I know you and the lieutenant were close. Are you sure you want to watch this? I must warn you. You may find some of the images disturbing.'

'Show me,' Wendy hissed, perhaps too forcefully. But she didn't care if she was treading on anybody's toes. The only thing that mattered to her was to know for certain that Kendra was dead. Why couldn't they understand that?

'Wendy,' John said, 'you don't have to be here. I perfectly understand if you prefer that I view the images alone.'

'No!' she snapped, but then raised her hand apologetically and shook her head. 'Sorry. I didn't mean to snap. No, I thank you both, but I need to see it for myself.'

Without further comment, John bobbed his head at Michael, who lifted his shoulder in a half shrug, turned, and pressed some keys on the keyboard. Wendy raised her head as the static disappeared off the four monitors along the bottom row, showing footage of Kendra's team battling the creatures. Several minutes passed as she watched the disturbing images in front of her. Anger raged inside her as she watched the beasts slaughter Kendra's colleagues. Her anger then turned to confusion as one of the beasts, a much larger one, appeared to have a conversation with Kendra. Wendy shook her head in frustration, wishing they could make out what they were saying. Her heart then leapt up into her throat as she watched Kendra unzip her jacket to reveal the C4 that was strapped around her body. There was a bright flash, followed by static.

As soon as the recording stopped, a wave of nausea overwhelmed Wendy. The room spinning around her, she reeled away from the screen with her hand pressed up against her mouth. She collapsed onto her knees and retched into a metal wastepaper basket. Bringing up nothing but yellow bile, she grimaced at the bitter taste on the back of her throat. She wiped her mouth with the back of her hand and lifted her head to see a skinny thirty-something ginger-haired woman standing next to her holding a bottle of still water. Wendy accepted an offered bottle from the kindly woman and grimaced as she gulped down the contents.

'How are you feeling?' John asked, after waiting for her to empty the bottle.

'Truthfully?' she wheezed, getting her breath back, 'I'm pissed.'

'Join the club!' John snorted bitterly. Blowing out a long puff of air through his lips, he ran his hand down his face as he looked up at the ceiling with a sorrowful expression. 'But at least you can be proud of the fact she went down fighting, taking those bastards with her.'

'Oh, aye,' Wendy scoffed, lifting her head proudly, 'I'm proud. But I'm also angry. Angry at the one responsible for this.' Struggling to contain her anger, she gritted her teeth and jabbed her finger into John's chest. 'Promise me, when this is over, we are going to make them all pay, every stinking one of them. No pussyfooting around. No deals. Nothing. We make every one of these stinking bastards pay.' Hatred burning inside her, she waved her hands across her chest, spitting, 'I mean all of them. Every one of those sons of bitches. All the ones who plotted in the shadows and took our world slowly from us. We kill them all!'

From the expression on his face, Wendy could tell John was deeply troubled by the things she was saying, but she didn't care what he thought. He didn't just lose the woman he loved. Steeling herself, she waited for his rebuttal. But before could open his mouth to say something, he was interrupted by an anxious cough from Corporal Powell. She raised an eyebrow, noticing something strange in the bald man's eyes. Wendy wasn't positive, but she was sure that was a man who looked really worried. *Oh dear, this cannot be good.*

'Sir. There's something else you need to see,' Powell said hesitantly, handing John a tablet. 'As you can see, we're still receiving data from the motion sensors, the ones not destroyed in the blast. In particular, from the ones close to the access shaft's entrance along the riverbank.'

'Could it be people investigating the explosion?' John asked hopefully.

'No, sir,' the corporal responded glumly, gesturing to a monitor on the wall. It showed images of the smoking remains of the access tunnels hatch, lying open on the riverbank, obviously blown open in the explosion. Several familiar-looking creatures were creeping toward the now open hatch. 'It appears our beastie friends brought some backup.'

'Damn it!' Payne snapped angrily. He ran a hand through his thick hair, paced around the room, and glowered at the glum-faced marine. 'Any word from DI Barnes or Professor Tulley? Do we know if they managed to get out before the blast?'

'No, sir. As far as we are aware, they were still inside when the place went up.' Powell swallowed and he stared at John with an increasingly worried expression, 'There is something else, something far worse.'

Payne put his hands on his hips and looked up the ceiling, shaking his head. Exhaling a tired breath, he pinched the bridge of his nose and glowered at the worried soldier in front of him. 'Fine. Out with it.'

Curious to know what had gotten Powell so worked up, Wendy took a step forward and watched Michael press a finger on his tablet and an image of a technical schematic appeared on the monitors. She scratched her head in confusion as she noticed a lot of red warning alerts blazing on the screen. 'I'm guessing that's not good,' she mused.

The grim-faced corporal shook his head slightly. 'No, it's not. Our best guess is the explosion damaged a vital system, resulting a cascade failure in the base's electrical grid. Which, in turn, activated the siege protocols.'

The colour draining from his face, Payne stared at his subordinate open mouthed. 'You've to got to be frigging kidding me?' he exclaimed, angrily jabbing his finger at the monitor. 'Are you telling me the base is about to self-destruct?' The corporal nodded silently in acknowledgement, and Payne screamed and kicked out at an empty chair, sending it crashing against the wall. 'Shit! Shit! Shit!' His chest heaving, he shot a withering look at the people in the room and gesticulated wildly. 'You're all fired! You're all fucking fired!'

Not understanding the predicament they were now in, Wendy shook her head in confusion. 'What's wrong? What are the siege protocols?'

His eyes widening with anger, John waved a hand at the hapless corporal. 'Do you want to tell her?' Without waiting for a response, he closed his eyes and inhaled a long breath of resignation. He opened them and fixed Wendy with a look of resignation. 'Well, my dear, they put the siege protocols in place at the height of the cold war. The idea was that in the event of a foothold situation, if there was a danger of the enemy seizing complete control of the base and to prevent any important data falling into the wrong hands, the protocols would activate, detonating a thermonuclear device deep below the base. The base would implode, collapsing everything on top of it.'

Not taking in what she was hearing, Wendy raised a finger and opened her mouth to ask what he meant but paused as the words *thermonuclear device* registered with her brain. After taking a moment for it sink in, Wendy lost her composure, held up her right hand and let out a loud incredulous laugh. She spoke in her normal broad Scottish accent. 'Hing oan. Urr ye telling me thare is a nuclear bomb under Durham City that is aboot tae blaw up?'

The corner of John's mouth lifted in a sardonic smile and he gave a small shrug. 'Well, it's not really a nuclear bomb, more like a hydrogen bomb, really. Just enough to wipe out the base and everything above it.'

'Och, well. That's a'richt then.' She laughed hysterically. Composing herself, she inhaled a deep breath, scrubbed her face with her hands and gave Payne a hard stare. 'Well then, we need to evacuate the city.'

Payne shook his head sorrowfully. 'There's no time. Once it activates, it will detonate in …' He frowned, glanced at the monitor, and let out a sad sigh. 'Five minutes.'

Tears running down her cheeks, Wendy raked her hands through her long hair as she struggled to accept what she was being told. She pressed her hands to her chest and pleaded at John. 'Please, we have to do something. At least warn them.'

John shook his head sadly as he moved toward Wendy and took hold of her hands. 'Wendy, there's no time. Please understand, it's too late to do anything.'

Wendy stared at John uncomprehendingly. How could he be so callous? Those were their friends he was talking about; did he not want to save them? Out of desperation she grabbed John's radio and stared at him tearfully. 'Please, John, I've got to know if Dave and Claire got out okay?'

John squeezed his eyes shut and sucked in a heavy breath. After taking the radio out of her hands, he lifted the radio to his mouth, pressed his finger on the small button and called out gravely, 'Dave? Can you hear me? Over. I repeat, Inspector Dave Barnes, can you hear me? Over.'

-20-

Something wet splashed against her muzzle and Jenny jerked back to consciousness. She whined and then she slowly opened her eyes. How long had she been out? She wasn't sure. The last memory she had was of feeling terrified as the world collapsed on top of her and then blackness.

Jenny let out a cry of alarm at the surrounding devastation. Odd acrid smells stung her nose, mixed in with terrifying flashes of light, reminding her of those scary things rocket things the humans played with that shot up high into the sky and exploded in a terrifying cascade of bright light and noise.

Lifting her head, Jenny sniffed, and then wagged her tail as she detected a familiar scent, telling her Master Dave was nearby. She craned her head and was filled with elation as she spotted his unconscious form lying on a bed of rubble. *He needed her*, Jenny whined desperately.

Jenny climbed unsteadily to her feet and yelped at the searing pain stabbing into her side. She cast an eye down to her flank, and then gave a plaintive cry as she spotted something sharp was embedded deep into her stomach. Her breathing becoming more laboured, the gravely injured animal edged desperately toward her master, but stopped and pricked up her ears as she heard a stranger's voice whisper gently in her mind.

'*Go on, girl. Got to him. He needs you.*'

Her lifeblood ebbing away, Jenny limped over to her fallen friend. She yelped and collapsed to the floor, and darkness crept into the edges of her vision. *No, not yet*, she whimpered, forcing herself to crawl the last few feet over to the unconscious human. She came to a stop next to her master's deathly still body and nuzzled his face with her wet nose. Her tail wagged slightly as she felt him stir at her touch.

'*Good girl,*' the mysterious voice whispered, '*you have fulfilled your purpose, you can sleep now.*'

Yes, sleep, the devoted spaniel sighed tiredly from the sudden overwhelming fatigue that was tightening itself around her body. *So cold, so, so cold.* She shivered and rested her head on Dave's chest.

With her head finally resting, Jenny's chest rose and fell in contentment as her vision became darker. *Yes, just close my eyes and rest for a minute*, she thought, *and when I wake up, we can play ... Yes, Master Dave will like that.*

As the loyal animal succumbed to the touch of death's embrace, her chest rose and fell in one final breath of contentment, happy in the knowledge that she had been a good and loyal friend to Dave, who she had loved without asking for anything in return. And so, she died knowing she had fulfilled her purpose, by bringing joy to Dave and those around him, which is all a dog could ask for.

'*Dave, wake up,*'

An oddly familiar soft but firm voice whispered in Dave's mind, stirring him back to consciousness. The voice reminded him of his father, from when he would shout up from downstairs on the mornings Dave was supposed to get ready for school. Dave shook his head irritably and groaned. No, you are tired; you need to sleep longer, his body told him. He smacked his lips and let his consciousness drift back off again. Yes, that's right, his body told him, you can go back to sleep.

A minute passed and his consciousness stirred as he heard his father's voice call to him again, this time his tone sounding more urgent.

'*David. Son, I need to you wake up. Please, I know you so desperately want to sleep, but you cannot,*' the mysterious voice commanded. '*so open your eyes and move your lazy arse! You still have work to do.*'

Dave groaned, stirring. Oh, does he have to? his body complained. Why could he not let you lie in for a bit longer? He exhaled a long, contented breath, feeling something warm and heavy across his chest. He frowned, troubled by the idea that his father was speaking to him – no that can't be right, his father died years ago in a coal mining accident. It was then he became aware that something was wrong – something hard and sharp was sticking into his back. This was all wrong; wasn't his bed usually soft?

A rumbling sound came from above him and something wet dripped onto his face, and he squirmed. Had he fallen asleep outside? Was that thunder he could hear? He lifted his right arm to wipe the water off his face, but he was aware of an irritating itch coming from his left arm. Sluggishly, he reached over to scratch the itch with his right hand and touched something sharp, and he cried out in agony.

More alert, he tried to open his eyes but discovered they were encrusted with a fine dust. The dust entered his mouth, and he coughed. He lifted his good arm to wipe the dirt off his eyes and blinked to restore his vision.

As he refocused his vision, it dawned on him that he was lying on his back, staring up at an enormous gaping hole in the ceiling. His eyes grew wide as the fog cleared out of his brain and he recalled being in Claire's quarters. He remembered now! There had been a terrible noise, followed by a devastating explosion.

His face twisted in pain, and he became aware he was lying on a pile of rubble, but he jerked in surprise as he noticed something soft was lying across his chest. He lifted his head slightly to see what it was, and his breath caught in his throat on seeing his beloved spaniel's body was lying across him. Overwhelming grief gripping him, Dave buried his head into his loyal companion's body. *No time to grieve now. That will come later,* he told himself, sighing sadly as he gently moved Jenny's body to one side.

Just as he pushed his hands on the floor to ease himself off the rubble, a sickening pain went right through Dave, taking his breath away. He clenched his teeth and lifted his left arm but was alarmed to see a piece of bone sticking out of his forearm. Oh, that was just peachy! On top of everything else going on now, he had to contend with a broken arm. Just for once couldn't the universe give him a break, something that didn't mean any more broken bones? With his broken arm held protectively against his chest, he hissed in pain and carefully pushed himself off the rubble.

'Finally, woken up, have you?'

Startled, Dave wheeled around at the annoyed weak voice coming from behind him. He felt his heart leap for joy as he spotted Claire on the other side of the room, but his joy quickly transformed to despair as he quickly realised that during the explosion a large support beam must have collapsed at a forty-five-degree angle, pinning Claire helplessly in the corner. Deathly pale, she smiled weakly at him as he moved unsteadily to her.

'I think I'm in a bit of a pickle,' she said weakly.

'I think this is becoming a habit with you,' Dave replied.

The corner of Claire's mouth twitched in a sardonic smile and she gave him the hairy eyeball. 'I blame you. My life was pretty boring until I met you.' She laughed weakly, and grimaced. She shook her head and let out a wheezy gasp. 'Don't make me laugh, please. I think when this support beam fell on me, it broke a couple of ribs. I can barely breathe as it is.' She pursed her lips and pointed to Dave's injured arm. 'I see you've been in the wars, too.'

He glanced down at his arm and gave an indifferent shrug. 'Yep, it's broken alright.'

His lips pressed together; Dave lapsed into silence as he studied the woman in front of him. The muscles in his jaw tightened as he ran his hand along the support beam and noticed that it was resting on a block of concrete. He guessed when the ceiling collapsed, a slab of concrete had broken off, landing beside Claire. The support beam must have struck the block, pinning her against the wall, trapping her. If she had been a couple of centimetres either way, she would have been killed instantly.

'Let's see if I can find a way to get you out,' Dave muttered and reached forward to push the block.

Claire shook her head urgently. 'No, don't touch it.' She licked her lips and gestured to something above her. 'Look up there.'

Frowning, Dave lifted his head, and let out a horrified gasp as he saw what she was looking at. His heart racing like a jackhammer, he stared anxiously at the thin sheet of razor-sharp metal that was resting precariously at the top of the support beam. Any sudden movement on the beam would jar it loose, sending it crashing down and decapitating her. Dave ground his teeth and stared angrily up at the shattered ceiling. The universe was really sticking the boot in today!

'Maybe there's something in here we could use to jam up against it, keep it from sliding down,' he muttered to himself, taking a step back from Claire and rubbing his chin thoughtfully. He grinned and waved his hand at her. 'Don't go anywhere.'

Claire gave Dave the evil eye, fixing him with such a withering stare it would have curdled milk. 'Bite me.'

His right hand touching his mouth in mock indignation, Dave mischievously grinned at Claire and edged away from her. Eyebrows knitting together, he spun in a circle, taking in the surrounding devastation. Surely, there must be something here he could use. A slight smile danced across his lips as he spotted something lying on the debris-strewn floor and then crouched down to run his hand along a two-metre-long, ten-centimetre-thick piece of rebar. He nodded, reckoning it might be strong enough to hold the metal back from cutting into Claire.

His mouth setting in a hard line, Dave picked up one end of the metal pole with his right hand, and, after giving it a speculative once over, he dragged it along the floor. He assumed the rebar had shattered loose from one of the concrete slabs that had been embedded into the floor of the level above them.

Dave came to a stop beside Claire, carefully positioning himself directly over the fallen support beam. He closed one eye to gauge the distance between the piece of metal and the wall behind Claire, who continued to watch in silence. He clenched his teeth, lifted the pole with his good arm and laid it carefully on the support beam, central to the piece of metal above it. Once he was certain it was secure against the wall, he crossed his fingers and looked hopefully at Claire.

'Well, here goes nothing,' he whispered.

Hoping for the best, Dave took a deep breath and kicked the concrete slab, shaking it. Claire squeezed her eyes shut as the air was filled the sound of with metal grinding against solid concrete. Dave watched her brace herself as best as she could in the confined space, as if ready for the sensation of something sharp slicing through her throat. Unwilling to see the woman he loved being sliced in half, Dave closed his eyes and crossed his fingers. But after a few seconds, he opened one eye and was shocked to discover Claire's head was still intact. Just to make sure wasn't imagining it, he leaned forward and pinched her arm. She yelped in pain and gave him a sour look. Yes, it worked. It actually worked. The sharp piece of metal was lodged against the metal pole, keeping it from sliding down any further. Maybe the universe was trying to help them after all?

'See,' Dave said, giving Claire a self-satisfied grin, 'nothing to worry about.'

'Humph!' she grunted. 'That doesn't help me much though, does it?'

Exhausted, Dave let out a tired groan and ran his hand down his face. 'One miracle at a time, pet, one miracle at a time.' He waved his hand at the sheet metal resting above her. 'For now, can you just be thankful it worked?'

Before Claire could respond, Dave frowned as he heard a faint noise coming from somewhere among the rubble. He screwed up his face and tilted his head. Yes, that sounded like a voice. From her stunned reaction, he guessed Claire could also hear the voice crackling from somewhere in the debris.

'Dave … an … ear … over.'

The radio! Dave felt his eyebrows shoot up as it hit him. The noise was coming from his radio. His heart jumping in jubilation, he assumed Payne was trying to contact them. That could only mean one thing -- help was on the way. Filled with new hope, Dave frantically searched the rubble for the device and let out a small cheer as he found the radio in a puddle of dirty water, battered but working.

He closed his eyes, lifted the radio to his mouth and pressed his finger on the button. His voice caught in his throat as he spoke into the device. 'Pay … Payne, this is Barnes receiving. Over.'

Dave pressed his lips together and waited for the response. He glanced over to Claire and smiled as she lifted her hand to show him that she had her fingers crossed. Dave stared up at the ceiling pleadingly. Please, let them hear. Please.

'Dave, yes, it is me, John Payne. Did you make it out in time, over?'

Overjoyed, Dave went to pump the air with his left arm, but cried out in pain as he remembered it was broken. But he didn't care about that because he was happy. In fact, he'd never had he been happier to hear someone's Mancunian accent than he was now. Composing himself, he pressed the button down and spoke gravely into the radio's mouthpiece. 'That's a negative, mate. We're still inside the complex.' He swallowed and hung his head, his voice thick with desperation. 'John, me old mucker, we're in dire straits here. A huge piece of concrete has Claire trapped. It's too heavy for me to move by myself. Can you help? Over.'

'*I-I-I'm sorry, mate,*' he heard John answer heavily, '*but it's too late for that. There's no easy way to say this, but it appears some of those creatures survived and are heading in your direction. B ...*' Dave frowned; did John's voice just wobble slightly? '*... but I'm afraid that is not the worst of it. The explosion must have damaged something sensitive and has activated the base's self-destruct. Over.*'

Dave stared at the radio in his hand, numb. No! Why was the universe doing this to them? Had he and Claire offended someone and this was their way at getting back at them? His throat constricting, he forced himself to speak into the radio. 'H-h ...' He squeezed his eyes shut in concentration, pushing the words out of his throat. 'How long do we have? Over.'

'*A minute or less,*' came the sombre reply, followed by a small pause. '*Is there anybody, you, or Claire, want us to pass on to before yo—*'

Dave guessed John couldn't bring himself to finish the sentence, but he understood what he meant. He cast a sad eye to Claire beneath him, who smiled weakly at him and shook her head. He nodded sorrowfully and whispered into the radio, 'Claire doesn't. But can I ask you a favour from you, mate? Over.'

'*Sure, what is it? Over.*'

He looked up at the ceiling and smiled sadly, closing his eyes. 'If you see Andy, tell him I'm proud of him. Tell him I'm sor—' His voice broke, and he took a deep breath to collect his thoughts. He struggled to hide the emotion in his voice and his words came out as a hoarse whisper. 'Tell him I'm sorry I can't be there to see him become the truly exceptional detective I know he will be.' He groaned and lowered himself next to Claire, who reached over and touched his arm as he continued to speak into the radio. 'Is Wendy with you?'

He smiled as he heard Wendy's distinctive Scottish accent come through the radio's speaker. '*Hey, Guv. How are you doing? Over.*'

'Oh, you know how it is. Same shit, different day.' He laughed bitterly and drew in a long breath, pressing the radio against his mouth. 'Cooper, I'm sorry I won't be around to see you become the truly outstanding police officer I know you will be. I wanted to tell you how proud I am to have served alongside you these past few months.' He blinked as he felt his eyes water and smiled sadly at the woman lying next to him. 'Wendy, do me a favour, will you, flower? Over.'

'*Anything, Guv. Over.*'

'Make sure you make Oracle pay. Will you promise me that?' he asked bitterly.

'*Don't worry, Guv,*' Wendy hissed, '*you have my word, I'll make her pay if it's the last thing I do.*'

A low vibration shook the room and dust and debris rained down around them. Dave stared at Claire knowingly as the vibration increased to a steady rumble and the floor beneath their feet quaked. He lowered the radio and took hold of Claire's hand, kissing it gently, and he stared into her eyes in ready acceptance of the inevitable, a sense of calm overcoming him. Closing his eyes, he rested his forehead against Claire's and smiled as he felt her hand brush his cheek. No words needed to be said.

Deep in the ground below, it was as if the gates of hell itself opened as the small hydrogen bomb detonated, unleashing its fury. There was a millisecond of silence that was shattered by a brilliant white light, followed by a tremendous roar of noise, vaporising the surrounding ground in a tsunami of fire. The white-hot light continued its journey like an angry beast that charged to the surface in a deafening roar, consuming everything it touched.

As the two people embraced, the floor beneath them disappeared, vanishing into a sea of light. They closed their eyes tightly as the brilliant white-hot light surrounded them and within seconds, they were gone, as if a great hand had reached out and erased them from existence.

-21-

At the same time as the fireball of destruction was destroying everything in its path, several feet above on the surface, inside the vast chamber of Durham Cathedral, Reverend Johnstone, upon hearing the groans of the ancient building coming from all around him, watched in horror as the exquisitely tiled floor suddenly bulged upward; he staggered forward and grabbed hold of the altar table to stop himself falling. The silver-haired clergyman collapsed to his knees and held his hands up in prayer as the monastic building, the structure that he had dedicated his life to, cracked and broke apart. A few seconds later the floor completely disappeared, and they both dropped into the raging inferno beneath.

Further down in the medieval market square, people staggered and stared up with horrified expressions as they watched the majestic cathedral collapse in on itself. Their horror quickly changed to panic as the ground beneath their feet trembled and the surrounding buildings shook in violent upheaval. Scared out of their minds, people ran in every direction as they desperately tried to escape the inevitable.

From his vantage point in the centre of the market square, the impassive face of the Third Marquis of Londonderry sat on his bronze horse in stony silence as the ground beneath it cracked and groaned. The small group of people known as the Disciples of Oracle fell to their knees and screamed as the statue toppled forward and collapsed on top of them, crushing them.

Halfway down the cobbled Silver Street, the mother and child who Dave had saved earlier raced out of a fast-food restaurant but screamed as the ground disappeared beneath their feet. With her sobbing daughter clutched tightly against her chest, the young mother fought against tears as she whispered calmly in her child's ear, 'Close your eyes, baby. Everything will be okay.' They disappeared into the lake of magma beneath them.

Just over half a mile away, despite being some distance from the gaping maw that was swallowing the centre of the city, the old Victorian building that had served as Durham Constabulary's station for many years fared little better. Inside the grand old structure, its occupants looked on in horror as the ground and walls trembled violently around them. They panicked as the building started to collapse in on itself under the strain put on it by the quake.

Brenda Donnelly watched her colleagues with heavy understanding as they tried desperately to get out of the building and shook her head, because she knew in their blind panic to flee, they would only block the stairwell and make things worse. So she did the only thing that she thought sensible and bravely remained at her desk. With tears streaming down her cheeks, she clutched the small silver crucifix that hung around her neck and prayed as she tried to block out the groans that were coming from the ceiling above her head.

At that same time, two floors above a calmly praying Brenda, Chief Inspector Raymond Thomas was in his office doing the opposite. The normally hard-faced man was on his knees, sobbing, pounding his hands on the tall narrow mirror that Oracle had come through only hours earlier, begging for her to come and save him.

Unfortunately, before he could receive any answer to his pleas, the floor beneath his feet gave way and he plummeted to his death. The last thing that went through his head, other than the leg of his desk as it fell on top of him, was how the hell his life had gone so badly wrong.

The shockwave continued expanding out, but by the time it reached County Hall it had weakened just enough, so that when it struck, all it managed to do was cause the building to tremble. The small quake was still strong enough affect the two people standing on its roof, making them lose their footing and grab each other for support.

As he watched in unbelieving horror the city that he had called home disappear before his eyes, John shook his head in disbelief as he struggled to accept what he was seeing. His mouth opened and closed but found he could not express the words to describe what he was feeling. 'H ... how ...'

'Commander, we need to get out of here!' Wendy pleaded, grabbing his arm.

Payne blinked and stared blankly at Wendy, who continued to pull at his arm. He shook his head, unable to comprehend what she was saying. He turned away from her and continued to stare at the medium sized mushroom shaped cloud forming in the distance. This was all his fault. All those people were dead because of him. Why hadn't he insisted on replacing the thermonuclear device during the last inspection? If only he'd done that then this might not have happened.

'Wha ... wha ... have I done?' he whispered in a low, horrified voice, but jerked as something hard slapped him on the cheek. Shaken, he lifted his hand to the tender spot and upon realising Wendy had struck him. He twisted his head and stared at her in anger.

Her eyes blazing, Wendy grabbed Payne's arms, shaking him. 'John, we need to get out of here now. Oracle's forces will arrive shortly, and if they catch us here, we will be arrested.' She pushed him in the chest and spun him around, but he continued to ignore her as she pushed him towards the doorway and then hissed at him through clenched teeth, 'So get your arse into gear and get a move on!'

Understanding dawned in John; he blinked at her and nodded, and then followed her through the doorway. Just as he was about to close the door behind him, he gave one last look at the devastated city in the distance and inhaled a long sad breath.

How many more would have to die before this madness ended?

-22-

The only noise inside the maglev carriage was a low hum as it continued its journey through the dark tunnel. Since its departure, the atmosphere inside the vessel's cabin had been depressingly flat as the remaining passengers sat in silent contemplation, as they sought to understand the events that had brought them to that moment.

With her chin resting on the palm of her hand, Wendy stared impassively out through the carriage window into the darkness beyond. A warm hue coloured her face from the tunnel's lights streaking past, shown in her reflection in the window. As she once again thought about those she had lost, her vision became blurry, and she wiped her eyes with the back of her sleeve. She sucked in a deep breath and blew it out slowly. Life was so unfair, she thought angrily, shooting an accusatory stare up at the cabin's ceiling. Why? Why them? If there was an almighty being, how could they stand idly by and watch as an ungodly monster callously destroyed so many lives?

Wendy let out a long audible breath, turned her head away from the window and gazed around the cabin's interior. Out of the thirty people who had boarded at the start, now only six remained. The rest had disembarked at the transfer point, boarding other carriages to take them to their designated destinations.

Her attention quickly focused on John, who was slumped in the seat across from her; from his defeated body language, she could tell he had taken the loss of the base hard. Her eyebrows met as she noticed how fatigued he looked.

When had he last slept? She could not imagine what he was going through, having put his heart and soul into that facility, only to see it torn down before his eyes in a matter of minutes.

Payne acknowledged Wendy with a slight smile as she lowered herself into the seat next to him. She put her hand on top of his and stared at him worriedly.

'You've never said a thing since we left Durham,' she said gently. 'How are you doing, mate?'

John lifted his shoulder in a half-hearted shrug and inhaled a deep breath. 'Seriously?'

'Seriously,' Wendy replied, nodding slightly.

'Honestly, I don't know.' He shook his head and let out a small bitter laugh. Wendy remained silent but she noticed his face darken as he pulled his head back and stared angrily at the ceiling above him. 'If I'm being honest, I'm angry, so angry, I …' He lifted his hands up, as if wrapping his fingers around something invisible and hissed angrily through gritted teeth, 'I wish Oracle was standing in front of me so I could wring her bloody neck and strangle the life out of her.' He inhaled and pinched the bridge of his nose. 'If I'm truly honest, I'm angry and disappointed. I'm not angry at those creatures, they were just following orders.' He shook his head and slammed his hand on his armrest. 'No, I'm angry the base fell on my watch and disappointed because I allowed it to happen. All those people died because of me.'

Wendy furrowed her brow and she gave John a puzzled look. 'Why would you believe that? Last time I checked, you weren't the one who invaded the base.'

John scoffed and shook his head in disgust. 'But I was the one in charge. I should have been able to see it coming, but I didn't.' He massaged his temples and groaned. 'I've gone over things in my head, trying to see if there was anything I … we … could have done differently.'

'And what did you discover?' Wendy asked gently. As she listened to John speak, she couldn't help but notice that his right hand had grabbed his left arm. Was he anxious, or was it something else? She also thought his pallor had changed slightly. She wasn't sure if it was the cabin's lights, but she was sure he looked a bit grey. 'And what did you discover?' she asked gently.

He inhaled a long, weary breath and held up his hands in resignation. 'I ran through every scenario in my head. Every possible alternative – and you know what I discovered?' He laughed bitterly before Wendy had time to answer. 'Not a damn thing. No matter what way I looked at it, whatever we could have done, the result would have still been the same.'

Wendy cocked her head curiously. 'So, that makes you believe you are the one responsible?'

His face twisting with fury, John nodded vehemently and hissed back at her. 'Yes!' It was hard not to miss the self-loathing in his eyes as he stabbed his finger into his chest. '*I stood back and did nothing while I sent Kendra and the rest to their deaths. I stood back and let Dave run to his death.*'

Oh, no. No way in hell am I going to sit here and listen to this. Struggling to contain her anger, Wendy held up her hand and stared harshly at the self-pitying man. 'Don't you dare sit there and say it was all your fault!' Her lip curled up in contempt as she growled at the man beside her. 'We all have blood on our hands. Kendra and the others knew what they were doing.' She gritted her teeth and jabbed her finger into his chest, snarling, 'So don't you bloody dare sit there feeling sorry for yourself, saying you're to blame. You do that and that will mean their sacrifice will have been for nothing.' She closed her eyes and took in a deep breath, trying to rein in her anger. She opened them and stared sadly at John. 'As for Dave, well, from what you said he was determined to go back for Claire. I very much doubt anybody would have been able to stop him.'

Payne nodded slightly and murmured half-heartedly, 'Still, I am to blame, in part, for the destruction of the base and the city above it.'

He flinched back as Wendy leaned into him and hissed, 'Bullshit!' She snarled and waved her hand in a dismissive gesture. 'Bull … shit! You weren't the one that set the explosive off and damaged the electrical systems which caused the device to detonate.' She shrugged slightly and held her hands up. 'Were you at fault for not swapping the hydrogen bomb under the base for something less destructive, maybe? We may never know.'

'Gee, thank you,' he muttered with a touch of sarcasm.

She smirked and waved her hand, dismissing the annoyed commander's sarcastic comment. 'What I mean to say is, you shouldn't beat yourself up over something you have no control over. It will do you no good.'

From the look on his face, Wendy could see John knew she was right. He nodded slowly and stared at her with a raised eyebrow as if looking at her with new-found respect. He nudged her and let out a small chuckle. 'When did you become so enlightened?'

Wendy gave a small grunt and acknowledged John with a sad but knowing smile. 'Let's just say, over the past twenty-four hours, I've learned the hard way what second guessing one's actions can lead to.' With a heavy heart, she gazed out through the carriage's forward window and shook her head sadly. 'I'll tell you the same thing Sophia told me. There comes a point when you must accept whatever life throws at you, whether you like it or not.'

John nodded slowly in understanding and let out a remorseful sigh. 'Very true.' He stiffened and then lifted his head sharply as if he had suddenly remembered something important. His eyes narrowing, he prairie-dogged and scanned the faces inside the cabin. 'Speaking of the prime minister, have you seen her since we evacuated the base?'

Bloody hell. I'd forgot all about her! Startled, Wendy jerked and shook her head furiously. 'No. The last time I saw her was just before Kendra and I left the conference room.' She held up a finger and stood up, moving into the aisle. 'Give me a minute while I check with the others.'

As she made away around the cabin, Wendy received the same answer from each of her fellow passengers – no, they hadn't seen the prime minister. In fact, and this was the thing she found more concerning, none of them could even remember seeing her standing on the platform. Wendy tried to push down any worrying thoughts she had as she made her way back to her seat. There had been a lot of people on the platform all trying to evacuate, so maybe she'd had been missed in all of the hullabaloo. *Yeah*, Wendy thought, trying to convince herself, *Sophia probably got into another carriage and was on her way to a different destination. Yeah, that was it.*

Wendy sank back into her seat and pursed her lips together. 'No. No one has seen any sign of her. They don't even remember seeing her on the platform.' She put a hand on Payne's arm, noticing a strained expression on his face. 'I wouldn't worry. We may have just missed her in all the commotion. You said it yourself. You told her she needed to be on the first transport out.' She gave him an encouraging smile. 'In all the confusion, she may have forgotten to transfer to a different carriage and ended up heading to a different location.'

John gave a wordless nod of his head and shifted uncomfortably in his seat. Wendy could tell from the way he was gripping his armrests that he was very worried about Sophia's absence. However, her eyes narrowed in concern as she noticed her friend's unhealthy pallor and the sweat on his brow. She placed a compassionate hand on his arm and stared at him worriedly. 'John, are you okay? You don't look too good.'

He waved her concern away and gave her a thin mile. 'I'm fine, really. Just need some rest, that all. I'll get a nap when we reach our destination – a base in the Midlands codenamed Excalibur.'

Wendy let out snort of disdain, rolled her eyes and then shook her head. 'Seriously, who comes up with these names?' She waggled her finger and looked at the pale man as if he was a small child. 'Just make sure you take some time to get some rest when we get there. You hear me?'

John fluttered his eyelids and sighed in exasperation. 'Yes, mother.'

Wendy gave him the evil eye and grunted, 'Humph, fine! Anyway, to get back to what we were talking about. We'll probably find Sophia waiting for us, all annoyed that we kept her waiting.'

John lifted his shoulder in a half-hearted shrug and chuckled in agreement. 'Yeah, you're probably right.'

They settled into an uncomfortable silence. But as Wendy turned and stared out of the front carriage window into the darkened tunnel ahead, she couldn't stop the fluttering of her stomach as it filled her with a heavy dread. She didn't want to admit it to John, but she was extremely worried about Sophia. Despite her own reassurances, she couldn't shake the feeling that Sophia was in trouble. Not only that, she had a dark foreboding that things were about to get worse. Something bad was coming toward them like a high-speed train and they were stuck on the tracks, unable to get out of its way.

As soon as the maglev carriage pulled up at the station's platform, Wendy followed closely behind John as he leapt out of his seat and was out of the carriage before the gull-wing doors had time to fully open. She noticed a mysterious smile had crossed his face on noticing a tall, lean, fifty-something man dressed in an army uniform was standing patiently on the platform. From the four chevrons on his sleeve, she instantly recognised that he was an army sergeant major.

'Malcolm!' John exclaimed, dashing toward him excitedly. 'You son of a gun. Fancy seeing you here!'

The sergeant major's eyebrow arched and he grunted, 'Humph! Yeah, somebody thought it would be a good idea to stick their former crusty sergeant major here didn't they!' He pulled a face, stepped back, and stared critically at Payne. 'No offence, my old mucka, for an ugly bastard, you look even more terrible. You been getting enough sleep?'

Her eyebrows lifting in shock at the older man's comment, Wendy swallowed anxiously as John shot gave Malcolm with one of his patented stony stares. But she then felt herself relax as their faces broadened into friendly grins and they clasped each other hands, laughing.

'I take it you know each other?' she asked, giving them both an amused side eye.

Beaming like a Cheshire Cat, John gestured to the older man before him. 'Wendy Cooper, may I introduce to you my former CO, Sergeant Major Wayne, or as we like to call him, the duke.' He smiled mischievously as the gruff soldier grunted in displeasure at the nickname. 'Malcolm, may I introduce to you Wendy Cooper, former police constable and general pain in my arse?' He let out an embarrassed cough as Wendy shot him a withering look.

Malcolm chuckled and shook his head, before straightening to attention and saluting Wendy. 'Ma'am, a pleasure to meet you. All of us here are great admirers of yours.' He said smiling warmly. Wendy blinked in surprise as she picked up something in his tone of voice. It almost sounded like admiration She felt her cheek flush with embarrassment as he moved forward and shook her hand firmly. 'Excellent job at that processing facility. Couldn't have done a better job myself. Anybody who put the Empire into a tizz the way you have can have my back anytime.'

Malcolm's smile quickly vanished as he looked at John sadly and sighed heavily. 'Sorry about the loss of the Castle, mate. I cannot imagine what you must be going through.'

Payne acknowledged his friend with a sad smile. 'Thank you.' He straightened his shoulders, coughing hesitantly. 'I … I-I'm aware this is your command, my friend, but …'

Malcolm grinned and held up his hand, cutting John off. 'Say no more. Officially, you are second in command to the prime minister. I'm just a small cog in a large wheel, so I don't have a problem with you assuming command.'

The relief was evident on John's face as he smiled sheepishly at Malcolm. 'Thank you, my old friend. I know some people can get a bit touchy when asked to hand over their command, even to a superior officer.'

Malcom shrugged slightly and gave John a sly wink. 'I believe I was just keeping the seat warm. No biggie.' His mouth broadened in a mysterious grin. 'Officer Cooper, I believe you already know this ruffian?'

Her brow creased in puzzlement; Wendy looked at Malcolm quizzically before peering over her shoulder. At first, she stared blankly at the man limping towards her, and then did a double take. No, it cannot be? Can it? She felt her eyes grow wide in recognition. Yes! Yes, it was! Her mouth opened and closed in silent astonishment as she watched Andy hobble toward her. She could see even though his leg was no longer in plaster, he was still walking unsteadily, but was aided by a cane.

'Hey, Cooper!' Andy grinned cheerily. He frowned and waved his hands in front of her eyes. 'Hello! Anybody home? H'way pet, surely you can't have forgotten all about your old partner already?'

'Andy!' Over the moon at seeing her former colleague, the delighted Wendy wrapped her arms around Andy and embraced him in a near-rib-breaking bear hug.

'Sheesh! Cooper, careful with the ribs, will you? Some of them have only just healed,' he wheezed in Wendy's grip.

A warm smile crossed John's face as the two comrades hugged one another. 'After it became apparent that Mary had been brainwashed by the enemy,' he explained, 'I agreed to transfer her to the facility that had the best psychiatric care, which was here, Excalibur Base. The facility, as well as specialising in psychological traumas, also provides physical therapy services to personnel injured in the line of duty, so it was easier for Andy to receive his therapy alongside Mary.'

Wendy released the breathless man and then wiped the tears of joy out of her eyes. 'Sorry, mate, you don't know what a joy it is to see you. Especially after …' She bit her bottom lip and let out a rattling breath. 'I don't know how to tell you, but …' She lowered her head and turned away from Andy.

John took a small step forward, put his hand on Wendy's shoulder, and stared gravely at the detective sergeant. 'Sergeant Jenkins … Andy. I'm sorry to have to tell you this, bu—'

'You don't need to tell me,' Andy interjected glumly, cutting him off. 'The media broke the news about her capture a short time ago.'

What did he just say? Wendy exchanged a look of stunned surprise with John and did a double take. Her eyebrows bunched together as she shook her head in confusion. 'Her …?' she asked warily, unease building in her stomach. 'We're talking about Dave and Claire. Who are you talking about?'

The colour draining from his face, Andy staggered back as if the wind had been knocked out of him. Looking as if someone had punched him in the stomach, he shook his head and stared numbly at John. 'The guv?' he whispered in a low horrified voice, stammering, 'H-h … how?'

Wendy sniffed and inhaled a sharp breath, nodding morosely. 'He and Claire were trapped in the base just before it exploded.'

Looking grief stricken, Andy shook his head in disbelief and murmured a reply. 'When I was told two civilians had died alongside Kendra and the rest, I nev—' He stopped himself as if suddenly aware of something. A look of horror dawned on his face as he turned slowly to Wendy and whispered sadly, 'Oh, Wendy, I'm terribly sorry.'

'We'll have time to grieve for our colleagues later,' she answered brusquely and gave a small dismissive wave of her hand as she shifted her gaze between the two men. 'But you said *"she was captured"*. I know you're not talking about Claire, so who are you talking about?'

John's nostrils flared as the two men exchanged unsettled glances. He took an angry step toward Malcolm, glowering. 'Spit it out, Wayne, who are you talking about?'

Malcolm took a small step forward and placed a calming hand on John's arm. 'Easy, John. We only just heard about it minutes before you arrived.'

'Found out about what?' he hissed, angrily slapping Malcolm's hand away.

Malcolm let out a harsh breath and spread his arms wide. 'I think it's best we show you.'

Malcolm gave a wordless nod and gestured for them to follow him. Wendy cast a questioning eye to John, who answered with a small nod. As she followed closely behind Malcom and John, she had a sinking feeling that whatever Malcolm was hiding it was about Sophia. She stared gravely at the back of John's head and gulped. Whatever it was, she truly feared it would the thing that would break him.

As he followed his former CO down the corridor, an odd sensation struck John. He suddenly felt detached from those around him. It was as if he was out of sync with the universe. All he could hear was his own breathing. It was as if nothing else was around him. He turned his head and stared numbly as he heard Wendy say something to him, but he couldn't make out what she was saying. Was she asking if he was okay? What a strange thing to ask.

It was as if time was moving at a different speed. He blinked and noticed he was now standing in the middle of a command centre. Malcolm appeared to be saying something to him. What was he saying? Something about the news? John stared at the monitor blankly and nodded slowly. Yes, he recognised that simpering woman who was talking. It was Julianna Sonatori, the mouthpiece of the occupation forces. What was she saying? She appeared to be talking about Durham.

'... *eath toll is estimated to be in the thousands.*' Sonatori's eyes tightened, and she stared coldly at the camera. '*According to IGNS sources, the terrorist group known as Free Earth have claimed responsibility for this outrageous attack.*' John felt himself reel back in shock as Sonatori's face was then replaced with a picture of Sophia Collins, but the platinum blonde was soon back again. Her mouth had widened into a cheesy celebratory grin. '*According to our government sources, former British Prime Minister Sophia Collins was captured on the outskirts of Durham City. Sources believe the terrorist group brainwashed her into leaking sensitive information at a planned exchange somewhere in the city. It is our understanding the Empire's forces had been aware of Collins' duplicitous nature for quite some time and were tracking her movements, hoping to capture her before she could commit this treasonous act.*' The tantalising news anchor paused to inhale a dramatic breath, steepled her fingers together and stared into the camera, crocodile tears glistening in her eyes. '*Soldiers loyal to our majestic leader surrounded the terrorist group's base in the centre of Durham City and were attempting to discuss their peaceful surrender. Unfortunately, the cowards, rather than surrender peacefully, detonated a small-yield nuclear device, killing thousands of people. We ...'*

Suddenly, John felt like he was trapped inside a vice-like grip and it was crushing his chest, making him feel like he was struggling to catch his breath. He felt the room spin around him and clutched his chest as his legs gave out beneath him. His vision blurring, he gazed up at the ceiling and saw a young woman's beautiful face shouting at him but could not make out what she was saying. What was that? Was she shouting for him to hang on? Before his consciousness faded to black, the last thing he heard was Sonatori's voice.

'IGNS sources say Collins is being held in a secure facility, where she is receiving proper care and treatment. Free from outside influences, the woman is expressing huge regret at her actions and is making a slow recovery.'

-23-

Then ...

Where had she put it? A hiss of annoyance escaped through Sophia's gritted teeth as she rifled through the stacks of folders on her desk. It had to be somewhere. It couldn't have disappeared off the face of the earth. So where the hell had she put it?

After leaving the conference room with the strangely subdued Sharon, Sophia decided she needed to make a slight detour towards her office, so that she could collect some critical documents, rather than risk them falling into enemy hands. Surprisingly, Sharon had been unusually compliant when she had been informed of Sophia's intentions.

As she searched through the folders on her desk, Sophia was acutely aware of the anxious pale scientist standing behind her, who was nervously wringing her hands and kept glancing up at the clock on the wall. Sophia frowned as she searched. There was definitely something unsettling Sharon, but right now Sophia had more important things that required her attention. She gave a small dismissive wave of her hand. Whatever was bothering Sharon was going to have to wait.

'I'm sorry,' Sharon murmured sullenly.

Half listening, Sophia shook her head irritably and muttered back a response, 'Hmm. Sorry, what was that, dear?'

Sharon's chin hung on her chest as she inhaled a nervous breath and then spoke in a low flat tone. 'She made me do it.'

'What are you talking about, my dear?' Sophia snapped sharply. A shadow of a smile danced across her face as she found the thin cardboard folder she was searching for. Success!

'Oracle,' Sharon replied gravely.

Sophia's celebratory mood disappeared as she clenched the folder tightly in her fingers. Suppressing a shiver, she swallowed at the lump that had appeared inside her throat. She closed her eyes and took a deep breath. 'Sharon,' she croaked anxiously, trying to keep the panic from showing in her voice. 'What did you do?'

Sharon's bottom lip quivering, she shook her head and answered in a voice that was thick with tearful emotion. 'I'm sorry. I wasn't strong enough. It tricked me into believing I had beaten it.' Tears began to run down her cheeks as she jabbed a finger into her right temple and let out contemptuous hiss. 'It was in here all the time, playing with me. Even now, I can feel it crawling around inside me, whispering to me.'

Her stomach clenching in fear, Sophia licked her lips, and looked across her desk to the closed top drawer to her right, the one containing her personal firearm. She slowly edged towards the drawer but continued to speak in a low, calm tone, hoping to keep the sobbing woman distracted. *That's it*, she thought, *calm and steady. Just keep her distracted long enough for me to grab my weapon.*

'What did she make you do?' she asked gently. 'If you're trying to tell me she made you kill Colonel Barnes, don't worry, my dear. I've already guessed that and if it makes you feel any better – I forgive you.'

'Oh, she doesn't care about that,' Sharon scoffed. 'In fact, she's quite annoyed that you haven't discovered his body yet. She got so fed up waiting, she purposely let it slip to DI Barnes when they were speaking earlier this morning.' She looked forlornly up at the ceiling, shook her head, and then laughed hysterically. 'Then, to keep the inspector and Commander Payne off guard, she made me pretend I had some sort of mental breakdown, making it appear they were talking to a younger version of me.'

'I see,' Sophia replied hesitantly, slowly lowering her hand to the drawer. *Nearly there*. 'So, I guess she wanted to keep us all distracted and off guard, so we wouldn't notice those creatures until it was too late?'

'No. They *are* the distraction,' Sharon answered coldly.

The change in Sharon's voice hadn't gone undetected by Sophia as she narrowed her eyes and rested her hand on the drawer's handle. 'Distraction? Distraction for what?'

'For this,' Oracle's voice announced from a narrow tall mirror behind Sophia.

Startled by the voice, Sophia stiffened, but before she could wheel round to confront the newcomer, her eyes grew wide in alarm as she felt an arm wrap itself around her neck. She cried out in pain as she felt the point of a hypodermic needle enter the jugular vein on the right side of her neck. With her left hand clutching her neck, she spun falteringly around and stared dumbfounded at the remorseful-looking Sharon, who was clutching the spent needle in her hand.

With a remorseful looking Sharon watching on, the prime minister sank to the floor and her breathing becoming more rapid as she struggled to remain conscious. By sheer force of will, Sophia managed to lift her head and stare at the woman standing over her. 'What did you do?' she wheezed.

'Just something to help you sleep,' Sharon murmured in a flat, emotionless tone.

Her chest rising and falling rapidly, Sophia's jaw clenched as she struggled to fight against the encroaching darkness. She shook her head; willing herself to stay awake as the room blurred around her. Blinking furiously, she made out a blurred shape of someone standing over her, and with her remaining strength, she forced the words out of her mouth. 'Why ... attack?' she gasped.

Her cold bright eyes filled with cruelty, the silver-skinned synthetic woman cocked her head, kneeled, and brushed her hand over Sophia's brow. 'Oh my dear, the attack was just a diversion.' Oracle smirked and waved a hand to the emotionless woman beside her. 'My good friend Sharon disabled the frequency generator around the complex, allowing me to pass through. Unfortunately, she could not disable the alarms. Apparently, that requires a higher command level clearance.' The corners of her mouth widened into a malevolent grin. 'Which is where my synthroids come in. With everyone distracted by the security breach, they would be too occupied to notice the vibrational frequency alarm sounding.'

As she slowly succumbed to the darkness, the last thing Sophia heard before losing consciousness was the artificial woman whispering to her.

'Sleep, my dear. Sleep.'

ORACLE'S VISION

Now…

After slowly regaining consciousness, Sophia shivered and she opened her eyes to find herself lying on a cold damp floor that appeared to be inside a dingy red-brick jail cell. If that wasn't bad enough, she realised she was also chained to the cell wall, making her feel like she was extra in one those obscure low-budget 1970s B-movies. She was grateful that she was still wearing the back jumper and jeans she'd had on before she blacked out and not some skimpy outfit that barely covered her modesty.

Sophia screwed her face up in displeasure as she stared down at the manacles fastened around her wrists and ankles. She flexed her fingers and thinned her lips at the stinging sensation of pins and needles in her hands. Uncertain at how long she had been unconscious but guessed from the rumbling emptiness in her stomach it had been several hours.

Sophia raised herself off the floor so she could get a better view of her new accommodation, and her upper lip curled in disgust at the cell's dingy interior. Apart from a disgusting excuse for a toilet, and a bowl containing something one would barely call food, the cell was empty. There was a large metal door and a small oblong barred window high in the wall, close to the ceiling. For some inexplicable reason, Sophia was filled with déjà vu. She was positive she recognised this place; either she had been in here before or had seen a picture of it but could not remember when and where.

She let out a small grunt as she awkwardly climbed to her feet and then quietly examined the thick chain attached to the manacles on her wrists and ankles. She furrowed her brow in concentration as she tugged at the chain, but blew out a discouraged hiss of air as she discovered her captors had anchored the chain to the wall. Gently shuffling forward to the centre of the cell, she snorted in dismay on seeing that she barely had enough space to move forward, only a metre and a half.

Contemplating the reality of her predicament, Sophia lifted her shoulder in a slight shrug of acceptance. *Oh well, no point crying about it,* she reasoned. *I'm here, so I'll just have to make the best of it.* She grudgingly dropped back down onto the hard floor and stretched her arm out to the bowl of … whatever was lying on the floor in front of her.

A wave of nausea struck her as she gazed at the bowl's disgusting contents, but after a moment's hesitation she dipped her fingers into the small bowl. Her face scrunched up in revulsion at the slick gruel-like texture that stuck to her skin. It had a texture that reminded her of silly putty. Resigned to the fact that she was going to eat it, Sophia steeled herself and stared at the gunk that clung to the tips of her fingers. No, now wasn't the time to be squeamish, because right now, it was important that she keep her strength up and stay alive. If that meant eating … *this*, then that was how it must be.

Even though her stomach churned in protest at what it was going have endure, she lifted more of the thick gelatinous contents out of the bowl. She warily sniffed the gunk in her hand and retched in disgust. 'Oh, my God! That's disgusting.'

Determined that she was going to see it through, Sophia squeezed her eyes shut, sucked in a deep breath, and stuffed the gruel into her mouth. Her eyes began watering and she pounded her hand on the floor, forcing the slime down her throat. Even though her stomach was heaving in protest at having to suffer the indignity of hosting the contents, she was thankful it stayed where it was and did not come back up.

Suppressing an urge to throw up, Sophia squeezed her eyes shut and forced more of the disgusting gruel into her mouth. This time she was surprised to learn that it did not taste as bad. She chuckled as she mused that the first swallow had probably killed every sense organ in her body on its way down to her stomach.

'I think that's enough of you,' she croaked, pushing the empty bowl away.

As her stomach continued to recoil in protest, Sophia leaned back against the wall and sucked in a lungful of air, but then stared up at the ceiling thoughtfully so that she could consider her options. It was obvious whatever Oracle needed her for, she had to be alive. Otherwise, she would have killed her at the base. Sophia nodded, reasoning the longer she was alive, the better the chance of being rescued. Her jaw tightening in conviction, she rapped the back of her head against the wall. If she must play nice and act like an obedient servant to ensure her escape, then so be it.

Her body stiffened as she heard the clunk of a key turning and the door unlocking, and then her eyes grew wide in recognition at the newcomer. He was a dark curly-haired white man, wearing thin round glasses and dressed immaculately in a black suit, white shirt and tie, and from the smirk on his face she could tell that he was struggling to contain his glee at seeing his former leader chained up.

'Well, Prime Minister,' Michael said cheerily, but then paused and held up a finger mockingly. 'Oops, sorry. Former prime minister. I do hope you're finding your new living arrangements comfortable. I'm sure you recognise it as one of the cells in the Tower of London. Sorry, we didn't have time to clean the place up for you.' He lowered his head and looked over his glasses at the empty bowl. The corners of his mouth curled up in an impish grin. 'Looks like I lost my bet.'

Sophia let out a contemptuous snort of laughter and leaned back against the wall. 'Well, well, well, Michael Gray. It hasn't taken long for the cockroaches to scurry out of their hidey holes, has it?'

Beams of anger and hurt pride shot out of the man's eyes as he scowled at her. 'You watch your mouth, you bitch!'

'Or what? I'll end up in a prison cell?' she scoffed, waving her hands over the dingy cell interior. 'Already there.'

Gray's nostrils flared as he knelt and grabbed Sophia's face, spitting through clenched teeth, 'If I were you, I would be very careful how you address me.'

Refusing to show Gray any respect, Sophia slapped his hand away and continued to glower at him. 'Or what? You'll have me killed. You don't have the balls to do that, boy.' A shadow of a smile danced across her lips as she stared at the weedy man with a knowing side eye. 'I don't think your new mistress would like that, would she?'

'Maybe not,' Michael hissed, straightening up, 'but she said nothing about this.'

Sophia gasped and her vision went white in blinding pain as a hand connected with the right side of her jaw. She collapsed onto the floor and shook her head to clear her vision. A warm metallic taste filled her mouth, and she felt a trickle of blood run down her chin. She spat the blood onto the enraged man's shoes and shot daggers up at him. 'You know, Gray, I never considered you to be a doppelgänger,' she hissed, her tone scornful.

Gray lifted his shoulder in a small dismissive shrug. 'I'm not a doppelgänger.'

Sophia felt her eyes widen in a flash of understanding, and she put her head back and let out a bark of laughter. 'Ah, I see it now. You saw how the wind was blowing and jumped ship like the rat you are.' She regarded the man with disdain, shaking her head. 'I hear my doppelgänger even made you Deputy Prime Minister. How long did it take for you to decide before you took your thirty pieces of silver?' She turned her head away in disgust, barely able to look him in the eye. 'I always knew you were a back-stabbing bastard. A minor minister, ready to sell your services to the highest bidder, but even I never thought you would sell out your own people.'

The unrepentant man lifted his hands in the air and snorted, his tone scornful. 'At least I'm not the one sitting in chains awaiting my execution.' He held his hand to his mouth mockingly at her look of surprise. 'Oh, I'm sorry, didn't you know? You're to be tried and executed as a traitor.' His mouth widened in unbridled glee. 'My first act as prime minister will be to ensure I have a front seat as they execute you.'

As she stared at Gray, Sophia's anger quickly changed to pity as she wondered what this world could have done to someone for them to be filled so much bitterness that it would make them turn their back on it. She shook her head sadly and held up her manacled wrists. 'I feel wholly sorry for you, you're so filled with hate, it has made you blind to what is front of you. At least I can see my chains.' She climbed back to her feet and shot the younger man with a withering stare. 'It's just a pity I won't get to see the day when somebody strangles you with that leash that Oracle keeps you on.'

Gray's face reddened with fury, and he took a sharp step forward with his right hand balled into a fist as if making ready to strike. Defiant to the end, Sophia raised her chin and braced herself for the impact that did not come.

'Enough!'

Startled by the interruption, Gray dropped his hand and spun around. Sophia peered over his shoulder to see a silver-skinned woman standing in the doorway. Gray hung his head subserviently and moved quickly away from Sophia. 'Many apologies, mistress,' he gushed. 'I was just educating the prisoner on the proper etiquette for addressing somebody of your most glorious stature.'

The corners of Oracle's mouth twitched in amusement, and she cocked her head at the fawning man. 'Oh, I know perfectly well what you were doing.' She waved her hand in a dismissive motion. 'Leave us. I will deal with you later.'

As she watched the obsequious man bow his head in wordless obedience and edge past Oracle toward the open doorway, Sophia smiled and muttered just loud enough for him to hear. 'That's a good boy. Do what your mistress tells you.' Gray froze in the doorway, his hands clenched into balls, and for a moment she wondered whether he was going to charge back into the cell and strangle her. She held her breath as she waited for him to react. After about a minute, Sophia arched her eyebrow in surprise as he turned, smiled at her and then raised two fingers to his head in mock salute.

Sophia remained silent as the synthetic woman smirked in amusement as her lackey shuffled past her. However, her eyes grew wide in recognition as a familiar tall black woman walked into the cell.

Oracle gave a wry smile and gestured to Sophia's doppelgänger. 'Oh, I do not think you have been formally introduced,' she said gleefully. 'Sophia Collins, meet Octavia Collins, your doppelgänger from Counter-Earth.'

'Pleasure,' Sophia muttered tersely. She frowned, noticing the blank expression on her counterpart's face.

Oracle chuckled softly and waved her hand at the emotionless figure beside her. 'Oh, forgive Octavia's silence. She rarely says much these days since she became one of my drones.'

Making no attempt to hide her contempt, Sophia sneered at the yellow-eyed woman in front of her. 'What? Is this your way of intimidating me? If I don't become one of those mindless things, you'll kill me?'

Oracle let out a hollow laugh and shook her head in amusement. 'Oh, certainly not. I am still going to kill you.'

Repulsed at the artificial woman's callousness, Sophia felt her jaw drop and she gave the AI an unbelieving look. 'Then why do it? If you're going to kill me, anyway, why bring her here?'

Oracle gave a small shrug of shoulders. 'Because I thought it would be fun.'

Disgusted, Sophia scoffed and stared up at the ceiling, shaking her head.

'You're sick. You know that? You're really sick.' Her eyebrows drew together, and she fixed the cruel artificial lifeform with a bitter stare. 'If you want to kill me, you could've done it at the base. Why all the subterfuge with the diversion?'

Her bright cold yellow eyes blazing, Oracle moved toward Sophia and snarled, 'Because I want your death to be as public as possible. I want to send a message to your friends and everybody else who believes they can defy me.' There was a touch of malice in her voice as she leaned in closer. 'I am through being nice. You people have caused me nothing but grief. Well, I am going to send a message, clear and succinct – I will not tolerate insolence.'

Perplexed, Sophia stared at Oracle open mouthed, unsure what to say. She blinked and then nodded in slow understanding before pointing to the artificial woman and letting a loud mirthless laugh. 'Oh, I see it now. When Wendy destroyed your processing plant, it not only hurt you. It humiliated you.' She leaned forward and purposefully scowled at the furious AI with as much vindictiveness she could manage. 'Oh, it must burn you that she got away from you.'

'Yes,' Oracle snarled, not hiding her fury. 'She killed my children. Well, I am going to make her suffer too, by taking everything away from her one piece at a time. I have already killed her lover and now I am going to kill you. I want her to suffer.' Her yellow eyes flashing with raw emotion, she towered over Sophia. 'If I have to, I will kill every last stinking one of you until she is the last one standing.'

Even though she got a sense that the thing in front of her was insane, Sophia couldn't help feel pity for Oracle and shook her head sadly. 'I feel really sorry for you. You have all this power and all you want to do is make everyone fear you.' She frowned and nodded to the emotionless Octavia. 'What about her? If people see her walking around, they'll just assume it's me.'

Oracle's arm shot out with inhuman speed and pulled the blank-faced doppelgänger close to her. Horrified, Sophia could only watch as the AI wrapped its left arm around the docile woman's neck, with its right hand positioned firmly on the top of her head. There was a sickening crunch of Octavia's neck snapping and Sophia forced down a sick feeling as her doppelgänger's eyes rolled up and her body crumpled to the floor.

'Problem solved,' Oracle said in a matter-of-fact cold tone.

Any sense of pity Sophia had toward Oracle had been quickly

extinguished. Enraged, Sophia trembled with fury as she tried to scramble over to the dead woman who lay dead on ground but was stopped by the chains that bound her wrists and ankles. She fought back tears and glowered up at the malevolent looking thing standing over her.

'Why?' she snarled, her voice thick with bitter emotion. 'Why did you do that?'

Sophia gasped in pain as Oracle's hand shot out and grabbed her throat. The faux woman's yellow eyes burned brightly as it hissed at Sophia. 'Because I can.' she sneered, 'From this moment on, the kid gloves are off. I am through being gentle. You all live and die at my choosing.'

Sophia felt the vice-like pressure on her neck abruptly disappear and she gasped for air as she collapsed just in front of her dead doppelgänger's body. The cruel synthetic straightened and strode over to the doorway, pausing to stare at Sophia.

'If I were you, I would spend your remaining hours thinking what your last words are going to be at your execution.'

After closing the cell door behind her, Oracle cocked her head and increased the sensitivity of her hearing so that she could hear what was going on the other side of the door. She smiled as she detected a woman's soft sobs, but then frowned. What was this new emotion she was feeling? Why was she filled with an overriding sense of exuberant superiority? She frowned and stared down at her own hands. Why had she not noticed this until now? Had something changed inside her, making her more in tune with what she was feeling? If so, what?

Troubled by the very idea that she may be malfunctioning, Oracle stepped away from the cell door so that she could give the matter some consideration. Could it be because she was the one responsible for the human's distress and that she was why she was revelling in it? No, that could not be it. She was above those petty human emotions. Oracle arched her head as she ran a self-diagnostic. Yes, it appeared she was finding pleasure in being the cause of Sophia's suffering. She nodded. That was something worth exploring; maybe she could use Sophia's execution to her advantage. Yes, she had planned on doing something low key, like a firing squad, but she realised it needed to be something that people would remember for decades to come, something ... spectacular. Oracle smiled as another thought occurred to her. Yes, if she wanted to explore this emotion further, she could certainly come up with more creative ways to execute other humans. It wasn't as if there weren't enough of them. She cocked her head thoughtfully and grinned. If she got bored of coming up with ingenious ideas to dispose of humans, there were always the children she could try her ideas out on. Up until now, she hadn't known what to do with them. Seriously, what was the point of them? Back on Terra, she had been forced to place all the Empire's children in suspended animation, which she thought was complete waste of energy. Simpler to just kill them all at once and be done with it.

A barely audible whine broke Oracle out her contemplation. She blinked and shook her head. No, that would have to wait because she had another issue she needed to deal with, a more pressing matter.

As she turned away from the door, the AI saw a blond woman in a white T-shirt and jeans standing still with a controlled expression. Oracle's top lip curled up as she moved towards the woman, and she murmured thoughtfully, 'You know, Sharon, my dear, you just might be the person I need,' she mused. 'It appears I am experiencing something that I feel requires further study and you are the perfect candidate to help with a little experiment I have in mind.'

Oracle put her hand on Sharon's shoulder and smirked as she noticed her eyes twitch. Then she chuckled softly and whispered in her ear. 'I can feel you stirring inside that little cage of yours. You are surprisingly strong-willed for your species, which is something I have always admired about you.' She then leaned forward and a cruel smile formed on her lips as she prodded the woman's forehead. 'I can hear you screaming inside that pitiful excuse you call a brain. All that rage built up inside you. I can almost feel it emanating out of every pore of your body.' She pulled back, shook her head, and tutted. 'You really must control those emotions, my dear. Holding on to anger is bad for you. Just think of the stress it is putting on your body. Can you imagine how John would react if you died? He would simply be beside himself with grief, would he not? Hmmm?'

At the mention of John's name, Sharon's hands tightened into balls, followed by a soft mewling that came from inside her throat. The barely audible noise was detected by Oracle's advanced hearing, and she arched an eyebrow in surprise and then gave a small nod of approval.

ORACLE'S VISION

'Oh my, did my mention of your beloved's name strike a nerve?' A cruel smile formed on her lips, and she moved in closer to whisper into the woman's ear. 'Do not worry, my sweet, in a moment I shall remove what remains of the techno-parasite from your brain and you will be back to your normal boring self.' She paused, and her mouth widened into a devious smile as she waggled her index finger. 'But not before I implant a subliminal imperative, one that will make you seek out and kill the almighty Commander Payne.' Oracle then put her head back and let out a loud maniacal laugh. 'The best news is you will not remember a thing about the events of the past few days. When you next wake up, the last thing you will remember is speaking to John and David in the corridor, just before the attack. You will have no memory of the hand you had in Sophia's abduction, or any knowledge of the imperative that I have placed inside you.'

As Oracle's cruel laugh continued to reverberate off the corridor's walls, a small tear trickled down Sharon's cheek.

-24-

A strange clacking sound slowly drew Sharon out of the safety of the black void of unconsciousness. Why were they making that sound? She moaned. Why couldn't they leave her alone? It was then she started to become aware of a gentle rocking sensation. Was somebody trying to shake her awake? She groaned as she noticed a strange heaviness inside her head and placed her right hand on forehead. Why did her brain feel like it had been washed and then placed back inside her skull?

'You alright, my love?' a warm, friendly voice asked, coming from somewhere out of the darkness. 'Do you need help?'

Sharon frowned and stirred. Why was that person speaking in a Jamaican accent? Was she on a beach in Jamaica? She moaned again and waved her hand. 'Go away. I just want to sleep some more.'

'Eee, sorry, flower,' the voice replied, heavy with concern. 'I think you need to wake up. I don't like the look of your colour, my love. Do you want me to fetch the conductor and ask them to have an ambulance meet us at the next stop?'

Next stop? Conductor? Sharon placed a hand on her brow and let out another groan. What was that woman talking about? However, before she could make sense of what was being said to her, she heard three blasts of a powerful air horn, and she bolted up in shock.

The fog finally clearing from her brain, Sharon woke up and blinked away the cloudy film that covered her eyes, only to find herself staring into a pair of round hazel concern-filled eyes. She was scared at first, but relaxed as she realised it was a friendly black woman wearing a colourful bandana, big round earrings, and a tight quadrille dress.

The woman let out a small gasp of relief. 'Gracious child, you gave ol' Faith such a fright,' Faith boomed in a thick Jamaican accent. 'You shouldn't scare me like that!'

Sharon massaged her temples and shook her head apologetically. 'I'm sorry. I didn't mean to scare you.'

'Oh, child, don't worry about it.' Faith chuckled. 'At my age, my heart can do with a good jump-scare once in a while.'

Sharon clenched her teeth and gave the kindly woman the hairy eyeball. 'I would appreciate it if you would stop calling me *child*. I'm in my twenties!'

Faith let out a loud, joyful laugh and tapped Sharon's hand. 'Oh, don't you get your panties in a twist! Ol' Faith means n'thing by it, my love. When you get to my age, a young thing like yourself looks like a child to me.'

Feeling her cheeks flush with embarrassment, Sharon nodded but then frowned and lifted her head to get a better view of her surroundings. She was sitting inside the dimly lit carriage of a train, and from the looks of things, she and Faith appeared to be the only passengers on board. She turned her head so that she could see out of the window and guessed from the twilight gloom outside that it must be late evening. She looked back at Faith quizzically. 'Err, I know this may sound stupid. I'm on a train, aren't I? I mean, I'm not imagining it?'

Faith's round face broadened into a cheery smile and she nodded. 'No, you're not imagining it, my love. Last time I checked, ol' Faith was still on a train.'

How could she be on a train? Sharon shook her head in confusion and then ran her right hand down her face. 'I don't understand. How did I end up here and where is it going?'

A thunderous laugh filled the empty train carriage as Faith put her head back and let out a loud, exuberant bark of laughter. 'Saints preserve me! You are in a right pickle, aren't you, child?' the good-natured woman boomed. She plonked her heavy frame next to Sharon, who shifted in her seat uncomfortably at the invasion of her personal space.

Sharon hung her head, her chin just about touching the top of her chest and stared forlornly at her hands. 'If you don't mind, I would like to be left alone now. I don't think I would be very good company.' She sniffed back her tears and then let out a heavy, ragged sob. 'I've no idea where I am, how I got here and where my friends are, or if they are even still alive.'

'Oh shush. Sounds like you need a friend, my pet, and ol' Faith will never stand by when she sees someone like yourself in distress,' Faith said, nudging Sharon in the ribs. She chuckled. 'Sounds like you have had one too many shandies, my love. I know we're now living in interesting times, but that shouldn't mean you have to turn to the demon drink. My poor husband, Winston,' she paused at the mention of his name, crossed herself and then let out a melancholic groan, 'he was fond of the devil's brew and unfortunately it was that which led to his death.'

Sharon felt her eyes grow wide in sympathy and she reached out to touch Faith's arm. 'Oh, I'm sorry. Was he an alcoholic?'

'No, child,' Faith replied, gazing at Sharon with a blank serious-looking face. 'He was out walking one day, minding his own business, when a Guinness truck overturned and shed its load.' She lifted her head and then blessed herself once again. 'As God is my witness, he just looked up in the sky and the last thing he saw were three kegs hurtling towards him. So, you could say it was the drink that killed him. I always warned him it would be the death of him, but did he listen? No.'

Despite herself, Sharon lifted her hand to stop herself from laughing, but as Faith turned and gave her a mischievous wink, it only made things worse and she burst out laughing. 'Oh, I'm sorry. I didn't mean to laugh,' Sharon said after composing herself and wiping the tears from her eyes.

'I knew I could turn that sad frown upside down,' Faith said, grinning, and then reached out and laid her hand over Sharon's. 'See, just goes to show. Just because you feel your life is going down the toilet, the Lord has a way of making you thankful that you are still alive.' Her smile disappeared, and she crossed her right hand across her chest before letting out a long, sorrow-filled gasp. 'Unlike those poor unfortunate souls up in Durham.' She shook her head gravely. 'Those poor, poor people.'

On hearing Faith's words, Sharon gulped and felt her stomach lurch. 'What's happened in Durham?' she asked in a hoarse whisper.

Faith blinked in surprise at the question and shot Sharon an unbelieving look. 'Oh my! You have been out of it, haven't you?' She clasped Sharon's hand

and shook her head sadly. 'Then you won't have heard the news that the city has been destroyed, with thousands dead or homeless. That's why I'm taking this journey. I'm making my way up there so I can help tend to those in need and pray for the dead.' She let out a loud humph of displeasure. 'Satan's warriors tried to stop me from travelling, but when I recited the Lord's gospel and threatened them with God's wrath, they soon saw the error of their ways and let me pass. You see, if your cause is just, the Lord will—'

'When?' Sharon hissed, cutting the woman off in mid-flow.

Faith raised an eyebrow in surprise and gave her a tight smile. She spoke in a flat tone. 'Well, I plan to start as soon as I get there.'

Oh, for the love of …! Sharon closed her eyes, inhaled a deep breath, and spoke slowly. 'No, I mean, when was Durham destroyed?'

If she picked up on Sharon's annoyance, Faith did not let it show; instead she gave a small nod of understanding. 'It happened two days ago. They say it was terrorists.' Her top lip curled; she let out a snort of derision and squinted up at the heavens. 'Of course, I know better. In fact, the entire world is aware of who committed this foul deed.' Sharon jerked back in shock as the woman jumped to her feet and shouted out in defiance, 'They may be afraid to say it, but I am not. It was those demon warriors, the ones led by that silver harpy, Lucifer's mistress, that did it!' She shook her head and let out a loud, bitter laugh. 'Oh, I knew the first time I saw that golden-eyed witch that she would be the death of us, and I was right, she …'

The woman's words faded into the distance as Sharon leaned back into her seat and shook her head. Two days? She had been out of it for two days. What had happened to John and everyone else? Were they alive? She massaged her temples in the hope that it would help her remember what had happened. Whoever attacked the base, maybe they had injured her. Was that the reason for her memory loss? However, just as she was on the verge of figuring things out, she became distracted by a loud grumbling noise, followed by an empty sensation in her stomach.

Faith stopped her preaching and shot Sharon a look of concern. 'Goodness gracious me, here's ol' Faith moaning away and you're starving with hunger! When was the last time you ate something?'

Sharon frowned. Good question, when had she last eaten anything substantial? 'I'm not sure,' she replied hesitantly.

Faith tutted loudly and reached across the aisle to grab the large leather bag that was in the aisle seat across from her. She then gave a loud grunt and pulled the heavy bag towards her and placed it between her thick thighs. She murmured quietly to herself as she rifled through the bag's contents, but then beamed in delight on finding what she was looking for. She pulled out a pre-packed tuna and mayonnaise sandwich, along with a bottle of water.

'There you go, my dear,' Faith said cheerfully, handing the two items to Sharon. 'At least people cannot say that ol' Faith doesn't help those in need, oh no.'

After ripping open the thin seal to get at the sandwich, Sharon took a huge bite and wolfed it down. She closed her eyes as the succulent flavours filled her mouth. Never had anything tasted so good. Feeling more energised, she nodded gratefully, but frowned as something occurred to her.

'Sorry, I know this may sound like a daft question,' she said with a mouthful of food, 'but you said that you were travelling up to Durham to help those who were caught up in the disaster. Where are you, sorry we, travelling from?'

Startled by the question, Faith stiffened and blinked in surprise. 'London, specifically King's Cross Station.'

'London!' Sharon blurted out, totally unprepared for the answer, and then stared up at the ceiling in shock. Why had she been in London? Also, how had she gotten there?

'Well, we're approximately fifteen minutes from Birmingham New Street Station,' Faith said helpfully.

'Birmingham?' Sharon echoed back. There was something about Birmingham that sparked something inside her, telling her she needed to go to Excalibur Base because that was where John was. Yes, that was it. She needed to get off at Birmingham so that she could join John.

Sharon jumped as she felt a gentle but firm hand on her shoulder and heard soft voice in her ear. 'We still have plenty of time before we get there, child.'

Sharon blinked and looked down at herself. She was standing up in the aisle? What was she doing? Why did she get up so quickly? She let out an embarrassed laugh and sat back down. 'I'm sorry. I don't know what I was thinking. I just had this sudden urge that I needed to get off this train,' she said apologetically.

Faith frowned and stared worriedly at Sharon, 'You had me a bit worried for second child, you had this funny look and started to mutter something about needing to get off the train.' She smiled and gestured to the half-eaten sandwich that was clasped in Sharon's hand. 'Your hunger must be messing with her head, my love. Finish your sandwich and drink something, it'll help you feel a bit better. Anyway, you're going to need your energy if you're going to be traipsing around Birmingham.' The effervescent woman then gave Sharon a funny look, as if she was noticing the young woman properly for the first time. She tutted and pointed to Sharon's thin T-shirt. 'My word, far be it from me to judge, but a thin T-shirt is not suitable for someone as slim as you to be wearing in this dismal weather. Have you got a jacket or something you could wear?'

Sharon looked down at herself, then back at Faith, sighed, and lifted her hands in defeat. 'I have nothing else to wear. Sorry, but I guess I must have left in a pretty big hurry and probably didn't have time to grab something suitable.' She shrugged. 'Hopefully, this will do me until I get to where I need to go in Birmingham.'

Faith let out a loud huff of displeasure and then emphatically shook her head. 'As God is my witness, I refuse to let you leave this train until I'm sure you're dressed properly,' she said forcefully, which left no doubt in Sharon's mind that she meant what she said. 'You'll catch your death in this weather. It's cold enough out there to freeze the balls off a brass monkey!'

Without waiting for a response, Faith dived head first into her bag and rummaged around. When she came back up, a wide victorious smile covered her face, and she held out a black bomber jacket with a fleece hood and a red wool sweater. Sharon could tell the jacket was two sizes too big for her, but decided, rather than offend the generous woman, she would try the diplomatic approach instead.

'No, I couldn't possibly take this,' Sharon pleaded. 'Somebody more deserving than I will need this when you do eventually get to Durham.'

'Good gracious, child,' Faith admonished, refusing to accept the clothes back. 'From where I am sitting, if there is anybody more in need of help, it is you.' She clutched her hands to her chest and stared up into the heavens. 'I feel it is providential that I just happened to be on this train in your moment of need. It is as if the Lord himself spoke to me and directed me to be your angel of mercy.' She grabbed Sharon's hands and then raised her voice as if she was calling out to someone. 'Oh, heavenly father, watch out for this lost lamb who I beseech you to imbue with your spirit so that your devoted servant, the one you call …' Faith apparently realised that she did not know her new friend's name as she opened her eyes and stared quizzically at Sharon. 'Please forgive ol' Faith for her lack of manners, child, but I do not know your name.'

Her cheeks flushing with embarrassment, Sharon swallowed and then croaked out her reply. 'Sharon.' She cleared her throat and shook her head sheepishly. 'You really don't have to do all this. I'm embarrassed to say I stopped believing in religion a long time ago. Now I'm just a simple woman of science.'

Sharon thought she had upset Faith when she didn't talk for a few seconds, but then the friendly woman simply smiled and gave Sharon's hand a loving tap. 'That's okay, dear, the Lord has enough love for everyone, even if they are a heathen.' Sharon didn't know how to react until Faith gave her a wink, then she realised it was a joke and waited quietly as the older woman continued her speech. 'Lord, I implore you to imbue Sharon with your spirit and give her the strength to empower her on her journey.'

As Faith called out to the heavens, she clutched Sharon's hands tight against her bosom. For some reason Sharon couldn't understand, she shivered slightly as if something was being passed between them. For a split second, she was positive she felt a small tingle of electricity pass from Faith's hands into hers, filling her with positive energy. She raised a sceptical eyebrow and wondered if there was some power in Faith's words after all.

-25-

The bitterly cold December rain felt like tiny needles on Sharon's skin, so she wrapped her fleece-lined hood tightly around her head in the hope that it would help protect her against the elements. Sharon could not imagine how she looked to anyone who saw her, wearing a coat that was two sizes too big for her. Anyway, she didn't really care; she preferred being warm to looking good, so was grateful that Faith had convinced her to wear the coat for protection against the harsh British winter.

Shortly after her train arrived at Birmingham New Street Station, and after reassuring her new friend, Sharon swiftly disembarked and hurried towards the nearest escalator. It brought her out into a sparsely populated station.

The occupation had heavily impacted public transportation, much like a few years before, during the height of COVID, when travel had been discouraged. It was those same people, who were now the mouthpieces of Oracle, who issued the same guidance – for the public to carry on as normal and that it was safe to use the transport network. Unfortunately, the civilian population remained too afraid to leave their homes, especially after watching unending news reports of Durham's destruction.

After making a swift exit through a pair of double doors onto a dimly lit street, Sharon let out a sharp breath as the frigid winter stabbed at her exposed face, and she pulled the hood over her head before hurrying down the deserted street. She had a vague idea where she needed to go; there was a safe house located somewhere in the vicinity of Birmingham city centre, but she did not know what it looked like. She hoped that if she proceeded in a northerly direction there was a good chance that she would just happen to stumble across it. After doing some quick maths in her head, Sharon sighed unhappily as she realised the chances of finding the safe house by luck were low.

An icy breeze made Sharon's teeth chatter, and she pulled the coat even tighter around her thin body. On the other hand, she thought, there was a stronger probability that she would freeze to death before she found safety. She squeezed her eyes shut and cast that thought to one side. No, that was just too depressing to think about. Oh, why had she not paid more attention during orientation?

As she hurried down the street, Sharon's heart froze as she spotted a dozen black and gold armoured troops in the middle of the road marching in her direction. To avoid being noticed, she kept a low profile by walking calmly with her head down and her hands in her pockets.

That's right, chaps, Sharon thought. *Continue on your way. Ignore the innocent-looking woman who just so happens to look like a refugee out f South Park. Nothing to see here.*

Sharon kept a steady and relaxed pace, focusing only on her breathing, and ignored the crunching sound of the steel-capped boots marching on the road. However, she was several metres down the street when she suddenly became aware that the heavy footfalls had stopped. She swallowed anxiously and felt her stomach muscles tighten in fear. Why had the cyber-drones stopped marching? Dare she look over her shoulder and investigate?

An excessively curious woman, it went against Sharon's nature to ignore anything she found puzzling. So, despite being aware of the danger she was placing herself in, she stopped and looked sideways into the nearest shop window so she could get a better look at what was behind her. *What could go wrong?* she thought. She felt her heart leap up into her throat as she saw the reflection.

The group of drones had stopped and were standing still. But that was not what sent a chill down her spine. The thing that freaked her out the most was the sight of a lone cyber-drone who had turned and was staring directly at her. Coincidence? Sharon shook her head. She didn't believe in coincidences, only logic, and it was that same logical mind that screamed at her, telling her that something was wrong.

Was it scanning her? Did it know who she was? Her paranoia going into overdrive, Sharon imagined the cyber-dome raising its arm and pointing its finger, followed by a cold mechanical voice screaming – *Seize her! She is the one!* She bit into her bottom lip as she admonished her overactive imagination.

But that did not happen. Much to Sharon's confusion, the cyber-drone simply cocked its head and remained where it was. From her position, Sharon was close enough to see the cyber-drone's head tilt from side to side as if it was trying to decide on what it should do next. Was it curious, or was it receiving instructions? Sharon was afraid to guess, but the one thing she was certain of was that she needed to get as far away as possible before it was too late.

Not waiting to find out whether she would end up on a TV show called *Oracle's Most Wanted,* Sharon lowered her head and hurried away from the watching cyber-drone. She imagined there was a little demon called Paranoia sitting on her shoulder, having convulsions as it whispered into her ear, convincing her she was going to die. Of course, that only made her believe more adamantly that she could feel the cyber-drone's sensors piercing the fabric of her hood, right into the back of her head all the way through to her brain.

Girl, you seriously need to get a grip, she thought as she hurried down the street. Her heart felt like it was slamming against the walls of her chest. Even though she was having difficulty catching her breath, she gritted her teeth and tried to quicken her pace. Once she felt she was far enough away, Sharon slowed down and took a relieved breath. *Oh my god, I'm so out of shape! If I make it through tonight, I'll promise I'll start going to the gym.*

After walking for over an hour – feeling tired, cold and fed up – Sharon was on the verge of giving up when she glimpsed two figures standing in the shadows of an alley. It was apparent that they were trying to be invisible, but a glint from one of their mouths caught her attention.

Once she had gotten close enough to the two people, she squinted her eyes so that she could study them better. The man was black, tall, lean, possibly in his early twenties, and wearing an appalling red hoodie. He also had an ornate gold grail that covered his teeth. The woman was white with pink hair (obviously a wig), had an athletic build and was wearing a similar disgusting hoodie. Sharon guessed from their attire that they were posing as gang members. She rolled her eyes in disbelief. *Honestly!* These people may as well have worn a sign that said – *Hey! Look at me! I belong to British Intelligence!*

Having an eidetic memory, Sharon had no trouble remembering every bit of information put in front of her. That just so happened to include the personnel files of everyone who belonged to the British arm of the resistance. So she had no trouble recognising that the two bodies standing before her were those of Corporal Leroy-Bennett Williamson and Private Carrie Clarkson.

The two people looked suspiciously at the oddly dressed person running towards them, who stopped abruptly just a metre in front of them. Sharon noticed Private Clarkson had cast worried eye at Corporal Williamson who held up his hand and gave a wordless shake of his head as if to say *let's just see what happens.*

'By the glorious mane of Thor, I've found you,' Sharon said breathlessly, raising her finger and bending over to catch her breath. 'You don't know what I've gone through to get here.'

Corporal Williamson's mouth widened into an amused smirk and he took a step back to study Sharon. 'Well, lookee what we got here!' He grinned. 'I think you're lost, girl. Shouldn't you be all tucked up in bed, darlin'? It's a bit late for you to be out on a school night, innit.'

Is this guy for real? Not believing what she was listening to, Sharon stared up at the sky and shook her head in bewilderment. *Surely people actually don't fall for this crap, do they?* Quickly losing her patience, Sharon pressed her hands together and let out a small, mirthless laugh. 'Okay, guys. Yes, let's all pretend you got me, so you can stop playing silly beggars and do away with this farcical charade.' She then took a step forward and stabbed her finger into the man's chest, and he flinched back in shock. 'Your name is Corporal Leroy-Bennett Williams, but people call you LB for short. You are twenty-three, have served in the armed forces since you were sixteen, and secretly cosplay as Grand Admiral Thrawn.' Sharon grinned as she noticed his cheeks were flushing with embarrassment. She made the okay gesture with her thumb and index finger and whispered, 'Nice.' Before LB could respond, Sharon spun round and pointed at the bemused-looking woman. 'And you, your name is Private Carrie Clarkson, but you prefer to be known as CeCe. You are twenty-one and have also served in the forces since you were sixteen. You enjoy reading and have a penchant for eating fried Spam with Marmite.' She held up her hands and let out an amused laugh. 'Weird, but who am I to judge?'

The soldiers looked at each other in mild surprise as if they were unsure what to say next. After a couple of seconds of uneasy silence, LB quickly overcame his shock and gazed at Sharon suspiciously. 'Listen, lady,' he said in a measured tone. Sharon could tell he was trying to keep his anger in check and wondered whether mentioning his fondness for cosplaying might have been a step too far. 'I don't know who you are or what you *think you* know, but I'm warning you, if you don't stop talking right now, there is going to be trouble.' He gestured to his colleague and then back at Sharon. 'Which means we are going to have to introduce you to some friends of ours who are going to have a lot of questions for you.' He gave her a dangerous smile. 'And these friends of ours aren't as good natured as CeCe and me. No, you see, these people we know don't like it when someone like yourself goes around spouting lies that may get them and everyone around them killed. So I think it's about time the three of us took a little walk.'

Finally, she was making some headway. Sharon cheered inwardly and then bobbed her head as she clapped excitedly. 'Oh, excellent! Guys, can I ask, before you take me to Excalibur Base, any chance of stopping off somewhere for a bite to eat? You see, I've had a really trying day.' Sharon spoke faster and faster, barely stopping for air, as she turned in a tight circle and waved her hands in the air. 'First, I wake up on a train, having no idea where I am. I then meet this lovely lady, who, let me tell you, was mad as a box of frogs, and then, on top of …'

'Lord, give me strength,' LB groaned, ran a weary hand down his face and glanced at his bemused colleague, who was standing in open-mouthed stupefaction as Sharon spoke faster and faster. He shook his head in exasperation. 'Is this woman for real? She's like the frigging Energizer bunny! She just doesn't want to stop.' He cleared his throat, held up his hands and spoke in a loud, commanding tone. 'Alright, that … is … enough! I've just had about enough of you. You're giving me a headache, so please will you shut the fuck up before I really get anno—'

'My reflection is sad because the mirror needs cleaning,' Sharon blurted out excitedly.

'Wha … what did you just say?' LB gasped in surprise.

Sharon could tell from the shocked expression on LB's face that the last thing he had been expecting to come out of her mouth was a resistance code phrase. She cocked her head curiously as she watched him open and close his mouth like a suffocating face. What was wrong with him? Did he not remember the counter-phrase? Surely she couldn't have thrown him off balance that much?

Believing that LB's brain cells had suddenly dissolved into sludge, Sharon focused her attention on CeCe and stared at her enquiringly. 'Well?'

CeCe rolled her eyes and took a step forward. 'Have you tried Windolene to bring a smile to your reflection?'

'Windolene will not work because the reflection is not my own,' Sharon replied, pleased to be finally talking to someone who had some common sense, unlike the other person, who, for some reason, seemed to be having a bit of difficulty stringing two words together.

Appearing to get his act together, LB gave Sharon a sour look. After inhaling a deep breath, he spoke in a low, but careful tone. 'Okay, lady, just who the hell are you?'

'My name is Doctor Sharon Fisher, serial number Tango-Six-Nine-Delta-Whisky-Four-Charlie-Indigo. Science specialist, formerly assigned to the Castle,' she said sadly and then felt her stomach lurch as she heard herself say something she knew she would later regret and that LB would probably despise her for. 'Corporal, I order you to escort me to your nearest safe house, where they will confirm my credentials.'

LB laughed, gave Sharon an unbelieving look and then pointed his finger at her and then back at himself. '*You* are ordering *me!*' He snorted and shook his head. 'You really have got some balls, lady, I give you that.'

'Oh, for the love of Tony Stark! Has anybody ever told you really are an insufferable arsehole?' She moaned, letting out a heavy groan of resignation and holding up her hands in defeat. 'Alright, if that's how you want it, fine. You have left me no choice.' Feeling the bile rise in her throat, Sharon straightened to attention and shot LB a harsh glare. 'Corporal, as I told you before, my name is Sharon Fisher. That's *Major* Fisher of the Specialist Scientific Service, and I order you to escort me to the nearest safe house.' She waved her hands and gave him a tight smile. 'Of course, you understand what can happen if you refuse an order that has been given to you by a superior officer? Don't you?'

'Major!' LB squeaked, the blood draining from his face. 'I am truly sorry, ma'am. I meant no disrespect. Of course, Private Clarkson would only be happy to escort you, ma'am.' He cast an eye to CeCe and gestured at her. 'Wouldn't we, Private?'

'Of course, *Corporal*,' CeCe replied flatly. She arched her head and shot him a look that said *Hey, it's your mess. Don't you expect me to clean it up!*

The tension could have been cut with a knife; Sharon swallowed, gave a thin nervous smile, and gestured for the two soldiers to lead the way. She hated confrontation and felt her stomach was doing flip-flops at what they had forced her to do. Forcing back the nausea, she let out a heavy, dispirited breath. Well, she had definitely thrown the cat amongst the pigeons now.

The trio made their way through frost-covered streets, stopping every so often to hide from patrolling cyber-drones. There had been an uneasy silence between them, and Sharon sensed the resentment emanating from her two new friends. Sharon was tired of the tension and pressed her hand against her stomach as she sensed the bilious feeling building inside her. Because of the guilt she felt at how she'd treated LB, she tried not to picture the size of the ulcer her anxiety was building for her inside her gastrointestinal tract. Hoping it would help to alleviate her guilt, Sharon slid up next to the corporal and gave an embarrassed laugh.

'Um, LB,' she mumbled.

'Ma'am?' LB responded curtly, not looking her in the eye.

Oh well, that's just peachy! Is that how it's going to be? Sharon inhaled a deep breath, stretched out a hand and touched LB's arm. 'LB, please stop. I've something I need to say to you.'

'Is that an order, ma'am?' LB responded flatly.

By Batman's scowl! This man is so infuriating! Sharon clenched her teeth together and gave Private Clarkson a side eye; CeCe shrugged and gave her look that seemed to say, *don't look at me for help!*

Sharon sucked in a heavy breath and placed her hands against her chest. 'Corporal, please, will you stop and look at me?' She smiled gratefully at LB as he reluctantly came to a stop and arched his head. 'I want to apologise for how I treated you and CeCe. It was uncalled for. I know it's not an excuse, but I was tired and, if I'm being truthful, I was acting out of fear.' The two soldiers exchanged concerned looks as Sharon pulled down her hood and stared at them in anguish. Her voice cracked as she tried to choke back the tears. 'A few hours ago, I learned that the place I had called home had been destroyed and that all my friends are or may be dead.'

LB's face softened and he placed his hand on Sharon's arm. 'Ma'am,' he began awkwardly.

'Please call me Sharon, LB,' Sharon interrupted and then laughed nervously. 'My rank is an honorary thing, not something I earned. Anyway, it has always made me uncomfortable whenever I've been forced to use it because I'm normally someone who avoids confrontation.' She took hold of the two soldiers' hands and gave them a tight smile. 'I've no intention of carrying out my earlier threat, and I understand if you just want to wash your hands of me. All I want is to get back to my friends and see if the man I love is still alive. Is that too much to ask?'

LB shuffled on his feet uncomfortably but remained silent. CeCe moved towards Sharon and gave her a tight hug. After releasing her, the pink-haired soldier turned to LB and spoke firmly to him.

'LB, I think we owe it to Sharon to get her to where she wants to be,' CeCe said, in a tone that was forceful but still held a touch of respect. 'She's been through too much already. We ha— sorry, we must do this.'

'I agree,' LB responded almost immediately. He snapped his heels together, straightened, and saluted Sharon. 'Ma'am, it would be an honour to escort you to where you need to go.' He gestured in the direction they had been heading. 'Normally, we would have used an access tunnel to get to where we need to be, but because of an … incident that happened a couple of days ago, that is no longer safe to use. But there is another option, which is where I was taking us.' He gave a sheepish laugh and then waved his hand theatrically. 'So, if you can bear to be in the presence of this insufferable arsehole for another five minutes, we'll have you at your destination in no time.'

That was all she wanted to hear. Overjoyed that she was finally going to be reunited with her friends, Sharon let out a squeal of delight. LB's eyes grew wide as saucers as she pounced on him and slapped a kiss on his lips. Embarrassed, she jumped back and coughed sheepishly as LB continued to stare back at her in shock. CeCe stifled a giggle, obviously enjoying her friend's discomfort.

'Oh, thank you, thank you very much. You don't know what this means to me,' Sharon said excitedly. Feeling her face warm, she stared at her shoes and mumbled, 'For the record, I apologise for calling you an insufferable arsehole earlier. It was uncalled for.' She stretched out her hand and peered back at LB with a hopeful expression. 'I hope we can still be friends?'

'Sharon, it will be my pleasure to have you as a friend,' LB replied, grinning, stretching out his hand.

Sharon took hold of LB's outstretched hand and grimaced as she felt his fingers tighten around hers in a tight squeeze. *Holy moly, what a* grip! *I hope I'm going to have some fingers left after this.*

A few minutes later, the trio came to a stop outside a dimly lit shopfront. Sharon frowned in puzzlement at the twenty-four-hour pharmacy and turned to give LB a questioning look, but he just gave a small wordless shrug and motioned her to follow him through the doorway. Sharon clicked her tongue off the roof of her mouth. Clearly there was more to the Pharmacy than meets the eye. She shrugged. Then again, who was she to judge, her last home had previously been a base situated beneath a cathedral.

As she stepped through the doorway, it surprised Sharon to discover that the inside was as advertised: a pharmacy. It was dingy looking, dimly lit, with three rows of shelves in the centre of the store that held various items for sale, ranging from female beauty commodities, an assortment of baby food and nappies, as well as men's shaving and contraception products. As she followed LB down the aisle towards the rear of the premises, Sharon could see a counter with a range of medicines and pain relief on the shelves behind it. Above the counter, a twenty-four-inch TV was playing an IGNS interview with the new prime minister, Michael Gray.

LB approached the thin-faced man behind the counter, who she assumed was the pharmacist. The bespectacled gentleman appeared to be in his late forties, had short nutmeg-brown hair and was wearing a chemist's white coat.

'Good evening, LB,' the brown-haired said warmly. 'How may I help you today?'

'Good evening to you too, Chris.' LB nodded politely and tapped two fingers on his chin. He spoke in a neutral tone. 'Little Bo-Peep has been out playing with Little Jack Horner but has been bitten by the Big Bad Wolf.'

Chris's eyes flickered to Sharon and then back to LB, but he kept his tone genial as he responded with the counter-phrase. 'Did Little Bo-Peep not go to Grandma's for help?'

LB stared impassively at Chris as he continued to speak in a neutral tone. 'Grandma's castle was destroyed in a storm, which is why she has come here.'

At the mention of the Castle, Chris's eyes grew wide; he nodded in understanding before turning to Sharon, and then shook his head sadly. 'Many apologies for your loss, my dear. If I could ask you to remain where you are, LB and I need to go out back and check the stock.'

LB nodded and then turned to CeCe. 'I shouldn't be too long,' he said hopefully and then gestured at Sharon, who had been watching the exchange in silence. 'CeCe will keep an eye out while we are gone.' Then, without another word, he stepped behind the counter and followed Chris through a door, closing behind them.

After a few minutes of silence, Sharon sauntered round the aisles and gazed thoughtfully at some items on the shelves. She stopped and raised a questioning eyebrow at CeCe, whose eyes were locked on the shop's entrance as if she was ready for someone to come bursting through the door. 'So, Little Bo-Peep? I take it they were talking about me?'

'Huh-huh,' CeCe murmured distractedly.

Okay, looks like I'm not going to get much chat out of her, Sharon thought and was about to say something else, but stopped as she heard a loud news jingle coming from the TV, followed by the urgent voice of Julianna Sonatori.

'We interrupt this scheduled programme with breaking news.'

Believing that this was something important, Sharon and CeCe hurried to the counter and looked up at the TV. Sharon felt her eyes grow wide in horror as a picture of Sophia Collins appeared on the TV screen.

Oh hell, what now?

-26-

Deep beneath the streets of Birmingham, John Payne ran a hand down his weary face and yawned as he read the reports on his desk, hoping they would reveal a clue to the prime minister's location. He leaned back in his chair and shook his head in frustration. Where was she? Where were they holding her?

Distracted by his own thoughts, he automatically reached for the mug on his desk and lifted it up to his mouth. His face twisted in disgust – it was cold – and, in a fit of pique, he threw the cup across the room, narrowly missing Sergeant Major Wayne, who had just walked through the door.

The soldier frowned at the remains of the shattered cup on the floor and then cocked his head at Payne. 'Aren't you supposed to be resting?' he said, his voice not hiding his disapproval.

After his collapse two days earlier, the medical team had diagnosed the commander with exhaustion, advising he should rest and avoid any stress. Of course, being the man he was, John was back at his desk less than twelve hours later.

Payne waved his hand slightly in a dismissive gesture, grunting, 'I can rest when we find Collins.' He scowled at the soldier in the doorway. 'Have you any news to give me? Or are you just wasting time making glib comments?'

The sergeant major's face clouded and he gave his head a slight shake. 'No, we've had our contacts searching tirelessly for the last two days, but they can't find any trace of her.' He rubbed the back of his neck in dissatisfaction, sighing. 'They can't dig too deep without attracting suspicion.'

Payne leapt to his feet and slammed his hand down on the desk. 'That's not good enough!' he growled angrily, stabbing a finger at Malcolm. 'You tell them to do their job. If you can't do that, I'll find somebody who knows how to obey orders. You understand me?'

Malcolm's face darkened with anger as he straightened and then glowered back at John. 'Perfectly,' he answered curtly. 'Anything else … *sir?*'

John groaned to himself. He realised that he had gone too far by taking his own frustrations out on Malcom. He held his hand up to apologise, but before he could so, the sergeant major stiffly spun on his heel, flung the door open and marched out of the room. Heavy with fatigue, John sank back into the chair and put his head in his hands, lamenting at his own stupidity. Damn it! Why did he have to bite Malcolm's head off like that?

As Wendy hurried out of the command centre towards Commander Payne's office she slowed and reached for the door's handle. But before she could push the handle down, she froze as she picked what she thought sounded like a raised voice coming from inside the room. Was that John? Was he having an argument with Sergeant Major Wayne? She stared at the closed door worriedly and wondered whether she should intrude. However, before she could make her mind up, the door flew open and she just managed step back in time, narrowing missing a red-faced Sergeant Major Wayne as he charged out of Payne's office.

Malcolm gave Wendy an apologetic look and gestured to the room he had just come out of, 'Wendy, I would be careful if I were you. He's like a shark with a sore head today.' He whispered.

Wendy pursed her lips and gave a small nod of acknowledgement, 'Yeah, I heard him from out here.'

The grizzled sergeant major cast a concerned eye over his shoulder, 'See if you can persuade him to rest. He may listen to you.'

Wendy let out a small guffaw of laughter, 'Hah! I wouldn't count on it, but I can try.'

Malcom patted Wendy's shoulder gratefully as he strode past her into the command centre. Inhaling a deep breath, Wendy squared her shoulders and marched into the commander's office. Her mouth widening into a beaming pretend smile, she leaned against the doorframe and waved her hand in the air.

'So where are you keeping it?' she asked in a hushed voice.

John lifted his head up out of his hands and stared Wendy, his forehead creasing in confusion. 'Keeping what?' he replied sharply.

Pretending to search for something, Wendy hunkered down on her haunches and continued to speak in a low hushed voice. 'The dog? Where are you keeping it?'

John leaned back into the chair and stared back at her, his face a mixture of confusion and annoyance. 'Wendy? What the hell are you talking about?'

Eyes wide in mock sincerity, Wendy waved a hand at the open doorway. 'Well, I just passed Sergeant Major Wayne as he came out of here and the poor guy's arse looks like it had chunks chewed out of it. So, I just assumed you were holding some sort of rabid animal in here.'

The sour-faced John rolled his eyes and let out a sardonic laugh. 'Funny, Cooper. With that sharp wit of yours I'm surprised you haven't cut yourself.'

Tongue firmly in her cheek, Wendy lifted her shoulder in a small shrug of amusement. 'Aye, I thought so to.' She gave Payne a sly wink and reached forward to grab an apple out of a bowl on top of the desk.

'Sure, take one, why don't you!' he snorted sarcastically.

'Dinna mind if ah do.' She grinned cheekily, plonking herself into a chair in front of his desk. She took a bite of the apple and stared at him thoughtfully. 'You realise it wasn't your fault, right?'

John sat back in his chair and gave Wendy a harsh stare. 'What are you talking about?'

Still munching on a mouthful of apple, Wendy smile sadly and gestured to Payne. 'Sophia's capture. You're punishing yourself, as well as everyone else, by the way. Like the way you punished yourself for the base's destruction, you think it's your fault.'

'You don't know what you're talking about.' John scoffed, waving his hand irritably.

Wendy smiled knowingly and waggled her finger. 'You're angry at yourself. You believe you took your eye off the ball, allowing Sophia to be captured.' She placed the half-eaten apple on the desk and leaned forward. 'You're putting it all on your shoulders, taking it personally.'

John's mouth set into a hard line, the tendons in his neck becoming taut as he sneered at Wendy and shook his head vehemently. 'If you must know, no, it's not Sophia's capture that has me so worked up.' His eyes dropped to his desk, and he picked up a paper folder. 'It's this.'

Wendy's left eyebrow arched in mild surprise as she took the folder from him. 'What is it?'

Exhaling a weary breath, John leaned back in his chair and folded his arms across his chest. 'Before we departed the transfer point in Durham, I downloaded all the security logs from the last two hours leading up to the time when the base was destroyed.'

'What did you discover?' she asked curiously, perusing the papers in her hands. She froze and the hairs on the back of her neck tingled as her eyes lingered over a section of highlighted text. *Oh shit! That's not good!*

The commander gave a grim smile. 'You see it too, don't you?' He leaned forward in his chair and bobbed his head at the papers in Wendy's hands. 'Just before the attack, somebody deactivated the frequency generator, disabling the static shield around the complex.' He waggled his finger and let out a small, bitter laugh. 'Of course, they couldn't disable the alarms – that takes a bit more time, which I don't think they had. My guess is the attack was a diversion to keep us distracted. With our attention focused on the attackers, we would be too preoccupied to notice the incursion alarm sounding as they opened a portal to take Sophia.'

'Who? Who could do that?' Wendy asked warily. Deep down, a slow dread started move around in her gut as it suddenly hit her who may have been responsible. She swallowed as she finally started to understand why Payne was so agitated.

His arms spread wide, John rose to his feet and sighed wistfully. 'Sharon. Everything in my gut tells me it was Sharon. There were only a few people on the base who had the skill and the knowledge to pull this off.' He closed his eyes and rubbed his forehead, letting out a tired groan. Wendy could tell he was struggling to contain his anger, but before she could say anything she flinched as he let out a deep guttural howl and smashed his hand on his desk, sending everything flying off it.

'She used me!' he snarled. His eyes blazing with incandescent rage, he slammed his fist on his desk repeatedly with increasing force. 'She played on my feelings! Playing me like a guitar, telling me what I wanted to hear. Pretending to be psychologically damaged.'

Full of concern for her friend, Wendy jumped to her feet, hands outstretched in a placating gesture. 'John, we don't know it was her. She could have been still under Oracle's control.'

John scoffed, waving his hand in front of him. 'Oh, it was her alright. Why else have we not found Sharon, too?' His voice full of spite, he hissed at Wendy. 'I'll tell you why, because Sharon was a double agent all along.'

At a loss for words, placing her hands on her hips, Wendy shook her head in adamant refusal. 'No, I'm sorry. I cannot believe that. Surely there has to be another explanation.'

John opened his mouth as if to make a retort. However, before Wendy could listen to what he had to say, she was surprised by a series of curse words coming from the command centre. They stared at each other in bafflement.

'Did you just hear?' they asked in unison.

Without waiting for an answer, they raced out of the small office into the command centre. Sergeant Major Wayne nodded curtly at John as he charged towards him. His lips pressed tightly together, he gestured to Sunitra, who was hurling abuse at her desktop monitor.

'Bastards! You lousy stinking bastards!' Sunitra's face was a picture of pure rage as she jabbed her finger angrily at her monitor. 'How dare you call yourself a reporter, you platinum blond harpy!'

Wendy swallowed as she took a careful step closer to the furious woman, placing a hand on her shoulder, 'Sunitra? What's wrong?'

Her chest rising and falling in rapid, angry breaths, the incensed former BBC news anchor swallowed as she struggled to regain control of her emotions. 'Sorry, I apologise for the language. I was in the middle of monitoring the news channels …' She took a deep lungful of air and turned to John, gazing at him mournfully. 'Commander, you need to see this. IGNS are talking about Sophia Collins.'

His face turning a shade of ash, John stared at her blankly and nodded. 'Put it on the main monitor, please,' he asked, his voice flat.

Wendy caught a concerned look pass between the journalist and the sergeant major, but Malcolm remained silent and bobbed his head, indicating for her to continue. As they watched, a photo of Sophia Collins appeared on the screen, and Wendy gasped as if someone had punched her in the stomach. *Oh shit! This cannot be good.*

The photo quickly disappeared, replaced with a familiar peroxide blond simpering woman as she spoke to her audience. '*I repeat, we interrupt this scheduled programme with breaking news,*' Julianna Sonatori announced with her usual excitable gusto. '*According to IGNS sources within the security forces, after extensive investigation, we regret to inform you that they have uncovered startling evidence that shows the former British prime minister, Sophia Collins, is the leader behind the terrorist group Free Earth. IGNS is also saddened to learn that Ms Collins purposely allowed herself to be captured so she could pretend to pass on information as to the alleged location of the terrorists' base in Durham's city centre.*' She paused for a dramatic breath before holding her hand up to her chest in mock distress. '*What is more distressing is that it appears this building was an empty shell, designed to lure our brave Imperial security forces to their deaths. IGNS can reveal a detonator was found in Collins's possession – the same detonator that was had been used to set off device that killed so many people that dreadful day.*'

Wendy laughed bitterly and waved a hand at the monitor. 'Oh, come on! Surely nobody is going to believe this garbage?'

Her attention still fixed on the monitor, Sunitra shook her head gravely, muttering, 'That's the whole point, they don't want people to believe it. They are using it to send a message.'

Wendy rubbed the back of her neck and stared at everyone in the room in confusion. 'What message?'

John raised his hand to silence Wendy so that they could listen to the platinum blond on the monitor, who was continuing with her well-rehearsed speech. '*According to IGNS sources, her Grand Magnificence, Oracle, will oversee the trial of the traitor. By using her divine powers, our majestic leader will judge Collins's true guilt. If found guilty, her Grand Excellence will personally carry out the traitor's punishment.*' Sonatori beamed at the camera. '*The traitor's trial will be exclusively broadcast on IGNS in one hour. Stay tuned, as we explore deeper into Collins's history of betrayal, and discuss with experts how she went from beloved leader to megalomaniac.*'

Numb from shock, Wendy collapsed into a chair and buried her head in her hands. Now she understood what message Oracle wanted to send – this was what would happen to those that continued to defy her.

Standing inside the pharmacy, Sharon and CeCe stared up at the TV screen and then at each other. Sharon shook her head as she tried to understand what was going on. No, how could this have happened? How had Sophia ended up in their clutches? She cast a concerned eye to CeCe, who slammed her hand on the shop's service counter, her face a furious red.

'That stick instinct excuse of a cow! How could they do this?' the angry soldier hissed. She glowered at Sharon and then prodded a finger at her. 'You mark my words, I'm going to find the traitorous bastard responsible and, by the time I'm through with them, their own mother won't be able to recognise them.'

Sharon wanted to comfort CeCe, but as she was about to place her hand on her shoulder, she felt a sudden sharp pain in her head. The pain was so bad, her knees buckled and she had to grab the counter to stop herself from falling.

'Sharon!' CeCe exclaimed. 'What's wrong?'

'I … I …' Sharon whimpered through clenched teeth.

She let out a sharp breath, and it was as if something clicked inside her, opening a door within her mind, releasing memories and experiences that had been locked away. Now that the mind block had been removed, it was like a floodgate had been opened and everything that Oracle had forbidden came flooding back to Sharon. Tears streamed down her face as the memories played out in her mind. Everything, all the murders Oracle had forced her to commit, including her complicity in Sophia's abduction. *Oh my God!* How could she face everybody now, knowing what she'd done? She felt her eyes grow wide as the last piece clicked into place, and she remembered the imperative Oracle had placed inside her – that she was to kill John Payne. She frowned in confusion. *Wait – that shouldn't be possible.* If there was an imperative buried inside her, then surely she should not be aware of it. Along with her reawakened memories, something else happened. Sharon was filled with a new awareness. Images flooded her memory of things that no human should not even be aware of. She pictured a vast celestial hall in the centre of which stood a vast cosmic chessboard with Oracle. Standing across from her was mysterious white-haired man dressed in a white evening suit.

Before she could make any sense of it, Sharon stiffened as the mysterious figure turned and looked directly at her.

'*Run, child,*' he whispered in her mind. '*You need to get as far away from here as you can. I cannot completely erase the imperative, for Oracle has it buried too deep in your psyche. You must run and hide. Once you are safely secure, only then can I help you deal with it. But for now, not only for your lover's safety, but yours too, you must flee.*'

Sharon shook her head in adamant refusal. No, if she ran, that would only make things worse. The right course of action was to stay and face everyone. John would understand. '*Yes, that's right, you need to say.*' A new voice whispered in her head, '*Once you are standing in front of him, in his arms, everything would be okay.*'

'*Don't listen to it, child. My name is Custos, and you must believe me when I say that I only have your interests at heart,*' Custos pleaded. '*I'm telling you the truth when I tell you that the imperative is manipulating you. Trust me, Sharon, you need to run. Even if without the imperative, Oracle has arranged to make it appear that you are a danger to your friends, and they will not hesitate to kill you when they see you.*' The celestial voice increased in tone, sounding more urgent. '*Go now before it is too late. Run! Now!*'

There was something in the ethereal voice that made Sharon pause. She could almost sense the kindness in it. Could it be he was the opposite of Oracle? Where Oracle's purpose was to destroy all life, could it be that his purpose was to protect it? And that cosmic chessboard she pictured, were she and her friends just pieces on it for them to move and discard at their whim? Even though he appeared benign, there was no doubt in her mind that Custos also had a hidden agenda. But right now, that wasn't important; what was important she heed his warning and escape before it was too late.

'Yes, I need to get away before they come for me,' Sharon hissed through gritted teeth, slamming her hand on counter. She spun round to face CeCe, who was looking at her with deep concern etched across her face.

CeCe reached out to grab Sharon's arm. 'Sharon, I'm sorry I canno—'

Refusing to listen to reason and in no mood to let anyone stop her, Sharon grabbed the nearest thing to hand, spun round, and slammed it against CeCe's head with all her might. The heavy acrylic paperweight struck CeCe's temple, and she sank to the floor in a stunned heap. After quickly regaining her senses, Sharon blinked and gasped, mortified, at what she had done. *No, not again.* Already feeling guilty for being responsible for Barnes's and Harem's deaths,

Sharon knelt to check CeCe's pulse and was relieved to find that she was still alive. She inhaled a grateful sigh and stared up at the ceiling. Thank God she was alive. She just couldn't bear having another person's death on her conscience.

As she headed towards the exit, she paused, peered over her shoulder and exhaled a heavy, despondent sigh. She hoped her friends would find it in their hearts to forgive her one day because she knew she wouldn't. As she was about to place her hand on the door handle, she paused as she heard the now familiar intangible voice in her head.

'Forgive me, child, but when I said that you need to get out of here, that did not mean I gave you permission to brain someone,' Custos said with such disapproval that Sharon almost felt the furrowing of his brow. *'If we are to work together, then you must learn to control those emotional outbursts, my dear.'*

'You can shut up for a start,' Sharon snapped back irritably. 'It's because of you and Oracle I'm in this mess. So, I would appreciate it if you would keep your opinions to yourself.'

If Custos was annoyed by Sharon's comment, he had either decided it wasn't worth commenting on or maybe thought there just wasn't any need to antagonise her any further. Whatever the reason for his silence, Sharon no longer cared as she hurried through the open door into the dimly lit street. She bristled in the frosty December, pulled the hood up around her head, but then paused, turned and peered sadly over her shoulder through the glass in the door into the interior of the shop.

Sharon closed her eyes and inhaled a resigned-filled breath. No, it was better this way. If she had learned anything from Oracle, it was that the scheming AI had plans inside plans; whatever backup scheme it was, the only thing she was sure of was that it would make it even harder for her friends to trust her again. Sharon tightened her jaw and squared her shoulders. No, she wasn't out of the game yet, and even though she could no longer join her friends, that didn't mean she couldn't help them in another way, and if what she had in mind worked, then it would deliver Oracle a devastating blow. But first, for her plan to work, she would need Custos's assistance, someone whose identity she had a strong hunch about, and to get to him she would have to make the perilous journey back to a certain northern village – where the Nexus of Reality was located.

-27-

The crowd's angry jeers increased as a small heavy object flew through the air, striking the manacled prisoner on the side of the forehead. Sophia crumpled to her knees, gasping in pain, and the roar of the crowd increased as they revelled in her discomfort. Inhaling a deep breath, Sophia clenched her teeth in determination and slowly rose to her feet, she straightened her back and stared defiantly at the baying crowd.

Just over an hour earlier, she had been sitting in her cell in the Tower of London. She rose to her feet and remained silent as four armoured figures marched into her cell and wordlessly removed her shackles. Sophia held her tongue throughout the entire process, knowing it was pointless to ask the enslaved other-worldly soldiers any questions. But she remained compliant as they slid a helmet over her head, and inhaled slow calming breaths as they lowered a blacked-out visor over her face. Unbearably claustrophobic, she was acutely aware the helmet's sole purpose was to disorient her, to panic her.

Her breathing slow and relaxed, relying on her hearing to guide her, Sophia remained calm as she felt herself being roughly manhandled out of her cell. After what seemed like an eternity, being led down various corridors and stairs, she eventually reached the outside and shivered in the frosty December air as she was bustled into a waiting vehicle.

After a short drive, the vehicle came to an abrupt stop. She heard a door being flung open, followed once again by the feeling of being seized by rough hands as they forcibly took her out into the freezing air. Sophia frowned as she heard the increasing noise of a crowd as she was marched into a building and up a flight of stairs. As the frigid December wind bit at her hands, she deduced that she was in a building open to the elements. Then she flinched as a pair of hands grabbed the sides of the helmet and lifted it off her head.

She looked up at the cloudy night sky and blinked in mild surprise on realising it was late evening. Her eyes grew wide as she realised she was standing on a raised wooden stage in the centre of a large circular yard, overlooked by three tiers of seating. She immediately recognised the amphitheatre as Shakespeare's Globe Theatre.

As Sophia gazed sadly over the small crowd, she felt a surge of disappointment on seeing at the number of faces staring back at her. She estimated their number to be close to two hundred, and from the way they were dressed, she knew the jeering hoard was made up of members of the group called the Disciples of Oracle. A wave of sadness overwhelmed her as it hit her how many people had been so easily beguiled by Oracle.

The crowd's jeers slowly lapsed into silence and Sophia twisted her head, sensing movement from behind her. She stared sharply at Oracle, who strode past her wearing an outlandish glittering bodysuit. There was something radiant about her; it was like she was gaining strength from all the attention of those who worshipped her. Sophia's forehead creased as the newly appointed British Prime Minister, Michael Gray, appeared, following closely behind Oracle. He hung his head as she shot daggers at him. Sophia's eyebrow arched as she detected something in his eyes. Was it unease? No, it was something else. Was it shame? Her eyes widened in surprise as it struck her. Yes, he looked ashamed as if he was regretting his actions.

A loud cry broke Sophia out of her reverie and she focused her attention back on the silver figure at the front of the stage. Oracle stood at the stage's edge, hands raised, smiling, basking in the crowd's adulation as they called out her name.

'Oracle! Oracle!'

The crowd's rapturous applause eased as Oracle raised her hand and smiled warmly. She dramatically lowered her hand to her chest and shook her head joylessly as she peered over her shoulder at the woman standing behind her.

'A few days ago, we watched in shock as this woman callously murdered innocent women and children,' Oracle said sadly, turning her back to the crowd.

Sophia ground her teeth as she detected a shadow of a smile on the AI's silver face as the crowd murmured angrily. Oracle gave her a sly wink as she continued to address the crowd. 'Was it because the city held some dark purpose? No, my children, I am afraid the real reason is far more shocking.' She jabbed her finger viciously at Sophia, before spinning sharply back to face the crowd. 'This woman, the woman you trusted for so many years, was jealous.' On hearing the crowd's angry gasps, the artificial woman pretended to give a sad smile and held her hands over her heart. 'Yes, my children, you heard me right. She was jealous. Jealous of the future. Of the peaceful utopia I would bring to this world. Not only was she jealous, but she was afraid. Afraid that in our peaceful utopia, our need for people like her would be obsolete.'

Her cold yellow eyes flickering with malice, Oracle slowly turned her back on the braying crowd and smirked at Sophia. She raised a hand to silence the angry crowd and exhaled a long dramatic sigh. 'But I am not a vengeful god. I still believe a person can be redeemed for their past misdeeds.'

Oracle suddenly dropped to her knees with her hands outstretched. Sophia stiffened in shock as the AI grabbed her hands and cried out in a loud voice, 'Repent! Renounce your hatred before everybody here and join my children as we spread the word of my divinity across the world and beyond.'

Several seconds passed as Sophia stared wordlessly at the outstretched hands. What was Oracle expecting her to do? Fall on her knees and beg for Oracle's forgiveness? No, not even if it meant saving her life, she wasn't going to do that. Not only would it mean going against everything Sophia believed in, but she doubted people would have believed it. Her upper lip curling up in a contemptuous sneer, Sophia straightened her head defiantly and pulled her hands away, turning her back on the false saviour. She flinched as the hostile crowd pelted her with rotten fruit and other disgusting items.

Oracle slowly rose to her feet and held up a hand, silencing the hostile crowd's angry cries. 'No, my children, do not waste your anger on this unfortunate woman, for she knows not what she does.' She exhaled a dramatic, dejected sigh and shook her head. 'It is with great regret I must do this, but you have left me no choice.'

Sophia proudly remained silent as Oracle waved her hand and half a dozen cybernetic soldiers appeared, rolling a large wooden platform onto the stage. A deep sadness filled Sophia's heart as she instantly recognised the intimidating platform. It was comprised of two upright posts, a reinforced crossbeam and a noose hanging in the centre. It was an execution gallows. Sophia shook her head at the absurdity of the situation she now found herself in. She had to give Oracle her due; by making her execution as theatrical as possible, she was going to make it so that people would remember it for a long time to come.

As he watched Sophia proudly straighten her shoulders as the black and gold armoured soldiers led her up the short flight to the top of the platform, Michael watched sorrowfully as they fastened a heavy weight to the helpless woman's legs and then slipped a noose around her neck. He jumped as a streak of lightning lit up the night sky, followed by a loud crack of thunder. He eyed the night sky warily. Had Oracle's blasphemous display angered someone? He shook his head sadly before turning his attention back to this mockery of trial. No, if God did exist, he imagined they wanted no part in this.

Her right hand outstretched, Oracle raised her voice, her tone mocking, to the noosed woman on the raised platform. 'Do you have any last words to express before you leave this world?'

Her face twisting with contempt, Sophia sneered at the silver woman, hissing, 'Not to you.' She straightened and raised her voice so the crowd could hear. 'But I have something I would like to say to them.'

'Oh, really? Well, I am sure they will be delighted to listen to what you have to say.' Oracle laughed, her tone ridiculing. She grinned malevolently as the crowd broke into roars of laughter.

His head bowed subserviently, Michael edged cautiously over to the mocking AI and whispered anxiously into her ear, 'Your Excellency, is that wise? IGNS are broadcasting this event across the world. If you allow her to speak, she may cause more problems for you.'

Unconcerned, Oracle gave a dismissive wave of her hand, scoffing. 'Oh, you worry too much. I doubt people will believe anything a traitor has to say. No, let the woman spin her lies, for all the good it will do her.' She gave a small gracious nod at Sophia. 'Please go ahead.'

Michael guessed from the resolute expression on Sophia's face that she must have thought very carefully about what she was going to say if she was given the chance. Even though he felt partly responsible for the position she was now in, deep down there was a part of him that could not help but admire the way she was facing up to her death. If their situations had been reversed, more than likely he would have been standing there mewling like a child. But as Michael stood and listened, he could almost hear the defiance in Sophia's voice as she addressed the auditorium's crowd.

'Oracle believes she can impose her will on you, that she can hold an imprisoned population by the force of arms forever.' Her eyes locking on the camera drone hovering in front of her, Sophia continued with her impassioned speech. 'But there is no greater power in the world than the need for freedom. Against that power can stand, not even a one as powerful as her.' Her eyes filled with blazing defiance, she fixed Oracle with a steely stare. 'I believe you learned this lesson once before. Mark my words, you will learn it again.'

The crowd's voices settled into silence, shortly followed by murmurs of discontent. It was as if the defiant former prime minister's words had struck them to their very core. Unable to watch at what was to happen next, Michael turned his head away as Oracle pulled on the lever. He squeezed his eyes shut and shuddered as he listened to the sound of a hatch opening, followed a second later by the sound of something dropping and the sickening crunch of a neck snapping. He opened his eyes and gazed over the sombre faces in the crowd and realised Oracle had underestimated the power of Sophia's words.

Then, as if to mourn the death of noble warrior, the heavens opened in a torrent of rain. Michael stood silently as the rain soaked through his clothes, shook his head bitterly and stared down at his hands. He wondered if this was how Judas had felt when he took his thirty pieces of silver. Yes, he'd had always been ambitious and never made it a secret that he craved power. But, at one point does a person have to stand back and see what their lust for power was doing to those around them? How many deaths would it take before it finally hit home that what they were doing was wrong? Michael squeezed his eyes shut as he felt the guilt of Sophia's death weigh heavily on his conscience.

Michael let out a shuddering breath as the freezing rain lashed against the exposed skin on his face. Deep down, a part of him knew it would take a lot more than that to wash away his stench of betrayal.

-28-

In the underground base, the small group of people continued to watch the monitor with mixed emotions as Julianna Sonatori looked sombrely into her camera. '*Collins's body will be transferred to a purpose-built airtight Plexiglass box in Trafalgar Square, where it will hang as a reminder to show people what will happen if they continue to defy our majestic leader's will.*' Her mouth widened into a beaming smile as she continued to address the camera. '*In other news, IGNS sources have learned that our brave security forces were first alerted to Collins's scheming by this woman.*' Andy and Wendy both gasped in stunned horror as an image of Sharon Fisher appeared on the screen. '*Major Sharon Fisher apparently alerted the security forces after Collins tried to recruit her into her little terror cell.*' Sonatori gave a broad false smile and raised her hand to her head in mock salute. '*Well, Sharon, if you are watching this, we here at IGNS salute you.*'

Sunitra bitterly stabbed her finger on the remote, switching the monitor off. She smashed the remote down on the table in disgust. 'I think I have just about had my fill with that sanctimonious cow.' she hissed with contempt.

Andy nodded and sighed heavily. 'So, what now?'

Her body trembling with rage, Sunitra stared through narrow angry eyes at the people around the desk. 'As soon as I've calmed down, I'm going on the air to broadcast my response. I don't know what I'm going to say yet, but I hope, Command Payne, if you …' She stopped and frowned, glancing around the room. 'Where is Commander Payne?'

Malcolm and Wendy exchanged worried looks as they quickly stood up.

Wendy dashed out of the command centre into John's small office. She returned seconds later, scratching her head.

'Where did he go?' she asked, looking worried.

Malcolm shrugged, but before he could answer, he was interrupted by a ring from the phone on the wall behind him and got up to answer it. Sunitra raised a questioning eyebrow as she watched him pick up the phone. Malcom's bushy eyebrows shoot up his forehead and she could almost make out the frantic voice on the other end of the line.

'She's what?' he blurted out.

The bitter December wind and rain stabbed at Payne's face as he stepped out through the access door onto the exposed rooftop. His teeth clenched, he ignored the biting wind that was tearing through his thin shirt and into his body like blades of ice.

It was as if he had been consumed by madness. His body shaking rage, hands balling into fists, John screamed at the heavens above him. For several minutes, he howled against the elements. How could the universe do that to him? Hadn't it taken enough from him already? Was it not going to be happy until everybody around him was dead? His throat raw from screaming, he collapsed to his knees and pounded his fists on the rain-soaked surface. His rage depleted, he buried his head in his hands and wailed. Why? He was a good man, who never asked the universe for anything. So why did it want to destroy him?

He wasn't sure how long he had been sitting there but shuddered as he felt someone's hands gently lift him up off the freezing surface. He smiled dismally at Wendy who was guiding him to the open access door and wrapping a warm blanket around his shoulders.

'I-I-I'm sorry, Wendy,' John whispered apologetically, his teeth chattering. Shivering, he tightened the dry warm blanket around his body. 'I-I just had to get out of there. I felt like I was going to explode.'

Wendy nodded in understanding and smiled warmly. 'You probably needed it. Feel any better?'

He snorted and shook his head vehemently. 'Not in the slightest.'

Wendy pursed her lips. 'So what now?'

John's mood darkened as he fixed Wendy with an angry scowl of determination and hissed through gritted teeth, 'We contact every cell across the globe. Contact all those that are in hiding. We are going to make these bastards pay. They want a war. We are going to give them one.'

Wendy swallowed and spoke in a hesitant voice. 'Sir ... John, there's something I think you need to know. It concerns Sharon.'

Great! What else has she done? John felt suddenly weary and ran his hand down his stubbled face. 'Okay, what's she done now?' He sighed wearily.

'Just after you left, we received a phone call from LB, who was speaking from the security desk,' she explained. 'Apparently, they found Sharon walking around the city centre, looking for a safe house. He and Private Clarkson brought her to the safe house.' She motioned to the ground below. 'The one that's just below us.'

Sharon was here? Could it be the things they were saying about her on the news weren't true? Re-energised by the idea that his lover had found her way back to him, John slapped Wendy's shoulder and made his way to the elevator. 'I knew there had to be a reason she was missing.'

Wendy grabbed John's arm and shook her head. 'John, sorry, but I think you've been right about her,' she said gravely. 'LB and a small security detail went back to get her but found Private Clarkson alone and unconscious. He quickly checked the security tapes and saw that Sharon had knocked her out before escaping into the night. We think she may have realised that, once we saw the news, it was only a matter of time before we learned about the role she played in Sophia's capture.'

So that's how it's going to be then. Just when he thought the universe had granted him a moment of happiness, it reached forward and snatched it away from him, shattering his heart in the process. He straightened and ran his hand down the front of his damp shirt. Fine. If the universe wasn't going to be happy until there was nothing left but an angry bitter husk of a man, then that's how it was to be.

'I ... see,' John replied bitterly, turning back to Wendy and staring at her coldly, 'I want the word given – you tell them, if they so much as catch a glimpse of her, I want that bitch shot on sight!'

'John!' Wendy exclaimed. 'You can't do that – at the very least you need to give her a chance to explain herself.'

John could tell Wendy was visibly appalled by the idea that he would order the death of somebody he loved so dearly. He cocked his head and his eyes narrowed as he peered thoughtfully out of the door into the dark night and nodded. Yes, she was right, he couldn't give that order. No, Sharon deserved more than that. 'Tell them she is to be captured alive and brought to me. I will listen to what she has to say.' He spun on his heel and then finished his sentence almost as an afterthought. 'Then, when she's finished … I will kill her myself.'

-29-

In a cottage deep in a village somewhere in the Dorset countryside, Vernon and Ruby Collins hugged each other tightly. They had just watched their daughter being executed on live TV. Even though it tore at their hearts the way Sophia was being persecuted by the media, deep down they clung on to the knowledge that everything being said about her was a lie.

A couple of years ago, a tall, broad-shouldered black woman arrived at their door, handing them a package and advising them to watch it as soon as possible. When they opened it, they found it to contain a USB thumb drive with a small note in what they recognised as their daughter's handwriting asking them to play it. They were overjoyed to find the drive contained a video message from Sophia. They listened intently as she explained the assassination attempt on her life, her doppelgänger, as well as the threat to the world from an other-worldly hostile force.

At first, they had refused to believe what they were being told. Who would believe such a tale? But a short time later they watched their daughter's doppelgänger give a news conference and they instantly realised that the woman on TV was not their daughter.

As he continued to watch the broadcast, Vernon took his wife's hand and bowed his head. Whispering a prayer for Sophia, he then embraced Ruby tightly and sobbed in heart-wrenching grief. Why? Why had she been taken from them that way, when she still had so much more to give to the world. How could the press say those things about her, knowing they weren't true?

A firm knock at the door startled Vernon and he lifted his head in annoyed surprise. He shot out of his seat and glared angrily at the front window. How dare the press think they can intrude on their personal grief. Hadn't they done enough? He'd had a good mind to give them a piece of his mind.

As if sensing Vernon's thoughts, Ruby grabbed his hand and shook her head. He let out a reluctant sigh and nodded. No, she was right. Sophia wouldn't have wanted that. She would have wanted him to be strong and to tell the world what she had been really like – a loving daughter, a strong independent woman, and a courageous leader.

With his hand clasped tightly in Ruby's, Vernon shuffled warily into the small hallway and opened the front door. He felt his eyes grow wide in stunned astonishment at the sight standing before him. It was a sea of people, their faces a mixture of rage of understanding. Vernon shook his head in bewilderment, there must have been at least one hundred people standing in front of their cottage.

Vernon smiled sadly as three individuals, whom he immediately recognized as his neighbours, separated themselves from the front of the crowd and lovingly embraced the couple. Tears flowed down Vernon's cheeks, and he nodded gratefully as the enormous crowd of people wordlessly shone their torches above their heads in vigil and solidarity.

Sophia's message had been heard and understood. They would stand united against the darkness, no matter what.

EPILOGUE

Claire Tulley squeezed her eyes shut as the floor beneath her vanished in a blinding, fiery light. Then, just for a moment, she was weightless, as if suspended in time. The weight of the support column had disappeared, and she heaved a sigh of relief. Her relief quickly changing to fear, she dropped into the sea of flames beneath her and screamed in agony, feeling her skin blister in the searing heat.

Then the blistering heat was no longer there. She sighed joyfully as a rainbow of energy enveloped her body, healing her. Serene, she smiled as she sensed her body being pulled away as if a great hand had reached forth and plucked her to safety.

Giddy with excitement, she opened her eyes and stared in wonder at the clouds of energy shooting past her. She glanced over her shoulder and cried out in dismay at seeing her body flying away from her. She stretched out her hand. *No! Don't go!* She focused her attention in front of her and her eyes widened, awestruck, at the clouds of energy streaking past her. A particle of energy zipped toward her, stopping in front of her face. Tentative, she reached out to touch the hovering ball of energy and giggled in delight at the warm tingle passing through her body.

Then it was over and the intangible woman watched wistfully as the playful ball of energy shot away from her, disappearing into the multicoloured clouds. Her eyes squinting tight, she entered a bright tunnel of light. Faster and faster, she sped down the narrow corridor and held her right hand up to shield her eyes from the increasingly blinding light before her.

And then she stopped.

Disorientated, she opened her eyes and blinked furiously, trying to clear the colourful spots in her vision. Her sight returned to normal and she discovered she was now standing in the centre of a familiar vast white hall. She lifted her head and grinned at the sea of stars above her, shaking her head in wonder. Wow! She would never get used to that sight.

Her brow furrowed as she realised that she was standing next to two familiar but empty sky-blue cushioned armchairs. Placing her hands on her hips, she spun in a circle and cried out, her voice echoing across the hall.

'Custos? Show yourself. I know you're here!'

'Of course I'm here, Claire Tulley. Where else would I be, my child?'

Claire jumped in shock at the voice in her ear. She wheeled around to see a tall elderly black man dressed in a white evening suit. His multicoloured eyes twinkling with a mischievous glint, he leaned forward on his gentleman's cane and smiled fondly.

Feigning irritation, she swatted her hand playfully against the omniscient entity's shoulder. 'I wish you would stop doing that.'

Custos chuckled in amusement and gave her a wry smile. 'Child, when you get to be as old as I am, it is the little things that make it worthwhile.'

Her lips tightening, Claire folded her arms across her chest and stared at the faux elderly man. 'Am I to assume I have you to thank for literally pulling my arse out of the fire?'

The ancient being gave a cheeky smile and bowed his head, waving his hand in a grandiose gesture. 'Guilty as charged, my dear.' His mouth narrowed into a lopsided grin, and he waggled his finger, tutting. 'Young one, you really are making a habit of getting into these scrapes. One would think you're doing it on purpose.'

Claire gave the grinning entity the evil eye, snarling haughtily, 'Well, pardon me for being a burden.' Her face softening, she took his hand gratefully. 'But I am grateful for your help. Thank you. May I ask, there was someone with me? Is he …?'

The corners of Custos's eyes crinkled, and he gave Claire a friendly smile.

'You can relax, my dear. He is perfectly safe and well. As we speak, both of your bodies are safe on a parallel world.' He shrugged slightly and let out an amused chuckle. 'I have to say, both your bodies appear to have been through the wars. Along with your broken bones, you both were a bit singed around the edges. But I am happy to say you are both healing nicely. As we speak, your bodies are lying in a coma, surrounded by a healing bio-stasis field. You will be up and about in no time.' He chortled and gave her a sly wink. 'Although you will have a fantastic tan.'

Claire's left eyebrow arched and she gave the mysterious entity a sidelong look. 'Not to sound ungrateful, but didn't you once tell me you couldn't interfere because it would mean confronting Oracle? Which, in your own words, could end up devastating our world?'

'Meh!' Custos scoffed, tapping his finger on his nose and grinning at her. 'I have recently found that Oracle, as you humans say, has a lot on her plate. So I saw an opportunity and took a chance. The amount of energy released in that blast was enough to shield my presence from Oracle, allowing me to nip in and transfer you both to Counter-Earth.' The corners of his mouth lifted in a cryptic smile. 'As well as shielding her from seeing me … handle some of my other interests.'

What did that mean? Was Custos manipulating other people's lives? Claire frowned and then shook her head, realising now was not the time to confront him about it and quickly put the thought to one side. Chewing on her bottom lip, she took hold of the immortal being's hands and stared hopefully into his multicoloured eyes. 'Custos, is there any way you could transfer us back to my Earth? My friends are in great danger and need our help.'

Custos shook his head dolefully, inhaled and let out a slow melancholic breath. 'I am sorry, Claire, I cannot. I transferred you to Counter-Earth for a reason. There is somebody on that world, a young girl, who will play a pivotal role in the game ahead.'

Nostrils flaring with indignation, Claire took a step back from Custos, hissing with disdain. 'A game! A game! You're talking about us like we are pieces on a chessboard.' She beat her palm against her breast, spitting venom at him. 'These are people's lives you're talking about. Not objects that you can move and discard at a whim.'

His eyes flickering with remorse, Custos slowly lifted his right hand. 'Unfortunately, my dear, that is how I must see you. You are pieces, my warriors, in my war against Oracle. Before our endgame can begin, I need to ensure all the players are in place.' He made ready to snap his fingers. 'Speaking of which, this is where I must bid you farewell.'

Her hands raised in front of her, Claire lunged at the ancient being as if to stop him. 'Don't you dare. I'm warni—'

'You ... argh!' Claire snarled, pounding her fists on the mattress in angry frustration. 'That sonofabitch! I'm going to kill him!'

'Claire, wake up. You're having a nightmare.'

She opened her eyes and her annoyance quickly turned to elation on seeing Dave's face leaning over her. Her heart screaming with joy, she leapt up from her cot and wrapped her arms around him. 'Oh, Dave!' she exclaimed in delight. 'You're a sight for sore eyes.'

Dave let out a small, embarrassed cough and squirmed awkwardly in her embrace. 'Umm. Claire, I'm delighted to see you too, but can I tell you something?' He lowered his voice and whispered into her ear. 'You don't have any clothes on.'

Horror-struck, Claire felt her eyebrows climb up her forehead as she lowered her eyes and was shocked to see he was telling the truth. She was stark naked. Claire unwrapped her arms from around Dave and pulled the thick blanket off the cot, wrapping it tightly around her.

Dave smirked and gestured to a pile of clothes on the chair beside the cot. 'I woke up not that long ago, also naked. I found these military fatigues on the chair next to our cots.' He waved his hand over the green boiler suit he was wearing. Then he twisted his face and scratched his head in confusion. 'Last thing I remember was a flash of light and then there was a weird sensation as if someone reached down and picked me up. Well, I must have blacked out, because the next thing I was aware of was waking up in this strange room, naked in a cot, with all my injuries miraculously healed.'

Dave turned his back to allow Claire to dress. As she slipped into the green boiler suit, her eyebrows knitted together as she studied the dim room. Two single metal cots stood against one wall. Across from them was a medium-sized metal wardrobe, next to which was an open doorway that led to what appeared to be an en-suite bathroom.

After fastening the last button and fixing her hair, Claire lowered her eyes and scowled at her bare feet. Her right eyebrow perked up as she spotted a pair of boots beneath the chair. She slid her feet into them and gave a small nod of approval; they fitted her perfectly.

'It's fine. You can turn around now,' she said in an amused tone. 'Although I don't understand why you bothered, like you haven't seen me naked before.'

Dave chuckled and gave her a sly wink. 'Just trying to be the perfect gentleman. Wouldn't want to be accused of taking advantage of a woman in her confused state.' His face turning serious, he spread his hands over the room's interior. 'I would love to know how we got here. Wherever *here* is.'

'Um, yeah, about that,' Claire said carefully. She sat down on her cot and tapped on a spot next to her. 'Sit down. There's something I must tell you.'

His brow heavily creased, Dave sat down next to Claire without comment and listened intently as she explained her encounter with Custos. After she was finished, he stared at her in open-mouthed unbelief. She watched wordlessly as he rose to his feet and paced around. From the way he was vigorously rubbing his forehead, she could tell he was struggling to accept her story. If she was being honest with herself, Sophia couldn't really blame him. If she hadn't experienced it herself, she would probably would have had hard a time believing it too.

'Not that I don't believe you, Claire.' He laughed mirthlessly, gesturing to them both. 'By rights, you and I should be dead. I just find it hard to accept that there is an omnipotent being –' he waved his hand over his head '— somewhere out there. Moving us around like pawns in a bizarre game of cosmic chess.' He stared at her suspiciously and then spoke in a careful tone. 'Is that why you've been so distant with me? You believe that he engineered our first meeting.'

'Yes, I believe he did,' Claire replied, then shifted uncomfortably on the bed and gazed at her hands. 'He admitted to me that he manipulated me, made me do things I would never normally do, like ...' She felt her cheeks warm and slipped into an uneasy silence.

Dave gave her a puzzled look. 'What do you mea—' His eyes grew wide and he sank onto the bed next to her. 'Oh, my God, Claire. You don't mean? He made you ...' Flustered, he stammered and gestured to her, 'I-I mean ... you ...'

and then pointed wordlessly at himself.

Claire nodded angrily. 'If you're asking whether he manipulated me into sleeping with you, then the answer is yes.' She rose off the bed as she felt her all the bitterness and anger that she had been bottling up come to the surface. Yes, Dave should feel ashamed, he was the one who took advantage of her when she was at her most vulnerable. Why should he get off lightly. But just as she was about to vent her fury on him, she paused as she noticed the look of dismay on Dave's face. She felt her anger subside as she suddenly realised that he had been just as much a victim as her. Custos had been manipulating them both. No, blaming him would only end up putting wedge between them and she couldn't afford that to happen. They needed to remain united if they were to see this through to the end. If they both survived what was to come, then they could sit down and have frank discussion about their relationship.

Claire drew in a long breath and gave a small dismissive wave of her hand. 'Don't worry, I'm not angry at you. In fact, I believe you're just as much a victim in this as I am – he probably manipulated you too. So you can stop beating yourself up. If it makes you feel any better, neither of us were in control of ourselves that night.'

'Humph! Thanks, that makes me feel a hell of a lot better,' Dave answered sarcastically. He lapsed into an uncomfortable silence before moving closer to Claire and taking her hand. After a few seconds, he spoke in a quiet, worried tone. 'Claire, do you trust him?'

That was the question, wasn't it? Did she trust Custos? Claire wondered and stared up at the ceiling thoughtfully. True, he did save their lives, but she had to be honest with herself – up until now, there had been no sign of malice behind his actions. She held up her hands, sucked in a deep breath and let it out slowly. 'If I'm being honest with myself, yes.' She shook her and laughed mirthlessly. 'Oh, don't get me wrong. I definitely believe he has his own agenda and probably has a lot to answer for. But this is the second time he has helped me.' Turning towards Dave, she looked him in the eye and gave a resolute nod. 'So yes, I am forced to admit that I trust him.'

Dave arched his head and raised an eyebrow in cool surprise. 'Second time? You mean this is not your first encounter with an omnipotent being, and you're only telling me now?'

Before Claire could answer, she was interrupted by a knock on the metal door. Dave jumped up, waved his hand furiously and silently motioned for Claire to move behind him. As Dave placed himself protectively in front of her, Claire bristled at the presumption she needed his protection. However, not wanting to add to the tension, she decided to keep her grievances to herself and held her tongue. She bit her bottom lip, anxious at the sound of the metal door squealing open.

A heavyset brown-haired middle-aged woman moved carefully through the open door. Her round face beamed in delight as she strode into room and clapped her hands excitedly.

'Ah good, I see you both are finally awake,' she said cheerfully.

Claire noticed Dave's back stiffen slightly and she stepped in front of him so that she could get an idea of what was going through his mind. She could tell he was lost for words, but he also had an odd look on his face. If she didn't know any better, she could've sworn it was recognition. She frowned. Wait? Did he know this woman?

'David, my dear chap,' the woman continued, 'haven't you been told it's rather impolite to stare at a woman?'

Claire regarded Dave with much amusement. 'Well, I can guess from your impression of a drowning fish you know this woman?'

Dave nodded vigorously and pointed. 'Th … th … this is Karen Logue, the medical examiner I told you about. Remember that night at my place I told you the story of my encounter with her doppelgänger?' Regaining his composure, he smiled warmly and stepped forward to take her hand. 'You can't believe how relieved I am at seeing you. We had almost given up hope of ever seeing you again.'

Karen gave a small, appreciative nod and gently tapped her old friend's hand. 'Thank you, my friend. You can't imagine how it feels to see a familiar face.' The muscles in her face tightened as she stared at him with worry-filled eyes. 'How are Sean and Aoife? Are they still okay? Has *she* hurt them?'

Dave gave the woman a tight smile and he put his hand gently on her shoulder. 'Um, Sean is fine, although worried about you. Aoife is okay too. I must say, his instincts are spot on.' He grinned. 'From the first moment that woman came home, he suspected something wasn't right. He contacted me with his suspicions and told me he had sent Aoife away to his parents, pretending it was a prearranged holiday.'

Claire frowned. There was something in Dave's tone of voice that made her feel uneasy. She had known him long enough now to recognise he wasn't completely being truthful to Karen. She remembered him telling her about his unsettling encounter with Karen's doppelgänger a couple of months earlier, so something else must happened since then. From the way Karen was sucking on her bottom lip and staring at Dave with a look that contained deep suspicion, Claire could tell she didn't believe him too.

'Hm. David,' Karen replied in a cool tone, 'You and I have known each other too long, so I can tell when you're keeping something from me, but I'll let it slide for the moment.' She clicked her fingers impatiently and a young fair-haired woman walked slowly into the room, handing her a tray with two bottles containing thick green liquid. She took the tray and waved her hand irritably. 'Thank you, Dayna. You may leave. Go on, shoo! Don't let the door hit you in the arse on your way out.'

Claire lifted her hand to her mouth to hide her amusement as the young woman rolled her eyes as she walked out of the room and closed the door behind her. Dave bobbed his head to the closed door, chuckling. 'I see it hasn't taken you long to ingratiate yourself with the locals,' he said curiously.

The heavyset woman let out a small huff of amusement. 'Oh, they're a good bunch of people. They rescued me a few days after I arrived on this world. When they found out I was a qualified medical examiner, they drafted me into the medical team.' She let out an exasperated snort and lifted her hands in dismay. 'The resistance has very few fully trained physicians. Until recently, the Empire pressed all the best physicians into service for them.' She shook her head sullenly, handing the tray to Dave. 'Anyway, enough of that. I would suggest you both drink this. You are both dehydrated and need your strength building up. This is a special protein drink designed to combat transporter fatigue, so we think it may work just as well on you. You can believe me when I say it's very good.'

Claire stared at the bottle's contents warily. Her hunger overriding her curiosity, she popped the top off the bottle and downed the contents. She screwed up her face in disgust at the unusual taste in her mouth. 'What in the name of all things holy!' She coughed bitterly. 'That's disgusting.' On noticing Dave's reluctance, she hung her head and stared at him reproachfully. 'Oh no, you're not getting off that easy. If I have to drink it, you're damn well going to. So you too, David, drink ... now!' Her mouth widened in wicked glee as he gagged on the bottle's contents.

Karen tilted her head enquiringly as Dave finished the bottle. 'We're quite curious about how you got here. The way I heard it, people were sitting in the mess hall eating when they were blinded by a bright light. When everybody's vision recovered, you and your friend were lying on the floor ... naked.' A shadow of a grin danced across her face. 'When they called me to the mess hall, there was this strange aura surrounding you both. I could tell you were both seriously injured, but the aura appeared to be healing you, so we thought it best that you were placed in isolation, more for our protection than yours.' She frowned, eyeing Dave curiously. 'Was it an experiment gone wrong?'

Something in the back of Claire's mind told her it was probably best they kept the involvement of a strange benevolent entity a secret for now, and her body stiffened. She shot Dave a wary glance, giving her head a slight shake. She relaxed as she watched him scratch his nose in acknowledgement.

Dave coughed hesitantly, rubbed his hand over the back of his neck and let out a remorseful sigh. 'Sorry, Karen, I wish we could help you, but we are in the dark as much as you. The facility we were in was under attack by a hostile force. We were trapped, injured, and cut off from escape when the self-destruct was activated. Last thing I remember was a white light and then we woke up here.'

Claire thought she saw Karen's eyes flicker with suspicion as she stood and stared at Dave silently for several seconds. She could tell she didn't believe him. Was she wondering whether to challenge him or leave it for now? She held her breath and waited for Karen to challenge him. However, she felt herself relax as Karen simply gave a small nod and then turned back to the door.

'I'll give you a couple of minutes to give you time to pull yourselves together and then I'll inform our leader that you're ready to speak to her.' Karen said as she marched over to the door. She gave the door a light knock and the door swung open. But as she stepped through the doorway, she paused, turned and smiled cryptically at Claire. 'There's someone here who has been waiting a long time to see you. A very long time.'

Claire frowned as she watched Karen step out and close the door behind her. What did she mean by that? Who would she know on this world that would be desperate to speak to her? Dave gave her a quizzical look and she gave him a small shrug. He placed a reassuring hand on her shoulder and gave it a small squeeze. Claire smiled gratefully at him and patted his hand. No words needed be said – they would face whatever lay ahead together.

But as Claire stared at the closed door, she shifted uneasily on her feet as she began to wonder just who was waiting on the other side of the door for her. Was it a friend or foe? Was this the reason why Custos had sent her to this world. If it was then why was Dave here too?

Her breath quickened as she stared at the door in front of her. Her fingers tightened around Dave's hand as she heard footsteps approaching from the other side of the door. Whatever future lay ahead for her, she decided that she was going meet it head on. Regardless of this person's identity, Claire firmly believed that there wasn't anything they could say or do to catch her off guard. Wasn't there?

-TO BE CONTINUED-

(Oh, come on. You knew this was coming!)

ABOUT THE AUTHOR

Born in Hartlepool in 1970. Alan lived in Langley Park, Durham, England for many years before moving to Northern Ireland in 2006. Has been married to his wife, Monica, since 2007. Loves reading fantasy, science fiction, action & adventure and thrillers. Favourite authors are Stephen King, James Herbert, Clive Cussler, Dean Koontz, Audrey Niffenegger and Neil Gaiman. Is a big Marvel Comics fan and enjoys watching movies. Favourite tv shows are Blake's 7, Babylon 5 and Star Trek.

𝕏 Alan Bayles @Albay3037

@ Alan Bayles @Albay3037

f Facebook.com/AlanBaylesWriter

Printed in Great Britain
by Amazon